PENDRAGON

JOURNAL OF AN ADVENTURE THROUGH TIME AND SPACE

Book One:

The Merchant of Death

Book Two:

The Lost City of Faar

PENDRAGON

JOURNAL OF AN ADVENTURE THROUGH TIME AND SPACE

PENDRAGON

JOURNAL OF AN ADVENTURE THROUGH TIME AND SPACE

Book One:
The Merchant of Death

Book Two:
The Lost City of Faar

By D. J. MacHale

Aladdin Paperbacks
New York   London   Toronto   Sydney

ALADDIN PAPERBACKS
An imprint of Simon & Schuster Children's Publishing Division
1230 Avenue of the Americas, New York, NY 10020
Pendragon: The Merchant of Death copyright © 2002 by D. J. MacHale
Pendragon: The Lost City of Faar copyright © 2003 by D. J. MacHale
These works were previously published
individually by Aladdin Paperbacks.
All rights reserved, including the right of reproduction
in whole or in part in any form.
ALADDIN PAPERBACKS and colophon are registered
trademarks of Simon & Schuster, Inc.
Designed by Debra Sfetsios
The text of this book was set in Apollo and Helvetica.
Manufactured in the United States of America
This Aladdin Paperbacks edition June 2005
2 4 6 8 10 9 7 5 3 1
ISBN-13: 978-1-4169-1224-8
ISBN-10: 1-4169-1224-X

PENDRAGON

JOURNAL OF AN ADVENTURE THROUGH
TIME AND SPACE

Book One:
The Merchant of Death

For Evander

DENDURON

I hope you're reading this, Mark.

Heck, I hope *anybody's* reading this because the only thing that's keeping me from going totally off my nut right now is getting this all down on paper so that someday, when it's all over, it'll help prove that I'm not a total whack job. You see, two things happened yesterday that changed my life forever.

The first was that I finally kissed Courtney Chetwynde. Yes, *the* Courtney Chetwynde of the bites-her-lower-lip-when-she's-thinking, stares-right-into-your-heart-with-her-deep-gray-eyes, looks-unbelievable-in-her-volleyball-uniform, and always-smells-a-little-like-roses fame. Yeah, I kissed her. It was a long time coming and it finally happened. Woo-hoo!

The second thing was that I was launched through a wormhole called a "flume" and got jacked across the universe to a medieval planet called "Denduron" that's in the middle of a violent civil war.

But back to Courtney.

This wasn't your average "nice to see you" peck on the cheek. Oh no. This was a full-on, eyes closed, starting with tight lips but eventually morphing into a mutual open-mouth probe thing that lasted for a good thirty-second lifetime. And we were close, too. Like *real* close. I was holding her so tight I could feel her heart beating against my chest. Or maybe it was my heart. Or maybe our hearts were bouncing off each other. I have no idea. All I know is that it was pretty cool. I hope I get the chance to do it again, but right now it's not looking so good.

I guess it's kind of dumb to be fixating on the glorious Courtney Chetwynde when the real problem is that I'm afraid I'm going to die. Maybe that's why I can't get her out of my head. The memory of that kiss is the only thing that feels real to me right now. I'm afraid that if I lose that memory I'm going to lose everything, and if that happens then . . . well, I don't know what will happen then because I don't understand *anything* that's been happening to me. Maybe by writing it all down, it'll start to make some sense.

Let me try to piece together the events that led to my writing this. Up until yesterday I was living large. At least as large as any normal fourteen-year-old guy can live. School came pretty easy; I kicked ass in sports; my parents were way cool; I didn't hate my little sister, Shannon, usually. I had excellent friends, with you sitting right on top of the list, Mark. I lived in this major house where I had my own private space to play music or whatever and nobody bugged me. My dog, Marley, was the coolest golden retriever there ever was; and I had recently macked with Courtney Chetwynde. (Did I mention that?) How much more goin' on can you get?

The thing is, I also had an Uncle Press.

You remember him? He was the guy who always showed up at my birthday parties with some special surprise. He wouldn't just bring a pony, he'd bring a *truckload* of ponies for a minirodeo. He's the guy who turned my house into that laser-maze game. Was that great or what? He's the one who was throwing the pizzas at my party last year. Remember that guy? Every once in a while he'd show up, out of the blue, and do something amazing like take me flying in a private plane. Yeah, he was a pilot. Another time he gave me this computer that was so advanced, it wasn't even in stores yet. You know the calculator I have that you input numbers by talking to it? That was from Uncle Press. I gotta tell you, he was the coolio uncle everybody wished they had.

But there was always something a little mysterious about Uncle Press. He was my mom's brother, but she didn't say much about him. It was almost like she felt weird talking about him. Whenever I asked, she'd shrug and say something like, "Oh, you know him, he's his own man. How was school today?" Basically, she'd dodge the question.

I don't know what he did for a living, but he always had boatloads of money. I figured he probably had some top-level government job, like doing research for NASA or something and it was all hush-hush. So I didn't ask too many questions. He wasn't married, but sometimes he'd show up at the house with some odd character. One time he brought this lady over who never said a word. He said she was his "friend," but I got the feeling she was more like his "girlfriend." I think she was African or something because she was real dark-skinned. And beautiful. But it was strange because she'd just stare at me and smile. I wasn't scared or anything because she had soft eyes. And maybe she didn't talk because she didn't know English, but still it was kind of creepy.

I'd have to say that my Uncle Press was the coolest guy I'd ever met. That is, until yesterday.

The county semifinal basketball game was last night. You know how important I am to that team. I'm the highest scoring point guard in Stony Brook Junior High history. I'm not bragging; that's just the way it is. So for me to miss that game would have been like Kobe Bryant missing a Lakers playoff game. Okay, maybe I'm not *that* important, but it would not have been cool for me to bail on that game. Mom and Dad had already left for the gym with Shannon. I had a ton of homework and I knew I'd be fried afterward, so I had to get it done before leaving. I had just enough time to scarf down a banana and some Pop-Tarts, feed Marley, jump on my bike, and blast over to school. At least that was the plan. I can't help but think that if I had done my homework just a little bit faster, or decided not to throw the tennis ball with Marley, or even waited till I got to school to take a leak, none of this would have happened. But it did.

I grabbed my pack, headed for the front door, threw it open and came face to face with . . . Courtney Chetwynde.

I froze. She froze. It was like somebody hit the pause button on two lives. Except there was nothing static about what was racing through my brain. The crush I had on her dated back to when we were in grade school. She was always so . . . perfect. But not in that unattainable she's too good for everybody way. She was beautiful and smart and great at sports and she laughed and told jokes. I think that was the key. The fact that she told jokes. Maybe that sounds stupid, but if you tell jokes it shows you're willing to look stupid. And if you've got the whole package going on and still willing to let people laugh at you then, man, what *else* do you want?

Of course I wasn't the only one who felt this way about Courtney. I was one in a long line of admirers. But she was standing at *my* front door. Instantly, every synapse in my brain started firing to try and find the perfect, spontaneous thing to say. The first words out of your mouth in a time of crisis can color someone's opinion of you forever. It either shows that you're totally in charge and ready to handle any situation with composure and wit, or that you're a blundering idiot whose mind will freeze at the first sign of pressure. This all flashed through my brain in the few nanoseconds while we were on "pause." Now it was my move. She came to the house, it was my turn to respond. So I hitched my pack up on my shoulder, leaned casually against the doorjamb, gave her a little smile and said: "Yo."

Yo??? That's not even a real word! Nobody says "Yo" unless they're impersonating Sylvester Stallone, which I was definitely *not* doing. I was all set for the smile to drop off her face in crushing disappointment as she turned and left without saying a word. Instead, she bit her lower lip (which meant she was thinking) and said:

"Hi."

That was good. "Hi" isn't much higher up on the cool scale than "Yo." I was back in the game. It was time to start playing.

"What's up?" I said.

Okay, maybe I wasn't ready to play just yet. It was easier to lob the ball back into her court. It was then that I noticed something weird. Courtney looked nervous. Not out of her mind scared or anything, but a little bit uncomfortable. My confidence soared. She was just as tense as I was. That was good.

"I know you've got to get to the game and all, I don't want to make you late," she said with a little embarrassed smile.

What game? Oh, right, the county semifinal. Somehow it had slipped my mind.

"I've got plenty of time," I lied casually. "C'mon in."

I was recovering nicely. As she walked past me to come inside I got that faint hint of rose fragrance. It took every ounce of willpower not to do a huge-old sucking inhale to try and grab every ounce of that wonderful smell. That would have been dumb and this was definitely not the time to do something dumb because Courtney was now inside my home. She was on my turf. I closed the door behind her and we were alone.

I had no idea what to do next. Courtney turned to me and I made contact with those amazing gray eyes. My knees went soft. I prayed she didn't notice.

"I wasn't sure if I should come here," she said tentatively.

"I'm glad you did," I shot back with perfect timing. I kept the ball in her court, yet still managed to make her feel at ease. I was on fire.

"I'm not really sure why I picked now to come. Maybe it was to wish you good luck in the game. But I think it's more than that."

"Really?" Perfect comeback.

"I'm not exactly sure how to say this, Bobby, but since we were kids, I've had this . . . feeling about you."

Feeling? Feeling is good, unless she feels like I'm an ax murderer or something.

"Oh?" I shot back. Noncommittal, nonaggressive, perfect.

"Man, I feel like such a geek saying this." She broke eye contact. I was losing her. I didn't want her to chicken out so the best thing I could do was throw her a bone.

"Courtney, there are a lot of words that come to mind when I think of you, but 'geek' is definitely not one of them."

She looked back to me and smiled. We were back on track.

"I'm not really sure how to say this, so I'll just say it. There's something about you, Bobby. I know you're a brain and a jock and popular and all, but it's more than that. You've got this, like, I don't know, this aura thing going on. People trust you. They like you. And it's not like you're trying to show off or anything. Maybe that's part of it. You don't act like you think you're better than everybody else. You're just this really good guy"—she paused before going on, then the bombshell—"who I've had this incredible crush on since fourth grade."

Nothing in my wildest fantasy could have prepared me for that. I was speechless. I hoped my mouth wasn't hanging open in stupefied shock.

"I'm not really sure why I'm telling you this now," she went on. "But I have this weird feeling that if I didn't, I might never get the chance again. And I wanted to tell you how I felt . . . and do this."

That's when it happened. The kiss. She stepped forward, hesitated a second to see if I'd stop her, (yeah right, like there was danger of *that* happening), and we kissed. I won't rehash the details, but suffice it to say I was a happy guy. It was the most amazing thirty seconds of my life.

It was the thirty-first second when it all came crashing down.

My eyes were closed, but I could see a whole future full of Courtney and Courtney's kisses. I don't know if it's possible to kiss and smile at the same time, but if it is, I did. And then I opened my eyes, and it was over.

"Hi, Bobby."

Uncle Press was standing there! Where did *he* come from? I pulled away from Courtney so fast that she still had her eyes closed. Actually, she looked kind of goofy for a second like she was kissing air, but she recovered fast and believe me, I didn't laugh.

"Uncle Press! Hi!" I probably should have said, "Yo!" that's how stupid I felt. I'm not sure why, either. We weren't doing anything wrong. We were just kissing. Granted, it was the big-league kiss of all time, but it was still just a kiss. Once Courtney realized what was happening, she went from zero to full-tilt embarrassed. She wanted to be anywhere but there, and I wanted to be there with her. She backed toward the door.

"I . . . uh . . . I better go," she stammered.

"No, don't go." I didn't want to take the heat alone, but Uncle Press had other things on his mind.

"Yes. You should go." Short, blunt, simple as that. Something about the way he said it made a red flag go up in my head. This didn't sound like Uncle Press. Normally he's the kind of guy who would think catching his nephew macking was pretty funny. In fact, that's exactly what happened when he caught me making out with Nancy Kilgore on the back porch. He just laughed. I was embarrassed as hell, but he got a real charge out of it. He'd bring it up every once in a while, just to jazz me. But not in front of anybody else, which made it okay. This time was different though. This time he wasn't laughing.

"Good luck tonight. I'll be cheering," said Courtney as she took a step . . . and walked square into the door. Ouch. Uncle Press leaned over and opened it for her. She gave him a quick, embarrassed nod of thanks, then shot me a look with the slightest hint of a sly smile. Then she was gone. Uncle Press closed the door and looked at me.

"I'm sorry, Bobby, but I need your help. I want you to come with me."

Again, this didn't sound like Uncle Press. He was a loose kind of guy. My guess was he was in his fifties, but he didn't act like a geezer. He was always goofing around, never seemed to take things all that seriously. But tonight, he was dead serious. In fact, it almost seemed as if he looked a little . . . scared.

"But, I got a game. County semis. I'm already late."

"You didn't seem too concerned about that a few seconds ago," he shot back.

Good point. But I really was late, and it was a big game.

"Mom and Dad are already there with Shannon. If I don't show up—"

"They'll understand. I wouldn't ask you to do this if I didn't think it was more important than a basketball game . . . or kissing that beautiful girl who just left."

I was prepared to argue on that last point, but man, he was acting pretty intense. It was weird. Then, as if he were reading my mind he said, "Bobby, you've known me all your life. Have you ever seen me like this?"

I didn't need to answer. Something was definitely up.

"Then you know how serious this is," he said with absolute finality.

I didn't know what to do. At that very minute there was a team waiting for me to help them win a county title. Not to mention a family, friends, and an almost-girlfriend who would be expecting me to trot out onto the court. But standing in front of me was a guy who was my own flesh and blood who needed my help. Uncle Press did a lot for me as I was growing up and never asked for a single thing in return. Until now. How could I turn him down?

"You promise to explain things to my coach, Mom and Dad, and Courtney Chetwynde?"

Uncle Press actually gave a small smile, just like he used to, and said, "They'll understand."

I tried to think of any other reason why I shouldn't go with him, but came up empty. So with a sigh I said, "All right then, let's go."

Instantly Uncle Press opened the front door. I shrugged and started out.

"You won't need that bag," he said, referring to my pack. I'm not sure why, but that sounded strange, and a touch ominous.

"What's this all about Uncle Press?"

If he had answered the question truthfully, I would have run upstairs to my room and hid under the bed. But he didn't. All he said was, "You'll find out."

He was my uncle. I trusted the guy. So I let my pack fall to the floor and headed for the door. Uncle Press didn't follow right away. I looked back and saw that he was looking around the house. Maybe I imagined this, but he seemed a little sad, as if this was the last time he was going to be here. After a few seconds he said, "You love this place, don't you? And your family?"

"Well . . . yeah. Of course," I answered. What a dumb question.

He took one more wistful look around, then turned to face me. The sad look was gone. In its place was the determined look of a guy who had business elsewhere.

"Let's go," he said.

He walked past me and headed down the front walk to the street. Uncle Press always dressed the same way, in jeans, boots, and a dark brown work shirt. Over this he wore a long, tan, leather coat that reached down to his knees. It flapped in the wind as he walked. I'd seen that look many times before, but for some reason, this time it gave him the air of someone for whom time has stood still. In another time and place he could have been a dusty cowboy striding into town, or a military emissary carrying vital documents. Uncle Press was indeed a unique character.

Parked in front of my house was the sweetest looking motorcycle I ever saw. It looked like one of those multicolored Matchbox racers that I had played with not too long ago. But this bike was very big and very real. Uncle Press always did things in style. He grabbed the extra helmet from the seat and tossed it to me. I buckled up and he did the same. He then gunned the engine and I was surprised to hear that it wasn't very loud. I was expecting some growling, gut-churning hog sound. But this bike was almost quiet. It sounded like, well, a rocket that's about to ignite. I hopped on the seat behind him and he glanced back to me.

"Ready?" he asked.

"No," I replied honestly.

"Good. I'd be surprised if you were," he shot back. He then kicked the bike into gear, hit the gas, and the two of us flew down the quiet, suburban street that had been my home for fourteen years.

I hope I'll see it again someday.

◉ SECOND EARTH ◉

. . . I hope I'll see it again someday.

Mark Dimond looked up from the stack of parchment papers in his hand and took a deep breath. His heart was racing. The words on the pages before him seemed as if they were written by his best friend, Bobby Pendragon, but the story they contained was impossible. Yet there it was. He glanced at the pages again. What he saw was frantic writing. Bobby's writing in smudged black ink on some kind of old-fashioned yellow parchment. It looked real, it felt real, but so much of the story these pages contained felt about as close to reality as a fevered dream.

Mark sat safely locked in the second stall from the door of the third floor boys' bathroom at Stony Brook Junior High. It was a rarely used bathroom because it was at the far end of the building, near the art department, way off the beaten track. He'd often come here to think. Occasionally he even used the toilet for its intended purpose, but mostly he came here to get away. At his feet were a pile of carrot ends. He'd been nervously gnawing on them as he scanned the pages. Mark had read somewhere that carrots improved your vision. But after months of almost constant carrot intake, he still had to wear glasses and only had a mouthful of yellow teeth to show for his efforts.

Mark knew he wasn't a full-on nerd, but he wasn't running with the cool kids, either. His only contact with the world of "the accepted" was Bobby. They grew up together and were about as tight as two friends could be. As Bobby started to grow up and become popular, Mark kept one foot firmly planted in kid-world. He still read comics; he still kept action figures on his desk. He didn't really know popular music, and his clothes were, well, functional. But that didn't matter to Bobby. Mark made him laugh. And Mark made him think. The two would spend hours debating issues as diverse as First Amendment rights and the relative merits of Pamela Anderson before and after cosmetic surgery.

A lot of Bobby's jock friends would dump on Mark, but never in front of Bobby. They knew better. Mess with Mark and you'd be messing with Bobby, and nobody messed with Bobby. But now, somebody was indeed messing with Bobby. Mark held the proof right there in his hands. He didn't want to believe what the pages told him. Under normal circumstances he would have thought it was some goofy joke that Bobby thought up. But some things had happened that made Mark think this might not be a joke. He leaned back against the cool tile wall and his thoughts brought him back to something that had happened the night before.

Mark always slept with a night-light. He was afraid of the dark. This was his secret. Even Bobby didn't know. Though sometimes Mark thought the night-light was worse than no light at all, because a night-light made shadows. Like the dark jacket hanging on the back of a door that looked like the Grim Reaper. That nasty vision happened more than once. It didn't help that without his glasses, Mark could barely see things clearly beyond the end of his bed. Still, the occasional rude awakening was much better than sleeping in the dark.

The night before, it had happened again. Mark was lying in bed, drifting in and out of sleep. He opened one groggy eye and in his stupor he thought he saw someone standing at the foot of his bed. His mind tried to tell him it was just the shadow cast by a passing car, but his gut told him to wake up. Fast. A surge of adrenaline shot through him and his brain went on full alert. He tried to focus his nearsighted eyes on the interloper to confirm it was just his backpack. No go. He couldn't tell what it was. So he groped his bedside table, knocked over a mug full of pens and his Game Boy, but managed to grab his glasses. When he finally jammed them onto his nose, he looked to the end of his bed . . . and froze in fear.

Standing there, lit by soft moonlight streaming in through the window, was a woman. She was tall and dark-skinned. She wore a colorful wrap that draped off one shoulder, revealing an incredibly taut, muscular arm. She looked to Mark to be a beautiful African queen. Mark dug his heels in and pushed his back against the wall behind his bed in the futile hope that he'd crash through and escape out the other side.

The woman simply raised a finger to her lips and gave a soft "shhh" sound. Mark froze in absolute, paralyzing fear. He looked into the woman's eyes and something strange happened. He grew calm. As he thought back on this moment, he wasn't sure if she was hypnotizing him or casting some kind of spell because, oddly, his fear slipped away. The woman had soft, friendly eyes that told Mark he had nothing to be afraid of.

"Shaaa zaa shuu saaa," she said softly. Her voice sounded like warm wind through the trees. It was pleasant and soothing, but it made no sense. The woman then walked around the bed and sat next to Mark. Mark didn't jump away because, for some reason, this all felt . . . right. A leather pouch hung from a cord around her neck. She reached into it and pulled out a ring. It looked to Mark like one of those school rings you see on college kids. It was silver with a slate-colored stone mounted in the center. There was some sort of inscription engraved around the stone, but it was written in no language Mark had ever seen before.

"This is from Bobby," she said softly.

Bobby? Bobby Pendragon? Mark had no idea what was happening, but the last thing he expected was to hear that this strange woman who appeared in his bedroom in the middle of the night had something to do with his best friend.

"Who are you? How do you know Bobby?"

She gently picked up Mark's right hand and slipped the ring onto his finger. It fit perfectly. Mark looked at the strange ring, then back at the woman.

"Why? What's this?" he asked.

The woman touched a gentle finger to Mark's lips to quiet him. Mark immediately felt his eyes grow heavy. A second before he had been about as wide awake as anyone can be, but now he felt weary enough to fall asleep on the spot. He felt the world slipping away. In an instant, he was out.

The next morning Mark woke up at the usual 6:15 with the alarm clock blaring. His first thought was that he hated alarm clocks. His second thought was that he had had the strangest dream. He chuckled to himself, thinking he should cut down on the raw vegetables before bedtime. He then reached over to hit the snooze button . . . and saw it.

There, on his finger was the ring the woman had given him. Mark sat up in bed quickly and stared at it with its gray stone and strange inscriptions. It was real. He could feel it. It had weight. It wasn't a dream. What was going on?

He dressed quickly and left the house without telling his parents what had happened. There was only one person who could explain this to him. Bobby Pendragon. But something had already happened with Bobby that gave him a queasy feeling. Last night was the county semifinal basketball game . . . and Bobby hadn't shown up. His parents were there, his sister was there, but not Bobby. After the first half he went over to ask the Pendragons where Bobby was, but they had already left. Very strange.

And Stony Brook lost. Bad. Everybody at the game was buzzing, wanting to know what happened to their star. Nobody knew. When Mark got home he called Bobby's house, but there was no answer. He figured he'd see him in school the next day and get the story. Then he went to sleep and had his strange night visitor. Now Mark wanted to know a lot more from Bobby than why he hadn't shown for a basketball game.

When Mark got into the school building, the number one topic of conversation was The Game.

"Hey Dimond? Where's your superstar pal?"

"He blew it!"

"This better be good, Dimond!"

"What's the story?"

Everyone was yelling at him about Bobby. That could only mean one thing. Bobby hadn't gotten there yet. Of course, Mark didn't have any answers, so he shrugged and kept walking. He went to Bobby's locker, but Bobby wasn't there. Instead there were more angry kids waiting to ambush him.

"He chickened out, didn't he?"

"Couldn't take the heat!"

Mark dodged them and went to Bobby's homeroom. Bobby wasn't there, either. Where was he? Something was definitely wrong.

And then it happened. It started as a twitch at first, but quickly grew. It was the ring. It was moving. It felt like it was squeezing and releasing, squeezing and releasing.

"Dimond! Hey, Dimond! Where is he?" More kids were closing

in. This was not a good time. Mark didn't know what to do, so he grabbed the ring with his other hand and ran. He blasted through kids, bumping into more than he dodged. A couple of older guys pushed him back, nearly sending him sprawling, but Mark somehow stayed on his feet. The bell rang and everyone headed for homeroom, but Mark didn't stop until he reached his own personal Fortress of Solitude—the boys' bathroom on the third floor.

He ran to the center of the room and held his hand out as if it didn't belong to him. The ring was still moving, squeezing and releasing like a heartbeat. Then the gray stone started to sparkle. An instant before it had been a solid gray mass; now it sprang to life like a brilliant diamond. Beams of light shot from the ring and filled the room.

Mark couldn't take it anymore. He yanked off the strange ring and threw it. It hit the tiled wall and bounced to a stop in the center of the bathroom. The beams of light continued to shoot from the stone and dance across the ceiling and the walls, making the room look as if it were alive with beautiful, dazzling stars.

Then Mark watched in awe as the circular band started to grow larger. It slowly got bigger and bigger until it was about the size of a Frisbee, and in the center of the now impossibly large band was a black hole where the floor should have been. The ring had opened up a dark portal to . . . somewhere. From deep within this portal, Mark could hear the faint sound of musical notes. It wasn't a melody; it was a jumble of sweet sounding tones that grew louder and louder.

Mark backed away from the strange ring, not sure if he should turn and run or stay and watch the show. He was fascinated and terrified at the same time. The musical notes coming from the portal got so loud that Mark had to cover his ears. Whatever was happening, he didn't want any part of it anymore. So he turned and ran for the door. He was just about to throw it open when . . .

Everything stopped. The musical notes ended so abruptly it was like somebody threw a switch to cut the power. The dazzling light show ended also. The only thing that didn't stop was Mark's pounding heart. Whatever had just happened, it was over now and Mark tried to calm down. He took his hand away from the door and looked back into the bathroom. What he saw was the ring on the floor, right where he had thrown it. It was back to its normal size and the stone had returned to its original solid gray color.

But something else was there too. Lying on the floor next to the ring was a scroll of paper. It was yellow parchment that had been tightly rolled and tied with a thin leather strap. Whatever the event had been with the ring, the result was that it had deposited this scroll here on the bathroom floor.

Mark approached the scroll cautiously, bent down, and picked it up with a sweaty hand. It was indeed rolled paper. Nothing scary about it. Just odd. Mark tugged on the leather cord that kept it together and gently unrolled the paper. There were four sheets, all filled with writing. Mark looked at the first line of the first page, and what he read hit him like an electric charge. He couldn't breathe. He couldn't think. This strange parchment was a letter . . . to him.

It began: *I hope you're reading this, Mark.*

DEПDVRОП

There wasn't much I could ask Uncle Press from the back of a speeding motorcycle. Between the whine of the engine, the blast of wind rushing by and the fact that both of us were wearing these high-tech helmets, conversation was impossible. So I was left with my own imagination to try and figure out where we were going and why.

One thing was clear though. We were leaving town. I lived in a quiet, peaceful, okay *dull* suburb of New York City. I'd been into the city a few times with my parents, mostly to go to events like the holiday spectacular at Radio City or the Macy's Thanksgiving Day Parade. Then there was that one time you and I, Mark, hopped the commuter train to catch that James Bond flick. Remember? Other than that, the city was pretty much a mystery to me.

On the other hand, it didn't take a New York cabbie to realize Uncle Press was steering us into a section of the city that by anybody's standards would be defined as . . . bad. This was not the New York I'd ever seen, except maybe on a TV news report about some nasty crime that had just gone down. Once we shot off the Cross Bronx Expressway we were smack in the middle of the badlands. Burned-out buildings were everywhere. Nobody walked on the streets. It all looked empty and desolate, yet I had the eerie feeling that many sets of eyes were locked on us from the dark windows of the derelict buildings as we cruised by. And of course, it was nighttime dark.

Was I scared? Well, judging by the fact that I wanted to puke and I held on to Uncle Press so hard I expected to hear one of his ribs crack, I'd say yeah, I was scared. Uncle Press guided the motorcycle toward one of those old-fashioned kiosks that marked the stairs leading down to the subway. We bounced up onto the curb and he killed the engine. As we glided to a stop, suddenly everything became quiet. Granted, I'd been riding on the back of a motorcycle for the past half hour and after that *anything* would seem quiet. But this was *really* quiet, like a ghost town. Or a ghost city.

"This is it," he announced and jumped off the bike. I jumped off too and gratefully removed my helmet. Finally, I could hear again. Uncle Press left his helmet on the bike and headed for the subway entrance.

"Whoa, hold on, we're going to leave the bike and the helmets?" I asked with surprise. I couldn't believe it. He didn't even take the keys out of the ignition. I'm no expert on crime, but I could pretty much predict that if we left this gear here, it would be gone before we blinked.

"We don't need it anymore," he said quickly and started down the subway stairs.

"Why are we taking the subway?" I asked. "Why don't we just stay on the bike?"

"Because we can't take the bike where we're going," he answered with a matter-of-fact tone. He turned and headed down a few more steps.

I didn't move. I wanted answers, and I wasn't taking

another step until I got some. Uncle Press sensed that I wasn't following him, so he stopped and looked back at me.

"What?" he asked, with a little bit of frustration.

"I just blew off the most important game of my life, my team is going to crucify me tomorrow, and you want me to follow you into the subway in the worst part of New York City? I think I deserve to know what's going on!" This had gone far enough and if I didn't get some answers, I was walking. Of course I wasn't exactly sure of where I would go if Uncle Press left me there and went on alone. I figured it was a safe risk, though. After all, he was my uncle.

Uncle Press softened. For a moment I saw the face of the guy I'd known all my life. "You're right, Bobby. I've asked you to do a lot on faith. But if we stop for me to explain everything, we may be too late."

"Too late for what?"

"There's a group of people who are in trouble. They're relying on me to help them, and I'm relying on you to help me."

I was flattered and freaked at the same time. "Really? What kind of trouble?"

"That's what would take me forever to explain. I'd rather show you."

I didn't know what to do. Even if I wanted to run away, I had no clue of how to get out of there. And here was this guy, my uncle, staring me straight in the eye and saying he needed me. There weren't a whole lot of options. I finally decided to divulge the single overriding thought in my head.

"I'm scared." There, I said it.

"I know. But please believe me, Bobby, as long as it's in my power, I won't let anything happen to you." He said this with such sincerity, it actually made me feel better . . . for about a second.

"What happens when it's *not* in your power?" I asked.

Uncle Press smiled, and said, "That won't be for a while. Are you with me?"

They say that just before you're about to meet your doom, your life flashes before your eyes. Surprisingly, that didn't happen. I didn't think of the game. I didn't think of my family. I didn't even think of Courtney Chetwynde. I just thought about me and Uncle Press. Here and now. I took that as a good sign. So I mustered all the bravura I could and said, "Hey, ho, let's go."

Uncle Press let out a laugh like I hadn't heard from him in a long time, then turned and rushed down the stairs. As I watched him disappear into the dark hole of the subway, I did my best to pretend I wasn't being an idiot by going along with him. When I got to the bottom of the stairs, I saw Uncle Press standing in front of a wall of graffiti-covered plywood that blocked the entrance. The station was closed and by the looks of the old wood, it had been closed for a long time.

"Well, that's a problem," I said glibly. "No go, right?"

Uncle Press turned to me and with the sincerity of a sage teacher imparting golden words of wisdom, he said, "There are no problems, only challenges."

"Well, if the challenge is to catch a subway at a station that's closed," I countered, "then I'd say that's a problem."

But not for Uncle Press. He casually reached toward the wall with one hand, grabbed one of the boards and gave it a yank. It didn't seem as if he pulled all that hard, but instantly four huge boards pulled loose in one piece, opening up an avenue into the darkened station.

"Who said anything about catching a subway?" he said with a sly smile.

He effortlessly dropped the large section of boards on the

stairs and stepped inside. I had no idea Uncle Press was that strong. I also had no idea why we were stepping into a closed subway station, at night, in the worst section of the city.

Uncle Press then poked his head back out. "Coming?"

I was half a breath away from turning, running up the stairs, and giving myself a crash course in motorcycle driving. But I didn't. Chances are the bike was already stolen anyway. I had no choice, so I followed him.

The station had been closed for a long time. The only light came from street lamps that filtered down through grates in the sidewalk. The soft glow cast a crisscross pattern against the walls that threw the rest of the station into darkness. It took a while for my eyes to adjust, but when they did I saw a forgotten piece of history. At one time this was probably a busy station. I could make out ornate mosaic tile work on the walls that must have been beautiful when new, but was now a mess of grimy cracks that looked like a giant, dirty spiderweb. Garbage was everywhere, benches were overturned, and the glass around the token booth was shattered. In a word, it was sad.

As I stood on top of the cement stairs, the derelict station began to show signs of life. It started as a faint rumble, that slowly grew louder. The station may have been closed, but the subway trains still ran. I saw the headlight first as it beamed into the opening, lighting up the track and the walls. Then the train came—fast. There was no reason to stop at this station anymore so it rumbled through like a shot, on its way to someplace else. For a brief moment I could imagine the station as it had looked in better days. But just as quickly, the image was gone, along with the train. In an instant, the place was deathly quiet again. The only sign that the train had been through was the swirling pieces of crusty paper caught in its slipstream.

I looked to Uncle Press to see if he were appreciating this forlorn piece of old New York history the same as I was. He wasn't. His eyes were sharp and focused. He quickly scanned the empty station looking for . . . something. I didn't know what. But I definitely sensed that he had just notched up into DefCon 2. He was on full alert, and it didn't do much to put me at ease.

"What?" was all I could think of asking.

He started quickly down the stairs. I was right after him. "Listen, Bobby," he said quickly, as if he didn't have much time. "If anything happens, I want you to know what to do."

"Happens? What do you mean happens?" This didn't sound good.

"Everything will be fine if you know what to do. We're not here to catch a train, we're here because this is where the gate is."

"Gate? What gate?"

"At the end of the platform are stairs that lead down to the tracks. About thirty yards down the track, along the wall, there's a door. It's got a drawing on it, like a star."

Things were going a little fast for me now. Uncle Press kept walking quickly, headed for the far end of the platform. I had to dodge around pillars and overturned garbage cans to keep up with him.

"You with me?" he asked sharply.

"Yeah," I said. "Stairs, door, star. Why are we—"

"The door is the gate. If for some reason I'm not with you, open the door, go inside and say, 'Denduron.'"

"Denda-what?"

"Den-du-ron. Say it!"

"Denduron. I got it. What is it, some kind of password?"

"It'll get us where we're going."

Okay, could this have been any *more* mysterious? Why didn't we just say "abracadabra" or something equally stupid? I was beginning to think this was all some kind of big old joke.

"Why are you telling me this?" I asked nervously. "We're going together, right?"

"That's the plan, but if anything—"

"Stop right there!"

Uh-oh. We weren't alone. We both stopped short and whipped around to see . . . a cop. Busted. For what I'm not sure. Trespassing, I guess.

"You boys want to tell me what you're doing down here?" The cop looked confident—no, cocky. He was a clean-cut guy, with a perfect khaki-colored uniform, a big badge, and an even bigger gun. At least it was still in its holster. Even though we were busted, I was actually kind of relieved to see him. To be honest, Uncle Press was starting to freak me out. I didn't think he'd gone off the deep end or anything, but this adventure was getting stranger by the second. Maybe now that a cop was here, he'd have to explain things a little better. I looked up to Uncle Press, expecting him to answer the cop. I didn't like what I saw. Uncle Press was staring the cop down. I could sense the wheels turning in his head, calculating. But what? An escape? I hoped not. The gun on the cop's hip looked nasty. There was a long moment of silence, like a standoff, and then somebody *else* joined the party.

"Can't you leave me in peace?"

We all shot a look over to a dark corner where a pile of garbage sat. At least it looked like a pile of garbage, until it moved and I saw that it was a homeless dude. Correction, he had a home and we were standing in it. He was a big guy, and I had no idea how old he was because all I saw was a tangle of hair and rags. He didn't smell so good either. He pulled himself to his feet and shuffled toward us. When he spoke, it was with a kind of slurred, crazy-speak.

"Peace! That's all I want! Little peace, little quiet!" he jabbered.

Uncle Press squared off and stood firm, glancing quickly back and forth between the cop and the homeless guy. He was thinking fast, calculating.

"I think you two better come with me," the cop said to us calmly. He wasn't rattled by the new arrival.

I looked to Uncle Press. He didn't move. The homeless guy got closer.

"Castle! This is *my* castle! I want you all to—"

"What?" asked Uncle Press. "What do you want us to do?" I couldn't believe he was trying to talk to this crazy guy. Then the platform started to rumble. Another subway train was on its way.

"I want you all to go away! Leave me alone!"

For some reason this made Uncle Press smile. Now I was totally confused. Whatever he was trying to calculate, he had his answer. He turned away from the homeless guy and faced the cop.

"You don't know this territory, do you?" he said to the cop.

Huh? What was that supposed to mean? Behind us, the light from the subway train started to leak into the station. It would be here in a few seconds.

The homeless guy started waving his arms for emphasis. "You! I'm talkin' to you! I want you out of my castle!" he yelled at the cop.

I was afraid the cop would pull his gun on the guy for his own protection. But he didn't. He just stood there, staring at Uncle Press. They looked like two gunslingers, each waiting for the other to blink. Then he gave a little smile and said, "What was your first clue?"

"The uniform. City cops in this territory wear blue, not khaki," answered Uncle Press.

This guy wasn't a cop? Then who was he? The train horn blared and the screeching of metal wheels on track grew closer.

"I'm flattered though," said Uncle Press calmly. "You came yourself."

Uncle Press knew who this guy was! The homeless guy kept getting closer to the cop, or whoever he was.

"That's it! That's it! If you don't git now I'm gonna—"

Suddenly the cop snapped a look to the homeless guy. It was a cold look that made me catch my breath. It stopped the homeless guy in his tracks. The cop stared at him with an intensity I'd never seen. The guy froze, and then began to shake like he had a fever.

The subway horn blared. The train was almost in the station.

The homeless guy looked as if he wanted to get away, but the cop's laserlike gaze had him locked in place. Then, something happened that I won't forget as long as I live, though I wish I could. The homeless guy opened his mouth and let out a horrifying, anguished cry. Then he ran. But he didn't run away, he ran for the tracks! The train entered the station in a blur, and this guy was running toward it.

"No! Stop!" I shouted. But it didn't matter. The homeless guy kept running . . . and jumped in front of the train!

I turned away at the last second, but that didn't stop me from hearing it. It was a sickening thud, and his scream was suddenly cut off. The train didn't even stop. I'll bet no one onboard knew what had happened. But I did and I wanted to puke. I looked to Uncle Press, who had a pained look. He wiped it away in the next instant and looked back to the cop, who stood there with a smug little smile.

"That was beneath you, Saint Dane," said Uncle Press through clenched teeth.

Saint Dane. That was the first time I heard the name. I had the grim feeling it wouldn't be the last.

The cop, Saint Dane, gave an innocent little shrug and said, "Just wanted to give the boy a taste of what is in store for him."

I didn't like the sound of that.

And then Saint Dane began to transform. I couldn't believe what I was seeing, but it was real. His face, his clothes, everything about him changed. I watched in absolute, stupefied awe as he became a different person. His hair grew long and straight till it was over his shoulders. His body grew until he was nearly seven feet tall. His skin became ghostly pale white. His clothes changed from the khaki brown cop uniform, to an all-black suit that vaguely reminded me of the Far East. But none of that mattered as much as his eyes. His eyes grew icy blue and flashed with an evil intensity that made me understand the sheer force of will he possessed that could make someone jump to their death in front of a speeding train.

There was only one thing that didn't change. He still had a gun. And I was surprised to discover, so did Uncle Press. With an expertise that made me feel as if he had done this sort of thing many times before, Uncle Press reached into his long coat and pulled out an automatic. Saint Dane went for his gun as well. I stood frozen. Ever hear the term "deer in the headlights"? That was me. I couldn't move. The next thing I knew I was on my butt on the floor. Uncle Press had shoved me down behind a wooden bench. We were protected from Saint Dane, but for how long?

Uncle Press looked at me, and in a voice that was way

more calm than the situation warranted, said one simple word, "Run."

"But what about—"

"*Run!*" He then dove out from behind the protection of the bench and started shooting. I stayed there long enough to see Saint Dane dive behind a pillar for protection. Uncle Press was a pretty good shot because the tiles on the pillar splintered and shattered as they were slammed with his bullets. It was clear what he was doing. He was keeping Saint Dane occupied to give me time to run. But run where?

"Bobby, the door!"

Right! The door with the star and the abracadabra. Got it. I started to crawl away, when Uncle Press called to me, "Watch out for the quigs!"

Huh? What's a quig? Bang! A tile shattered right near my head. Saint Dane was now shooting back, and I was the target! That's all the encouragement I needed. I ran. Behind me the sound of the blasts from the gun battle rang through the empty station. It was deafening. I ran past a pillar and *bang*! A bullet pulverized another tile. Pieces of flying tile stung the back of my neck. That's how close it was. I got to the far end of the platform and saw the stairs leading down to the tracks, just as Uncle Press described. I stopped for a second, thinking I'd have to be crazy to crawl down onto subway tracks. But the alternative was worse. It would be easier facing a subway train than that Saint Dane guy. So I took a quick breath and climbed down the stairs.

Once I was down on the tracks, the gun battle seemed far away. I still heard the occasional crack of a gun, but I was now more concerned about what was in front of me than behind. For a moment I thought I should go back and help Uncle Press, but jumping into the middle of a blazing gun battle didn't seem like such a hot idea. I could only hope that he could handle the situation. The only thing I could do was follow his instructions.

It was dark. I had to feel my way along the greasy wall to make sure I didn't accidentally step on the tracks. I'd heard about the infamous electric "third rail" that powered the trains. If you stepped on that thing, you were bacon. So I stayed as close to the wall as I could. Uncle Press said this door was about thirty yards down from the platform. I tried to picture a football field to visualize how far thirty yards was. It didn't help. I figured I'd just keep moving until my hand hit this mysterious door. My biggest fear was that I'd miss it and then . . .

Grrrrrr.

A grumble came from behind me. What was that? Was it a train? Was it power surging through the third rail? It was neither, because I heard it again and it came from a different direction.

Grrrrrr.

It sounded like growling. But I didn't think rats growled, so it couldn't be rats. Good thing. I hated rats. I looked around slowly and in the dim light, I saw something that nearly made my heart stop. Across the tracks, looking straight at me, were a pair of eyes. They were low to the ground and caught the light in such a way that it made them flash yellow. It was some kind of animal. Could this be the "quig" Uncle Press had told me to watch out for? Or maybe it was a wild dog. Whatever it was, it was big, and it had friends, because more eyes appeared. It was a pack of animals gathering, and their growling told me they weren't friendly. Gulp. My plan was to do everything I could not to threaten them. I decided to move very slowly, very deliberately and make my way toward the door and . . .

GRRRRRRR!

Too late! The entire pack of dogs, or quigs, or whatever they were leaped from the shadows and charged me! Suddenly the third rail didn't seem all that dangerous. I turned and ran. There must have been a dozen of them. I could hear their teeth gnashing and their claws scratching on the metal rails as they bounded over one another to get to me and . . . and I didn't want to think of what would happen if they did. I remember having a fleeting thought that maybe they'd hit the third rail and vaporize, but that didn't happen. My only hope was finding that door. It was so dark I kept tripping over stones and garbage and railroad ties and everything else down there, but I kept going. I had no choice. If I fell, I was kibble.

Then, like a lifeline to a drowning man, I saw it. The only light came from dirty, old bulbs strung above the tracks, but it was enough for me to see. Recessed into the cement wall was a small door with a faint star shape carved into the wood. This was it! I ran up to the door, only to discover there was no door handle. I couldn't open it!

I looked back and saw the pack of animals nearly on me. I only had a few more seconds. I leaned my weight against the door and it opened! The door opened in, not out! I fell inside and quickly scrambled back to close the door just as—*slam slam slam!*—the animals hit the door. I leaned back on the door, desperate to keep them out, but they were strong. I could hear their claws feverishly scratching at the wooden door. I couldn't keep them out for long.

Now, I'm going to stop my story here, Mark, because what happened next was far more important than those animals who were trying to get me. I know, hard to believe, but it was. Obviously the wild dogs, or the quigs or whatever they're called, didn't get me. If they had, I wouldn't be writing this.

Duh. I think what happened next was the single most important event of this whole nightmare. As scary and as strange as everything was that had happened up till then, there was no way I could have been prepared for what was waiting for me beyond that door.

While I was trying to keep the animals out, I looked at the space I'd just entered. What I saw was a long, dark tunnel. It wasn't big, maybe about six feet high. The walls were made of craggy, slate gray rock. It didn't look as if it were drilled out by a machine, either. It was crude, like somebody dug the tunnel with hand tools. I couldn't see how far the tunnel went back, because it dropped off into blackness. It could have gone on forever.

I didn't know what to do. If I tried to run down the tunnel, the instant I left the door the animals would burst in and be on me. Not a good move. I was stuck. But then I remembered what Uncle Press had told me. There was a word. He'd said to go inside and say this word. He'd said it would get us to where we were going. What was that word? Dennison? Dandelion? Dandruff? I couldn't really see how saying a hocus-pocus word could get me out of this predicament, but it was the only choice I had.

Then I remembered it. Denduron. It meant nothing to me, but if it was going to get me out of this, it would be my favorite word in the world. So I put my back to the door, planted my feet, looked into the dark tunnel, and shouted out:

"*Denduron!*"

Instantly the animals stopped beating against the door. It didn't sound like they ran away; they were just suddenly not there. I took a chance and stepped away from the door and . . . nothing happened. At least, nothing happened with the door. The tunnel was another thing altogether.

It started as a hum. It was low at first, but the frequency started to grow. I looked into the tunnel and watched in wonder as the walls started to twist and move. I was looking down the barrel of a huge, flexible, living pipeline. Then the walls started to change. They went from solid gray to clear! These craggy walls suddenly looked as if they were made of crystal, or diamonds. Light was everywhere, as if it were coming right from the walls themselves.

It was truly an amazing sight. So amazing that I didn't stop to wonder what it all meant. That's when I heard the music. It wasn't a recognizable tune or anything; it was just a bunch of soft, sweet notes that were all jumbled up. It was almost hypnotic. The mixed-up notes got louder and louder as if they were coming closer.

The thing that brought me back to myself was a strange sensation. I stood at the mouth of the tunnel and felt a tingling throughout my body. It wasn't horrible, just strange. The tingling grew stronger, and I felt an odd but unmistakable tug. I didn't realize it at first, but it soon dawned on me that I was being pulled into the tunnel! Some giant, invisible hand had gotten hold of me and was pulling me in! I tried to back away, but the force grew stronger. Now I started to panic. I turned and tried to find something, anything to grab on to. I fell down and dug my nails into the ground, but nothing worked. I was being sucked into this horrible tunnel, and there was nothing I could do to stop it.

This is the point. This is where my life changed. What happened next turned everything I had ever known, everything I had ever believed in, everything I had ever thought to be real, totally inside out.

I got sucked into the rabbit hole, Mark. And I was headed for Wonderland.

☻ SECOND EARTH ☻

Mark had to get out of this bathroom. The little stall was closing in on him. He tried to jump up off the seat, but a loop on his pack was caught on the flusher handle and all he managed to do was fall back and flush the stupid toilet. He pulled his pack free, jammed the parchment papers into it, then fumbled for the lock to spring himself from the stall. He was so flustered he couldn't even work the simple latch. Finally, mercifully, he slammed it back and threw the door open to see . . .

Standing there was Andy Mitchell. He was leaning casually against the wall, smoking a cigarette. "Jeez, you been in there a long time, Dimond. Everything come out all right?" Mitchell gave a stupid grin like this was a truly clever line.

Mark froze for a second, feeling as if he had been caught doing something wrong.

"I'm f-f-fine." When Mark got nervous, he had a little stutter. It wasn't a horrible thing, just something that came out under stress.

Mitchell expertly flipped his cigarette across the room and it landed in one of the urinals. Bull's-eye. Ordinarily Mark would have been grossed out by that, but his mind was on other things right now.

"It's cool," said Mitchell. "What you do in the privacy of the can is your business. What's in the pack?"

Mark clutched the pack to his chest as if it contained precious papers. Which in fact, it did. His mind raced. What was the one thing he could say that Mitchell would accept and not ask more questions? The answer was clear.

"P-Playboys."

Mitchell gave a lascivious grin. "You dog. Lemme see." He reached for the pack but Mark yanked it away and backed toward the door.

"S-Sorry. I'm late." Before Mitchell could say another word, Mark turned and ran from the room. He didn't know where he was going, but he ran anyway. The words from the pages kept running through his head. Could this story be true? This was the kind of stuff you saw in the movies or read in graphic novels. People made this stuff up for entertainment. It wasn't real.

He probably would have dismissed the whole thing as a work of fiction, except for the strange visitor he had the night before and the ring on his finger that made these pages appear on the bathroom floor. They were both real as can be. There was no logical explanation for what happened, so therefore all the normal rules of reality had to be tossed out the window. He needed to talk to Bobby. But if this story were true, Bobby was indisposed at the moment and not available for questioning.

It was nine thirty in the morning. Mark and Bobby should have been in geometry class. Of course, Mark wasn't there because he was too busy running frantically through the empty halls of Stony Brook Junior High like a nutburger. Somehow geometry didn't seem all that important right now. But he swung by the classroom anyway, praying that he'd find Bobby sitting at his desk.

Mark approached the door warily. He took a breath and looked in to see that Bobby's desk was empty. Not good. Mark didn't know where to turn. He had to talk to somebody, but who? He wanted to share what was going on, but more important, he needed confirmation that he wasn't totally out of his mind. That's when the answer came to him. There was one person who could verify part of the story. Courtney Chetwynde.

The gym classes at Stony Brook were normally segregated, boys from girls. The only time the classes were coed was for gymnastics when they had to share the apparatus. The rest of the time there was a huge, collapsible wall drawn between the boys' gym and the girls' gym. However, there was one other exception to the rule.

That was Courtney Chetwynde. When it came to team sports, Courtney didn't play with the girls. She was tall and strong, and the advantage she had over most girls was unfair. So even though it went against every rule of the school system and the county and the state, Courtney was allowed to play with the guys. No one complained, either. The girls were just as happy not to have to deal with her whupping up on them all the time. And after she proved herself to the guys, which took all of thirty seconds, they welcomed her. And they didn't cut her any slack either. In fact, most of the guys feared her. When Courtney played, it was full speed all the way around.

And her game was volleyball.

Wham! Courtney leaped high over the net and spiked the ball off the head of her poor opponent. The guy was stunned silly and Courtney landed gracefully before the ball hit the ground.

"Point break," she said with a smile. Courtney never showed mercy. It was her serve now and the ball was bounced to her.

"C'mon, C. C."

"Let's go!"

"Game point!"

Courtney had a killer serve and everyone expected this to be the final nail in the coffin. But as she walked to the service line, something caught her eye. It was Mark Dimond. The little guy was waving at her frantically from outside the gym door. As soon as he got her attention, he started motioning for her to come over. Courtney raised a finger as if to say, "Wait one second," but that made Mark wave even harder. He would not be denied.

Courtney frowned and tossed the ball to one of her teammates. "You serve," she said and headed toward Mark.

"What?" the teammate yelled in shock. "It's game point!"

"I know. Don't blow it."

The guys watched her in wonder for a moment, then turned back to the game with a shrug. Though none of them would admit it, the guys from the other team breathed a little sigh of relief.

Courtney headed straight for the door and threw it open to find Mark waiting in the empty hallway.

"This better be good," she said impatiently.

Mark waffled back and forth nervously, shifting his weight from foot to foot. Courtney watched him for a second and then said, "You have to pee?"

"N-No. I . . . I . . . it's about Bobby."

Courtney's gray eyes focused. "Where is he? Why didn't he play last night?"

Mark hesitated as if not wanting to ask the next question. But he did. "D-Did you guys make out at his house last night?"

Courtney stared at him, not exactly sure she heard what she thought she just heard. Then she blew a gasket. "That's what you got me over here for? He missed the biggest game of the year and . . . wait a minute . . . did Bobby tell you about us? I'll kill him!"

"C-Courtney . . . wait . . . it's not like that." Mark tried to stop her angry tirade, but Courtney was on a roll.

"I don't care who he is. He can't go around telling private stuff that—"

"Stop!" shouted Mark.

Courtney did, mostly because she was so surprised Mark had made such a bold move. That wasn't like him. They both looked at each other, not sure of where to go next.

Mark now had her attention and it was up to him to make the next move. When he spoke, it was slow and thoughtful. He didn't want to stutter and he didn't want to make a mistake. So he pushed his glasses back up on his nose and said, "I think something strange happened to Bobby. What went on between you two last night was a part of it. I . . . I'm sorry if it upsets you, but I've got to know. Did you two make out at his house last night?"

Courtney tried to read Mark. He was a shy guy and the fact that he'd ask a personal question like this was hugely out of character. Clearly there was more going on here than guys bragging to each other about getting to first base with a girl. She could see it in his eyes. Mark was scared.

"Yeah," she said. "We did. Where is he?"

"I . . . I don't know," he said, downcast. "I hope he's at his house. Will you come with me and talk to him?"

The two held eye contact for a long time. Courtney was trying to read Mark's thoughts, and Mark was praying that Courtney would come with him so he could share some of the burden of what he knew. Maybe she could even help him figure things out.

Courtney walked past Mark and gave him a simple, quick, "Let's go."

Courtney was now on a mission. She wanted to talk to Bobby. If she had to go to his house to find him, so be it. Mark was relieved that he now had an ally, but he had no idea how to tell Courtney what he knew, or if she'd believe him. For now though, he was happy just to have someone to talk to.

The Pendragons lived on a quiet cul-de-sac not far from school. It was lunchtime, so Courtney and Mark figured they could reach Bobby's house, get to the bottom of what was going on, and be back at school before anyone missed them. As they hurried up the sidewalk, Mark had to walk quickly to keep up with Courtney's long, purposeful strides. He wanted to tell her about the visitor he had had the night before, and the ring, and the parchment with Bobby's story, but he was afraid she'd dismiss him as a mental case. He had to choose his words carefully.

"Do you know Bobby's Uncle Press?" he asked cautiously.

"Yeah."

"Did, uh, did you see him last night?"

"Unfortunately. He's the guy who caught us making out."

Mark's heart sank. Not that it mattered if Bobby and Courtney made out, or that they were caught by Bobby's uncle. The problem was, Courtney's answer confirmed more of the story contained on the parchment papers. Mark feared that if some of the story were true, then maybe all of it was true. The thought made him sick.

They were nearly at Bobby's house now. Mark hoped that Bobby would be there to settle everything. He imagined walking up to Bobby, holding out the parchment paper, and seeing Bobby bust out laughing. Bobby would say it was all a goof and that he never expected them to think it was real. It was a prank, like Orson Welles's "War of the Worlds" radio broadcast that made everybody think the Earth was being invaded by Martians. That's what Mark was hoping for, but what they both saw in the next instant dashed that hope entirely.

Two Linden Place. That was the address. Mark had been there a thousand times. Ever since kindergarten they'd trade off playing at each other's house. Bobby's house was like his second home. Mrs. Pendragon called Mark her second son. That's why nothing could prepare him for what he was about to see. Courtney and Mark walked up the sidewalk that led to the split-rail fence that surrounded Bobby's front yard, and stopped cold. They both looked at 2 Linden Place, stunned.

"Oh my god," was all Courtney could whisper.

Mark couldn't even get that much out.

Two Linden Place was gone. The two of them stood together, wide-eyed, looking at a vacant lot. There were no signs that a house had *ever* been there. Not a single piece of wood, brick, stone, or blade of grass existed in the space. The ground was nothing but dirt. Mark looked to the huge maple tree where years before Mr. Pendragon had hung a tire swing for the boys. The tree was there, but there was no swing. Even the branch that had been rope-scarred by years of swinging was clean. No marks. Nothing.

Courtney broke first. "It's the wrong address."

Mark said softly, "It's not the wrong address."

Courtney wouldn't accept it. She stormed onto the empty lot. "But I was here last night! There was a sidewalk to the house right here! And the front door was here! And Bobby and I were standing . . ." Her voice trailed off. She looked to Mark with dread. "Mark, what happened?"

Now was as good a time as any. Even though he had no idea what had happened, seeing the empty lot confirmed his worst fears. Everything he had read on the pages from Bobby was true. He had more questions than he had answers, but he did have some answers, as strange as they were. He wanted to share them with Courtney. Knowing all this by himself was too tough. So he reached for his backpack and took out the yellow parchment papers.

"I want you to read something," he said. "It's from Bobby." He held out the pages to Courtney, who looked at them, then back to Mark. Reluctantly, she took the pages from him and sat down. Right there. Right in the middle of the empty lot at Two Linden Place, not far from the spot where she and Bobby shared their first kiss.

She looked down at the pages and started to read.

DENDURON

I thought my life was over. All that was left was to wait for the pain. Would it come fast and hit me hard? Or would it start at my feet and gradually work its way up my legs, over my body, and zero in right on my head in a brilliant, searing flash of agony before everything went dark?

I was voting for fast. But it didn't come fast. In fact it didn't come at all. There was no pain. I didn't die. Instead I found myself falling through this snaking tunnel. It was like sailing down one of those water-park rides. But the water-park rides are actually more violent than this. Now that it's over, I can look back on it and actually say it was kind of fun. But that's now. At the time, I was freaking out.

Once I realized I wasn't being sucked into some giant garbage disposal, I opened my eyes and looked around. It felt like I was moving fast.

Like I wrote before, the walls of the tunnel were craggy, like rocks. But they were translucent, too, as if they were crystal. The strange thing was, it wasn't a bumpy ride. I was flying along, feet first like on a playground slide, but it felt like I was floating. I couldn't feel the walls of the tunnel. There were many twists and turns, but I didn't get slammed against the walls or anything, like you do when you hit the turns on a water slide. It felt like I was floating on a magic carpet that knew exactly where it was taking me.

There were sounds, too. They were soft notes, like from a tuning fork. All different notes. Pretty notes. They were the same kind of notes I heard when the tunnel came to life, but much further apart. That's one of the reasons I could tell I was going so fast, because I was sailing past the notes. The sound would come up fast from up ahead, and then flash past me and disappear behind. It was a strange sensation.

I looked back the way I came and there was nothing but crystal tunnel for as far as I could see. I looked down between my feet and it was the same thing. Snaking tunnel. Infinity.

After a while I got used to it, sort of. There was nothing I could do to stop anyway, so I figured why fight it? Now, here's the freaky thing (as if everything up to this point wasn't freaky enough). I could look out beyond the crystal walls to see that it was dark out there. I figured that made sense, I was underground, after all. But when I looked harder, it seemed as if the blackness was broken up by thousands and thousands of stars.

I know, screwy, right? I had started in an underground subway and was going deeper underground from there, so how could I be looking at stars? But that's what it looked like. Why should this make any more sense than anything else?

I don't know how long I was flying. Three minutes? Three months? My normal sense of relativity had long since gone bye-bye. I'd given myself over to the experience and wherever it took me, and for how long, it just didn't matter.

And then I heard something different. It wasn't one of the soft notes that had been my guides on this bizarro journey.

This sounded, well, solid. It sounded craggy. It sounded like I was coming to the end of the line. I looked down between my feet and saw it. The end. The twisting, bright tunnel ended in darkness, and I was headed for it, fast. All around me the walls of the tunnel started to change. They were transforming from the translucent crystal back to the slate gray craggy rocks that I had seen at their start near the subway.

The panic returned. Was I about to hit the center of the Earth? Wasn't there supposed to be a core of molten magma there? Was this magical flight just a prelude to a fiery death? Whatever was going to happen, it was going to happen now. So I did the one and only thing I could think of to prepare myself for the end. I closed my eyes.

But the end wasn't a fiery crash at all. I got the same tingling feeling that I had felt at the mouth of the tunnel. Then there was a shower of sound. All the sweet notes I had been hearing gathered together the way they did at the beginning of my journey. I felt as if a heavy weight were pressing against my chest. The next thing I knew, I was standing up. The musical notes faded away. I had been gently deposited somewhere by the magic carpet.

It was strange having to support my own weight after having been weightless for the journey. I was like an astronaut returning from space who needed to get used to gravity again. I opened my eyes, looked back, and saw the tunnel. It looked exactly like the mouth I had entered back at the subway. It was gray and dark and stretched out to nowhere.

I had arrived safely. But where was I? Another subway station? In China maybe? I turned around to know where the tunnel had deposited me and saw that I was at the entrance to some sort of cave. Now that I had my wits back, I realized that I was cold. The sharp sound I had heard during the last stretch of my journey was a howling wind. Wherever I was, I wasn't underground anymore.

I took a few shaky steps away from the mouth of the tunnel and entered the cave. As I walked into this larger space, I noticed that the cave was marked by the same star symbol that was on the door in the subway. It was carved into the rock at about eye level. Weird.

I then saw light pouring in from an opening on the far side of the cavern. It was so bright that it made the rest of the cave seem pitch black. I was suddenly overcome by the feeling that I had been in the dark way too long. I wanted out, and that light showed me the way, so I stumbled along to reach it. When I got there, I knew that it was indeed the way out of the cave. The light also told me that it was daytime. How long had I been in that tunnel? All night? Or was it daytime in China? My eyes weren't accustomed to the light, so I had to cover them and squint. I stepped outside and immediately realized it was even colder out here. All I had on was my Stony Brook warm-up top over a T-shirt, so the wind cut through me instantly. Man, it was freezing! I took a few steps and looked down to see—snow! The ground was covered with snow! That's another reason it was so bright. The sun reflected off the snow and blinded me. I knew it wouldn't take long for my eyes to adjust, so rather than duck back into the cave to get warm, I waited till I could see. I wanted to know where I was.

After a few seconds, I gingerly took my hands away from my eyes. My pupils had finally contracted enough to let me see, and what was there waiting for me nearly knocked me off my feet.

I was standing on top of a mountain! And this was no small ski mountain like we go to in Vermont. This was like

Everest! Okay, maybe not that big, but I felt like I was on top of the world. Craggy snow fields stretched for as far as I could see. In the far distance, way down below, I could see that the snow gave way to a green, lush valley, but it was a long, steep trip between here and there.

One question kept running through my head. "Where in heck am I?" Good question, but I had no one to ask. So I turned to go back into the safety of the cave to get my act together and figure out some kind of plan. Just before I turned back I saw, scattered several yards away from the mouth of the cave, these yellowish, kind of smooth, pointed rocks about two feet high. They jutted up out of the snow like stalagmites. Or stalactites. I can never remember which is which. They stuck up and came to a sharp point. I had no idea what they could be, but the word "tombstones" kept creeping into my head. I shook that particularly morbid thought out of my brain and trudged through the snow back to the cave.

That's when I saw the strangest thing of all. The sun was just rising up over the rocks that formed the cave. But I had just been shielding my eyes against the sun that was shining from the other direction! How could that be? I looked behind me to see that there wasn't just one sun. There were three! I swear, Mark, there were three suns in opposite corners of the sky! I blinked, thinking my vision was just screwed up or something, but it didn't help. They were still there. My mind locked up. I didn't know what to think, but there was one thing I knew for sure—I wasn't in China.

I stood there on top of this mountain, all alone, sneakers getting wet in the snow, staring up at three blazing suns. I'm not ashamed to admit this, I wanted my mom. I wanted to be sitting in front of the TV fighting for the remote with Shannon. I wanted to be washing the car with Dad. I wanted to be shooting hoops with you. Suddenly the things I had taken for granted in life felt very far away. I wanted to go home, but all I could do was stand there and cry. I really did. I cried.

Then the sound came again, from inside the cave—the same jumble of musical notes that had sucked me into the tunnel and dumped me here. Someone else was coming. Uncle Press! It had to be! I ran back into the cave, overjoyed that I wasn't going to be alone anymore. But then another thought hit me. What if it wasn't Uncle Press? What if it was that Saint Dane guy? The last time I had the pleasure of hanging with that dude, he was shooting at us. And I gotta tell you, getting shot at isn't like what you see in the movies, or with Nintendo. It's real and it's terrifying. I could still feel the sting on the back of my neck where I got hit by the shattered pieces of tile.

I didn't know what to do, so I stopped in the middle of the big cave and waited. Whoever it was would be coming out of the tunnel. Would it be Uncle Press or Saint Dane? Or maybe those freakin' dogs that wanted to eat me. Wouldn't that be just perfect? Who was it going to be? Friend or foe?

"Bobby?"

It was Uncle Press! He walked out of the tunnel with his long leather coat flapping against his legs. I could have hugged him. In fact, I did. I ran over to him like a little kid. If this were a movie, I'd have been running in slow motion. I threw my arms around him with the feeling of pure joy and gratitude that I wasn't alone anymore, and that my favorite guy in the world wasn't shot dead by that Saint Dane guy. He was safe.

This feeling lasted for about, oh, three seconds. Now that my fear of impending doom was gone, reality came flooding back. And there was only one person responsible for my being here. Uncle Press. Someone I trusted. Someone I loved.

Someone who yanked me from home and nearly got me killed about eight times over.

I pushed away from him with a shove that was hard enough to knock him off his feet, because that's what I wanted to do. I wanted him to feel how angry I was. But as I saw before, Uncle Press was strong. It was like trying to push over a wall. All I managed to do was knock myself off balance and fall on my butt.

"What the hell is going on!" I shouted as I scrambled back to my feet, trying not to look like an idiot.

"Bobby, I know you're confused about—"

"Confused? Confused doesn't begin to cover it!" I stormed over to the mouth of the tunnel and screamed, "Denduron. *Denduron!*" I'd say *anything* to get out of there. But nothing happened.

"This is Denduron. We're already here," he said as if that were supposed to make sense.

"Okay then," I looked into the tunnel and screamed, "Earth! New York! The subway! There's no place like home!" I ran into the tunnel, hoping the magical notes would pick me up and fly me home. But nothing happened. I came back out and got right in Uncle Press's face.

"I don't care what this is about," I said with as much authority as I could generate. "I don't even care where we are. I care about going home and going home now! Take . . . me . . . home!"

Uncle Press just looked at me. He had to know how angry and scared I was, so I think he was trying to choose his next words carefully. Unfortunately no matter how carefully he chose his next words, there was no good way of saying what he then told me.

"Bobby, you can't go home. You belong here right now."

Boom. Just like that. I backed away from him, stunned. I

didn't know what to do. I didn't know what to think. I wanted to cry. I wanted to hit him. I wanted to reason with him. I wanted to wake up and find this was all just a horrible nightmare.

Uncle Press didn't say anything. He just watched me and waited for me to get my act together. But with all the confusing information that had been so rudely input into my poor little skull, all I could squeak out was a single, simple question. "Why?"

"I told you. There are people here on Denduron who need our help," he said slowly, as if to a little kid, which made me even more angry.

"But I don't know these people!" I shouted. "I don't care about them. I care about me. I care about getting me home. What is it about that, you don't understand?"

"I understand perfectly. But that can't happen," he said firmly.

"Why? What's so important about these people? And where is here anyway? Where is this . . . Denduron?"

"That's hard to explain."

"Try," I said. I was getting fed up with all the mystery.

Uncle Press sat down on a rock. I took that as a sign that he was ready to start helping me understand things.

"We are far from Earth, but this isn't a different planet in the sense you're thinking. It's a territory. Like Earth is a territory."

"Territory, planet, what's the difference? It's just words."

"No, it's not. If we had a spaceship and blasted off from here and went to the place where Earth is, it wouldn't be there. At least not the way you know it. When you travel through the flumes—"

"Flumes?" I repeated.

"That's how you got here. Through a flume. When you

travel to the territories through flumes, you're not just going from place to place, you're moving through space and time. I know that's hard to comprehend, but you'll get it."

I was not so sure I wanted to get it. Maybe it was better to stay ignorant. I looked at Uncle Press and for the first time it hit me that this guy wasn't the person I thought he was. I always knew he was a mysterious character, but now he was way more ozone-esque than I could ever have imagined.

"Who are you?" I asked. "Really, you're not a normal guy."

Uncle Press smiled and looked down. Somehow I had the feeling that this wasn't going to be an easy answer either.

"I'm your uncle, Bobby. But I'm also a 'Traveler.' Just like you are."

Another new word. "Traveler." I didn't want to be a "Traveler." I wanted to be Bobby Pendragon, point guard on the Stony Brook basketball team. But that life seemed pretty far away right now.

"So if we're not on Earth, why is it like Earth? I mean, I can breathe and there's snow and normal gravity and all."

He answered, "All the territories are pretty much like Earth, but not exactly."

"You mean, like the three suns here?"

"Good example."

"And those weird yellow stone things sticking up out of the snow?"

Suddenly Uncle Press got tense. "Where? Outside? How many are there?"

"Uhh, I don't know. Ten. Twelve."

Uncle Press shot to his feet and started pulling off his coat.

"We gotta go!" He dumped his coat on the ground and hurried to the far side of the cave where there was a pile of dried branches. He started pulling at them.

"What's the matter?" I said, confused and more than a little worried.

He turned to me and raised a finger to his lips to "shush" me. He continued pulling branches off the pile and spoke quietly, as if not wanting to be heard.

"Quigs," he said.

Uh-oh. Quigs. Not a new word. I hated that word.

"Those aren't quigs. Quigs are like dogs, right?" I asked hopefully.

"Depends on the territory," he whispered. "On Second Earth they're like dogs. Not here."

"So what are . . . quigs?" I asked, but I wasn't really sure I wanted to know.

"They're wild animals that are special to each territory," he explained. "Saint Dane uses them to keep the Travelers away from the flumes."

There was that name again. Saint Dane. Somehow I knew he'd factor back into this equation. But how was it possible for a guy to "use" a wild animal to do anything? Before I got the chance to ask, Uncle Press pulled off the last branches to reveal a jumble of fur and leather. Animal pelts. He then started taking off his shirt.

"We can't wear Second Earth clothes in this territory. Put these on," he said as he lifted up a nasty looking piece of skin.

"You gotta be kidding!" was all I could say.

"Don't argue with me Bobby. These will keep you warm."

"But—"

"No buts. Hurry!" He said this in a stage whisper. He really was afraid of the quigs. I figured I should be too, so I started taking off my clothes.

"Even my underwear?" I asked, horrified at what the answer would be.

"They don't wear boxers on Denduron," he said, which is exactly what I didn't want to hear. This was going to be uncomfortable. I followed Uncle Press's instructions and dressed in the leather and fur. There were even leather boots that were kind of soft, which was good because they didn't wear gold-toe sweat socks on Denduron either. As we took more of the clothing off the pile, something else was slowly revealed. I picked up one last furry pelt, and saw a two-man sled! It looked sort of like the sled you see in Alaska for sled dogs, but there was nothing modern about this thing. The runners were slats of wood, the sides were made of branches, the seats were woven out of some kind of cane, and the steering mechanism up front was fashioned out of huge antlers. Fred Flintstone would have been proud. But there was something else about this sled that made me nervous.

Lashed to either side were long, deadly-looking spears. The shafts were carved from smooth tree branches. The tips were made of hammered-out metal and looked surgical sharp. The tails had some sort of feathers attached for stability. As crude and low-tech as the whole rig was, these bad boys looked pretty lethal. They hung on either side of the sled like prehistoric sidewinder missiles, ready for launching.

"What about your gun?" I asked hopefully. "Can't we use that on the quigs?"

"There are no guns in this territory," he answered, then stopped working for a moment and looked me dead in the eye. "We can only use what the territory offers. That's important. Remember that. Okay?"

"Yeah, sure, whatever."

He then shoved something into my hand. It was a small, carved object that hung from a leather cord. It looked like . . .

"It's a whistle," he said, reading my thoughts. "Keep it handy."

I wanted to ask why, but at this point it didn't really matter. I just hoped Uncle Press was as good with a spear as he was with a gun, because a little whistle sure as heck wasn't going to protect us if things got hairy. I followed orders and put it around my neck.

"You ready?" he asked.

"No," was my usual reply. Though honestly, I was. I felt a little like a caveman, but the strange clothes fit me fine. Where they were too big, I tied them tight with leather straps the way Uncle Press showed me. I was actually pretty comfortable. The only bad thing was I really wished I could have kept my underwear. There was going to be some major league rash action going on here and they probably didn't have talcum powder on Denduron either.

Uncle Press started dragging the sled toward the light and the entrance of the cave. I helped him pull.

"When we get the sled in the snow, hop on and sit in back," he instructed. "I'll get us going and steer from the front. If we're lucky we'll be gone before the quigs wake up."

"What if we're not lucky?" was the obvious next question.

"We can't outrun them. Our only hope is to get one of them."

"Get? Define 'get.'"

He didn't. We were at the mouth of the cave. Uncle Press looked at me.

"I'm sorry for this, Bobby, I really am. All I can say is that sometime soon you'll understand why it had to be this way."

He said this with such conviction that I actually believed him. The thing was, I was afraid to believe him. Because if what he had been saying was true, I'd have no choice but to face whatever trouble lay ahead. And based on what had happened so far, it wasn't going to be fun.

"I hope you know how to drive this thing," I said.

"Hold on tight," was his answer. Yeah right, like I planned on waving my hands in the air like on a roller coaster. Give me a break.

We pulled the sled out of the cave and onto the snow. It took a few seconds for my eyes to adjust to the light again, but when I did, the first thing I saw were the ominous looking yellow pointed rocks sticking up out of the snow. In spite of Uncle Press's fear, I didn't see how these things could be dangerous. Uncle Press motioned silently for me to get in. He then went to the back and started pushing. For a clunky prehistoric bobsled, it moved pretty smoothly. In front of us was the field of yellow stones. I counted twelve of them, spread out over several yards. We glided closer to them with almost no sound. I looked to Uncle Press. He winked at me and put a finger to his lips as a reminder to be quiet. After a few more yards, we were right in the middle of them. Uncle Press maneuvered the sled carefully so as not to disturb anything. That's when we started to pick up speed. The slope was growing steeper. I looked ahead and suddenly I wasn't worried about the quigs anymore. We were about to set sail down a steep, craggy, boulder-strewn, snow-covered mountain on a rickety piece of wood that was held together by leather straps. Compared to that, how horrible could some two-foot-tall animals be?

I was about to find out.

We were nearly out of the field of yellow stones, when right in front of us the snow started to shake. There was only one stone left, but one was enough. Suddenly, right in front of us, the snow cracked and the yellow, pointed stone started to rise up. But it wasn't a pointed stone at all. This was a spike made of bone that stuck out of the back of the most hideous beast I had ever seen. The quig rose up out of the snow until its entire body was free. It looked like a huge, dirty-gray grizzly bear. But its head was giant, with fangs like a wild boar. Upper and lower. Spiky sharp. Its paws were oversized too, with claws the size of piano keys. Sharp piano keys. And its eyes looked like the eyes of the dogs in the subway. They were yellow, and angry, and focused on us.

Uncle Press maneuvered the sled around the quig and ran while he pushed, trying to get more speed.

"Get the spear!" he shouted.

I couldn't take my eyes off the beast. It reared up on its hind legs and let out a horrifying bellow that I thought would wake the dead. Or at least wake the other quigs. And that's exactly what happened. Behind us, the snow around the other yellow spikes started to boil. The rest of the quigs were waking up.

"Bobby move!"

Uncle Press jumped onto the sled and I snapped to my senses. I dove forward to grab one of the spears. We were moving faster now, bouncing over the snow. It was tough to keep my balance. I stayed low and leaned over the side to try and untie one of the two spears.

"Hurry please," came from the back. He was calm, but insistent. I turned to look and saw that there were now a dozen quigs behind us, shaking off the snow.

I shouldn't have looked. The trouble was I had almost finished untying the spear and just as I looked back, the sled hit a bump. Before I realized what was happening, the spear worked itself loose and fell off! I tried to grab it, but it was too late. It clattered to the snow, just out of my reach. Gone.

"The other one! Now!" shouted Uncle Press.

I dove across the sled to get the other spear. I grabbed it and held it tight with one hand while fumbling to untie it with the other. There was no way I was going to let this one get away. Finally I worked off the strap and the spear was loose.

"Got it!" I shouted. I fell back, holding it up for Uncle Press to grab. Once he had it I got to my knees and looked behind us. To my horror, I saw that the quigs were now charging. It was like a stampede of snarling, vicious bears that had us in their sights. I had no idea what one little spear could do against this deadly onslaught.

"Steer!" shouted Uncle Press. "Keep it steady."

I scrambled to the front of the sled and grabbed hold of the antlers. The sled responded perfectly. Whoever built this thing knew what they were doing. Still, Uncle Press was right. We weren't going fast enough to lose the quigs. They were getting closer.

The first quig was far ahead of the others, and it was getting dangerously close. I kept glancing back over my shoulder to see what was happening. Uncle Press was amazing. He stood on the sled, backward, with spear in hand. I was getting used to seeing Uncle Press pull off stunts like this. Nothing surprised me anymore. Like Captain Ahab hunting Moby Dick, Uncle Press waited for the quig.

"Come on. Come on. Little closer," he growled, taunting it.

The quig obliged. It was nearly on us. It charged forward with a bloodlust, ready to snap its jaws shut on Uncle Press.

"The whistle!" Uncle Press shouted back. "Blow it! Now!"

The whistle? What was a whistle going to do? But I wasn't about to argue. While keeping one hand on the steering antlers, I fumbled for the carved whistle around my neck. The beast was almost on Uncle Press. I finally managed to grab hold of the whistle, pulled the leather cord over my head, put it to my lips, and blew.

It didn't sound like anything. The thing must have been

designed like one of those silent dog whistles where the sound was so high pitched that only dogs could hear it. Well, only dogs and quigs, and quigs didn't like it. The beast suddenly opened its hideous mouth and let out another bellow that made the hair on the back of my neck stand out. It was a roar of pain, as if the high-pitched sound from the whistle was piercing its head.

That's when Uncle Press struck. He hurled the spear like an Olympic javelin thrower. The deadly missile flew straight at the quig and stabbed into its open mouth! The beast let out a choked howl as the spear plunged into the back of its throat. It stopped short, kicking up a spray of snow as it fell to its side. Blood spewed from its open mouth like a gruesome fountain.

It was disgusting. But not as disgusting as what happened next. The other quigs caught up with the first one, and rather than come after us, they all stopped and pounced on their fallen brother. It was a frenzy feed, like you see with sharks when there's blood in the water. I can still hear the sound they made as they tore into it, ripping it apart. The sound of flesh being torn away from cracking bones is not one I care to hear again. It was still alive, too. Its pained screams were horrifying. Thankfully, they didn't last long.

I took one last look back and wished I hadn't. At that moment one of the quigs looked up at us, and I saw that its mouth and fangs were smeared with the blood of its living meal. Now I knew what Uncle Press meant by "getting" one of the quigs.

"Look out!" he shouted.

I quickly looked ahead and saw we were seconds away from slamming into a boulder the size of a car. I turned the antlers, hard. The sled turned, but the back fishtailed into a skid that slammed us into the boulder. We kept moving, though the shock was so strong it threw Uncle Press to the floor of the sled. It nearly knocked me off too, but I grabbed the antlers in a death grip. It would take a heck of a lot more than a little bumping around to pry me loose. The only problem was, when I grabbed the antlers, I dropped the quig whistle. If the quigs came after us again, we'd be in deep trouble. We had no spears and no whistle. Why hadn't I left the strap around my neck?

Now we were going fast. The slope turned double-diamond steep. I could see that we were about to reach the tree line. Up to this point we only had to maneuver across snow and avoid some boulders. Now we were headed into a forest.

"I got it!" shouted Uncle Press. He had made his way to the front of the sled and I was only too happy to let him take charge.

"I don't suppose we've got brakes?" I shouted.

"I wish," came the shouted answer. Bad answer. This wasn't a nicely groomed ski slope. Oh, no. We were headed full-tilt boogie into the trees. The only thing that was going to stop us now was something solid. I didn't want to find anything solid. That would hurt.

"Right! Lean right!" shouted Uncle Press. I did and he skirted us around a tree. "Stay with me! Watch where we're going! Left!" he shouted.

It was like riding on the back of his motorcycle. We both had to lean into the turns to help make them. But the motorcycle had brakes and we didn't have to drive it through a minefield of trees. This was terrifying. We were rocketing down on a rickety bobsled through a slalom course of rock-solid pine trees.

We flew past trunks with inches to spare. Left, right, right again. We were going too fast for Uncle Press to tell me which way to lean. I had to look ahead and anticipate what turns he was going to make. Branches slashed at our faces. We were so close to some trees I could hear them as we sailed past. The further down we dropped the more dense the forest became.

"There's a clearing ahead!" he shouted. "When we hit it, I'm going to turn sharp right. Hopefully we won't flip."

Yeah, hopefully. And hopefully we won't launch ourselves into a rolling tumble that'll land us into a tree! Not that I had a better idea.

"When I make the turn, lean hard right!" he yelled. "We're almost there."

I looked ahead and saw it. Through the trees there was a field of white. That must be the clearing. But we still had a lot of trees between here and there, and we were still moving fast. Left, left, right. A few more turns and we'd hit the clearing.

"We're gonna make it!" I shouted.

We didn't. Our left runner hit a snow-covered root that kicked us up on our right side, but we kept going. Now we were on one runner and out of control. There were only a few trees between us and the safety of the clearing when we crashed. The sled hit a tree and spun us around. The force of the collision was huge. I mean, it rocked me. But I stayed with the sled. Uncle Press wasn't so lucky. He was ejected.

And I kept going. The sled fell down off the right runner and now ran flat again, but I was lying in the back, miles from the controls. I was nearly at the clearing and for an instant I thought I'd make it. But then the sled hit a rise and suddenly I was airborne! If there was any time to abandon ship it was now, so I bailed. The sled went one way and I went the other. For a moment I was airborne, and then I beefed. Hard. The snow wasn't as deep anymore, so instead of a nice cushy snow landing, I hit hard ground. It knocked the wind out of me and slammed my head against the ground. The world became a spinning mass of white. I couldn't think. I couldn't breathe. But I wasn't moving any more and that was good.

I'm not sure how long I lay there because I was drifting in and out of consciousness. Then I remember hearing something odd. It was far off at first, but it was coming close very fast. I feared that the quigs had finished their lunch and caught up with us for dessert, but this didn't sound like them. This sounded like horses. Galloping horses. More than one.

And then I heard Uncle Press calling to me. "Bobby! Bobby, if you can hear me, don't move. Stay where you are! The Milago will find you. They'll help you."

What did he mean? What were the Milago? I had to see what was happening. I rolled over on my side, which really hurt by the way. I must have smashed a couple of ribs in the fall. I didn't stand up though. I'm not sure I could have, even if I wanted to. My head hurt and I was really dizzy, but I clawed at the snow and crawled toward Uncle Press's voice. There was a little rise of snow, probably the one that launched me into space, and I painfully crawled toward it on my belly. When I got to it, I cautiously peeked over the top.

I was relieved to see Uncle Press standing on the edge of the clearing, not far from me. He was okay. Come to think of it, he looked a lot better than I felt right then.

To the far right of the clearing, closing fast on him, were the horses I heard. And there were riders on the horses, four of them. They looked to me like ancient knights. They wore black armor made of heavy leather. They had black leather helmets with faceplates as well. Even their horses had similar leather protection. They all looked the same, as if the armor were some kind of uniform. I also saw that they had swords. They looked to me like something out of the Knights of the Round Table.

Uncle Press gave them a friendly wave as they circled him.

"Hello!" he called out in a friendly voice. "How are you this fine day?"

We weren't in America. We weren't even on Earth. Why did Uncle Press think these guys spoke English?

"Buto! Buto aga forden," shouted one of the knights brusquely. I was right. They didn't speak English.

"No!" answered Uncle Press. "I am hunting rabbits. For my family."

"Soba board few!" barked another knight. This was weird. They were speaking some bizarro language and Uncle Press was speaking English, yet they both seemed to understand each other. I, on the other hand, understood nothing. What else is new?

The first knight pointed a finger at Uncle Press and started shouting, "Buto! Buto aga forden ca dar!" This looked bad. Whatever "Buto" meant, I didn't think it was a compliment. Uncle Press raised his arms innocently and shrugged, as if he didn't know what they were talking about.

"No!" he said with a smile. "Why would I spy on Kagan? I'm a miner who only cares about feeding his family."

Spy? Miner? Kagan? My head started to throb.

And then things turned sour. The first knight pulled a nasty-looking bullwhip off his saddle and slashed it at Uncle Press! Whap! It wrapped around his arm. Uncle Press let out a yelp of pain and the knight yanked on the whip, pulling him to his knees.

I tried to get up and run to him, but the pain in my side shot through my body and I lost my breath again. My head started to spin. I was seconds from losing consciousness. But I kept my eyes riveted on Uncle Press. Two of the other knights took ropes from their saddles and lassoed him like a steer in a rodeo. Then they kicked their horses and took off across the field, dragging Uncle Press along on his back!

That's the last thing I saw—these laughing, black knights on their horses dragging my uncle across the snow. As they disappeared into the woods, I lost it. My head was spinning out of control. I was going down. The last thing I remember thinking was that what seemed like only a few hours before, I had been standing in my kitchen throwing the tennis ball for Marley to fetch. And I hoped somebody remembered to take her out for her nighttime walk.

Then everything turned white, and I was gone.

END OF JOURNAL #1

◉ SECOND EARTH ◉

Mark Dimond paced nervously as Courtney Chetwynde sat on her backpack in the empty lot at Two Linden Place, reading the parchment pages. He wanted her to read faster. He wanted her to look up and tell him that everything was okay. He wanted her to find a clue somewhere in the pages that proved none of this could be real. But most of all, he wanted to turn around and see that Bobby's house was back where it should be.

Courtney took her time reading the pages and when she finally finished she looked up at Mark with a curious expression.

"Where did you get this?" she asked with no emotion.

Mark dug into his pocket and pulled out the strange ring with the gray stone. After what happened in the boys' bathroom, there was no chance he was going to put the cursed piece of jewelry back on his finger.

"It came from this thing," he said while holding the ring out gingerly. "It was like, alive. There were flashing lights and it got big and opened up this hole and there was a sound and suddenly the pages were just . . . there."

Courtney looked at the ring, looked back at the parchment papers. Mark could tell the wheels were turning in her head as she tried to make sense of everything he had just thrown at her. Finally, she stood up and tossed the parchment pages over her shoulder like yesterday's news.

"Gimme a break," she said with a sneer.

"Hey!" squealed Mark as he frantically ran after the pages. There was a slight wind that scattered them across the empty lot so he had to scramble before they blew away.

"What do you guys think I am?" Courtney barked. "Some kind of idiot?"

"N-no! It's n-not like—" Mark's stutter was back.

"You tell Bobby Pendragon that I'm not dumb enough to go for such a stupid joke."

"B-but—"

"What happens next? Am I supposed to get all worried and tell everybody that Bobby missed the game last night because he got flumed into another dimension and had to battle cannibal beasts and unless he rescues his uncle from some dark knights on horseback he might miss the next game too?"

"W-well, yeah."

"Oh yeah, that's perfect," shouted Courtney. "Then Bobby jumps out and yells, 'Surprise!' and I have to move to another state because no one will ever let me forget that I was dumb enough to fall for the most ridiculous practical joke in the history of practical jokes. I don't think so!"

With that, she snatched up her pack and started to walk away.

"Courtney, stop!" shouted Mark.

Courtney wheeled back to Mark, throwing him a look of total disdain. When you get a look like that from Courtney Chetwynde, it's really hard not to quickly dig a hole and bury yourself in it. It took every bit of strength for Mark to go on. When he spoke, it was sincere and without a trace of a stutter.

"It's hard for me to believe it too," he began. "But this isn't a joke. I don't know if everything in those pages is true, but I've seen some things that I can't explain. I swear I have. And it's enough to make me believe something totally bizarre happened to Bobby."

Courtney didn't move. Was she starting to believe him? Or was she just waiting for him to finish so she could tell him, again, what an idiot she thought he was?

Mark took the chance and continued, "I know it's a lot to swallow. But if this is all just some big old practical joke, then where's Bobby's house?"

Courtney looked past Mark to the empty lot. Mark wondered what she was thinking. Was she remembering how she had come to this spot last night, gone inside a house that was no longer here and kissed Bobby Pendragon?

"I'm scared, Courtney," added Mark. "I want to know what happened, but I don't think I can figure it out by myself."

Courtney stared at Mark for a moment more, as if trying to read his mind. She then walked past him to stand in the center of the empty lot. She did a slow 360 around to take everything in. But there was nothing to take in. There wasn't a shred of evidence to show that a family of four, with a dog, had lived there not twelve hours before. Courtney was the kind of person who was always on top of things. It didn't matter if it was a game of volleyball, or an argument with her parents, Courtney always knew how to handle difficult situations and turn them to her advantage. But this was different. She couldn't control this situation because she didn't know the rules. Yet.

"All right," she said thoughtfully. "We can't go crazy trying to figure out everything at once. It's just too . . . too much." She was half talking to Mark and half thinking out loud. "I don't know anything about quigs or Travelers or plumes—"

"Flumes," he corrected her.

"Whatever," she snapped back. "That's all fantasy to me. But this house . . . this house being gone is about as real as it gets. If we can find out what happened to the house, maybe that'll point us toward Bobby."

Mark smiled for the first time in forever. He had an ally, and it was somebody he knew could make things happen.

"Where do we start?" he asked.

Courtney started to walk toward the street with her long, bold strides. She was now on a mission. "We've got to find his parents. No way they disappeared too."

"Excellent!" shouted Mark. They were moving forward.

Courtney suddenly stopped, whirled around, and went nose to nose with Mark.

"And I swear, Dimond," she said while jabbing him in the chest with a strong finger. "If you're pulling my chain about all this, I'll slam you so hard you'll have to reach up to tie your shoes."

"So noted," gulped Mark.

Courtney continued on toward the street. Mark followed while stuffing the parchment papers into his pack. As he was about to step onto the sidewalk, he took one last look back at the empty space where his best friend's house used to be. He could understand where Courtney's disbelief was coming from. The story contained in the parchment papers was tough to believe, even though some of it had proven to be true. At least the part about Courtney, that is. That was the easy part. The rest was just plain incredible. And there was a mystery too. Nowhere in the pages did Bobby say anything about his house disappearing. If everything had played out the way the pages said, when he and his uncle Press took off on the motorcycle, the house was still here. Something happened to it after they were gone, which meant Bobby didn't know that his house was history. Oddly enough, this gave Mark some hope. Courtney was right. If they could figure out what happened to the house, then maybe they could make some sense out of what happened to Bobby.

There was another thought that nagged at the back of Mark's mind, and it was one he didn't feel comfortable sharing with Courtney. At least not yet. It had to do with the ring, and the fact that Bobby sent the pages to him. The question that Mark kept asking himself was: "Why?" If all that Bobby wrote about were true, and he was on a most incredible adventure, then why would he take the time to write down everything that happened and send it to him? Sure, they were best friends, and Bobby wrote that he hoped the pages would someday prove that he wasn't making everything up. But that didn't seem to be enough to justify doing it. Mark felt that somehow there was an important reason that he should know about what was happening to Bobby.

For now, he was happy just to be on the road to making sense of what had happened to his best friend. The logical place to start would be to find Bobby's parents, and ask them what happened to the house. So with that positive thought in mind, Mark turned his back on the empty lot and ran to catch up with Courtney. They were both sure that their questions would soon be answered, they would find Bobby, and life would return to normal in time for school the next day.

They couldn't have been more wrong.

Their investigation first took them to Mark's house. They figured it would be easier to track down Bobby's parents over the phone than by racing around town on their bikes, or by taking the bus. Mark lived on a cul-de-sac about a half a mile from Bobby's house. Rather, half a mile from where Bobby's house used to be. Of course, when he left for school that morning Mark hadn't anticipated that the fabulous Courtney Chetwynde would be paying a visit to his bedroom that afternoon. The odds of that happening were roughly the same as . . . well . . .

his best friend being launched across the universe.

"Wait here," commanded Mark as he ran into his bedroom and closed the door in Courtney's face. Courtney rolled her eyes, but respected his privacy.

Mark took one look at his room and wanted to faint. He wasn't sure which was the most embarrassing: the dirty underwear and socks that were scattered everywhere; the cartoon superhero posters that he hadn't gotten around to taking down; the *Sports Illustrated* bikini posters that he had just gotten around to putting up; or the rancid smell that seemed to permeate the whole squalid mess. Mark went into overdrive. He threw open a window, scooped up an armload of the offending Fruit Of The Looms and jammed as many as he could fit behind the pillow of his unmade bed.

Then the door opened and Courtney charged in.

"Look, I've got two older brothers. It's not possible to gross me out—" She took a look at the room and stopped dead in her tracks. Mark stood frozen holding a bunch of dirty gray socks that in an earlier life had actually been white. Courtney sniffed the air and had to try hard not to gag. "I was wrong. I am totally grossed out," she managed to say. "Did something die in here?"

"S-sorry," he said in complete embarrassment. "It n-needs a little air."

"It needs fumigation. Open another window before I pass out," gagged Courtney.

Mark tossed his bunch of socks out of one window and quickly threw open another. Courtney surveyed the room, stopping in front of two posters on the wall. One was a colorful anime superhero cartoon, the other was a gorgeous girl lying on a tropical beach in a leopard-print thong.

Courtney said, "Looks like you've got kind of a conflicted puberty versus playschool thing going on."

Mark stood in front of the posters, blocking them. "Can we f-focus on the important problem, please?" he said curtly.

Courtney got the message. Now wasn't the time to be giving Mark grief. She sat down at his desk as he quickly cleared off the F-117 model plane he had been building in order to give her room to work.

"Phone book," she said. All business.

Mark went to his closet in search of one. Courtney found a scratch pad of paper and opened a desk drawer to look for a pen. Big mistake.

"Well, I solved one mystery," she announced.

"What?" asked Mark hopefully.

Courtney reached into his drawer and pulled out a revolting-looking block of yellow ooze.

"I know why your room smells like a shoe," she said, holding out a rotten piece of moldy cheese as if it were diseased. It probably was. Mark instantly grabbed it.

"Hey, I've been looking for that," he exclaimed.

Courtney rolled her eyes and grabbed the phone book Mark had found. The plan was to call Bobby's parents at work. Mr. Pendragon was a writer for the local newspaper and Mrs. Pendragon was the assistant librarian in town. Courtney found both numbers and called both places. Unfortunately she got the same disturbing information each time. Neither of Bobby's parents had shown up for work that day and neither had called in to say why. That was bad. She then called Glenville School where Bobby's sister, Shannon, was in the third grade. Again, she got the same answer. Shannon hadn't come to school that day. After hearing this last bit of information, Courtney slowly put the phone back down in the cradle and looked to Mark.

"They're *all* missing," she said soberly.

Mark quickly grabbed the phone and dialed a number.

"Who are you calling?" asked Courtney.

"I'm dialing Bobby's number." He did, and what he got was a recorded message from the operator that said: "The number you have reached is not in service." Mark slammed the phone down.

"That's impossible!" he shouted. "I just called him yesterday! A whole family can't just vanish!"

On a hunch, Courtney took the phone book and flipped through it. She got to the "P" section and searched for "Pendragon." She checked, double-checked, triple-checked and then announced: "It's not here. Their name isn't here."

Mark grabbed at the book and looked for himself. Courtney was right; there was no listing for "Pendragon."

"Is their number unlisted?" asked Courtney.

"No," answered Mark quickly. This seemed to upset him more than anything else. "And I'll tell you something else. Bobby and I looked up his number in this very book about a year ago. I was goofing around and next to 'Pendragon' I wrote 'Sucks.' I know, lame joke, but I did it. And now it's n-not there. It's n-not erased, it's n-not cut out, it's just . . . not there, like it was never there!"

This had gotten out of hand. A whole family was missing. There was only one thing to do. They had to report it to the police. This wasn't the kind of thing they wanted to do over the phone, so the two of them headed right for the Stony Brook Police Station.

Stony Brook was a little town in Connecticut that wasn't exactly a center for criminal activity. There was an occasional robbery, or fight, but most of the time the Stony Brook Police Department kept itself busy by making sure people obeyed the traffic laws and cleaned up after their dogs.

When Courtney and Mark walked into the police station, they weren't exactly sure what they were going to say. They decided that they would stick to the obvious facts, which were that Bobby and his family were nowhere to be found and that their house was gone. Telling them about the ring and the parchment and the wild story that supposedly came from Bobby would be a bit much to throw at them at first. They spoke to a policeman by the name of Sergeant D'Angelo sitting behind the large front desk. Courtney did the talking. Mark was too nervous. She explained how Bobby hadn't shown up for the game last night and didn't come to school today. She told him how they had gone to the Pendragon's house to find that it wasn't there anymore, and none of the other family members were where they should have been. Sergeant D'Angelo listened to everything they had to say and took notes on a form. Courtney had the strange feeling that the policeman didn't believe a word they were saying, but he had to go through the motions because it was his job. After he finished the form, he walked away from the front desk and went to his computer. He clicked away on the keyboard, read the screen, and occasionally glanced back to Mark and Courtney. Was he scowling? Finally, he stood up and came back to the desk to face them.

"Look kids," he said with a frown. "I don't know what you're trying to pull here, but you're wasting my time and taxpayers' money."

Mark and Courtney were stunned.

"What are you talking about?" asked Courtney. "Didn't you listen? A family is missing. Isn't that the kind of thing the Stony Brook Police should be worried about?"

This didn't impress Sergeant D'Angelo. "Pendragon, right?" he said. "Two Linden Place?"

"That's r-right," answered Mark.

"I just went through the town registry," said the sergeant with force. "There is no family by that name living in Stony Brook. There is no house on Two Linden Place. There has never been a house on Two Linden Place. So the only possible explanation is that you're either pulling some kind of joke, or you're talking about a family of ghosts and no, the Stony Brook Police are not interested in tracking down a family of ghosts!"

With that, he tore up the form he was filling out and tossed it in the wastebasket. Courtney was livid. She was all set to leap over that desk, grab the smug cop and force him to go to their school where everybody knew Bobby. She might have done it too, except for one thing.

The ring in Mark's pocket started to twitch.

Mark's heart instantly leaped into his throat.

Courtney leaned closer to the desk, looked up at the cop and said angrily: "I don't care what your computer says. I know the Pendragons! Bobby is my—"

Mark grabbed Courtney by the hand and pulled her back with such force it actually made her stop talking.

"We gotta go," was all Mark could say. In his pocket, the ring was starting to shake harder.

"No way! I'm not going until—"

"Courtney! Let's go!" He shot her a look that was so intense she got the message. She didn't know what was going on, but she knew Mark was serious.

Mark backed toward the door, pulling Courtney with him. But Courtney wanted the last word with D'Angelo.

"I'm coming back!" she shouted. "And you better hope those people are okay or it's going to be on your head!"

Mark pulled her out of the door, leaving Sergeant D'Angelo alone. The policeman sniffed, shook his head, and went back to reading the newspaper.

Outside of the station, Mark pulled Courtney into an alley to get away from the main street. Though Courtney was bigger and stronger than Mark, he would not be denied.

"What is your problem?" she shouted.

Mark dug into his pocket and pulled out the ring.

"This," he said while holding it out in front of him.

The gray stone had already turned crystalline and rays of light once again shot from its center. Courtney watched in wonder as Mark placed the ring on the pavement and took a few steps back. The ring twitched, flipped over, and started to grow.

"Oh . . . my . . . god." Courtney breathed, dumbfounded.

Within the growing circle was a black portal where the road should have been. From this portal came the musical notes that Mark had heard in the boys' room at school. The sparkling lights flashed against the walls of the buildings and even though it was daytime, they shone so brightly that Courtney and Mark had to shield their eyes. The musical notes grew louder, the stone gave off one last blinding flash, and that was it. The lights ended, and the music stopped.

"Is that it?" asked Courtney.

Mark walked cautiously over to the ring. It sat on the road, right where he had left it. It was once again back to normal size and the stone had returned to its original gray color. But something else was there too. Lying next to the ring was another scroll of parchment paper tied with a leather cord. Mark reached down, picked it up gingerly, and turned to Courtney.

"Mail's in," was all he could say.

DENDURON

Uncle Press is going to die tomorrow.

So much has happened since I wrote to you last, Mark. It's been strange, scary, confusing and sometimes even sort of—dare I say it—fun. But the bottom line is, Uncle Press is going to die tomorrow.

Right now I'm sitting in a small cavern that must be two hundred feet underground. I'm writing this by the light of a candle because there's no electricity. I'm looking around and all I see are rocks. Tons and tons of black rocks that look as if they might collapse on my head at any second. I better stop thinking about it because I'm freaking myself out. The cavern isn't going to collapse. I'm safe here, at least for now. The guy who is in trouble is Uncle Press.

I'm telling you this because I need your help. I'm going to ask you to do something for me that is pretty dangerous. Under normal circumstances I'd never ask you to do something like this, but it's the only thing I can think of that might help me save Uncle Press. I'd understand if you didn't want to do it, but before you decide I want to tell you all that's happened since the last time I wrote you. Once you know everything, then you can decide.

I ended my last letter right after Uncle Press was dragged off by Kagan's knights, and I blacked out. Have you ever blacked out, or fainted? It's not like falling asleep at all. When you fall asleep, you never know the exact moment it happens. You just kind of lie there, waiting, and the next thing you know, bang, it's morning. But when you pass out, you can feel yourself slipping away. It's not a good feeling. Waking up afterward isn't much better. There's a moment where you're not really sure where you are and what's going on, then suddenly everything rushes into focus and you're snapped back to reality. It's a pretty rude experience.

Of course, in this case, even after I snapped back to reality I still didn't know where I was and what was going on. The first thing I saw was a face. A girl's face. For a second I thought it was Courtney. But once my brain started to click I realized this girl didn't look anything like Courtney. She was totally beautiful. (Whoa, that sounded bad. Not that Courtney isn't totally beautiful, but this girl was, well, different.) I'd say she was my age, maybe a little older. She had dark skin and eyes that were so brown they looked black. Her hair was dark too. It was tied in a long, tight braid that reached halfway down her back. She wore the same kind of weird leather skins that Uncle Press had made me put on, but on her they looked pretty good because she had an amazing body. She had to be an athlete or something. Seriously, this girl was cut like an Olympic sprinter. No fat, all muscle, totally awesome. And she was tall. Maybe a few inches taller than me. If I saw her at home I'd guess she was of African descent. But this wasn't home.

I lay flat on my back as she looked down at me with absolutely no expression. I couldn't tell if she was glad I was alive, or getting ready to finish the job the quigs started and kill me once and for all. We stayed that way for a few seconds, with neither of us moving. Finally I swallowed to make sure my voice would work and croaked out, "Where am I?" No points for originality but hey, I wanted to know.

The girl didn't answer. She stood up and walked to a table that had a couple of wooden bowls. She picked one up and held it out for me, but I didn't take it. Who knows what she was trying to give me? It could have been poison. It could have been blood. It could have been some vile-tasting liquid that they consider a delicacy here, but would make me puke.

"It is water," she said flatly.

Oh.

I took it. I was thirsty. The girl then walked over to the door and stood with her arms folded. I took a drink and looked around to get my bearings. I was inside what looked like some kind of hut. It wasn't big, maybe the size of my living room at home. There was only one room with six walls. Is that a hexagon? The walls were built of stones that were held together by dried mud. There were a few holes which passed for windows and one big opening for a door. The ceiling rose to a center point and was made of interwoven tree branches. The floor was dirt, but it was so hard it might as well have been concrete. I was lying on a low bench-thingy that was made out of lashed-together logs. The top was woven out of straw or something. It was comfortable enough, but I wouldn't want to spend a whole night there. There was a bunch more of these beds lined up in the hut, which made me think this might be some kind of hospital. It made sense. After what I'd been through, I belonged in a hospital.

It was like I had stepped into a time machine and been sent back a few thousand years to an age when people built their world out of anything they could get their hands on . . . and didn't care much for personal hygiene. Oh, yes, did I mention the place smelled like a locker room for goats? It made me wonder if the mortar holding together the stone walls was really mud, or something disgusting that would make me retch if I knew what it was.

I looked over at this amazing girl. She stood there, staring back. Was she a friend? An enemy? A guard who was standing watch until one of those knight guys came in to drag me off like they did Uncle Press? A million thoughts ran through my head, but one thought stood out above all others.

I had to pee.

The last time I took a leak was before Courtney showed up at my house. When was that? A million years ago? Judging by how my bladder felt, it was at least that long. So rather than lie there and wet my leather pants, I started to get up.

"Hey," I said. "I gotta—"

As soon as I moved, the girl flew into attack mode. She instantly crouched down and whipped out a wooden pole that must have been strapped to her back. It was about five feet long and well-worn from use. She held the weapon steady with both hands, and I saw that each end was stained shiny black from hitting things I didn't even want to imagine. Scarier still were her eyes. They were dead-set focused on her target, which happened to be me.

I froze. No way I was going to stand up or she would have whacked me so fast my head would hit the ground before my feet did. I didn't want to move at all for fear of setting her off. We both stayed that way, waiting for the other one to make the next move. One thing I knew for sure, it wasn't going to be me. And if she took a step toward me, I'd be off that bench and out the window headfirst.

Then a voice called from outside, "Buzz obsess woos saga!" At least that's what it sounded like; I'm not exactly sure of the spelling. Someone stepped in through the door. It was a woman dressed in the same crusty leather clothes that apparently were fashionable in this neighborhood. She actually looked like an older version of the girl who was about to brain me. But as powerful as this woman looked, there was something about her that made me feel as if she could possibly be my savior. I think it was her eyes. They were kind eyes. No anger there at all. When she looked at me, I knew it was going to be okay. She looked familiar, though I can't imagine where I could have met her before. She gave the younger girl a stern look and the girl reluctantly responded by putting her weapon away. Whew. Disaster averted.

The woman then turned to me and said, "Forgive my daughter. She often takes herself too seriously."

New info. This was a mother-daughter team. I guess I shouldn't have been surprised. They looked alike. I wondered what Dad looked like. He must have been a linebacker. I still didn't feel comfortable moving. This woman seemed cool, but after what I'd been through I wasn't taking any chances. She walked up to me, knelt down by the bench and gave me a kind smile.

"My name is Osa," she said softly. "My daughter's name is Loor."

"I . . . I'm Bobby and I'm not from here," was all I could think of saying.

With a smile, Osa said, "Neither are we. And we know exactly who you are, Pendragon. We've been waiting for you."

Whoa! She knew who I was! A million thoughts flashed through my brain, but one in particular jumped out. If they knew who I was, then why was amazon girl over there ready to beat my brains out? I figured I better not ask. I didn't want to tick Loor off. She might decide to yank out her stick and start wailing on me anyway.

"How do you know me?" I asked.

"From Press, of course," she answered. "He has been telling us about you for quite some time."

That's right! Now I remember where I'd seen her before. Uncle Press had brought her to our house. We had met before! I remember thinking how beautiful she was, and how odd it was that she didn't speak. The mystery was over: She was a friend of Uncle Press's. But that realization was quickly replaced with another. Man, I'd almost forgotten. Uncle Press was in trouble. At least I think he was in trouble. Those knight boys who lassoed him and pulled him off didn't exactly look like his pals. A rush of adrenaline shot through my body and I sat up fast.

"He's in trouble!" I shouted. Bad move. Not the shouting part, the sitting up fast part. My body was one big black-and-blue mark from our bobsled crash in the forest. A wave of pain hit me like, like, well, like that stick would have hit me if Loor were taking batting practice on me. I don't know why I didn't realize it before, but I was really hurt. It felt like every one of my ribs was cracked. The pain was so intense it took my breath away. My legs went weak and I had to lie back down or I would have passed out again. Osa quickly grabbed my shoulders and gently lowered me back on the bench.

"It is all right," she said in a soothing voice. "The pain will not last."

How could she know that? Unless maybe she thought I was about to die. Nothing short of death was going to stop this burning pain anytime soon. But what happened next was nothing short of amazing. I lay there taking short quick breaths because deep breaths made the pain even worse. Osa then reached out and gently put her hand on my chest. She looked into my eyes and I swear, Mark, it was like I melted. The tension totally flew out of me.

"Relax," she said softly. "Breathe slowly."

I did. Soon my heart stopped pounding and I could take a deep breath. But most amazing of all, the pain went away. I swear. A second before I was hurting so bad I couldn't even cry. Now it was gone. Completely.

Osa took her hand away and glanced over to Loor for a reaction. Loor turned away. She wasn't impressed. But I sure was. It was some kind of miracle.

"How did you do that?" I asked while sitting up and feeling my ribs.

"Do what?" was Osa's innocent reply.

"Are you kidding?" I shouted. "My ribs! I was like, dying. You touched me and poof, I'm off injured reserve."

Osa stood up and said, "Perhaps you were not hurt as badly as you thought."

"Yeah right," I shot back. "I know what pain is, especially when it's mine."

That's when Loor decided to join the party.

"We are wasting time," she said in a peeved voice. "Press is being held by Kagan."

I didn't care much for Loor's style, but she was right.

"Who is this Kagan dude?" I asked.

"There are many things you must learn," said Osa. "Press was to begin teaching you, but until he returns the task will be mine. Come."

She walked over to the hole in the wall that was a door and stood next to her daughter. They both looked at me, which I took as my cue to follow. I stood up, ready to feel the pain in my ribs shoot back. It didn't. Amazing. I then looked at Loor to see if she would spring into attack mode again. She didn't. So far so good.

"Shouldn't we find Uncle Press?" I asked.

"We will," responded Osa. "But first you must learn about Denduron."

Denduron. Right. That's where I was. There wasn't much I liked about Denduron so far, and I couldn't imagine finding out anything else that would make me like it any more. But I didn't have a whole lot of options, so I followed the others toward the door. I took two steps and then stopped, remembering something very, very important.

"Uhhh, where do I go to, uh, you know, I've got to—"

"Relieve yourself in there," Loor said coldly, pointing to a far corner of the room where there was a wooden screen separating a small space from the rest of the hut.

"Great, thanks," I replied and hurried toward it. When I looked behind the screen I learned two things. One was that these people didn't have indoor plumbing. The toilet was nothing more than a hole in the ground surrounded by a circle of stones. Not exactly comfy. The second thing was that the mystery of why this place smelled so bad was solved. I guess these people hadn't figured out that an outhouse should definitely be "out" of the house. Man, it smelled like a sick elephant had been using this thing. But what the heck, it wasn't my house and I had to go bad. So I held my breath against the stink and then took about five minutes to figure out how to undo the leather clothes. I guess these people hadn't yet discovered zippers, either. It was during this that I realized the furs I had been wearing were gone. I guess somebody took them while I was unconscious. That was fine by me because if I'd had to get through another layer, I would have wet myself for sure.

After I finished, I hurried across the stone hut to catch up. I didn't know what I was expecting to find outside, so I guess no matter what I saw it would have been a surprise. But when I stepped outside, I had to stop and catch my breath because I had just stepped into another world, and it was like nothing I had ever seen before. The hut I had just come from was in the middle of a village of stone huts. They all looked the same, more or less, with stone walls and roofs made of woven branches and straw. There were no decorations of any kind to distinguish one from the next. Some had smoke curling up from stone chimneys, which meant there were fires burning inside for cooking and for heat. The roads and pathways that snaked between the huts were dirt, well-worn and narrow. And why not? It's not like they had to worry about cars or anything. All the huts were built around a big grassy area kind of like a town square, with a large, round platform about ten feet across at its center. The base of the platform was made of stones like the huts, and it was topped by a surface made of lashed-together logs. The setup reminded me of those towns that have a gazebo in the center of a park for concerts and stuff. But the stage was empty now. No shows today.

The village was busy with people doing whatever people do in a village like this. They were hurrying here and there, some carrying baskets of food, others moving a herd of goats. They all wore the same kind of leather clothes I was wearing, so even though I felt out of place, I probably didn't look it. The people who looked out of place were Osa and Loor. As I described them to you, they were both tall, dark-skinned, and athletic looking. There were no other people of color in this village. Just the opposite. The people of Denduron were the palest people I had ever seen in my life. It was like they never saw a day of sun in their lives. That was strange because even though it happened to be overcast just then, I had seen three suns in the sky from on top of the mountain. Could it be that the suns here didn't give you a tan? Or was it mostly always overcast, like Seattle or something? Whatever the reason, it was pretty obvious that Osa and Loor were not from Denduron, just as they had said.

The village had been cut out of a forest. Looking one way, beyond the huts, was vast farmland. I could see many people working out there, tending to crops. Looking off in the opposite direction I saw the mountain where Uncle Press and I had made our idiot bobsled run to escape the quigs. Any other direction showed nothing but forest. Not that I'm an expert anthropologist or anything, but this first brief look at the village made me think of books and movies I'd seen about Europe back in medieval days. The only thing missing was some huge castle that loomed over the village.

Osa and Loor let me stand there for a few minutes so I could take in the surroundings. I was about to join them, when suddenly I was grabbed from behind and spun around.

"Ogga ta vaan burr sa!"

It was a little guy with long scraggly hair, an eye patch over one eye, and a smile that showed more spaces than teeth. On each of his fingers was a different ring that looked to be braided out of rope. Ten fingers, ten rings. The guy was grubby, but he sure liked jewelry. I had no idea what he wanted until he shoved a furry-looking thing at me. I jumped back, but then realized it was some kind of woolly shirt, like a sweater.

"Ogga ta vaan," he said again with a smile as he shoved the piece of clothing at me. I figured he was harmless and that he wanted me to take the thing. Hey, what the heck? Maybe it was a local "welcome" custom. It was kind of chilly and this leather shirt thing I was wearing wasn't keeping me all that warm. So I smiled back at him and reached for it. But just as I was about to take it, the little guy pulled it back, held out his hand, and rubbed his fingers together. Yes, he was giving me the international sign, no, I guess it was more the intergalactic sign for "you want it, you pay for it." This weird little guy was trying to strike a deal for the sweater.

"Figgis, leave him be!" said Osa as she stepped between us.

"Mab abba kan forbay," said the little guy innocently. At least I think it was innocently. His language made no sense to me.

Osa looked at Figgis and said, "He has only just arrived. Go sell your wares somewhere else."

The guy was a salesman. He seemed to deflate in disappointment and started to walk away, but then he turned back and gave me a sly, toothless smile. From out of his grungy shirt he held up a shiny red apple, trying to tempt me. It looked good.

"Go!" commanded Osa.

Figgis snarled at her and ran away.

"Figgis would sell you his breath if he could," she explained. "They say he wears that patch because he sold his eye to a blind man."

Nice. That's a fairly disgusting image.

"Osa," I asked. "Are you from Earth?"

Osa laughed and looked to Loor to share the joke that I didn't get. Loor didn't laugh back. Big surprise.

"Why do you think that?" she asked.

"You know English," I said.

"You are wrong, Pendragon," she said. "I do not understand a word of English. Come." She left me there and continued walking with Loor.

Huh? I could be mistaken, but I thought sure we were

speaking English. I should know. Aside from a little classroom Spanish, it's the only language I know. This was getting frustrating. Every time I thought I was starting to get a handle on things, something would come along and pull the rug out from under me. I figured I better get used to it.

Osa and Loor were already way ahead of me, so I had to run to catch up. I had to jog to keep pace with their long strides while making sure to keep Osa between me and Loor. I liked the mom, but I didn't trust the daughter. I kept catching her throwing me these "you aren't worthy to breathe air that could go to someone more deserving" looks. She was giving off a major cold vibe. I figured it would be best to stay out of her way.

"I don't understand," I said to Osa. "How can you say you don't know English if you're speaking it?"

"I am not speaking English," she answered. "You are speaking English. I am speaking the language from Zadaa, which is our home territory."

"Sounds like English to me," I said.

"Of course it does. That is because you are a Traveler."

This was getting more confusing by the second.

"So, you're saying that Travelers understand all languages?" Logical question, right?

"No," came the illogical reply. "Travelers hear all languages as their own. And when they speak, others will understand them no matter what their native language."

Cool. If this were true, maybe I'd have a shot at getting better than my usual lousy C in Spanish class. Still, something didn't fit.

"Okay, so how come when that Figgis guy spoke it sounded like blah, blah, blah to me?"

Suddenly Loor jumped in front of me. I had to put on

the brakes or walk into her. That would have hurt.

"Because maybe you are not a Traveler!" she said with a challenging snarl.

Ahhh! Suddenly it all came clear. Loor didn't think I was who I was. That's why she was acting all strange and aggressive. Of course, I wasn't even sure myself who I was supposed to be, so there wasn't anything I could say to convince her that I was me. Or I was who I was. Or . . . you get the idea.

Again Osa came to my rescue saying, "The reason you did not understand Figgis is that you have not yet learned to hear. You understand us because we are Travelers, but Figgis is not. You must learn to hear, without trying to listen."

Say what? Hear without listening? That sounded like fortune cookie logic.

"How can he be a Traveler? He is just a boy!" Loor said to her mother vehemently. "He is soft and frightened. He will do more harm than good."

Wow. How's that for an ego pounding? Ouch. Unfortunately though, she was right. I *was* soft and frightened. Maybe I wasn't a Traveler after all. Frankly, it wouldn't kill me to find out I wasn't, no matter how much it would have helped my Spanish grades. I was beginning to think that maybe this was all some big mistake and they would send me home.

Osa looked at me with those dark, knowing eyes, but spoke to Loor saying, "No, Pendragon is a Traveler. But he has much to learn." Then she looked at her daughter and said, "And you seem to forget that you are but a child yourself."

Loor stormed off in a huff. I got the feeling she didn't like being told she was wrong. Osa turned to me and said, "You will find that she is not always so angry."

"Hey, no big deal," I shot back. "Just so long as she isn't angry at me!"

Osa smiled and walked on. I followed, and she began to tell me about Denduron.

"The people who live in this village are a tribe called the Milago," she began. "As you can see they live a simple life. They grow all of their own food and live peacefully with the other tribes of Denduron."

Milago. Uncle Press had used that word just before those knights showed up. He said they'd find me, so I guess they are the good guys.

"What about those knight-looking guys who attacked Uncle Press?" I asked. "Are they Milago too?"

"No," answered Osa. "That is what I want to show you."

We continued walking out of the village and along a path in the woods for about a quarter of a mile. (I judge all distances by the track at Stony Brook High. It's a quarter of a mile around, and it felt like we walked about the distance of that track.) We broke out of the woods into a clearing and I was yet again hit with an amazing sight. Remember how I said the only thing missing from this medieval village was a big old castle looming over it? Well, as it turns out there was a big old castle, it just wasn't doing any looming.

Here's what I saw: When we emerged from the path through the trees, we came upon a huge, open field of grass. We walked across this rolling field until we came to a cliff on the far side. Down below the cliff was water. Yes, we were at the edge of an ocean as vast and as blue as the Atlantic. The sea was to my right, and I turned to look down the coast—an uneven, craggy shoreline with big, rocky cliffs. I saw that the cliff we were on was actually one side of an inlet. Looking down over the edge, I saw wave after wave of seawater crashing on the rocks below. Far below. We were so high above the water I started getting sweaty palms. I'm not good with heights. I looked up and straight ahead to the cliff on the far side of the inlet to see that the land on top was covered with more lush sea grass that waved in the ocean breeze. Then what I saw *below* that grass took my breath away.

Built right into the face of the cliff was a monster fortress. It looked as if it were literally carved out of the rock that made up the bluff. I could see several levels of stone balconies where knights like the ones who attacked Uncle Press were keeping guard. They marched back and forth with lethal-looking spears over their shoulders. I'm not exactly sure what they were guarding against. Marauding fish, I suppose.

I counted five levels of balconies, so this fortress was big. Osa must have read my mind because she said, "You are only seeing the outside wall of the palace. It is built far into the cliff. It is a village in itself."

From what I saw so far, these people didn't have any heavy-duty construction equipment, so this place was chiseled out of the rock by hand. It must have taken centuries to dig such a huge building out of hard rock using simple tools.

"There have always been two tribes here," she continued. "The Milago work the land, the Bedoowan are the soldiers and rulers. At one time many of the tribes of Denduron were at war. The Bedoowan protected the Milago from marauders, and in return the Milago provided food. Each tribe relied upon the other, while they remained very much apart. It lasted that way for centuries, with both tribes living in relative harmony. But the Bedoowan were powerful and power can lead to arrogance. It was forbidden for a Milago to marry a Bedoowan, or even to become friends. As so often happens in situations like this, the Bedoowan began to look upon the Milago as their slaves."

"But still, they protect the Milago, right?" I asked.

"There have not been invaders here for many years. The need for protection no longer exists," said Osa.

"So the Milago guys still do all the work and the Bedoowan guys do . . . what?"

"That is a good question. The Bedoowan are ruled by a royal family, with the role of monarch passed down to the eldest child. There was a time, not too long ago, that the Bedoowan monarch wanted to break down the barriers between the two tribes and allow them to become one. But he died and left the monarchy to his firstborn. There are some who believe that the father was murdered by those who did not want the Bedoowan to give up their superior position."

"And let me guess: The new monarch likes having slaves and wants to keep the two tribes apart," I said.

"Yes," she said. "The Milago are afraid to even say the name . . . Kagan."

There was that name again. I was beginning to get the picture, and I didn't like it.

"The knights who attacked Uncle Press thought he was spying on Kagan," I said. "But Uncle Press pretended that he was a miner. Are there mines here?"

"Yes," she said with a sad breath. "That is the worst part of the story."

Oh great, it gets worse. Just what I wanted to hear. But before Osa could continue, I heard the sound of a far-off drum. It was a steady, booming sound that came from the direction of the Milago village.

Loor ran up to us and said breathlessly, "It is the Transfer. Hurry." She took off, running back the way we came.

Osa looked at me and said with concern, "Stay close to me. Do not let them see you." With that she took off after Loor.

As I told you, these two were athletes. But I didn't care

how fast they were, I was going to keep up with them. I caught up and kept right on Osa's tail as we beat feet along the path back to the Milago village. Good thing it was only about a half mile away, or I would have bonked for sure.

As we approached the village, I saw that everyone was gathering toward the central area with the stage in the middle. I guessed there was going to be a show after all. People came in from the fields, emptied from their huts, and generally left whatever they were doing to crowd around the platform.

I was all set to join the crowd when Osa grabbed my hand and pulled me in another direction. The three of us climbed on top of one of the stone huts and positioned ourselves on the roof so we could get a good view of the show.

"They must not see us," cautioned Osa. "We are not a part of this."

Whatever. No biggie. We had the best view in the house anyway. So I settled in and wondered what the performance was going to be. Maybe some Milago musicians, or some school play thing.

I looked out on the meeting ground, and saw the Milago villagers gathered in a wide circle around the central platform, which wasn't empty anymore. On top of it was some kind of contraption that looked like a seesaw. On one end was a seat, on the other was a big, wide-mouthed basket. Standing on the platform next to the gizmo was one of Kagan's knights, beating on a drum. I hoped the purpose of this guy was to signal for everyone to gather, because if this was the whole show, I wasn't impressed. The deep booming sound echoed across the village. His rhythm was pretty lousy too. Standing next to the platform were six more knights. They stood at attention, each holding a nasty-looking spear in front of them. The Milago villagers gave these guys a wide berth. I would have too. They didn't look friendly.

It started to dawn on me that none of these people looked as if they were getting ready for a good time. There wasn't an excited air of anticipation that comes before a fun event. No one spoke, or laughed or joked. Except for the booming drum, it was deathly quiet. These people all had a look of dread on their faces.

Osa then tapped me on the shoulder and pointed to the far side of the clearing. I looked to see a group of four Milago villagers walking slowly toward the assembly. They were all men who were covered with dirt from head to toe. Not that any of these Milago people were all that clean to begin with, but these guys were pretty gnarly. The black dirt really stood out boldly against their pasty-white skin. The four men were carrying a large basket filled with craggy rocks of all sizes. Some were as large as bowling balls, others were much smaller. But the thing that really stood out about them was that they were blue. And I mean bright blue, like dazzling sapphires. I had never seen anything so stunning.

"The stones are called 'glaze,'" whispered Osa. "There are mines throughout this area. The Milago mine for glaze day and night."

"I guess it's valuable," I said, stating the obvious.

"Very," she answered. "Glaze is the foremost reason why Kagan wants to keep control over the Milago. Glaze has made the Bedoowan wealthy. They trade with merchants from all of Denduron. So long as the Milago mine for glaze, Kagan remains a powerful monarch."

So Kagan and the Bedoowan weren't only lazy bullies, they were greedy bullies who forced the Milago to do their dirty work. Nice guys. I wanted to ask more questions, but suddenly the drummer stopped pounding and an ominous silence fell over the village. The four miners brought the basket of glaze to the platform and carefully placed it down. The whole thing was starting to take on the air of a ceremony. The Transfer is what Loor called it.

That's when I heard the sound of a galloping horse. Someone was coming straight down the path where we had walked out to the ocean, and he was coming fast. The weird thing was, nobody turned to look. Nobody but me, that is.

As the horse came charging out of the forest, I saw that riding it was a guy who looked like he knew what he was doing. He was a big guy, with long dark hair, wearing some kind of leather armor similar to what the knights had on, but his armor didn't look like it had seen many battles. It was clean and unscarred, unlike the knights' armor, which looked pretty beaten up. As he galloped up to the circle of villagers, they parted to give him access to the platform. Good thing too, because he didn't slow down. I think if the people hadn't moved, he would have plowed over them. Already I didn't like this guy.

"Is that Kagan?" I whispered.

Osa and Loor exchanged secret looks, like there was something going on that they didn't want to tell me about. I caught the look and I didn't like it.

"His name is Mallos," answered Osa. "He is Kagan's chief advisor."

Mallos, Kagan, Osa, Loor, Figgis . . . was I the only guy around here who had a first and a last name? This Mallos guy rode his horse right up to the platform and stopped. My guess was the show was about to begin. He sat there on his horse and surveyed the assembled crowd like he owned them. None of the Milago returned his look. They all stood with their heads down, avoiding his gaze. It didn't take a genius to figure out that they were afraid of him. Mallos then turned in his saddle and looked right up to where we were hiding on the roof.

"Stay down!" ordered Loor with a strong whisper.

We all ducked down further, trying to press ourselves into the roof to make ourselves smaller. But I could still see Mallos. As his horse kicked at the dirt, he sat there stock still, looking toward us. It was like he knew we were there. But that was impossible. There was no way he could have seen us.

That's when it happened. As I looked back at him, I was hit with a realization so shocking that it made me gasp in surprise. I think the thing that tipped it were his eyes. As far away as he was, I knew those cold blue eyes. How could I forget?

Osa and Loor both sensed my surprise and looked at me questioningly.

"Saint Dane," I said softly.

"You know him?" whispered Loor with total shock.

"Yeah, he tried to kill me back on Earth just before I got flumed here," I said. I couldn't believe those words had just come out of my mouth. There was a lot going on in that one little sentence. It would have sounded like fantasy about twenty-four hours ago, but right now it made all too much sense. Osa and Loor exchanged concerned looks again.

Then Loor whispered to me, "He followed you to Second Earth?" She said this as if it were an amazing thing to have happened. I shrugged and nodded a silent "yes." It was the first time she looked at me with something other than total disdain. Up until now, she acted as if I were less important than the dirt on her boots. But now her look was one of, well, curiosity. Maybe the fact that I survived an encounter with Saint Dane proved that I wasn't so soft after all. Of course I wasn't about to tell her that all I did was run for my life. I wasn't an idiot.

Looking down at Saint Dane, or Mallos, or whatever he called himself, I got hit with a strong wave of "I want to go home." But that wasn't going to happen anytime soon. I was stuck here looking at a guy who had tried to kill me. Could he see me? Was he going to kick that horse into gear and come charging toward the hut? We'd be trapped up here on the roof. All I could do was hold my breath.

It felt like a lifetime, but Saint Dane finally turned away. I could breathe again. With a wave of his hand he said sharply, "Begin!"

Whoa. He spoke English. Did that mean he knew English, or that he too was a Traveler and that's why I could understand him? That question would have to wait, for the main event finally began. One of the miners who had carried in the basket of glaze stepped forward. He was a big guy and something about the way he carried himself told me he was in charge. Whatever was about to happen, this guy didn't seem too happy about it. Every move he made was stiff and forced, as if the pressure of doing what he had to do was physically painful.

"That is Rellin," whispered Osa. "He is the chief miner."

Guess I nailed that one. Of course, he was another one-name guy.

Rellin stepped up onto the platform and turned to the crowd. He then held out his hand and gestured to someone. The crowd parted and a man stepped forward to join him on the platform. He was a tall skinny guy, which I point out only because of what happened next. The skinny guy walked over to the seesaw thing and sat down on the end with the seat. Since there was no weight on the other side, he tipped his end down to the floor of the platform. Rellin gestured to the other miners and the three guys lugged the basket of glaze up onto the platform, placing it near the opposite end of the seesaw. What were they going to do? Measure the guy's weight in glaze?

"They make a Transfer every day," explained Osa. "Mallos chooses one of the Milago, and that determines how much glaze they must mine for Kagan the next day."

I was right. Measuring the guy's weight in glaze was exactly what they were going to do. The big seesaw was a scale. The miners reached into the basket of glaze and were about to pick up the first few stones to begin the process when Saint Dane barked, "No!"

The miners stopped. Everyone held their breath, waiting for Saint Dane's next move. Saint Dane surveyed the crowd, then pointed.

"Him," he said with no emotion.

There was a general rumbling of discontent within the crowd. Two of the knights pushed roughly past a few of the villagers and grabbed the man Saint Dane had pointed to. He was a much bigger man than the first guy. The rules had just changed, and Rellin didn't like it.

"Mallos ca!" he shouted. He was ticked and started yelling angrily at Saint Dane. I won't write the words as I heard them because, as you know, his language made no sense to me. I'll just tell you the translation that Osa gave me.

"Mallos has chosen a different subject for the Transfer and Rellin is telling him that it is not fair," Osa explained, though I pretty much figured that out on my own. "He is pleading with Mallos to use the choice he made yesterday."

I could see why. This new guy was much heavier than the original guy. If they had mined enough of the glaze to balance with the first guy, there was no way they'd have enough to balance with the second guy. Rellin begged Saint Dane for fairness. Saint Dane didn't flinch. He looked at Rellin like he was a bug. Then one of the knights stepped up to Rellin and slapped him on the side of the face with his spear. Rellin spun around and I could see the fiery anger in his eyes. He was already bleeding from the smack on his cheek. I could tell he was a breath away from leaping at the knight's throat. But he didn't. That was smart because the other knights were standing right there, ready with their weapons. He would have been hammered.

"Look at me, Rellin," commanded Saint Dane.

Rellin looked up at his enemy on the horse.

"Being a loyal subject, you should want to do more for Kagan than is expected of you," Saint Dane said with an arrogance that even made *my* blood boil. "Are you telling me that you are doing the least amount of work that is necessary?"

Rellin answered with a seething yet controlled tirade that Osa translated for me.

"He is arguing that mining glaze is difficult and dangerous. Every ounce they pull from the mines comes at a huge cost. He says they mine as much as they possibly can."

Saint Dane snickered and said, "We will see."

He then gestured to the knights. One of them jumped up onto the platform, grabbed the skinny guy who was sitting on the end of the seesaw and pushed him off the platform. Then the other two knights dragged the heavyset guy up onto the platform and jammed him down into the seat. This guy was scared. He looked to Rellin with pleading eyes, but there was nothing Rellin could do.

"Now," said Saint Dane. "You may begin."

The miners looked to Rellin, who gave them a slight nod. They had no choice, so they went to work taking the glaze from their basket and putting the stones on the opposite end of the seesaw.

"What happens if they don't make the weight?" I asked Osa.

"Let us hope you do not have to find out," came her ominous answer.

The miners quickly placed the glaze stones on the scale, starting with the larger ones and working their way down to marble-sized ones. The villagers' eyes were all focused on the scale. My guess is that no one was breathing. I know I wasn't. When the miners were about halfway through, the seesaw began to move. Ever so slowly, the heavy man on the opposite end of the scale began to rise. As soon as he felt himself move, a look of relief came over his face. Maybe there would be enough glaze stones to balance him after all. With renewed hope the miners continued to pile the stones on the scale. Slowly the scale moved and the heavyset man rose into the air.

I could feel the mood of the crowd beginning to turn. They were going to do it. They had mined more than enough glaze that day, just as Saint Dane had demanded. With the last few small stones, the scale rose until it was perfectly level. It took every last one they had, but they made it. If this had been a World Series game, the crowd would have erupted into a cheer. But this was no game. Even though I could sense their joy and relief, no one made a peep. I saw them secretly exchanging little smiles of joy. There were even a few quick, secret hugs. It was a good moment. Even Rellin looked relieved, though he tried not to show it. Throwing victory back in Saint Dane's face would not have been a smart thing to do.

Saint Dane didn't react. I couldn't tell if he was happy they had mined so much extra glaze, or ticked that the Milago had met his unfair challenge. He swung his leg over and jumped down from his horse. He climbed up onto the platform and looked at the level scale with a slight smile. Suddenly the mood of the crowd grew tense again. What was Saint Dane doing? He looked to the heavyset man who was swaying on the end of the scale. The man looked down, afraid to make eye contact. Saint Dane then walked to the end of the scale where the glaze stones were piled into the basket.

"Well done, Rellin," he said. "You have mined quite a large amount of—" He suddenly stopped talking, and leaned in closer to the basket of glaze stones. Throughout the crowd people started holding one another's hands for strength.

Saint Dane gazed into the basket of stones and said, "Rellin! I am surprised at you. There is a stone in here that is not pure glaze!"

Uh-oh. Rellin made a move to run to the basket, but two of the knights held him back. Rellin yelled something at Saint Dane, but it didn't matter what he said. Saint Dane reached into the basket, grabbed the largest glaze stone, and picked it up. Instantly, the scale tipped and the heavyset man slammed down onto the platform, hard. Saint Dane carried the stone over to Rellin and held it up to his face.

"You know that Kagan only accepts stones of pure glaze," he said through smug, clenched teeth.

Not that I'm a geology expert or anything, but that stone looked just like every other stone in the batch. Saint Dane was changing the rules again.

"You know what must happen now," he said with mock sadness.

Apparently the heavyset men knew it too. He scrambled to his feet and jumped down off the platform. He wanted out of there, fast. But the knights grabbed him and held him tight.

"What's happening?" I asked Osa.

Osa didn't answer. She kept staring at the scene with sad

eyes. I figured I was going to find the answer soon anyway and turned back to watch the last act of this drama.

One of the other knights quickly grabbed a heavy chain that was attached to one end of the wooden platform. He pulled on it and half of the platform top lifted up like a trap-door. Underneath there looked like . . . nothing. The platform was built over a huge hole.

"It is the first mine shaft that was dug here in the Milago village," Osa said without taking her sad eyes off the scene. "It is a pit that reaches down farther than the eye can see. I am afraid there are many lonely bones resting on the bottom."

My mind was racing. I couldn't believe what I was seeing. They were going to toss this guy down the mine shaft!

"Why don't the Milago do something?" I said. "There are hundreds of them! Why don't they stop it?"

The knights dragged the heavyset man closer to the open pit.

"Bagga! Bagga va por da pey!" he cried. It was horrible.

No one in the crowd moved. No one tried to help the poor guy. Even Rellin. It was like they knew it was futile. I noticed that next to me, Loor reached to her back and grabbed hold of her wooden weapon. But Osa put her hand over her daughter's.

"You know it is not the time," she said softly.

Loor didn't release her weapon at first. I could feel her tension. One push, and she would be down there, swinging away. But today was not that day. She kept her eyes on the scene and released her grip on the weapon.

The knights dragged the screaming heavy man up to Saint Dane, who looked at the poor guy without a trace of sympathy and said, "If you weren't such a glutton, you may have lived to see another day." Saint Dane then nodded at the knights, and they dragged the poor, screaming man toward the open pit.

"Ca . . . ca!" he pleaded. "Maga con dada pey! Maga con dada! Moy fol wife, and two children! Please! I must take care of them! They will be alone!"

The scene was so horrifying that it wasn't until later that it hit me . . . I could understand him. It sure sounded like English, but it didn't make sense that he suddenly would have switched languages. Osa said that the Travelers had the ability to understand all languages, and since I was suddenly able to understand this man, maybe I was a Traveler after all.

But I didn't think about that until later. Right now I was witnessing the most gut-wrenching moment I could imagine. The two knights dragged the heavy man closer to the open pit. Suddenly a woman jumped out of the crowd and tried to pull him away from his executioners. She was in tears and begging for mercy. She must have been the man's wife, but her brave effort didn't help. She was quickly grabbed by another knight and thrown to the ground. She lay there in the grass, sobbing.

The knights finally got the man to the edge of the pit and were about to push him in, when the man suddenly stopped wailing. Up until this point he had been crying and begging for his life. But now he stopped fighting and stood up straight. I swear, there was a look on his face that was almost calm. The knights didn't know how to react. They weren't used to someone being calm during the worst moment of their life.

The heavy man turned and faced Saint Dane, and in a distinct, strong voice he said, "My only regret is that I will not live long enough to see Kagan suffer the way we have all suffered."

Saint Dane chuckled and said, "None of you will live that long, for that day will never come." He then gave a quick, almost imperceptible nod and the two knights pushed the doomed man backward into the pit. His wife screamed, but the guy didn't let out a sound. One second he was there, the next he was just . . . gone. Hopefully his death would be quick and he'd now be in a better place than this horrible village.

The knight holding the chain let it go and the wooden platform fell down with a boom. Saint Dane walked up to Rellin, who looked him right in the eye. Saint Dane then pointed to the man's sobbing wife.

"We will use her for tomorrow's Transfer," he said with pleasure. "She seems quite light. It should make for an easy day. Please thank me for being so considerate."

Rellin looked at Saint Dane and for a second I thought he was going to spit in his face. But he didn't. Instead, he gritted his teeth and said, "Thank you."

"You're welcome," Saint Dane said with a smile. With that he strode to his horse, jumped into the saddle and was just about to ride off when he once again looked back toward us. Actually, it was more like he was looking right at me. I could feel it. He knew I was there. Was all of this a show for me? Saint Dane laughed, kicked his horse and rode off through the stunned crowd back toward the Bedoowan palace.

The knights pushed a few of the miners toward the basket of glaze with their spears. The valuable stones had to be delivered to Kagan and it was clear that they weren't the ones who were going to carry them. That was a job for their slaves. The miners picked up the basket from the seesaw and started the long walk toward the palace. The rest of the villagers slowly started to disperse. Not a word was spoken. A few people went up to console the poor woman who had just lost her husband, but most simply headed back toward their homes. They had been through this horror before, and they probably would go through it again.

But I hadn't. I was frantic. I had just witnessed a man

murdered in cold blood. It was even more horrible than the poor homeless guy who Saint Dane hypnotized into running into the subway train back in New York. That was awful, but it didn't seem real. This was very, very real and I didn't understand it. My emotions were all over the place. And yes, I'm not ashamed to admit it, I was crying. They were tears of anger, and fear, and sadness for a man I didn't even know. And for his family. I didn't care that I was crying in front of Loor or anybody else. I was out of control.

"Why didn't they do something?" I shouted at Osa. "They could have ganged up on the knights. They could have pulled the guy away. Why didn't they stop it?"

Osa was as calm as I was upset. She said, "If they had done anything, Kagan would have sent an army to punish them. They had no choice."

I looked to Loor and was surprised to see that she too looked upset. She may not have been ranting the way I was, but her icy calm was cracked. I even thought I could see a tear in her eye. Maybe there was a heart beneath that tough exterior after all.

Still, I didn't buy what Osa was saying. "So what? They should have done something," I cried. "If they don't do something, it'll never stop."

Osa put a hand on my shoulder, and I could feel myself starting to calm down. But what she said next was the last thing I wanted to hear.

"They are going to do something, Pendragon. They are going to take destiny into their own hands and rise up against Kagan. That is why we are here. We are going to help them. *You* are going to help them."

These words hit me like a bolt from the blue. Uncle Press had told me there were people who needed our help, but I had no idea he was talking about an entire village of people who were at the mercy of a vicious army that didn't think twice about killing people in cold blood. This was crazy. I felt bad for these people, but there was nothing I could do to help them. I didn't care how tough this Loor person was, those knights were killers. And there were only three of us . . . four if you counted Uncle Press. What good could we do against an army? No, this was crazy. I made up my mind right there that the first chance I got, I'd get away from these nutburgers and get back to that flume thing. If it brought me here, then there had to be a way for it to get me back home. Yes, that was the answer. I was going to get myself out of here and kiss this place good-bye—with or without Uncle Press.

◉ SECOND EARTH ◉

"Hey, you kids!"

Mark and Courtney looked up from their reading to see Sergeant D'Angelo calling to them from the front of the building. The two had been sitting there the whole time, reading the pages from Bobby.

"Run!" yelled Mark. He started to get up, but Courtney grabbed him by the seat of the pants and pulled him back down.

"Why?" she asked him calmly. "We're not doing anything wrong."

Mark had to think about that for a second. She was right, all they were doing was sitting in the alley, reading. Nothing illegal about that. So then why was this policeman yelling at them? Courtney looked to the cop, but didn't budge.

"What do you want?" she yelled.

"I want to talk to you," came the reply.

"Then you come to us," Courtney yelled.

Ouch. Mark winced. Courtney was being pretty disrespectful. Okay, so maybe the guy dissed them before, but he was still a cop. Mark was sure he was going to arrest them.

D'Angelo took a few steps toward them with his hands on his hips, and said in a downright civil tone, "I want to talk to you about the Pendragons."

"Why?" asked Courtney, oozing skepticism.

"Because I believe you," answered D'Angelo.

Mark and Courtney shot each other a look. Victory! He must have found Mr. and Mrs. Pendragon. They both jumped up to go to the cop. Mark made sure that Bobby's half-read journal was tucked securely in his pack, and the two followed D'Angelo back into the station house.

Once inside the sergeant led them past the lobby and continued on through the back offices. Mark thought this was kind of cool. He had never been behind the scenes at a real police station. The experience wasn't exactly what he had expected. On TV, police stations had a lot of activity. There were always cops leading handcuffed perps toward interrogation rooms, and detectives taking statements and SWAT teams hurrying to some mission and generally a ton of cop-type hubbub. But not here in Stony Brook. Here a guy was making a phone call to Domino's for pizza, and another guy looked bored while playing FreeCell on an old computer. Not exactly a beehive of electrifying police activity. Very disappointing.

"I gotta be honest," said D'Angelo as he led them through the station. "I thought you two were pulling a number on me until I spoke with Captain Hirsch."

"What did he say?" Mark asked.

"Ask him yourself," said the sergeant as he opened a door and motioned for Mark and Courtney to enter. The two walked into a conference room with a large metal table surrounded by eight chairs. It was a plain room with a huge mirror that covered most of one wall. Sitting at the head of the table was a pleasant-looking man wearing a suit. When the kids entered he stood up and smiled, but both kids sensed that he was troubled. Good. He should be. There were troubling things going down.

"Hi, guys. I'm Captain Hirsch," the man said. "Thanks for coming back."

Courtney went right up to the mirror and stuck her nose to the glass while cupping her eyes to block out the light.

"This a two-way mirror?" she asked. "Who's back there? You interrogating us?"

Hirsch looked to D'Angelo and the two chuckled. "Yes, it's a two-way mirror," said Hirsch. "But nobody's back there and we're not interrogating you."

Courtney kept trying to look through the mirror. She didn't believe him.

"Why don't you two sit down and relax," said the sergeant.

Mark and Courtney took seats next to each other at the table. D'Angelo stood by the door. Hirsch sat down and looked at the kids. The kids looked back at Hirsch. Hirsch nervously pulled at his eyebrow. It seemed as if he didn't know where to begin, so Courtney being Courtney, decided to kick things off herself.

"So how come you suddenly believe us about the Pendragons?" she asked Hirsch.

"Mr. and Mrs. Pendragon are good friends of mine," he said. "My son Jimmy plays basketball with Bobby."

"Jimmy Hirsch!" shouted Mark. "I know him. Strong forward."

Captain Hirsch nodded. This was good. Now they had an adult on their side. And he was a cop. A captain, no less. Now things were going to start happening.

"When was the last time you saw Bobby?" he asked them.

Mark knew the answer, but it was up to Courtney to give it.

"Last night at his house," she answered. "About an hour before the game."

"Did he say anything that would make you think he was going away?" came the next question.

Courtney and Mark looked at each other. They knew exactly where Bobby had gone. If the story on the parchment were true, then they knew how Uncle Press had taken him on the back of his motorcycle and left for a place on the far side of the universe called Denduron. But neither of them were sure if the outlandish story was really true, and they didn't want to sound totally insane. Besides, the pages didn't explain what had happened to the Pendragons' house. Mark and Courtney had decided before going to the police that they'd stick to the facts that could be proved. And it was pretty easy to prove that the house was gone. So without discussing it again, they both decided to stick with the original plan.

"I was talking to Bobby at his house," answered Courtney. "His uncle Press came in and I left. That's the last I saw him."

Captain Hirsch looked down at a piece of paper where he had written some notes.

"Right. Uncle Press," he said out loud, though it seemed like he was thinking it more than saying it. Hirsch looked like he wanted to say something, but wasn't sure if it was a good idea or not. He looked to Sergeant D'Angelo for guidance.

"I think you should tell them, Captain," said the sergeant.

"T-Tell us what?" asked Mark.

Obviously these policemen had some disturbing information. Captain Hirsch stood up and paced nervously.

"After you spoke with Sergeant D'Angelo, he told me about your visit," began Hirsch. "Frankly, he didn't believe you because he couldn't find any information on the Pendragons."

"But you know them," interjected Courtney.

"Yes, I know them," said Hirsch. "I've been to their house many times."

"And the house is gone!" added Mark.

Hirsch didn't continue right away. He looked at the two kids, then to Sergeant D'Angelo. Finally he said, "Yeah. The house is gone. This may be a small police department in a small town, but we have access to pretty much any piece of information that's part of the public record," he said. "After you came in here, we did a computer search for the Pendragons . . . and found nothing."

"What do you mean 'nothing'?" asked Courtney. "No police record?"

"No, I mean absolutely nothing," said Hirsch. A hint of frustration was creeping into his voice. "No birth certificates, no driver's licenses, no social security numbers, no bank accounts, no deeds, no electric bills, no school records, no credit cards, no nothing! The Pendragons didn't just disappear—it's like they never even existed!"

Hirsch paced faster. He was getting upset because what he was saying didn't make sense, yet it was true.

Finally Mark said, "B-But they do exist, don't they? I mean, we know them."

"I know!" snapped Hirsch. "I've had dinner at their house. I've driven Bobby to Boy Scouts. Here's another one for you: We scanned back copies of the newspaper where Mr. Pendragon works and couldn't find a single article he had written. But I remember reading them. I've discussed some of those articles with him."

This was getting stranger by the second. Disappearing is one thing. But having someone's whole history vanish seemed downright impossible.

"W-What about Uncle Press?" asked Mark nervously.

"Again, nothing," answered Hirsch. "There is nothing we can find to prove that any of these people ever existed. . . ."

"Except in our memories," added Courtney.

That was a chilling thought. If what the captain said were true, the only thing left of Bobby and his family were the memories they all held . . . and the parchment papers in Mark's bag. Captain Hirsch sat back down at the table and looked to the kids with pleading eyes. This had turned his orderly policeman's mind inside out.

"Kids," he said with a touch of desperation. "Help me out here. If there is anything you can add, anything that might help us figure out what happened to the Pendragons, please tell us."

Mark and Courtney had plenty to add. It was all sitting in Mark's backpack on the table in front of them. All they had to do was slide it over to Captain Hirsch. He would read the pages and take over. That's what adults did. They took over and fixed things. It wasn't Courtney's call—the letters were to Mark. If they were going to tell the police about the pages, it would have to be Mark's decision.

Courtney saw that he was staring at the pack. She knew exactly what was going through his mind. He was debating whether or not to give over the pages. He then looked to her and they made eye contact. Courtney wished that she had some way of helping him make the decision, but she honestly didn't know the right thing to do. So she gave him a slight, helpless shrug that said, "You're on your own."

"Well?" asked Hirsch. "Can you guys think of anything else?"

Mark took a deep breath, turned to Hirsch and said, "No. We're just as confused as you are."

Decision made. Courtney picked up on Mark's lead and added, "Yeah. We're pretty freaked out."

Hirsch took a deep, tired sigh and stood up saying, "Okay, we're going to start an investigation. Tell your parents, tell your friends, tell anybody who'll listen. If they hear anything about the Pendragons, have them call me. Okay?"

Courtney and Mark nodded. Hirsch then gave each of them a business card with his phone number on it. Mark grabbed his pack and they headed out.

Once they were out of the building, they walked silently for a long while. The police station was right near Stony Brook Avenue, which was the main business street in town. Most of the shops and restaurants were there. Since there was no mall in Stony Brook, the "Ave" as they called it was where everybody hung out. But Courtney and Mark weren't interested in any of the temptations that the Ave held that day. They walked by the CD Silo without even a glance into the window; they weren't tempted by the smell of the best french fries in the world coming from Garden Poultry Deli; they had no interest in ice cream from The Scoop; and they didn't even think of going to the library. The front steps of the library was where everyone stopped first on a trip to the Ave because you were sure to find someone you knew there.

But not today. Not for Courtney and Mark. Somehow these familiar haunts didn't seem so familiar anymore. Everything looked the same, but the last few hours had opened their eyes to the possibility that the world didn't work exactly the way they thought it did. Between Bobby's adventure and the strange disappearance of the Pendragons, everything they'd ever believed was thrown into question. With thoughts like this running through their heads, somehow grabbing a box of fries at Garden Poultry Deli didn't seem all that appetizing. So the two walked past the usual places where their friends hung out and went into a small, quiet pocket park that was sandwiched between two buildings. They sat down on a park bench and stared at the ground.

Finally Mark looked to Courtney and asked softly, "Should I have told them about Bobby's letter?"

"I don't know," was Courtney's reply. "I don't know what to think anymore."

Mark tried to put his feelings into words. "I have a feeling," he began, "that there's an important reason Bobby is sending me his story."

"Why? We haven't even read what he wants yet," said Courtney.

"Yeah, I know. But I think it's more than that. I've got a feeling that something big is going on and Bobby's only one part of it. There's some serious stuff going on here. I mean like, cosmic stuff. Am I being weird?"

"Weird?" chuckled Courtney. "How could anything sound weird now?"

"Exactly! The idea of Travelers who understand languages, and territories, and flumes that send you across space and time . . . that stuff changes everything we know about how things work."

This made Courtney fall silent. Mark was right. Up until now she was only thinking about Bobby and the Pendragons. But the implications of what they were reading were totally huge. Too huge to comprehend.

Mark continued, "As we were sitting with the police, I thought about what might happen if I gave them Bobby's story. I came up with two possibilities. One was that they'd announce it to the world, there'd be a huge furor and we'd be smack in the center of it. Remember, I might still get more pages. I don't think Bobby would want that kind of uproar, especially if he wants me to help him. If he did, he would have started right off by telling me to take his story to the newspapers."

"What's the other possibility?" asked Courtney.

"The exact opposite might happen. The stuff Bobby wrote about might be so disturbing to the world that they'd bury the whole thing and pretend it never happened . . . kind of like the aliens from Roswell, or the Kennedy assassination. People don't like to hear that their nice, orderly world isn't what they thought it was. I wouldn't blame them; I'm not so thrilled about it myself."

"There's a third possibility," added Courtney. "People may think we're responsible. Everyone always wants easy answers and the easiest answer is that we made the whole thing up. It would be easier for people to think it's all a hoax than to believe there are people who jump through wormholes and travel through the universe."

It was hard to believe that only a few hours ago their biggest concern was that Bobby Pendragon had missed a basketball game.

Courtney looked to Mark and asked, "What do you think we should do?"

Before he could answer, someone reached in from behind, grabbed his backpack and yanked it out of his hands! Courtney and Mark looked up in surprise.

"What'cha got, Dimond? More magazines?" It was Andy Mitchell, the kid who caught Mark in the boys' room reading Bobby's first journal. He fumbled with the clasps on Mark's pack, trying to open it.

Mark jumped to his feet, shouting, "M-Mitchell. G-give it back!"

Mark lunged at him, but Mitchell danced away.

"Aw, c'mon," laughed Mitchell. "Don't you want to share?"

He held the pack out toward Mark. Mark swiped at it, but Mitchell pulled it away and laughed.

"How bad you want it back?" Mitchell taunted. "Bad enough to swim with the rats for it?" He backed toward a storm drain in the curb. It was plenty big enough for the pack to fit through.

"Don't!" Mark shouted desperately.

Mitchell dangled the pack over the drain. "What'll you give me for it?"

"What do you want?" asked Mark nervously.

Mitchell thought for a moment, then spotted something on Mark's hand. "I'll trade the pack . . . for that big old ring"

Mark couldn't give up the ring, no way. But he didn't want to lose the pages, either. He hadn't read what Bobby wanted him to do yet.

"Think fast, Dimond," snickered Mitchell as he dangled the pack over the storm drain. "The pack or the ring . . . pack or the ring."

Mark didn't know what to do. Suddenly, a steely-strong hand clamped down on Mitchell's wrist. He looked up and came face to face with Courtney. She had been calmly watching the scene from the bench. She might not have known how to deal with the mysterious disappearance of Bobby and the Pendragons, or the fact that the world had just turned upside down, but the one thing she knew how to handle was a bully like Andy Mitchell. She squeezed his wrist and stuck her nose in his face.

"Drop that in the sewer," she said through clenched teeth, "and you're going in after it . . . headfirst."

They stood that way for a long moment. Finally, after what seemed like a lifetime, Mitchell smiled.

"Jeez. I was just kidding around," he said.

Courtney reached over with her other hand and grabbed the pack. Once she had it, she let Mitchell go. He pulled away quickly, while rubbing his wrist to get the circulation flowing again.

"It was just a goof," he said, trying to save face. "Where'd you get that butt-ugly ring anyway?"

Mark and Courtney stared at the guy until he felt so uncomfortable that the only thing he could do was leave.

"Jeez, lighten up," he said as he turned and jogged away. Courtney tossed the pack to Mark.

"Thanks," said Mark with a bit of embarrassment. Now that the crisis was over, he knew he hadn't handled it well.

"I hate that weenie," she said.

"We've got to go somewhere and finish reading this," Mark said seriously. "I'm nervous about having these out in public. Let's go back to my house."

"Uh-uh," Courtney said uncomfortably. "No offense, but your room is like . . . rank."

Mark looked down, embarrassed.

"Hey, don't sweat it," she said with a smile. "All guys' rooms are rank. It's just the way it is. Let's go to my house."

It was a short walk to Courtney's house, and neither of them said much along the way. Both had their minds on the pages. There were a lot of questions to be answered, but one stood out above all others: What was the dangerous favor that Bobby wanted Mark to do for him? Courtney was dying to know. So was Mark, but he wasn't all that sure he liked the idea of having to do something dangerous, no matter how important it was. Up until now, Mark's idea of doing something dangerous was to ring somebody's doorbell on Mischief Night and run away. Given what Bobby was going through, the stakes here were a wee bit higher than that.

They arrived at Courtney's house, which was very much like Mark's. They both lived in a quiet, suburban neighborhood. But rather than go to Courtney's room, Courtney took Mark down to the basement where her father had a workshop. Mark had a fleeting moment of disappointment that he wouldn't get to see the inner sanctum of the glorious Courtney Chetwynde, but there were larger problems to deal with.

The two sat down on an old, dusty couch and Mark opened

his pack. He laid the precious pages out on a coffee table in front of them. The two hesitated a moment. As much as they were dying with curiosity about what happened next to Bobby, they were also a little bit frightened about what the pages contained and what new and disturbing wonders they would reveal. They each took a breath.

Then Courtney looked to Mark and said, "You ready?"

"Yeah."

They looked down at the pages and picked up where they had left off.

I was going to get myself out of here and kiss this place good-bye—with or without Uncle Press.

DENDURON

My plan was to climb back to the top of the mountain, get past those cannibal quig beasts, find the gate that leads to the flume, and get the hell out of here. Simple, right? Yeah, sure. I'm not even sure I could *find* that stupid cave again, let alone survive the climb through the snow and the quigs. Still, my mind was made up. It was better than staying here.

But it wasn't going to happen today. The suns were going down and it was getting dark. Yeah, that's right. Suns. Plural. Remember I told you there were three suns? Well, they all set at the same time, but in opposite parts of the sky. North, south and east . . . or whatever they use for directions around here. I figured I had to spend the night and sneak away once it got light. Besides, I was hungry. I hadn't eaten anything since I had a banana and some raspberry Pop-Tarts before the basketball game I never made it to.

Loor brought me to a hut that was like the one I woke up in, only smaller. In one corner was a pile of furry animal skins.

Loor pointed to them and gave me a simple command. "Sit."

I did. It was smelly, but comfortable. There was a small stone fireplace where Loor quickly and expertly made a fire that gave us light and took the chill off. Osa arrived soon after with a cloth sack that I quickly found out was full of food. Yes! We all sat around the fire and shared loaves of crunchy bread; some weird fruit that looked like an orange but you ate like an apple; and some soft nutlike things that tasted like licorice. Maybe it was because I was so hungry, but this odd meal was delicious. I would have preferred some fries from Garden Poultry Deli on the Ave, but this did just fine. While we ate, Osa gave me some strange instructions.

"Is there someone back on Second Earth whom you trust above all others?" she asked.

It didn't take me long to come up with the answer. I told her it was you, Mark. Sure my family's cool, and of course I trust them, but a friend is someone who gives you trust because they want to, not because they have to.

Osa handed me a stack of blank parchment paper that was all yellowed and crunchy. She also gave me a crude pen that looked like it was carved from a tree branch, along with a small bowl of black ink.

"It is important that you write down all that is happening to you," explained Osa. "Every chance you get, write your thoughts, your feelings, and describe the things that you see. Think of it as a journal."

"Why?" was my obvious question.

"Because you will send them to your friend for safekeeping," she answered. "I will not lie to you, Pendragon. This is a dangerous journey. If anything should happen to you, this journal will be the only record of what you have done."

Yikes, that sounded grim. It was like she was asking me to write out my last will and testament. Part of me wanted to refuse because doing what she asked made me feel like I was going along with the program. And I definitely was not. On the other hand, what she said made sense. If anything happened to me, nobody would know the real story. I didn't like that. If I was going to go down, I wanted everybody to know why.

"How are we going to get it to Mark?" I asked.

"Write first," she said. "When you are ready, I will show you."

That was interesting. If she could get these pages to you, that meant she knew how to use the flume in the other direction. Maybe this would be my chance to find a way home. So with that in mind, I took the pen and went to work. I set myself up next to the fire, using a piece of wood on my lap as a desk. It took a while to get the knack of using the pen because it wasn't exactly a Bic Rollerball. I had to dip the pointy end in the ink and scratch the words out on the paper. It was a pain, but after a while I got to where I could write a whole sentence without having to re-dip.

Across from me, Loor was doing the same thing. It felt like we were doing homework together. As she scratched out her thoughts on the same kind of parchment paper, I couldn't help but wonder what she was writing about me. I knew she thought I was a toady boy, but maybe having survived a brush with Saint Dane gave me a little more credibility. On the other hand, who cares? Tomorrow, I was out of here.

That's how I spent the rest of the night. I wrote for a while and when my eyes got heavy I sacked out on the animal skins. I'd sleep for a little bit, then wake up and write some more. Loor did the same thing. Osa was in and out of the hut. She'd come in to put some wood on the fire, then leave again. I wondered if she was getting any sleep at all. I got as far as writing about Uncle Press being captured by Kagan's knights, and then I crashed for good. The next thing I knew, Osa was gently shaking me to wake up.

"It is morning, Pendragon," she said softly.

I was sleeping deeply and had to force my eyes open. There was light in the hut, but I could tell it was early because there were no shadows and the birds were singing. I looked around to see that the fire had gone out and Loor was gone.

"Give me your journal," she commanded.

I sat up and gathered the pages I had written. She took them, rolled them up, and tied them with a leather cord. She then walked to the center of the hut, sat down cross-legged and placed something on the floor. It was a big old clunky silver ring with a gray stone mounted in the center. From where I was sitting I could see there was some kind of inscription engraved around the stone, but I had no idea what it meant. Osa looked to make sure I was watching, then reached down to the ring, touched her finger to the stone and said, "Second Earth."

What I saw next sent a bolt of adrenaline through me so quickly that I was shocked out of any last remnant of sleep. The gray stone in the ring started to glow. It acted like the flume had when it brought me here. The flume was made of gray rock, just like the ring. When I said, "Denduron," the gray rock of the flume had started to glow, just like the ring. Bright light shot from the facets of the stone and washed the walls of the hut, just like the lights in the flume. And like the flume, I started to hear the strange musical notes.

Then the ring started to twitch . . . and grow! The band actually stretched out and got bigger until it was about the size of a Frisbee. But inside the circle, where the floor should have been, was a hole. It was like this ring opened up a miniflume to . . . where? Osa took the rolled-up parchment pages and dropped them into the ring. The pages disappeared as if they had been dropped into a hole in the floor. Then the ring snapped back to normal size and everything ended. No lights, no sound, no hole. Just the ring. Osa picked it up and put it into a leather pouch that hung from around her neck.

"Your friend Mark has your journal," she said and got up to leave. That was it. No explanation, no nothing.

I jumped to my feet to head her off. "Whoa! You can't pull that hocus-pocus number and not tell me what happened!" I demanded.

"I told you what happened," she said calmly. "I sent your journal to Mark Dimond."

She tried to continue out of the hut, but I got in front of her.

"But how? Is that like a portable flume?" Obviously my mind was in overdrive.

"There are many things to know about being a Traveler, Pendragon," she said patiently. "Once you are more comfortable, this ring will be yours and you will be able to send your journals to Mark Dimond yourself. Until then, be satisfied to know that the power contained in the ring is similar to the power found in the flumes."

I wasn't going to give up that easily. "But how can it find Mark?"

Osa took a deep breath like she was getting tired of my questions. Too bad. She knew how this stuff worked. I didn't.

"I gave another ring to Mark Dimond," she said.

"What? You saw Mark? No wait, you went to Earth? When? How? Did you tell him I'm here? Did you see my parents? Did you—"

Osa put a hand to my mouth to shut me up. She was gentle, but firm.

"I went to Second Earth and gave Mark Dimond the ring," she explained. "That is all. I saw no one else. No more questions."

She took her hand away and started out of the hut.

"Just one more," I called after her.

Osa turned back to me, waiting to hear.

"Does this ring thing work both ways? I mean, if we can send things to Mark, can he send things to us?"

Osa smiled. It was the kind of smile I'd see from my mother when I thought I was being clever about trying to keep something from her. That smile said "I know exactly what you're thinking, smart guy. You can't fool me."

"The rings can transport small objects, but they only work for Travelers," was her answer. "Mark Dimond would not be able to send you anything. Now if you wish to bathe yourself, there is a river that runs a few hundred feet south of the village."

She left and my mind went into hyperdrive. This ring business had just opened up a whole new world of possibilities. Maybe I didn't need to get all the way to the top of the mountain after all. Maybe the ring could grow big enough for me to jump into it. And if I'm a Traveler, then the ring will work for me! Yes! For the first time in a long while, I felt as if I had a shot at taking control of my life again. When the time was right, I'd get the ring from Osa and punch my ticket out of here. That was the new plan and it felt good. Heck, anything would be better than climbing that mountain and getting past the quigs. So with a new sense of hope, I left the hut to start the day.

The suns were just creeping up over the horizon and I saw it was going to be a clear day. The first thing I wanted to do was find that river and wash up. Not that I'm a clean freak or anything, but the animal skins I was wearing weren't exactly cottony fresh. I'm not sure which smelled worse: me or my clothes. A quick splash of water would be a good thing, so I picked my way through the Milago village in search of the stream.

The village was just waking up. Smoke drifted up from chimneys in all the huts. A few women scurried along carrying firewood. In the distance I saw farmers already working out in the fields. I also saw a pretty depressing sight. A group of men trudged into the village on a path that led from the woods. I figured they were miners since they were covered with dirt, like the miners who had brought glaze to the Transfer ceremony the day before. Could these guys have been working all night? I then saw another group of miners pass them going in the other direction. I realized this was some sort of change in shift. The day crew was taking over for the night crew.

As bleak as this scene was, it wasn't the depressing part. The thing that really hit me was that nobody talked. Nobody. They didn't even make eye contact with one another. They just went about their business, doing their work or their chores or whatever it is they probably do every single day, but with absolutely no human interaction. I guess it didn't surprise me. After what I had seen the day before, I realized that these people were prisoners. Kagan's army had stolen everything they could from them, including their souls. There was no joy in this place. No hope. They probably didn't want to make friends with anyone because they never knew who might be Kagan's next victim. So they kept to themselves, living in their own personal, tortured world.

It feels kind of weird to admit it, but as I stood there watching these people going about their dreary lives, I started to cry. Normally I'm not a crying kind of guy. Yeah, a couple of times I got weepy during a movie when somebody's dog died or something. But this was different. This was real. I stood in the center of this village and it was like I could feel a huge weight of sadness press down on me. The thing is, no matter how bad somebody's life gets, it can always get better. Things pass and life goes on. Like for me. As bad as things were for me right then, I had a shot at getting home. There was hope. But for these people, there was no escape. Their future was just as bleak as their present. This was their life, and the hopelessness of it brought tears to my eyes. For that one brief instant, I could feel their pain.

But you know something? It didn't last long. If anything, it made me want to get out of there even more. Yeah, I felt bad for them, but it wasn't my problem. This struggle had been going on for a long time and nothing I could do was going to change it. I had to worry about myself right now, so I wiped away the tears, put my head down, and started to look for the path that led to the river. I had only walked a few feet when somebody grabbed my shoulder and whirled me around.

"Crabble nectar?" It was Figgis, the strange little guy who tried to sell me the sweater before. He was holding up a leather pouch that looked full of liquid. "Very delicious. Very rare. Only four quills."

I assumed quills were like Denduron money.

"Thanks, no," I said and walked on. But Figgis jumped in front of me. This time he held out a thing that looked like a crude fanny pack that was woven from dried straw.

"Twenty quills!" he announced while tying it around his waist to demonstrate.

Even if I wanted to buy it, I didn't have any quills, so this was a waste of time. I tried to push past him but he blocked my way again.

"Ten quills, since you are new!" he offered.

He could tell that I wasn't interested, but he was desperate to make a sale so he quickly yanked off one of the ten rings that he wore on his fingers.

"Two quills!" he shouted.

"I'm sorry, dude, I don't have any quills," I said.

This guy seemed to be all about cash, so I figured that telling him I didn't have any would make him back off. It didn't. He grabbed my arm and pulled me toward him so fast that I didn't have a chance to stop him. He leaned in close and whispered something in my ear like he was giving me some information of dire importance.

"Tak is the way. It is the only way. Rellin knows this." I could feel his hot breath on my ear. He smelled like a goat. I wanted to retch. "Remember tak. Remember me." He then let go and scampered off and disappeared into the activity of the village.

That was weird. What was tak? He spoke about it with such passion that it made me think it must be something pretty special. It was like he was tempting me with it. Maybe it was illegal and he had to be careful about selling it.

It also felt kind of weird that I understood what he was saying. The day before his words made no sense. Now I heard them as if he were speaking English. But according to Osa, he wasn't speaking English. He was speaking the Denduron language, but I heard it as English. Still, there were some words that didn't translate into English like "quill" and "tak" and "crabble." I guess those are things that are special to Denduron, and therefore don't have an English translation. Whatever it was he was selling, I didn't want any. So I continued on toward the river.

A path snaked out of the village in the opposite direction from the ocean. Since I hadn't been there yet, I figured it must be the way to the river. After walking about a hundred yards through the forest, I began to hear the sound of rushing water. A few yards further along, I hit it. The path ended at the bank of a river that looked to be about twenty yards across. I knelt down on the bank and dipped my hand in. Yeow! It was like sticking my hands into a bucket of ice. I'm sure it was fed by snowmelt from the mountain, and rivers fed by snowmelt are frigid. But I was feeling all crusty from sleeping in animal skins and breathing smoke from the fire, so cold or not, I had to get wet. I took a deep breath and splashed water on my face. Wow. It was like a thousand needles stinging me, but it actually felt pretty good. I took a big gulp and swished out my mouth. I wished I had my toothbrush, but this would have to do.

That's when I heard the *crack* of a broken branch. Somebody was nearby! I heard someone humming a sweet tune. It was coming from just a few yards away. I think under normal circumstances I would have turned and left, but something compelled me to investigate. Remember how I described the people of this village? There was no joy here. There was only the sad business of survival. So hearing a pleasant tune being hummed felt out of left field. It made me want to see who it was. As strange as this seems, knowing that one of the Milago would actually want to hum a song made me feel that there might be some hope left in these people after all.

I remember going on a hike with my dad once through a forest that had been recently destroyed by fire. We were surrounded by nothing but the burned and black remains of what had once been a wonderful, green thicket. It was sad, until I saw that growing out from beneath a fallen log was a single, green fern leaf. As horrible as the devastation was, this one leaf was proof that one day the forest would return to normal. Hearing this tune coming through the woods made me think of that single fern leaf and I wanted to see who was singing it. So I quietly snuck through the brush toward the sound. When I pushed back the final branch between me and the singer, I saw that it wasn't one of the Milago after all.

It was Loor. She was kneeling on a rock with her back to me, washing out some clothes. I was disappointed at first, but this posed another interesting puzzle. As I told you, Loor is a hard case. I don't know much about the territory where she and Osa came from, but it didn't take a genius to figure out that these two were warriors. Osa had a calm way about her. She reminded me of one of those Black Belt guys who are so confident in their fighting abilities that they are actually gentle people. Of course, if you messed with them, they'd kick your ass. Loor, on the other hand, didn't have that calm thing going on. She seemed ready for a good ass kicking all the time. Maybe it was because she was young and hadn't gotten that wisdom comes with age thing. It didn't matter though, all I knew was that she scared the hell out of me. But seeing her on this rock, with her hair undone and humming a sweet tune seemed completely against character. Maybe there was a soft side to her that she kept hidden somewhere below all that macho stuff. Way below. She was facing away from me and had no idea I was there. Her long hair fell across her shoulders. It was deep black, and beautiful.

Now before you go thinking I was some kind of perv watching her from the bushes, you gotta realize that I was stuck. If I made a sound, she'd turn and see me watching her and probably pick up her stick and start playing Bobby the piñata boy. I wouldn't blame her. My only hope was that she'd finish washing up and walk back along the river toward the path without ever knowing I was there. So I stood rock still, doing my best to look like a tree.

After what felt like a lifetime, Loor stood up and started to braid her hair . . . and that's when I heard it. Another crack of a branch told me that somebody was walking up behind me. My heart pounded. I thought for sure that Loor would hear this, turn around, and catch me standing there like a doofus. I also thought that whoever was behind me was about to see me doing a peeping Tom number on Loor. But I was afraid to leave because Loor would surely catch me. None of these scenarios was very good.

What I didn't realize was that there was another scenario that was worse than all the above.

"I've been looking for you, Pendragon," came a deep voice that made Loor turn quickly in surprise. I turned too, and what I saw made my knees buckle. Standing behind me was one of Kagan's knights! He towered over me holding a spear in one hand and a rope in the other.

The guy had me. In that instant I felt sure that Saint Dane, or Mallos, or whatever he called himself had sent this guy to bring me in, the same way they got Uncle Press. And I knew one other thing—I wasn't going to go easily. So before the knight could make a move, I made my own move. I turned and ran for the river.

Loor didn't have time to react and I made another snap decision. She was coming with me. As she scrambled to her feet, I launched myself into a full-on, horizontal, flying tackle. I hit her and we both went sailing off the rock into the river.

Cold? You don't know cold until you jump into a river swollen from melted snow. The only reason it wasn't frozen solid was because it was moving so fast. But the truth was, I didn't care. If this river could get us away from that knight, it didn't matter to me if it froze the blood in my veins. I could always get warm later.

We hit the river in a tumble of arms and legs. The water was flowing so fast that it swept us downriver and away from the knight. There was no way he could catch up with us. I looked back and saw him standing on the shore looking stupid. He wasn't even going to try and catch up.

My attention went from getting away from the knight to surviving the river. You know when you first jump into the ocean you get a jolt of cold, but then your body quickly adapts and you get used to it? Well, not here. The river water was too cold for that. It felt like my body was actually freezing stiff. But I had to fight it, because we were in rapid whitewater, and that meant there were rocks. I heard once that if you're caught in rapids like this, the best thing to do is point your feet downriver and go with it until you hit a calm patch where you can swim to the side. That was the plan, but Loor was making it tricky. She held on to me so tightly that I was having trouble moving my arms to maneuver. I had to get away from her or we'd both drown.

"Feet first!" I yelled. "Float on your back!" I tried to push away, but Loor wouldn't back off. Then she said the three words I never expected to hear from this macho warrior girl. They were the three worst words you could hear in this situation, but she said them just the same.

"I cannot swim."

Oh, great. No wonder she was clinging to me. This was bad. The river was swirling us around and every time we hit a drop, both our heads went under. Each time we came up sputtering, and I didn't know how long our luck would hold out. I had to take control somehow or we were going to drown, or bash our heads into a rock and then drown. I thought maybe we could make a train with both of us on our backs. She'd go feet first and I'd cradle her from underneath while using my arms to guide us like a rudder.

"Feet downriver!" I shouted. "Face up, lie on me!"

She didn't move. She couldn't. It wasn't that she didn't want to, it was because she was paralyzed with fear. I can't imagine what it's like not being able to swim, but it must be terrifying. And with her strength, there was no way I could pry myself loose. We hit another drop and both went under again. No sooner did we come up for air than we both slammed into a rock. I barely felt it because Loor took most of the hit with her back. It must have been crushing, because it made her loosen her grip on me. Instantly I grabbed her and flipped her onto her back.

"Grab my legs," I commanded. She did. I was on my back too, with Loor between my legs. My arms were now free to steer and keep us afloat. My train idea was working. Now if we could only ride this out until the rapids stopped.

"Use your legs to keep us off the rocks," I said. Loor was scared, but she had enough of a grip to start thinking again. While I paddled frantically, she kicked us away from a few sharp rocks. We then hit another drop and went under again. I could feel Loor starting to squirm away from me, but I held her tight with my legs. In a few seconds, we were above water again.

Then I was hit with a terrifying thought. What if these rapids led to a waterfall? There was no way we could survive that. I had to force the idea out of my head, because there was nothing I could do about it now.

We hit a few more drops, bounced off another rock or two, and then mercifully, the river grew calm. We made it through the rapids and there was no waterfall waiting. But we weren't safe yet because Loor still couldn't swim. My junior lifeguard training took over at this point and I began to tow her to the side. She was so tired and beaten that she didn't have enough strength left to fight me, so it wasn't all that tough to bring her along. Soon we were dragging ourselves out of the freezing water and crawling up onto the bank. We lay down on the gravel, totally exhausted, totally beaten up, but alive. Luckily the three suns were now higher in the sky and they were starting to give off some warmth.

After I caught my breath, I sat up on my elbows and looked at Loor. She lay flat on her back, still breathing hard. I have to admit, now that we were safe, I was feeling pretty good about myself. Not only did I save the big, bad warrior girl from one of Kagan's knights, I also saved her life a dozen times over on the river. I couldn't wait for her to admit that I wasn't the lame wad she thought I was. But of course I wasn't going to fish for a compliment. That wouldn't have been cool. It had to come from her. So I waited. And waited. And waited some more. But she didn't say a word. What was up with that? I was getting kind of ticked off. Not that I was expecting a full-on "Oh, Pendragon, you're my hero!" but a simple "Thank you" would have been nice. Still there was nothing. Finally I decided to break the ice.

"You okay?" I asked.

"No thanks to you," came the reply.

"What?" I shouted and sat up straight. "I saved you from drowning!"

"But if we had not been in the river, I would not have needed help," she said as if she were totally ticked off at me.

"But if we weren't in the river, we would have been attacked by Kagan's knight!" I shot back.

Loor finally sat up and looked at me. She didn't say anything at first, but her hard look made me feel like some sort of lower life-form.

"You were hiding in the bushes, watching me," she said. Gulp. *Busted.* "If you had come out to speak with me," she went on, "I would have told you that I was waiting for that knight."

Huh? I couldn't get my mind around this. "You were waiting for one of Kagan's knights?" I asked, dumbfounded. "Why?"

"Because he is the Traveler from Denduron and he was coming to give me information about Press. You nearly killed us both to escape from the most important friend we have here on this territory. What am I supposed to say to you, Pendragon? Thank you?"

DENDURON

I had reached a new low. The more I learned about this world the less I understood. Worse, when I finally tried to take action, I screwed up. Loor and I nearly died on that river and it was my fault. I wanted to go home. I wanted to be in my bed. I wanted to feel Marley's nose nudging me and smell her fishy dog breath. Instead I was lying cold and bruised on the bank of a river on the other side of the universe.

"Loor! Are you all right?" I heard the voice first, then saw the guy crashing through the woods. It was the knight who scared me into our whitewater adventure. As he appeared from out of the brush I could see that he wasn't much older than me. He was tall, and the leather armor made him look even bigger. He wasn't very agile though. The other knights I saw were trained, dangerous dudes, kind of like ancient marines. This guy had the gear and the look, but he acted more like a big puppy who was all floppy arms and legs. He wasn't exactly the fighting machine one would expect. He stumbled out of the woods, tripped over a root, nearly did a face plant in the dirt, then looked at us with wide, frightened eyes.

"We are fine," assured Loor.

"This was my fault," whined the knight. "I am so sorry."

Loor felt herself for broken bones. "Pendragon," she said, "this is Alder."

"Alder what?" I asked, though I think I already knew the answer.

"Just Alder," answered the knight.

Yup, another one-name guy. When does a society progress far enough to start using two names? Whatever.

"I cannot tell you how happy we are that you have arrived, Pendragon," said Alder enthusiastically. "Now we can begin."

Uh-oh. What did he mean by "begin"? I was getting sick of being one step behind everybody else.

"Begin what?" I asked.

Alder looked at Loor like he was surprised I didn't know what he was talking about. He should get used to it. I looked at Loor too. Obviously they hadn't told me everything. Loor gazed across the river. I could tell she was debating whether or not to answer. Her jaw was clenching. She looked back to me, stared me down for a second, and then let it out.

"You have seen how the Bedoowan tribe treats the Milago," she began. "There is more you have not seen. There is torture and starvation and disease. The Bedoowan treat the Milago worse than dogs. They do not have enough food or medicine. Half of the babies born do not live past the first few months. The glaze mines claim lives every day. If this horrible treatment is not stopped, the Milago will die out. The time has come to stop it."

I didn't like where this was going. Sure, these people had it pretty rough, and things needed to change. But what I didn't get was what my part was supposed to be in all this. I wasn't so sure I wanted to know, either.

Alder said, "The Milago are a gentle people. They are not

warriors. It has taken years of hardship to convince them to take action. If it were not for Press, they may never have been ready."

"What's Uncle Press got to do with it?" I asked.

"Press has been their inspiration," said Alder with reverence. "He has given the Milago the strength to fight back."

Things were happening fast. This was the first time I heard the word "fight," and I didn't like it. "What about you?" I asked Alder. "You're not a Milago. You're a Bedoowan. How come you're so concerned about them?"

Loor stared me right in the eye. "He is a Traveler, Pendragon," she said forcefully. "Just like I am, and Press, and my mother. That is what Travelers do. They provide help where it is needed. Are you ready for that responsibility?"

"Well . . . no," I said honestly.

"I did not think so," spat Loor with disgust.

Alder gazed at me with a look of confusion, and maybe a little desperation. "But Press has spoken of you for some time now," he insisted. "He told us that if anything happened to him, you would take his place."

"Whoa, whoa!" I said, backing away from him. "Uncle Press didn't fill me in on any of this! All he said was that there were some people in trouble who needed our help. I figured all we had to do was give somebody a ride someplace, or maybe help move some furniture. I didn't know he was talking about leading some freakin' revolution!"

Loor spun to me with fire in her eyes. "That is the word exactly," she said with passion. "Revolution. The Milago have been preparing to revolt against the Bedoowan. Press has made them believe they can succeed. Without him, they will not have the strength to fight and they will all die. I do not know why, but he has made the Milago believe that you are able to lead them as he would. That is why you are here, Pendragon. That is what you must do."

I felt like I was in the river again, being swept along with no control. My heart was beating about as fast as it had in the river too. I'm not a revolutionary, Mark. The closest I ever came to being in a fight was the time you and I wrestled over who was gonna bat first in Wiffle ball. That doesn't exactly qualify me to lead a revolution.

"Look," I said, trying hard not to let my voice crack. "I feel bad for these people and all, but I'm not up to this. You say I'm a Traveler? Fine, whatever. But up until two days ago I had no idea any of this even existed! How can I suddenly lead a revolution?"

"But you must," said Alder seriously. "The Milago believe that you will take over for Press."

"Then go get Uncle Press!" I shouted. Alder then looked down at the ground. Obviously something was wrong.

"Where is Press now?" she demanded.

Alder kept his eyes on the ground and said, "He is being held in the Bedoowan fortress. Kagan has sentenced him to death. He will be executed tomorrow at the equinox."

Oh, man! Uncle Press was going to die! Could things get any worse? Loor spun away from Alder and picked up a rock. With a roar of anger, she reached back and threw it across the river. It was like she was channeling her anger and frustration into this one, mighty throw. She stormed toward me like an enraged bull. I took a few steps back, expecting her to take a swing at me. But she didn't. Instead she stuck her nose in my face and seethed. "I do not understand why Press believes in you. You are a coward, you are weak, and you do not care for anyone but yourself. But you are a Traveler, and you will begin to act like one. It is time you saw the truth," and with that she gave me a shove backward.

I had to pinwheel my arms to keep from falling over.

Alder said meekly, "You know I cannot go with you."

"I know," answered Loor. "Meet us after dark."

She gave me another shove and walked off. I didn't know what else to do, so I followed her. We didn't say much on our walk back to the Milago village and it gave me a chance to digest all that I had just learned. I guess that Travelers are some kind of cosmic do-gooders. That's very noble and all, but I didn't volunteer for this particular honor. Just the opposite. I didn't want any part of it. Everyone kept telling me that I was a Traveler and that I had a responsibility, but who the heck made me a Traveler? I don't remember signing up. Maybe it's like the army where you get drafted. But if I were the guy in charge of drafting Travelers, I sure as heck wouldn't pick somebody like me! They should have picked a Navy SEAL or a SWAT guy or better still, one of those WWF muscle heads. They shouldn't have picked a fourteen-year-old gym rat. Even if I wanted to help the Milago, the second I opened my mouth they'd know I was a fraud. No, the best thing I could do was stick to Plan A, and that was to get to the flume and get out of here, ASAP.

There was one thing that bothered me though. Uncle Press was in trouble. No, worse. He was going to die the next day. But what could I do? If I went after him, Kagan's knights would cut me to ribbons and we'd both be dead. I was in a horrible situation.

When Loor and I got back to the village we were greeted by Osa, who looked at us with concern. My guess is she could tell that things were going badly. Before Osa could ask what had happened, Loor said, "He must see the mines."

Osa didn't ask why, she just looked at her daughter and gave a weary sigh.

"Come with me, Pendragon," said Osa and started to walk off.

"What if I don't want to see the mines?" I asked, because I didn't.

Osa looked at me with these intense, piercing eyes. She wasn't scolding me. She wasn't trying to intimidate me either. This is hard to describe, but the look she gave me was one of absolute certainty. The look said: "You will come and see the mines because that is what you must do." Maybe it was a kind of hypnotism, but the instant she looked at me, I knew I had no choice. So I followed her. Weird, huh?

Loor didn't come with us and Osa didn't invite her. It was just the two of us and that was fine by me. As we walked through the Milago village, I started to notice something I hadn't seen before. Whenever we passed one of the Milago, they would give me a quick glance. We'd make eye contact and then they'd quickly look to the ground and continue on their way. It was weird. It was like they were watching me, but afraid to acknowledge that I was there. Up until now, I thought they didn't even know I existed. Nobody talked to anyone else and they certainly didn't talk to me. That is, of course, except for Figgis. He was the only Milago who spoke to me. Everybody else kept to themselves. Yet here they were, checking me out. I was betting these villagers were looking at me and thinking: "How can this be the guy who's going to lead our revolution? He's a wussy kid!" And they were right.

I followed Osa back to the path that led to the ocean. We walked a few yards into the woods and I saw that there was another, smaller path that led off to the right. This is the path we took and it led us to a clearing where there was a large foundation made of stone. It looked much like the stage in the center of the village where the Transfer ceremony took place, but there was no wooden platform covering it. There was a huge wooden frame built over the foundation with a large pulley attached. A thick rope looped over the pulley and dropped down into the hole. Two burly men were hauling on the rope, bringing up something from below. The setup kind of reminded me of one of those old-fashioned wishing wells where the bucket would be dropped down on a rope and then hoisted out with water. But in this case, they weren't hoisting up water, they were hoisting up glaze. The two men brought the large basket to the surface, grabbed it, and emptied it onto the ground. A few craggy glaze stones tumbled out. The two looked at each other and sighed. Apparently this wasn't a very good haul. I remembered that they had to bring out enough glaze to balance with the wife of the man who was killed the day before. They added the new stones to a larger pile next to the foundation. There wasn't much there. If they didn't bring up more glaze, the poor woman would join her husband at the bottom of the pit. A cold chill went up my spine.

Osa walked to the foundation, sat down, and swung her legs over the side. "Be careful," she commanded. And with that, she lowered herself over the side. Where was she going? Did she jump? I walked up to the edge, looked down, and saw that there was a ladder attached to the side. Osa was climbing down into what looked like a bottomless pit. In no time she disappeared into the gloom. I looked over at the two miners. Sure enough, they were looking at me. But the second we made eye contact, they looked away and went back to work. I'm not sure what was creepier: Knowing that everyone was checking me out, or climbing down a rickety ladder into the dark unknown.

"Now, Pendragon!" echoed Osa's voice from below.

I reached over the side and tugged on the ladder to make

sure it was sturdy. I swung my legs over, grabbed the ladder and started down. It was a good thing the pit was dark, because if I could have seen all the way to the bottom, I'm not sure I would have had the guts to climb down. The ladder itself was crudely made from saplings lashed together, but it was strong. After climbing down several feet, I found that the foot of the ladder rested on a stone ledge. But this wasn't the bottom. The top of another ladder was leaning on the ledge next to this one and since Osa wasn't there, I figured I had to climb down it as well. In all, there were fifteen ladders. Unbelievable. This pit was deep. Every third ledge had a tunnel that led horizontally away from the pit. I figured that these were abandoned sections of the mine. Probably when the glaze ran out on each level, they would tunnel deeper and deeper and deeper.

Finally I reached the bottom, where Osa stood waiting for me. There was light down here too. Small candles were everywhere. It wasn't exactly bright, but once my eyes adjusted, I could see just fine. There was one tunnel leading away from the pit, and that's where Osa went. I followed her obediently. The tunnel was carved out of the rock; I could stand up straight, but Osa had to crouch down a bit. It was a good thing I wasn't claustrophobic.

"The main shaft was built generations ago," she explained. "But when they discovered a rich vein of glaze at this level, the miners decided to do things differently."

"What did they do?" I asked.

Osa didn't have to answer. After a few more yards the tunnel emptied out into a humongous cavern. The ceiling must have been thirty feet high. It was spectacular. Leading off from the cavern were many other tunnels. It was like we were at the center of a wagon wheel and the tunnels, like spokes, led out from the center in all directions. Down each tunnel was a set of miniature tracks. I had seen pictures of gold mines before and I figured these tracks were for the ore cars.

"Once it was discovered that this was the level to find glaze, the tunneling started to spread out in all directions," she explained. "There are miles and miles of tunnels. It is so complex that miners have lost their way and wandered for days."

I had to admit it was pretty impressive, especially because these guys did all of the work by hand. We stood to the side of the cavern and watched the activity. There were no powerful mining machines here, just the strong backs of Milago miners. Some were pushing carts full of dirt, others emptied the carts in the center of the cavern and sifted it for bits of glaze. I also heard the distant sound of pickaxes ringing against stone as the miners labored to stretch the tunnels in their search for more glaze.

"The miners work day and night," Osa explained. "It is the only way they can possibly meet Kagan's unreasonable demands."

She reached down and picked up one of the miners' tools. It was a metal pickax with a wooden handle. "These tools are forbidden on the surface because they are made of metal," she told me. "The penalty for using a metal tool on the surface is death."

Now that she mentioned it, I didn't remember seeing anything made of metal on the surface. All the tools that were used above were made from wood or from stone. It was like the Bedoowan were trying to keep the Milago back in the stone age, except for when it came to getting their precious glaze, of course.

I began to notice that there was an odd smell to the mine. It wasn't a horrible smell, in fact it was kind of sweet. "What is that smell?" I asked.

Osa didn't answer, but motioned for me to follow her. We walked across the large cavern, stepping across the railroad tracks. As we approached the far side I began to make out something that made me shudder. I hadn't seen it before because the light was so dim, but now that we were here I could see things plainly. To be honest, I wished I still couldn't see, but I did. Lying on the floor of the cavern were dozens of miners. They looked horrible. Some moaned in pain, others just sat there with blank looks.

"They look sick," I said.

"They are," came the sad reply. "The smell is a gas that is released when the glaze is separated from the rock. It is a poison that slowly destroys your ability to breathe."

"We're breathing toxic fumes?" I asked, ready to bolt back to the ladders.

"Do not worry," she said calmly. "You must breathe it for years for it to be of concern."

I looked at the sick miners and said, "These guys have been breathing it for years?"

Osa nodded sadly. "It is a painful death."

"Why don't they go up into the fresh air?" I asked with horror.

"They have no strength left," was the grim answer. "These poor souls are in the final stages of the disease. They will die here."

I took a few steps back from the sick miners. I'm ashamed to admit it, but I was afraid I might catch this nasty disease from them. Suddenly the huge cavern didn't seem so huge anymore. The walls felt like they were closing in and I wanted out of there in a bad way. Maybe I had a touch of claustrophobia after all.

"Why did you have to show me this?" I demanded to know.

"Because it is very important that you understand how

desperate the situation is for the Milago," Osa said.

I wanted to scream. Osa was setting me up. She was showing me how bad these guys had it so I'd feel sorry for them and agree to lead their revolution. But why? Osa didn't seem like a fool. She could see that I wasn't the kind of guy who could lead a revolution. Her daughter figured it out pretty quick. Why wasn't Osa with the program? I didn't want to argue here in front of these poor miners, so I headed for the tunnel that led to the ladders.

"Where are you going?" she asked.

"Home!" was my simple reply. I hurried across the cavern, hopping over the railroad tracks and dodging the ore cars. Then just as I was about to enter the tunnel that led to the ladders, somebody ran in front of me. It was Figgis. But this time he didn't stop to try and sell me something. He was in a hurry and I'm not even sure he knew it was me who he cut off. I watched the little guy run down the tunnel toward the ladders and was about to follow him when I felt the ground start to shudder. Uh-oh, was this an earthquake? Or a cave-in? A second later there was a huge explosion! I spun to look where the sound came from and saw black smoke billowing out from one of the tunnels. Many of the miners were looking at the smoking tunnel with confusion.

Now, I'm no expert, but these guys have been doing this mining thing for a long time. Surely they had been through an explosion like this before. You'd think that they would have instantly kicked into emergency gear and either evacuated the mine or started damage control. There could be miners trapped in there who needed to be rescued. But that's not what happened. The miners just looked to each other with a mixture of fear and confusion. It was like they didn't know what to do.

Finally Osa called out, "Are there men in there?"

One of the miners shouted out, "Rellin!" This seemed to wake the others up. They quickly came to their senses and headed for the smoking tunnel to rescue their leader. One of the miners tied a rope around his waist, boldly fought the smoke and entered the tunnel. Another few miners held the other end of the rope. I guess the idea was that if he passed out, they could drag him back to safety. Brave guy.

The ground didn't shake again. Whatever damage the explosion caused was only in that one tunnel. I didn't feel I was in any danger and I wanted to stay and see if Rellin was okay.

"How often do they have explosions like that?" I asked. Osa kept staring at the smoking tunnel and then said something I never expected to hear.

"What is an explosion?" she asked.

Huh? How could she not know what an explosion was? This woman knew everything there was to know. It couldn't have been a language thing because Travelers understood all languages.

"You know," I continued. "Explosion. That big bang. From dynamite or something."

Osa looked at me with confusion and said, "I have never seen anything like that happen here, nor in my home territory. You are saying that loud noise caused the damage? Like lightning?"

This was deeply weird. Though maybe it explained why the miners reacted the way they did. They probably had no idea what happened either. But then what had caused the explosion? Maybe they tapped into some underground gas pocket.

Before we could talk more about it, the miners holding the rope began to frantically pull on their end. Other miners gathered to watch with concern. They stared into the smoky tunnel, waiting to see what came out. After a few seconds, the miner on the other end emerged from the smoke and in his arms . . . was Rellin. The chief miner was full of black soot and there were traces of blood around his forehead, but he was okay. Dazed, but okay. He was helped to sit down and brought a leather skin full of water to drink. Rellin took a long drink, swished it in his mouth, and spit.

Then an odd thing happened. Rellin looked up at the other miners, gazing at each one in turn, and began to laugh. The other miners didn't know what to make of this. Maybe the total relief from his brush with death came out in nervous laughter. Or maybe he was crazy. I sure didn't know and from the confused looks of the miners, they didn't know either. I have to admit, it was kind of creepy. I think Osa felt the same way because she put a hand on my shoulder and said, "We should go to the surface."

She didn't have to tell me twice. I was down that tunnel and up those ladders in an instant. As I climbed, I looked up at the circle of blue sky that grew larger and larger the higher I got. It was the light at the end of a long, dark tunnel and I couldn't get to it fast enough. When I poked my head out into the fresh air, I took a deep breath and promised myself that I would never go down in that hell hole again. One of the miners who hoisted up the basket of glaze was leaning against the wooden frame of the pulley system, watching me. The other miner was gone.

Then I sensed something strange. For some reason the miner didn't turn away after we made eye contact. He kept on staring at me.

Osa poked up out of the hole, jumped onto the ground, and said, "Tell me more about this thing you call . . . explosion."

Before I could answer, Osa's attention was caught by something behind me. I turned to look and saw the miner who had been staring at me. Osa walked past me with her eyes fixed on the man. He just stood there, still looking at me with a dumb expression on his face. Osa walked right up to him, stared at him for a moment more, then quickly spun back toward me and shouted, "Pendragon, run!"

"Huh?"

Before Osa could say another word, the miner toppled over and fell at her feet. My eyes fixed on the wooden arrow that was sticking out of his back. Yeah, the guy was dead. That wasn't a dumb look on his face, it was a dead look. I had never seen a dead man before. I couldn't move. Osa ran to me, grabbed my hand, and started to drag me toward the forest. We had only gone a few steps when four of Kagan's knights leaped out in front of us. Now I knew what had happened to the miner.

"We've come for the boy," they announced. There was no mistaking it this time. Unlike the knight named Alder who I mistook for an enemy back by the river, these guys were not on our side. They carried clublike weapons and, judging from the poor dead miner with the arrow sticking out of his back, they wouldn't hesitate to use them for whatever mayhem they thought fit.

Osa didn't move, but I could feel her tense up. She let go of my hand and slowly turned sideways. I knew what this meant. It was exactly what we were taught to do in karate class. Turning sideways made you a smaller target. Yeah, there was going to be a fight and I was in the middle of it. Osa wasn't about to make the first move. She was too smart for that. If something was going to happen, it would be the knights who would start it.

One raised his club and took a step toward us. I froze. Osa bent her knees, ready to defend herself. The knight let out a bellow, began to charge and . . . whack! He suddenly went down in a heap as if he had been shot. The other knights were just as surprised as I was, but I saw the reason for it before they did.

Standing behind them was Loor, holding her wooden stave. Nice shot. She had another weapon and quickly tossed it to her mother. Osa caught it and crouched into attack mode. Now they were both armed and the odds became a little better. But still, these knights were professional fighters. I wasn't so sure how these warrior women would do against them.

Things happened fast. Before the knights could recover from the surprise of seeing their buddy do a face plant, Loor grabbed the club from the hand of the knight she had just whacked and in one quick movement she threw it to me. I caught it just as Loor took up position next to her mother. It was now three-on-three. Well, two-and-a-half-on-three because the chances of me using that club to attack one of those hairy knights were about the same as me sprouting wings and flying out of there.

"Fight, Pendragon," commanded Loor.

At that instant the three knights charged. Osa and Loor ran to meet them. I stood frozen. My prediction about Osa and Loor being warriors turned out to be a hundred percent correct. These two were awesome. They swung their long wooden weapons like martial arts experts. If I weren't so terrified, I probably would have enjoyed the show. They spun and twirled the long staves so quickly they were nothing more than blurs. The knights, on the other hand, fought awkwardly. They would swing their clubs, but the women would either bat the attack away with a deft flip of their stave, or dodge out of the way and answer the attack with a ringing smack to the body. If this were a toe-to-toe slugfest, I would have bet on the knights. But Osa and Loor never stood still long enough for the knights to get a solid shot at them. It was like watching lumbering bears being attacked by vicious bees. And the bees were winning.

The only problem was that the knights were armored. It was going to take more than a few defensive blows to stop these guys. But I was certain that Osa and Loor were going to take care of them, so I began to relax.

Bad move. That's when one of the knights charged me. He had his club held high and screamed like he was getting up the energy to take my head off. I didn't know what to do. I should have held out the club to protect myself. I should have ducked and then attacked. I should have thrown the club at him to slow him up. But I didn't do any of those things. All I did was take a few steps back in fear, trip, and fall down on my butt. I was dead meat. The knight was almost on me. I could see the rage in his eyes. This was going to hurt. A few more steps and he would be within swinging range.

But then, Osa threw her wooden stave at the guy like a javelin and it hit him right in the knees. His legs buckled and he fell to the ground, hard. Loor was on him instantly. She gave him a ringing whack with her stave, and the knight crumpled unconscious. Two down.

Loor looked at me and I could see the fire of battle in her eyes. "Fight, you coward!" she commanded.

Osa ran up and shouted, "No! Take him. Hide him!"

Loor wanted to stay and fight beside her mother, but Osa was in charge.

"He must not be taken. Go!" commanded Osa.

There wasn't time for argument because the other two knights were back on the attack. Reluctantly Loor grabbed me by the arm and yanked me to my feet. I have to tell you, Mark, I never felt so helpless and embarrassed in my life. I was a complete wuss. You always wonder how you might react in times of danger. You always have these visions that you'll rise to the occasion and be the hero and save the day. Well, let me tell you, that fantasy couldn't be any further from the truth than what was happening to me. I'm ashamed to admit it, but I was like a frightened baby.

As Loor pulled me away toward the forest, I glanced back to see what was happening with Osa. What I saw was incredible. She was even better on her own. This amazing warrior woman fought both knights at the same time. She spun, thrust, parried, and rarely missed the mark. It seemed almost easy.

Loor and I dove out of the clearing into the woods, then turned back and hid to watch the end game. I knew that Loor wanted to be in there fighting beside her mother. It was killing her to be here, baby-sitting me.

"Your mother is amazing," I whispered to Loor.

Loor didn't comment, but I knew she felt the same way. A few moments later, it was all over. The knights had been losing steam and after a few more ringing blows, they both collapsed to the ground either unconscious, or too exhausted to move. Osa remained in a crouch and swept the air with a quick 360 to be sure the fight was over. She then straightened up, spun her wooden stave like a ninja master and slipped it into its leather strap that ran across her back. The battle had been won.

"You don't deserve this, Pendragon," Loor spat at me.

She was right. I didn't. These two women had risked their lives for me, and there was no way I was capable of living up to what they expected of me in return. But as bad as I felt, the real horror of the situation hadn't yet hit. Loor and I stood up and started back into the clearing. Osa saw us. She took a few steps toward us, then suddenly stopped. Loor saw this and quickly put her hand out to stop me as well. Something was wrong. Were the knights waking up? I looked at Osa, who slowly returned to her fighting stance. She was back on full alert and started to reach for her wooden stave. I looked around the clearing, but there was no movement at all. The knights lay unconscious where they had fallen. Why was everyone so tense?

A second later I had my answer—a moment that will forever haunt me. I first heard a rustling and thought someone was coming through the bushes. I soon learned it wasn't in the bushes. It was coming from above. It was in the trees. I looked up and saw to my horror that perched up in the trees were four more knights. These knights weren't armed with clubs. They had bows and arrows. I had forgotten that the miner was killed with an arrow. These knights had been there the whole time, watching the spectacle. And now they were about to make their move.

Osa stood in the middle of the clearing, unprotected. Loor was about to run to her, but Osa yelled out, "Hide him!"

This made Loor stop. It must have taken every bit of willpower to go against her instincts and obey her mother, but that's what she did. She backed off, grabbed my hand, and that's when it started.

The knights let loose with their arrows, all aimed at Osa. The brave woman wore no armor. There was nothing to protect her from this deadly rain. All four arrows hit their mark, and Osa crumpled to her knees. Loor let out a pained little sound and started to run for her, but I grabbed her. By now the knights had already reloaded, and if Loor had run to her mother, she would have met the same deadly fate. We stood there for a second, looking into the doomed woman's kind eyes. Maybe I was imagining things, but as I write this now I could swear that she gave us a little smile.

The knights unleashed another volley of arrows. But these weren't meant for Osa. These were aimed at us. Luckily we were protected by trees and they all ended up missing us or slamming into branches. But it was enough to throw Loor back into action. She grabbed my hand and off we ran into the forest, leaving behind her mortally wounded mother.

Loor knew the forest well. Keeping up with her was like running with a deer. She leaped over fallen trees, skirted boulders, and blasted through a thicket. We weren't going in a straight line either, and I realized that this journey was all about shaking the knights who might be trailing us. I was getting tired and had a nasty stitch in my side, but there was no way I would complain. Not after what these women had done for me.

We eventually made our way around to the far side of the village, where Loor brought me to a stone hut. I wasn't exactly thrilled with her choice of hiding places. All it would take for a knight to find us was a quick search of the village. But I soon found out that Loor had other things in mind. She quickly dove on the pile of animal skins that was lying along one wall and pulled them aside. Beneath was the same hard-packed earth that all the hut floors were made of. Loor took her wooden stave and started to scratch at the dirt. With a couple of quick digs, she unearthed a wooden ring. She threw her stave down, grabbed the ring and pulled. It was a trapdoor!

"This leads to the mines," she said in explanation.

Oh, great. I had promised myself never to return to those mines. It was a promise that lasted a good twenty minutes.

"The Bedoowan are afraid of the gas," she said. "They

never go into the mines." She threw open the trapdoor to reveal another crude ladder leading down. Here we go again. She motioned for me to go first. Loor followed quickly and closed the door behind her. We climbed down only one ladder. It led to a small tunnel that we had to crouch down in to walk along. I could tell that it was angled downward.

"There are many of these small tunnels," she said. "They bring air to the miners."

So basically we were walking along a ventilation shaft. Made sense. But since this was only for ventilation, there were no candles to show us the way. It was like walking through ink. I kept one hand out in front of me in case a wall decided to jump out. But I wasn't going fast enough for Loor. She barged ahead and took the lead. She moved much faster and it was easier to follow her than it was to follow nothing. I just hoped she knew where she was going.

This ventilation tunnel led to a much wider tunnel with some ore car tracks. I figured this must have been one of the early mining tunnels that was dug before the Milago built the big cavern. We followed this tunnel for several minutes until it emptied out into a familiar space. It was the mine shaft where Osa and I first climbed down. When was that? It felt like a century ago, but it was more like an hour. We came out on one of the rock ledges and I saw that we were only three levels down from the surface. The familiar circle of blue light beckoned from above.

Loor stood out on the ledge and looked up. She was obviously debating with herself about something and it didn't take long for me to find out what it was.

"Go to the bottom," she commanded. "I will meet you there. Go!" She stared at me until I started to climb down the ladder. As soon as I started down, she began to climb up. Just as I figured. She wanted to go to her mother. I hung on the ladder and watched her climb to the surface. I know I should have kept going down as I was told, but I couldn't. Osa had put her life on the line for me, and I had to find out how she was. So after wrestling with the decision for a few seconds, I started to climb up.

When I reached the last ladder before the surface, I heard something coming from outside. I didn't know what it was at first, and when I finally recognized it, it made my heart sink. It was Loor. She was humming the same sweet song that I'd heard her humming by the river. I pulled myself up out of the mine shaft and what I saw then, broke my heart.

Loor was sitting on the ground next to the stone foundation. She cradled Osa's head in her lap and stroked her hair while slowly rocking back and forth as if lulling a baby to sleep. I didn't know if Osa was dead or alive. Lying next to her were the four arrows that had hit her. Loor had pulled them out. I stayed where I was because I didn't want to intrude. Loor was a proud girl and I was sure she wouldn't want me to see her cry.

I glanced around the clearing and saw that the knights were gone. The archers in the trees probably dragged off their unconscious buddies. The body of the Milago miner was still there though. He lay on his back, staring up sightlessly into the sky.

That's when I saw Osa's hand move. She reached out weakly and took her daughter's hand. She was alive! I quickly ran over to see if I could be of any help. Loor didn't acknowledge that I was there, except that she stopped humming her song. But Osa knew I was there, and she looked up at me with tired eyes.

"Do not be sad," she said with a weak voice. "Either of you. This is the way it was meant to be."

I had trouble holding back my tears. Osa wasn't going to make it.

"I . . . I'm sorry, Osa," was all I could get out.

Osa then took her hand away from Loor and reached for the leather pouch around her neck. It was the pouch where she had put the silver ring.

"Take this, Pendragon," she said. "Use it as you see fit."

I took the pouch and pulled out the ring. Osa nodded encouragement, so I put it on the ring finger of my right hand. Oddly enough, it fit perfectly.

"You are both at the beginning of a long journey," said Osa as she grew weaker. "Pendragon, I know you do not feel you are up to the challenge. You are wrong."

I nodded, but I didn't believe her.

Osa continued, "Halla is in your hands. Remember that. Let it be your guide. Together you two will—" Osa caught her breath, gave a little shudder and closed her eyes. They would never open again.

This was a painful moment. Of course, I felt sympathy for Loor. The girl had just lost her mother. But I, too, felt loss. In the short time I had known Osa, I had developed an affection for her. She was the one voice of reason in the storm of confusion that I had been swept into. I trusted her. I felt safe with her. And my trust had proven to be well placed, for she had sacrificed her own life to save mine. That's a debt that can never be repaid.

I wanted to comfort Loor but I didn't know how. I struggled to find the right words, but Loor spoke first. "Go down into the mine, Pendragon," she said. "I will meet you there."

I wasn't about to argue. I just nodded and stepped away. Before I climbed down onto the ladder I said, "I'm sorry, Loor."

Loor didn't acknowledge me. She just sat there, still

cradling her mother. As I climbed down the ladder, I could hear that she was once again humming the tune from the river. I had to fight back my tears.

I climbed all the way down to the bottom of the mine and found my way into the giant cavern. Once there I saw that it was business as usual. There was no day here and no night. All signs of the excitement from the explosion were gone. I didn't know what to do, so I found a quiet corner and sat down to try and think. To say that my mind was a jumble of conflicting thoughts was an understatement. I spun the silver ring on my finger. This strange piece of jewelry might actually be my ticket home. But as much as I wanted to use it, the idea of bolting out of here made me feel incredibly guilty. For some reason that I still didn't understand, everyone was expecting me to help these poor people fight for their freedom. Stranger still, an amazing person had just given her life so that I could live to carry out that mission.

I wished I knew what to do. If there was something these people needed that I could deliver on, I'd gladly do it. But lead a revolution? That's insane! I sat there for a while and even got a little bit of sleep. Finally Loor arrived carrying a basket.

"Come with me," she ordered. So I got up and followed her. She led me down one of the mine tunnels that didn't look as if it were active. A few feet along we came to an opening to a small room that had been cut from the rock. It was set up like one of the huts with animal fur bedding, a table, and candles for light.

"This is where we come when Kagan is looking for us," she explained. "You will be safe here." She then handed me the basket and I saw that it was full of bread and fruit. I needed to eat, but I didn't have much of an appetite.

I took a chance and asked, "Where's Osa?"

"She was taken to the village," said Loor with no emotion. "Tomorrow I will take her to Zadaa."

Zadaa. That was the territory where Loor and Osa came from. So that meant Loor knew how to use the flumes to get around. And if she was going to bring her mother's body back home, I couldn't imagine she planned to climb back to the top of that mountain to get there. There must have been another way to use the flumes.

There was some serious tension in this little stone room just then. Loor was angry, but I wasn't sure how much of that anger was aimed at me. I was upset and sad and to be honest, a little scared of her. She had a nasty temper and if she decided to take it out on me, there'd be nothing left of poor Bobby Pendragon except a stain on the wall. I decided not to push Loor by talking. So I sat down on the animal fur and tried to act invisible.

Loor was like a caged cat, pacing back and forth. What I feared was that her anger would build to a point where she'd explode and take me apart. In a strange way, that was exactly what happened. But it happened in a way that I never expected. She didn't hit me. She didn't insult me. She didn't even scream at me. All of those things would have been understandable. But what she did hurt much more.

"I am taking you home tomorrow," she said flatly. "You do not belong here."

Whoa. That was the *last* thing I expected to hear.

"But . . . what about the revolution?" I asked lamely.

"You think you cannot help these people because you are not a warrior," she said. "But the Milago do not need a warrior. They need someone they can trust. You are not that person."

This took me by surprise. Obviously I was not a fighter like Loor, and I was not exactly the brave, hero type. But trustworthy? Come on! I could be trusted. I was a good guy. Where did she get off calling me untrustworthy?

"Why do you say that?" I asked.

She looked me right in the eye and said, "How can someone be trusted who only thinks of himself? From the moment you arrived, you have plotted to get away. It did not matter how much the Milago need help. It was always about getting home."

I was feeling a little defensive at this point. I thought she was being unfair and said, "Okay, maybe you're right. But I was kind of thrown into this mess without a whole bunch of warning. It's a lot to ask someone to turn their life upside down in a day!"

"I know, Pendragon," she said. "The same thing happened to me. But there is a difference between you and me and it has nothing to do with fighting."

"And what's that?"

That's when she let me have it.

"You saw how my mother died," she said, trying to hold back emotion. "I would have done anything to save her. But you . . . I do not understand how you can only think of yourself when your uncle is about to die."

Those words hit me hard. She was right. Uncle Press was in trouble. I knew it ever since that sled had landed us in the snow bank. Yet I was planning on leaving without even trying to help him. I had been so worried about saving myself that I didn't think for a second that Uncle Press needed me. Loor was right and I was ashamed.

"That is why you are of no use here, Pendragon," she said with finality. "The Milago need someone to have faith in. You are not that person." She turned and headed for the door, but just before she left she said, "After you get some sleep, I will bring you home. You can go back to the life you miss so dearly and forget that any of this ever happened. I suppose in time you will also forget about Press." And she left.

I had just learned something about myself and I didn't like it. Could I really be that selfish? Everything Loor said was dead on. Sure I cared about Uncle Press, but I convinced myself that there was nothing I could do to help him. But was that true? Or was it just an easy way to get out of trying? Did I even let my mind think of the possibility of trying to rescue him? I spent the next few hours questioning myself. Memories of the past few days played over and over in my head. I was haunted by the vision of the guy who was coldly thrown to his death because the Milago hadn't mined enough glaze. I continued to see the horror of Osa fighting for her life and ultimately losing to a shower of arrows. I remembered the look on Loor's face when she wanted to help her mother, but chose instead to protect me.

But most of all, I remembered Uncle Press. I thought back to my first memories of him. He was always there for me. It was sad testament that my last memory of him was going to be the sight of him dragged off by Kagan's knights. That wasn't right. That was not the way it should end. And that's why I need your help, Mark.

After I finish writing this journal, I'm going to put down some instructions on a separate piece of parchment. That way you can keep it with you. I think you should keep my journal separate and in a safe place. Osa was right. It's important that I write down everything that's going on. If I never get back, these words are the only record of what happened to me. Treat them like gold, buddy.

I don't know if it's fair of me to ask you to do this. I'm beginning to think that I don't deserve it. If you can't help,

I'll understand. No harm, no foul. I'm still going to do what I have to do anyway. I'm not even sure if the help I'm asking for will do any good. I'm winging it here. The real wild card is Loor. She may not give me a chance, and without her help the odds are going to be really against me. But you know, it doesn't matter. One way or another, with or without her, I've made up my mind.

Tomorrow I'm going after Uncle Press.

END OF JOURNAL #2

● SECOND EARTH ●

Courtney finished Bobby's second amazing journal and placed it down on the table. Mark had finished a few minutes earlier and was already looking over the additional piece of parchment paper that Bobby had included with his latest missive. It took a while for her to say anything. The story contained on the pages from Bobby was getting more fantastic with each new paragraph, and she had to let it sink in. Finally she looked at Mark and asked, "What does he want you to do?"

Mark stood up and paced Courtney's dad's workshop as his mind tried to work its way around the task at hand. On the additional piece of parchment, Bobby had outlined a job for Mark to do that was fairly simple, yet still dangerous.

"It's a list," explained Mark. "He wants me to put together a bunch of stuff and get it to him."

Courtney grabbed the paper and looked over the list. "Get it to him?" she exclaimed. "How?"

Mark grabbed the list back and shook it at her. "Th-That's the hard part," he declared nervously. "He wrote out instructions. First I'm supposed to try and use the ring the way Osa did. But if that doesn't work, which it shouldn't because I'm not a Traveler, then he wants me to find the gate to the flume in the subway station."

"You mean the abandoned subway in the Bronx with the killer dogs?" asked Courtney in disbelief. "That's like . . . suicide."

"Y-Yeah, tell me about it," Mark exclaimed.

Courtney and Mark fell silent. It was a dangerous favor that Bobby was asking.

Finally Courtney asked, "But you're gonna do it, right?"

"Of course!" Mark answered quickly, as if he were insulted that she even had to ask. "You think I'd blow off my best friend? Gimme a break."

"Then I'm going with you," said Courtney without a hint of doubt.

"N-No way," said Mark quickly.

"Yeah way!" Courtney shot back. "You need somebody to cover your butt."

"Who'll cover *your* butt?"

"I can cover my own butt," said Courtney with her usual cockiness.

It was hard to argue with that. Courtney *could* cover her own butt. But Mark doubted that she ever had to do it in a place like the badlands of the South Bronx against a pack of vicious quig-dogs and a demon killer by the name of Saint Dane. No, he was pretty sure Courtney hadn't encountered that particular challenge before. But then again, he didn't want to do this alone. The idea terrified him. He thought over the dilemma for a good five seconds and then asked, "You sure you want to help?"

"Absolutely," she said as she grabbed Bobby's list back. She looked it over and then announced. "I get why he wants some of this stuff . . . a flashlight, a watch . . . but what's he gonna do with a CD player?"

"You're asking me like I should know?" Mark said sarcastically. "None of this makes any sense to me."

Courtney scanned the list again and then said, "Uh-oh, he wants some stuff from his house."

"Yeah, I saw that," said Mark. "But I can substitute other things."

This raised another tough issue. Courtney threw a sober stare at Mark and said, "If we can get things to Bobby, that means we can tell him his family disappeared."

Mark had to think about this. Courtney's instincts were right. Bobby had to know what was going on, even though they didn't really know themselves. The only thing they knew for certain was that the Pendragons had vanished.

"Bobby should know," said Mark cautiously while still working out his thoughts. "But not yet. There's nothing he can do about it now."

"But it's his family," countered Courtney.

"I know," said Mark. "But so is Uncle Press. I don't know what Bobby's got planned, but he has a shot at saving his uncle. I'm not sure there's anything he could do here to help find his family."

Courtney realized that Mark was right. Bobby needed to do what he had to do on Denduron. There would be plenty of time after that to find his family. Besides, the police were already working on the case. What more could Bobby do?

"We'll tell him after he's back for good," said Mark with finality.

"And what if he doesn't come back for good?" asked Courtney. "Mark, I think we should tell our parents what's going on."

"N-No! We can't!" shouted Mark.

"Why? Maybe they can help!" said Courtney hopefully. "It would be much safer if we *all* went to the subway with the stuff! Right?"

Mark really wanted to agree. He wanted to dump this all on an adult who had more authority than he had. But he felt certain he knew what would happen if they did. He chose his words carefully and said, "Courtney, I'd love to tell our parents and get their help and go to this subway station with Captain Hirsch and armed cops from the Stony Brook Police. But you know what would happen if we told them? They'd stop us. They'd probably lock us up. Then they'd all sit around and try to logically figure out what's going on and by the time they came to any decisions it could be too late for Bobby . . . and for Press."

Courtney let Mark's words sink in. The guy was kind of a dweeb, but he was a smart dweeb. If they told their parents it would be all over. They had to do this on their own. Mark quickly gathered up the parchment papers and started rolling them up.

"We can get this stuff together in a couple hours," he said. "The trick will be to sneak out without our parents knowing—"

"Whoa, whoa," interrupted Courtney. "You're not thinking of doing this tonight, are you?"

"Well, why not?" said Mark innocently.

Courtney spoke to Mark slowly and deliberately, as if he were a child. She wanted him to understand exactly what she was saying. "This is important," she said. "But by the time we get this stuff together it'll be dark and something tells me that going where we have to go isn't too safe after dark."

This made Mark think. They were headed into a rough part of town and rough parts of town got rougher after dark. They definitely had a better chance of pulling this off in the daylight. It was more important to get it done than to get it done fast.

"You're right," said Mark. "I'm not thinking straight."

"Yeah, you are," said Courtney. "You're just excited. Let's split the list, get the stuff, and then meet back here tomorrow morning."

That made sense. Tomorrow would be the day. Courtney

searched for a piece of paper and a pen so she could write them each their own list. She picked up the piece of parchment paper with Bobby's instructions and looked at the yellowed paper with the blotchy writing for a long time. Mark could see that something else was on her mind. He waited for her to pull her thoughts together. Finally Courtney turned to Mark and asked, "What was she like?"

"What was who like?" asked Mark.

"Osa. She gave you the ring, right? What was she like?"

It was true. Mark had almost forgotten. He had actually met one of the characters from Bobby's adventure. She was in his bedroom. Mark put the rolled parchment pages down and allowed his thoughts to drift back to the night before.

"She was like a dream," he said softly. "But the thing I remember most is that when she looked at me, I felt . . . safe." Mark looked down to the ring on his finger and continued, "And now she's dead. I guess she wasn't able to make things safe after all."

The two took a moment to grieve silently for a woman they only knew through the pages of Bobby's journal. Then Courtney picked up her pen and began to write. There was work to be done. They went over Bobby's list and picked the items they felt they could each find most easily. Courtney made out the two lists, then with the plan of meeting back at her house at seven A.M. the next day, they split up and went to work.

Mark went home and brought Bobby's parchment papers with him. Bobby had asked him to treat them like gold and that's what he planned to do. Mark had a hiding place that no one in his family knew about. His attic was full of old furniture. Tucked way in the back was an ancient rolltop desk that hadn't been moved since before Mark was born. The drawers of the desk were locked and his parents never tried to open them because they didn't have the key. But Mark did. He had found it hidden on a lip under the desk when he was eight years old. He never told his parents because they didn't really care, but for him it was the perfect place to hide his most treasured possessions. His special stash included mint condition *Mad* magazines; baseball cards for rookie Yankees Derek Jeter, Bernie Williams, and Mariano Rivera; some Star Wars action figures that were still in their original packaging; a report card from the seventh grade that had two Ds . . . just to remind him how easy it is to screw up; and an assortment of other small items that had special value to him alone.

Every so often Mark would go up in the attic to look over these treasures. It always made him feel good, like visiting old friends. He especially liked to check out the toys. He was too old to be playing with them, but they always brought him back to a fun time in his life, if only for a moment. It was a pleasure that no one had to know about.

When he opened the drawer this time, he wasn't hit with the familiar warm wave of nostalgia. As he looked down at all his good junk, he had the strange feeling that it belonged to someone else. And in a way, it did. It belonged to the old Mark, the innocent Mark of yesterday, whose biggest concerns were about finishing homework on time and battling the acne that was running wild on his nose. But that was yesterday. Today he had to deal with issues that not only affected life and death on the far side of the universe, but raised serious questions about the reality of life in his own backyard. It wasn't until Mark opened that drawer that he realized how much he had changed in the past few hours. He wanted to pick up the Chewbacca figure and let out a Chewie roar. He wanted to flip open a *Mad* magazine and laugh at "Spy vs. Spy." He wanted to walk the dog with the whistling yo-yo he had kept since his day at the state fair when he was six. Instead he found a cardboard box, pulled out the drawer and dumped everything into it. He closed the box and shoved it under the desk alongside all the other dusty, long-forgotten boxes full of long-forgotten stuff. It was like putting aside his old life to make room for the new one.

This desk drawer was still going to be the place for Mark's most valued possessions, but they were no longer the trinkets that held warm memories of childhood. This would now be the place to hold Bobby's story. He carefully placed the rolled scrolls in the wooden drawer. They fit perfectly, front to back. Mark made a mental note that there would be room for many more scrolls. He usually kept the desk key in his bedroom desk, but that didn't feel secure enough anymore. His mother had given him a silver chain that she used to wear when she was his age. It had a peace symbol on it and Mark had it hanging from his bedroom mirror. Mark took the chain down and replaced the pendant with the key. The chain then went around his neck, never to be away from him again. He now felt reasonably secure that Bobby's pages were safe. Or at least as safe as he knew how to keep them.

At seven A.M. sharp Courtney's doorbell rang. When she opened the door, Mark was standing there wearing a large backpack from L.L. Bean.

"Did you sleep?" he asked.

"No," she answered. "Did you get any more pages?"

"No," he answered. "Let's get this party started."

They went down to Courtney's dad's workshop, where Courtney had laid out all of the items from her half of the list.

"Where are your parents?" Mark asked her.

"They left for work."

"You know we have to cut school to do this," Mark said.

"Do you care?" asked Courtney.

Mark didn't have to answer. The two stood there looking at the items, not sure of what to do next. Courtney broke the tension.

"Try the ring thing," she said.

Mark scanned the items and picked out the flashlight. It was roughly the same size as the rolled parchment pages and as good a candidate as any. He then took off the ring and put it on the floor. He knelt down, put his finger on the gray stone and looked at Courtney.

"Go for it," she encouraged.

"Denduron," whispered Mark. Nothing happened. "Denduron," he said again, this time a bit louder. Still no reaction from the ring.

"Let me try," said Courtney and knelt down. She touched the ring and shouted, "Denduron!"

They both looked at the ring, but it lay motionless on the ground.

"I g-guess we're going to the subway," Mark said soberly.

Courtney jumped up and started to pack the gear into Mark's backpack. She moved fast, as if she were afraid she might chicken out if she stopped to think too much about what lay ahead.

"I got a train schedule," she said efficiently. "We can take the commuter train to 125th Street, then catch a subway from there." When she finished packing, she closed up the buckles on the pack and looked at Mark. It was time to go.

"Courtney," said Mark sheepishly. "I'm scared."

The two let that admission hang in the air for a moment, then Courtney straightened up and said, "You know something? I'm not. We're gonna do this."

It may have been a bold bluff, but seeing Courtney being her usual confident self gave Mark hope. Maybe they could do this. So he hoisted the pack onto his back and the two started for the train station.

Stony Brook Station was at the bottom of the Ave. It was early so the platform was still packed with business commuters in suits who were on their way to work in New York City. Courtney and Mark had to keep one eye out for any parents who might know them and question why they weren't in school. They saw one guy who Mark knew from Boy Scouts, but they saw him in time to make sure they boarded a different car when the train pulled into the station. They didn't need to be so cautious. All the commuters had their heads buried in their newspapers and didn't look at anyone else on the platform.

The train ride into New York was a quiet one. The commuters who weren't reading were asleep. It would have been hard for Courtney and Mark to discuss their mission for they definitely would have been overheard. Mark looked at the commuters reading their morning papers and had to laugh to himself. They were all reading articles about the stock market, or about sports, or about a speech the president had given at some parade. But whatever news they were reading about couldn't compare to the very real story that he and Courtney were living out right in front of their noses. Mark could imagine the headline: LOCAL BOY FLUMED ACROSS THE UNIVERSE TO LEAD REVOLUTION. Now *that's* a news story.

All Courtney wanted to do was take these few minutes to relax. She knew that once they stepped off this train their adventure would begin and she wanted to be calm enough to handle whatever came their way. So she laid back in her seat, closed her eyes and tried to keep her heart from beating as fast as it was.

In no time they arrived at their stop, 125th Street in Manhattan. The train would continue on from there to Grand Central Station, where most of the commuters were headed. But 125th Street was much closer to the Bronx, so with a silent nod Courtney and Mark got off the train.

They had always heard their parents say that this was a bad section of town. They weren't entirely sure what was meant by bad, but they were nervous just the same. One thing was certain.

This wasn't suburban Connecticut. They were in New York City with all the traffic, noise, and people congestion that New York is famous for. Courtney had a map of the New York City subways and had carefully plotted out a route to get close to Bobby's abandoned subway station. It was a short walk from the 125th Street commuter trains to the nearest subway stop and they made it with no problem. They descended into the underground station, bought their tokens, and hit the trains.

The subway trip to the Bronx was uneventful. The neighborhoods of New York that they traveled through were filled with people from all different nationalities and ethnic backgrounds and none of them were monsters. They were all just people going to work or going to school and generally living their lives. Under other circumstances, Courtney and Mark might have enjoyed this. But these weren't other circumstances. They were on a mission.

After changing trains twice, they arrived at the subway stop that was nearest to the abandoned one that Bobby had described. They climbed back up into the sunlight to see a Bronx neighborhood that was just as busy and diverse as the one where they had first gone underground.

According to their map, Bobby's subway stop was three blocks east from where they were. As they walked those few blocks, neither of them said it but each secretly wished that the subway station where Bobby and Uncle Press had gone, wouldn't be there. They each held a slim hope that none of this was true and that Bobby was making the whole thing up. Those hopes totally disappeared when they reached the corner of a busy intersection and looked across to the far side.

"Th-That's it, isn't it?" asked Mark nervously.

Courtney didn't have to answer. The station was exactly what Bobby had described. It was a small kiosk covered with cracked green paint. Mark gave a nervous look to Courtney, but

Courtney kept her eyes on the building. She didn't want Mark to see that she was starting to get nervous. Instead, she stepped off the curb and headed for the building. Mark had no choice but to follow. When they got to the kiosk, they looked down to see a cement stairway that was covered in garbage and debris. This was definitely an abandoned station. After a quick glance around to make sure nobody was watching, they ran down the steps. They hit a landing, turned, and were faced with the boarded-up entrance that Bobby had described.

Courtney reached out, grabbed hold of one board, and pulled it aside as easily as Uncle Press had done. She had just opened up a dark doorway into the underground. Before they had the chance to change their minds, Courtney ducked in and disappeared. Mark took a scared breath and was right after her. He had to squeeze through with the pack, but he made it and closed the board up behind him. Everything was playing out exactly as it had for Bobby. But Courtney and Mark were now hoping that this is where the similarity would end. Neither of them wanted to run into Saint Dane or the quigs. They walked down the last few steps into the abandoned station and stood shoulder to shoulder, with every sense on full alert.

"I feel like I've already been here," Mark said in awe. Indeed, everything was just as Bobby had described. It was a lonely station that hadn't seen passengers in years. Then they heard the distant rumble of an oncoming subway train. In a few seconds the train blasted into the station and thundered through without slowing down. This seemed to kick them back into gear.

"C'mon," said Courtney, and headed for the far end of the platform.

"Wait," said Mark and quickly took off the pack. He opened it up and dug deep down inside.

"What are you doing?" asked Courtney.

As he dug through the pack Mark said, "I brought a little insurance." He found what he was looking for and pulled out a package wrapped in brown paper.

"Was that on the list?" asked Courtney curiously.

"No, it's a little something I added." He unwrapped the paper to reveal two huge, succulent steaks. He held them up proudly. "A bribe, just in case we run into some hungry quigs."

Courtney had to smile. "I don't care what anybody says, you're good." She then grabbed the steaks and walked off. Mark smiled proudly at the compliment, but then the smile dropped when he realized it wasn't exactly the greatest compliment in the world. He picked up the pack and hurried after her.

They reached the end of the platform and saw the small set of stairs leading down to the dark tracks.

"This looks hairy," declared Mark. "What if the gate door isn't there?"

"Everything he described so far has been true," said Courtney. "I gotta believe this will be too."

Just then they heard another train approaching. They took a few steps back from the edge of the platform and a few seconds later, the train flashed through, moving fast. The idea of being down on those tracks when a train came through was a frightening one.

"Gulp," said Mark.

"Don't think, move!" shouted Courtney. She ran to the edge of the platform and disappeared down onto the tracks. It was kind of like jumping into cold ocean water. The longer you thought about it, the more reasons you'd come up with to wait. It was better just to do it and that's what she did.

Mark was right behind her. He ran across the platform and hurried down the stairs to find Courtney below, pressing her back against the wall.

"I can't believe I did that," she said, panting hard.

"Yeah, me neither, but don't stop now," he added.

With Courtney in the lead, the two made their way cautiously along the tunnel. It was dark and they didn't want to risk wandering out onto the tracks so Courtney kept one hand on the grimy, greasy wall.

"How far did he say the door was?" asked Courtney.

"I don't remember," was Mark's answer. "Just keep—" That's when he heard it.

"What was that?" he asked.

"What was what?"

"I heard something, like a growl." Mark grabbed one of the steaks back from Courtney and held it out. "Gooood doggy! Goooood doggy!"

Then Courtney heard it too. It was faint, but unmistakable.

"That's not a growl," she said. "That's a train! Another train is coming!"

A blast from the train's horn told them she was right. Another train was coming and the two were caught. They didn't know which way to run.

"I'm going back!" shouted Mark and turned to run back for the platform. But Courtney grabbed him by the pack and held him tight.

"No!" she commanded. "We can't be far!"

She turned and continued to make her way along the wall as Mark pushed her from behind. It was getting hard to see because the train had just rounded a curve ahead and its headlight was shining right in their eyes. And it was coming fast.

"Hurry!" pleaded Mark.

Courtney desperately felt at the wall, then tripped over a switch and fell to her knees. Mark quickly pulled her to her feet and pushed her forward. The train was now getting dangerously close. The racket from the wheels on the track was deafening. There wasn't much space between the wall of the tunnel and the track.

"We're not gonna make it!" Courtney shouted. "Press against the wall!"

Mark pulled off his pack and flattened his back against the wall. The train was only a few yards away. The two held hands tightly. Mark closed his eyes. Courtney pressed against the wall and slid her hand out in one last desperate attempt to find the door. She leaned forward a few more inches . . . and her hand found something.

"I got it!" she shouted.

The train was right there. Its horn blasted. Courtney held on tight to Mark's hand and dove for what she hoped was the gate. She pushed against the dark recess and it gave way. Courtney and Mark tumbled inside just as the train flashed by. In seconds it was gone and all was as quiet as it had been only a few moments before. Courtney and Mark lay on the ground, totally out of breath. It took a minute for them to get their heads back together, and when they did they both looked up and saw it at the same time.

"Whoa," was all Mark could say in awe.

It was the rocky gray tunnel. With their eyes fixed on the craggy portal, they both stood up. Courtney then hurried back to the wooden door they had just come through and poked her head outside.

"It's here," she announced. "The star, just like Bobby said."

She came back inside to join Mark, who kept staring into the tunnel.

"This is it," he said with growing excitement. "It's all true. Everything Bobby wrote is true."

This was as far as Bobby's instructions took them. In his letter, he wrote for them to come to the gate and wait. But wait for what? They stood there for a few minutes, not exactly sure of what to do next. Finally Courtney looked at Mark with a mischievous smile and said, "I'm gonna try it."

She took a step toward the mouth of the gray tunnel, but Mark pulled her back.

"Don't!" he yelled nervously.

"Why not? If Bobby can do it, I can do it," was her typical Courtney-esque response. She shook Mark off and stepped into the mouth of the flume. Mark backed away and watched nervously as Courtney faced the depths of the endless, dark tunnel. She stood up straight, gave a quick glance to Mark, then turned back toward the darkness and said, "Denduron!"

Nothing happened. Zero. They could hear the word echo back from the tunnel, but besides that, nothing.

"It's gotta be the same as the ring," said Mark. "If you're not a Traveler, you don't have the power."

Courtney backed out of the tunnel with a look of definite disappointment. She was psyched to take the magic carpet ride of light that Bobby had described, but it was not meant to be. "So why is it that Bobby has the power?" she asked, a little bit peeved. "What makes him so special that—"

"Shhh!" Mark held his hand up to quiet Courtney.

"What?" asked Courtney.

"Do you hear that?"

Courtney listened and then said, "It must be another train coming."

"No," said Mark as he strained to listen harder. "It's not a train. It sounds like . . . like . . . music."

Courtney listened harder, and soon she heard it too. It *was* music. Far off music. But it wasn't a tune. It was more like a jumble of sweet, high notes.

"I've heard that before," exclaimed Mark. "When the ring opens up." He glanced down at the ring on his finger, but the gray stone wasn't glowing. No, this music wasn't coming from the ring. Courtney looked into the tunnel, and what she saw made her jaw drop open in surprise.

"Uh, Mark," she said numbly. "You looking at this?"

Mark was also looking down the tunnel and what he saw made his jaw fall open as well, for there was something coming toward them. It was a pin spot of light, like the headlight on the front of a far-off train. As it drew closer, the light grew larger and the sweet music grew louder.

"D-Do we want to run?" asked Mark with a shaky voice.

"Yeah," answered Courtney. "But we can't."

As the light came nearer, they saw that the gray walls of the tunnel were beginning to change. It was like they were disappearing. The gray, craggy rock walls were transforming into clear crystal, just as the gray stone of the ring had done. Beyond the clear walls was a vast star field. The light grew so bright that Mark and Courtney had to shield their eyes. The music grew louder as well. Without thinking, the two backed away until they hit the far wall. They were trapped. It was too late to find the door and get out of there. All they could do was cover their eyes, crouch down, and hope that it would soon end.

With one final burst of light, the room fell dark and the music stopped. All was quiet and calm. Slowly Mark and Courtney lowered their arms from their faces to see what had happened. What they saw seemed more impossible than anything they had seen so far. Yet there he was, plain as can be.

It was Bobby. He stood at the mouth of the tunnel looking a little dazed. He glanced around to get his bearings, then saw Mark and Courtney cowering against the far wall. Nobody knew what to say. They all just stared at each other for a good long time. Finally Bobby let out a simple, calm, "Yo."

That broke the ice. Mark and Courtney jumped up, ran to him and all three threw themselves into a tight group hug. They didn't need to say anything. This one unplanned action said it all. It was a release from all the fear, uncertainty, and sadness that had been building up in them since the adventure began. They stayed this way for some time, until Bobby finally said, "Okay, I'm choking here."

Reluctantly they all let go and took a step back from each other. They waited a second and then all three ran at each other again for another hug. This time they all started to laugh.

"You guys are the best," said Bobby, but then something dawned on him and he pulled away from the group. He looked right at Courtney and said, "Wait, what are you doing here?"

"I showed her the journals," admitted Mark. "I'm sorry. I couldn't deal on my own."

Bobby had to think about this. He thought that he was writing to Mark and Mark alone. But it was a big responsibility that he threw at his friend and Bobby realized that maybe sharing it was a good idea. If there was anybody who could help him deal, it was Courtney. So he smiled reassuringly at his friend and said, "It's cool, Mark. I'm glad you did. Does anybody else know?"

Courtney answered, "No, just us."

"That's good," said Bobby. "At first I was thinking everybody should know, but now I'm not so sure. This is all pretty heavy."

"That's what we thought," said Mark.

Bobby added, "There's gonna be a time when everybody should know, but not yet, okay?"

Courtney and Mark nodded. There were all on the same page.

"Are my parents freaking out?" Bobby asked.

There it was. The question they didn't want to answer. Mark and Courtney gave each other a quick glance. They had already decided it wouldn't be a good idea to tell Bobby that his family had disappeared. He had enough to worry about as it was. But they didn't want to lie to him. Mark didn't know what to say, so Courtney jumped in, saying, "Everybody's real worried about you."

It wasn't a lie; people were definitely worried about him. It just wasn't the whole truth. But it was the right thing to say because Bobby then said, "I hate to keep them in the dark, but I think they'd be more worried if they knew what was really going down. So don't tell 'em anything, okay?"

Both Courtney and Mark nodded quickly. Whew. They just dodged a bullet. Bobby then spotted the L.L. Bean pack that Mark and Courtney brought.

"Did you get everything?" he asked as he quickly poked through the contents.

"Every bit," answered Mark.

"Any trouble getting here?" Bobby asked.

Courtney answered, "No sweat."

Bobby looked back to his friends as if he were seeing them for the first time. What he saw were two people who came through for him in a big way when they really didn't have to. "I don't know how to thank you guys," he said sincerely. "I don't deserve friends like you."

Courtney and Mark answered with smiles.

"Bobby," said Mark sheepishly. "Is it true? I mean, what you've been writing about?"

"Yeah," was Bobby's answer. "Weird, huh?"

Courtney and Mark started to ask more questions but Bobby cut them off by saying, "Guys, I don't know any more about what's going on than what I wrote. I don't know why I'm a Traveler. I don't know where Denduron is. I don't know *when* Denduron is. I've got a million questions and no answers. And I'm scared as hell."

Yes, there were many questions but none of them had any answers. Finally Courtney took a step toward Bobby. She hesitated, as if what she was about to say would be difficult. She finally gathered the strength and said, "Don't go back. That's not your world back there. It's not your life. You belong here. All you have to do is walk out that door with us. Nobody would know. Please, Bobby, stay here."

Bobby looked at Mark. Mark nodded to him as if agreeing with Courtney. "You're home now, Bobby," he said. "Stay here."

Bobby hadn't thought about the possibility. It would be so easy. All he had to do was walk away. He was home now. He was safe. It was so tempting. He didn't answer at first because this was the most important decision he ever had to make in his life. He looked around him, looked down into the dark tunnel, and then to the L.L. Bean pack full of stuff his friends had brought him. He had made up his mind.

"There are a ton of things I don't know," he said soberly. "But there's one thing I do know for certain. Uncle Press is going to die unless I do something."

The others dropped their heads. Bobby was right. If he stayed, Uncle Press was doomed.

"But there's more," Bobby added. "I'm not the guy to help those people fight their revolution. I don't know why they think I am, but I'm not. The guy to help them is Uncle Press. If he dies, they don't stand a chance. I gotta go back and get Uncle Press for the sake of the Milago, too."

Bobby picked up the pack and swung it onto his back.

"What're you gonna do with that stuff?" asked Mark.

"I'm not exactly sure," answered Bobby, "but I better think of something fast." He tightened up the straps on the pack and took a step back toward the flume. "I'm no big hero," he then said. "I'm gonna try to save Uncle Press and then get out of there. I'd just as soon not stick around for the real fireworks."

"We'll be waiting for you," said Mark.

Everyone looked at each other, not entirely sure of what to say. It was time for Bobby to go.

"There's nothing I can say to thank you guys for doing this and for hanging on to my journals," Bobby said.

"Just keep 'em coming, dude," said Mark with a smile.

Bobby smiled and then the three once again joined in a group hug.

"I'll write as soon as I can," said Bobby and pulled away. Everyone was holding back tears. Bobby had turned to the flume when Courtney asked, "Is Loor really as gorgeous as all that?"

Bobby winced. Busted. "You weren't supposed to see that," he said sheepishly. "She's not my type."

"No?" said Courtney with a sly smile. "I think she and I have something in common. We can both kick your ass."

Bobby laughed at that. Of course she was right.

"Get home safe," she added.

"Soon as I can," was his reply. Mark gave him a wave and Bobby turned back to the flume. He stepped in, took a breath, and said, "Denduron!"

Instantly, the flume reactivated. The walls started to shimmer, the musical notes grew loud, and bright light blasted out from somewhere far inside.

Bobby turned back to them and gave a quick wave. "Later!" he said.

Then, in a flash, Bobby was gone. The light and the music trailed away inside the tunnel, transporting Bobby to his far-off destination. Soon all was quiet once again. The two stood there, staring into the dark, empty tunnel. There was nothing left to do now except to start the long journey home.

"Uh-oh," Mark said.

"What?" asked Courtney nervously.

Mark held out his hand and they both saw that the gray stone in the ring was starting to glow. Mark quickly took it off and placed it down on the ground. They each took a step back and watched as the ring grew larger and light blasted out of the stone. The familiar musical notes were heard again as the light built in intensity. There was a flash, and just as quickly as it started, it was over. The ring lay still on the ground. Next to it was another rolled-up parchment.

"How could he have written so fast?" asked Courtney.

Mark picked up the pages and started to unfurl them.

"Something tells me that time here and time there aren't relative," said Mark.

"Huh? English please," demanded Courtney.

"I think Denduron might not only be in another place," explained Mark. "It might be in another time. It could be thousands of years ago, or a million years from now. The flumes not only travel through space, I'll bet they travel through time as well."

Courtney didn't quite get this, but then again she didn't get much of anything that was happening. Mark unfurled the pages, gave them a quick glance, then looked up at Courtney with a smile.

"I was right. It's from Bobby."

DENDURON

I messed up big time, guys.

I tried to take charge and do the right thing, but I'm afraid I only made things worse. It's been a wild ride since I saw you two in the subway, but the bottom line is that as I write this journal, we are on the verge of a catastrophe that could rip Denduron apart. It's not all my fault, but I'm afraid I pushed it closer to the edge. First I gotta backtrack to what happened since I wrote last. I finished my last journal before I saw you two, so I should tell you what happened before the trip I took to Second Earth where you gave me the backpack. As much as I was over-the-moon psyched to see you guys, I wish I had never made that trip, because that trip is one of the reasons we're on the edge of disaster.

When Osa was killed, something snapped in my head and I was able to think clearly. It wasn't anything dramatic like I suddenly realized I had to fulfill my destiny as a Traveler and lead the Milago to victory or anything like that. No way; gimme a break. It was about Uncle Press. I was ashamed of myself for not trying to help him. My only defense is that I had a whole lot of wild stuff thrown at me all at once and I was having a tough time keeping my head on straight. But when Osa died, it was like a wake-up call. And my loss wasn't even on the same scale as the loss was for Loor. Osa was her mother. I imagined what it would be like to lose my own mom. I take that back. I couldn't imagine what it would be like to lose my mom. The thought was just too horrible.

Osa didn't deserve to die. All she was trying to do was help some people find a better way of life. So was Uncle Press. He was trying to help the Milago and because of it, he was going to be put to death. Was that fair? I didn't think so, and I realized that somebody had to step up and say so. Unfortunately I also realized that the only person who could do something was me. I say "unfortunately" not because I didn't want to help him, but because I knew I wasn't exactly the best candidate to stage a Schwarzenegger-style commando assault on the Bedoowan palace and fight my way out with Uncle Press in tow. That particular fantasy was going to stay a fantasy. Still, I had to do something. And if I was going to have any chance at all, I needed help. That meant Loor. There was nothing I could say to Loor that would make her feel any better about what had happened to her mother. Man, she must have hated me. But she was the only person I could go to for help, so I had to take a shot.

I wandered out into the main cavern of the mine to look for her. I found her sitting cross-legged on the far side of the cavern, alone, carving a small piece of wood. It looked like she was sculpting a small face that was half sun and half moon. She was really concentrating on the work and I didn't want to disturb her, so I waited until she said something first. For several minutes she ignored me and continued to carve. Finally I think she figured out that I wasn't going to leave so she said, "This is a szshaszha. On my territory it symbolizes the end of one life and the beginning of another. I will give it to my mother for it is said to bring luck in the next life."

"That's pretty cool," I said.

"It is an old fairy tale that has no meaning," she spat back sharply. "But my mother believed in these things and I will respect that."

I guess I said the wrong thing again. I was ready to chicken out and leave her alone. I had to force myself to stay and go through with this.

"I'm not going home tomorrow," I said trying to sound stronger than I felt. "I'm going after Uncle Press."

This made Loor stop her work and look up at me. I did my best to hold eye contact without blinking. I wanted her to know how serious I was. But then she burst out laughing. Obviously the idea of my going up against the Bedoowan knights was pretty funny to her.

She stopped laughing and said sarcastically, "Why, Pendragon? So you can watch him die the way you watched my mother die?"

Ouch. That was cold.

"No, I'm going to rescue him," I said trying to make it sound like I could make it happen.

"Go to sleep," she said dismissively. "I am tired of looking at you."

She was starting to tick me off. Yeah, she had been through a lot, but she didn't have to treat me like a turd. I stood my ground and said, "You told me I didn't care about my uncle. You're wrong. I care enough to go in that fortress and get him out."

She scoffed and said, "The Bedoowan knights would shred you before you got close to your uncle."

"You're probably right," I said. "That's why you're going to help me."

Loor shot me a surprised look. Uh-oh, maybe I was coming on too strong. She slowly stood up to her full height and looked down at me. It was all I could do to keep myself from backing off because if I did, I'd be lost.

"Why should I help rescue your uncle when my mother died trying to protect you?" she said with a seething intensity I'd never seen before.

"That's exactly why you should help me," I said, trying to keep my voice strong. "We both know that I'm not the person to lead the Milago against the Bedoowan. But Uncle Press is. I want to rescue him because he's my uncle. And if you care about the Milago as much as you say you do, then you should want to rescue him because these people need him."

Loor didn't move right away. I thought I saw something in her eyes. Was it a moment of doubt? She backed away from me and picked up her wooden weapon from the floor of the cavern.

"There is a meeting," she said coldly. "I will allow you to come."

A meeting. Cool. I didn't know what it was about, but at least she had thawed enough to include me. That was a start. She stepped forward and pointed the end of her weapon at me threateningly. "I will not protect you, Pendragon," she said. "If you come with me, you are on your own."

With that sweet little promise delivered, she walked off. I wasn't sure what to do until she turned back over her shoulder and barked, "Come. Now!"

I wasn't sure where we were going, either, but I was willing to follow her and find out. She led me back up the ladders to the surface. Night had fallen and the stars made it bright enough to see clearly. Loor glanced around quickly, probably looking for any knights that might still be hanging around looking for us. Good idea. I looked around too, but all was quiet. I followed her back into the Milago village and straight to the hut where I first woke up. When we ducked inside, I saw that I was right about this being a hospital, sort of. Two of the wooden benches now had occupants. But these two weren't here to get well. It was Osa, and the miner who was killed at the mine shaft. This is where they were keeping the bodies until doing whatever they were going to do with them. I supposed I should have been creeped out, but I wasn't.

There were two other people there as well, only these two were alive and well. It was Alder, the knight who Loor said was the Traveler from Denduron, and Rellin, the chief miner. They were sitting cross-legged in front of a fire that was burning in the hearth. Loor walked right over and sat down as well. I figured this was the meeting Loor had invited me to, so I sat down across from Loor.

Rellin started the meeting by saying, "I am sorry about your mother, Loor. She was a good person. I speak for all the Milago when I say how grateful we are to you and your people for coming here to help us. It saddens me that it had to end this way."

Loor was quick to respond and said, "I thank you for your sympathy, but my mother's death does not end things. We will still lead the Milago to their freedom."

Rellin looked nervous. Suddenly there was tension in the air. I felt it and Loor felt it. I'm not sure what Alder felt because I didn't know him well enough.

"No," Rellin said with finality. "It is over. There will be no fighting." With that declaration he got up to leave. But Loor jumped up and stopped him. Rellin's comment had taken her by surprise.

"How can you say that, Rellin?" she asked. "If the Milago do not break free of the Bedoowan, you will all die!"

"And if we fight them we will die much sooner," said Rellin. "My people are not warriors. You know that, Alder." He looked to Alder, who dropped his head. Rellin then looked back to Loor and said, "And you know that too, Loor. We would have no chance in a fight with the Bedoowan knights. We would be slaughtered."

Loor didn't give up. "Remember what Press said? You may not be warriors, but you are strong. He said the Bedoowan do not have the character to resist if the Milago stand up for themselves. He said—"

"Press is gone!" shouted Rellin. "And now Osa is gone as well. Who is left to lead us in this mad quest? You? Him?" He said this while pointing at me. "You are children. Your motives are noble, but it is time to end these foolish dreams."

With that he turned and stormed out of the hut. The meeting was over. I could tell that Loor wanted to go after him, but she didn't. She may have been a warrior, but she didn't have the words to change his mind.

"He is wrong," said Alder softly. "The Bedoowan are not as strong as Rellin thinks."

Loor walked slowly toward the body of her mother. She looked down at the fallen woman, then touched her arm as if trying to gain strength from her. She took the wooden szshaszha she had been carving and placed it in her mother's lifeless hand. Man, this was tearing my heart out. I can only imagine how Loor felt.

"He is lying," she said with finality.

Alder looked up quickly. This surprised him as much as it had me.

"Say what?" was all I could come back with.

"Rellin has wanted to fight the Bedoowan all of his life," she explained. "His anger and hatred are far greater than his fear. I do not believe that he has changed his way of thinking so quickly."

Alder stood up. He looked as confused as I felt.

"Then why did he say there would be no fight?" he asked.

Loor kept her eyes on her mother and answered, "I do not know, but something has changed. Something he has not told us about. Maybe he does not trust us because we are so young."

I thought back to the other two times I had seen Rellin. The first was at the Transfer ceremony. Though I was far away, I felt his hatred for the Bedoowan. The other time was in the mines after the explosion. After he was rescued, he had that strange laugh that felt so out of place. Loor was right. Something odd was happening.

"He trusted your mother, didn't he?" I asked.

"Of course," came her quick reply.

"Then he would have told her if things had changed and she would have told you, right?" I asked.

"Are you saying that I am wrong?" she asked.

"No," I answered quickly. "I'm saying that if you're right, then something strange is going on and the fact that he didn't tell your mother about it makes me kind of nervous."

We all let this hang in the air for a while. Finally Alder said, "So what do we do?"

I knew the answer to that. So did Loor, but I wanted to say it first.

"We rescue Uncle Press," I announced. "We gotta get him back here."

I shot a look at Loor. She didn't have to say a word. I knew what she was thinking. Rescuing Uncle Press was exactly what we needed to do and she had decided to help me. She then looked to Alder and said, "This will be a difficult fight, Alder. You will have to reveal to them that you are a Traveler."

Alder stood up proudly and said, "I knew this day would come. I am ready."

"Whoa, whoa!" I said while stepping between them. "Who said anything about a fight?"

Loor scoffed and said, "If you think we can get into the Bedoowan fortress, find Press, release him, and get out without a fight, you are not only a coward, you are a fool!"

Loor's macho act was starting to get old, but I didn't want to make her angry by telling her so. I had to stand up to her or she'd walk all over me.

"Yeah?" I said trying to match her bravura. "The goal here is to get Uncle Press out, and if you think the three of us have any chance of doing that by fighting Kagan's knights, then maybe *you're* the fool!"

Loor didn't have a comeback. Alder put the icing on the cake for me by saying, "He is right, Loor. If we charge in fighting, we will be killed before we find Press."

This bothered Loor. It was obvious that her first reaction to problem solving was to come out swinging. But she wasn't an idiot, and she was beginning to realize that her way might not have been the best way in this case.

"Then what do we do?" she asked. "Ask Kagan politely to release Press? Maybe if we said *please* it would happen."

Whoa, the muscle head was capable of sarcasm. Maybe she had more going on than I gave her credit for.

"The only chance we have is to sneak in there without them knowing," I said. "The longer we can stay invisible, the better chance we have of getting Uncle Press out."

Alder was getting excited. He said, "Yes! I know a way to get in. And I know every corridor of that fortress. There are passageways and tunnels that are rarely used."

Loor didn't like being told she was wrong, especially by someone she didn't respect, which was me. But I think she was smart enough to know that my way made more sense.

She said, "And do you have a plan for what to do after Alder gets us into the palace?"

The fact is, I did. Sort of. It wasn't really a plan as much as it was a bunch of ideas. Unfortunately all my ideas needed things that didn't exist here on Denduron. I needed a bunch of stuff from back home.

"If I got a message to my friends back home," I asked, "is there a way for them to send me something from there?"

Loor stepped away from me. She knew the answer, but I think she was reluctant to tell me. I was still pretty new to this whole Traveler thing. Maybe she wasn't sure she could trust me with all the secrets yet.

But Alder didn't have the same concerns. "Of course there is," he said innocently. "You can flume back to your territory and get whatever you want."

I was beginning to like this guy. Could it be as simple as that? All I had to do was go back to the flume and I could get home? Cool. But there was still the tricky issue of having to climb back to the top of that mountain to get to the gate. There's no way I could do that in time to get home, then get back here to rescue Uncle Press before he was executed. Besides, I'd probably get eaten by those quigs anyway.

"That's no good," I said. "Is there another way?"

"You do not need to go to the mountain," said Loor. "There is another gate in the mines that is not guarded by quigs."

Oh, yeah! This was getting better by the second. And maybe best of all, by Loor giving me that piece of information, she was allowing herself to trust me. Maybe we could work together after all. Now that I was certain I could get home, my mind started to calculate all of the things I could get that would help us sneak into the fortress. The thing that was so cool is that the people of Denduron knew nothing about life at home. They would be blown away by something as simple as a flashlight. Man, talk about power! I wasn't exactly sure how it was going to work, but I was beginning to think that we might really have a chance of getting Uncle Press out of there.

Loor took me back down to the mine. It was an uneasy truce that we had going. We both knew we needed each other, but neither of us was too happy about it. The first thing I did was go back to the small cell-like room where Loor made me wait before, and finish my journal. I also wrote out the list of items and the instructions that I sent to you. Once they were ready, I rolled them up and did exactly what Osa had done when she sent you my first journal. I took off the ring, put it on the ground, touched the gray stone, and said, "Earth!"

But nothing happened. I tried again. Nothing. I was suddenly hit with a terrible thought. Osa told me that the power only worked for Travelers. What if I wasn't really a Traveler? I was doing exactly what she did, but the ring didn't work. Maybe I wasn't a Traveler after all!

Loor had been watching from the doorway. Before my panic got any worse she said, "You are not from Earth. You are from Second Earth."

Oh. Right. That's what Osa said. Second Earth. Did that mean there was a First Earth? I made a mental note to ask that question later. There were more important duties at hand. I touched the stone and said, "Second Earth!" Sure enough, that was the ticket. The stone began to glow, the ring grew, the musical notes played, and I dropped the journal with my list into its center. It disappeared and all returned to normal. Cool. But then I was hit with another thought.

"Loor," I asked. "How will I know when to flume back to Earth . . . uh . . . Second Earth? It could take a long time for my friends to get the stuff together."

Loor gave me the straightest answer I'd had since my arrival. And she seemed unsure of herself, like it didn't make sense to her, either.

"I do not fully understand how," she began. "But when Travelers fly through the flumes, they will always arrive when they need to arrive."

It was then that I realized that Loor didn't know much more about being a Traveler than I did. Sure, she put on this tough front, but I think she was still trying to get her mind around the concept.

"My mother began to explain it to me," she added. "She said the flumes travel through time as well as through space. But why a Traveler always arrives at the time they need to arrive was not made clear to me."

"So you're telling me that when I flume to Earth—"

"Second Earth," she corrected.

"Yeah, whatever. When I flume to Second Earth I'll arrive at the same time that my friends arrive at the other end?"

"Yes."

"Does that work both ways? Forward and back?" I asked.

"What do you mean?"

"I mean, if I left right now, would my friends be waiting for me already? Even though I just sent the list a minute ago?"

"I think so," she answered.

"Then let's go!"

Loor led me back into the large cavern and then into a tunnel on the far side. This was an ancient tunnel, more so than the others. There were some loose rocks scattered over the ore-car tracks, which told me there hadn't been any miners through here in a long time. The walls also looked to be a bit rougher than the others, as if they hadn't quite perfected their digging techniques when this tunnel was gouged out of the earth.

We had walked for quite a while when I asked, "How do you know we're going the right way?"

Loor answered by raising up her hand. She was wearing a ring that was identical to mine. I couldn't believe I hadn't noticed it before. I guess when you're in the Traveler Club, everybody gets the special ring. But the thing was, the gray stone was letting off a very slight glow.

"My mother showed me this gate a few days ago," she explained. "She also showed me how to tell if a gate is nearby. The stone will tell you."

Sure enough, I looked at my own ring and saw that the gray stone was starting to glow. Then as we rounded one more bend, I saw it. Embedded in the rock was a wooden door.

Several yards farther down the tunnel was another opening. There was a pile of stones in front of that, as if it had just recently been dug out. Beyond this opening was an old ore car on the tracks. The thing probably hadn't been moved in decades.

"How do you know it's this tunnel and not that one?" I asked.

Loor pointed to the wooden door. There was a star symbol carved in it, just like the door in the subway back in the Bronx. We walked inside and I saw the familiar tunnel that led to nowhere and everywhere. I took a few steps toward it and then turned back to Loor.

"What do I do?" I asked.

"I think you know," she answered.

Yeah, I did. I walked a few steps farther into the mouth of the tunnel when Loor called to me, "Pendragon?" I turned back and she said, "Your uncle is a good man. I want to rescue him too."

I thought that was pretty cool. I nodded to her, then turned to face the darkness and said, "Second Earth!"

You know what happened next.

DENDURON

I didn't want to leave you guys. When I took the flume back to that subway station, my thoughts were all about Uncle Press and the mission ahead. But once I got there and saw you both, I remembered how much I missed my real life. The small time I had spent on Denduron put my head in an entirely different place, but when I saw you two I suddenly felt like I had never left home. There was a moment where the idea of stepping into that flume and jumping back to Denduron was impossible. You were right, Courtney; it would have been easy. All I had to do was walk away.

But then I remembered Uncle Press and I knew what I had to do. I had to come back. Maybe it would have been better if I had stayed with you because I've made things worse than they were. Good intentions aren't always enough. You have to be smart and sometimes I think that I'm not that smart. I'll tell you what happened and you be the judge.

When I took the flume back to Denduron, I was greeted by Loor. The first thing she said was, "I was not sure if you would return."

I got all indignant and said, "Hey, give me a little credit, would you?" Of course she was absolutely right. I almost stayed on Second Earth, but I didn't want her to know that. I wanted her to think that I was confident in our mission.

She said, "We are both tired. We must get some sleep before we begin."

"Do we have enough time?" I asked. I knew that Uncle Press was to be executed at "the equinox," whatever that was. It could have been in ten minutes for all I knew.

"The equinox is at midday tomorrow," she explained. "When the three suns are one in the sky. We have enough time for a short rest."

Now I understood. The equinox was noon. Loor and I walked back to the small room in the mine. She didn't ask me about what was in the backpack and I wasn't about to start explaining. That would come later. But there was one item I wanted, so I took it out. It was my digital watch. I had no idea what time it was, but if we were going to sleep, I didn't want to end up sacking out for ten hours and waking up too late. I set the alarm to go off in two hours. That's just a long nap, and my tank was empty. Still, a few hours of sleep was better than nothing.

Loor watched me curiously as I set the watch alarm. She even jumped back with surprise when it beeped. I assumed they didn't have watches where she came from. It made me feel like I had one up on her for a change. But more important, her surprise at the beep meant my guess was right. To the people of Denduron, the simple things I could pull out of this pack would seem like huge magic. Throwing someone off balance, even for a short time, might mean the difference between success and failure. Or between life and death.

When I dug the watch out of my pack, I also found the extra surprise you put in there, Mark. You are the best. You know how much I love Milky Ways and the one you stuck in that pack was the most delicious treat in the history of treats. Thanks. I even offered a piece to Loor. I thought that was pretty nice of me, since I didn't have much hope of finding another Milky Way around these parts. She took the bite-sized piece, popped it cautiously into her mouth and instantly spit it out. What a waste! I guess they don't have candy bars on her territory either.

"Next time you wish to feed me poison, warn me first," she demanded.

"What are you talking about? Where I come from this is a major treat," I said, still laughing.

"Then you come from a strange place, Pendragon," she said while taking a swig of water to wash the taste out of her mouth. It was like I had given her a brussel sprout or something.

This was the first time Loor and I weren't totally tense around each other. We were like two normal people doing normal things. Believe me, it wasn't like we were suddenly buds or anything, but it gave me the courage to ask her a question.

"What else did your mother tell you about being a Traveler?" I asked. I figured the more information I had, the better chance I had of getting out of here alive.

Loor didn't answer and busied herself arranging the animal pelts on her side of the cell floor. I knew she heard me, so I didn't ask again. I had just about given up on her when she said, "You may not like what I have to say."

Oh, great. More good news.

"If it's important," I said, "I should hear it whether I like it or not."

Loor sat down on the pelts and leaned her back against the wall. In spite of what I had just said, I wasn't so sure I wanted to hear this. But I had to.

"I have only known for a short time that I am a Traveler,"

she began. "I do not know much more than you do. But there is something my mother told me that is important. Maybe more important than saving Press and helping the Milago."

This sounded big. She had my full attention.

"I know you want to know why we are Travelers, but I do not know. That is the truth. My mother said that I would understand someday, but for now it was not important. What she did tell me though, is that we must understand our mission."

"Mission? You mean there's more to this than helping the Milago?" I asked.

"Yes," she said. "My mother explained that there are many territories, and they are all about to reach an important time. A 'turning point' she called it. It is a time when the outcome will either send the territory toward peace and prosperity, or plunge its people into chaos and destruction."

"So the battle between the Milago and the Bedoowan is some kind of turning point for all of Denduron?" I asked.

"That is what my mother said," she continued. "If the Milago break free of the Bedoowan, then Denduron will continue to exist in peace. But if the Bedoowan triumph it could be a disaster that will destroy the entire territory."

That was huge. This struggle wasn't just about helping these poor miners, it was about saving the whole territory.

"How did she know all this?" I asked. "That's like predicting the future!"

Loor shrugged and said, "It is part of being a Traveler. Someday we will understand this. But for now we must know that the Travelers' mission is to go to the territories that are about to reach their turning point and do all we can to help guide events in the right direction. That is why my mother was here; that is why Press is here. That is why you and I are here."

This was all a little cosmic for me. I thought I was finally getting my mind around how things worked, but I was only scratching the surface.

"Then who is Saint Dane?" I asked.

"Saint Dane is a Traveler like us," she said. "But he has been working against us. He wants the territories to turn the wrong way and create pandemonium."

"But . . . why?"

"When we find that answer, we will know all there is to know," she said. "Right now, I do not have those answers. Now go to sleep."

Yeah, right. Sleep. She just revealed that we have the future of Denduron in our hands, not to mention other territories that might be headed for trouble, and I was supposed to nod off to dreamland? And to make things just a little bit more interesting, there was a killer out there trying to stop us. I saw what this Saint Dane dude was capable of. Sweet dreams, Bobby boy! I was on the verge of a major brain hemorrhage and had to try and calm down. I told myself that none of this had anything to do with me. I had one goal and one goal only: to rescue Uncle Press. After that, I was out of here. If Uncle Press wanted to stay and try to change the course of history, that was his choice. But for me, I was catching the next flume home.

This gave me a little comfort and I tried to get some sleep. But before I put my head down I asked, "Is that it? Is there anything else you're not telling me?"

Loor didn't even open her eyes. She was nearly asleep. But she managed to say, "That is all I know, Pendragon. Is that not enough?"

Oh, yeah. That was plenty. It was time for lights out. I thought I would have trouble knocking off, but the truth was I was so exhausted, I didn't even remember my head hitting the fur. That was great, except that it felt like I had just closed my eyes when my watch alarm went off. Two hours felt more like two seconds. Man, did I go out hard! I had one of those weird waking-up moments and didn't know where I was. It seemed like I was in my bed at home and my first thought was, "I gotta walk Marley." But in no time, the reality of my situation came hurtling back. I sat up and tried to clear my head.

Loor wasn't there. After a stretch and a yawn, I went to my pack to do inventory and saw that the clips were undone. Somebody had been going through my pack! I quickly threw it open and did a quick scan. It looked like everything was still there, though it was definitely rummaged through. I was pissed. I clipped the pack shut and went looking for Loor.

I walked back into the now familiar main cavern of the mine. It was business as usual out there. These poor guys never stopped. I briefly wondered what had happened with the latest Transfer ceremony and if they had mined enough glaze to balance with the woman Mallos had chosen. I hoped so, but there was nothing I could do about that. I needed to find Loor and get the rescue show on the road.

I scanned the cavern and something caught my eye. Walking out of a tunnel to my left was Rellin. He walked along quickly while speaking with another one of the miners. The weird thing was, these guys actually looked happy. Rellin slapped the guy on the back like they had just shared some joke and the guy took off running someplace. Now, these guys had nothing to be happy about. The last time I spoke with Rellin he had pretty much condemned his entire tribe to a slow death by refusing to stand up against Kagan. Why was he happy all of a sudden? When he got farther away, I went to take a look down the tunnel they had just come from.

I entered to find that it was another abandoned avenue. The ore-car railroad tracks were old and rotten. This must have been one the first tunnels they dug off the main cavern. I wondered how long ago that was. Years? Decades? Centuries? I also wondered why Rellin and the other miner were down here. I found my answer a few yards in. As with many of the other tunnels, there was a chamber dug out of the rock off to the side. But unlike the cell where I had just slept, this one had a wooden door to it. I took a quick look around to see if I was being watched, then opened the door and went inside.

It was a room about twice the size of the one I had just slept in, and this one was packed full of equipment. At first I thought this was where they kept their mining tools, but on closer inspection I saw the truth. This wasn't digging equipment, this was an armory loaded with weapons! There were hundreds of spears like the ones Uncle Press had lashed to the side of the sled we rode from the top of the mountain. I was surprised to see their sharp metal tips gleaming in the light. The Milago weren't allowed to use metal tools except in the mines, but I was sure they weren't allowed to make weapons, either.

One side of the room was full of these spears. Below them were stacks and stacks of arrows. There must have been thousands. Across from them were the bows for the arrows. Probably a hundred in all. This looked to be a pretty formidable arsenal. Then I saw something that didn't quite make sense. There were large baskets placed along the back wall. I recognized them as the baskets they used to bring the glaze to the surface. These baskets were full, but not with glaze. I walked over to them and picked up one of the items inside. It was a small, sturdy stick about six inches long.

Attached to one end were two thin, leather straps about eighteen inches long. At the other end of the strap, a leather pouch the size of a baseball card was attached. I looked at the strange contraption trying to figure out what it could be. And then I got it. It was a slingshot! An old-fashioned slingshot! These guys didn't have rubber, so it wasn't the kind that you could stretch back and snap to propel stones. With this thing you had to hold the wooden stick and kind of fling the stone. There must have been a couple hundred of these babies in the baskets.

As I stood there holding the slingshot, I was struck with a sad thought. Rellin was right. The Milago were not prepared to do battle with Kagan's knights. These slingshots were pitiful. Sure, we all knew the story about David slaying Goliath, but that was just a story. How did these guys think they could stand a chance against trained, killer knights in armor by using these toys? The spears looked a little more dangerous. The arrows did too, but did the Milago even know how to use them? Suddenly Rellin's concern seemed very real to me. If they tried to fight the Bedoowan, they'd be slaughtered.

I was just about to drop the slingshot back in its basket, when somebody reached out and grabbed it from my hand!

I turned in surprise to see Figgis. He danced away from me, swinging the slingshot over his head.

"Changed your mind, have you?" he chirped. "Ready to make a trade?"

"I don't want anything from you," I said as strongly as I could.

"No? I have many things you may need," he said with a toothless smile. "How about this?"

He took something from his waist pouch and held it up to me. It was a red Swiss Army knife.

"That's mine!" I shouted and grabbed it away from him. "You went through my pack! What else did you take?" The mystery of why my pack was worked over had been solved. Figgis didn't put up a fight for it. He just cackled out a wheezy laugh.

"I know what you really need," he said slyly. "I know, I know."

"What do I need?" I asked, losing patience.

"You need tak," he announced. "I am the one, the only one who can get it for you."

Tak. There was that word again.

"What is tak?" I asked.

Figgis laughed again and reached into his waist pouch.

"Tak is the answer," he said reverently. "Tak is the hope."

Whatever tak was, it couldn't be very big because it fit in his pouch. He was just about to pull it out . . . when Rellin walked in.

"Figgis!" he shouted.

Figgis instantly pulled his hand out of the pouch, empty. He looked incredibly guilty.

"You should not have brought him here, old man," Rellin chastised.

Figgis cowered and ran out of the room like a guilty puppy. Whatever tak was, it was clear he did not want Rellin to know that he was trying to sell me some.

"I am sorry you saw this room," he said, sounding tired. "I do not want you to think we still have hope of fighting the Bedoowan. These weapons will soon be destroyed."

Something wasn't right. Rellin wasn't telling me the whole truth. I figured since he wasn't being totally up front with me, then I should be careful about what I said to him. So I didn't mention the tak thing that Figgis was trying to sell me.

"I guess you gotta do what you gotta do," was all I could think of saying.

I didn't like being there, especially since there was something going on that I wasn't clear on. The best thing for me to do then was leave. So I walked past Rellin and out the door. He didn't say another word to me.

Once away from there, my thoughts went back to the problem at hand, which was Uncle Press. So I ran back to the cell where my gear was. When I stepped inside that room, I saw that Loor and Alder were there and they were going through my stuff! They had it spread out all over the floor. Wasn't there any such thing as privacy around here?

"Hey!" I shouted.

Alder jumped back, embarrassed. But Loor kept right on rummaging.

"I am looking for the weapons you brought back," she said without a hint of apology. "I see no weapons here." She said this while shaking one of the yellow walkie-talkies you sent.

I grabbed it from her and said, "I didn't get any weapons. I wouldn't even know how to use a weapon."

"Then this is all useless," she spat out.

"That's what you think," I said and handed her back the walkie-talkie. I then found the other walkie-talkie and stepped to the far side of the room. I put it up to my mouth, hit the send button and said, "Boo!"

Both Loor and Alder jumped in surprise. Loor threw the walkie-talkie away like it was hot. Alder caught it and then he threw it too. Man, how excellent was that? It was the exact reaction I was hoping for.

"What is this magic?" asked Alder with wide eyes.

"It isn't magic," I said. "You gotta understand, my territory is way more advanced than here. Things like this are pretty common where I come from. It's not magic, it's science."

I picked up the small CD boom box you sent and hit Play. Instantly the first track started to play. It was a headbanger rock song with thrashing guitars that sent Loor and Alder into a panic. They covered their ears and ran to the far side of the room like frightened rabbits. It was awesome. I didn't want to prolong their agony so I turned the music off quickly. The two sat there staring at me with wide, frightened eyes.

"Still think we need weapons?" I asked with a sly smile.

Then I saw something that totally blew me away. Loor looked to me and, believe it or not, she smiled.

"I like this science," she said.

"Me too," added Alder.

So far so good. Their reactions gave me hope that my ideas might work. The trick was to use this stuff the right way and the time to do that was coming fast. I took a quick inventory and saw that you were able to get everything except for the flashlight. You guys are amazing. I was a little surprised to see that none of the stuff was mine though. I didn't mean for you to go out and get new stuff, or to send your own, Mark. But after I thought about it, I realized that it would have been hard for you to go to my house and get my stuff. My parents would have asked questions and that would have been tricky. So as soon as I can, I'll repay you for everything.

I gave one of the walkie-talkies to Loor and showed her how to use it. If we got split up, these would be crucial. The rest of the equipment I put back in the pack. Alder then added something that was a little surprising. He gave us each clothes that the Bedoowan wear inside the palace. They were simple pants and jackets with long sleeves. The pants had pockets and were tied with a drawstring. The jackets closed with buttonlike pieces of wood. They were light, almost pastel colors of green and blue. But the thing that really jumped out at me was that they were soft. The material was some kind of cotton and they were really comfortable. Even the leather shoes were comfortable. If I didn't know better, I'd guess that the Bedoowan did their shopping at The Gap. It really struck me how the Milago lived their lives wearing rough, smelly caveman skins while the Bedoowan wore these coolio, comfortable clothes that were like pajamas.

Loor didn't want to wear them. She wanted Alder to get us armor from the knights. But Alder explained that the knights were not allowed to wear their armor in the palace. If we were seen inside wearing armor, the Bedoowan would instantly take notice and we'd be lost. Wearing the clothes he gave us was our best chance of blending in. Loor didn't like it, but she couldn't argue with the logic, so we quickly dressed in the Bedoowan outfits.

Alder also had something else of value—a map of the palace. It was crude and drawn roughly on some parchment paper, but it was good enough. It didn't show everything, but it had the key areas we needed to worry about: the cell area where Uncle Press was being held and the guard quarters where the knights stayed. Everything seemed in place except for one small detail. Maybe the most important detail of all.

"This is all good," I said. "But how are we going to get in?"

"There is a way," Alder said. "The Bedoowan do not know of it and very few of the Milago are aware. My brother showed it to me the day before he died."

Now there was some new information. Alder had a brother who died. I wanted to know what that was all about, but now was not the time for chitchat.

"Then let's go," I said.

I put on the pack and followed the others out of the cell. Rather than turn for the main mine shaft to climb to the surface, Alder led us to one of the ore cars.

"No sense in all of us walking," said Alder. "Jump in."

Wherever we were going, it was underground. Loor and I climbed into the ore car and Alder started to push. We headed down the track of yet another tunnel off the main cavern. As we passed some miners, they barely took notice of us. These poor guys were like the living dead.

Alder was a pretty strong guy and he pushed us along with ease. Luckily the tunnel was flat, so maybe it wasn't all that hard anyway. We traveled for a long time and went pretty deep into the mine. After a while it got totally dark, but it wasn't like we had to make a turn or anything, so Alder kept on pushing. As the tunnel started to grow brighter, I looked ahead and saw a small spot of light way in the distance. Before I could ask what it was, Alder said, "The tunnel leads to the sea. The end is not far from here. You cannot enter from the outside because the opening is high in the bluffs. It is to bring fresh air into the mines."

Fresh air, yeah, right. Not fresh enough to get rid of the poisonous gas that was killing all the miners. I then noticed something else weird. Throughout all the tunnels, the walls looked the same. They were made of solid, craggy rock that had been chiseled out by hand. But here it was different. Along one side of the tunnel were round, stone columns. They were wide too, maybe three feet in diameter, and looked to me like big ancient columns from Greek ruins.

"The miners uncovered these by accident many years ago," Alder said. "They are the foundation of the Bedoowan palace."

Whoa! That meant we were directly under the fortress!

"The Bedoowan do not know that the Milago have tunneled

under their palace," Alder added. "If they did, they would have closed this tunnel off and killed some miners in punishment."

There must have been about twenty of these pillars and they were roughly ten yards apart. I saw off to the side, between two of the stone pillars, another tunnel. Actually it was more like a small recess, because just inside it was a ladder. Obviously this ladder led up into the palace. Gulp.

"No one knows why this secret entrance was created," said Alder as we climbed out of the ore car. "It is older than any of the miners who are alive today."

I stood at the bottom of the ladder and looked up. I then looked back at the others. It was show time.

"Let's make sure we're all on the same page," I said. "Our plan is to get to the cell where they're keeping Uncle Press as quietly as possible. If this becomes a fight, we'll lose." I said this while looking straight at Loor. She looked away from me. I knew she agreed, but it was killing her.

"Alder," I said. "Can you get us to the cell area?"

"Yes, I think so," was his answer.

"You think or you know?" I didn't want anything left to chance.

"I know," came his more confident reply.

"Good," I said.

"But it is not going to be as easy to get back unnoticed," he added.

"And that is when we fight," said Loor.

"Yeah, whatever," I said, and turned for the ladder. Jeez, she had a one-track mind. It wasn't until I got halfway up the ladder that I realized I didn't want to be the first one up. What was I thinking? I had no idea what might be waiting for me on top. But it was too late now; we weren't about to change places while dangling in the air. So I continued to climb and ended up on a dark shelf of stone. The ceiling was also stone and it was so low that I couldn't stand up straight. The others quickly joined me.

"Now what?" I asked.

Alder knew exactly where to go. He walked a few feet along the stone ledge and then raised his hands. I looked to see that above him was a wooden door. A trapdoor! Alder pushed it up easily, then hoisted himself through it. Loor was next. She easily pulled herself up. It wasn't as easy for me. Not only was I shorter, but I had the pack on. I stood below the open trapdoor looking up and said, "Uh, excuse me? Little help, please?"

Loor and Alder both reached down, grabbed my out-stretched hands and hoisted me up as easily as if I were a child. We were now in another dark room.

"This leads to a storage room off the kitchen," Alder whispered. I figured that since he was whispering, we were getting close to where we might come across some Bedoowan.

Alder led us across the small room and then felt along one of the walls. I wasn't sure what he was looking for until he found it. There was a small notch carved into the stone. Alder stuck his fingers in and pulled. Suddenly, the wall opened up as if it were a door! We quickly went through and Alder closed the secret door behind us. When I looked back, I saw that once it was closed, you could barely see the seam where the door was. The wall was smooth, as if it were made out of plaster. That seemed weird. Everything I had seen so far on Denduron was crude and rough. This wall seemed almost modern.

I looked around to see that we were in a storage room. There were baskets of food and rough, burlap bags full of stuff. There were also stacks and stacks of earthen pots. I was hit with a bunch of new smells. For the last several hours I had been smelling that nasty, sweet smell in the mines. But now I got the definite aroma of cooking food. I had no idea what it was, but it was making my mouth water. All I could think of was how my house smelled at Thanksgiving. My stomach rumbled. So did Loor's, I'm glad to say.

On the far wall was a wooden door. Alder crept quietly to it and gently eased it open. Instantly, the sounds of banging pots and sizzling food filled the room, like a busy restaurant kitchen. Again my stomach rumbled. I wanted to get out of here as soon as possible because this was torture. Alder waved for us to come and look. Loor and I joined him at the door and peered out. What I saw gave me a total shock.

This was a busy kitchen. Several cooks scurried around carrying large, succulent roast turkeys cooked to a golden brown. Other cooks were peeling vegetables and cutting potatoes on large wooden tables. Others were stirring pots of fragrant soups that bubbled on fiery stoves. But that wasn't the shocking thing. What surprised me was how modern this kitchen was. Believe me, by our standards it was still pretty ancient looking, but not compared to what I'd seen so far on Denduron. The pots were crudely shaped and hammered out of black metal; the ovens were made of stone with fires burning inside. The chefs slid the turkeys and other roasts in and out of these ovens with long paddles. Their other utensils didn't exactly look as if they came from the mall. They were crudely made and very simple but still, this setup was light years ahead of anything the Milago had.

I saw a device that looked like a dumbwaiter. The chefs placed platters of sumptuous, steaming food into a hole in the wall, then pulled on a rope that raised the small elevator and its cargo up into the palace. They even had running water! I saw iron sinks with hand pumps that produced clean, fresh water. Unbelievable. The Bedoowan had running water while the Milago had disgusting sewerholes in their crude huts!

It was then that I noticed the kitchen workers. As they went busily about their chores, they had a different look than anyone else I had seen on Denduron. Their features were all very small and delicate, like perfect dolls. Everything about them was small. Their hands, their feet, and even their height. Their eyes were different too. They slanted down, which gave them kind of an Asian feel. They all wore outfits like we had on, but theirs were white. But the thing that jumped out the most about them was their skin. It, too, was pure white. I don't mean pale-skinned like the Milago, I mean white. Believe it or not, it wasn't creepy. In some strange way, they were beautiful people. They just happened to look like porcelain dolls.

Alder must have been reading my mind because he whispered, "The workers in the palace are not Bedoowan. They are brought from a place across the ocean called 'Nova.'"

"Why don't they use the Milago to do their work?" I asked. "They make them do everything else."

"Because they do not want the Milago to see how well they live," answered Alder with a trace of venom. "They are afraid it would cause unrest."

That was an understatement. If I were a Milago and saw this I'd be downright pissed. Heck, I was getting pissed anyway. And hungry. Those turkeys smelled good.

"Look," said Loor as she pointed across the kitchen.

Standing in the doorway was a guy who was definitely not from Nova. He was so big that he filled the opening. He wore the same kind of clothes we had on and stood with his hands on his hips, surveying the kitchen. Around his waist was a leather belt from which dangled a nasty-looking club. I could feel Alder tense up.

"It is a Bedoowan knight," he whispered. "I do not like this. The knights never come to the kitchens. He must be looking for something."

"You think they know we're here?" I asked nervously.

"I do not know," answered Alder. "But if he catches us, we are finished before we even begin."

The knight stepped into the kitchen and slowly walked around to survey things. The Novans paid no attention to him and he didn't acknowledge them either. His eyes slowly scanned the room, taking everything in. We were trapped. In a few moments he would certainly enter this closet and find us.

Alder said nervously, "We should go back to the mines. We can wait until he's gone and then return."

"There isn't time," snapped Loor. "When he enters the door, we will overpower him and throw him into the mine."

That wasn't a good idea either. We weren't about to kill the guy; at least I wasn't about to. And he'd be sure to wake up and sound some kind of alarm. And who knew what the Novans would do if a knight entered their pantry and never came out? No, beating up on the guy wasn't the answer. I quickly pulled off my pack and dug into one of the side pouches, looking for a better solution.

"What are you doing?" demanded Loor.

"I've got an idea," I answered. "If it doesn't work, we'll do it your way."

I found what I was looking for and quickly moved back to the door. The knight was only a few yards away. There wasn't much time. He looked into a large pot of soup and reached in to take a taste, the slob. That's when I took my shot.

The thing I pulled out was the laser pointer you sent. I clicked it on and aimed the red beam at the pot of soup. From where we were it was easy to see the red laser dot against the black pot. I could only hope that the knight saw it too. He pulled his hand out of the pot and started to suck on his finger to taste the soup, but still he didn't see the laser. Alder and Loor watched the scene over my shoulder. Of course, they had no idea what this laser thing was, but now wasn't the time to ask.

I jiggled the beam a little so that the red dot danced on the pot. The knight stood there sucking on his tasty finger. He was just about to reach back into the pot for a double dip . . . when he saw it. He looked at the jumping dot curiously, without even taking his finger out of his mouth. The idiot. Then I slowly moved the dot off of the pot and let it travel across the stove. The knight, with his finger still in his mouth, followed it. This was like the game I play with Marley and a flashlight. I'd shine the beam on the floor and Marley would jump at it. The poor dog never got the idea that the spot of light wasn't something she could get her paws on. But that didn't stop her from trying.

That's exactly what happened with the knight. I slowly moved the red laser dot over loaves of bread, past bubbling pots, across wooden tables, down along the floor and back up on the wall. The curious knight never took his eye off of it. He followed the magical red light like, well, like a dog following a flashlight beam. What he didn't realize, is that I was moving him farther and farther away from us.

Once his back was to us, I silently motioned to the others to get moving. They slowly but silently opened the pantry door and crept out into the kitchen. I was right on their tails, while still concentrating on holding the beam steady to keep the dumbfounded knight entertained. We quickly moved across the kitchen to the exit. The Novans didn't even give us a second look. I was the last one out. My body was already out of the door, but I leaned back in, directing the beam. Then, I turned the laser off and couldn't resist waiting one last second to see the befuddled knight's reaction. It was perfect. He stood still for a moment, then started looking around frantically. Sheesh, even Marley wasn't stupid enough to do that. I wanted to laugh out loud, but I couldn't stay to enjoy the show. We had to get moving, so I followed the other two into the palace.

We had made it. We were in. The next step was to make our way to the cell where Uncle Press was being kept. Alder was already checking the map. All Loor and I could do was follow him and try to blend in. As it turned out, it wasn't all that difficult. The palace was busy with Bedoowan people who all more or less looked and dressed like us. Yes, Loor's skin was a bit darker than most, but not so much that she stood out. If no one recognized us for who we really were, we might just make it. As we made our way through the corridors, what I saw was not only surprising, it made an anger grow inside of me that I never thought possible.

The fortress was nothing like I expected. From the outside it looked like an ancient stone castle like they had in medieval times. I had seen pictures of those castles that still stood in England and the interiors were just as crudely simple as the exteriors. Here I expected to see corridors of stone and tiny cell-like rooms. I expected the floors to be of dirt and the light to come from windows or torches. You know, your basic Robin Hood–style castle. But this is not at all what we found inside the Bedoowan fortress.

The kitchen had been my first hint that all was not going to be what I thought. I'm telling you, Mark and Courtney, this place was beautiful! The walls were smooth and painted with light colors. Near the ceilings were elaborate decorative paintings done right on the walls. Some corridors had paintings of vines and flowers that stretched the whole length of the wall. Other corridors had paintings of people who were probably famous Bedoowans from the past. The ceilings were decorated with colorful chips of glass that were sculpted into beautiful patterns. The floors were all tiled with intricate marble work. And the place was totally clean. Every so often we'd pass one of the Novan servants on his hands and knees scrubbing the floors, or dusting the statues that stood on tables like this was some kind of museum.

Loor and I exchanged glances. We were both thinking the same thing. How could these people live in such elegance at the expense of the Milago people? I saw that Loor's jaw was clenching. She was angry too.

We heard music coming from a room we were about to pass. As we went by I glanced in to see a small concert going on. Three musicians sat on chairs playing oddball instruments like I had never seen before. They were string instruments, but they were shaped like human forms. It was really bizarro. The music they played was sweet and soothing. Several Bedoowans lounged around listening on big, cushy pillows. Pillows! These people had pillows! And to top it all off, they had Novan servants scrambling around serving them fruit from large platters.

The more of the Bedoowan people I saw, the more I realized that they were a pretty soft bunch . . . except for the knights, of course. All the others had this kind of baby fat thing going on. The men, the women, even the kids . . . all looked as if they needed to hit the gym. I guess that's what happens when you have nothing to do except lie around, eat stuff, and listen to lame music.

And here is the wildest thing. In every corridor along the walls there were thin glass tubes about the diameter of a nickel.

These tubes stretched the whole length of every corridor, and they gave off light! Light! They didn't have electricity here, but they figured out some way to make artificial light! The bottom line is that these guys were incredibly advanced. By our standards they were still back in the dark ages, but compared to the Milago they were the Jetsons!

I was amazed at first, but my amazement was replaced by anger. The Milago were dying and living in squalor so that these people could get fat and live in such luxury. It was just flat wrong. The more I saw of how these people lived, the more determined I grew to get Uncle Press out of there so he could help the Milago even things out a little.

All the while I was taking in the rich surroundings, Alder had been leading us through the maze of corridors. The kitchen was on the lowest level of the palace. We had climbed one set of wide, circular stairs to the next level. According to the map, this was the level where the prisoners were kept. Finally we came to an area that was a little less fancy than the rest of the fortress. The walls didn't have paintings on them and the floors and ceilings were bare. I guessed this was where they kept their prisoners, though it was still a lot nicer than where the Milago lived. At a turn in the corridor Alder motioned for us to stop. He took a cautious peek around the corner, then turned back to us.

"There is good news and bad news," he said. "The cell where Press is being held is being guarded. That means he is still there."

"Okay," I said. "What's the bad news?"

"The bad news is that there are six knights keeping guard."

Uh-oh. I took a peek around the corner to see for myself. Alder was right. There were six guards there. And these weren't fat and sassy Bedoowans, either. These were solid-looking knights. Each was dressed the same as we were and had the same club-weapons hanging from their belts as the knight in the kitchen. This was bad. There was no way we were getting past those guys. I snuck back to the other two, looked right at Loor and said, "Don't even think about taking those guys on."

"We must do something," countered Loor. "Or this was all for nothing."

Alder added, "And the equinox is fast approaching."

"We gotta get the knights away from the door," I said. "You know how this place works, Alder. What can we do that would make them leave their post?"

Alder thought and then said, "It would take some sort of emergency. Something they had to respond to quickly."

"Keep going," I said. "Think."

Alder looked around. He had no clue. But then his eye caught something near the ceiling. He stared at it for a moment, and smiled. Loor and I both looked up to where his gaze was fixed. What we saw was something that looked like a pipe. It was about six inches in diameter and ran along the wall right by the ceiling.

"What's that?" I asked.

"You have something in your bag," said Alder. "It has a handle, with a jagged metal blade."

I knew exactly what he meant. I dug into my pack and pulled out the camp saw. This one was even better than the one I asked you for, Mark. All I wanted was the small saw from my dad's workshop. But you gave me this coolio thing that folded in half to fit in the pack. Alder opened it up, locked the saw blade and felt the sharpness of the teeth.

"This is for cutting?" he asked.

"Yeah," I answered. "What are you thinking?"

Alder looked back up at the pipe in the ceiling and said, "That carries water throughout the fortress," he answered. He then looked at us with a devilish smile. It took me a second, but I figured out what his plan was and smiled back.

"You can cut through that thing?" I asked.

"Like soft fruit," was his confident answer.

Loor still didn't get it. "Why would you do that?" she asked angrily. She was ticked that we were a few steps ahead of her.

Alder answered, "I will go a few corridors over and cut out a section of the water carrier."

"It'll make a mess," I said, enjoying the thought.

"Yes, it will," he said, enjoying the idea as much as I was. "And of course the missing piece will not be found anywhere."

"That's perfect, dude. Go!" I said. Alder took off running in the opposite direction, away from the prison corridor. Loor and I hid ourselves in a small room around the corner, waiting for the excitement to begin.

"I did not think we would get this far," she said.

"Neither did I," I replied.

We waited a few minutes, but nothing happened. I was getting nervous. Loor seemed calm. She had her game face on. Maybe she was used to this prebattle moment, but my stomach was a knot of tension. I couldn't take it anymore and jumped up.

"I gotta see how he's doing," I said.

"Pendragon, no!" she hissed and tried to grab me. But there was no way I could wait there any longer. I moved quickly in the direction that Alder had gone, peeking down the corridors at each junction, expecting to see him. Finally I rounded a corner and there he was. Alder was standing on a table, sawing away at the pipe. He had already sawed all the way through once and water was leaking down on him. There was a pool of water growing on the floor. But the best was yet to come. With a few final pulls on the saw, he sliced through a second time and pulled down a chunk of pipe about two feet long. The second he pulled it down, water starting gushing out like a berserk fire hydrant. Alder got doused and was nearly knocked over by the force. I sure hoped this was fresh water and not sewage. That would have been nasty. Effective, but nasty. Alder got his bearings, caught sight of me and held up the hunk of pipe triumphantly.

Then suddenly, "*Ahhhhhh!*" A Bedoowan woman had rounded the corner on the far end and saw the waterworks. The alarm had been officially sounded. Alder tucked the pipe away like a football and ran in the opposite direction from me. I was now in the wrong spot and started back to Loor. I had to force myself to walk. I didn't want anyone thinking that I was running away from the scene of the crime . . . which is exactly what I was doing. It was a good thing too, because no sooner did I slow down, than I saw the team of knights that had been guarding Uncle Press come running toward me. Or should I say, toward the screaming woman. They ran past me as if I wasn't even there. I really wanted to stay and watch the madness as they tried to stop the water. But that's not why I was here. It was time to spring Uncle Press.

When I got back to Loor, she was up and peering around the corridor toward the cell. She sensed I was near and turned to face me.

"There is only one guard left," she said. "It is my turn." She reached behind her back and from underneath her jacket she pulled a smaller version of her wooden stick weapon. I had no idea she had it. Sneaky. She was all set to charge, but I stopped her.

"No," I said as strongly as possible. "They don't know we're here yet. The longer we can be secret, the better chance we have of getting out."

"There is no other way, Pendragon," she said seething. She wanted to fight.

I took a quick glance around the corridor to see the guard standing there. Further down, the corridor ended at a balcony. My guess was that this balcony overlooked the ocean.

I had an idea.

"Can you get to that balcony without him knowing?" I asked.

Loor took a quick look, turned to see that there was a parallel corridor behind us, and said, "Yes."

"Then go. I'll send him to you."

Loor wanted to ask how, but I pushed her to go before she had the chance. I figured if the laser pointer trick worked once, it would work again. So I waited a few minutes to make sure Loor was in position, then took the pointer out of my pocket. When I clicked it on, the beam didn't work! I clicked it a few more times, I banged it, I took out the battery to clean it, but nothing worked. It was dead and so was I. I didn't know how much longer the other knights would be occupied with the water geyser, and Loor was waiting for me to do something.

I dug back in my pack, looking for an answer . . . and I found it. It was the radio-controlled stunt cycle. If the batteries failed on this baby, then we were out of luck. I wasn't as good with the stunt cycle as with my four-wheel humvee, but I understand why you guys couldn't go to my house to get it. It was going to be the stunt cycle or nothing. I still remember the day you got this for your birthday, Mark. We both picked up on the radio controls pretty quick and had that cycle taking air off ramps in no time. The plastic helmet on the driver still had the scars from all the times he landed on his head. But I wasn't planning any tricks with him today. All I wanted him to do was drive straight and smooth. If I could pull that off, then we might have a chance.

So I took the little motorcycle out of my pack, reached around the corner of the corridor, and put him on the floor. My plan was to send it slowly past the guard, but I didn't want him to see me standing there with the radio controls. I had to do this blind. I took a breath, then pushed the forward stick. The motorcycle hummed to life with that familiar whine. I wasn't sure how fast it was going, but I couldn't take the chance of looking too soon. If I sent it off course, I was dead. If I sent it too slowly, the guard might just bend over and pick it up. So I forced myself to count to ten, then I peeked an eye around the corner.

I saw exactly what I wanted to see. The guard was standing at the door, dumbfounded, staring at the little man on the motorcycle. I can't imagine what was going through his mind. I couldn't tell if he was curious or scared. Probably a little bit of both. I had the motorcycle moving on a perfectly straight line, headed for the far end of the corridor. So far so good. But just as the cycle was about to roll past him, the guard took a step forward and reached down to pick it up.

I quickly hit the throttle and the cycle shot ahead, just barely out of his grasp. Maybe I was better at this than I thought. This seemed to get the guard's curiosity up even further, and he walked after the cycle. Perfect. This was like playing a fish on a line. I teased him by slowing up. When he would bend down to pick it up, I shot it forward. The whole time he kept moving closer and closer to the balcony on the far end of the corridor where Loor was lying in wait.

With one final push on the throttle, I accelerated the motorcycle forward and it shot out onto the balcony. The guard walked out behind it. He looked down, then hesitated because he expected it to move again. But it didn't. He stared at it for a second, then suddenly bent over and snatched it up with one quick move. But his victory was short-lived because he never stood up again. Loor jumped out and whacked him with her ministick. With two quick moves she slammed the guy, pivoted, and sent him sailing over the rail into the ocean. Mission accomplished and we hadn't given ourselves away.

I quickly reached into my pocket and pulled out my walkie-talkie. "Get Alder," I commanded into the yellow walkie. Loor definitely heard me, because she took off running along the balcony and out of sight. I put my walkie-talkie away and looked to the cell door. There was nothing left between me and Uncle Press but that door. So I quickly grabbed my pack and ran for it.

It was too much to expect that the door would be unlocked, and it wasn't. There was an old-fashioned keyhole, but of course I had no key. So I dug into my pack to look for something that might help me open the door. All I could come up with was the Swiss Army knife that I had nabbed back from Figgis. I opened up the awl blade and stuck it into the keyhole, figuring I might be able to turn the lock somehow. But it didn't work. I jammed the awl up and down desperately. If I couldn't open the lock then maybe I could break it. I think that's exactly what happened, because with one final twist, the latch moved and the door opened. I was in! Or should I say, Uncle Press was out.

"Uncle Press!" I shouted as I ran in. "It's me! We gotta get—"

The small cell was empty. Uncle Press wasn't there! I didn't understand why it would be guarded if there was no one to guard. The answer came quickly.

"Ahhhhh!" Somebody jumped me from behind. He leaped up on my back, wrapped his legs around my waist, and tried to wrestle me to the ground.

"Let me outta here, ya filthy Bedoowan pig!" he shouted. The guy wasn't very heavy, or very strong for that matter. All I had to do was spin once and he went flying off. He landed on the hard floor with a loud thud that must have knocked the wind out of him. I looked down and saw that this definitely wasn't Uncle Press. It was a grimy little guy dressed in Milago skins. His hair and beard were incredibly long, which meant he'd been here for a long time.

"Where's my uncle?" I shouted.

The strange little man looked up at me with confusion in his eyes. "You . . . you are not Bedoowan?" he asked.

"No! I'm here to get my uncle. Where is he?"

The guy took a while to answer. I guess he wasn't used to this much excitement. Join the club, neither was I.

"You must be . . . Pendragon," he said.

"Yes! And I'm looking for my uncle. Do you know where he is?"

"They took him," answered the Milago prisoner. "Early, before the suns came up. He is to be executed today."

Yeah, I knew that. This guy wasn't helping much. I didn't know where to turn. Uncle Press could be anywhere. My mind raced but I didn't come up with a single answer. I was in total brain lock when my walkie-talkie came to life.

"Pendragon," came Alder's voice. "I found Press. He is not in his cell."

I grabbed my walkie and said to him, "Yeah, I know. Where is he?"

"I am with him now," he came back. "I will direct you to us. Hurry."

We were back in the game. I glanced at the Milago prisoner and said, "Now's your chance. Get out!" Then I turned and ran out of the cell. I quickly ran back toward the mayhem that Alder had caused. The water was still gushing out of the pipes and the corridor was totally flooded. Knights and Novans worked together trying to stop the flow, but they were doing a lousy job. Good. It kept them busy.

Alder then came through the walkie-talkie saying, "Go back to the stairs and climb two more levels."

Got it. I did what I was told. But when I entered the stairwell I saw something down below that nearly made my heart stop. Coming up fast from the lower level were a dozen knights. And these guys were in full battle gear, carrying spears. I think some kind of alarm must have finally sounded. They knew we were here.

One of them looked up and saw me. "There he is!" shouted the knight.

Yep, they knew we were here. The knights began to run. There was no way I could outrace these guys, so I played my final card. I pulled the CD boom box out of the pack, held it in front of me, cranked the volume and hit "Play." Instantly the thrashing rock guitar blasted out of the speakers.

It was like I had thrown a bomb at these guys. They froze in their tracks with a look of total shock on each and every face. They had never heard anything like this before and probably never would again. They turned and fled back down the stairs in total panic. Under other circumstances I would have thought this was pretty funny. Right now it just felt like victory. I left the boom box on the stairs, figuring this would be as good as putting up a gate to keep them down there.

"Pendragon, hurry!" came Alder's voice through the walkie.

As I started to run back up the stairs, I grabbed my walkie and called to him, "I'm almost on the fourth level."

"Turn left at the top and go to the end of the corridor," he instructed. "We're hiding in the last room to the left, before the balcony."

I tucked the walkie away and ran to where he told me. My mind was working ahead to the next few moves. We had to find Loor and get out. But we couldn't get back out through the kitchen because I had the knights trapped down there. There had to be another way out. Hopefully Alder had one, because I sure didn't.

I got to the top of the stairs, made the turn and ran down the corridor. I realized briefly that this corridor was more ornate than any we had seen so far. There were huge sculptures and giant paintings on the walls. It would have been pretty cool, if I weren't so scared out of my mind. But I had reached my destination. The last room on the left was where Alder and Uncle Press were waiting for me. Hopefully Loor was there too. I ran into the room and skidded to a sudden stop.

It took all of a half second for me to realize that this had gone terribly wrong. I turned to run back out, but two Bedoowan knights jumped in front of me, blocking the door. I was trapped. Slowly I turned back to see Alder standing there holding the walkie-talkie. A knight had a spear to his throat. Alder looked as if he were about to cry.

"I . . . I am sorry, Pendragon," he cried. "They were going to kill her."

Two other knights were holding Loor. One had her arms, the other held a knife to her throat.

"You should have let them," she spat out in defiance. There were a few other people in the room too. Seeing them is why I knew all was lost. One of them was Saint Dane. Or Mallos, as he calls himself here. He stood with his arms folded and a smug smile on his face. But it was the final person in the room who gave me the biggest surprise of all. This person was seated on a large, ornate throne that was decorated with cut pieces of glaze. I didn't need to be told who it was. This was the heir to the throne of the Bedoowan. This was the monarch who had their father killed so they could begin their tyrannical rule over the Milago. This was the person who ordered the deaths of Milago as easily as ordering more glaze. This was Kagan's throne room, and seated on the throne was Kagan.

The thing that surprised me though, is that Kagan was a woman.

"Hello, Pendragon," said Saint Dane. "Lovely day for an execution, don't you think?"

The one person missing from the room was Uncle Press.

DENDURON

"This is the Milago boy I have heard so much about?" said Kagan with a sneer. "His odor offends me."

Gee, thanks, lady. Nice to meet you, too. I have to describe to you guys what Kagan looked like because she was a real piece of work. First off, she was fat. Not just baby fat chubby, we're talking gordo. I'll bet she kept that kitchen downstairs pretty busy. She wore a flowing yellow toga dress that didn't do much to hide her rolls of chub. Luckily the dress went to the floor and had long sleeves because I didn't think her arms and legs would be a pretty sight. The dress didn't hide her feet, though. She wore these sandals that her toes poked out of like stuffed sausages. Not a pleasant picture. She also had a double chin of fat that hung down over the neck of her dress. Ick.

I have no idea how old she was. She could have been eighteen or thirty or any age in between. The fat stretched her skin so much that it gave her a smooth, baby look. Of course, she wasn't a baby; she was a monstrous, evil queen with fat toes. Everything about her was big. Her hands, her feet, her head, even her eyes. Oddly enough, with all of the size she had going on, her mouth was tiny. Such a little hole didn't belong on this immense, doughy face. She had long hair too. But it wasn't shiny and combed; it hung down over her shoulders and looked like it hadn't been washed in a few months. Nice, huh? She was like some kind of bizarro cartoon sumo wrestler woman.

She had multiple drapes of silver necklaces, bracelets that traveled halfway up her arms, and rings on every finger. She also had a tiara perched on top of her head that looked kind of stupid because it was too small. On any normal head it would look fine, but her big, old, round, greasy-haired dome made it look like a doll crown on a giant. Of course, all of the silver jewelry was adorned with glaze. The precious blue stones were cut in every shape and size imaginable. It must have taken the Milago miners a week to dig up this much glaze. Her throne was decorated with glaze as well. There were baseball-sized stones mounted all over the golden chair.

As I took all of this in, I kept thinking about the Transfer ceremony where that miner died because they hadn't brought up enough glaze. I can honestly say that I have never hated anyone in my life. But this lady was in line to be the first.

"Show me the toy," she commanded. Her voice was high and squeaky, like fingernails on a blackboard.

The knight who was holding Alder grabbed his walkie-talkie and handed it to Kagan with a subservient bow. She took it and inspected it from all angles.

"What sort of magic is this?" she asked.

I couldn't resist. I took my walkie, hit the send button and said, "Put it down!"

Bad move. Kagan let out a yelp and dropped the walkie like it was alive. It hit the floor with a clatter and a knight immediately crushed it with his boot like an annoying bug. I stood there holding the second walkie (which was now totally useless) wishing I hadn't pulled that stunt. Kagan hoisted herself up out of her throne and waddled toward me, her jewelry jangling as she walked. She stared down at me with those big, round black eyes, raised a meaty hand, then hauled off and slapped me across the face.

Yeow. That stung. But I wouldn't give her the benefit of letting her know how much, so I clenched my teeth and forced back my tears. I looked to Kagan and oddly enough, it seemed as if she were holding back tears too. She looked at her hand, then looked at me with genuine surprise and exclaimed, "You hurt my hand!"

Say what? Whose fault was that? I guess it was mine, because instantly two knights ran up to me and jammed the points of their spears in my neck.

"Whoa, whoa!" I yelled. "Sorry. It won't happen again!" What I wanted to say was: "Gee, sorry I hit your hand with my face, chubby." But I figured it wouldn't be a good idea to be a wise ass. Especially when I had two spears at my throat.

"Let him go," commanded Mallos/Saint Dane.

The knights pulled their spears away, but stayed on either side of me. Kagan fell back into her throne, sobbing like a pouting baby. Mallos comforted her by saying, "Shall I call the surgeon, Your Majesty?"

Surgeon? You gotta be kidding me.

"No," sniffled Kagan. "I will be brave."

Give me a break. This lady was a piece of work all right.

"He will be punished." Mallos added, "Along with his uncle."

This was bad. We came to rescue Uncle Press, and now it looked as if I was going to join him in whatever horrible fate they had planned. Some rescue, huh? Mallos then left Kagan and walked to me.

"Press will be so happy to see you," he said to me with an oily smile.

"Where is he?" I asked, trying to sound like I wasn't totally petrified.

Mallos answered me with a laugh. He turned to Kagan saying, "This boy is a spy like his uncle, like this girl"—he walked to Alder and stared him square in the eye—"and like this traitor Bedoowan." Mallos leaned close to Alder until their noses nearly touched. Alder was scared, but tried not to flinch. Mallos said, "I always knew you were a traitor, but I needed you to deliver Pendragon."

Alder dropped his head in shame and embarrassment.

Loor struggled in anger to pull away from the two knights who were holding her, but as strong as she was, these huge knights held her tight. To stop her from struggling, one of the knights gave a quick jab with the knife he was holding to her throat. My stomach turned when I saw a trickle of blood flowing down her neck. But Loor wouldn't flinch. She wouldn't let the guy know he had hurt her. I wasn't surprised.

Mallos then walked to the throne saying, "They are all conspiring to incite the Milago into a revolt against us, your majesty. And for that they should be put to death."

Things were falling apart, fast. "What do you mean 'us'?" I shouted at Mallos. Then to Kagan I said, "He's not a Bedoowan! Ask him where he comes from!"

Kagan looked at Mallos. Was there a hint of doubt in her mind? If I could expose Mallos as being a Traveler from a different territory, maybe Kagan wouldn't buy everything he had to say. It was a long shot, but the only thing I could think of.

"It's true and I can prove it. Who thought of the trick to

get me here? It must have been Mallos. Nobody else knows how those walkie-talkies work, right? A Bedoowan wouldn't know how to use that magic."

Kagan looked at the crushed walkie on the floor, then to Mallos. I was getting through to her.

"Mallos isn't a Bedoowan," I said with authority. "You can't trust him!"

She sniffed back her tears, looked at Mallos, smiled, and said, "Of course, Mallos is not a Bedoowan. He came to us many years ago from the far side of the ocean and has been my most trusted advisor ever since. Why do you tell me things I already know?"

Oh well, so much for my brilliant plan. She already knew. Kagan reached to the table next to her throne and grabbed a piece of purple fruit. It must have been past her feeding time, which was probably every five minutes. She took a big sloppy bite and a river of purple juice ran down her chin and landed on her ample chest. I wanted to puke. When she spoke, it was with a mouth full of fruit goo. Did I mention I wanted to puke?

"Why are you trying to get the Milago to make war with us?" she asked in her squeaky, annoying voice. It was weird; she sounded all innocent, like a three-year-old asking why the sky is blue. Was it possible that she didn't know how bad the Milago had it? Was Mallos really the guy who was calling the shots and using this creepy, child-woman like a puppet? I figured I'd better answer carefully.

"Because they have horrible lives," I said. "They live in dirty, mud huts and they don't have enough food. If they don't mine enough glaze, they are murdered. But the worst thing is, they're dying. The air in the mines is poisoning them. They want to fight because they are desperate for better lives."

That about summed it up. I didn't want to accuse the Bedoowan of taking advantage of them, that might get her mad. But I wanted to paint a picture of how bad the Milago had it. If Her Royal Chubness didn't know these things before, maybe now she would think twice about what her people were doing and have a little sympathy.

She took another juicy bite from her purple fruit and stared at me. What was she thinking? Alder and Loor watched her, waiting for her reaction. Mallos looked bored. Kagan then tossed the juicy wet fruit pit on the floor. Instantly a Novan servant appeared from behind the throne, cleaned up the pit, then disappeared again. No wonder this woman was so fat. She didn't have to lift a finger to do anything.

Kagan then said innocently, "That is how it always has been. The Milago dig for glaze so that the Bedoowan can trade it for lovely things. It has been this way forever."

Wow. Could she really be so clueless? She didn't think there was anything wrong with the Milago suffering and dying for them. I glanced to Loor and she had the same look of dumbfounded surprise on her face that I'm sure I had. Alder just kept looking down at the floor. I think he already knew where Kagan's head was. I wasn't sure of what to do next, but I had to say something.

"And what do the Bedoowan do for the Milago in return for their hard work?" I asked.

Kagan cocked her head in surprise, as if I were asking something she had never thought of before. It reminded me of the way Marley turns her head and her ears go up when she hears a strange sound. Before answering, Kagan reached for another piece of purple fruit and started gnawing on it. She made these little grunting, slurping sounds that turned my stomach. What a pig. The whole while she gazed off into the distance, as if she were giving some serious thought to the question I had asked. I couldn't wait to hear the answer because from what I saw, the Bedoowan do nothing for the Milago except abuse them. Alder and Loor waited for the answer as well. Even Mallos looked at the queen in anticipation.

Kagan took another messy bite of her fruit, swallowed, then looked right at me and said, "Your questions make my head hurt." She then looked at Mallos and said, "Kill them."

Whoa, bad response. Instantly the knights grabbed me and started dragging me and Loor and Alder toward the door.

Loor put up the best fight. She screamed back at Kagan, "It does not matter what happens to us! The Milago will not be slaves forever!"

That was very bold and all, but I was kind of thinking it *did* matter what happened to us. The knights dragged us out into the corridor and toward the stairs when I heard Mallos calling from behind.

"Wait," he shouted. "I wish to speak with that one!"

That meant me. The knights stopped dragging me along and Mallos approached us. He looked at me for a long while, as if sizing me up.

"Remember what happens here today, Pendragon," he said seriously. "This is how it will be. There is no hope for you. Halla will fall, and you will fall with it."

He then looked at the knights and ordered, "Take them to the box." As the knights dragged me away, Mallos called, "Remember, Pendragon!"

What was he talking about? I expected him to say something like: "The Milago are doomed!" or "You will all die a horrible death!" or some other nastiness. But instead, what he said made no sense. What is Halla? Osa had said something about Halla before she died, but I had no idea what she was talking about. More important, if I was about to die, then why did he tell me to remember what was going to happen? The way things were going, I wasn't going to live long enough to have time to forget. Believe it or not, as scared as I was, Mallos's words gave me hope. They reminded me that this was actually a larger battle than it seemed. It wasn't just about the Milago and the Bedoowan. It was about the future of the whole territory of Denduron. If Mallos threatened that he would always defeat me, then he must expect there to be more battles. And maybe that meant he wasn't planning to kill us after all. At least that's what I hoped.

The knights dragged the three of us to the circular stairway. I expected them to bring us down to the prison area, but instead we went up. We climbed one more flight of stairs and were then hurried down a wide corridor to a wooden door with a heavy lock. One of the knights pulled out a big old key, opened the door and shoved us inside. Behind us, the door slammed with a booming crash and we found ourselves in the dark. I think we were all too stunned and scared to look around. Not that there was anything to see.

"Is this it?" asked Loor, sounding bold as ever. "Is this where we will die?"

"No," said Alder. "This is not where we will die." Alder seemed pretty calm about the whole thing. It was strange. Alder was a pretty nervous guy in general, but now he acted all casual in the face of certain death. I guess of the three of us, I was the only one who was actually scared. No fair.

"How come you're so calm?" I asked.

I didn't like his answer. He said, "Because this is the holding area. Nothing will happen to us here. When they are ready, they will bring us to the horror."

I guess that meant Alder wasn't being casual, he was in

a state of shock. He knew this was the calm before the storm. Something was coming and the thought of it was so horrible that it frightened him far beyond the point of showing nervousness.

"What will they do to us?" asked Loor.

She didn't have to wait for an answer. A door creaked open on the far side of the room and bathed the place in bright sunshine. Once the sun came in I saw this was a cell, with shackles on the walls and leg irons on the floor. Two knights in full battle gear stood at the open door. One of them motioned for us to come outside. We knew we had no choice, so we walked toward the sunlight. Loor took the lead, but before she went she turned to us and said, "I will not die without taking some of those Bedoowan animals with me." She then turned and left, with Alder and I close behind.

When we stepped into the sunshine, I was blinded and had to shade my eyes. Before they adjusted, I got a strange feeling. I think maybe it was the sound, but I had the feeling we weren't alone. Once my eyes adjusted I realized that not only weren't we alone, we were standing in a huge stadium along with thousands of other people. This was the Bedoowan version of a sports arena. It was open air. Above our heads was blue sky—we were on the top level of the Bedoowan palace. Two days before when I had looked across the inlet to the bluff above the palace, I thought it was just barren land. But now I realized that from where I was I couldn't look down into this arena that was dug below the surface.

The stadium was square. It reminded me of one of those arenas where they play tennis matches. My guess was that the place could seat a few thousand people. And it was packed. Each side of the arena held a different tribe. One side was all Bedoowan. They sat on cushioned seats with pillows for their backs. The next section was taken up by the Novan servants who sat on long bleachers. It was odd seeing so many of these pure white doll people in their white uniforms. The next section was full of Milago. It was obvious they were Milago because of their filthy leather clothes and the fact that they weren't even allowed to sit. They had to stand on stone tiers. My guess was they entered the arena from above, since they weren't allowed to walk through the palace. The fourth side was nearly empty. Halfway up the stands there was a box with a throne. Obviously this was where Kagan sat.

There were high walls with spikes built between the sections so there was no way the tribes could mingle. But even if the Milago wanted to get a little rowdy, they couldn't because there were armed knights ringing the top of the stadium. They stood as sentries, lining the entire top tier with their spears at the ready.

We stood in a section right next to the playing field below Kagan's box. There were no seats here, only a low barrier between us and the field. At least, I thought it was a playing field, but I wasn't exactly sure what game they played here. The flat area was about the size of a baseball diamond. The surface was grass, but there weren't any lines or markings that would show the boundaries for a game. It was just a plain, grass field.

I looked up at the various tribes in the stands and saw that each group acted very differently. The Bedoowan were chatting and seemed relaxed. Some smiled, others laughed. There were kids, too. It had the feel of a baseball stadium before a game. The Novans sat quietly looking down at the field. Most had their hands crossed in their laps politely and didn't move a muscle. Their faces were blank. I couldn't tell if they were happy to be here or not. The Milago were much easier to read.

They were restless. They kept glancing up at the guards that surrounded the stadium. It was obvious that they weren't here by choice, and it wasn't for entertainment.

Unfortunately I was afraid that Loor and Alder and I were the main attraction. I leaned over to Alder and asked, "What kind of game do they play here?"

Alder's eyes were riveted on the playing field. "This is no game, Pendragon," he said softly.

Before I could ask any more, I heard chimes. They were three simple notes that sounded like they came from a loud, but pleasant xylophone. All eyes turned to the empty viewing box above the playing field. I looked up too and saw two knights walk out into the box, followed by Mallos, who was followed by Kagan. She didn't wave to the crowd or anything the way you would expect a queen to acknowledge her subjects. She just lumbered to her throne and plopped herself down like a bored, spoiled little kid. She was eating again too. Big surprise. It looked like she was gnawing on a turkey leg. The entire stadium was now quiet except for the slurping and grunting sounds as Kagan finished off her latest snack. I really would have been grossed out, except for the fact that I knew whatever was going to happen, was going to happen soon. My heart started racing. I'm not sure what would have been worse—knowing our fate or not. The fear of the unknown was terrifying. Either way though, the show was about to begin.

Kagan looked up to Mallos and said impatiently, "Well?"

Mallos took a few steps forward and motioned down to the playing field. Instantly I saw a small door open on the opposite side of the field. A few seconds later somebody was pushed out from inside and tumbled down onto the grass. Obviously this guy didn't want to be here. In a few seconds I realized who it was—the scrawny Milago prisoner who was in

Uncle Press's cell. I guess he didn't get away when he had the chance. The poor guy looked scared. He pulled himself to his feet and looked around the stadium while shielding his eyes from the suns.

As if on cue, the Bedoowan spectators let out a loud, football-like cheer. This startled the guy and he stumbled away from them to the center of the field. At the same time, the Novans applauded politely. There was no yelling or whistling from them, just polite applause that ended as quickly as it began. The Milago didn't do anything but watch in silence. The guy backed to the center of the field because it was the one place where he could be the farthest away from everybody. He stood in the center, alone, his eyes darting around the stands with confusion and fear. He seemed to be looking for help. Then, his eyes finally fell on me. That's where he stopped. It was creepy. I didn't know what to do. Was I the only familiar face in the crowd? Did he want me to wave or something? I looked back at him, feeling helpless.

Then something strange happened. He was a bent over, old guy who had a rounded back that I assumed came from working in the mines his whole life. But as he stood staring at me, the fear left his face. He stood up straight, pushed his shoulders back, then touched his heart and held out his hand toward me. He even gave me a small smile. I know this sounds bizarro, but I felt that somehow by seeing me, he got some kind of strength. Believe me, I have no idea why it happened. It's not like I did anything or could help him, but after he saw me, it was like he transformed. Whatever was about to happen, he was now ready, and I played some small part in that.

We didn't have to wait long to find out what was in store

for the guy. On the right side of the arena from where we were sitting was a door that was larger than the one the Milago just came through. Two knights ran across the grass field toward it. There was a big brass latch that was so heavy it took two of these big knights to release it. Once the latch was undone, they threw the door open and ran for the stands. The scene reminded me of movies I'd seen of bullfights. I looked into the dark recesses beyond this large open door and expected to see a bull come charging through.

As it turns out, I wasn't that far off. I heard movement and snarls beyond that door. All eyes were riveted on the opening, including Loor's and Alder's. Even the Bedoowan stopped their socializing for a moment to look with anticipation.

A quig beast leaped through the doorway and crouched down on all fours. The Bedoowan section let out a cheer. The Novans applauded again and the Milago cringed. Some hid their eyes, others stood straight as if the least they could do for their fellow tribesman was to honor him by having the courage to watch.

The quig scanned the arena with yellow hunter's eyes, ready to spring as soon as it found quarry. It curled its black lips back from its teeth to reveal sharp rows of deadly fangs. Even from where I was I could see drool dripping down its chin in anticipation of the hunt. My mind quickly flashed back to the quig that Uncle Press nailed with the spear and of how the other ravenous quigs devoured one of their own, ripping its flesh from the bone while it was still alive.

I glanced up at Kagan, who stared intently at the quig with a smile on her face. Without taking her eyes off the animal, she took a huge bite out of her turkey leg. At once the idea of a bullfight left me. This wasn't like a bullfight at all. This was like one of those Roman Coliseum spectacles where they threw the Christians to the lions. The Bedoowan wanted to see blood. Their wish was about to come true.

The Milago prisoner had remained still ever since the quig had entered the arena. And why not? There was nothing for him to do. He was too frail to fight and had no place to run. Mallos made a gesture to one of the knights near the arena floor and the knight threw something to the Milago. It was one of those stick weapons like Loor used. But there was no way the Milago miner could use this puny weapon to defend himself. I think it was given to him in hopes of having the battle last more than a few seconds. That's the best the guy could hope for. He picked up the weapon, but just from the way he held it I knew that he had no clue how to use it. He might as well have had a pillow to fight off the quig.

The coiled quig sniffed the air. It had caught scent of the Milago. Its body tensed, zeroing in on its prey.

I looked up to Kagan and saw that she had put her turkey leg down and was leaning over the rail in anticipation. Mallos stood behind her with his hands clasped behind his back. He turned and looked right at me. I looked away. I didn't want to see this guy anymore.

Then the quig attacked. It crouched back on its legs like a cat and sprang at the poor Milago miner. The Milago turned and ran. It was heartbreaking and horrifying. He ran to the side of the arena, but there was no safety there. So he started to run around the circle with the wooden weapon dragging behind him.

Loor couldn't take it. She made a move to jump out and rescue the doomed miner, but the instant she took a step, Alder stopped her. It was a good thing, too. She wouldn't have much more of a chance against this beast than the scraggly miner.

The Milago in the stands watched silently. I could see the agony on their faces. The Novans watched silently as well. I couldn't tell how they felt about what was going on. Then I looked to the Bedoowan. The horrible thing was, these people were laughing. The sight of a Milago miner running for his life was a big joke!

The quig kept its distance from the Milago miner, almost playing with him like a cat plays with a mouse before killing it. After a few moments, the Milago miner realized it was futile to run around the ring, so he stopped and turned back to face the beast. He raised the wooden stick, but there wasn't a person watching these events who thought it would help him beat back the vicious animal. Time seemed to stand still. The Milago stood with the stick weapon at the ready. The quig crouched a few feet away, swaying its massive head. Everyone in the stadium held their breath.

And then the quig jumped. The Milago miner held up his stick to defend himself. The last thing I saw was that the quig swept it out of the way with a mighty swing of his clawed paw. The stick flew across the arena and when it landed, I was horrified to see that the Milago miner's hand was still clutching it.

I looked up toward Kagan and the other Bedoowan. What I saw there was almost as horrible as the carnage that was taking place in the arena. Kagan sat forward on her chair and clapped her hands with glee like a little girl watching clown tricks. The other Bedoowan were laughing uproariously as if this were some kind of slapstick comedy. And through it all, I could hear the sounds of the quig tearing at the flesh of the Milago miner. The doomed man gave one quick yelp and then he was silent. Luckily he died quickly. All that was left was the feeding. It turned my stomach and made me hate the

Bedoowan even more for their total lack of compassion for another living being.

Mallos looked at me and smiled. This may have been the most horrible moment of all, because I felt in that second that he had staged this whole spectacle for my benefit. The idea that I may have been responsible for this, in any way, made my stomach hurt.

The show was over quickly. I knew it was done because the Bedoowan applauded as if the quig had just staged a fine performance. The Novans applauded politely as well, though with much less enthusiasm than the Bedoowan. The Milago just watched in horror. A few of them were crying.

Then a few more chimes sounded. Instantly six knights rushed into the ring with ropes. Three of them held spears on the quig, while the others lassoed its neck and began to drag it back toward the large door. Now that it had fed, it was much more calm than before. It actually went without a fight. I saw the blood dripping from its jaws as it was led back to the door leading to the quig pens. I looked back to the spot where it had attacked the Milago miner. All that was left of the poor man was a wet, red spot on the grass. A Bedoowan knight filled a wooden bucket with water from a faucet near the quig pen, then quickly rushed over to the spot of the kill and poured it on the blood. The water and blood sank into the grass as if they had never been there.

Then two more chimes sounded and a terrifying thought came to me. We were next. We had been shown what our fate would be and now it was our turn. I looked around, expecting the knights to prod us into the arena. But they didn't. I looked up to Mallos to see what he was doing. He looked back at me and pointed to the sky. I looked up and realized what would happen next.

In the sky the three suns were about to converge on each other. It was the equinox. Then I heard another door open inside the arena. It was the same door where the doomed Milago miner tumbled out before. But there were no more Milago to be executed today. What I saw at that door made my heart sink. A man stepped out into the sunlight standing up straight, with his head held high. I think I actually gasped when I saw him.

It was Uncle Press. It was the equinox, and he was the next to die.

DENDURON

Uncle Press walked defiantly to the center of the killing ring. It was only a few days since I had seen him last, but with all that had happened it felt like it had been months. It was strange to see him dressed in the leather skins of the Milago. I was used to seeing him wearing jeans and his long coat that would flap in the wind as he rode his motorcycle. But things had changed. Though he was still Uncle Press, he also looked like any other Milago miner with his three-day-old beard and messed-up hair. But unlike the other Milago, Uncle Press had an air of confidence. The Bedoowan stopped talking and laughing. There was now tension in their section of the stands, as if this newest gladiator was going to prove to be more of a match than the last.

I looked to the Milago spectators and saw that they were watching his arrival in pretty much the same way. But rather than the look of fear they had for the poor Milago prisoner who had just been devoured, they now seemed to have hope that maybe, just maybe, the visiting team might have a shot here. Only the Novans reacted the exact same way as before. They gave Uncle Press some polite, emotionless applause.

Even though Uncle Press looked all sorts of confident, it was going to take more than confidence to beat a charging, hungry quig. Still, something about the way Uncle Press carried himself gave you the feeling that if any man could beat a quig, it would be this one. He stood in the center of the field and looked up at all the spectators. He did a 360 turn, and stopped when he laid eyes on the Bedoowan section. I could see that he was shaking his head and knew what he was thinking. It disturbed him to think that these people were gathered to watch blood sport.

In the royal box Kagan didn't sense any of this tension. She was being her normal, oblivious self as she sat on her throne, gnawing her turkey leg. Mallos leaned down and whispered something in her ear. Kagan answered with a shrug that told me she didn't care one way or the other about what Mallos had asked her. Mallos bowed to Her Royal Chubness, then stepped to the front of the box and surveyed the people in the stadium. He raised his hands and all eyes immediately went to him. Even Uncle Press looked up to see what this evil puppet master had to say.

"People of Denduron," he bellowed. "The man you see before you has been accused of the high crime of treason. He is guilty of plotting to destroy the peaceful balance of our society and of inciting the Milago into overthrowing the great reign of our beloved Queen Kagan." When he said this, he looked to Kagan. Kagan acknowledged his look with a loud, deep belch. What a class act.

Mallos didn't react and continued, "For this crime he has been sentenced to death at the equinox, when the light is the strongest so we can all bear witness to his punishment. Let this execution serve as a reminder that the natural order must never be disrupted. To try and change the normal course of events is a crime against humanity, and punishment will be harsh and swift. Long live Denduron. Long live Queen Kagan. Death to those who oppose the throne."

Mallos then made a motion to the field and two knights ran across the grass to open the door to let in another quig. It was clear what this was all about. Mallos was using Uncle Press as an example to scare the Milago out of their rebellion. The Milago trusted Uncle Press. In seconds another quig would leap out of that dark door and attack. It would mean the end of the rebellion and the death of my uncle. And the way things were going, Alder, Loor, and I would be the next victims in the ring.

As scared as I was, I realized that there was an even bigger picture unfolding here. Uncle Press had brought us here to try and bring peace to the Bedoowan and the Milago. It was a tribal feud that Mallos (or Saint Dane) was doing a fine job of fueling. By eliminating Uncle Press, and us, there would be nothing to stop the Bedoowan from destroying the Milago. The territory of Denduron would fall into chaos, and Mallos's evil mission would be complete.

That is, unless I did something to stop it. I knew exactly what I had to do. I was scared out of my mind, but still, I knew what had to be done. Before I had the chance to chicken out, I jumped over the barrier that separated our box from the field and ran toward my uncle.

"Pendragon!" shouted Loor with surprise. I think she was totally shocked that I was the first one to take action for a change. I hadn't told her what my plan was. There wasn't time. But she must have figured I had something in mind, so she and Alder quickly followed after me. I know what you're thinking, Mark, and you're wrong. I hadn't gone delusional. I hadn't suddenly gotten all hero macho and figured I could whup up on a quig. It wasn't like that at all. But I had an idea and if I was right, it might give us all a chance of getting out of there alive.

I ran up to Uncle Press and stood beside him. I expected him to see me and be totally surprised and shout something like: "Bobby, no! Go back! Save yourself!" But he didn't. Instead he looked down at me as if he were expecting me to show up all along and calmly said, "I forgot to tell you, that Courtney Chetwynde is pretty cute."

I gotta hand it to the guy, he was cool. Maybe a little crazy, but cool.

Loor and Alder quickly joined us. Loor had scooped up the wooden weapon that the Milago prisoner had used and was ready to wield it. I was glad to see that she had separated it from the guy's severed hand first.

Then suddenly a cheer went up from the Bedoowan crowd. I knew what that meant. I looked to the animal entrance and saw a huge quig lumber out of the darkness. This one was even bigger than the first. The spines on its back grazed the top of the doorway as it came through. It seemed slower, too, but that may be just because it hadn't gotten its blood boiling.

Yet.

Loor jumped between us and the quig and shouted, "I will go for its eyes."

I guess she felt that fighting was the only chance we had. Big surprise. So she squared off against the beast, prepared for it to charge. She must have realized that fighting this thing would be suicide. But fighting was what she knew, so she was ready.

Uncle Press seemed oblivious to the impending danger. He turned to me and said, "I'll bet it's been an interesting few days."

Was he kidding? Here we were about to be attacked by a

vicious beast with three-inch fangs and an appetite for human flesh and he was making small talk! Maybe he didn't think we stood a chance against the monster and decided to spend his last few moments in peace.

I had one last trick left from the stuff you two sent me and it was time to use it. I have to admit, this was the one item I didn't think you could come up with. I knew there wouldn't be a problem getting the laser pointer or the Swiss Army knife or the wristwatch or any of the other stuff, but I knew this last item would be tricky to find. I was thrilled when I saw it in the pack. To be honest, I hoped I wouldn't have to use it, but here I was and it was in my pocket and it was the only chance we had. Thank you, guys.

The quig spotted us. Or maybe it had smelled us. It didn't matter which because either way, it was starting to circle for the attack. Its ghastly yellow eyes were trained on us, looking for the right moment to spring. We crowded together, trying to look bigger than we were. I glanced up at the stands and saw that every eye in the stadium was on us. They were ready for the show. Only this time they were expecting a killing frenzy because there were four tasty morsels being served to the quig, not just one.

Loor said, "When it attacks, get behind me."

"No," I said with as much authority as I could gather.

Loor gave me a quick glance of surprise, then focused back on the quig. "Do not be foolish, Pendragon," she said. "I am the one with a weapon."

Before I could tell anyone what I had planned, the quig reared up on its back legs, bellowed, then galloped toward us. Loor started to run to meet the beast, but I grabbed her belt with one hand and held her back.

"Pendragon!" she yelled at me.

I didn't let go. I held her tight and with my other hand I pulled out my last trick . . . the silent dog whistle. I put it to my lips, and blew for all I was worth. Instantly the quig skidded to a stop and cried out in pain, just as the quig had done on the mountain when Uncle Press and I were speeding away on the sled. But this modern dog whistle must have produced a sharper sound than the hollow wooden whistle I used on the mountain because the reaction from this quig was much more dramatic. This quig crashed to its knees and screamed so loud I thought its head was going to explode. But I wasn't about to cut it any slack. As soon as I emptied my lungs, I took another breath and blew harder than the first time.

The quig screamed in pain. I glanced around the stadium and saw every single person staring back in openmouthed shock. Every person except for Mallos, that is. Mallos simply cocked his head to one side as if this latest development were nothing more than a minor, interesting surprise.

"What is happening?" shouted Alder.

Loor stood stunned as well. Only Uncle Press wasn't surprised. Finally he kicked into gear.

"The quig pens, go!" he commanded. Then as an aside to me he said, "Cutting it a little close, aren't you?"

He knew I had the whistle all along! How could he have known that? Maybe he didn't know I had dropped the one he gave me in the mountains. Either way, he was calm because he knew I would use the whistle to stop the quigs. I gotta say it again, the guy is cool. And I'm glad he was back in action now because my plan didn't go beyond blowing the whistle to stop the quig. I had no clue of what to do next, but Uncle Press did. That was good. His plan had us escaping through the only avenue open to us . . . the holding pen where the quigs were kept. That was bad. But he was right, there was no other way, so we all ran for the door.

The crowd watched in stupefied awe. It was Kagan who made the first move. She jumped off her throne, ran forward still clutching her turkey leg and squealed out, "Stop them!"

One of the Milago spectators yelled out an impassioned, "Run!" The other Milago spectators took his lead and started to cheer for us too. It was like they had all suddenly snapped into delirious football fan mode as they cheered for us like we were running a hundred-yard kickoff return. It was the most life I had seen from these people since I got here. Maybe seeing us escape from that ring was the first time their side had a chance of winning. For those few moments it was like every one of those Milago were down on that field with us, running for freedom.

But what lay ahead was every bit as deadly and dangerous as what we were escaping from. As we ran I continued to blow the whistle and the quig kept writhing in agony. Suddenly I felt a hand on my shoulder and I was jerked to a stop. It was Uncle Press. It was a good thing he stopped me because if I had taken one more step I would have walked right into the path of a spear that was thrown from the top of the stadium by one of the knights. The spear screamed down and stuck into the ground like a javelin in the exact spot where I was headed. I had been so focused on the quig that I forgot there were Bedoowan guards swarming the place. I looked up and saw them all running down the stadium steps toward us. Worse, several had unleashed their spears and the dark, deadly shafts were raining down on us from above.

"Keep your head up, keep moving," commanded Uncle Press.

Uncle Press had the presence of mind to grab the spear that had barely missed me. Loor took one as well. I didn't grab one. That little metal whistle was every bit as powerful a weapon as those spears and I wasn't about to lose this one the way I lost the whistle on that sled. I'd leave the sharp stuff to those who knew how to use it.

With the Milago miners cheering deliriously and the spears stabbing the ground around us, we made it across the field and into the dark tunnel. Just before ducking in I glanced up at the royal box and at Mallos. I didn't like what I saw. I expected him to be leaning out of the box, shouting commands at the knights to stop us. After all, this was his big demonstration to the Milago and it was falling apart before his eyes. But that's not what I saw. Instead I saw Mallos standing next to the throne with his arms folded, looking calm. I could swear that he had a smug smile on his face. Maybe I was reading too much into it, but it was almost like he wasn't surprised by what was happening. No, it was like he was enjoying it! Could he have anticipated this? Were things playing out the way he wanted them to? I remembered his words to me back in the palace. Though he was sending us to certain death, he spoke as if this wouldn't be the last battle between us. Of course, the question was, if this wasn't the last battle, what was?

I couldn't think about it too long, for we were in the process of jumping into the fire outside of the frying pan and I needed to keep my head on straight. I was the last one into the tunnel and away from the falling spears. But before I got too far along I heard a command barked from behind, "Stop!"

I looked back and saw two Bedoowan knights standing in the large open doorway. They each had their spears drawn back, ready to throw, and I was way too close for them to miss. The others had already disappeared into the gloom of the quig pen ahead of me, so it was just me and the knights. It looked as if after all I'd been through, it was going to end with one of these knights skewering me with his harpoon.

As I stood there staring back at the knights who were about to kill me, I froze . . . and stopped blowing the dog whistle. It was still in my lips, but there wasn't any blowing going on. I was too scared. That's what happens when you are seconds away from death.

The knights cocked their arms ready to throw their spears. All I could do was hold my breath and brace against the impact. My only thought was: "Oh man, I hope this doesn't hurt too bad."

That's when my savior arrived. With a screeching howl the quig from the ring came back into play. It charged the knights from behind and slammed them both to the ground with a giant paw on each. When I stopped blowing the whistle, the quig had gotten its act back together . . . and now it wanted revenge. I actually felt bad for the two knights because they were seconds away from a bloody death. The quig let out an angry bellow that shook the ground. Though the two knights had been about to kill me, I couldn't stand seeing anyone die the way they were about to. So I took a breath to blow the whistle and stop the quig. Before I could blow, Uncle Press grabbed my hand.

"Save them and they'll kill you," he said soberly.

He was right. If the knights got away, they wouldn't be grateful, they'd try to kill me again. Then they'd go after the others. No, this was war, and the knights were going to be the next victims. I nodded to Uncle Press and he let me go. He walked further into the dark pen and I turned to follow. I don't think I will ever forget the sounds I heard behind me as I ran. I won't even describe them to you because it was too horrifying. I will say this: Their deaths weren't as quick as the Milago prisoner's. That's because the quig had to work its way through the knights' armor first.

For a moment I felt a surge of guilt. Not about the two knights who were being devoured, but for the poor Milago miner who had died in the ring earlier. I had been so stunned by the quickly unfolding events that I hadn't thought to use my whistle. Could I have saved him? I don't know for sure. I'll never know. My only solace came from the fact that if I had tipped my hand back then, we wouldn't have gotten together with Uncle Press, who was now helping us make our escape. Maybe all things happen for a reason.

But our escape was not yet complete. We now faced a different danger. We were in the bowels of the quig pen. I could only hope that there was another door somewhere that would lead us out. There had to be another way out. The trick was to stay alive long enough to find it. Sunlight snuck in through the cracks in the rock walls, sending bright slices of light throughout the place. Because these light beams were so bright, they created deep shadows everywhere. That's what I feared. The shadows. There could be quigs lurking there, ready to spring.

The quig pen was nothing more than a big cave that had been dug out of the rock. The cavernous space was broken up by low walls made of stone that acted as corrals for the quigs. I figured that out because a few of the pens had heavy metal chains attached to the walls that I was sure were used to restrain a quig. In each of the large pens there was some kind of haylike material spread out, I guessed to soak up whatever the beasts decided to deposit. It wasn't doing a very good job, though. The place smelled vile. Remember how I described the smell that came from the latrine hole in the Milago hut? Well, multiply that by about a thousand and you'll have the smell of the quig pen. It was a combination of quig waste, rotten meat, and death.

Uncle Press turned back to me and said, "Keep that whistle handy."

Yeah, right, like he needed to remind me of that. If I held that metal whistle any tighter it would have snapped in two. Uncle Press walked on cautiously, with his spear at the ready. I walked close behind him, though I didn't like being last. I kept glancing back over my shoulder to make sure nothing snuck up from behind. After walking for a few moments, I heard something that made me stop short. It was a growl and it was coming from the pen to my right. I snapped a look and saw a quig lying there on its side. It must have been the quig that just ate the Milago prisoner, because it was looking all sleepy and relaxed. This monster had no interest in us. It was grooming itself by licking its giant paw. The blood it licked off was the final clue that it was indeed the quig who had just feasted. Gross. I continued walking while keeping my eyes on the bloated quig . . . and tripped over something. When I looked to see what it was, I swear I almost barfed. It was a leg bone. A human leg bone. I knew it was human because the skeleton foot was still attached. I scanned more of the floor and saw that there were tons of bones scattered about. It became disgustingly clear that feeding time for the quigs meant the death of more Milago.

We continued to walk along and I saw that there were many quig corrals, but no more quigs. I guess they didn't keep many down here at one time. That was fine by me. Maybe the two quigs I saw today were the only quigs down here. But looking around this dark labyrinth I saw many tunnels that led off to places unknown. There could very well be a quig down any one of them who would catch a whiff of us and come running. I wasn't about to relax until we were out of there.

Then Uncle Press stopped and held out a hand to still me.

He had heard something. I listened and heard it too. Something was coming toward us. Fast. I put the whistle to my lips, ready to blow my lungs out, but Uncle Press stopped me. He wanted to make sure what it was first. Good thing too, because as it turned out it wasn't a quig. It was Alder. If I had blown the whistle, I might have woken up a napping quig.

Alder ran up to us out of breath and said, "Loor has found the way out. This way!" He then turned and ran back the way he came.

Excellent. We were one step closer to getting out of there. Uncle Press nodded to me and took off running after Alder. I followed close behind. We ran through the dark tunnels as quietly as possible so as not to sound the dinner bell. After a few turns I began to see light up ahead. We were headed toward a section of the quig pen that was brighter than where we'd been. We made one last turn around a rock outcropping and I saw why.

There was a large, round hole in the rock ceiling. I saw blue sky above. I even heard the sound of crashing waves. We were right on the edge of the bluffs. The hole was big, maybe about the size of your above-ground pool, Mark. It was just about the right size for a quig to fit through. I now saw how the Bedoowan managed the quig pen. All they had to do was shove a quig into the hole from above and it would fall into this cavern and be trapped. The only way out was through the door to the stadium. I guess once a quig was down here, it never left because the hole was too high for an animal to crawl back out. Of course, that also meant it was too high for *us* to climb out of too. Our freedom was a mere thirty feet away, but it was thirty feet straight up and out of our reach. I had no clue how we could possibly make it.

But Loor did. When Alder and Uncle Press and I arrived at the hole, she was busily tying a long vine to the end of her stolen Bedoowan spear.

"There is a rope up there," she explained quickly. "I will get it down for us to climb out."

I looked up and saw that sure enough there was a thick rope that looped down below the hole. My guess is that this was an emergency escape route for any unlucky Bedoowan who happened to stumble down here. One of his buddies could drop the rope from above for him to climb out.

"Make it fast," said Uncle Press. "We gotta get out before the knights catch up."

He was right. Even if we got out of here, that didn't mean the Bedoowan knights wouldn't be waiting for us on top. They may have been barbaric, but they weren't idiots. If this were the only way out, they would be headed for this hole for sure. The faster we got out, the better chance we had of getting away. Suddenly I was less concerned about the quigs than about what we might find above.

Loor expertly tied the long vine to the spear and stood up. She tested its weight since it was now imbalanced because of the vine. Then she looked up at her target. To be honest, I had no doubt that she would nail this on the first shot. That's how good she was. With a grunt of air, she javelin tossed the spear up at the dangling rope. It flew toward the ceiling with the long vine trailing behind like a contrail. The spear made a perfect arc through the loop of the hanging rope and careened back toward the ground. Loor had just threaded a needle thirty feet in the air. The trailing vine draped over the loop of rope with both ends now touching the ground. Alder quickly grabbed the vine and gave it a yank, pulling down the rope. Our escape route was set. Loor had done it. I told you, she was good.

Now as I looked up at that rope, all that came to mind was the dreaded rope climb in gym class. I hated that. Some guys could climb that rope like monkeys. I wasn't one of them. Sure I could get up, but it wasn't quick. And right now, speed was a good thing. But what choice did I have? None. All I could do was hope that adrenaline would help me climb this thing.

Loor started up first. I wasn't surprised to see that she climbed it like one of the aforementioned monkey boys. I don't think she even used her legs. She muscled up the rope as if gravity weren't an issue. She got to the top in seconds and climbed up through the hole. She scanned the outside and leaned back down to say, "We are alone. Hurry."

That was good. The knights hadn't figured out what we were doing yet. Maybe they *were* idiots after all. Loor then threw something down to us. I had to duck out of the way or it would have hit me. When I looked back, I smiled with relief. It was a rope ladder. I guess not all the Bedoowan were as strong as Loor. Some of the weenies had to take the easy way up, like me. I had no problem with that.

Uncle Press grabbed the bottom of the ladder and held it taut.

"Alder, go," he commanded.

Without hesitation our Bedoowan friend began his climb. He was kind of a big, clumsy guy so he wasn't as quick on the rope as Loor. Still, he was on his way up and that was good. As he climbed, Uncle Press looked to me and for the first time he smiled.

"That was a brave thing you did, Bobby," he said. "Jumping in the ring like that."

I was feeling pretty good about myself. Granted, I was pretty sure the whistle would work, but still it was a scary thing to do. Maybe I even impressed Loor. But even though I was feeling all proud, I had to act the way all good heroes act at a time like this.

"No big deal," I said with as much humility as I could muster. "You would have done the same thing."

I looked up and saw that Alder was struggling, but he was almost at the top. I took the few seconds left before it was my turn to ask something that was bugging me.

"You weren't surprised to see me," I said to Uncle Press. "How come?"

"I know you, Bobby," was his answer. "Maybe better than you know yourself. I knew you'd come after me. And since you had the whistle, I knew you'd use it."

I don't think Uncle Press realized how close I was to *not* coming. I thought back to where my head was when I first arrived on Denduron and I was ashamed to remember how rescuing Uncle Press was pretty low on my list of concerns. But you know, the bottom line is that I made the right decision. So maybe it's okay to think like a weenie sometimes, so long as you don't act like one. There's a grand philosophy in there someplace. I'll leave it up to you guys to figure out what it is.

"You were right," I said. "Except for one thing."

"What's that?" Uncle Press asked.

"This isn't the whistle you gave me. I lost that when we hit that boulder."

Uncle Press gave me a quizzical look. It was the first time I saw doubt in his face since we started this adventure.

"I don't get it," he said. "Did you make another one?"

I held up the silver whistle and said, "No, this is from home."

Uncle Press quickly let go of the rope ladder, then swiped the whistle out of my hand.

"How did you get this?" he demanded. "Did you bring it with you?"

Uh-oh. Something told me I had done a bad thing.

"N-No," I said nervously. "I wrote to my friends and told them I needed one. Then I took the flume back to the subway and—"

Uncle Press did something stunning. He took the whistle, whirled, and threw it up and out of the hole in the ceiling!

"Throw it in the ocean!" he shouted to Loor above. "Now!"

Loor obeyed without question. She picked up the whistle and threw it. Uncle Press then spun back to me and stared me down with a look of intensity that made my knees buckle.

"I told you," he seethed. "We can only use what the territory has to offer! That's why I didn't bring the gun with me."

My mind was spinning. That's exactly what he had warned me about, but frankly, I forgot.

"Did you get anything else from home?" he asked.

Uh-oh again. Not only had I gotten some other things, I left them scattered all over the Bedoowan palace. I wasn't sure why this was such a bad thing, but from the look on Uncle Press's face, I had made a grave mistake. Before I fessed up we heard a noise. It came from deep down in one of the tunnels that stretched out behind us. Uncle Press and I both whirled toward the sound. We listened a moment . . . then heard it again. Yup, it was a growl. Turned out there were more than two quigs in the cavern after all and from the sound of things, our new company had just woken up.

"Climb," commanded Uncle Press.

He didn't have to tell me twice. I grabbed the rope ladder and started up. I tried to go fast, but climbing a rope ladder is not like climbing a regular ladder. A regular ladder is solid. A rope ladder is soft and swings. As soon as you put your foot on one rung, it bends down under your weight. If you're not completely balanced the ladder will twist. And if you aren't careful where you put your foot, it can easily slip off and that would be disaster. So I tried to climb fast, but the faster I climbed, the tougher it got.

Alder called down from above, "Hurry, Pendragon."

Yeah, thanks for the tip. My foot nearly slipped off a rung and I had to hang on for my life. The movement caused the ladder to swing and I had all that I could do to get my balance back. Uncle Press wasn't holding the ladder at the bottom either, which made it more tricky. I looked down and saw that he was staring off into the depths of the cavern. He must have sensed that I was watching him because without looking up he shouted, "Climb!"

Another bellow came from deep within the cavern. Only this was louder and closer. The quig had definitely picked up the scent and was on its way.

"Come on!" I shouted down to Uncle Press.

"No!" yelled Loor. "It is not strong enough for two."

"There it is!" said Alder, pointing into the cavern.

As I kept climbing I glanced back. A quig appeared from out of the shadows, stalking closer. It was hunched down like a hunting cat, with its belly grazing the ground. Any moment now it would pounce. All Uncle Press had to defend himself was the Bedoowan spear. Why had he thrown away the whistle? If I still had it, he would be safe. Now he was back in the same position he was in at the stadium, only this time I couldn't help him. I was near the top and stole a quick look down to see that Uncle Press was sliding a heavy, flat rock toward the bottom of the ladder. What was he doing? I climbed up two more rungs and was high enough now to reach up for Alder and Loor. They each grabbed one of my hands and hoisted me up.

"I'm up!" I shouted down to Uncle Press. I quickly scrambled around and the three of us looked back down into the cavern. The quig was only a few yards from Uncle Press and stalking closer. Its horrible yellow eyes were focused on him. If Uncle Press started to climb, the quig would pounce and easily pick him off. His only choice was to fight, and fighting a quig could only end in death. Not for the quig, but for Uncle Press. History was repeating itself. Someone I cared for was about to die so that I would live.

The quig stopped advancing as if it sensed that Uncle Press was more dangerous than the average Milago miner. It crouched, facing Uncle Press, who stood holding his spear at the ready.

I was surprised to see that the first one to make a move was Uncle Press. But he did a curious thing. He relaxed. He lowered the spear and held it down at his side. Why was he doing that? It was like he was giving himself up. He stepped over the heavy rock that he had pushed under the ladder and held his hands out in surrender. To the quig it must have looked as if Uncle Press were opening himself up to be eaten without a fight. The quig didn't move. It must have been just as confused as I was. But its hesitation didn't last long. It was suppertime. The quig coiled, wagged its butt, and with a snarl it launched itself at Uncle Press.

Uncle Press barely moved. As soon as the quig had committed itself, he jammed the tail of the spear against the rock that was now behind him. At the same time he dropped to one knee and angled the spear up toward the flying quig. The quig realized too late that Uncle Press had set a trap and that it was now sailing toward a six-foot spike! Yes!

The quig landed on the spear. It impaled him through the

chest and came out his back. The weapon didn't move because it was anchored by the heavy rock. Uncle Press let go of it and did a dive roll to the side just before the wounded quig fell to the ground. But the battle wasn't over. The quig was injured, but the spear didn't seem to have pierced anything major. The angry animal squirmed and screamed and writhed on the ground like a fish out of water, but it was still very much alive . . . and dangerous. Uncle Press had to get out of there fast.

He leaped for the rope ladder. The quig saw this and swiped at him, but his claws bit into the air below his feet. Uncle Press was much better at climbing than I was. He flew up the ladder as if it were rock steady. Yet the quig wasn't done. Judging from its pained bellows it was in horrible agony, but it still wanted a piece of Uncle Press. It squirmed over to the rope ladder and with a sweep of its mighty paw, grabbed on to it and began to pull. The quig must have been eight hundred pounds. There was no way this flimsy rope ladder could withstand that kind of pressure. I looked next to me to see that the top of the rope ladder was tied to a tree. The point where it was tied was dangerously frayed as if it had been rotting in the rain.

"Look!" I shouted.

Loor and Alder looked to see how the rope ladder was going to break right on top. Loor didn't stop to think. She jumped over me and grabbed on to the rope. This was crazy. The rope ladder was going to break and if Loor were hanging on when it went, she'd go down with it. Alder realized this and ran to Loor. He sat behind her, grabbed her waist and dug his heels in. Maybe the strength of two would be enough. Or maybe the strength of three. I had to help. It was crazy, but it was the only thing to do. I dove behind Alder and grabbed him around the waist. That's when I heard the *snap!* The rope ladder broke from the tree. Loor held on tight and became the only link that kept it from falling into the pit. I could see the muscles in her arms bulge as she fought desperately to hang on. Alder held on to her and I held on to Alder but we all started to slide toward the edge of the hole. We dug our heels in, desperately trying to stop. I felt the tension in both of their bodies as we strained against the weight of the ladder, of Uncle Press, and of the quig that was pulling from below.

It felt like we were hanging on for hours, but it was probably only a few seconds. Where was Uncle Press? Did the quig get him? Were we hanging on just so that the quig could pull its bad self out from the hole and eat us? It didn't really matter, because we weren't going to be able to hang on much longer.

Then, finally, just as we were about to go over the edge, I looked up and saw the welcome sight of Uncle Press's head poke up from below. He crawled to the surface, rolled away from the rope and shouted to Loor, "Let it go!"

She did. The rope whiplashed away and we all fell back. A second later I heard the heavy sound of the quig hitting the ground below. It let out a yelp of pain. Good. Served it right.

As we all lay there, trying to catch our breath, I looked down the bluff toward the stadium. It was about three hundred yards behind us. We had traveled quite a way in the quig pen. It was hard to believe that a huge stadium was dug below the surface, and even more amazing was how, beneath the stadium, was an elaborate, multileveled palace.

A moment later I realized that we weren't safe yet. The Bedoowan knights had finally figured out what we were doing. Several of them were now climbing up out of the stadium to come after us.

"We gotta move," I announced while pointing back to the palace.

Without another word we all jumped up and ran for the woods. Our best hope was to lose them in the dense forest that surrounded the Milago village. Compared to what we had just come through, this was going to be a piece of cake.

Loor led the way again. She took us on another romp through the forest, but this time I knew what to expect. I was in for another grueling cross-country trek, but I didn't care. The further we got away from the palace, the more I realized that we had done exactly what we had set out to do. Uncle Press was running next to me because we had saved him. We went in, we found him, and we got him out. How cool was that? Better still, my adventure was almost over. As soon as we got him back to the Milago village, he could take charge of their rebellion and I could go home. So even though we were running like scared deer through the forest, I began to relax because my job was nearly complete. I already started plotting how I would go back down into the mines, make my way to the flume, and launch myself home, for good.

Loor ran us a long way around. We were on the far side of the farmland, maybe a half mile from the Milago village.

"Can we rest awhile?" asked Alder.

I was happy that it wasn't me who burned out first, for a change. So we stopped and the four of us stood together to catch our breath. After a few seconds I looked to Loor and smiled, but she didn't smile back. Neither did Alder. I looked to Uncle Press and he scowled back at me. What was going on? Was it because I had used the dog whistle from home? Okay, maybe it was against the rules, but if I hadn't done it, we'd all be on the inside of some quig by now. I think I deserved a little more credit than I was getting. Before I had the chance to say something about it, we heard a sound. It was a loud, sharp *pop,* like a firecracker. No, it was louder than that. It was more like a cherry bomb. Both Loor and Alder tensed. Uncle Press shot a glance in the direction of the sound too. From the look on his face I could tell that something was wrong. It didn't seem out of the ordinary to me, though. I hear sounds like that at home all the time. It could be a car backfiring, or fireworks, or even somebody's TV. But we weren't at home. Whatever made that sound was something out of the ordinary for Denduron.

There were two more pops. *Crack. Crack.* Uncle Press jogged toward the sound. The rest of us followed.

We traveled a short distance through the woods until we came upon the edge of a clearing. This was an area I hadn't seen before. It was past the Milago farmland and not exactly on the beaten track. Uncle Press hid behind a tree to watch what was going on. We all followed his lead. What we saw seemed to be some kind of target practice. On one side of the clearing was a line of scarecrow-type figures that were crudely made out of straw. Opposite them was a group of Milago miners, each holding one of the slingshots I had found down in the mines. The miners were practicing throwing stones at the scarecrows. They each had a pile of rocks at their feet that were about the size of walnuts. They would put one of the stones in the slingshot, spin it overhead, and release it. They were pretty accurate, too. But still, a small stone being flung from a slingshot wasn't going to do much to stop a knight in full armor.

I then found out how very wrong I was.

Someone stepped forward holding a small basket. It was Figgis, the crafty little salesman. He walked up to each of the throwers and held the basket out to them. The throwers reached inside and took out another kind of rock. These new stones looked very different. They were about the same size as the stones they had been flinging, but they looked soft and rusty red colored. It seemed to me these new rocks would do even less damage than the rocks they had been flinging, yet the shooters held them gingerly as if they were precious. The first shooter loaded a new stone, spun the slingshot over his head and let it fly. The rust-colored stone shot across the clearing toward its target. When it hit the scarecrow, the scarecrow exploded in a ball of fire!

Whoa! The Milago had some kind of explosive that detonated on impact! Those were the loud pops we were hearing. I looked to Loor and Alder. They were just as shocked as I was. Uncle Press watched intently. Nothing surprised him.

The next miner flung his stone at a scarecrow and it too erupted in a ball of fire. Figgis jumped up like a child and clapped with delight.

"Where did they find such a thing?" asked Loor.

"They didn't find it," answered Uncle Press. "He did," he said, pointing to Figgis.

The odd little man held the basket of explosives over his head and danced a jig. He was having a great time.

"I knew that little guy was up to something," said Uncle Press. "But I didn't know what . . . until now. He must be selling the stuff to the Milago."

One word sprang to mind. Tak. That's what Figgis was trying to sell me. It was a weapon. An explosive. He said that "tak was the way" and maybe he was right. If there was enough of that stuff around, the Milago could use it against the Bedoowan and the odds of beating them would suddenly be very good. Maybe there was hope for them after all. Tak may indeed have been the way.

But Uncle Press looked worried. He didn't like what he saw.

"What's the matter?" I asked him.

"If the Milago use that, it will be the end of Denduron," he answered soberly.

We all looked to him in surprise.

"End of Denduron?" I said. "Am I missing something here? That stuff could help the Milago beat the Bedoowan. Isn't that the point?"

Before Uncle Press could respond, all hell broke loose. We were attacked. But it wasn't the Bedoowan knights who caught up to us, it was a group of Milago miners. They jumped us from behind and wrestled us to the ground. One put a knee to my back and jammed my face into the dirt.

"Hold them," someone commanded.

I struggled to look up and see who was giving the orders and saw Rellin stride up past the miners. What was happening? These were the good guys, right? Why were they attacking us? Did they think we were Bedoowan? Rellin surveyed the scene to make sure that none of us could escape, then his eyes fell on Uncle Press.

"Hello, Press," he said. "I wish I could say that I was happy to see you."

Two miners pulled Uncle Press to his feet and held him opposite Rellin.

"You can't do this, Rellin," said Uncle Press.

"I am glad that you are alive," said Rellin. "But do not try and stop us."

"Listen to me," said Uncle Press with passion. "I want you to defeat the Bedoowan. You know that. But using that weapon is wrong. It will change everything."

"Wrong?" spat Rellin. "How could it be wrong to end our misery? Without tak we have no hope of defeating the Bedoowan. But with it, we can return centuries of pain and torture to them in a few short seconds."

"But at what cost?" asked Uncle Press.

Rellin smiled at him and then said, "Let me show you something." He walked toward the clearing and motioned to the miners to follow with us. The miners pulled us to our feet and we were dragged along after him. There was no use in fighting; there were too many of them. I wasn't really sure we should be fighting them anyway. Up until a few minutes ago they were on our side. Now, well, now I didn't know what was happening. Same old, same old.

Rellin entered the clearing and the Milago miners instantly stood at attention. That was a surprise. Maybe these guys were more organized than I knew. Could all of the cowering and silence have been an act to make the Bedoowan think they were pushovers? Rellin walked over to something that looked like a big box that was covered with a large, brown blanket. He stopped there and turned to us.

"Soon we will begin the battle of our lives," he said proudly. "But it will not last long thanks to you, Pendragon."

Me? What did I have to do with any of this? Uncle Press shot me a look. So did Loor and Alder. All I could do was shrug. I had no idea what he was talking about.

Rellin continued, "Tak is powerful, but it is delicate." Figgis appeared next to him and held up his basket. Rellin reached in and took out a piece of tak that was no bigger than a pea. "All it takes to release the power is a small impact."

Rellin threw the pea down on the ground and it exploded with a huge bang that echoed through the forest. There was a blast of flame and smoke that left a deep, jagged hole in the ground the size of a water barrel. Man, that stuff really *was* powerful. Figgis giggled. I wondered how much he charged for each piece of tak.

"It is dangerous to use any more than a small amount,"

said Rellin. "But we had to find a way to use more. We had to find a way to release the power of enough tak to deliver a single, crushing blow to the Bedoowan. We have not been able to find that way, until now."

He reached under the brown blanket and pulled something out that made my heart sink. It was a heavy-duty twelve-volt battery, the kind you use in big flashlights. At first it didn't make sense to me. Where did he get that? Then it hit me. I guess you guys sent me a flashlight after all. The reason I didn't find it was because Figgis must have stolen it from my pack when he took my Swiss Army knife.

Rellin held the battery up and said, "Such an interesting device you brought to us, Pendragon. I do not know why, but it too gives off power. And it is a power that can be controlled."

He then reached under the brown blanket and pulled out the flashlight. He looked at it admiringly and played with the on-off switch. I looked to Uncle Press. I wanted to apologize, but it was too late for that. Uncle Press didn't look at me. His jaw was set and he stared at Rellin.

Rellin then continued, "We can now use the power of this strange device to release the awesome power of tak." He said this while switching the flashlight on and off. "One little push will unleash as much tak as we desire. The Bedoowan will fall, and they will suffer greatly for how they have treated us."

I now realized where this was going. They were going to make a bomb. They weren't satisfied with throwing little bits of explosives in slingshots. No, they wanted a big bang, and I had delivered the means for them to do it. They were going to use the electricity in the battery to set off a huge bomb. Nice going, Bobby.

With a flourish Rellin pulled away the brown blanket that

was covering the big box. What lay beneath wasn't a box at all. It was one of the ore cars from the mines. To my horror, I saw that it was filled with tak. There must have been a few hundred pounds of it. Judging from the big explosion that came from a very small bit of tak, if this load blew up it would be like a nuclear bomb going off.

"This is a mistake, Rellin," Uncle Press pleaded. "You think this will save the Milago? You're wrong. If you use this weapon, you may find yourselves free of the Bedoowan, and slaves to a new power. The power of tak."

I immediately realized what Uncle Press was worried about. The Milago were on the verge of creating a weapon of horrible power. If they used it, it would alter the course of Denduron forever. Not only would there be devastating destruction, but once these simple people used the power of this explosive, where would it end? Already they weren't satisfied with using small bits of tak. They wanted more power. It was like the Milago skipped over gunpowder and jumped right into the nuclear age . . . and Armageddon.

The crazy thing was, this all came about because of two people who never could have foreseen the outcome of their actions. There was me, who stupidly brought the last piece of the bomb puzzle from home. And there was Figgis, this strange little man who lived by scrounging things and selling them to whomever had the coin to pay. Figgis had struck the big time now. He wasn't selling sweaters and knives anymore. No, Figgis was now a merchant of death, and the people he was selling to were eager to buy.

It was clear to me now. The turning point for Denduron wasn't the battle between the Milago and the Bedoowan. It was the introduction of this strange and horrible new power into the territory. As I looked at that deadly load of explosive in the ore car, there was something else that became clear. I wasn't going home. Even if I could get to a flume, there was no way I could go back now. No way. Not after the damage I had caused. I had no idea what to do, or how to stop this horror from happening, but I resolved then and there to stay and see this through to the end . . . even if the end meant my own death.

This may be the last journal I write to you, Mark and Courtney. If it is, then please know that it wasn't your fault about the flashlight. All you did was help out a friend. The blame is all mine. If you don't hear from me again, then please know I did everything I could to undo the mess I created. I may not be successful, but at least I tried. Thank you for reading this, and for being my friends.

Hopefully this isn't a final good-bye.

END OF JOURNAL #3

◉ SECOND EARTH ◉

Mark threw the parchment pages down onto his bedroom floor angrily.

"We should have known!" he shouted. "It was as much our fault as it was Bobby's!"

Courtney and Mark had waited until they got back home to Stony Brook before reading Bobby's latest journal. After saying good-bye to Bobby in the abandoned subway station, their journey back home was uneventful. They traveled the same route as the one that brought them to the flume in the Bronx, taking the subway to 125th Street and catching the first commuter train back to Connecticut. Once back in their hometown, they went straight to Mark's house and locked themselves in his bedroom where they could read Bobby's journal in private.

"It's not our fault!" argued Courtney. "The Milago are like a step above primitive. How could we know they'd figure out how to make a bomb with that stuff?"

"Because we read the journal," countered Mark. "We knew the same things Bobby did. Press told him never to bring anything from one territory to the next. We read that, but we did it anyway!"

Mark paced the floor out of sheer nervous energy.

"We helped Bobby," argued Courtney. "And maybe we helped the Milago, too. To be honest, I hope they do make a bomb that'll blow those Bedoowan creeps away. They deserve it!"

"You don't get it," argued Mark. "The Milago aren't ready for this kind of power. They don't know how to control it."

Now Courtney was getting angry. She jumped up and said, "What are you saying? Only socially evolved, brilliant people are allowed to blow themselves up?"

"No," Mark shot back. "It takes socially evolved brilliant people to figure out how *not* to blow themselves up. Look at it this way. The Milago are pissed off and they should be. The Bedoowan have been torturing them for centuries. Now suddenly they're given a weapon that's so powerful they can wipe out their enemies with the push of a button. They don't really understand it. They really don't know how to control it, but they're angry enough to use it anyway. If that tak stuff is as powerful as Bobby wrote, then they could end up killing themselves as well."

This made Courtney stop. "Is it really possible to use a battery to set that stuff off?" she asked thoughtfully.

"I don't know," answered Mark. "I suppose so. If tak is that volatile then a small electric charge could set off a chain reaction and . . . boom."

The two fell silent for a moment, imagining the consequences.

"I guess the trick is to be somewhere else when the button gets pushed," said Courtney. "I don't think they're smart enough to figure out how to make a timer."

"It wouldn't matter," said Mark soberly. "Tak isn't like anything I've ever heard of. If a little bit can make an explosion that big, then the amount Bobby described in that ore car would not only destroy the Bedoowan palace, it would level the Milago village too. And if the explosion makes fire the way it did with those scarecrow targets, then it could create a firestorm. Every living thing for miles around would be torched . . . the Bedoowan, the Milago, the farm, the forest . . ."

"And Bobby, Alder, Loor, and Press, too," said Courtney slowly. "I guess this Figgis guy really is a merchant of death."

Mark picked up the latest journal and scanned it, looking for something. It didn't take him long to find it.

"Listen to this," he said. "This is what Loor said to Bobby." Mark read from the journal. *"My mother explained that there are many territories, and they are all about to reach an important time. A 'turning point' she called it. It is a time when the outcome will either send the territory toward peace and prosperity, or plunge its people into chaos and destruction."*

Courtney said, "Yeah, and if the Milago beat the Bedoowan then everything will be okay."

"I don't think that's it," said Mark. "I think it's all about tak. Think about it. The Milago have been slaves of the Bedoowan for centuries. If they fight them and lose, then it will be business as usual. But if the Milago tip the balance by using something as horrible as that explosive, then who knows what it could lead to?"

"Then we've got to try and undo it!" countered Courtney.

"How?" was Mark's obvious question. "It's not like we can go through the flumes. It doesn't work for us, remember?"

Courtney paced, her mind kicking into overdrive.

"Then maybe we can send something to Bobby," she said. "Like a . . . like a . . ."

"Like a what?" shouted Mark. "We can't send anything to him. It would only make things worse! The only thing we can do is—"

Ding dong. Mark was interrupted by the doorbell. The two instantly fell silent.

"You expecting somebody?" asked Courtney.

"We skipped school today," Mark said nervously. "Maybe they're coming to check up on me."

The doorbell rang again.

"L-Let's hide," said Mark.

Courtney gave him a sarcastic look and said, "Hide? Gimme a break, I think we have bigger things to worry about than getting caught for skipping school. Answer the dumb door."

Courtney was right, thought Mark. Who cared if they got busted for skipping school? Whoever was at the door he'd deal with them and get back to the bigger problem at hand. When he got downstairs, he hesitated a second and tried to look sick in case it really was somebody from school coming to check up on him. He gave a little sick cough and then called out with a weak voice, "I'm coming."

He got to the door, unlocked it, swung it open, and then shouted out, "Bobby!"

Indeed, Bobby Pendragon was standing at the front door wearing the same clothes he had worn the night he disappeared. The Milago leather clothes were history.

"Hey, Mark," he said casually. "Can I come in?"

Courtney came running down the stairs on a tear. "Bobby?" she shouted.

Bobby stepped into Mark's house and gave Courtney a little smile.

"Miss me?" he said.

Courtney grabbed him in a hug and Mark hugged the two of them together. Bobby was home. He was safe. Everything was going to be okay. When they finally pulled away from the group hug, Mark and Courtney looked at Bobby in disbelief. This was too good to be true. A few seconds ago they were worried about never seeing him again. Now here he was standing right in front of them. But Bobby looked different. Both Courtney and Mark noticed it. It was still Bobby, no doubt about that. But he looked tired, like he had gone through an ordeal that took a lot out of him.

"Are you okay, man?" asked Mark. "You look kind of . . . sick."

"I'm not sick; I'm totally beat," was Bobby's answer. "I gotta lie down."

Mark and Courtney quickly led Bobby up the stairs to Mark's bedroom. They watched him as he walked and saw that he was a little unsure on his feet. They also noticed streaks of blood on his cheeks that came from many tiny cuts all over his face. Obviously a lot had happened since they saw him leave through the flume on his way back to Denduron. To Mark and Courtney only a few hours had passed. But as they had already figured out, time here on Second Earth and time in the other territories weren't relative. Bobby could have been gone for much longer than a few days for all they knew. Bobby looked as if he'd been through a war, but neither Mark nor Courtney wanted to ask him about it. They both figured that he'd tell them when he was ready. So without another word, they followed Bobby into Mark's room and watched as he lay down on the bed.

"I gotta get home," said Bobby weakly. "But I want to rest up first. Is it okay?"

"Absolutely," answered Mark. "Whatever you want."

"Thanks, man," said Bobby and put his head down on the pillow. Mark cringed, wondering how he was going to explain the streaks of blood on the white pillowcase to his mother. But then he felt bad for even thinking so selfishly and put the thought out of his head.

"Will you guys come with me?" asked Bobby without opening his eyes.

"Sure, Bobby," answered Courtney. "Uh . . . where?"

Bobby spoke weakly, as if he were nearly asleep. "To my house. Everybody must be going nuts looking for me. I'm gonna need you guys to help explain things."

Mark and Courtney exchanged looks. Both knew what the other was thinking. Bobby's house wasn't there anymore. His family had disappeared and along with them so had any history of the Pendragon family ever having existed. His parents, his sister, even his dog were just . . . gone. The police had launched an investigation to try and figure out what had happened to them, but so far they had come up empty.

"Whatever it takes," said Courtney. "We'll be there for you."

Bobby smiled.

Mark, on the other hand, was dying with curiosity. He didn't want Bobby to nod off before finding out what happened on Denduron.

"So tell us what happened!"

Courtney gave Mark a punch in the arm.

"Ow!" yelped Mark and grabbed his stinging arm.

"Go to sleep, Bobby," said Courtney. "Tell us later."

Bobby didn't open his eyes, but he chuckled at his friend's curiosity. "Oh yeah, I almost forgot," he said while reaching up to his shirt. He unbuttoned a few buttons, reached his hand in and pulled out a roll of parchment paper.

"It's all there," he said fading fast. "Everything that happened since I wrote last. Wake me up when you're finished."

That was the last thing he said. Bobby was in dreamland, the roll of parchment paper still in his hand. Mark glanced to Courtney, hesitated a moment, then took the precious journal. Courtney took the folded-up comforter from the bottom of Mark's bed and laid it gently over Bobby, right up to his chin. This was probably the first time he had slept in a bed in a long time and she wanted to make sure he was as safe and comfortable as possible. Then the two of them walked quietly to the far side of the room.

"Should we go downstairs and leave him alone?" whispered Mark.

"No," was Courtney's reply. "Nothing we could do would wake him up now."

Mark nodded. He didn't want to leave either. He slipped the familiar leather twine off the rolled-up scroll and opened it enough to read the very first line.

"Journal Number Four?" asked Courtney.

"Journal Number Four," answered Mark.

The two sat down next to each other on the floor and began to read the final chapter in Bobby's adventure.

DENDURON

I can't believe I'm still alive. At least I think I'm still alive. Every muscle, every bone, every hair follicle I've got is sore as hell, which pretty much tells me I'm still among the living. As I write this final journal to you guys, I've still got one major task ahead of me before I can come home. But right now I don't even feel like moving. Even the effort of pushing this pen across the paper is painful. I'm going to try and rest up, write this journal, and then get myself psyched for the final push.

As hurting as my body is, it's just as painful to remember the events of the past few days. But I've got to do it and write it all down because once it's on the page, I'm going to do my level best to forget it all.

I should warn you that some of the things I'm going to write about I didn't see for myself. It has been an incredible few days and there was no way I could be everywhere at once to see it all. But I'll do my best to re-create those events in my journal as accurately as possible based on what others have told me. I don't have a problem doing this because I'm sure everything they described is true. So sit down, take a breath, and hold on. It's going to be a wild ride.

I finished my last journal right after we rescued Uncle Press, then got recaptured by the people whom we thought were our friends—the Milago. Their leader, Rellin, showed us the huge bomb of tak they planned on using to vaporize the Bedoowan. There is something you should understand here. The Milago are not our enemies, but they were afraid we would try to stop them from using that nasty weapon. And they were right. If they exploded that bad boy, the destruction would be horrible. If we could stop them, we would. So we were in the weird position of being friendly enemies.

They brought us back to the hospital hut I'd been to a few times and locked us up with guards at the door. They said that as soon as the battle was over, they'd let us go. Great. If they detonated that bomb, there wouldn't be any place *left* for us to go. So the four of us—me, Uncle Press, Loor, and Alder—were prisoners again.

As soon as we entered the hut, Uncle Press looked around quickly. "Osa isn't here," he said. "She must be in hiding."

Uh-oh. We hadn't gotten the chance to tell Uncle Press what had happened to her. I also realized that Osa's body wasn't there any longer.

"What happened?" he asked quickly.

Loor pointed to me and said, "She was killed while protecting him from the Bedoowan knights."

Perfect. As if I didn't have enough guilt going on at the moment, she had to remind me about my part in Osa's death. I guess I couldn't be angry with her. Osa was her mother. She deserved to be angry. But I wished she didn't have to lay all of the blame on me. Mallos and the Bedoowan knights had a little something to do with it too.

We all looked to Uncle Press for his reaction. It was a

strange one. Rather than show any sign of grief, he simply nodded as if the news of Osa's death were nothing more than a simple fact to file away. I think he realized that the three of us were taking it harder than that, because he put his hand on Loor's shoulder and said, "Don't be sad. This is the way it was meant to be."

That was exactly what Osa said just before she died. Was that some sort of Traveler motto? If so, it was a lousy one. It didn't make me feel any better, and I doubted if it helped Loor at all.

"Everyone get some rest," Uncle Press ordered. "Tomorrow's going to be a tough day."

He was right; we all needed rest. So we took places apart from one another in different corners of the hut. This is when I wrote the last journal that I sent you. Loor wrote too, as did Alder. We were all documenting our experiences as Travelers, though I'm pretty sure we all had different opinions about how things were going. The only one who didn't write was Uncle Press. He laid down on one of the benches and closed his eyes. I wondered how much sleep he had gotten while a prisoner in the Bedoowan palace. Not much, probably.

As I wrote I sensed that there was tension in the room. Maybe it was just my own paranoia, but I had the feeling that the others were blaming me for the tough position we were in. Whenever I looked up, both Alder and Loor would quickly look away. The truth was, I didn't blame them. As I played out the events of the past few days in my mind, the sickening realization came to me that the situation on Denduron was much worse because of me. If Uncle Press hadn't brought me here, then he probably wouldn't have been captured by the Bedoowan. And if he hadn't been captured then he wouldn't have needed to be rescued, and I wouldn't have written to you guys to send me the stuff from home. And if I hadn't gotten that stuff from home, then the Milago wouldn't have the ability to explode that huge bomb. And if I weren't here, Osa would still be alive because . . . if, if, if. Whenever you look back and say, "If," you know you're in trouble. There's no such thing as "if." The only thing that counts is what really happened, and the truth was that every chance I got, I screwed up. Even when I thought I had done something good, it always turned out bad.

Then, just to rub salt in everyone's wounds, my watch alarm started to beep. I had totally forgotten about my Casio. Alder and Loor shot a look at me. They had no idea what it was. Uncle Press just cracked an eye open and gave me a deadly look. Without saying a word I jumped up and ran to a corner of the hut where I pulled the watch off and threw it into the latrine. I think it was a safe bet that nobody would go down there after it. I even pulled my Swiss Army knife out of my pocket and dumped it in the ooze. I looked back at the others to see they were all staring at me. I couldn't take it anymore.

"What?" I yelled. "So I messed up! Yeah, I got that stuff from home, but it was the only way I could think of to get Uncle Press out. And it worked, didn't it?"

Nobody said a word. They just stared back at me. It was making me crazy.

"It's not like you tried to stop me, Loor . . . Alder," I added. "You used the stuff too!"

"But we did not know it was wrong," said Loor quietly. "You did."

I couldn't argue with that, but I was still in an arguing mood so I yelled, "I didn't ask to come here, you know! It's not like I had a choice. I'm not a warrior like Loor or Osa. I'm not a knight like Alder. And I'm not a . . . not a . . . I don't know *what* you are anymore, Uncle Press, but I'm sure as hell not like you! You never should have brought me here." I was ready for a fight. I wanted them to say what a loser I was because I had a great comeback. I'd agree with them. I never claimed to be anything more than a junior-high kid from the suburbs. That's it. I wasn't a revolutionary, or a fighter, or anything else they wanted me to be. It wasn't fair to blame me for not living up to their expectations. I was doing the best I could. If that wasn't good enough, well, too bad.

But that's not what happened. Instead Uncle Press sat up on the bench and softly said, "Come here, all of you. Sit down."

We all kind of awkwardly exchanged glances and walked over to him. I had no idea where this was going. Uncle Press then spoke to us in such a calm manner that it took all of the tension out of the room. It kind of reminded me of the way Osa always seemed to have the ability to chill everybody out.

"I understand how tough this is for all of you," he began. "You haven't known about being Travelers for very long, and it's gotta be confusing."

"I do not understand why this has happened to me," said Alder. "Why must we be Travelers?"

"I was not given a choice," added Loor. "It does not seem fair."

I then realized that I wasn't the only one who was freaking out. Loor and Alder hadn't known about being Travelers for very long either. The only difference was they were better equipped to handle the assignment than I was. The closest I ever came to that kind of training was in Saturday morning karate class when I was ten. I usually ended up getting a bloody nose and running home crying. That's not exactly elite warrior training. I was definitely out of my league here.

Uncle Press smiled warmly and said, "If you want to know why you are Travelers, all you have to do is look back on what you've already done. The way the three of you rescued me from that palace was an amazing thing. You proved yourselves to be smart and brave and resourceful. But more important was the fact that you willingly put your lives at risk because it was the right thing to do. Ordinary people wouldn't do that. You want to know why you're Travelers? Look first to yourselves."

"But what are these powers?" asked Loor. "We understand words that we should not."

"There's a lot for you to learn," said Uncle Press. "But the best way for that to happen is for you to experience it. As time goes on everything will come clear, but you need to learn it on your own."

"Come on," I said impatiently. "You gotta give us more than that. Are there others? I mean, are there more Travelers?"

"Yes," said Uncle Press. "Every territory has a Traveler. When you arrive in a new territory, always find the Traveler. They know best about the customs and history of their home territory and can help you along."

"Like Alder," said Loor.

"Yes, like Alder," confirmed Uncle Press.

"And what about Mallos . . . Saint Dane?" I asked. "He's a Traveler too, right?"

Uncle Press's expression grew hard. "Yes," he said coldly. "This is something you should know about now," he said. "Every territory is in conflict. There are always wars and disputes and battles. That's the nature of things. Always was, always will be. But no matter what the conflict of a territory is, the true enemy is Saint Dane. Here on Denduron it's not the

Bedoowan, or Queen Kagan, or even the quigs. The real threat is Saint Dane. He's the one who must be stopped."

"What's his deal?" I asked. "Why is he so dangerous?"

I could tell we were getting into hairy territory, because Uncle Press had his game face back on. "He's dangerous because you never see him coming," was Uncle Press's answer. "He changes himself. On Denduron he has become Mallos, advisor to the queen. Bobby, you saw him back on Second Earth. He took on the form of a policeman. I'm not sure if he physically changes, or if he uses some kind of mind control to make you think he looks different, but the bottom line is you don't always see him coming. And make no mistake about it, the guy is evil."

Uncle Press paced faster. We all listened closely because it was clear we needed to hear what he was now telling us. "But his evil isn't obvious," he continued. "He doesn't murder, or cause floods or fires. His methods are much more devious. He will go to a territory and move himself into a position where he can *influence* events. He's smart and convincing. He'll appear to be your friend while the whole time he's pushing you toward disaster."

"Like with the Bedoowan?" I asked.

"Exactly," shot back Uncle Press. "The Milago and the Bedoowan have been in conflict for centuries, but Saint Dane has pushed it to the edge. Before he got here things were rough for the Milago, but nowhere near as bad as they are now. He worked his way into the trust of Queen Kagan—"

"Who isn't exactly a rocket scientist," I added.

"No, she isn't," he agreed. "For a while it was looking as if the Bedoowan might cut the Milago some slack, but it was Saint Dane's influence that convinced the Bedoowan to push harder. He's the one who started the unreasonable demands for glaze and the Transfer ceremony and the horrible quig slaughters in the stadium. It looks to the Milago as if the Bedoowan wanted all this, but it was really Saint Dane, or Mallos as he calls himself here. He whispers suggestions to Kagan, and she makes them law."

"But . . . why does he do this?" asked Alder.

"To push the territory toward chaos," was Uncle Press's firm answer. "Saint Dane doesn't care about the Bedoowan or the Milago. He's using the Bedoowan to push the Milago into getting so desperate that they will fight back. He wants a war. But not just any war, he wants the Milago to use tak. I see that now."

"He wants them to blow everybody up?" I asked.

"Not exactly," he continued. "Yes, using that bomb will cause terrible damage, but the long-term effects are what Saint Dane is after. I should have seen it coming, but I didn't. I didn't know about tak."

"Could Saint Dane have brought it from another territory?" I asked.

"I doubt it. My guess is that it's natural to Denduron and somehow Figgis stumbled across it . . . and Saint Dane is taking advantage. Tak now represents power to the Milago. They've been held down for so long that they'll grab at anything to pull themselves up. But once they start using tak on the Bedoowan, where will it stop? They could create weapons that would make them the most powerful tribe on Denduron. There are thousands of tribes here. None of them have a weapon like this. Putting the power of tak into the hands of one tribe is like tipping the balance. The Milago may be a peaceful bunch now, but they've got years of pent-up anger. Put that kind of power in their hands and they could overrun Denduron. That's the kind of chaos Saint Dane is looking for."

There it was. Loor had told me about the mission of the Travelers, but Uncle Press had now spelled it out pretty clearly. If this war began and the Milago used tak, it would be disaster. It really was a bigger deal than just a battle between two warring tribes. But there was something else that was bugging me.

"What is Halla?" I asked Uncle Press.

Uncle Press shot me a surprised look. "Where did you hear that name?"

"From Saint Dane," I said. "Before he took us to the stadium he told me that Halla would fall and we would fall with it. What is Halla?"

"Halla is everything," he answered. "Every territory, every person, every living thing, every *time* there ever was. Halla is what separates order from chaos. If Halla crumbles, there will be nothing left but darkness. Everywhere. For everyone."

Whoa. Now there was a concept to try and get my mind around. None of us spoke for a long while. We had just shifted into a new gear here. Was it possible? Could it be that the battle between the Milago and the Bedoowan was not only about the future of Denduron, but about the future of *all* territories? If things turned sour here, could that somehow affect things back home? This was the most devastating thing I had heard so far. The stakes had become so huge that it was hard to comprehend. Before any of us had the chance to ask another question, the wooden door to the hut flew open and a Milago miner stormed in.

"Rellin wishes to see you," he announced.

Uncle Press stood, but the miner held his hand up to stop him.

"Not you," he said. "Pendragon."

"Rellin wants to see *me*? What for?"

"Go with him, Bobby," said Uncle Press. "Listen to what he has to say. You know how important it is."

Yeah, this was important all right. It was so important that I wished somebody *else* were going. But I got up to follow the miner out of the hut. Before I left, I looked at Uncle Press. "I messed up," I said. "I'm sorry."

Uncle Press smiled and said, "It's okay, Bobby. Mistakes will be made."

That actually made me feel better. We were still in deep trouble and it was still my fault, but at least I didn't feel like a total nimrod for what I had done. One thing I could say for sure though: I wouldn't do it again. I guess that's what Uncle Press meant by telling us we would have to learn about being Travelers by experiencing it ourselves. You don't truly learn something until it's real, and the bomb that was about to blow us all into dust was very real. It's a tough way to learn a lesson.

I followed the miner out of the hut. Night had fallen, though I had no idea what time it was. My watch was floating in the latrine, remember? The village was empty. I could see lights coming from the huts, but nobody was walking about. It felt like the calm before the storm. The miner walked quickly until we came to one of the larger huts. He motioned for me to enter. It wasn't like I had a whole lot of choices, so I went in.

Rellin was waiting for me. He sat near the fire and offered me a cup of some kind of liquid. I wasn't sure if I should take it or not. Maybe it was poison. Or maybe it was a peace offering and by not taking it I'd be insulting him. I decided to take the cup and only pretend to drink. Of course if it was poison and I didn't clutch my throat in agony he'd pretty much know I faked taking a drink. Maybe I was overthinking this.

Once I had taken the cup and faked the drink (with no reaction from Rellin) he stood up and walked to a wooden table. Lying there was the battery from my flashlight. But something was attached to it. I looked closer and my stomach twisted when I saw that it was a small piece of tak. The wires and the switch had been pulled out of the flashlight and were used to connect the tak to the battery. These guys learned fast. They had made a little bomb. If they flipped the switch from the battery, it would complete the circuit and send a jolt of electricity through the tak. It may be a small jolt, but probably enough to detonate the unstable explosive. Rellin picked it up and examined it. I wanted to shout for him to be careful, but I could see that he appreciated the power and was handling it with caution.

"We have been trying to find a way to control tak," he said. "But until now we have been unsuccessful."

My mind flashed back to the moment down in the mines when there was an explosion and Rellin had to be rescued. He was probably experimenting with tak and something had gone wrong. Slowly the pieces of the puzzle were coming together.

"This is how we will ignite the tak," he continued. "Tomorrow this small device will explode and that will set off the larger load. When my army hears the explosion it will be their signal to attack. They will then overrun what is left of the Bedoowan. It will all be so very simple, because of you."

Gee, thanks. I'm thrilled that I could help us all move closer to Armageddon. Rellin put the small bomb down and sat back by the fire. He motioned for me to sit across from him.

"You have seen our lives," he said sadly. "We are dying. The Bedoowan will never allow us to be free. Tak is our salvation. With tak the Milago can pull themselves up from the dirt and become the proud people we were destined to be."

He was absolutely right. The Milago had it bad. They lived like tortured animals. Nobody deserved that. They had every right to fight back, but they didn't understand that they were going about it the wrong way.

"You and your people want to help us," he continued. "For that we are grateful. But there is one thing we need from you that will be more helpful than you can imagine."

"What's that?" I asked warily.

Rellin stood up and walked quickly back to his little homemade bomb. He picked it up and held it out as if it were the Holy Grail.

"Bring us more of these devices," he said with passion. "If we had more we could become the most powerful army on Denduron. Once the Bedoowan are defeated, the Milago would never have to live in fear again. We could turn our miserable lives around to become the leaders of Denduron!"

Oh, man. Uncle Press was absolutely right. Now that the Milago had a little taste of power, they weren't going to be satisfied with just beating up on the Bedoowan. They hadn't even won yet and they already had visions of taking over the rest of Denduron. The good guys were going to become the bad guys, and the result would be chaos.

"Will you help us, Pendragon?" asked Rellin sincerely.

This was my chance. Maybe my *only* chance to try and talk Rellin out of his plan. I couldn't argue against centuries of hatred, so the best thing I could do was try and make him see the downside to his plan. I had to choose my words carefully.

"I'm not an expert on these things," I said. "But if you blow up that big load of tak, there may not be much left of the Bedoowan to conquer. Heck, there may not be much left of the Milago, either. Where I come from, there are many weapons like this. But the biggest fear we have is that they will be used. You don't understand what you're doing, Rellin. Your lives may be horrible now, but you may be worse off after the explosion. There must be a better way."

"No!" he shouted angrily.

I hadn't chosen my words carefully enough.

"You do not understand!" he yelled at me. "You have not lived your life in fear, in pain, in hunger. This is the only way. This is how the Milago will defeat the Bedoowan. Now, will you help us?"

Key moment.

"I'll help you," I answered as firmly as I could. "We'll all help you. But not if it means using tak."

Rellin stiffened and said, "Then go back to your friends. You will not be harmed. When the battle is over you will be free to leave."

My mind was racing. I wanted to come up with something to change his mind, but I was drawing a blank. The truth was I didn't know how the Milago could possibly defeat the Bedoowan without the help of something like tak. I couldn't offer a better solution. I had one chance and I blew it. But then a thought hit me.

"How will you explode the bomb?" I asked. "If someone pushes that switch, then they'll go up with it."

Rellin straightened up proudly. "It will be an honor to die in the name of freedom for the Milago."

Oh, man. Rellin was going on a suicide mission. This wasn't about personal glory or power. This was a good man who cared about the future of his people more than he cared about his own life. There was nothing more for me to say, so I left the hut feeling sorry for him, but also feeling incredible respect . . . and fear. If someone was ready to die for his cause, a dweeb like me had no chance of talking him out of it. That bomb was going to explode tomorrow and there wasn't anything I could do about it.

The miner led me back to the hospital hut where I quickly told the others about my meeting.

"So then it is true," said Loor. "The Milago will become a powerful, warring tribe and destroy all of Denduron."

"That's if they don't blow themselves up with that humongous bomb first," I added.

There was still a big question to be answered. Where were the Milago going to explode the bomb? They couldn't very well do it around here or their own village would be vaporized. They may have been primitive but I'm sure they figured that little detail out. No, they must be planning on exploding it near the Bedoowan palace. But how could they pull that off? It's not like they could drop it off on the palace doorstep, ring the doorbell and run away. As soon as they got within a hundred yards of the place the Bedoowan knights would stop them. They must have a plan, but what?

The answer turned out to be so simple I probably should have figured it out myself.

The next morning we were all awakened by the same thing. It was a deep, constant booming sound. I was still asleep and at first it had worked itself into my dreams. I dreamed that I was in a battle. Explosions were going off all around me. No matter which way I turned, another explosion would go off in my face. It was like I was trapped in a minefield. As I began to wake up I realized that I wasn't in a minefield, I was in the hospital hut of the Milago village. But the deep booming sound continued. What was it? I lay there for a few seconds, trying to remember where I'd heard it before. Then suddenly, it hit me. I knew exactly where I had heard it before and the realization shocked me wide awake. I sat up quickly to see that the others were already awake and looking out of the small windows of the hut. I didn't have to ask what they were looking at. I already knew.

The sound I heard was the sound of the drum calling the Milago to a Transfer ceremony. I could picture the single drummer standing on the wooden platform in the clearing of the Milago village, slowly but steadily hitting that drum. The memory wasn't exactly a pleasant one, because it ended in the horrible death of a Milago miner. I truly hoped that this Transfer wouldn't end the same way.

I jumped up and joined Uncle Press at one of the windows. Loor and Alder peered out of the other one. The hut wasn't far from the central clearing of the Milago village. We were going to see all that we needed to see.

The scene in the clearing was painfully familiar. The Milago villagers slowly gathered around the central platform; the seesaw device was in place, ready to weigh the next poor victim; the lone drummer stood on the platform, beating out the summons; and a handful of Bedoowan knights stood next to the platform with spears in hand. The drummer suddenly stopped pounding his kettle and an ominous silence fell over the village. Then, as if on cue, I heard the sound of a galloping horse. Mallos was on his way. The crowd parted and Mallos charged up to the platform and dismounted before his horse had come to a stop.

How could anyone be this evil? What was it that drove him to spread terror and chaos wherever he went? Was it because he enjoyed it? Did it give him some kind of thrill? Does evil exist just for evil's sake? There had to be answers to these questions, but they would have to wait for another time because the curtain was about to go up.

"Where is the glaze?" Mallos bellowed. "Why was I summoned before the glaze was ready to be transferred?"

He scanned the crowd waiting for an answer, but none was coming. Nobody could even look him in the eye. I was afraid he would blow a cork and send the knights on a rampage, but that didn't happen. Instead, Rellin stepped forward. The chief miner looked calm and in control.

"Mallos," he said. "I truly hope you will be happy with the news we bring you."

Mallos shot a suspicious look at Rellin, then stepped up to him and stuck his nose in the chief miner's face.

"Where are they, Rellin?" he seethed. "I know they are here. If you hide them from me, you cannot begin to imagine the punishment that will come down upon you."

Mallos was talking about us. He seemed incredibly ticked that we had gotten away and was accusing the Milago of hiding us. The four of us exchanged looks, but none of us were about to give ourselves up. Rellin was cool. He didn't back down.

"That is the news I bring you," he said. "We are sorry for all the trouble the outsiders have caused you. We thought they were our friends, but they are not. And knowing that they have caused distress to Queen Kagan, well, that now makes them our enemies as well."

Was he for real? Was he going to turn us over to Mallos and the knights after telling me he'd let us go? I didn't think Rellin was a liar, but this sounded bad. I could tell that Mallos wasn't sure where Rellin was going with this either. He looked at the miner suspiciously and asked through clenched teeth, "Where are they?"

"I do not know," answered Rellin. "But when we find them we will bring them to you immediately."

Okay, maybe he was a liar after all, but at least he hadn't

lied to me. He wasn't going to turn us in. What was he up to?

"In the meantime," continued Rellin. "As an apology for the trouble we have caused you and Queen Kagan and all the Bedoowan, we would like to present you with a gift." He made a motion and the crowd parted. Three miners stepped forward carrying their load of glaze. But this was no ordinary load. They carried an entire ore car full of glaze! It was spectacular. The cart was piled high with the biggest, most brilliant glaze stones I had seen yet.

"Yesterday we struck a promising new vein of glaze," said Rellin proudly. "That is our good news. There is more glaze in this new vein than we could hope to bring up in a lifetime. It took us a full day and night to load this one car and I predict that there are hundreds of more cars to come that will be just as full."

Mallos seemed impressed. He should have been. It was a lot of glaze.

"This is our gift to you," said Rellin. "I ask only one thing in return."

"What is that?" barked Mallos.

"I wish to be able to present this to Queen Kagan myself," said Rellin. "I realize that a lowly Milago miner would never be allowed into the palace, but perhaps I could bring this carful of glaze to the Bedoowan stadium? I would be honored to present this to Queen Kagan along with the promise of much more to come."

Rellin was brilliant. He was playing Mallos like a fish and the fish was about to bite the hook. Of course we all knew the truth. That ore car wasn't full of glaze at all. My guess is that if you dug about a quarter of the way down, the glaze would stop and the load of tak would begin. Yes, Rellin had figured out a way to smuggle his monstrous bomb right into the heart of the Bedoowan palace. It was like the story of the Trojan Horse where the Greeks were at war with the Trojans and gave them a gift of a giant wooden horse. Only the horse was loaded with Greek soldiers. As soon as the big horse was wheeled inside the city of Troy, the soldiers jumped out and gave a big helping of whup-butt to the surprised Trojans.

But this Trojan Horse wasn't full of soldiers. This was loaded with a deadly explosive that would level the Bedoowan palace and probably most of the Milago village. The plan was insane, and brilliant. The question was, would Mallos fall for it?

Mallos looked at the carful of glaze. He walked to it and dug his hand down into the precious stones. I could sense Rellin tensing, but he didn't make a move. Mallos pulled his hand out and clutched a load of brilliant blue stones. He then looked to Rellin and said, "Why make your promise to only Queen Kagan? I believe all of the Bedoowan people should be in the stadium to receive this gift and to hear your promise."

Rellin did his best not to smile and only said, "Yes, you are a wise man."

Unbelievable. Not only was Mallos going to let Rellin bring the bomb in, he was going to gather all of the Bedoowan around it.

Mallos then climbed back on his horse and bellowed, "Bring the glaze now. I will prepare the stadium!" With that he kicked his horse and charged toward the palace.

Rellin looked to the miners who had brought in the tak bomb. Without showing a hint of satisfaction, he walked to the ore car. No words were spoken. The men knew what they had to do. They all reached down, lifted the heavy car and began the long walk to the Bedoowan palace. Their death mission was under way.

Uncle Press backed away from the window and said, "Mallos knows."

"No way!" I said. "Why would he let them bring a bomb into the Bedoowan stadium?"

"Because he wants the Milago to use it," was his answer. "He doesn't care who wins, or who dies. He wants the Milago to use the tak. If that bomb goes off, he'll have succeeded."

Maybe Uncle Press was right. If Mallos wanted to start a war that would throw Denduron into chaos, what better way to kick it off than by letting the Milago have their big bang right in the Bedoowan backyard? For Mallos it was perfect. We all knew exactly where this was leading but there was nothing we could do to stop it because we were trapped in this stupid hut.

But not for long. Without stopping to tell us, Loor ran for the window and in one quick, acrobatic move pulled herself up and out. In seconds she was climbing up onto the roof. It happened so fast that none of us could react. We just sort of stared at each other, wondering what she was doing. We heard her quietly scamper across the roof until she was above the door to the hut. What followed was the sound of a brief scuffle outside, followed by a few quick grunts. Loor then poked her head back inside the door.

"We may leave now," she said with matter-of-fact calm.

None of us were exactly sure of what had happened, but we all ran for the door and followed Loor out. Outside we saw all three guards had been knocked unconscious and were leaning against the hut. Loor had struck before they knew what hit them and had managed to free us all in less than twenty seconds.

That was pretty cool, but there wasn't time for praise. We had to get out of the Milago village without being caught. As it turned out, it wasn't hard. Rellin's plan was being carried out, which meant the rest of the miners were preparing for their attack. As soon as they heard the explosion they would charge the Bedoowan palace. Those miners had more important things to worry about than guarding us. So getting out of the village and disappearing into the woods was easy.

The four of us ran until we felt we were a safe distance away. Uncle Press then raised his hand and we all stopped to catch our breath. Uncle Press looked at Loor and said what was on all of our minds.

"You are unbelievable!" he said with a laugh. "Why didn't you tell us you were going to do that? We could have helped."

Loor gave a very Loor-esque response. "I did not need your help. The best weapon in battle is surprise. The miners were watching Mallos and Rellin. They were not thinking about us. If I had waited, they may have turned their attention back to guarding us. I did not want to give them that chance."

"I'm proud of you, Loor," said Uncle Press. "Your mother would be too."

"She taught me well," said Loor.

My mother never taught me anything like that. She spent a lot of time drilling good table manners into me, but we never got to the lesson on how to disarm and crack heads with three guys twice my size. My education was definitely lacking in that area.

"What about the bomb?" said Alder. "We must do something!"

Uncle Press spun back to us and said, "Okay, first thing we have to do is get to the palace. We aren't doing any good here."

I wasn't so sure that going to the palace was on the top of my To Do list. The palace was the target and unless we had a real chance of stopping Rellin from setting off that bomb, the only thing getting closer would do is guarantee that we'd be killed the instant it went off. But I wasn't about to say that. The truth was if there was any hope of stopping Rellin, we had to get there.

"Alder, I want you to go back to the village," said Uncle Press.

"No!" he exclaimed. "I want to stay with you."

"Look," said Uncle Press firmly. "I have no idea if we're going to stop this thing. So get back to the village, talk to anyone who'll listen. Warn them that this bomb is going to be bigger than they could ever imagine. Try to get them to go down into the mines. Maybe if they get underground they'll be safe."

"But I—"

"No buts, Alder," said Uncle Press. "I know you want to be with us, but if we fail, you still might be able to save some of the Milago."

Uncle Press was right. If Alder could save even one person from being killed by the explosion, then his mission would be successful. He had to go back.

Alder nodded to Uncle Press, which told me he understood how important his job was. There wasn't time for long good-byes. I hadn't known Alder for very long, but I had grown fond of him. He was kind of a goof, but I didn't doubt for a second that he would have put his life on the line for any one of us. I'd like to say that I would do the same for him.

"Good luck, Travelers," he said, and smiled at each of us.

"You too, Alder," said Uncle Press. "Hurry."

Alder then spun around and ran back toward the Milago village. Now it was just the three of us. The warrior, the boss, and the kid who was so scared he had to pee. Guess which one I was?

"Come on," commanded Uncle Press and ran deeper into

the forest. Our immediate goal was to get back to the Bedoowan palace. Beyond that, there was no plan. We would have to wing it once we got there, assuming we even got there. Since we were bushwhacking, it took us a long time. I could tell that Loor was getting impatient, but it was better to take a little longer to get there than to risk being captured again. We took a wide route and circled around toward the sea, then crawled along the bluffs until we were within eyesight of the outcropping that held the Bedoowan palace. Though we couldn't see it, we knew where it was because there was a long line of knights marching toward it. Behind them were the four miners carrying the ore car full of glaze and tak. They were almost at the palace. In a few minutes they would descend into the stadium.

We continued to move quickly along the bluffs, moving closer to the stadium. It was a smart thing to do because none of the knights expected anyone to be coming from the sea. They were ever vigilant, but always with their eyes toward the forest. We were able to quietly slip in from behind them and crawl the last several yards on our bellies until we reached the lip of the stadium. We had made it. Now the question was, what were we going to do?

The three of us peered down into the stadium to see that the line of knights was marching down the steep stairs toward the grass field below. Behind them came Rellin and the miners struggling with the heavy ore car. I glanced around the rest of the stadium and saw that two of the spectator sections were beginning to fill up. The Bedoowan people and the Novans were once again taking their seats in anticipation of a show. It was a horrible feeling. None of these people had any idea that the main event was going to be their own deaths. I looked to the section where the Milago were before to see that it was empty. Big surprise. These guys knew what was coming and didn't want to be any part of it. I then looked to Loor and to Uncle Press. Nobody said anything. That could mean only one thing. Nobody knew what to do. The thought ran through my head that we could run down the stairs screaming at everyone to run for their lives. But all Rellin would have to do is stop, press the button on his homemade bomb and it would be all over. That wouldn't work at all. But if we were going to come up with a better plan, we needed to do it fast, because Rellin and the miners had reached the grass field and were about to place the ore car dead center in the ring.

"If I had an arrow I could kill Rellin from here," said Loor.

"Then one of the others would press the button," said Uncle Press.

I then heard the three chimes that signaled the arrival of Queen Kagan. Sure enough, when I looked at the royal box a few knights marched in, followed by the chubby queen. True to form, she was munching on something that looked like a roast beef. What a piece of work.

"Mallos isn't there," said Uncle Press. "My guess is he's on a horse riding as fast as he can to get as far away from here as possible."

Indeed, Mallos was nowhere to be seen. That was further proof that everything was happening according to his plan.

And that's when it hit me.

"I . . . I've got an idea," I said without even thinking. Even as I said it I was still working it through my head, calculating the possibilities and the chances of it working.

Uncle Press and Loor looked at me, but I didn't respond to them at first. I still had to work things out.

"Don't take your time, Bobby," said Uncle Press. "We don't have much."

"Okay, okay," I said nervously. "There might be a way, but if it doesn't work, we're all dead."

"We are all dead anyway," said Loor.

Good point. I looked down to the stadium and realized that I was about to volunteer to do something crazy. If I did it, I'd probably die. If I didn't do it, we'd *definitely* die. Probably was better than definitely.

"I think I know how to stop this party," I said with as much confidence as I could muster, which wasn't much. Before I said another word, two more chimes sounded and the crowd fell silent. Rellin and the miners stood next to their wicked gift. Queen Kagan dropped her roast and leaned over the railing to look down on them.

"Tell me what it is you've brought me!" she shouted greedily.

If we were going to do something, now was the time.

DENDURON

"Good day, Queen Kagan!" shouted Rellin from the center of the stadium field.

This was probably the first time a Milago miner had addressed a Bedoowan monarch. Ever. It was probably going to be the last. Rellin had everyone's attention in the stadium. I hoped that he had a lot to say, because if he decided to keep it short and reach for the bomb button, my plan had no chance of working. But if he took this opportunity to say what was on his mind and make some kind of grand political statement for the history books, then maybe we'd have a chance.

For my plan to work, we each had a different task. Unfortunately my job was probably the most dangerous. It's not that I wanted the most dangerous task, but it was the only job I was capable of pulling off. Lucky me.

I quickly told my idea to Uncle Press and Loor. They didn't even stop to discuss it. The time for debate was over and since nobody had any better ideas, my plan was a "go." The plan called for the three of us to split up. Before we had the chance to share a "good luck" or a "good-bye," Loor was off and running. Typical. Uncle Press didn't run off as quickly. He stayed long enough to give me this look of unclelike concern. I felt like I needed to say something important, but the only thing that came to mind was, "I really wish you had let me go to that basketball game." Okay, maybe not the most eloquent last words, but it was how I felt.

Uncle Press smiled and said, "No, you don't." Then he took off running.

I hesitated a moment because, well, I was scared. But I also had to think about what Uncle Press just said. Sure, if I had gone to that basketball game I wouldn't be lying here facing certain death. But that's not where my head went. This is going to be hard to explain because I'm not really sure I understand it myself, but as dire as the situation was, it somehow felt right. Believe me, it's not like I was having fun or anything. Far from it. But when I took a few seconds to do a gut check, I got the strange feeling that this was the right place, no, the *only* place for me to be. What was that Traveler motto? "This is the way it was meant to be." Okay, stupid motto, but it really felt to me as if this is the way it was meant to be. I don't mean to make this sound any more dramatic than it was, but the word that came to my mind right then was "destiny." Maybe this was my destiny. Now I could only hope that I'd get the chance to play a basketball game again sometime. But that wouldn't happen if I didn't get moving. So I jumped up and ran to do my part of the plan.

As I ran along the top of the stadium, I wasn't worried about getting caught because all eyes were focused on Rellin. It must have been amazing for the Bedoowan people to see this Milago miner addressing their queen. It was a spectacle that never would have happened if Mallos hadn't orchestrated it. I guess that's the kind of thing Uncle Press was talking about when he said that Mallos never did any of his own dirty work. He said how Mallos would influence others to do it for him. Well, Rellin was definitely about to do some dirty work, courtesy of Mallos.

"People of Denduron," Rellin continued. "I come before you today with a gift that is more valuable than you can imagine."

It seemed as if Rellin was indeed about to give a speech. That was good. Hopefully he was long-winded because I had no idea how much time it would take to pull off my plan.

"My gift is more valuable than the glaze you see before you," he bellowed. "It is more valuable than all the glaze that has ever been taken from the mines. It is the gift of a wonderful future, and it is for *all* the good people of Denduron to share."

Was this guy dramatic or what? Well, why not? He wasn't planning on being around long enough to hear any bad reviews. This was his moment in the spotlight. Keep going Rellin, I thought, make it good and long.

As I ran I saw that Loor and Uncle Press had already managed to pull off the first part of their jobs. They had each snuck up on a Bedoowan knight from behind, whacked them and taken their armor. They needed to wear the armor so they could make their way down to the stadium field without being noticed. That's why I gave them the jobs I did. There was no way I was going to knock out a knight and steal his armor. And even if by some miracle I was able to do that, I was too small. If I put on the armor I'd look like a little kid wearing his daddy's clothes.

No, I had another job and I knew exactly where I had to go. It was only yesterday that I had been there. At the time I swore never to go near the place again but here I was, headed right back. It only took me a few minutes to get there. I was pretty fast, so running three hundred yards was nothing. But as I approached my destination I had a moment's hesitation. I thought that maybe if I ran fast enough and far enough, I could survive the blast from the tak bomb. But that thought lasted only about a nanosecond. There was no way I was going to bail on the plan.

At this point it wasn't even the bomb I was afraid of. That's because I had arrived at my destination: the horrible hole that looked down into the dark depths of the quig pens.

Yup, if my plan was going to work, I was going to have to climb down there and make my way to the stadium through a minefield of hungry quigs. And I didn't have my trusty whistle to protect me either. This could hurt. I stood on the edge of the hole trying to get the nerve to climb down. The rope ladder was in a heap at the bottom of the hole, right where it had fallen yesterday. But the thick rope that Loor had climbed to make her escape was still hanging there. That was my ticket down. I had to stop worrying and kick myself into gear because Rellin could hit that button at any second. So I grabbed the rope, swung my legs over, and slid down the rope into the pit of hell.

When I got to the bottom the first thing that hit me was the smell. It was as nasty as I had remembered it. Then I realized I had landed in a puddle of some kind of thick brown goo. I realized what it was and I nearly barfed. It was a congealed pool of blood from the quig that Uncle Press had skewered. I fought back the rising puke and quickly looked around. The injured quig wasn't there. Maybe it was dead. Better still, maybe it had been eaten by the other quigs. Can you believe this was the way my mind was working now?

My next goal was to get to the door that led to the stadium as fast as possible. I couldn't sneak quietly through the quig pen. No, I had to beat feet and get there fast, so I took off running in the direction I remembered traveling the day before. The run through the quig pen was terrifying. As I rounded each turn in the labyrinth, I kept expecting to see a monster quig waiting there with its mouth open, ready for dinner. My adrenaline was pumping so hard I don't think I could have walked slowly and cautiously if I'd wanted to. I should have been exhausted by now, but I wasn't. Fear will do that. If a quig didn't get me, then the bomb would. I wasn't sure which would be more painful. My guess is that the bomb would be quicker. But I forced those morbid thoughts away because the goal was to stay alive, not choose the least painful way to die.

After a few more turns I saw the door to the stadium. I had made it! Believe me, I never thought I'd get this far. I ran to the huge door and put my ear to it. I could hear Rellin still giving his speech. That was good. But there was another sound I wanted to hear as well. The job I had given to Loor was to get down to the stadium floor and unlock the door. That wouldn't be easy because as soon as she started to lift the heavy latch, somebody would certainly see her and try to stop her. Timing was everything. If she opened the door too soon, my plan would fail. If she opened it too late, my plan would fail. There was a small window of opportunity and it was getting close.

I listened again, and that's when I heard it. Two quick raps on the door. That was the signal. Loor had made it and was standing outside. Excellent! Now she had to wait for my signal before opening the door. Of course she had no way of knowing if I was on the other side or not. For all she knew I was being munched on by a quig who had a surprise treat fall into its lap. Still, I knew it didn't matter. She would stand there until I signaled for her to open the door, or the bomb blew up. Whichever came first.

Now came the hardest part of all. Talk about gut-check time. Everything that I had done up to this point was easy compared to what I had to do next. I looked around for something to help me and found a metal shield that one of the Bedoowan knights had dropped yesterday before he became quig food. I needed something else, too. I hoped to find one of the knight's spears, but for some reason they were gone. Time was running out, I had to move faster. I looked around again and saw the perfect thing. It turned my stomach to use it, but I couldn't let my squeamish belly stop me from doing what I had to do. So I picked it up. It was a leg bone. A human leg bone. As disgusting as it was, it was exactly what I needed. At least this one didn't still have the foot attached. I fought back my disgust, took a few steps back into the cavern, and rang the dinner bell.

Yes, I was using myself as bait. I used the leg bone to bang on the metal shield and hopefully wake up any napping quig that had missed my crazed run a few seconds before. "Come on!" I shouted. "Come and get it! Tasty meat, right this way!"

This was insane. Think about it. I was putting myself out there to be eaten by a beast that had already devoured three people. My hands were shaking with fear. Whose idea was this, anyway? Oh, right. Mine.

I banged on the shield a few more times and the annoying sound echoed throughout the cavern. Another horrible thought went through my head. What if they could hear this from the stadium? If there was even a hint of a problem, Rellin would hit the button and the game would be over. "Let's go!" I shouted. "C'mon, you losers! I'm the guy who killed your buddy up on the mountain! Come and get me!"

It came without so much as a warning. Yesterday when the quig attacked Uncle Press, it stalked him cautiously and slowly until it was close enough to pounce. That's not what was happening now. From far back in the depths of the rocky labyrinth I heard the bellow of a quig that was already charging! Maybe it was because of the annoying sound of the shield. Maybe it was my yelling. Maybe it was ravenously hungry. I'll never know, but whatever I had done, it worked. A quig was now charging toward me at a dead run. I could hear its giant paws pounding on the rocky surface as it rumbled closer, ready for the kill.

Now was the time. Now was the window of opportunity. Loor had to open that door fast or I'd be lunch. I dropped the shield, ran to the door and gave the secret, prearranged signal for Loor to do her thing.

"Open the damn door!" I yelled as loud as I could. How's that for a secret signal? Loor got the message. With my ear to the door I heard her fumbling with the heavy lock. This was the same lock that it took two knights to lift. I hoped that Loor had the strength to do it herself. Uncle Press could have helped, but he had his own job to take care of and was probably nowhere near the door. It was all up to Loor.

"Hurry!" I shouted. This was one time I didn't care about sounding cool or confident. I wanted her to know how close I was to being eaten. I heard a roar, turned back to look into the quig pens, and saw it. The quig. Its yellow eyes blazed as it charged through the pools of light, picking up speed, lusting for the kill. It was getting close enough that I could see bits of saliva flying from its open mouth. This thing was hungry and I was dinner. I threw my back against the door, hoping it would open. It didn't. I could hear Loor struggling with the lock. If she took any longer, someone would surely see her and stop her. Or Rellin would push the button. One way or another, this would all be over in a few seconds.

The quig crouched lower to the ground. It was getting ready to pounce.

"If you don't open the door," I shouted, "this quig is going to—" With a loud creak, the door swung open and I fell back. At that exact moment the quig sprang, but because I had fallen down it sailed over me and through the open door into the stadium. I swear I felt the breeze from its paws as they sailed over my head, inches from slicing me to pieces. I quickly jumped to my feet and ran into the stadium to see what was happening. The next few seconds were critical. It all came down to what the quig did . . . and Uncle Press.

The stadium was in total chaos. The quig was out of control. Several Bedoowan knights ran onto the field to try and capture it, or kill it. I saw that Loor had been attacked by two knights. But Loor wasn't their problem anymore. They let her go and went after the quig. I helped her to her feet and the two of us took cover next to the open door. The monster quig had taken a stand. It went from offense to defense as the knights attacked it with their spears. I'm not sure who was doing more damage, the quig or the knights. For every spear they threw at the wild animal, the quig must have slashed two knights. It was in a total frenzy of anger, pain, and blood. But the main thing is that the battle to contain the quig had done exactly what I hoped it would. It disrupted the events that were taking place in the ring.

I looked to the center of the ring to see what Rellin was doing. He must have been momentarily stunned by the sudden appearance of the quig, because he stood there with the other miners staring at the action. That didn't last long. He snapped out of it and went for the ore car full of tak. This was it. This was the moment. Rellin was going to push the button.

From the corner of my eye I saw a black streak headed toward Rellin. It was a flying spear. The missile flew at the chief miner and stabbed him right in the forearm, pinning him to the side of the wooden ore car. Rellin screamed out in pain, but I'm not sure if it was a scream of pain or of frustration because he couldn't get to the tak bomb. Then I saw a Bedoowan knight run up to the ore car. But I knew this wasn't a Bedoowan knight, it was Uncle Press. He was going for the detonator. Rellin couldn't move, but the other miners could. They realized what Uncle Press was doing and attacked him. These simple miners were no match for my uncle. Uncle Press was a blur of arms and legs as he took the miners on and knocked them down one by one. There was no way he was going to let any of them get to the detonator.

It was an amazing sight. The Bedoowan knights had all but killed the quig and Uncle Press was in full command of Rellin and the miners. I couldn't believe it. My plan had worked.

No sooner did I think that the worst was over than all hell broke loose again. I had forgotten there was another quig in the pen, and the door was still open. The second quig charged out onto the field with just as much fury as the first. But the knights were spent and they didn't have the strength or the will to kill another quig. This was going to be a slaughter. There was nothing to stop this murderous quig . . . except for Uncle Press.

Uncle Press had finished off the last miner, then quickly and carefully pulled the small homemade bomb out from under the ore car full of tak. Rellin tried to stop him, but he was literally pinned to the wooden car and could barely move. The quig crouched down on all fours and surveyed the scene.

It was looking for its first victim and it quickly made its decision. It wanted Uncle Press.

"Uncle Press!" I shouted. Uncle Press looked up to see the quig heading for him at a dead run. Without a second of hesitation he heaved the small bomb at the charging quig. I didn't know if he pushed the button as he threw or not, but whatever happened, the results were spectacular—and gruesome. The small bomb of tak hit the quig in midair and exploded. The force of the tak ripped into the beast and tore it apart, sending pieces of bloody quig raining down on the entire field. It was disgusting and beautiful at the same time. The quig was killed and the means to explode the bigger bomb was gone.

There was an odd calm in the stadium now. It was like no one understood what just happened, or what to do next. Many of the Bedoowan knights were injured or just plain exhausted from their battle with the quig. Kagan stood in her royal box looking down on the carnage. She must have been really confused because she wasn't even eating. The Bedoowan spectators watched in stunned silence. They had no idea if what had happened was planned, or some horrible mistake. Only the Novans reacted. They gave their typical polite applause. Gotta love those guys.

I looked to Loor and said, "What took you so long with the door?"

"I had two knights on my back," she answered. Not only had she lifted the heavy lock, she did it while fighting off two of the Bedoowan knights. Uncle Press walked over to Rellin and pulled the spear out of his arm, releasing him. He then gave him a rag to tie his wound. Loor and I joined them. Nobody knew what to say. I couldn't tell if Rellin was angry, disappointed, in pain, or all the above.

That's when Rellin started to laugh.

It was the last reaction I expected. It was the same kind of crazy laugh I heard from him down in the mines. It was like he knew something we didn't know. Again, it gave me the creeps.

Finally Rellin said, "You think this is over, but it is not."

"Yes, it is," said Uncle Press. "You have no way to explode this tak now."

Rellin laughed even harder. What was going through his mind?

"But this is not all the tak that was brought from the mines," he said. This grand weapon may have failed, but the signal has been given just the same. It was you who gave that signal, Press, my friend."

The three of us looked at each other, befuddled. What was he talking about? Then it hit me. I remembered what Rellin had said to me the night before. He said that as soon as his miners heard the explosion, it would be their signal to attack. And there had certainly been an explosion. Granted it wasn't the big boom everybody was expecting, but it was pretty loud just the same. There were quig guts all over the place as proof. Could the Milago miners have heard it? The answer to that question came right away. A horn sounded from on top of the stadium. All eyes looked up to see a lone Bedoowan knight standing there.

"The Milago!" he shouted for all to hear. "They're attacking!" Instantly the Bedoowan knights scrambled. Even the knights who had bravely fought the quig and were wounded jumped to attention. They grabbed their spears, straightened their helmets and quickly climbed up the stairs of the stadium.

"Look!" said Loor and pointed toward Kagan's royal box. What we saw were more knights, hundreds of them, all piling out from inside the palace to join their comrades. Queen Kagan stood on her throne, laughing and clapping like a child, cheering them on. To her, this was a game. She had no idea that these men were headed into a very real battle. Or maybe she just didn't care.

The knights were now several hundred strong. They looked like a formidable fighting unit. They marched up the stairs of the stadium to join with their comrades and begin the defense of the palace. Then an odd thing happened. The Bedoowan spectators began climbing the stairs to the surface as well. They were excitedly laughing and chatting with anticipation. They were followed in turn by the Novans. This was unbelievable. It was like they wanted to watch the battle for themselves. Did they think this was going to be a show put on for their amusement, like the quig battles? Did they have any idea what was about to happen?

Rellin said, "We may not have made our grand statement, but we will still have our battle. We are armed with tak and we will triumph. Your efforts have been in vain. The battle is about to begin."

DENDURON

Much of what I am going to write about now was told to me after the battle. As I wrote before, I have no doubt that it is all true and I have no problem adding it to my journal. I'll try to recount it in the order that it happened.

When Alder left us to warn the Milago villagers about the bomb, nobody listened to him as he ran through the village shouting, "Everyone! Into the mines! You must protect yourselves!" But I guess none of the villagers even knew about tak, let alone about the huge bomb that was supposed to blow away the Bedoowan. So when Alder came running through like a nut job, they slammed their doors in his face and ignored him. I don't blame them. If a guy ran around all Chicken Little screaming that the sky was falling, I'd probably ignore him too. Alder quickly realized that trying to save them was futile. His last hope was to find the one group of people who might listen to him: the miners who were preparing for battle. They knew about tak and they knew about Rellin's mad plan. So Alder ran out to the training area where Rellin and his miners had captured us the day before.

What he found there was a frightening sight. All the

miners of the Milago had assembled. There were hundreds of them. It never seemed like there were all that many miners living in the village, but that was because most of them were usually in the mines. Not today. All the miners were now on the surface and they were ready to rumble. According to Alder they had emptied the secret stash of weapons from down in the mines and each of them was armed with either spears or bows and arrows. But more important, several of the miners carried a much more lethal weapon. Around their waists were leather pouches full of small tak bombs.

As Alder ran through the crowd looking for someone in charge, he looked into the eyes of these hardened miners. He told me that what he saw gave him a chill. Even though they were about to begin a battle that could cost them their lives, these guys showed no fear. I suppose a lifetime of slavery will do that to you. They wanted blood. Bedoowan blood. They may not have been trained warriors, but what they lacked in fighting skills was made up for with pure hatred for the Bedoowan. They were confident, too. Once Rellin exploded his bomb, they figured that most of the Bedoowan knights would die instantly. Any of the knights who survived would be easy to mow down with their precious tak. They thought the battle would be short and sweet.

They were absolutely, totally wrong.

Alder finally found the leader. It was a miner who stood toward the front of the group giving orders. Alder ran up to him and said breathlessly, "The bomb . . . the tak bomb. It is more deadly than you could imagine! If Rellin succeeds, it could kill us all! We must get everyone down into the mines to—"

That's when it happened. That's the moment when Uncle

Press threw the small bomb at the quig and made quigburger. The miners all looked in the direction of the Bedoowan castle as the explosion thundered through the hills. Then just as the last echo died away, the leader shouted, "Death to the Bedoowan!"

There was a huge cheer and the miners began running toward the castle. Alder had to dive out of the way for fear of being trampled by the stoked-up miners as they rushed to their destiny. They had no idea that they were headed right into the full force of the Bedoowan army.

The stadium was almost empty. Even Queen Kagan had left to watch the show. Four Novans had lifted up her throne and carried her up the stairs and out to the battlefield. Those pale little guys must be a lot stronger than they looked because that throne and that fatso must have weighed a ton. The three miners who brought the tak bomb with Rellin were gone too. They had run off to fight with their comrades. The only ones left in the huge stadium were me, Loor, Uncle Press, Rellin, and a dead quig. Actually two dead quigs, but the second one looked more like Hamburger Helper.

Rellin struggled to get to his feet. Uncle Press gave him a hand. These guys weren't enemies. They both wanted the same thing, sort of. Their only disagreement was how to go about getting it.

"Your miners aren't prepared to battle those knights," Uncle Press said to him. "The tak may prolong the fight, but the Bedoowan will crush them."

"Perhaps," said Rellin. "But better to die fighting, than as a slave."

Those were powerful words. I had seen the horrible lives the Milago lived. If they were going to die, at least now they would die with some dignity. It was a terrible choice, but maybe it was the right one. Rellin then said, "Permit me to join my men?"

Uncle Press picked up the spear he had used to stop Rellin from exploding the bomb. He looked at it, then handed it to the chief miner. "Good luck," he said.

Rellin took the spear, gave a small nod of thanks, then took off running to join his doomed men. We watched him run across the stadium grass and bound up the stairs toward the battle that was about to begin. I wondered if I would ever see the guy alive again. Uncle Press then picked up another spear.

"What are you doing?" I asked.

"I'm going back to the Milago village," he answered. "The Bedoowan are going to suffer casualties. That's never happened to them before. I'm afraid they'll get angry enough to continue on to the Milago village and take it out on some of the villagers."

"But how can you stop that?" asked Loor.

"I can't," was his answer. "But I can help Alder get them down into the mines. The knights won't go down there and it'll give them a chance to cool off."

"We're coming with you!" I said.

"No," ordered Uncle Press and pointed to the ore car full of tak. "See what you can do about that bomb."

"Like what?" I asked.

Uncle Press started to run off, but turned back to us and shouted, "I don't know. Get rid of it. Dump it in the ocean. Just don't let the Bedoowan have it."

I watched as Uncle Press ran up the stairs. After a quick wave back to us, he disappeared over the lip of the stadium and was gone. I looked to the ore car, then to Loor.

"Is he crazy?" I said. "This is too heavy to carry up those stairs!"

Loor started grabbing the glaze stones from off the top and throwing them aside like they were common rocks. "Not if we make the load lighter," she said.

"And what if we slip and drop it down those stairs?" I countered. "It'll make just as big a bang now as before."

"Then we must be careful not to drop it," she shot back.

Yeah, no kidding. I walked over to the cart and tested the weight. It was heavy! It had four wheels that rolled on the rails down in the mines, and handles both front and back that were used to push or pull it. I didn't care how strong Loor was, the two of us were not going to lug this thing up the stadium stairs. I reached in and dug down beneath the glaze until I found the tak. It was soft, like clay. I was thinking maybe we could pull it apart into smaller pieces and take it up that way, rather than transport the whole thing at once. I scraped it with my finger and pulled out a small piece. For something so deadly, it looked pretty innocent. Like I wrote before, it was rust-colored and soft like Silly Putty. I easily rolled it into a marble-sized ball. The texture was kind of gritty and there was residue that stuck to my fingers as I rolled it.

"Are you going to help me?" asked Loor impatiently as she unloaded the glaze.

"I have an idea," I announced and ran toward the quig pen. Loor watched me as if I had lost my mind, but she needn't have worried. My plan didn't involve going back into quig world. No way. In fact, as an afterthought I stuck the little ball of tak into my pocket to free my hands and then closed the door to the pen just in case any more of those bad boys were wandering around inside. It was a smart thing to do, but it wasn't the main reason I went over there. I was looking for the water faucet where the Bedoowan knight filled the water bucket that he used to wash away the blood of the Milago miner. When I found it, I turned the handle so that water poured out slowly. I then checked my fingers to find that they were still covered with the rusty-colored tak residue. I stuck my fingers under the faucet, rubbed them together, and the tak dissolved! That was exactly what I hoped would happen. This stuff may be a powerful explosive, but it was still a natural mineral that would dissolve in water. Thank you, Mr. Gill, and eighth-grade Earth science. He thought I was asleep in class most of the time. I wasn't.

"What are you doing?" shouted Loor.

I quickly grabbed one of the wooden buckets that was near the faucet, filled one, and lugged it back to Loor and the ore car.

"We are wasting time, Pendragon," Loor said with growing impatience.

I ignored her and dumped the bucket of water into the ore car. Loor had this angry look on her face like I was being an idiot again. I stood back with the empty bucket and watched. In a few seconds my patience was rewarded. It was only a small drip, but the water had worked itself down through the tak and was running out between the wooden floorboards of the ore car. The water was rust-colored, which could mean only one thing . . . the tak could be dissolved!

"We don't have to lug this thing out," I announced. "We can dissolve the tak like dirt."

Loor stuck her finger under the drip of water and saw that it was indeed full of dissolved tak. She thought a moment, then said, "More water!"

She jumped to her feet and ran back to the faucet for another bucket. For the next ten minutes we ran back and forth between the faucet and the ore car, dumping water inside. Little by little, the tak turned into liquid and ran out of the car. When enough of the tak dissolved so that we could move it, we began taking turns pushing it around. My idea was to spread the tak around enough so that its power would be diluted all over the field. The rusty liquid ran out of the car, poured onto the field and sank down below the grass like some deadly fertilizer. I had no idea what kind of problems this would cause later on. For all I knew, once the tak dried this could be like a minefield. But I didn't care. The main thing was that the power of the huge bomb was gone forever.

Finally I took a look inside the ore car to see that most of the tak was dissolved away. There were still some remnants clinging to the wooden car, but there wasn't enough left to do any big damage. I guess you could say that we had success-fully "liquidated" the bomb. I looked to Loor and smiled.

"Or we could have tried carrying it out," I said with a touch of sarcasm.

I didn't get many chances to dig Loor, so I took them where I could. She looked as if she wanted to say something in return, but was having trouble finding the words. I expected her to point out how I had done something stupid after all.

"I am a warrior," she finally said. "I was raised to fight my enemies with force. That is not what you were taught."

Uh-oh. Here we go. I was sure she was about to tell me what a weenie I was and that we should have muscled the ore car out of the stadium.

"But maybe that is good," she went on. "Maybe that is why we are together. You are not a warrior, yet you have shown more bravery than any warrior I have known."

Whoa. That was out of left field! After getting slammed

by her at every turn, I wasn't expecting a compliment. I didn't know what to say.

I thought about what she said and realized that maybe she was right. I wasn't a fighter and wasn't planning on becoming one, so maybe our strengths complemented each other. I wrote to you before about the feeling I got that being here felt right. Well, as I stood there with Loor, I got the same feeling. The two of us being together felt right. We weren't exactly buddies, but maybe we were meant to be partners. It must have been hard for her to admit that I was her equal, at least when it came to the bravery department, and I wanted to say something back to her that let her know how great I thought she was. But I didn't get the chance. Before I could open my mouth, I saw something that I could barely believe.

"What is the trouble?" asked Loor.

All I could do was point. Standing in the royal box was Figgis, the little merchant of death who started this whole tak mess. What was he doing here? How did he get into the palace? Stranger still, he must have known what Rellin was trying to do with this bomb, so why did he hang around here knowing the whole place was going to blow up?

"This is strange," she said. "Why is he here?"

As if in answer, Figgis raised his hand to show us something he was holding. It was the yellow walkie-talkie that was taken from me in Queen Kagan's chambers. He held it up, and giggled.

"It is the talking toy," exclaimed Loor. "What is he doing with that?"

My heart sank. We had dodged a huge bullet, but here was another one aimed right at us. Loor looked at me and recognized how scared I was.

"Pendragon, what is the matter?" Loor shouted.

"The walkie-talkie works the same way the flashlight does," I answered. "It has a battery that gives off a charge of power."

"Could he use it to explode another bomb?" she asked nervously.

"Well, yeah," I answered soberly.

Now Loor looked sick as the reality of the situation hit her. "Do you think he has another bomb?" she asked soberly.

"I don't know," I answered. "But we better find out." I took a step toward the royal box and called out, "Figgis! We want to talk with you!"

In answer Figgis abruptly turned and ran back into the palace.

"C'mon!" I shouted and ran for the royal box.

Loor was right behind me. We both hit the stairs and ran up three at a time until we hit the royal box. Without hesitation we ran into the Bedoowan palace after the strange little man who was responsible for finding the power to destroy all of Denduron.

Outside of the palace the two armies were drawing closer. The Milago miners were making their way through the dense forest, while the Bedoowan knights massed along the far side of a giant, open field. This grassy, sloping field was where the long-awaited battle would take place. Behind the Bedoowan was nothing but ocean. Behind the Milago would be forest. Between them was a huge expanse of empty field with nothing to use for protection but sea grass. The Bedoowan knights knew what they were doing. They had trained to protect their palace from marauders. They lined up in rows with shield carriers first, followed by archers, followed by spear carriers on horseback. They were ready.

Alder later told me how he ran through the forest with the

miners, trying to get them to turn back. But no one listened. They were locked and loaded and primed for a fight. But when they got to the edge of the forest, the leader held up his hand and the miners stopped short of charging out into the open. It was a smart thing to do, for he saw something that the rest of the miners hadn't yet seen.

Standing across from them on the far side of this vast field were the Bedoowan knights. But they did not look like a straggle of injured survivors who were reeling from a devastating explosion. Just the opposite. There were more knights standing there than the Milago knew existed. They didn't look any worse for wear, either. They were strong and healthy and well armed. Obviously something had gone wrong. The explosion didn't do the damage they had hoped. This battle wasn't going to be the cakewalk they had anticipated. This was going to be a dogfight and they were going up against the best dogs in town.

The Milago leader held his army back, not entirely sure of what to do. The rest of the Milago miners had now seen the vast army of knights and it shook their confidence.

The only thing that Alder could do was watch, and pray.

When Loor and I ran into the palace, we found ourselves in Queen Kagan's empty chambers. We got our bearings, then dashed out into the corridor. I looked toward the stairs and caught a quick glimpse of Figgis scampering down.

"There!" I shouted and ran after him.

Loor was right behind me. We got to the stairs and started down. They were wide, spiraling stairs, and as we ran down we could see that Figgis was far below, headed for the lowest levels of the palace. We bounded down the stairs as fast as we could without taking a header and breaking our necks.

When we hit the bottom, I saw that my boom box was there, only it was in pieces. That's how the knights finally got it to stop playing. They smashed it. I guess no one knew how to use the on-off switch. Idiots. I had the presence of mind to dig through the debris for the batteries. It may have been too little too late, but at least nobody could use these batteries to blow anything up.

We both took a quick look around for Figgis and heard a familiar giggle coming from down the corridor. The thought came to me that he was playing with us. But it didn't matter. We had to stop him. So we took off down the corridor.

"He is going for the mines," she said. "He must know the secret entrance."

She was right. That's probably how he got into the palace in the first place. Since we knew the way, we didn't bother looking down every corridor for the little guy. We headed right for the kitchen, which led to the pantry, which led to the trapdoor and the tunnels that would drop us down into the secret passage of the Milago mine that stretched beneath the palace.

In the forest, the Milago leader didn't know what to do. This wasn't the way it was supposed to happen. They weren't supposed to fight the Bedoowan army at its best. Should he attack or retreat? His decision would clearly decide the future of his tribe. Luckily for him, the responsibility for making a decision was soon taken away from him. With a roar of excitement from the miners, he looked to see a familiar face making his way toward him through the crowd. It was Rellin. He was here to take charge.

The sight of their trusted leader sent a rumble of relief through the Milago miners . . . not to mention to the interim leader who no longer had to be in charge anymore. It must have been a stirring sight, seeing their leader walking confidently to the front of his troops to take command. He jumped on to a rock so that all the Milago could see him and announced, "My brave Milago brothers! Today is the day. Now is the time. This is where our slavery ends!"

The miners all gave a cheer. Rellin was stirring them up again.

"Bring the tak to bear!" he commanded and all of the miners who had the tak and slingshots came to the front of the group. "Are we prepared to take back our lives?"

Everyone let out a whooping cheer. They were no longer concerned about why he hadn't died. He was their inspirational leader, and they trusted him.

"Are we prepared to win our freedom?"

Another cheer.

"Are we prepared to make the Bedoowan pay for their crimes against us?"

That brought the biggest cheer of all. They were ready.

"Then do not stop until we have reached the throne room!"

That was it. The miners went nuts and the charge was on. With the tak throwers first, they charged out of the forest and onto the field to meet their enemy.

While this was going on, Loor and I dropped down the ladders into the Milago mine. No sooner did we hit the tunnel, than Loor stopped short, her ear to the air.

"Listen," she said.

I did, and after a second I heard what she was talking about. It was footsteps. Running footsteps. Figgis wasn't far away. But the strange thing was, they were coming from deeper in the tunnel. That didn't make sense because the tunnel didn't go on much farther. There was nothing beyond the end of this tunnel but a long drop to the sea. So where was that sound coming from?

Loor didn't stop to think, as usual. She headed deeper into the tunnel. Her senses told her that someone was back there running and she didn't bother to let logic stop her from following her instinct. All I could do was follow. We didn't go more than twenty yards before we came upon another offshoot from the main tunnel. It was a crudely dug side tunnel that was wide enough for one person to pass at a time. This is where Figgis went, so this is where we had to go too. As always, Loor went first. She ran into the tunnel, unafraid of what she might find. That was cool with me; she was the macho end of this duo, after all. Luckily the tunnel wasn't all that dark because there was enough light that seeped in from the main tunnel to let us see our way.

"I see the far end," Loor announced. "This tunnel connects with another tunnel."

I looked ahead and saw that she was right. This side tunnel connected with another large tunnel. But it soon proved to be more than just a shortcut. Before we reached the other end, the side tunnel grew wide and opened up into a large space. We stopped, trying to figure out why this cavern existed so deep inside the Milago mine. I took a step and felt something weird under my feet. It was a soft, springy sensation, like walking on tiny bits of rubber. I knelt down and scooped up a bit of the stuff to give it a close look. It had the feel of eraser dust. You know, the stuff you brush off your paper after erasing something. It didn't take me long to realize what it really was though, and my heart nearly stopped.

"What is it?" asked Loor.

"It . . . it's tak," I said with a dry mouth. "I think we just found out where Figgis got the tak. He mined it . . . from right here."

"That is right!" came a giggling voice from the tunnel ahead.

"Figgis!" shouted Loor and continued on to the end of the side tunnel.

I followed her out and into the wider tunnel on the far side. When I hit the intersection I saw that this next tunnel stretched out in two directions. Ore-car track was at our feet and an empty ore car sat on the tracks to our right. It was an ancient Milago mine tunnel. I looked at the floor and saw there was a lot more rusty tak dust coating everything. This must have been residue from when Figgis mined the stuff out of the rock. Like gold dust. A thin layer of the deadly stuff was everywhere. But there was something else strange about this place. It looked somehow familiar. The ore car, the opening to the side tunnel, the pile of rocks in front of the opening. I felt as if I'd been here before.

That's when my ring began to glow. I looked to Loor and she had already seen her own ring glowing. We had indeed been here before. This was the tunnel that held the gate to the flume. When we used the flume the other day, we had no idea that we were close to Figgis's source for tak. I looked to my left and sure enough, a few yards down the tunnel was the wooden door that led to the flume.

"Why does this whole setup give me the creeps?" I asked Loor.

She felt it too. Why would Figgis lead us down to the one place that he would want to keep secret? The answer came in the form of a rumble.

"What is that?" asked Loor nervously.

I listened. The rumble grew louder. It was either thunder, an earthquake, or . . .

"Cave-in!" I shouted.

I grabbed Loor's hand and ran along the track in the direction that would take us back to the main cavern of the mine. We passed the door to the flume and got only a few steps further when the ceiling in front of us collapsed! Tons of rock and gravel fell down, blocking our way out. My first thought was to go for the gate and jump into the flume, but we couldn't leave Denduron. Not now. So we ran back into the tunnel and dove into the side tunnel that led to Figgis's tak mine.

No sooner had we entered the tak mine than another cave-in sealed off the smaller tunnel ahead of us. Rocks tumbled down from the ceiling and poured into the small cavern. I took a few steps back and fell down on my butt. When I turned to get up, I came face to face with something that had tumbled down in front of me when the ceiling collapsed. It was a skeleton. I'm not ashamed to admit it; I screamed. Yes, I screamed like an idiot in a *Scooby Doo* cartoon. I quickly scrambled away and Loor helped me to my feet. The two of us stood there holding each other, not sure of what to do. It seemed as if the cave-in had stopped, at least for the time being.

Loor looked at the skeleton and said, "It must be a miner who was trapped here."

That made sense. But then I saw something that threw her theory out the window. I took a closer look at the skeleton. He wore rotted-out leather clothing that marked him as Milago. But there was something else, something unique that made me want to scream all over again. The corpse wore an eye patch. The cloth was shredded and dangled down from the empty socket, but it had definitely once been a patch. And that's not all. On each of his bony fingers was a braided green ring. I had seen this only once before and remembered it all too well. This wasn't any miner.

"It's Figgis," I said, trying not to sound too freaked out.

"That cannot be!" exclaimed Loor. "Unless we have been chasing a ghost."

Then a voice came from behind us. "I am afraid it is indeed Figgis."

Both Loor and I spun to see someone standing in the opening to the tak mine. It was *Figgis*! Huh? The guy looked pretty healthy for a, okay I'll say it, for a ghost.

"The poor little man died a few years ago," he said. "Such a tragedy. He set traps to protect his little find here. That's why the ceiling collapsed. He didn't want anybody else to steal it from him. He died setting one of those traps. So sad. Such a visionary, and so . . . dead."

My mind was not getting around any of this. We stood there staring at Figgis, uncomprehending.

"I see you have not figured this out yet," he said with a smug smile. "Let me make things easier for you." And then, the little man began to transform. I had seen this happen once before, in a lonely subway station in the Bronx. His hair grew long and his body grew back to its normal height of seven feet. His leather Milago clothes changed into an all-black suit, and his eyes flashed with icy blue intensity. Yes, we were looking at Saint Dane, and he had us trapped under a ton of rock with no escape.

"I told you, Pendragon," he said with a smile. "You can't beat me."

DENDURON

The Milago miners charged out of the forest. The attack was on.

The Bedoowan knights didn't budge. They wanted to see what these bold peasants had planned. The first line of miners stopped and loaded their slingshots with tak. On command they flung their explosives at the waiting Bedoowan. The small tak bombs flew across the battlefield and exploded on impact. But they had fallen far short of the front line of the Bedoowan defense. If they were going to do any damage, they were going to have to get closer, which meant they had to put themselves within range of the Bedoowan archers.

The Bedoowan on the other hand, were surprised by the explosions that blasted down in front of them. Except for the quig that had been blown to bits in the stadium, they had never witnessed anything like this. There was a movement along the lines to retreat, but the Bedoowan commander wouldn't let them budge. They were going to hold their ground. The Bedoowan commander sent a line of shield carriers to the front. These brave men stood in line like a barrier of steel and flesh to protect their comrades from the incoming missiles. Behind them, the archers stood ready to release their arrows as soon as the Milago miners were in range. This was going to get real ugly, real quick.

But I didn't know any of this until afterward. Right now I had my own problem to deal with, which was Saint Dane. There was no way out. We were trapped by two cave-ins that were caused by Figgis's booby traps. The only way out of this seemed to be through the flume. But it might as well have been a mile away because standing between us and the gate was Saint Dane.

"You brought the tak here, didn't you?" I spat at the guy.

"I did no such thing!" he said, acting all innocent. "Tak is natural to Denduron. Figgis discovered this vein several years ago."

He walked over to one of the walls and scraped off a layer of dirt with his hand. As the dirt fell away, I saw beneath it the familiar rusty red color of tak. I looked to Loor and for the first time since we met, she looked scared. That's because she realized, as I did, that this entire cavern was made of tak. The bomb we had dissolved in the stadium was like a fire-cracker compared to this cavern . . . and we were standing in the middle of it.

"Figgis thought the miners could use the tak to help them tunnel through the rock," Saint Dane explained. "It was noble of him, but he was a merchant and he thought like one. He wanted to help the miners, but he also wanted to make a profit."

The evil Traveler walked over to the skeleton that used to be Figgis and nudged the bones with his foot. "I can't say that I blame him, but his greed proved to be his undoing. He set traps all over this cavern to protect his precious find. Unfortunately one of them backfired."

He kicked Figgis's skull and it rolled away from the body and landed at our feet. I wanted to kick it back just to keep it away from me, but that would have been gross.

"So you came to Denduron and took his place," I said. "And you showed the Milago miners how to use tak as a weapon."

"Of that, I am guilty," he said with a proud smile.

"But we stopped you," Loor shot back at him. "Rellin did not use the bomb."

Saint Dane answered this with a laugh. I didn't like that. When bad guys laugh it means they know something you don't.

"But it is better this way," he said with smug authority. "If that bomb had blown up it would have taken much longer for the Milago to regroup. Now, once they have won their little war they will still be strong enough to begin their march across Denduron. I suppose I should thank you, Pendragon."

Oh, man, was it possible? By preventing that bomb from going off, did I make things worse? "And what if they don't win the war?" I asked. "What if the Bedoowan win?"

Saint Dane brushed more dirt off the walls, revealing more tak. "No matter," he said with a shrug. "There is an endless supply of tak. It may take time, but the Milago will come back. They will find new ways to use this lovely weapon. It is inevitable, Pendragon. This will soon become a territory at war. Denduron will fall. And when it does, it will be the beginning of the end of Halla."

Halla. There was that word again. This was all about Halla.

On the battlefield above, the Milago miners had crept closer to the Bedoowan knights. They were now within range to slingshot the tak into the front line of shield carriers. The frightened Bedoowans huddled beneath their shields as the tak bombs smashed into them. With small explosions the tak burst on impact against the shields and threw a blast of fire into the ranks. Several of the Bedoowan knights died right there. Others got smart and realized it wasn't a good thing to let the small rock bombs hit their shields. They began to dodge out of the way rather than shield themselves as the tak bombs rained down, setting off explosions that tore up the ground.

That's when the next line of Bedoowan knights began sending their arrows. They were too far away to take direct aim, so they arched their arrows high into the air toward the Milago. The black little streaks shot across the sky and rained down on the Milago silently. Some found their mark, others stuck harmlessly into the ground. But there were enough arrows in the air to prevent the Milago miners from flinging their tak uncontested.

Watching this all from a safe distance from the battlefield were the rest of the Bedoowans and the Novans. They had spread out along the grassy bluffs to witness the spectacle as if it were a show put on for their amusement. Children played, musicians performed, and food was passed around as though at some kind of summer festival. Queen Kagan was positioned in the center of it all and stood on her throne to get the best view possible.

In the Milago village Uncle Press had found Alder, and the two of them tried again to warn the villagers to hide in the mines. The villagers knew Uncle Press, so at least they didn't slam doors in his face. But time after time they got the same response. To a person, the villagers were prepared to do battle with the Bedoowan. It didn't matter if they were women or children or the elderly or the sick. None of them feared death, nor did they fear the Bedoowan. Their only fear was having to continue to live the horrible lives they had been born into. No, these people were not about to run and hide. If the Bedoowan knights got past the miners, they would be ready, and they would fight.

Frustrated, Uncle Press and Alder ran quickly to the battlefield. Arrows rained down on the Milago while tak bombs scattered the front lines of the Bedoowan. Uncle Press and Alder were stymied. They wanted the Milago to defeat the Bedoowan, but not with tak. The true enemy here was tak. But if they somehow convinced the Milago to stop using it, the miners would be overrun by the Bedoowan. It was a no-win situation.

And speaking of no-win situations, Saint Dane had just said something that scared me to death. He said that the fall of Denduron was the beginning of the end for Halla. Uncle Press said Halla was everything that existed. Every place, every territory, every time that ever was. If Saint Dane succeeded in destroying Halla, did that mean that the entire universe would be destroyed? The thought was too huge to comprehend.

"Why do you want to destroy Halla?" I asked.

Saint Dane laughed. Great, more laughing. I hated that.

"You are young, Pendragon," he said. "There is much you do not know. But I will say this: When Halla crumbles, I will be there to pick up the pieces."

That sounded ominous. "I don't believe you," I said. "How can one man control the destiny of the entire universe?"

Saint Dane ran his hand over the wall of tak. "It is like lining up dominos," he said. "Pushing over the first domino takes almost no effort, but when it falls it knocks down the next and the next and the next until before long there is nothing left but a pile of toys in complete disarray. The territory of Denduron is my first domino."

It was true. Denduron was only the beginning. Saint Dane would then turn to the next territory and the next. It would only be a matter of time before he worked his evil on Loor's home territory of Zadaa and set his sights on our home. On Second Earth.

"Your mother is dead," Saint Dane said to Loor. "But what of the rest of your family on Zadaa? And you, Pendragon, what of your family on Second Earth? And your friends, what are their names? Mark and Courtney? When the dominos fall, they will all be caught in the crush."

I wanted to scream. It was like he had read my mind. This guy *was* evil.

"But this does not have to be a tragedy," he said with an oily smile. "Think of it as an opportunity. You two are strong. You have powers that you cannot imagine. If you joined me, I would teach you how to use them. Fighting against me is impossible, but fighting with me can bring you untold rewards. You could protect your loved ones, and live to rule Halla beside me. It is a wonderful thing I am offering you."

On the battlefield above, things were getting worse. The Milago had been able to keep the Bedoowan back while suffering only minor casualties. The Bedoowan side of the field was a mess. There were fires burning everywhere and the tak had chewed up the ground. However, the Bedoowan casualties were very few. They had mostly managed to avoid the incoming tak. Now the Bedoowan commander realized that the incoming bombs were slowing down. The Milago were running out of their strange and horrible weapon.

Rellin watched the action from behind the spear carriers. His worst fears were coming true. The Milago had used up most of their tak bombs, yet the Bedoowan were still a mighty force. Soon they would be out of tak altogether and the Bedoowan would overrun them. Their only hope of victory was to strike while the Bedoowan knights were still back on their heels. Rellin needed to summon every bit of courage he had in order to do what must be done. He stood up behind his miners, grabbed a spear, and shouted, "Freedom!"

The miners screamed in defiance and ran across the field toward their enemy. The Bedoowan commander seemed stunned that these peasant miners would have the audacity to challenge his vaunted knights. But if a fight was what they wanted, he was willing to oblige. He motioned for his spear carriers on horseback to come forward. With a sweep of his hand, he sent the knights charging toward the oncoming Milago.

Alder and Uncle Press watched in horror as these two tribes ran to meet each other in the center of the field. Queen Kagan jumped up and down, giggling with delight. Only one thing was certain.

It was going to be bloody.

In the mine below, Saint Dane waited for our response to his offer. He had asked us to join him in his mad quest to control all that exists and threatened that our loved ones would die if we refused. It seemed as if we had run out of options. The guy scared the life out of me. I hated looking at him, so I looked down at the ground.

What I saw there started me thinking.

I saw rusty tak dust stuck to the Bedoowan shoes I had been wearing. I kept my head down and looked around the small cavern to see that tak dust was everywhere. It coated the floor and the walls and even seemed to hang in the air.

That's when I remembered something. It was something I had done a while ago without thinking. I didn't know it at the time, but it might turn out to be the key to saving Denduron. My mind raced. If I was going to make a move, it had to be now. I had no idea what was happening in the battlefield above, but after what Saint Dane had said, it really didn't matter. This wasn't about the Bedoowan or the Milago. This was about a horrible weapon that would change the course of a peaceful territory and send it to ruin. If anything must be stopped, it would have to be the supply of tak.

To be honest, it scared me to think about doing what I was about to do. But I didn't see any other choice. I wasn't even sure if it would work. I might end up looking like an idiot. No problem there, I was used to that. But if it did work, there was a good chance that Loor and I would die. Neither outcome was exactly a good one, but it was clear that I had to give it a try.

"Saint Dane," I said, trying to keep my voice from cracking with fear. "I believe you."

Loor shot me a surprised look. She didn't know where I was going with this . . . yet.

"I can't explain why we're Travelers, or how it's possible to travel through flumes, or how you can do the things you do, but I've seen enough to know that it's all real. I don't know if you have the power to bring down the universe, or Halla or whatever you call it, but I do believe that you can cause a hell of a lot of trouble. If toppling Denduron is the first part of your plan, then I can't let you do it."

I could feel Loor stiffen next to me. She knew I had something in mind and she wanted to be ready.

Saint Dane watched me with a smug smile and said, "And how do you plan to stop me?"

"I'm not," was my answer. "I'm going to stop the supply of tak."

That's when I reached into my pocket and pulled out the little ball of tak that I had taken out of the ore car in the stadium. I had put it into my pocket before closing the door to the quig pen. Now this little piece of explosive clay could be the only hope for Denduron. As I wrote before, I wasn't sure if this would work. But what I saw next made me think that it just might. For as soon as I pulled it out, I saw something that I didn't think was possible.

Saint Dane blinked.

The smug smile dropped off his face and I saw something in his eyes that made my heart leap. I saw fear. Up until then he had orchestrated everything that happened on Denduron. But things were about to change and he knew it. Seeing this in his eyes gave me a shot of confidence. I looked to Loor. She nodded. She knew what might happen to us, but she also knew that it was the only way. We were seconds away from salvation—or doomsday.

The battlefield above had erupted into a clash of bodies and clubs and horses and steel. The Milago were driven by their hatred and anger, the Bedoowan by their training and strength. It was going to be an even fight, which meant both sides were going to suffer huge casualties. The worst of the fighting was about to begin.

Saint Dane made a move to stop me. "No!" he shouted in panic.

But before he could take a second step, I threw my little

ball of tak down at the ground. There was an explosion. Not a big one, but big enough. The small ball of tak erupted and shot out a blast of flame. The explosion didn't do much damage, but that didn't matter. It was the flame I was counting on. That small, hot burst of fire ignited the tak dust on the floor. Instantly, the tiny little bits of tak began to burn. It looked like a Fourth of July sparkler on the floor of the cavern as the dust ignited and shot up into the air. But more important, the eruption began to spread. With each passing second the fizzing and popping circle of sparks grew larger. There was so much tak dust on the floor and in the air that this fire had plenty of fuel to burn.

Saint Dane jumped at the expanding ring of sparks and desperately tried to stamp it out with his feet.

"No! No!" he shouted at me in anger.

For all his ability to manipulate people and twist them into doing his dirty work, he was powerless against this simple, growing fire. There was an unlimited amount of fuel and as soon as it grew big enough, the sparkling ring of fire would ignite the large vein of tak that ran through the mine. Once that happened, well, we'd all find out soon enough.

Saint Dane gave up trying to stop it and shot me a look of hatred that froze the blood in my veins. "This isn't the end, Pendragon," he seethed.

"Don't be sad, Saint Dane," I said. "This is the way it was meant to be."

Saint Dane looked as if he were about to erupt with anger. His icy blue eyes flashed with hatred. I must have pushed a pretty raw button to get him that ticked off. Loor thought he was going to attack us because she took a threatening step toward him, daring him to charge. I think he might have done it too, but he took a quick look around at the rapidly growing fire and decided to back off.

"Until next time," he said, then turned and ran out into the Milago tunnel.

The sparkling ring of tak fire was growing larger by the second. It was like a fuse that couldn't be stopped as it got closer and closer to setting off the mother of all bombs. I had no idea how much time we had, but if we had any hope of surviving we had to get out of there.

"The flume!" I said and ran toward the tunnel. Loor was right after me. We hit the mine tunnel and ran straight for the gate that led to the flume. The wooden door was already open because Saint Dane had the same idea. As I was about to turn into the doorway I heard Saint Dane inside.

"Cloral!" he yelled into the flume.

We ran inside the gate in time to see the sparkling light that was Saint Dane disappear into the depths of the flume on his way to . . .

"What is Cloral?" I asked.

"It must be another territory," Loor answered.

"Let's not go there, okay?" I said. "We should go—" Before I had the chance to say another word, we both saw something in the flume. The sparkling lights and musical notes were heading our way. Was Saint Dane coming back? As the lights grew closer, I heard a sound that didn't make sense. It sounded like . . . water. We took a curious step closer to the flume and saw that it wasn't a Traveler headed our way at all. It was an actual rush of water coming through the flume. What was Saint Dane doing? Was he trying to put the fire out?

The answer was no. He was trying to prevent us from escaping through the flume. But it wasn't just water he was sending back. There was something *in* the water, and it had teeth. Swimming toward us through the flume was a giant shark! As impossible as it sounds, the thing must have been twenty feet long and was headed straight for us, jaws first. There was one other thing I remember: It had vicious, glowing yellow eyes.

We didn't have time to move and were both hit with the crushing wave of water. The force hit us so hard that it sent us both hurtling back out of the gate and slammed us against the far wall of the tunnel. That force of water was the only thing that saved us. If we had stayed at the mouth of the flume, we would have been rudely introduced to shark teeth. I got my head together, grabbed Loor and pulled her to the side just in time because the huge yellow-eyed shark was propelled out of the gate and it smashed, head first, into the far wall of the tunnel. It was now a fish out of water, literally. It squirmed and thrashed in the mine tunnel and its giant jaws bit at the air only a few feet from our heads. I tried to crawl away, but saw that Loor was unconscious. She must have smashed her head when she hit the wall. I grabbed hold of her and was able to drag her farther back into the tunnel and safety.

Did I say safety? We may have gotten out of range of the monster shark, but the fuse was still burning on the tak mine. We had nowhere to go. We couldn't get to the flume because there was three thousand pounds of thrashing shark in the way. We couldn't get back through the small tunnel to the Bedoowan castle because of the cave-in. The only place we could go was deeper into the mine. To make things worse, if that was possible, Loor was unconscious.

I tried to shake her awake, but it was no go. Her lights were out and I was looking down at a deadweight. It's amazing what adrenaline will do, because I stood up and was actually able to pick her up and get her on my back in a fireman's carry. I had no idea how much time we had left, but moving slowly was not an option. I tried to run with her, but it was hard. I couldn't get very far this way. We got past the entrance to the tak mine and I glanced in to see that the entire floor was ablaze. The place looked alive with mad fireflies as the tak dust sputtered and burned. I didn't take the time to stop and admire it though. I had to get us farther into the mine.

That's when I saw something that could help. It was the wooden ore car. If this thing still moved I could put Loor inside and push her the way Alder had pushed us before. With Loor still on my back I gave the car a kick. It moved! Yes! Without worrying about being gentle, I dumped Loor into the empty car. I didn't think she'd mind a few bruises under the circumstances. I quickly jumped to the back of the car and pushed. It moved slowly at first, but with each turn of the small wheels it picked up speed. I kept both hands on the car while pumping my legs like a football lineman hitting a blocking sled. I went from a crawl, to a walk, to a jog, and finally to a run. I had no idea where this tunnel would lead, but we were on our way.

The thought flashed through my head that we might hit a piece of damaged track that would send the car crashing into the wall. I also feared that the tunnel would reach a dead end that we'd hit at full speed. That would hurt. Or a wheel could fall off. Or . . . or . . . I thought of a million other things that could derail our escape, but none of them mattered. This trip wasn't about caution, it was about speed. If we had any hope of surviving, we had to get as far away from that burning vein of tak as possible.

And then I heard it. It started as a rumble and quickly grew like an earthquake. It felt like a freight train was barreling up from behind, but I knew what it was. The burning dust had finally reached the large deposit of tak. The chain reaction had begun. The rumble was actually a series of small explosions, and those small explosions would set off bigger explosions. And bigger and bigger until . . . well, there would be a very big bang. I didn't stop to think about it. If anything it made me push harder. I could feel the ground shudder. The finale of this baby was going to be a thousand on the Richter scale.

On the battlefield the miners and the knights felt it too. Alder described it as the ground beginning to move under his feet. The fighting continued until they realized the shaking wasn't going to stop. One by one they dropped their weapons and backed away from each other. There was now a more frightening enemy.

Queen Kagan stood on her throne and threw a fit because the fighting had ended. Before she had the chance to order anyone to continue the battle, the ground shook and knocked her throne over. She tumbled down right along with it, and lay flat on the ground, scared to death. The rest of the Bedoowans and the Novans did the same thing. They all fell to the ground in fear. The fun and games were over.

Uncle Press and Alder didn't move. They knew it was futile to seek shelter, so they stood together and waited for the end. They weren't going to have to wait long.

The rumbling grew louder. It began to sound more like deep, booming explosions. As I pushed the cart with every bit of energy I had, I began to feel heat at my back. The tak mine was probably a blast furnace by now. I'm sure the shark was already roasted. It wouldn't be long before the whole mine blew.

Up ahead the tunnel was growing brighter. We were reaching the end, but I had no idea what that meant because I was crouched down behind the ore car pushing for all I was worth. Still, whatever was up there meant we had a shot at getting out, so I dug down even deeper and pumped my legs even harder. The faster we moved, the brighter the tunnel became. We were definitely nearing the end. Now the tunnel was shaking so violently that I was afraid it would throw the ore car off the track. If we didn't get to the end soon, it would definitely be the end for us.

I don't know why I realized what was about to happen when I did, but I did. It hit me about three seconds beforehand. Maybe it was some kind of survival instinct, but whatever it was, those few seconds prepared me. As we were hurtling down that tunnel with the force of the exploding tak at my back, I remembered about the layout of the mines. We were flying along a track that ran parallel to the tunnel under the Bedoowan palace. I knew where that tunnel ended, and that meant this tunnel would end the same way. This was a ventilation tunnel that led to the ocean bluffs. We were about to be launched out of the end where there was nothing waiting for us but a long drop to the sea.

And that's exactly what happened. Without breaking stride I pushed the ore cart off the end. One second I was running, the next second we were falling. I tumbled out of control, not knowing which way was up. I was desperate to see the water and get my body in a position to take the impact. If I hit head first, I'd break my neck. So I corkscrewed into a position to avoid that. Splashdown was a second away. Believe it or not, the last thought I had before hitting the water was, "Loor can't swim!"

There's only one word I can use to describe the feeling of hitting the water at that speed. Rude. It was just plain rude. I was able to twist myself around so I hit on my side rather than my head, but the impact still knocked the breath out of me. What a jolt! It was worse than when I beefed it off the sled into the snow after the crazy sleigh ride down the mountain. But I didn't lose consciousness this time. Good thing. I didn't want to drown. After all we'd been through, that wouldn't be fair. I came to the surface and looked back up at the opening to the mine. The fall was a big one, maybe thirty feet. But that's not what concerned me at the moment because I also saw that the entire wall of bluffs was shaking. Remember, these were cliffs. It was like looking up at a wall of skyscrapers. If this thing came down, we'd be buried.

I looked around quickly and was relieved to see that Loor was floating near me. She must've fallen out on the way down. I swam to her and listened to her breathing. She was alive, but I didn't know how badly she was hurt. All I wanted to do was swim as far away from the bluffs as possible. I also found the wooden ore car that had been our transportation out of there. It was floating right next to us. Luckily it hadn't hit either of us when we fell. So I got Loor on her back, brought her over to the floating ore car and grabbed on. We had a better chance of surviving with this lifeboat than by my swimming skills alone. I wasn't sure what direction to go in, but I soon realized I didn't have a choice. There was a swift current running parallel to the shore that swept us along. We weren't moving farther out into the ocean, but we were moving steadily away from the mines. It was a good thing too because that's when it happened.

Ignition.

The whole world exploded. The sound was like a deep, powerful growl from a giant demon trapped below ground and struggling to force its way to the surface. A second later, the ventilation shafts along the bluffs blew out, spewing huge blasts of flame that shot over our heads like rocket engines on full power. There must have been twenty openings, all breathing fire that streamed a hundred yards out over the ocean. The water began to churn and roil. It took everything I had to keep Loor and myself afloat. The bluffs themselves seemed to be out of focus. But that was because they were shuddering from an immense force that was tearing them apart from within. My thoughts went to Uncle Press and to Alder. They were up there somewhere. If the top blew off like a monster volcano, they'd be done.

Mark, Courtney, what I saw then will haunt me until the day I die. The eruption had begun a good thirty seconds before, but the powerful flames continued to jet from the holes in the bluff with incredible intensity. I allowed myself one small bit of hope that most of the force from the exploding tak would be funneled out through these openings. Maybe these man-made openings would act like release valves to get rid of the force of the explosion before it destroyed the land above, and every living thing on it.

That's when I heard the sound.

It was different than the rumble from the explosions. It sounded more like something was cracking. If you've ever heard the sound that a big tree makes in its last moments as it falls to a lumberjack's ax, that was what it sounded like. It's a horrible, screeching sound as the tree tries to hold on to the last sinews of its trunk. That high-pitched tearing sound was what I now heard, only multiplied by about a million.

I looked up to my left to see where the sound was coming

from. Imagine a huge, five-story castle carved into the bluffs. That was the Bedoowan palace, and it was about to fall down. The horrible creaking sounds were the palace's last desperate gasp at trying to hang on to its perch. But it was no use. The force of the exploding tak was tearing it apart. Cracks appeared like spiderwebs all over the stone castle. For a moment I thought it would dissolve into a billion pieces. But with one last groan the giant palace pulled free of the bluff and slowly began to lean over. In a final thunderous crack, the palace let go and toppled into the sea with a monstrous splash.

If the swift current had been running the other way, Loor and I would have been right under it. And though we were clear of the tumbling palace, we weren't safe yet. When the huge building hit, it created a monster surge of water that was headed right for us. If we didn't ride this thing, we'd drown for sure. So I faced the oncoming rush, prepared to ride it like a wave. We both rose with the huge swell and came down on the other side safely. Unlike regular wave sets, there was no second wave to worry about. This was a one-time phenomenon, and we had survived it.

Once the immediate danger had past, I looked at the castle. Or should I say, at what was left of it. The giant structure had hit the water and rolled over. One whole side was above water. I looked up to the bluffs to see a gaping scar that used to be the palace. The only thing left was the heavy columns it had been built upon.

I then realized that the flames had stopped shooting out of the mine airshafts. The rumbling had stopped too. The explosion was over—and we were still alive! Now all we had to do was get to shore. I tried to push the ore car along, but that was more trouble than it was worth. So I kicked the car away, but not without a nod of gratitude, for it had saved our lives.

It didn't take long for me to get Loor to shore. When I got us close enough for my feet to touch sand, I stood up and put her on my back with a fireman's carry again. It wasn't easy. My adrenaline surge was gone, and along with it, most of my strength. So after a difficult struggle I fell to my knees and slid Loor off of me onto the sand.

Then I collapsed. I figured that as soon as I got my breath and Loor woke up, we'd make our way up the bluffs to find Uncle Press and Alder. I feared for what we would find up there, but didn't have the energy left to worry. I wanted to enjoy being alive for a few moments, so I laid down on the sand, closed my eyes and crashed.

I think I had earned it.

DENDURON

I probably would have slept on that beach for weeks if I hadn't been gently nudged awake by something tapping at my foot. As I slowly pulled out of slumberland, I remembered that giant freakin' shark in the flume. I felt the tapping on my foot again and somehow made the connection between that feeling and the shark. Suddenly I was convinced that the shark had survived and was getting ready to bite off my feet. So I yelped and jumped up while pulling my legs closer for protection.

Of course it wasn't the shark. It was Loor. She was awake and trying to rouse me. She hadn't expected my dramatic reaction though, and when I jumped, she did too.

"I am sorry, Pendragon," she said sheepishly. "I did not know you were ticklish."

Ticklish? I was too embarrassed to tell her why I really jumped. "No problem," I said. "How do you feel?"

She rubbed the nasty black and blue mark on her forehead and grimaced.

"My head does not hurt as much as my pride," she said.

"What do you remember?" I asked.

"There was something coming at us from the flume, but what I remember does not make sense."

"Yeah, it does," I said. "It was a shark. Saint Dane didn't want us to follow him."

Loor thought about this for a moment. I think she was hoping that her memory was a bad dream. "After that I do not remember much," she continued. "But I do have memories of you carrying me. Was that a dream?"

"No, it wasn't," I said.

Loor frowned. At some point I would give her all the gory details of our escape, but now wasn't the time. Loor was a proud warrior. It hurt her ego that it took a weakling like me to save her. I didn't need to rub salt in the wound. Not yet anyway. Believe me, at some point I was going to get mileage out of this, but not now.

"You continue to surprise me, Pendragon," she said. "You have proven yourself to be brave and clever, and now it seems you react as a warrior would after all." She paused, and then said, "Thank you."

She had just given me the highest praise she was capable of. In her mind I was worthy of being elevated to the lofty status of warrior. I wasn't sure I agreed with her though. I was no warrior. Everything I did was out of total panic. I never felt as if I had a choice. In fact, I'd just as soon she didn't consider me a warrior because I didn't want her to expect any more heroics. As far as I was concerned, my Indiana Jones days were over. But I couldn't say that so I gave her the simplest, best response possible.

"You're welcome."

I wondered if she had also forgiven me for the death of her mother, but I wasn't about to go there. Loor looked out toward the water. The Bedoowan palace was a giant wreck that barely poked above the surface. Small waves lapped over it and a few seagulls explored its walls. In time the sea would eat away the stone and this mighty symbol of Bedoowan power would turn to sand. But right now it served as a reminder of the fall of the mighty Bedoowan. It was a perfect monument to their destruction.

"Do you think many Bedoowan died?" asked Loor.

"I don't know," was my answer. "I think most of them left to watch the battle. They're going to get a big surprise when they go back home though."

"It is sad," Loor said.

She was right. The Bedoowan were a pretty advanced culture for this place. They could have used their knowledge to improve all of Denduron, but instead they chose to use their power and knowledge to enslave others. The truth was, none of this would have happened if the Bedoowan hadn't abused the Milago. Saint Dane may have pushed it along, but the Bedoowan were already on the path. They had brought this on themselves.

"What of the tak mine?" Loor asked.

"It was a hell of a show," I said. "I'll bet that every ounce of tak was blown away. I don't think we have to worry about the Milago using it anymore."

Loor then turned and looked me right in the eye. "If the explosion did this to the palace," she said soberly, "then what of the Milago village?"

That was a good question. My thoughts went immediately to Uncle Press and to Alder. Had they survived? I looked up toward the towering bluffs.

"We've got to climb up," I said, not really wanting to.

We walked to the bluffs and searched for the best way up. This was going to be tough. It was steep and treacherous.

"I can climb rock," suggested Loor. "I will braid a rope

with vines and we will tie ourselves together for safety. It will be dangerous, but we can make it."

"That sounds good," I said while slowly scanning the bluffs. "Or we could take that path over there."

Loor looked to the path I was pointing to. It was narrow and there were dozens of switchbacks because it was so steep, but it was definitely a path.

"Oh," said Loor. "That could work too."

"C'mon," I said with a smile, and started for the path. Loor followed silently.

The hike up wasn't horrible. The switchbacks kept the path from getting too steep, but made the trek very long. We didn't talk much as we climbed. I can't speak for Loor, but the closer we got to the top, the more I dreaded what we might find. The last we saw of the Bedoowan and the Milago they were headed for battle. Was the fight over? Did one tribe win? Or would we arrive at the summit to find the tak explosion had created a burned out hole that looked like the bottom of a volcano? I tried to put the worst of those thoughts out of my mind. We would learn the truth soon enough.

When we were nearly on the top, I stopped and looked at Loor. I felt that she was just as worried about what we would find as I was. Neither of us said it, but we both wanted to wait one more second before having to deal with whatever horror was waiting there. After a few moments Loor took a deep breath and nodded. I nodded in agreement and the two of us climbed the last few yards to the summit of the bluffs.

What we saw on top was nothing like I had imagined. First off, it looked as if the surface had remained relatively intact after the tak explosion. There was no gaping volcano-like hole. That was good. Maybe the mine vents channeled away most of the power of the tak explosion after all.

But still, things had changed. It looked as if all the violent action from the explosion took place underground, and the result on the surface was like a huge earthquake had hit. What had once been relatively flat land now looked like a roller coaster of mounds and depressions. The large, flat battlefield of sea grass where the Milago and the Bedoowan fought had been torn apart. Huge boulders had forced their way up from underground and gaping holes had opened up elsewhere. The tak explosion had dramatically torn the terrain apart, changing it forever.

"We should get to the Milago village," I said.

The two of us walked cautiously back the way we knew would bring us to the village as quickly as possible. Though the terrain had become a tumultuous mess, there was something else that stood out even more dramatically. It was the people. There were hundreds of people wandering around in a daze. As we walked toward the village we saw Bedoowans and Novans and knights and miners. They all seemed to drift about in the same stunned haze. No one cared that they were among the enemy, either. Knights and miners passed each other without so much as a second glance. No one spoke, no one fought, no one was afraid. Everyone was just . . . stunned.

There were bodies, too. I didn't know if they were the victims of the tak explosion or the battle. They were being carried off the battlefield and laid next to each other. It didn't matter if they were Bedoowan or Milago, they were laid side by side. As horrible as this was, I had feared there would be way more bodies than this. Between the battle and the tak explosion, I expected everyone to be wiped out. But it now seemed as though most everyone survived. Only a few unlucky victims lay next to each other beside the battlefield.

Loor and I watched this strange scene silently as we made our way toward the village. We looked for the path that would lead us through the woods, but the path was gone. Most of the woods were gone too. Hundreds of trees had fallen and were piled up like pickup sticks. Finding our way through this maze of trees was tricky.

Then I saw something that made me stop and stare. An injured miner was sitting near the stump of a fallen tree. His head was bleeding and he had to lean against the stump for support. A woman knelt beside him, tending to his wounds. She had a bucket of water and some rags. She dipped the cloth into the water and gently dabbed at the miner's wound to clean it. She wasn't rough, she wasn't in a hurry. Her actions looked like a mother taking care of her child. Given all that had happened you wouldn't think this scene was out of the ordinary, but it was. That's because the woman taking care of the Milago miner was a Bedoowan.

"I do not understand," said Loor. "They are enemies."

"Maybe they found a common enemy," was my reply.

We picked our way through the toppled forest and found the Milago village. The place was a mess. Many huts were still standing, but most of them were badly damaged. Some were nothing more than a pile of rubble. The path that led through the village was now a mass of ruts, rocks, and rubble. I looked to the center of the village and to the platform where the Transfer ceremonies took place. It was destroyed. The large stone foundation was still there, but it was now scorched black. The platform was gone. I was about to suggest we look for Alder and Uncle Press when we heard a familiar voice.

"Loor! Pendragon!"

It was Alder. He was alive! The big bumbling knight came bounding toward us like a happy puppy. In his excitement he tripped over a rock and stumbled, and we caught him before he did a complete face plant. The catch turned into a hug for all of us.

"I feared you were dead!" he exclaimed. "How did you escape from the palace?"

"Long story," I answered. "What happened up here?"

"It was unbelievable!" he shouted. The guy was totally charged. "There was a battle. The Milago tried to defeat the Bedoowan with tak, but the tak ran out so the Milago charged and the two sides clashed and . . . and . . . that's when it happened!"

"What?" asked Loor, though she had a good idea what the answer was.

"The ground came to life!" he shouted. "The earth began to move like the sea! The Milago and the Bedoowan stopped fighting and turned to run, but there was nowhere to go! Trees began to topple and huts fell and the sound . . . the sound was like thunder under the ground. And then came the fire—"

He pointed at the charred remains of the platform in the center of the village. "Giant pillars of fire shot from the openings to the mines! The flames were like water geysers that shot high into the sky. And then . . . it was over."

Alder fell silent, letting us get our heads around all that he had said. After a moment he asked, "And where were you when this all happened?"

I looked to Loor and she gave me a shrug. That meant she wanted me to answer.

"Well," I said. "We blew up the tak mine. I think that might have had a little something to do with all the excitement."

Alder stared at us with his mouth open in disbelief. He was having trouble processing the information.

"Close your mouth," I said. "Where's Uncle Press?"

"Uhhh, Press," he said, snapping back to reality. "Right. Follow me."

Alder stumbled off and led us through the remains of the Milago village. As we approached a hut that was still fairly intact, Alder gave us the "shh" signal. Whatever we were going to see, he didn't want us to be disruptive. He stayed close to the wall and peered around the corner. Loor and I joined him and looked around the corner as well.

Several yards ahead was the hut that had once been Rellin's. I remembered it because I had been there when he asked me to go back home and get more batteries. But the walls of the hut were gone. It was bizarre. There were people inside who acted as if they were in the hut, but they were really outside and . . . well, you get the picture. There were three people who looked to be having a heart-to-heart meeting. I'm thrilled to say that one of them was Uncle Press. He was alive and looking fine. I wanted to shout to him, but I realized he was in the middle of something heavy, so I bit my tongue.

The second person I saw was Rellin. He looked like he had been through a war, which, in fact, he had. His leather clothes were in shreds and his bandaged arm was caked with dried blood, but he was alive. It was the third person in the hut that was the shocker.

It was Queen Kagan. The woman sat on the floor, hugging her knees to her chest, crying. I swear, she was crying like a two-year-old. I couldn't hear what they were saying, but it looked as if Rellin was speaking to her softly, like a father might speak to a sad child. Uncle Press wasn't saying anything. My guess was that he was there to act as a neutral peacemaker.

It was then that Uncle Press saw us and broke out in a big grin. He excused himself and ran to us. He threw his arms around me like a big old bear and laughed like it was

Christmas. I think he was even crying a little. To be honest, it made me laugh and cry a little bit too. How's that for a couple of tough-ass Travelers to behave? He pulled us back around to the other side of the hut so we wouldn't disturb Rellin and Queen Kagan, then threw his arm around Loor as well. I hadn't seen Uncle Press act like that in forever. For the first time since this adventure began, he was my old Uncle Press again. It was good to have him back. He then pulled away and gave us both a good hard look.

"What?" I finally said.

"Was it you?" he asked. "I mean, all this?" He motioned around to the destruction of the Milago village and I knew exactly what he meant. I looked to Loor. She shrugged, which was becoming our signal that she wanted me to do the talking.

"Well," I said. "Yeah."

Uncle Press burst out laughing. "I told you to get rid of the bomb, not set it off underground!"

"We didn't," I said, and gave him a quick rundown as to what happened from the time he left us in the Bedoowan stadium. Though everything I told him was the absolute truth, I have to admit that it sounded pretty fantastic. I think the most amazing fact of all was that all of this destruction started when I threw down a pea-sized marble of tak. Talk about knocking over the first domino. Wow.

Uncle Press listened closely. So did Alder. I didn't think it was possible, but I believe that the story of our adventure in the tak mine shocked my uncle. I knew it stunned Alder; he still couldn't close his mouth.

"What about Saint Dane?" Uncle Press asked.

"Gone," I answered. "He jumped into the flume. We would have followed him except he sent back this giant monster shark to stop us. It worked."

"Monster shark? That means he's on Cloral," said Uncle Press thoughtfully.

"Exactly!" I exclaimed. "How did you know?"

"Because the quigs on Cloral are giant monster sharks," was his simple answer.

Of course! I should have known! Quigs on Second Earth are monster dogs, quigs on Denduron are monster bears, and quigs on Cloral are monster sharks. It was so simple. Everybody knew that. Mental note to self: Stay away from Cloral.

"What's going on over there?" I asked, referring to the meeting with Queen Kagan and Rellin. I was tired of thinking about quigs, no matter what form they took.

We all looked back around the corner to see the two leaders were still in deep conversation.

"You're looking at two people who are very frightened," Uncle Press said. "They both got a glimpse of the apocalypse. Rellin came close to losing every last one of the Milago and Queen Kagan saw her palace fall into the sea. There's nothing left of their worlds, except for their people."

"What are they talking about?" asked Loor.

"A lot of things," answered Uncle Press. "But the bottom line is, they're talking about how to survive, together."

A few hours ago the idea of the Milago and the Bedoowan living together in cooperation was a joke. They had centuries of baggage to deal with. That kind of thing doesn't go away in an afternoon. But then I thought back to the Milago miner who was being cared for by the Bedoowan woman. They were still people, after all. And since the palace had been destroyed, they were pretty much in the same dire situation. Their best chance of survival was to help each other. It seemed like a lot to ask of mortal enemies, but I guess a cataclysmic event that nearly destroys every living thing in sight will make you rethink your priorities.

"They have a lot to offer each other," added Uncle Press. "The Bedoowan have an advanced knowledge of engineering and chemistry that can help bring the Milago out of the stone age. The Milago are farmers and builders. Now they can finally get something back for their hard work."

"What about the mines?" asked Alder.

"The mines are gone," answered Uncle Press. "When the tak blew, the mines collapsed. It would take decades to get back to where they were. It's not worth it. The Milago are out of the mining business . . . for good."

"That means no more glaze," I added.

"Yeah, no more glaze," said Uncle Press. "The Bedoowan used glaze to trade with other tribes. Now they'll have to be more self-sufficient."

"How do the Novans fit into all this?" I asked.

"They can go back to their own tribe," said Uncle Press. "Or they can stay and help rebuild. It's their choice, but I think they'll stay."

"What if the Milago try to use tak again?" asked Alder. "That is what Saint Dane wanted, is it not?"

"There *is* no more tak," I said with authority. "Rellin couldn't get his hands on any even if he wanted to."

"Rellin is a good man," Uncle Press said sharply. "But he was blinded by his concern for his people. Now he can channel that energy into something more constructive. He's going to be a great leader. But he's going to have his hands full with Queen Kagan. She's a piece of work."

As if he knew we were talking about him, Rellin looked up to us. We made eye contact and Rellin smiled. That one little smile spoke volumes. He had been humbled, and though he looked tired, he also seemed to be at peace. There was a huge task in front of him, but he was the right man for the job.

"There are no guarantees," said Uncle Press. "These people have to work through centuries of hatred and mistrust. But at least now they've got a shot at building a society that can benefit everyone. It's not often that you get a second chance."

As I looked around the ruined Milago village it was hard to comprehend that the best thing that could have happened to these people was the near-destruction of their world. But maybe Uncle Press was right. Maybe the only way they could change was to clean the slate and start over. They were certainly going to get that chance. I truly hoped that they'd make the most of it.

"I'm hungry!" announced Uncle Press. "Loor, could you and Alder head over to the hospital hut? They've set up an emergency supply station there."

Alder and Loor quickly left us to search for some food. But I don't think Uncle Press was really interested in eating. I think he wanted to talk to me alone.

"Let's walk," he said. The two of us left Queen Kagan and Rellin to their discussion and walked through the Milago village.

"How do you feel, Bobby?" he asked me.

Now there was a simple question that didn't have a simple answer. How did I feel? I felt a million different ways. I felt tired. I felt sore from my escape with Loor and our plummet into the sea. I felt proud of myself for having kept my head on straight when things were crashing down around me.

I felt as if I learned a few things. I learned that it's sometimes okay to think like a weenie, so long as you don't *act* like one—at least not all the time. I learned that it's okay to be wrong, as long as you can admit it and are willing to listen to those who may know better.

I also felt sad. Sad for Osa, Loor's wonderful mother. She was someone I wish I had gotten to know better. And I felt sad for Loor, who lost her. I also felt sad for the others who lost their lives here as well. There was so much I had seen over these few days and not all of it was good. I saw the horrible way that people could treat each other. That may be the saddest thing of all. I saw greed and anger and murder and a total lack of concern for human life. It was the wicked side of the human soul that I saw here on Denduron and it saddened me to know that such a dark place existed.

How did I feel? I was frightened of Saint Dane. Not because I thought he would come after me or anything, but scared of what one man was capable of. He used his evil influence to manipulate people into doing horrible deeds. His power nearly brought about the destruction of an entire world. I feared that he might try again elsewhere and hoped that by stopping him here, his plan would go no further. But what I was mostly scared of, was being a Traveler. I didn't want the responsibility. I mean, I'm just a kid. If there is something that truly scares me, it's my own future.

How did I feel? I also felt a little glad. I was glad that the people of Denduron were going to get a second chance. I was proud of Uncle Press. I wasn't entirely sure of what his deal was, but he cared enough to help bring about the resurrection of a society headed for ruin. I was also glad that I met the people I did. Alder had a good heart and I'll always remember him as a friend. Rellin may have been misguided, but what he did he did for the good of his people and I respected that. Now he has the chance to help them in a more positive way. I'm glad that I met Osa. I don't think I will ever forget her calm wisdom and I hope that some of it rubbed off on me. I was glad that I had good friends like you two, Mark and

Courtney. You helped me when I needed it most and I will forever be in your debt.

But I think I was mostly glad that I met Loor. She was fiercely loyal and willing to put her life on the line for what she believed. She was brave and caring and smart and beautiful as all hell. But beyond that, there was something about Loor for which I couldn't even begin to thank her. When this adventure fades in my memory, and it will, I will still be grateful to her for having pushed me to think outside of my own little world, and recognize my own strength.

So how did I feel? It was a complex question, but I had a simple answer.

"Uncle Press," I said, "I feel like I want to go home."

He was about to argue with me, but I cut him off.

"No," I said. "When you asked me to come with you, you said there were people who needed our help. I did everything you asked me to do. Now I want to go home."

He didn't even try to argue. How could he? "Okay, Bobby," he said warmly. "You're right. I am more proud of you than I can begin to say. Tomorrow, I'll take you home."

Now, *that's* what I wanted to hear! And that's what brought me to the place where I am right now, writing my final journal. We're spending the night in the hospital hut. Tomorrow we're going to make the long trek back up the mountain to the flume. Unfortunately the gate that was in the mines is now buried under a million tons of rock. Uncle Press assures me that the climb won't be hard. We will borrow some horses from the Bedoowan and take along a few whistles in case we run into any rogue quigs.

Alder and Loor are with me and they, too, are writing their journals. Alder filled me in on all that had happened during the battle, so that is how I know. I'm not going to send this journal to you through the ring. My plan is to hand it to you guys myself. I'm looking forward to seeing the expressions on your faces when I show up.

I'm also looking forward to seeing my family again. I'm not sure what to tell them, but I'll figure something out. I wonder if Marley misses me as much as I miss her?

Well guys, this is the last time I'm going to be writing to you. Thank you for reading. Thank you for being my friends. Tomorrow I'm going to leave Denduron for the final time. I can't wait to get home.

END OF JOURNAL #4

☢ SECOND EARTH ☢

Mark finished reading the pages before Courtney did, but didn't move until she looked up. They both looked at Bobby, who was lying on Mark's bed. They wanted to talk to him, but they wouldn't dare wake him up because he needed the rest. It was a strange feeling. This was their friend. They had known each other since they were little. Things were different now. Yes, this was still Bobby, but he wasn't the same Bobby who had kissed Courtney only a few days before. Could things go back to the way they were?

"I'm awake," Bobby said softly.

Mark and Courtney jumped up and went to him. Courtney sat on the edge of the bed. Mark paced.

"So I guess you got back to the flume on the mountain okay," said Courtney.

Bobby sat up, but it was a struggle. Obviously he was sore. Not hurt, just sore.

"Yeah, we got some Bedoowan horses and they took us most of the way."

"What about the quigs?" asked Mark.

"They didn't show, but I think that was because of the nasty ice storm." He pointed to the small cuts on his face. "The wind was blowing hard. It was like being cut by flying needles. Basically, it sucked. Sorry if I messed up your pillows."

"It's cool," said Mark. He meant it too.

"Who came back with you?" asked Courtney. "Uncle Press?"

"Yeah," answered Bobby. "But you know something weird? When we got to that subway station, his motorcycle was waiting for us right where he left it. The helmets, too. How strange is that?"

It was strange indeed, because when Mark and Courtney went to that station the motorcycle wasn't there. Someone must have been keeping it, waiting for Press's return.

Mark said, "Yeah, that's strange." He held up Bobby's last journal and added, "But you want to talk about strange?"

They all stared at the parchment pages, then burst out laughing. Mark was right. Compared to what Bobby had done on Denduron, a motorcycle mysteriously disappearing and reappearing was pretty low on the "strange" scale.

It felt good for Bobby to laugh and to be with his friends, yet he had the same awkward feeling that bothered both Courtney and Mark. A lot had happened. He was a different guy. Could he go back and pick up his life where he left off?

"What about Loor?" asked Courtney. "Did she stay on Denduron?"

Mark thought he caught a touch of jealousy in her voice, but he decided not to point it out.

Bobby stopped laughing. Courtney had touched a raw nerve. "She climbed with us to the top of the mountain," he said softly. "But when we got into the cave where the gate was, she just kept walking and jumped into the flume. No good-byes. No see ya around. No gee it's been swell. Nothing. I mean, it's not like we'd become best friends or anything, but we'd been through a lot. There were some things I wanted to say."

Obviously this hurt Bobby. He had grown to like Loor, but it didn't seem as if Loor cared about or liked him the same way. There was a long moment of awkward silence. Then Mark raised the key issue that was on everyone's mind.

"Bobby," he said tentatively. "There's some crazy stuff in your journals. The deal with the Milago and the Bedoowan is only part of it. What about this Traveler stuff; and flumes that shoot you between times and places; and people who live on territories all over the universe; and Halla? What is Halla? How can every *place* and every *thing* and every *time* still exist? And who is this Saint Dane dude? Is he gonna show up here someday and do what he did on Denduron? The stuff you wrote tears apart everything we know about how things work and I gotta tell you, it's freaking me out."

"I wish I could make you feel better," Bobby began. "But it's freaking me out too. I don't know anything more about it than what I wrote in those journals. I wish I could turn back the clock to the other night and tell Uncle Press to find somebody else to help him, but I can't. Part of me is okay with that. I learned some things about myself that are pretty cool. I also found out some things that I gotta change. That's all good. But as for the whole Traveler deal . . . I haven't got a clue."

"So, what are you going to do?" asked Courtney.

Bobby pulled himself across the bed and stood up. His legs were a little shaky, but otherwise he was okay. "I'm going to try to get back to normal," he announced with certainty. "If Uncle Press needs help again, he can find somebody else. Would you guys come home with me? It might make things easier."

This was the moment Mark and Courtney were dreading. How could they possibly tell Bobby that his family had disappeared? After what he had been through, he didn't deserve this. But still, he had to know.

"B-Bobby," said Mark nervously. "There's s-something you should—"

Courtney cut him off. "We'll go with you, Bobby," she said. "We want to be there for you."

Mark shot Courtney a look, but Courtney didn't back down. She felt there was only one way that Bobby should learn about what had happened and that was to see it for himself. If they told him, he'd want to see for himself anyway, so Courtney felt it would be better to get the news all at once.

It was a short walk to Bobby's house on Linden Place. As they walked along the familiar sidewalks of Stony Brook, Bobby looked around with a smile. He had walked these streets a thousand times before, but he now had a whole new appreciation for them. He took in every sight, every smell, every sensation that he could. He wrapped himself in the feelings like a comfortable blanket and it made him feel whole again. He felt so good that he even allowed himself to think that it was possible to pick up his life where he had left off.

Mark and Courtney sensed this. It broke their hearts to know that soon his happy homecoming was going to crash and burn. Then just before they rounded the final bend that would bring them to 2 Linden Place and the empty lot where Bobby's house used to be, Courtney grabbed Bobby and stopped him. She held him by the shoulders and stared him right in the eye.

"You gotta know something, Bobby," she said sincerely. "We're here for you."

"I know that, Courtney," replied Bobby.

Courtney didn't let go of him. She knew that as soon as she did, he'd turn that corner to see that the life he so desperately wanted back, wasn't there anymore.

"Hey, you okay?" Bobby asked her curiously.

Courtney nodded and let him go. Bobby glanced at Mark to

try and get a clue as to why Courtney was acting all strange, but Mark looked just as bad as Courtney did. Bobby knew right then that something was wrong. He spun and ran around the corner to get to his house. Mark and Courtney gave each other a nervous glance and followed.

When Mark and Courtney rounded the corner, they saw Bobby standing alone on the sidewalk, staring at the empty lot where his house used to be. He didn't move, he didn't shout, it didn't even look like he was breathing. He just stood there and stared. They didn't say anything. They had to let Bobby take the time to get his mind around what he was seeing. Or *not* seeing. Bobby walked forward and stepped onto the spot where his yard used to be. It was the yard he had played in since he was a toddler. It was the yard where he wrestled with Marley. It was the yard that led to the house he had called home for fourteen years. It was all gone.

"Hey there," came a familiar voice from behind them.

Everyone spun to see Uncle Press standing on the sidewalk. He was once again dressed in his jeans and long leather coat. Behind him was a small, black sports car he had just arrived in. A Porsche. Uncle Press always traveled in style.

"It's okay, Bobby," said Uncle Press softly. "Try to breathe."

Mark and Courtney took a few steps out of the way. Whatever was about to happen, it was between Press and Bobby. They saw that Bobby's eyes were red. He had started to cry. But the sad look turned to one of fury when he saw his uncle.

"Where are they?" Bobby said through clenched teeth. "And don't tell me this is the way it was meant to be. I don't want to hear that."

"They're fine, "Press said soothingly. "They're all fine."

Bobby took a few steps toward Press. He was angry, sad,

confused, and scared. But most of all, he wanted answers. "Then why aren't they here?" he demanded.

"This is the toughest part," said Press. "It was tough for me, it was tough for Alder and for Loor, too, but we all had to go through it. I would have told you on Denduron, but you had to see for yourself."

"See what? What is happening?" Bobby demanded.

Courtney reached out and grabbed Mark's hand for support. Mark didn't resist.

"Bobby, your family is gone because it was time for you to leave," said Uncle Press. "They raised you to be the person you are today, but it's time to move on."

Bobby took a few steps back as if Press's words had physically hit him. What was he saying? Was it planned for him to go to Denduron from the day he was born? Did his family know about this all along? How could that be? His life had been so . . . normal. Then a realization came to Bobby.

"You're not my uncle, are you?" he asked.

"No, not in the traditional sense," answered Press. "But I've always looked out for you and I always will."

Bobby turned back to the empty lot and ran to the center. He wanted to find a splinter of wood, a piece of glass, maybe even a piece of an old Wiffle ball. There had to be something that said he had passed through here. But there was nothing. Then Bobby heard something that came as another surprise.

"It will be all right, Pendragon," said another familiar voice.

Bobby spun back toward the sidewalk to see that standing next to the car was Loor. She was dressed in denim overalls and a tight pink sleeveless shirt that showed off her powerful shoulders and arms. She even had on Doc Marten black boots. Her long black hair was braided down her back and she wore a necklace made of small shells. She could have easily passed for a student at Stony Brook High. No one would ever guess that she was actually a warrior from a far-off territory.

Courtney looked at Loor and sized her up, head to toe. Mark saw this and made a mental note to give Courtney a hard time later for being jealous. But who could blame her? Mark thought that Loor was even more strikingly beautiful than Bobby had described. She may have been dressed like a suburban girl, but she had the powerful presence of a warrior. Courtney Chetwynde had finally met her match.

Bobby walked to Loor. If anyone could tell him the truth, it would be her.

"Does this make sense to you?" he asked.

"It is starting to," was her answer.

"What about your mother?" he asked. "Was Osa your real mother?"

"No. I was told the truth before I first went to Denduron," answered Loor. "Osa raised me, she taught me all that I know. She was my mother in every sense, except that she had not given birth to me. But that did not stop me from loving her."

Bobby looked down, letting this sink in.

"On the mountain," continued Loor, "I did not say good-bye to you because my mind was elsewhere. Osa's body was already back on Zadaa. I had to return for the burial ceremony. It was difficult for me. I hope you were not offended."

Bobby shook his head. He understood all too well because he now knew what it was like to lose your mother. He looked to Press and asked, "So that's it? Travelers don't have families? They don't have lives? They only bounce around the universe looking for trouble?"

Press smiled and said, "You trust me, Bobby, don't you?"

"I think so," said Bobby skeptically. "But I'm losing faith fast."

"Don't," said Press quickly. "Believe me when I tell you that as time goes on, this will make sense to you. And I'll make you a promise. You will see your family again. You'll see your mom and your dad and your sister, Shannon, too."

"What about Marley?" Bobby asked.

"You'll run with your dog again too," said Press. "But not today."

"When?" asked Bobby.

Press gave this thought. He may have had all the answers, but this one eluded him. "That's one I can't answer," he said.

Bobby looked to Loor who gave him a slight nod of encouragement, then back to the empty lot. He took a long time to collect his thoughts. Finally he said, "You asked me how I felt before. You want to know how I feel right now?"

"How?" asked Press.

"I feel like I just found out there's no Santa Claus," he answered. "It's not a good feeling."

"It'll get better," said Press.

"So what happens now?" asked Bobby.

"Now you come with us," answered Press.

Bobby walked over to Mark and Courtney. He looked at his two friends and the memories of his life in Stony Brook came flooding back. He wanted nothing more than to turn around and see his house standing there so he could go back to the way things were before. But that was not meant to be.

"I . . . guess I've got to go," said Bobby.

"We'll always be here for you," said Courtney as tears began to well in her eyes.

Bobby leaned forward and grabbed the two of them in a hug. He tried hard not to break out in tears. He didn't want to do that. Not in front of Loor. But he didn't want to let go of his friends, either, because as soon as he did it would be the final act of letting go of his life here on Earth. Second Earth.

"Time to go, Bobby," prodded Press gently.

Bobby pulled back from his two best friends and looked them in the eye. Mark wiped away a tear, smiled and said, "Hey, don't forget to write!"

The three of them laughed at this. That went without saying.

"Are you sure?" asked Bobby. "Will you keep my journals?"

"I'd be pissed if you sent them to anyone else," Mark replied as he held up his hand to show Bobby the ring that Osa had given him.

Bobby gave a smile of thanks and fought back tears to say, "See you guys soon."

"Good-bye, Bobby," said Courtney. "Good luck."

Bobby nodded, then turned and headed toward the car. He stopped in front of Loor and looked at the warrior girl who was destined to be his partner.

"I know you do not want to hear this, Pendragon," she said. "But this is the way it was meant to be."

"Yeah, we'll see," said Bobby with skepticism. He gave one last look to the empty lot where his house used to be, then slid into the back of the Porsche. Loor looked at Mark and Courtney. Courtney stood up a little straighter. Loor chuckled, then she too got into the car.

"Keep his journals safe," Press said to Mark and Courtney. "He may need them again someday."

Mark and Courtney nodded a promise. Press then jogged around the car and hopped behind the wheel. With a roar of the engine, the little sports car blasted away from the curb and flew down the street, headed for . . . somewhere.

Mark and Courtney watched it until it was out of sight and the sound died away. They stood there for a long time after, not sure of what to do next.

Finally Mark said, "There's no Santa Claus?"

Both of them laughed. It felt good, but it hid their true feelings.

Courtney said, "You'll call me if—"

"Soon as the next one comes in," promised Mark.

Then the two of them walked away from the empty lot, split up, and headed to their homes. Mark went right to his bedroom and waited for another journal from Bobby. The others had come pretty regularly and he expected his ring to start moving with the telltale quiver any second. But it didn't. He stayed awake most of the night, staring at the ring, willing it to move.

But it didn't.

Courtney called him twice a day to see if Bobby had written but kept getting the same answer, "Nothing yet." Whenever she saw Mark in school she would make eye contact as if to ask: "Anything?" But Mark would always answer with a shrug and a shake of his head.

Days passed. The days turned into weeks, the weeks into months, with nothing from Bobby. Mark and Courtney realized that they couldn't live their lives around waiting for his next message, so they drifted apart. Besides their friendship with Bobby, they really had nothing in common. Courtney went back to playing volleyball and led the Stony Brook team to the county finals. The men's team, of course.

Mark went back to being Mark. He still ate too many carrots and spent most of his time huddled over books in the library. There was one big change in his life though. Andy Mitchell didn't bother him anymore. Courtney didn't know it, but she became Mark's guardian angel . . . at least when it came to Andy Mitchell.

The investigation to find the Pendragons continued, but they found nothing. Sergeant D'Angelo and Captain Hirsch would sometimes call Mark or Courtney to ask if they had heard anything, but the answer was always the same. No. Even if they wanted to tell the truth, neither of them could begin to figure out what to say.

Mark and Courtney never forgot about Bobby. He popped into their thoughts at least once a day. But the more time that passed without a word, the less he stayed on their minds. It made sense. They had to get on with their own lives.

The times when they thought of Bobby were usually triggered by seeing things that reminded them of their friend. Mark would play Nintendo football and remember the times that Bobby kicked his butt at the very same game. Courtney would hear a comedian say something goofy on TV and she'd laugh because she knew it would have made Bobby laugh. One time Mark sat in the stands during gym watching the guys play basketball and it made him think of how great Bobby was at the game.

And that's when it happened. The ring twitched.

At first Mark didn't know what it was. But when he looked down, he saw the familiar glow coming from the stone. Mark nearly wet his pants with excitement. He ran out of the stands and right through the game. It didn't matter to him that he totally disrupted play and was getting yelled at by every guy on the court. He had to get out of there fast and he had to find Courtney. He found her in the girls' gym next door. She was taking a class on combatives and was in the middle of a judo match. With very little effort she picked up her opponent and threw her on her back with a loud, sickening *thud.* Then just as she was helping her victim to her feet, Mark ran into the gym and yelled.

"Courtney!"

Everyone turned to look at the mad dweeb. Courtney locked eyes with him and instantly knew the deal. She quickly bowed to her opponent and ran to Mark. They didn't have to say a word.

They knew what to do. The two of them headed right for Mark's fortress of solitude: the boys' bathroom on the third floor. Courtney wasn't shy, she barged in ahead of Mark. No sooner did they get inside than Mark took off the ring and put it on the ground. The ring twitched, the crystal lights flashed and the familiar process began. The little ring grew larger and with a final blinding flash, it was over.

On the floor was a roll of paper, but this one looked different than the others. It was a light green color, rather than the yellowed pages they were used to. There was a tie around the roll, but rather than a piece of brown leather, this looked like some kind of dark green plantlike material. Mark pulled it off and carefully unrolled the pages. They were roughly the same size as the others, but these were oddly shaped. There were no squared edges. Mark felt the texture—they didn't appear to be paper at all. These pages were some sort of large, dried leaves that were sort of rubbery . . . and waterproof.

"You ready?" asked Courtney.

"My hands are shaking," replied Mark.

Then the two of them looked at Bobby's newest journal.

to be continued

PENDRAGON

JOURNAL OF AN ADVENTURE THROUGH
TIME AND SPACE

Book Two:
The Lost City of Faar

This is for my mom, Ellie.

CLORAL

Hi, guys. I gotta apologize for taking so long to write. So much has happened since I left you two, Mark and Courtney. I'm not really sure where to begin. First off, one mystery is solved. Remember the giant shark that nearly ate me down in that mine shaft on Denduron? Well, now I know where it came from. The territory I'm on is called Cloral and it's entirely underwater. No kidding. Underwater. The quigs on Cloral are giant, flesh-eating sharks. Nice, huh?

Now let me tell you about some of the new trouble I've been getting into.

I was almost eaten, again; I came dangerously close to drowning; my arms were nearly yanked out of their sockets; and I think I cracked a couple of ribs—all in the first hour after I got here. Sounds like a fun place, no?

I'm writing this journal now because things have finally calmed down and I need the rest. I think it's best to start my story at the point when I last saw you two. Man, that already seems like years ago. Time sure flies when you're out of your mind.

I still have tons of questions about what's happened to my

life, but two jump to the top of the list. Why is it that I, Bobby Pendragon, have been chosen to become a Traveler? I don't think that's a lot to ask since I've had to risk my butt about a thousand times over while performing my Traveler duties. The second is that I want to know what happened to my family. I keep asking Uncle Press these questions, but getting info out of him is like squeezing blood from a turnip. (Not that I've ever tried squeezing a turnip, but it seems like a tough thing to do.) He keeps saying, "It will all come clear with time." Great. Meanwhile, we keep jumping from one disaster to the next, and the best I can hope for is that I'll stay alive long enough to figure out why the heck I'm in the middle of all this when all I really want to do is go home and hide under my bed with the dog. C'mon! I'm only fourteen! Is that too much to ask?

I guess it is, seeing as my home isn't there anymore. The last time I saw you two, you were standing in front of the empty lot where my house used to be. It's hard to describe the emotions that were banging around inside me back then. I was nervous about going on another adventure with Uncle Press and bummed to be leaving you two guys again. But the worst part was the fear of the unknown.

Uncle Press promised me I would see my family again. Mom, Dad, Shannon, and even my golden retriever, Marley. But he stopped short of telling me where they had gone. He told me that they had raised me and prepared me for the moment when I would leave home to become a Traveler, but he didn't tell me why. Was it planned from the moment I was born? Was my family part of some secret plot? He also told me that he wasn't my real uncle. Meaning, a blood relative. But he hadn't yet answered the single most important question: *Why?* Why are there Travelers who blast through time and space, helping the territories through dangerous times?

Who chooses them? Most important, why me?

To be honest, I've stopped asking these questions because his answers are always so freaking elliptical. It's like he's some kind of Jedi master who only drips out information on a need-to-know basis. Well, I need to know bad. But I guess I'll have to be patient and learn as I go along. I think Uncle Press is afraid if he lays it all out for me in one shot, the truth will make my head explode and I'll end up lying in a corner some-place, drooling. He's probably right.

When I said good-bye to you two, I got into the car with Uncle Press and Loor, my partner from the adventure on Denduron. I was leaving my two best friends to take off with my new friend and partner. At least I considered Loor a friend. We had been through hell together on Denduron and even though I wasn't the warrior she was, I think I had earned her respect. At least I'd hoped I had.

I squeezed into the back compartment behind the two seats of the Porsche without being asked. Obviously Uncle Press was going to drive, and since Loor was bigger than me, there was no way she could fit in the back. She may have been dressed like she belonged on Second Earth, but she looked like no classmate I'd ever seen. I'm guessing she was around six-teen, but with her zero-body-fat, muscular bod, she looked ready for the Olympic decathlon. Her cocoa-dark skin made her look as if she were African, but I knew the truth. She was a warrior from the territory of Zadaa, which exists in an entire-ly different time and place from here. I think one of the first requirements for the Olympics is that you have to be from Earth. She didn't qualify.

"Comfy?" asked Uncle Press.

"Not even close," I answered.

With a laugh, Uncle Press hit the gas and once again we

screamed away from my hometown of Stony Brook, Connecticut. I didn't even ask him where we were headed, because I knew. We were going back to the abandoned subway station in the Bronx to find the gate that led to the flume that would take us . . . somewhere.

The last time we traveled this route I was on the back of Press's motorcycle, with no clue of what lay ahead. This time I had a clue, but not much more.

We blasted along the turnpike, out of Connecticut, headed for New York City. Within half an hour we had gone from the leafy-green suburbs of Stony Brook to the concrete pavement of the borough of New York called the Bronx. It's the home of Yankee Stadium, the Bronx Zoo, the New York Botanical Garden, and a secret Traveler flume into the unknown.

As Uncle Press maneuvered the quick little sports car through the city streets, people turned to stare. This was a rough neighborhood. They weren't used to seeing a sleek sports car screaming through their 'hood. Or maybe they were staring in wonder at the guy riding in back who was turning blue because his knees were jammed into his throat. That would be me.

With a final spin of the wheel, Uncle Press brought us right up to the curb next to the small green kiosk that was our destination. As I looked at that little building and the peeled paint on the sign above it that said SUBWAY, only one thought came to mind.

Here we go again.

I hadn't expected to see this place again so soon. No, I had expected to *never* see this place again. Uncle Press and I had come through this way only a few hours before, having returned from Denduron. My plan was to get back home, and do my level best to forget about this whole Traveler business. But things changed. I discovered that my family was gone, along with the life I knew. I think Uncle Press brought me back to Stony Brook to see for myself. It was a smart move, because if he hadn't, I never would have believed it. I would always be thinking about how to get home. But there was no home to get back to anymore. The cold, hard reality hit me that my destiny was to go with Uncle Press and learn more about being a Traveler. What a difference a few hours can make.

So there we were again, back in the Bronx, on the verge of starting my new life. I wanted to cry. Yes, I admit it. I wanted to cry. If Loor wasn't there, I probably would have.

Uncle Press hopped out of the car first, leaving the keys in the ignition. Loor and I crawled out after him. Actually, I did most of the crawling. I was so mashed up in the backseat that my legs were now totally asleep, and when I tried to stand, I fell over. Loor caught me and held me up until I got the feeling back. How embarrassing is that?

Uncle Press didn't stop to see if I was okay. He headed right for the stairs that led down into the subway.

"Uh, Uncle Press?" I called. "You sure you want to leave the car here?" I remembered back to our first trip here. We had left the motorcycle and the helmets right where the Porsche was now. I thought for sure that somebody would pinch them, but when we returned that morning, the bike was right where we had left it. The helmets were there too. Unbelievable. Pure luck. But this was really pushing it. A hot sports car sitting alone with the keys in the ignition was too tempting a prize. Worse, it was in a no-parking zone. If thieves didn't get the car, the cops would tow it for sure.

Uncle Press said, "It's okay. The acolytes will take care of it."

Huh? Acolytes? That was a new wrinkle. I looked at Loor to see if she knew what he was talking about. She shrugged. Before I could ask any more, Uncle Press disappeared down into the subway.

I said to Loor, "Yeah, I know—we'll learn more as we go along."

"Don't ask so many questions, Pendragon," she said. "Save them for when it is truly important." She then followed Uncle Press.

Truly important? Wasn't all this bizarro stuff truly important? I wanted to know! But since I was now standing alone and feeling dumb out here all by myself, the only thing I could do was follow. I was getting good at that.

I hurried down the dirty stairs and squeezed through the opening in the wooden boards that were nailed across the entrance. To the rest of the world this was a closed and abandoned subway station that had outlived its usefulness. To us Travelers, it was the crossroads of Second Earth, my home territory, and our jumping-off point to all the other distant territories. Sounds romantic, doesn't it? Well, it isn't. It's scary.

The filthy subway station was all too familiar to me. Subway trains still flew by, but it had been a long time since any had stopped at this forlorn spot. When I hit the platform, I saw something that brought back a chilling memory. It was the pillar that Uncle Press had hidden behind during his gun battle with Saint Dane. It was a battle that had given me the time to escape and find the gate and the flume that sent me to Denduron.

Saint Dane. There's a guy I'd like to forget. Uncle Press says he's a Traveler, like us. But he isn't exactly like us because the guy is wicked. On Denduron he pushed two rival tribes to the brink of annihilation. But we stepped in and messed things up for him.

Unfortunately Denduron was only the beginning. Saint Dane promised to wreak havoc with all the territories in his quest to rule Halla. That's key. He wants to rule Halla. Now, I'm no genius, but since Uncle Press described Halla as "every territory, every person, every living thing, every *time* there ever was," then having a guy like Saint Dane be the ruler is not a very good idea.

What made it all so incredibly creepy was that Saint Dane enjoyed seeing people suffer. I saw that firsthand, too many times. This abandoned subway platform was the first. This was where he hypnotized a homeless guy into jumping to a gruesome death in front of a speeding subway train. It was a cold-blooded trick that Saint Dane said was "to give the boy a taste of what was in store for him."

The boy he referred to was me. Nice guy, huh? I told you before that the worst part about my new life as a Traveler was the fear of the unknown. Well, that's not entirely true. Right up there on my list of fears is knowing that somewhere, sometime, we would cross paths with Saint Dane again. The guy was worse than dangerous, and it was our job to stop him. Standing there on that platform, I was really wanting a different job.

"Pendragon!" called Loor.

I followed her voice to the end of the platform. I knew this route. We had to climb down onto the subway tracks, carefully avoid getting fried by the third rail, and make our way along the grimy, oil-stained wall until we came upon a wooden door. On this door would be a symbol that looked like a carved star identifying it as a gate. That was our destination.

With Uncle Press in the lead, we moved quickly along the tracks. We had to hurry because a subway train could come charging along at any moment. There wasn't much room between the tracks and the wall, and a train speeding past our noses would hurt.

As we got closer to the door, I noticed that the ring on my finger began to grow warm. I looked at it and saw that the slate gray stone was beginning to transform. The dark gray color began to melt away and the stone now sparkled. This was the sign that we were getting near a gate. It was amazing how many things I was taking for granted. Once upon a time, the idea of following a possessed, glowing ring to a mysterious door in an abandoned subway station would seem like an off-the-wall dream. Not anymore. Now it felt natural. Sort of.

Uncle Press found the door, opened it, and hurried us all inside.

The cave inside hadn't changed. I immediately glanced into the dark tunnel that led off into the unknown. This was the flume that would sparkle to life and take us . . . somewhere. Right now it was quiet, waiting for us to tell it where we were going. I'd only traveled through the flume between Second Earth and Denduron. I had to believe that this time we were going someplace else, and now was the time for Uncle Press to tell us where. Loor and I stood together, waiting for him to show us the way.

"We're going to split up," he said.

Whoa. Not a good start. Was he crazy? We shouldn't be broken apart! Uncle Press knew his way around the cosmos and Loor was a fierce warrior. The idea of fluming off to face Saint Dane by myself without any backup was not something I could get psyched up about. A million thoughts and possibilities flashed through my brain—all of them bad. But just as I was about to break into full panic mode, Loor spoke.

"Why?" she asked flatly.

Nothing like keeping it simple. She was good to have around.

"Since your mother died, you are the Traveler from Zadaa," he answered. "They'll need you there soon. I want you to go home and be ready."

"What about me?" I asked, immediately flying into protest mode.

"You and I are going to Cloral," was his answer. "Saint Dane went there for a reason and I want to know what it is."

Good news, bad news. Good news was Uncle Press and I were staying together. Bad news was we were going after Saint Dane. Really bad news.

"But if I'm the Traveler from Second Earth, shouldn't I stay here?" I asked hopefully. "You know, to take care of stuff?"

Uncle Press gave me a smile. He knew I was trying to weasel out.

"No, it's best you come with me," was his simple answer.

Oh well. I wasn't surprised that my lame attempt at getting out of this trip had failed miserably. But hey, it was worth a shot, right?

Loor then stepped up to me and said, "If you need me, I will be there for you, Pendragon."

Wow, that blew me away. I guess I had earned her respect after all. I nodded and said, "I'll be there for you, too."

We held eye contact for a moment. The bond the two of us had created during the war on Denduron was stronger than I realized. I felt safer with her around, but it was more than that. I liked Loor. In spite of her inability to give an inch on anything, Loor's heart was always in the right place. I didn't want to go on without her. And I really believe that if she'd had the choice, she'd have stayed with me. But before I could say another word, she turned and strode into the mouth of the flume. She stared into the dark abyss, took a deep breath, and called out, "*Zadaa!*"

Instantly the tunnel started to breathe. The rocky walls began to writhe like a giant snake slowly coming to life. Then there was the familiar sound—the jumble of sweet musical notes that came from somewhere deep in the tunnel and grew louder as they rushed toward us. The walls transformed from gray stone into brilliant crystalline gems, just as my ring had as we approached the gate. The light that shone from the tunnel was so bright that I needed to shield my eyes. Loor became nothing more than a dark silhouette standing before the brilliant display. She gave one last look back to us and waved good-bye. Then, in a flash of light, she was swept into the tunnel. The retreating light and music carried her away and back to her home, the territory of Zadaa.

In an instant the show was over and the tunnel returned to darkness.

"Your turn," said Uncle Press.

"Tell me about Cloral," I asked, stalling for time. As much as I knew a trip through the flume was kind of fun, I was nervous about what I'd find on the other end. I needed a few seconds to get my act together.

"You'll find out all you need to know once you get there," he answered as he nudged me closer to the mouth of the flume. "Don't worry, I'll be right behind you."

"Why don't you ever give me a straight answer?" I asked.

"I thought you liked surprises?" he answered with a laugh.

"Not anymore I don't!" I shouted back. Uncle Press

used to surprise me all the time with great birthday gifts and helicopter rides and camping trips and—basically all the coolio things a kid could ever want from an amazing uncle. But lately Uncle Press's surprises weren't as fun as they used to be. Especially since they mostly involved me being chased by hungry beasts or shot at or blown up or buried alive or . . . you get the idea.

"C'mon, you're no fun anymore," he teased as he pushed me into the flume. "*Cloral!*" he shouted, and stepped out as the tunnel sprang back to life. I didn't even look into the depths because I knew what was coming.

"Fun?" I shouted. "If you think this is fun, you're crazy!"

"Oh, one thing, Bobby," he said.

"What?"

"Remember the Cannonball."

"What 'cannonball'?" I asked. "What's that supposed to mean?"

The light grew brighter and the musical notes grew louder. I was seconds away from launch.

"Just before you drop into Cloral, hold your breath."

"What!"

The last thing I saw was Uncle Press laughing. Then the light grabbed me and sucked me into the tunnel. I was on my way.

☉ SECOND EARTH ☉

"What are you two doing in here?" shouted Mr. Dorrico, the chief janitor of Stony Brook Junior High. "This ain't a library. You can't sit here reading your—hey, you're a girl! Girls aren't allowed in the boys' washroom!"

Mr. Dorrico had been a janitor at Stony Brook for most of his illustrious fifty-year janitorial career. There wasn't much you could put past him and this time was no different. There was indeed a girl in the boys' lavatory. Mr. Dorrico may have been ancient and terminally cranky, but he could still tell girls from boys. Most of the time.

Courtney Chetwynde and Mark Dimond had been sitting on the floor, reading Bobby's first journal from Cloral. The washroom on the third floor was near the art department. It was rarely used by anyone, boy or girl. It had become Mark's fortress of solitude. When the world got too busy, Mark would come here to escape and think and eat carrots and be alone. If he received one of Bobby's journals at school, this is the place he would come to read it. And since Courtney was now part of the picture, she would join him. The fact that she was a girl never seemed to matter, considering how important the journals were. But now they were faced with an angry chief janitor who looked as if he were going to have a heart attack at the very thought of a girl being in the boys' washroom.

Mark jumped to his feet and quickly grabbed up the pages of Bobby's journal. "It's c-cool. W-We were just leaving," he stammered nervously.

Whenever he got stressed, Mark stuttered. Courtney, on the other hand, was at her best under pressure. She stood slowly, walked up to Mr. Dorrico, and stared him right in the eye.

"The only reason I came in here," she said confidently, "was because there were so many boys in the girls' washroom. It was getting way too crowded in there . . . and they never lift the toilet seats."

"What!" shouted Mr. Dorrico, his face turning three shades of red.

To him this was clearly an offense that threatened to crack the very foundation of etiquette that our society was founded on. He grabbed the mop that he was going to use to swab up the boys' bathroom and charged back out, ready to do battle with the rogue delinquents who mocked the sanctity of the girls' lavatory.

Mark stepped up to Courtney and said, "You are bad."

"Time to go," she replied with a mischievous smile.

They ran from the bathroom and down the hall, careful to avoid the girls' room.

Mark knew that he and Courtney Chetwynde made an odd pair. Mark was an introvert. He lived in a world of books and graphic novels. He didn't have many friends. His hair was always a little too long and a little too unwashed. Sports were a four-letter word to him and his mother still picked out his clothes, which meant he wore a lot of non-name-brand geek outfits that were always about two years out of date. But the thing was, he didn't care. Mark never wanted to be cool. In fact, being comfortable with his noncoolness made Mark feel pretty good about himself. Where everyone else was busy trying to impress their friends with the way they looked or who they hung out with or what parties they went to, Mark couldn't be bothered. So Mark considered himself cooler than cool—in a nerdy kind of way.

Courtney, on the other hand, had it all going on. She was tall and beautiful, with long brown hair that fell to her waist and piercing gray eyes. She got decent grades. Not world-class, but good enough. She also had a ton of friends. But the thing that defined Courtney was sports. Volleyball in particular. Courtney was so tall and strong that it was unfair for her to play against most girls, so she played on the guys' teams at Stony Brook. As it turned out, it was unfair for her to play against most boys, too. She absolutely crushed them. Guys feared her because they didn't want to be embarrassed by a girl, but more because they were afraid when they faced Courtney, they'd lose teeth. At fourteen she was already a legend.

So the differences between Mark Dimond and Courtney Chetwynde were so huge that a friendship wasn't something you'd expect. That is, except for one thing.

Bobby Pendragon.

Both Mark and Courtney had known Bobby since they were little. Mark and Bobby were best buds beginning in kindergarten. Bobby spent so much time at Mark's house that Mrs. Dimond referred to him as her second son. As they grew older their interests changed. Bobby was into sports and was incredibly outgoing. Mark . . . wasn't. But where most people who were so different would drift apart, Mark and Bobby had a friendship that didn't fade. Bobby often said that as different as they seemed, they both laughed at the same things, and that meant they really weren't so different after all.

As for Courtney, Bobby met her in the fourth grade and fell in love. From the very first second he saw her stunning gray eyes, Bobby got slammed with a crush that had yet to fade. Growing up, they were rivals in sports. Bobby was one of the few guys who weren't intimidated by Courtney. Just the opposite. Even though she was a girl, he never cut her any slack. Why should he? She was too good. When they played dodge ball, he'd go after her as hard as she went after him. When they ran the four hundred in gym, he'd make sure the two of them went head-to-head. Sometimes he won; other times Courtney took him. In Little League they were on opposing teams and both were pitchers. When the other came up to bat, they'd each dig down a little deeper to throw heat. Naturally there was the occasional brush-back pitch that sent the other into the dirt. No one ever got hit, though. They may have been rivals, but they were still friends.

The thing was, as strong as Bobby's crush on Courtney was, Courtney felt just as strongly about Bobby. But neither let the other one know until that fateful night when Courtney came to Bobby's house before a basketball game. That's when Courtney admitted to Bobby how great she thought he was. It was also the night the two kissed for the first time. For Bobby, it was one of those incredible moments that actually transcended expectations. It was downright magical.

Unfortunately it was also the night when Bobby's Uncle Press took him away from home to begin their adventure on the troubled territory of Denduron. Bobby's old life ended with that one sweet Courtney kiss.

It was out of concern for Bobby Pendragon that Mark and Courtney got together. Both were terrified that something horrible would happen to him as he flumed through the territories. It was Mark who first started receiving Bobby's journals through the magical ring that was given to him one strange night. It was presented by a kind, strong woman who Mark thought was part of a dream. But in the morning the dream was over, and the ring was still there. This woman turned out to be Osa, Loor's mother, who was doomed to die while protecting Bobby. This ring was the conduit through which Bobby could send the journals of his incredible adventures back to his friends.

Reading about Bobby's adventures was both exciting and frightening for Mark. The perils were more enthralling than any action flick he'd ever seen. But Bobby's stories weren't meant to be entertaining. They were real, and that's why they were so frightening. The idea that there was a group of people called Travelers who voyaged through the universe doing battle against evil was a concept that challenged everything Mark knew about how things worked. Stranger still, knowing that his best friend was one of these Travelers made it all the more tough to deal with.

The fact was he couldn't deal with it. Not alone, anyway. That's why he brought Courtney into his confidence. Together, the two would read Bobby's journals and try to help each other understand what was happening to their friend.

Their meeting place of choice was the basement of Courtney's house. Her dad had a workshop down there, but he never used it. Courtney always laughed at her father, saying how he got all these tools because they looked cool, but then had no idea of what to do with them. So the basement workshop was pretty much a dusty tool-museum, which was perfect for Mark and Courtney. There was a big worn-out couch down there where they would settle in to devour Bobby's journals.

Their run-in with Mr. Dorrico came toward the end of the school day, so the two didn't go back to class. Instead, they headed right to Courtney's house. Courtney even skipped volleyball practice. She never missed practice unless there was an emergency. The arrival of a journal from Bobby definitely qualified.

Courtney ran down the basement steps ahead of Mark and leaped into the old couch sending up a cloud of dust. "C'mon!" she shouted impatiently at Mark. "I'm dying! I want to know what happened on Cloral!"

Mark had Bobby's journal in his backpack. But rather than dig it out and sit next to Courtney so they could continue reading, he stood over her, looking nervous.

"What's the matter?" she asked, trying to sound as impatient as she felt.

"C-Courtney, I-I'm scared," he said softly.

Normally Courtney would bulldoze over guys like Mark if she wasn't getting what she wanted. But this was different. They were a team. They shared a secret. If one of them was having a problem, the other one had to respect that. So as eager as she was to rip the pack off of Mark's back and grab Bobby's journal, she took a breath and tried to relax.

"I am too," she said softly. "But I want to know if he's okay."

"I'm not talking about Bobby," Mark whined. "I'm scared for us."

Courtney sat back in surprise. Mark now had her full attention.

"Why?"

Mark paced. "Ever since he left a few months ago, I've been giving this a lot of thought."

"Yeah, no kidding. Me too," Courtney said. But obviously Mark's thoughts were more troubling than Courtney's because he was the only one worried just then.

"Think about what's at stake here," Mark continued. "Saint Dane is trying to rule Halla. That's everything. Every time and every place there ever was. Don't you think that's a little scary?"

"Well, yeah," she answered. "Until a few months ago the biggest thing I had to worry about was passing algebra. Going from that to sweating over the future of all space and time is kind of a leap for me."

Mark nodded. A problem this huge was kind of hard to get your mind around.

"Okay," he said while continuing to pace. "It's hard for me to understand too, but there's more. Uncle Press told Bobby that all the territories were about to reach a turning point. It was the job of the Travelers to help them get through the crises so they could continue to exist in peace. If they failed, the territory would fall into chaos, and that's when Saint Dane would step in."

"Okay, so?" Courtney said impatiently. She wanted to know where this was going.

"So think about it," Mark said, getting worked up. "Bobby and Press went to Denduron because that territory was on the verge of a civil war. We just read that Press told Loor she had to go back to her home territory of Zadaa because they would need her there soon."

Courtney listened carefully. Mark was leading to a point and she wanted to make sure she fully understood what it was.

"Saint Dane went to Cloral," he continued. "Bobby and Press followed him there. Cloral must be reaching its critical time too."

"I get all this. But why are you so scared?" Courtney asked.

"Think," he said quickly. "We're reading these journals like they're stories happening far away from our safe little town. Sure, Bobby is right in the middle of things, but nothing is touching us. Not here. Not in the safe suburbs."

Courtney was starting to catch on. "You're saying something big might happen here, too?" asked Courtney soberly.

"Exactly!" shouted Mark. "We're a territory too. Second Earth. We're not immune. We're part of Halla or whatever it's called."

Courtney turned away from Mark to let this sink in. If all the territories were about to reach a turning point, that had to include their own territory as well. This was definitely bad news.

"I'll tell you something else," Mark said. "We've been trying to figure out why Bobby is a Traveler. I have no idea why, but I'll bet I know *when*."

"Huh?" said Courtney. "When what?"

"It seems like Travelers only go where they are needed, *when* they're needed," reasoned Mark. "I'll bet the time has come for Second Earth to need a Traveler, and that's why we now have one. Bobby."

Courtney didn't ask another question. She didn't need to. What Mark said made all sorts of sense. Up until now, everything that Bobby had written was true. He wrote that Uncle Press warned him that all the territories were nearing a critical time. *All* the territories. That included this one. Second Earth. Home.

"You want to hear more?"

"Not really," answered Courtney nervously.

"I think we're part of it, you and I," he said. "Bobby is sending us his journals. Besides him, we're the only ones here who know what's going on."

"You think we're being prepared for a battle on Second Earth?" Courtney asked softly, as if she could hardly get the words out.

"I think that's exactly what's happening," answered Mark.

Suddenly Courtney was just as scared as Mark. He had finally made his point, but she wished he hadn't.

"So what do we do?"

Mark took off his pack and sat down next to her.

"That part I haven't figured out," he answered. He dug inside the pack and pulled out Bobby's journal. Unlike the first journal that was written on crude, yellowed parchment paper, these pages were light green and supple. Each page was roughly the size of standard printer paper, but the edges weren't square. These pages were oddly shaped, as if they had been hand-made. The green pages were like a light, thin rubber. The writing looked pretty much the same as the other journals though. The words were written in black ink, and the handwriting was definitely Bobby's.

"Until we get more of an idea of what to expect," continued Mark. "All we can do is read Bobby's journals and learn as much as we can so when the time comes . . . we're ready."

Courtney stared into Mark's eyes. His last comment sounded ominous. This wasn't a game happening to someone else. This was real. Common sense told them that sometime, somehow they were going to get sucked into this nightmare. Courtney was beginning to hate common sense. The question was, when would it happen? Those questions could only be answered by the words in Bobby's journal, so without any more conversation, Mark and Courtney looked down at the strange green pages and continued to read.

CLORAL

The flume.

It was my fifth time flying through this magical tunnel into the unknown, but I still wasn't used to it. Heck, I could travel like this a thousand times and I wouldn't get used to it. As I told you guys before, it's kind of like sailing down a huge water slide. But it's not as violent as a water-park ride. It's really more like floating on a cushion of warm air. The tunnel walls that were surrounding me looked like transparent crystal. But I knew this only happened when the flume was activated. Why does it do this? Haven't got a clue.

Beyond the walls I saw stars. Billions of them. I was in the middle of the universe traveling through space and time. At least that's how it was explained to me. I wondered if the flumes were actually solid. Was it possible to damage a flume? Could an orbiting satellite accidentally smash into one? What about a meteor? Or an asteroid? I figured I had enough to worry about without thinking about that kind of potential disaster, so I tried to think of something else.

Up ahead I could see the twists and turns of the tunnel. The first time I had done this I was afraid to bounce off the walls, so I tried to lean into the turns like one of those maniacs on a luge run, but as it turns out I didn't have to bother. Whatever force was speeding me along also prevented me from slamming into the walls. All I had to do was kick back and enjoy the ride.

Until now, I had only taken the flume between Second Earth and Denduron. This was the first time I was headed to somewhere else. I wondered if I was going to hit some kind of intersection and get shot in the new direction. The answer came pretty quick. There were no turns. There were no junctures. I was on the express line to Cloral.

How did I know that? I heard a sound. I was used to hearing the jumble of sweet musical notes as I shot along, so this new sound jumped out at me. It kept getting louder, which meant I was getting closer to it. It wasn't until I was almost to the end when I realized what it was.

It was water.

Suddenly the warning Uncle Press had given me before I got sucked into the flume made sense. He told me to remember the Cannonball and to hold my breath. In that instant I remembered the Cannonball. Do you remember, Mark? It was a ride at the water park in New Jersey that Uncle Press took us to a few years ago. It was a short, fast water slide that went underground, then shot you out for a fifteen-foot drop into an icy cold pool of snowmelt mountain water. I think the word you used to describe it was "rude." Well, if I was right, then Uncle Press's warning meant that I was about to be shot out of the flume into a pool of water. I quickly folded my arms in front of my chest, crossed my legs, and waited for the end.

It came quickly. I was fired out of the flume like a torpedo, feet first. One moment I was floating comfortably in the flume, the next moment gravity took control and I was falling through the air toward . . . what? Everything was a blur. I couldn't get my bearings or my balance. All I could do was hope to land on something soft. Or wet.

It was wet. With a graceless splashdown, I hit water. But thanks to Uncle Press's warning, I was ready. I hit feet first and plunged below. I even remembered to hold my nose so I wouldn't get a sudden brain-flush of water shooting up my nostrils.

The water was tropical warm, like swimming in Florida. As soon as I stopped driving downward, I kicked my legs to push back to the surface. I wanted to know where I was and what the territory of Cloral had going on. When I broke the surface I took a quick look around to check the place out. I was treading water in a large pool in an underground cavern. Not a big surprise. So far all the flumes were underground. But unlike the other flumes that I walked into, the opening to this flume was cut into the cavern wall about twenty feet above the water. That's where I had just been shot out like, well, like a cannonball. Thanks for the warning, Uncle Press.

A quick scan around told me that the cavern was completely sealed and the only light came from the water where I was floating. I figured the sun was shining outside and it reflected off the sandy bottom to create a luminous green pool that was bright enough to light up the entire cavern.

The place was about the size of two tennis courts, with a high arching ceiling that reached a peak far above. It kind of reminded me of being in a small church. The walls were craggy, sand-colored stone that looked to have been carved by centuries of erosion. There were also thousands of green, leafy vines that grew right out of the stone and draped down over the rocks like a curtain.

But the thing that really jumped out at me were the

thousands of colorful flowers that grew from the vines. The light from the pool of water must have been enough to let them grow, or maybe flowers didn't need light on Cloral. Whatever the case, they were like a spectacular tapestry of color all over the walls. There were vivid reds, deep blues and vibrant yellows. The flowers were all different shapes and sizes and looked nothing like Earth flowers. Some were trumpet shaped, others looked more like small helicopter blades. Stranger still, they seemed alive. No kidding, all the blossoms were slowly opening and closing like they were breathing oxygen. Seeing these thousands of moving flowers made the cavern itself seem alive. It was magical and creepy at the same time.

I had calmed down by now and floated lazily in the green pool. It was actually kind of cool. I also think I was mesmerized by this wondrous place. I probably would have kept floating there for a long time if I hadn't heard the familiar sound of musical notes coming from the flume overhead. It took a second for me to register what was happening. Uncle Press was about to arrive. That was good. But I was treading water on the very spot where he was going to land. That was bad. I instantly kicked and lunged for the side of the pool to get out of the way. No sooner did I touch the rocky edge when I heard, "Eeeehaaaa!"

Uncle Press shot out of the flume headfirst. The force of it sent him sailing out into the center of the cavern. He seemed to hang there for an impossible second until gravity kicked in. As he began his arc down, he thrust his arms out to form a perfect swan dive. Then just before splashdown, he brought his arms together and entered the water almost vertically. He barely even made a splash. A perfect ten all the way around.

I pulled myself up and sat on the edge of the pool as Uncle Press resurfaced. He had a huge, exhilarated smile on his face as he shook his head to throw his wet hair out of his eyes.

"Yeah! I love this place!" he shouted with joy. "Headfirst is the only way to go."

I was beginning to think that Uncle Press liked being a Traveler. At least he enjoyed it more than I did, that was for sure. With two quick strokes he swam to the side of the pool and hauled himself out. He was a little out of breath from his dramatic arrival, so he sat on the edge and looked at me with eyes that were alive with excitement.

"Welcome to Cloral," he said with glee. "This is my favorite territory. No contest."

He sounded like some kind of tour guide whose job it was to make sure I was enjoying my vacation. But this was no vacation. Not even close.

"So what's the deal here?" I asked, not really wanting to hear the answer. "Is there a war? Some impending disaster? Some evildoings that Saint Dane cooked up to make our lives miserable?"

Uncle Press gave a shrug. "I don't know," was his casual response.

Huh? Up until now Uncle Press had all the answers. He didn't always share them with me, but it was good to know that at least one of us wasn't totally clueless.

"Don't know?" I shot back. "Why do you keep stuff from me? If we're headed for trouble, I want to know."

"I'm not trying to hide things from you, Bobby," he said sincerely. "I really don't know what's happening here. On Denduron, I'd been living with the Milago and knew that there was civil war brewing. But I've only been to Cloral a couple of times. As far as I know, everything here is fine and dandy."

"So then why are we here?" I asked with frustration.

Uncle Press looked me right in the eye, suddenly all business.

"We're here because Saint Dane is here," he said soberly. "He hasn't tipped his hand yet, but he will."

Right. Saint Dane. Back on Denduron, moments before Loor and I had made our death-defying escape from the mine shaft, Saint Dane had jumped into a flume and shouted, *"Cloral!"* Since the mine was seconds away from blowing up, Loor and I would have gladly followed him, except that he sent a killer shark riding a wave of water back through the flume to stop us. We had two choices: death by shark-lunch, or flee deeper into the doomed mine. We chose to run and luckily escaped through a ventilation shaft before the entire place exploded.

It suddenly dawned on me that the reason we were here on Cloral was because of me. I was the one who knew Saint Dane came here. I guess I was playing more of a part in this whole saga than I really cared to.

"Tell me about Cloral," I asked. I figured I should at least know what to expect from this new territory.

Uncle Press stood up and glanced around the colorful, living, underground cavern.

"The whole planet is covered by water," he began. "As far as I know there isn't an inch of dry land anywhere. This cave is part of a coral reef that's about sixty feet underwater."

"You're kidding?" I interrupted. "Who lives on this territory? Fish?"

Uncle Press laughed and reached toward one of the vines that clung to the rocks. Behind the colorful flowers, attached to the same vine, were dark lumpy-looking things. He plucked one off like an apple from a tree and tossed it to me. I caught it awkwardly and saw that it looked like a small, dark green cucumber. It was kind of rubbery, so I guess it was really more like a pickle than a cucumber.

"Break it in half," he said.

I held both ends and snapped the strange tube in half easily. The green skin on the outside was so dark that it was nearly black, but the inside was bright red.

"Try it," he said while plucking another one for himself. He took a big bite and chewed. I figured if it didn't kill him, it wouldn't kill me, so I took a bite and it was delicious! It was like the sweetest little watermelon I had ever eaten. Even the skin was good, though chewier and a bit more salty than the sweet pulp inside. No seeds, either.

"I think there may have been a time when the people of Cloral lived on dry land," he continued. "But that was centuries ago. There aren't any records of it. Whatever happened to the planet, no one knows. But the land is long gone."

"So how do they live in water?" I asked while wiping the sweet juice from my chin.

"They don't," he answered. "They live on floating cities called 'habitats.' Whole communities are built on these monster barges. Some are so big you'd swear you were on an island."

"That sounds impossible," I said. "Where do they get food? And building materials? And—"

"Why don't I just show you?" Uncle Press interrupted.

Good point. We could sit here talking about it, or I could see for myself. I hated to admit it, but I was kind of interested by a world that was always floating.

Uncle Press wiped fruit juice from his mouth and walked carefully across the rocky ledge until he came to a thick mound of vines near the base of the wall. He pulled them away and I saw that the vines had been covering a pile of clothing and equipment. I immediately remembered the cave on top of the mountain on Denduron where Uncle Press gave me the leather clothes of that territory. It was against the rules to wear anything from other territories, so we needed some Cloral clothes.

"I don't get it," I said quizzically. "If you didn't know we were coming here, how did you know enough to have this little stash of stuff ready?"

"We aren't alone, Bobby," he said while picking up and checking out something that looked like a clear-plastic bubble the size of a basketball. "There are acolytes who support us on every territory. They brought this gear here."

Acolytes. That's who supposedly took care of the motorcycle back in the Bronx.

"Who are they?" I asked. "How come I've never seen one?"

"You won't," he answered. "At least not often. But they're around."

"If they're so helpful," I added suspiciously, "how come they didn't help us out a little more on Denduron?"

"It's not like that," he said. "They aren't Travelers. They can't play a direct role in our mission. All they can do is help us blend into the territory. Here!"

He tossed the plastic bubble to me. It was light, but solid. One section of the globe was open so it looked kind of like a big, round fishbowl. There was also a small gizmo attached to it that looked like a silver harmonica.

"Put your head in it."

Yeah, right. Sticking my head into that alien object is not something I'd do by choice.

"Just put it on," he said with a smile.

Why couldn't he just tell me what was about to happen for a change? Why did I always have to experience it myself? Oh well. Why argue? I reluctantly lifted the clear globe and slowly lowered it down over my head—until a freaky thing happened. As soon as the top of my head touched the inside of the globe, the clear dome started to change shape! I instantly yanked the cursed thing off. It immediately stopped moving and returned to its original round shape.

"What the hell was that?" I exclaimed, totally freaked out.

Uncle Press laughed and reached toward the pile of stuff to get another clear globe.

"The Clorans are pretty advanced," he explained. "They've got some pretty incredible toys."

"Like torture devices that clamp on your head and suck out your brain?"

"No, like anything to do with water. Water is their life. They've learned how to use it in ways you can't even imagine."

He put the second globe over his head. Instantly the clear dome began to writhe and change shape. In a few seconds the sphere went from totally round, to a perfect formfitting shell around his head. It was unbelievable. The thing had taken on the shape of Uncle Press's head. He smiled at me from inside the clear mask.

"They've figured out how to create solid material from water," he said while tapping the shell that had formed around his face. It was hard again. Amazing. I could even hear him clearly, though his head was encased in . . . whatever it was encased in.

"And this thing here"—he pointed to the silver harmonica thing attached at the back of his head—"this is a filter that takes in water, breaks it down atomically, and feeds oxygen into the mask so you can breathe. Cool, aye?"

Now I got it. This strange living mask was some kind of scuba gizmo. You could breathe underwater with this thing.

And the clear plastic would act as a mask to keep water out of your eyes so you could see. How cool is that?

Uncle Press pulled the clear mask up off his head, and by the time he placed it in his lap it had already become round again.

"Centuries of living on water makes you resourceful," he said.

"Absolutely," I added. "What else you got there?"

There were two gizmos on the pile that I can best describe as looking like the plastic floats lifeguards use when they make rescues. Uncle Press picked one up and held it out for me to see. It was roughly football shaped, bright purple, and had handle grips on each side. It was about a foot and a half long. One end had a round, open mouth. The other end came to a point. There were also rows of slits that ran across the top and bottom.

"Okay, I give up," I said.

"It's a water sled. When you're in the water, grab the handles, hold it out in front of you and pull the trigger."

I could see that hidden inside each of the handles was a trigger.

"The open end goes in front," he explained. "Point it where you want to go. Water gets sucked in through these slits for power and the whole thing pulls you along. The harder you squeeze the trigger, the faster you go. Easy peazy."

This was getting good. I was beginning to see why Uncle Press liked Cloral so much. He then threw me a pair of rubbery swim fins that needed no explanation.

"Get changed," he added.

It was time to dress like a Cloran. I had been through this drill before. So I walked across the stone ledge and began to dig through the pile of Cloral clothes. Uncle Press did the same. There were shirts and pants and even shorts that I guess were supposed to be used as underwear. Good thing. I didn't get to wear any underwear on Denduron and the rough leather clothes gave me a raging rash that was only now starting to calm down.

The material was soft and kind of rubbery. Cloral was all about water, so I guessed these clothes would be perfect for swimming and would dry fast. The colors were bright, too. All were on the cool end of the spectrum, blue, green, and purple. I knew from the times that Uncle Press had taken me scuba diving that the best colors to use underwater were in the blue family—they showed up best. Colors like red and yellow were quickly filtered away underwater so they ended up looking gray, but blue still looked like blue underwater. So did purple and green.

I had the feeling that there would be more opportunities for my scuba diving experience to come in handy here on this water territory. Uncle Press had taken me to diving classes last year and I got my open-water diver's certification. Uncle Press then took me on a great trip to Florida where we dove in the ocean and explored some of the fresh water springs. That was fantastic. We swam with schools of fish and hitched rides on turtles.

Uncle Press and I had done a lot of great things like that. I was beginning to think that maybe those adventures weren't so much about having fun as they were about preparing me for some of the challenges I would face as a Traveler. I guess I should be grateful—except maybe for the time he took me sky diving. It was a blast, but I really didn't want to think about what he may have been preparing me for with that little episode. Yikes.

I grabbed a light blue shirt and pair of pants that looked

sort of like the same color. Nobody knew me here, but I didn't want to look like a clashing, colorblind geek. I picked out some blue shorts, too. I wasn't sure if they were the right size, but when I put them on, it was like they were made for me! There weren't any zippers or buttons, either. I dumped my Second Earth clothes and stepped into the shorts and pants, then pulled the shirt down over my head. The stretchy clothes molded to my body perfectly. They weren't too tight, but were still formfitting enough that nothing would twist and get in the way in the water. There were even soft boots with hard rubber souls that slipped on easily and fit like they were custom-made. It was all very Star Trek.

"Put on a belt, too," said Uncle Press, and handed me a thin, soft strap.

"That's okay," I replied. "I'm not a belt kind of guy."

"It's not about fashion," he said. "It's a BC."

Cool. Going back to my scuba experience, I knew that BC stood for buoyancy compensator. Scuba divers have to wear a weight belt underwater or they'd float back to the surface. A BC is a vest that you fill with air from your scuba tank to help you adjust your buoyancy so you won't sink to the bottom, or shoot up to the surface. When everything is perfect, it's called "neutrally buoyant." It makes swimming feel like flying. But I wasn't sure how this little belt was going to keep anybody neutrally buoyant.

"It's automatic," Uncle Press explained. I think he was reading my mind again. "It takes on water for weight, or creates oxygen for lift, depending on what you need. I told you, these guys are pretty advanced."

I took his word for it and threaded the strap through the belt loops on my new pants. I was really eager to get in the water and try out these new toys. This was like old times with

Uncle Press, only better. Yes, so far I really liked Cloral. It was a major improvement over Denduron. It was warm, the clothes didn't suck, the local fruit was pretty tasty, and from what Uncle Press told me, this was a territory that wasn't at war with anybody and had advanced enough to create some pretty nifty gadgets. I was actually jazzed about getting out of the cavern and starting to explore.

That is, until I saw Uncle Press doing something odd. As soon as he finished dressing in his local outfit, he took one of the extra pairs of Cloral pants and tied a knot on the end of each leg.

"Grab a bunch of fruit," he ordered.

I started grabbing off pieces of fruit from the vines. Uncle Press took the pieces and stuffed them into the pant legs he had just tied off. I figured maybe he was using the pants as a makeshift bag to carry some fruit to the surface. That was cool. I liked the stuff. He filled the pants up until they looked like a lumpy pair of legs, then yanked down a piece of vine from the wall and used it as a rope to thread through the belt loops and tie off the waist.

"Hand me one of the water sleds," he asked.

Okay, now he lost me. What was he doing? I gave him one of the two purple sleds and he tied the other end of the vine that was holding the pants together to the handles. There was now about a three-foot length of vine between the water sled and the pants full of fruit.

"You gonna tell me what you're doing?"

"We've got to swim out of here," he explained. "Put on fins. We'll use the air globes to breathe. We're only about sixty feet down. There should be a skimmer waiting for us on the surface."

"A skimmer?"

"It's like a speedboat. Very fast. Easy to maneuver. You'll love it."

"Courtesy of the acolytes?"

"Exactly."

"What's with the fruity pants?"

"No big deal. Just a little quig bait."

Uh-oh. That was it. Fun time was over. He punctuated this last comment by digging down under the rest of the Cloral clothes and pulling out a nasty-looking speargun. I knew this was going too well. There were quigs lurking outside. If you remember, quigs were the nasty beasties that Saint Dane used to guard the gates to the flumes. On Second Earth they were wild dogs. On Denduron they were prehistoric, cannibal bears with spiny backs. On Cloral they could only be . . .

"Sharks," I said flatly. "You're saying there are giant sharks swimming around out there waiting for us to pop out in our spiffy new rubber outfits?"

"You saw one yourself, on Denduron."

I did. In the mine shaft flume on Denduron. I still remember its demonic, yellow quig-eyes as it rode the wave of water toward us. The memory made my knees buckle. The tropical vacation was over.

"Don't worry," said Uncle Press. "I'll send the water sled out first. Our smell is already on these pants. If there are any quigs around, and I'm not saying there *are*, mind you, they'll chase the smell."

"You think they'll be dumb enough to go for it?"

"They're vicious, not bright," he answered with confidence. "We'll have plenty of time to get to the surface and find the skimmer."

He handed me the speargun, which I took gingerly.

"You don't expect me to use this, do you?"

"Just hold it," he said. He then took another small piece of vine and looped it through the handle of the water sled. With a quick tug, he tightened it down so that it pulled the trigger, then tied a knot to keep it in place. The trigger supposedly kicked over the engine, but it wasn't making any noise.

"Why didn't it turn on?" I asked.

"I told you, it needs water for power."

Uncle Press knelt down next to the pool. He first placed the loaded pants into the water. They floated off to the length of the vine that was attached to the sled. Then with both hands on the sled, he lowered the purple engine underwater as well. As soon as the slits were underwater, I could hear the low whine of its motor kick to life. The trigger was pulled all the way so it was on full power. The little sled nearly yanked Uncle Press off the ledge. He had to struggle just to hang on to it.

"Told you," he said with a laugh. "This thing has some giddyap."

He was enjoying this way too much. He then released his grip and the sled jumped out of his hands. The vine attached to the pants snapped tight, and it was gone in an instant, dragging the pants o' fruit after it.

Uncle Press then sat down to put on his swim fins. I put the speargun down and did the same, quickly. I wanted to be up and out of the water before any quigs realized they were on a wild-fruit chase and came back looking for meat. Uncle Press then picked up one of the clear globes and tossed it to me.

"Let's go," he said with a smile.

I think he was actually looking forward to this. He was crazy. I put the globe over my head and it immediately began changing into the shape of my face. I developed instant claustrophobia and had to tell myself that it was going to be okay.

It worked for Uncle Press. It'll work for me. Either that or it will smother me and I'll die right here in this fruit-filled underwater cavern. Maybe that wouldn't be such a bad thing. It would definitely be better than getting chomped on by Jaws.

"Breathe normally," instructed Uncle Press. "It's easier than using a regulator from a scuba tank."

Breathe normally. Yeah, right. We were about to dip into shark-infested waters and he wanted me to breathe normally. Maybe I should try and stop my heart from pounding out 180 beats a minute while I was at it.

"I'll use the water sled," he said. "It'll be faster than swimming. When we go under, get on my back and hold on to my belt with your left hand, tight."

"What do I do with my right hand?"

"That's for the speargun."

"Oh, no," I said. "I'm not taking that responsibility. No way."

"Just hang on to it," he said, trying to reassure me. "Nothing's going to happen. But on the off chance it does, we'll stop and you can give the gun to me. Okay?"

I guess that made sense. If the choice was between having a speargun and not having it, I'd certainly rather have it. So I reluctantly reached down and picked up the weapon. The gun was made of what looked like bright green plastic. The spear that was loaded in the gun was actually clear, like glass. But it looked pretty lethal just the same. I'm guessing it was made from the same hard material as our air-globe helmets. I felt the tip. Oh, yeah, it was sharp. I had held a speargun once before, in Florida. So I knew how to be safe with it. But to be honest, I never shot anything. I couldn't bring myself to do it. I never even liked fishing with a rod and reel, let alone a high-powered weapon. Okay, so I'm a wuss.

"Once we submerge," Uncle Press instructed, "we have to swim under the rock ledge for about thirty yards. We won't use the water sled until we get out from under the ledge. Then we've got to travel about a hundred yards along the reef to where the skimmer is anchored. Understand?"

I understood all right. I understood that I didn't like Cloral anymore, no matter how nice and warm the water was. But I didn't say that. Time was wasting. Uncle Press grabbed the other water sled and slipped into the pool. I jumped in too and immediately felt the belt tighten around my waist. This thing really did work automatically. I found that I didn't have to tread water to stay afloat. The belt had compensated for my weight and kept me hovering in the water comfortably. I would have been really impressed, if I wasn't ready to puke out of fear.

"Is that decoy really going to lure the quigs away?" I asked hopefully.

"In theory."

"Theory! Don't give me theory! I want guarantees!"

"The sooner we go, the sooner we'll be safe," he replied calmly.

"Then let's get out of here!" I shouted.

With a wink and a quick swing of his arms, Uncle Press sank underwater. I took one last look around the cavern and spotted the mouth of the flume far overhead. I was sorely tempted to shout out "*Second Earth!*" so the flume would suck me up and bring me home. But I didn't. I was here now and I had to go forward, not back. Actually, I had to go down. Underwater. With a sweep of my arms and a kick of my legs, I thrust up out of the water, then sank back down below the surface. We were on our way. Hopefully it wouldn't be a short and painful trip.

CLORAL

Swimming underwater is a very cool thing.

My parents taught me how to snorkel in Long Island Sound when I was a kid and Uncle Press, as I told you, took me to get my diving certification. I never liked regular old swimming much. To me, doing laps in a pool was like jogging on a treadmill. There was nothing interesting to look at. But diving below the surface was a whole other story. That was like dropping in to a different world.

Of course, I had been dropping in to a few too many different worlds lately, so I wasn't as psyched about this dive as usual.

Once I sank below the surface, I was afraid to take a breath. I was used to breathing through a mouthpiece connected to a hose that was connected to a scuba tank. But there was no mouthpiece in this weird head-bubble thing. And there was no tank of compressed air strapped to my back either. All I had was a stupid little harmonica-looking doo-dad stuck near the back of my head that was supposed to take oxygen out of water. Suddenly the whole thing sounded pretty impossible. Even though I knew I was underwater and my head was still completely dry, I couldn't bring myself to let go and . . .

"Breathe!" commanded Uncle Press.

I spun around and saw that he was floating right next to me. How weird was that? I could hear him even though we were underwater with our heads encased in clear plastic. His voice sounded kind of high and thin, like the treble knob on my stereo was cranked all the way to ten and the bass was backed off to zero, but I could hear him as plain as if, well, as if we weren't underwater.

"Trust me, Bobby," he said. "Look at me. I'm breathing. It works."

I wanted to trust him. I also wanted to shoot back to the surface and breathe real air. But my lungs were starting to hurt. I didn't have any choice. I had to breathe. I exhaled what little air I had left in my lungs, then took in a tentative breath, to discover it worked. I had no idea how, but that little harmonica gizmo was letting me breathe. It was even better than using a mouthpiece and a scuba tank because there were no hoses to deal with. And because there was no mouthpiece, I could talk. We could communicate underwater!

"That's better," Uncle Press said reassuringly. "You okay?"

"Yeah," I answered. "How come we can talk?"

"It's the re-breather," he said, tapping the silver device on the back of his globe. "It carries sound waves, too. Cool, aye?"

Cool was the word.

"Let's go," he ordered.

With a kick of his fins Uncle Press took off swimming. He left a trail of carbon dioxide bubbles that came from the re-breathing device as he exhaled. Now that I was getting used to breathing in the air globe, I took a quick look around to get oriented. The pool of water we had flumed into turned out to be the opening to a passageway underneath a huge overhang of rock. Uncle Press was now slowly swimming toward a ribbon of light about thirty yards away that I could tell was the end of the rock ceiling, just as he had described. Behind me I saw that the ceiling only went back a few more feet before ending at a craggy wall. This was a pretty out-of-the-way place for a gate to be hidden. But I guess that was the idea. The gates were *all* hidden in remote places so ordinary people from the territories wouldn't accidentally find them.

Uncle Press was already several yards ahead of me and I didn't want to be left here alone, so I kicked off and started after him. The BC belt was doing a perfect job of keeping me neutrally buoyant. I kicked easily and swam perfectly level. I didn't have to worry about banging my head on the rock ceiling above or crashing into the sand below. Excellent. If only I weren't so worried about a quig sneaking up on us, it would have been perfect. I gripped the speargun and did a quick look right and left to make sure no bogey had wandered under the rock shelf to join us. The water was incredibly clear. I'm guessing I had about a hundred feet of visibility, which is amazing. If there were any quigs headed for us, at least we'd have a little bit of warning before we got chewed on.

Uncle Press stopped when he got to the end of the overhang. The ceiling was lower there, so the distance from the rock overhead down to the sandy bottom was now about five feet. Uncle Press swam a few yards out into open water then motioned for me to look at something. I joined him outside and saw that he was pointing back to the lip of the rock where we had just come out. There, carved into the stone, was the familiar star symbol that designated this as a gate to the flumes. I gave him an okay sign, which is the universal signal you use underwater that means you understand.

Uncle Press returned the okay sign, which is custom, then smiled and said, "We can talk, remember?"

Oh, right. We didn't have to use hand signals. I'd forgotten. Habit, I guess. I looked up and saw a wall of rock we'd been swimming under that extended straight up. This was the formation that housed the cavern and the flume.

"Now check this out," he added, and pointed behind me.

I turned around and was confronted with one of the most breathtaking sights I had ever seen. Beyond us was open, green-blue sea. The sandy bottom turned into a coral reef that spread out before us like a colorful blanket. It was awesome. I had been on tropical reefs before and seen all sorts of tropical fish and unique coral formations, but I had never seen anything like this. The colors of this reef were nearly as vibrant as the flowers in the cavern we had just left. There were intense blue fans the size of umbrellas that waved lazily in the soft current. Dotted around them were giant chunks of brain coral, which are called that because they look like, well, like brains. At home brain coral is kind of brownish and dull. Here on Cloral, it was bright yellow. Yellow! I told you before that water filters out red and yellow at this depth, but not here on Cloral. Every color of the spectrum could be seen. There was vibrant green vegetation growing all over the reef. Off to our left was a thick forest of kelp. The vines started on the reef and floated all the way to the surface like leafy ropes—and they were bright red! Other coral had grown up out of the rock bed and formed shapes that looked like a green topiary garden. If you used your imagination, they seemed like a herd of small animals grazing on the rocks. But they weren't; they were coral. Amazing.

Swimming among all this splendor were the most incredible fish I had ever seen. They traveled in schools, each seeming to know exactly what the others were thinking as they all changed direction at the exact same time. It always amazed me how there could be a hundred fish in a school, but none of them ever made a wrong turn or bumped into one another. One school looked like silver flutes with long delicate fins that fluttered quickly like the wings of a hummingbird. Another school of fish were perfectly round and thin, like a CD. Only they were bright pink! Still another school looked exactly like small bluebirds with beaks and feathers. I know they were swimming, but with each flap of their fins it sure seemed like they were flying. It was all a perfectly orchestrated ballet, and it was beautiful to watch them swim about the colorful reef, lazily enjoying their day.

I was totally in awe of the spectacular scene. The water was as clear as air. It was even more special because the air globes allowed me to look all around. Unlike diving goggles where you pretty much had to look straight ahead, the air globe gave me a perfect view of everything—and, man, it was worth it!

That is, until something happened that caught my eye.

"Uh-oh," said Uncle Press.

He had seen it too. One second there were hundreds of these weird fish gently dancing through the currents. The very next moment they all scattered. It happened so fast that if I had blinked I would have missed it. Every single last fish in my view had suddenly darted off in a different direction. There's a better word for it. They had fled. Something had scared them. And if they were scared, I was too.

"What's going on?" I asked, not really wanting to hear the answer.

"Something just spooked the fish."

"Yeah, no kidding," I said. "What do you think—"

"Look out!"

Uncle Press grabbed my arm and pulled me back down under the rock ledge. A second later I saw what caused the fish panic. Yup, it was a shark. A quig shark. It wasn't in a hurry though. The big beast drifted past us as we cowered back in the shadow of the ledge. It used no effort to propel itself along.

It was beautiful and horrifying at the same time. Most of its body was battleship gray, but its underbelly was jet black. And it was big. We're talking *Jaws* big. It was way bigger than the shark Saint Dane had sent back at us through the flume. One thing was the same though. Its eyes. The beast had the cold, yellow eyes that told me it was no ordinary shark. It was a quig, no doubt about it. The monster glided past, turned away from the rock, and started swimming directly away from us.

"Maybe it didn't see us," I said hopefully.

"It saw us," came the flat response. "It's just taking its time to—here we go!"

I quickly looked back outside and saw in horror that the shark had done a complete 180 and was now swimming directly at us! It had moved away from the rock overhang so it could get up a good head of steam to make its kill run at us. There was nowhere to run, or should I say, swim. We were trapped and this thing had us in its sights.

Uncle Press grabbed the speargun away from me, planted his feet, and took aim. The quig kept coming. It was almost on us. Its jaws were already open in anticipation of the big bad bite.

"Shoot!" I yelled. "Get him!"

Uncle Press waited to make sure he wouldn't miss. I hoped he was as good with this speargun as he was with the spears on Denduron. His finger tightened on the trigger, but he didn't fire.

Believe it or not, the shark being so big turned out to be a good thing. Its head slid underneath the ledge, but its dorsal fin hit the rock above. Yes! It was too big to fit under the ledge. It couldn't get to us! Uncle Press lowered the speargun because the immediate danger was gone. That is, unless the quig could figure out how to squeeze in sideways. I didn't think that would happen. Fish don't swim sideways.

"So much for your decoy theory," I said.

"It worked," replied Uncle Press. "But this bad boy was quicker than I thought. Look."

I saw that stuck in the shark's teeth was the decoy water sled, completely tangled up in pants and vines. The quig went for the bait all right, but it was just an appetizer. It now wanted the main course. Us.

The huge quig wriggled and squirmed, trying to force its way under the rock shelf. If it's possible for a fish to look angry, this thing looked major-league ticked. It writhed its body, swung its tail and gnashed its jaws, desperately trying to get at us. We were just out of its reach by a few yards. Too close, in my book, but no matter how furiously the quig pushed, its body was too big to squeeze any closer. Phew!

"If you've got a plan B, now's the time to tell me," I said nervously.

"I've always got a plan B," came the confident reply. "I'm going to swim over to the left and come out from under the ledge. When it sees me, I guarantee it'll come after me. As soon as I get a clear shot at it, I'll take it. Its skull is thin. One shot and he's gone."

"Why wait?" I shouted. "Do it here!"

"I can't get a good shot through the sand. I don't want to miss."

He was right. The quig's violent thrashing had kicked up a storm of sand and it was hard to tell which end was up.

"As soon as it follows me, swim out as fast as you can, and keep swimming straight ahead along the reef. About a hundred yards dead ahead you'll see an anchor line that'll lead you up to the skimmer. I'll catch up with the water sled. Got it?"

"No, I don't," I said with rising panic. "What if you miss? What if the spear misses the skull and all you end up doing is pissing him off more? I want a plan C."

"There is only a plan B." Then he added with a confident smile, "And I never miss."

"Uncle Press I—"

He didn't stay to listen. He kicked off forward, coming dangerously close to the snapping jaws of the quig, then shot off to the left using the speedy water sled to pull him along. He did a great job of tempting the quig, because it pulled its body back out from under the ledge and started to shadow him.

Now was the time. The quig was busy, and if I was going to get out of here, it had to be now. Unfortunately, I couldn't move. Panic had set in and I was frozen. The idea of swimming out into open water where that quig could turn around and chomp me like a Slim Jim had shut down all of my systems. I was absolutely, totally incapable of moving.

Then I spotted something. The billowing sand was starting to settle and I saw it lying on the bottom near the edge of the rock outcropping. It was the water sled Uncle Press had used as a decoy! The quig must have dropped it out of its mouth when it backed out. It gave me a flash of hope. If I could use the speed of that water sled, then maybe I had a chance of getting to the skimmer before Moby Dick came a-nibbling. That was it. I had to do it.

My legs worked again. I pushed forward and quickly swam to the tangle of pants and vines that engulfed the water sled. I picked it up to find that the pants were totally wrapped around the thing. The fruit stuffing was gone though. The quig had gotten a treat out of this after all. But there was a problem. I quickly saw that the sled wasn't going to work because the pants were totally wrapped around it. The pants kept water from entering the slits, and that's where it got its power. I had to get rid of the pants, or the sled would be useless. So I frantically began tugging at them.

While I worked I glanced up to where Uncle Press had gone, but there was no sign of him, or the quig. Had he speared it already? I had absolute confidence in Uncle Press. If he said he was going to shoot the quig, then the quig would be shot. But what if the quig had his *own* plan B and decided not to follow him? Then all bets were off. I had to think less and work faster. Finally I figured out how the pants had gotten twisted around the sled and with a final yank, I pulled them free.

Big, big mistake.

You know what it's like when you're walking in bare feet and stub your toe really hard? A weird thing happens. There's about a half-second delay between the time you crunch your toe and when the pain registers in your brain. That's just enough time to think "Uh-oh!" before you feel the hurt. I don't know why that happens, but it does. Well, that's kind of what happened to me right then and there. The instant I pulled the pants off the water sled, I realized I had made a huge mistake.

What hit me was that the little piece of vine Uncle Press

had used to tie the trigger down was still in place. The sled was still turned on. The only reason it wasn't moving was because the pants had prevented water from entering the slits. But as soon as I pulled the pants away, the slits were cleared and water could rush in to power the engine and—like when you stub your toe—I had about a half-second to think "Uh-oh!"

Oh, yeah. The sled was on and ready to go. I wasn't. Too bad.

Things happened fast. The powerful little engine sprang to life and jumped out of my hand. It only got worse. While trying to get the pants away from the sled, I had gotten the vine twisted around my wrist. It was the vine that had tied the pants to the water sled. It was the vine that was *still* tied to the water sled, and the other end was now wrapped around my wrist. Yeah, you guessed it. The vine snapped taut and an instant later I was yanked sideways and dragged through the water by the runaway sled, full throttle.

Worse still, it pulled me out from under the rock ledge, into open water and right in the same direction that Uncle Press had lured the quig. That was the *last* place I wanted to go, but I had no way of steering because the sled was out of my reach. I desperately tried to pull the vine off my wrist, but it was so twisted I couldn't free it. I was absolutely, totally out of control. I tried to look ahead, but I was moving so fast the force of the water kept spinning me around. No matter what I did to kick my fins or twist my body, I kept spinning helplessly. I felt like the tail on an out-of-control kite. I wasn't the one in charge, it was the runaway water sled that was calling all the shots, and right now it was pulling me toward an angry quig.

I twisted my neck to look up ahead and sure enough, there

it was. I saw the immense gray shape of the quig, lurking just outside the rock ledge, peering in at what I guessed was Uncle Press. I was traveling parallel to the rock ledge, further out than the quig. In a few seconds I would pass by the monster and unless it was deaf and blind, I would get its attention. I could only hope that between now and then Uncle Press would nail it with the speargun. But he would have to shoot fast because I was almost at the quig.

Then two things happened. When I flew by the quig, it heard me coming and it made a sudden, surprised turn to see me. It was a small turn, but enough to let something else happen that made me want to scream. I saw the glint of a spear come shooting out from under the rock ledge—and miss its mark. The missile sliced through the water just over the quig's head. Uncle Press assured me that he wouldn't miss, but he hadn't figured that I'd be flying by like an idiot to distract his prey.

The quig had dodged eternity, and now the prey was me.

I was traveling on my back now. My arm felt like it was going to rip out of the socket, that's how powerful the pull from the water sled was. But when I looked back, I realized the pain in my shoulder was the least of my problems. The quig was after me. As fast as this sled was pulling me, the quig was faster.

It took only a few seconds for the huge beast to swim right up beside me. We were traveling at the same speed with ten yards between us. I can't begin to tell you how helpless and vulnerable I felt. I knew that soon this bad boy would turn into me and clamp its jaws on my midsection. I saw its yellow eye staring at me. There was no emotion there, just calculation. It was measuring the perfect moment to turn and strike. This was going to be a bad way to die. I'm not exactly sure if there's a *good* way to die, but if so, this isn't it.

The quig didn't come any closer. It didn't need to. When it struck, it would need a little bit of distance to get a good run at me. In fact, it started to pull a little bit ahead. It made a few quick little head turns toward me, as if judging the exact right distance and speed for its attack. This was torture. I was at the point that I wanted to get it over with.

Finally it struck.

The shark opened its jaws and made a sharp turn toward me. I gritted my teeth, waiting for the pain.

But then I saw a flash of light just over the shark's head. Was it a flash of light? No, it was another spear! I thought for an instant that Uncle Press had reloaded, but that was impossible. There was no way he could have reloaded and got up above fast enough to be shooting from that angle. No, the spear had come from someone else.

Whoever the archer was, he was good. The spear flew directly down at the shark and struck it on top of the head, burrowing into its skull. The instant the spear found its mark the quig started to thrash. It was still headed toward me though, and as it spun I got slammed in the ribs by its tail. Yeow. It hurt, too. Bad. But I didn't care. It didn't hurt like its teeth would have.

The quig continued thrashing and sank down beneath me. A moment later it crashed into the reef. The sled kept pulling me away, but I looked back and saw that the monster was writhing uncontrollably. It was a horrifying sight. This fish was history. It wasn't going to eat me or anybody else.

I was saved from the quig, but I was still traveling out of control. I wondered how long this little engine would go before burning out. Now my arm was starting to hurt bad. Not to mention my ribs, which had taken a healthy whack of shark tail. I wasn't sure how much longer I could take this.

Then something caught my eye. It was a gray shape moving up alongside me. Uh-oh. Was there another quig? I spun around to get a better look and saw that it wasn't a quig at all. It was a guy being pulled by another water sled. But it wasn't Uncle Press. This guy wore black pants with a black top that had no sleeves. Through the clear air globe on his head I saw that his hair was kind of long and black. He had an empty speargun strapped to his leg, which meant he was probably the shooter who saved my life. I had no idea who this guy was, but I liked him already.

He knew how to handle a water sled, too. He eased over close to me until we were traveling side by side. He held on to his sled with one hand and let go with the other to reach back to his leg. What was he doing? He brought his hand forward again and I saw that he was now holding a very large, very nasty-looking silver knife. For a second I freaked. Was he going to stab me? But that didn't make sense. He wouldn't have gone through the trouble of killing the quig just to kill me himself. At least I didn't think so.

He reached forward with the knife and with one quick move he lashed out at me. Not knowing what he was doing, I closed my eyes. But what he did with that one strong swipe was cut the vine that attached me to the runaway water sled. The pull on my arm stopped instantly. The force of the water slowed me down. I looked ahead to see the runaway water sled continue forward on its crazed trip to nowhere. Good riddance!

I was dazed and hurt. I tried to move my legs to get some sort of control, but I was floundering. That's when I felt something grab the back of my shirt. It was the guy in black. He had come around and was now right next to me.

Without a word he grabbed the back of my collar and began towing me to the surface. I totally relaxed. Whoever this guy was, he was in charge now and I didn't care. All I could think about was breathing fresh air again.

The trip to the surface took about twenty seconds. The closer we got, the brighter the water became. I couldn't wait to get on top. Then just before we surfaced, the guy in black let go of my collar and let me float up on my own.

It was a great feeling. My head broke the surface and the BC belt kept me floating. That was a good thing because I didn't think I could tread water just then. I yanked the air globe off my head and took a deep breath of fresh air. The sun was warm, the air smelled sweet, and I was alive.

"Friend of Press's, are you?" came a voice from behind me.

I spun around to see the guy in black floating next to me. He had taken off his air globe and I now saw that he was a little older than me, and had a slight Asian look with almond-shaped eyes. He had deep, sun-colored skin and long black hair. He also had the biggest, friendliest smile I thought I'd ever seen in my life.

"Told me he was bringing somebody to visit," the guy said cheerfully. "Sorry 'bout the rude welcome. Them sharks can stir up a real natty-do sometimes. Easy enough to handle 'em though. Just gotta know the soft spots," he said, tapping his head.

"Who are you?" was all I could think of saying.

"Name's Spader. Vo Spader. Pleased to meet you."

"I'm Bobby Pendragon. You saved my life." I wasn't sure what else to add but, "Thanks."

"No big stuff. It happens. Never saw anyone caught up by a sled like that though. No sir, that was a real tum-tigger."

"Yeah, a real tum-tigger," I said. Whatever *that* was.

"Took us a might off course though," he added, looking around.

I looked around too and what I saw made my heart start to race again. Because what I saw was . . . nothing. Oh, there was plenty of water all right. But that was it. We were in the middle of the ocean with no landmass in sight.

If a tum-tigger was bad, this was definitely a tum-tigger.

CLORAL

Talk about feeling helpless. Here we were, two guys floating like corks in an endless ocean. A quick three-sixty scan showed no land, no boat, and no rescue of any kind in sight.

"Beautiful day, isn't it?" asked Spader.

Beautiful day? We were lost at sea and he was talking about nice weather? Either he was in strong denial, or he was crazy. Either way, he was starting to make me nervous.

That's when I felt a tug on my foot.

I screamed. The quig was back. Or he had a brother. Or he had *two* brothers. And they were both after me and they . . .

The water to my right began to boil and an instant later a bubble-covered head surfaced. It was Uncle Press. He yanked off his air globe and smiled at me.

"Have a nice trip, Bobby?" he asked. "That wasn't exactly plan B."

"You think I *tried* to get dragged like that?" I shot back, all indignant.

"Whoa. Relax. I was kidding."

"And I thought you never missed?"

I couldn't help but add that last dig. I knew it was my fault he missed hitting the quig with the spear, but still, he did say he *never* missed. No qualifications.

"Then it's a good thing Spader came along," he said calmly.

"Hello, Press!" exclaimed Spader. "Good to see your face again."

"Yours, too," said Uncle Press. "Lucky for us you were in the area."

"I was out doing a bit of fishin' and spotted your skimmer anchored a ways back," said Spader. "I have to say I was a might surprised. You know this is shark territory."

"Yeah, tell me about it," I threw in. "Maybe we shouldn't be here anymore."

"Right!" shouted Spader. "No sense in waiting for another nibbler to come a-callin'."

Spader looked at his big, black diver-style watch. I think it must have been some kind of compass because he checked it, looked up, changed position, then announced, "Off we go."

He popped the air globe back on his head, pointed his water sled, then shot off across the surface.

I looked at Uncle Press thinking that this guy must be crazy. There was nothing out here. Where was he going?

"I love that guy," he said.

"Where is he going? We're in the middle of an ocean."

Uncle Press put his air globe back on and swam close to me. "He'll bring us to our skimmer. You okay?"

"I feel like I was stretched on a medieval rack and beaten with a club. Other than that, I'm cool. But I don't think I can swim."

"You don't have to. Put your globe on and grab my belt."

I did as I was told. I put the air globe back on and it instantly conformed to my head. I then reached out for Uncle

Press's belt. I made sure to use my left hand. My right arm had taken a bit too much abuse. It was probably two inches longer now, too.

Uncle Press gently squeezed the throttle on his water sled and we started our journey toward the skimmer that would take us . . . somewhere. Luckily the water was calm so the trip was easy. Good thing, too. I needed to catch my breath. As Uncle Press pulled me through the gentle swells, I floated on my back and looked up at the sun. Yes, the sun. There was only one, unlike Denduron where there were three. It was a hot sun, too. So far everything about Cloral gave me the feeling of being someplace tropical. Both the water and the air were warm, but not so hot as to be uncomfortable. Of course, the whole quig thing made the place feel a little less like paradise, but you can't have everything.

We had only traveled for a few minutes when Uncle Press slowed to a stop. I let go of his belt and saw that bobbing on the water in front of us were two water vehicles—skimmers. Spader had actually found his way here with the help of his watch. Talk about finding a needle in a haystack. I was impressed.

Spader had already climbed aboard one of the vehicles. They looked kind of like Jet Skis. But these sleek vehicles weren't toys. They were way too high-tech for that. Each frame was about the size of a very shallow bathtub. They were pure white and looked to be made out of plastic. The bow was pointed and the stern was straight across. To control it, the driver stood at a column that looked like motorcycle handle-bars. Behind the driver's space was a molded seat for a second passenger. The sides only came up a few inches. I guess water getting inside wasn't a problem.

You'd think they'd be unstable, but that was taken care

of. The skimmers had wings. If you've ever seen an outrigger canoe with beams that project out to the side, with pontoons on the end, you'll know what I'm talking about. The skimmers had outriggers on either side. Right now they were lifted up out of the water, which gave them the look of a bird frozen in midflap. On the ends of each outrigger were torpedo-shaped pontoons. My guess was that when under way, the outriggers would be lowered into the water to make the skimmer stable.

Spader's skimmer was identical to Uncle Press's, except that he had a float thing that was attached to the back like a caboose. It was some kind of equipment carrier that floated behind the main skimmer.

No, these skimmers weren't toys. They looked more like those sleek, high-end corporate jets that big shots fly around in. I have to admit, they were way cool.

As Uncle Press climbed up on his skimmer, I watched this Spader guy. Who was he? Was he the Traveler from Cloral? Whoever he was, he was pretty confident in the water. But I guess you have to be if you come from Cloral. His skin was really dark, but I don't know if that was natural or because he was out in the sun so much. Probably a little of both. He was about six feet tall and looked pretty strong. Not a muscle guy, but definitely lean and mean. His black hair was long and shaggy and nearly came to his shoulders.

But the thing that stood out most about him was his personality. I know that sounds weird, especially since I had just met him and all, but right from the start I knew this guy had it all going on. He was concerned enough about Uncle Press that he went looking for him when he saw that his skimmer was anchored in quig waters, then risked himself to save my life. But he shrugged the whole thing off like it was no big deal. That was pretty cool. And the guy always looked like he was having fun. Whether it was flying underwater with his sled, or getting his skimmer ready to run, the little smile on his face made it look as if he always enjoyed whatever he was doing. You gotta like a guy like that. Bottom line, from what I had seen so far, I thought Spader was pretty cool.

"C'mon, Bobby," said Uncle Press.

I kicked my fins and slid over toward the skimmer. Uncle Press had to pull me out of the water because I had no strength left in my arms. I laid down on the deck of the skimmer, happy to be on something solid again, even if it was just a small high-powered boat.

"You okay, Pendragon?" called Spader from his skimmer.

I struggled to sit up and pretend that I wasn't totally out of my league here, which I was.

"I'm good," I shouted, not convincingly. Then added, "Real good!" as if that would make me sound better off than I was. I'm sure I didn't fool anybody.

Spader let out a big, warm laugh. For a second I thought he was laughing at me, but he wasn't.

"Don't you worry, mate, been there myself. Many times," he said. "We'll fix you up spiff soon as we get back, don't you worry."

"Get back where?" I asked.

Spader now stood at the controls of his skimmer, as did Uncle Press. I saw that they each began flipping toggle switches. As they did, the skimmers came to life. I heard a slight whine of engines, then in turn, each of the outriggers that had been sticking up in the air began their descent into the water.

I also saw that Spader and Uncle Press had both grown tense. They each stood stiffly at their control columns while throwing quick, furtive glances at each other. Something was up. I didn't like this.

"It's a wonderful place," continued Spader. "You're going to love it."

"I'll second that," added Uncle Press. "Spader lives on the most beautiful habitat on Cloral."

The two were speaking calmly, but their body language said they were anything but calm. What was going on? Was there another quig zeroing in on us? Each of the four outriggers was now underwater and I could hear the low hum of the skimmer's engines waiting to be told what to do.

"Nice of you to say, Press," replied Spader. "Last one to Grallion buys the sniggers?"

"Snickers?" I said. "They have candy bars here?"

"Sniggers, Bobby. It's a drink," answered Uncle Press. Then to Spader, "But I don't know the way."

"No worries," laughed Spader. "Follow me!"

With that Spader gunned his skimmer and shot forward.

"Hang on!" shouted Uncle Press and hit the throttle.

Our skimmer took off and I got rocked back on my butt. I wished he had given me a little more warning. Now it all made sense. These guys were playing with each other. They wanted to race. Okay, I could deal with that. I scrambled to my knees and got into the seat behind Uncle Press. Our two air globes were rolling around on the deck so before I could look to see where we were going, I grabbed them to make sure they wouldn't go flying overboard.

We were moving fast—faster than I've ever traveled over the water. I looked down at the pontoons and saw that they weren't just for balance. They were below the water and I saw a jet of water coming out of each one. They were the skimmer's engines. The skimmer didn't have a rudder or anything, so when Uncle

Press turned the control bars, it would send more or less power to either pontoon. That's how the thing was directed. Very cool.

I looked up ahead and saw that Spader had a pretty decent head start. Uncle Press was intense at the controls, but I could tell by the look on his face that he was enjoying this. I didn't blame him. I was too.

"What is Grallion?" I asked.

Oddly enough, I didn't have to shout. The engines of the skimmer weren't loud like a powerboat. Instead they gave off a steady, solid hum. Rather than the loud drone of an engine, most of what I heard was the hull flashing across the water. The water was amazingly smooth too, so we shot across it like ice skates on glass.

"Grallion is the habitat where Spader lives," said Uncle Press without taking his eyes off our adversary.

"What's his deal?" I asked.

"He's what they call an aquaneer. All the habitats have a crew that keeps them moving safely over the water. It's an important job. Spader's good at it. He's a good guy, too."

"Yeah, but is he the Traveler from Cloral?"

"Look!" he shouted.

He pointed ahead of us and there on the horizon I saw our destination. At first it was just a hazy gray smudge that could have been an island. But the closer we got, the more I saw that the outline was too regular to be an island. No, this thing was man-made. And it was big. This was Grallion.

Uncle Press gunned the throttle and easily caught up to Spader. I then realized what his strategy was. We had to lay back until we saw Grallion. But now that we knew where it was, the race was really on.

"You've got too much drag!" taunted Uncle Press at Spader. "We'll beat you at three-quarters!"

"But you've got the extra weight, mate!" Spader shot back. "Even up!"

Both guys gunned the throttle and the skimmers charged forward even faster. We hadn't been at full speed up till now. Unbelievable.

To be honest, I was less concerned about our race to decide who was going to buy sniggers than I was about our destination. Mark, remember the time we went to Manhattan on that school trip to visit the aircraft carrier *Intrepid*? It was pretty impressive, right? Well, imagine approaching the *Intrepid* on the water in a rowboat. Can you picture that? Takes your breath away, doesn't it? Well, now multiply the size of that aircraft carrier by about four hundred and you'd have Grallion.

I kid you not, this was a floating island. As we sped toward it, I kept thinking that we'd be there any second. But we weren't. With each passing moment this monster barge kept on getting bigger and bigger. It was about four stories high, but that's not where the size was. This thing they called a habitat spread out before us for what seemed like a couple of miles. Because we were approaching head-on, I couldn't tell how far back it went, but if the front end was any indication, this thing was the size of Stony Brook.

"We've got him now!" exclaimed Uncle Press with glee.

I looked over to Spader's skimmer to see we had pulled ahead by a few feet. Apparently the drag from his equipment caboose was a little bit more than the extra weight that I added to our skimmer.

"There's the marker buoy!" Uncle Press said, pointing ahead.

I looked to see there was a buoy floating about twenty yards off from the habitat. Beyond the buoy I saw that at the water line there was some kind of seagoing entrance to the barge. The opening was large enough to pilot small crafts inside. I could even make out other skimmers in there, along with a few small boats of various shape and design.

"The buoy marks the safety zone," added Uncle Press. "Once you pass it, you've got to slow down. That's our finish line."

We were only a few yards away from victory. I didn't know which excited me more, knowing that we were about to win or looking up at Grallion as it loomed over us. Spader wasn't giving up though. He coaxed a little more power out of his skimmer and pulled to within a few feet of us. This was going right down to the finish line. And . . .

We won! We passed the marker buoy first. With an exuberant "Yes!" Uncle Press killed the engine.

But Spader didn't stop. He kept on full throttle, headed toward the water dock. All we could do was watch him in wonder.

"Maybe he *is* crazy," I said.

Uncle Press gunned the engine and followed him in, though at a safer speed. What I saw in the next few seconds was amazing. As I told you before, Spader jammed into Grallion at full throttle and full speed for these skimmers were *fast*. I saw a handful of dock workers go wide-eyed and scramble out of the way in anticipation of the nasty crash that was sure to follow.

Spader didn't flinch. He drove his skimmer right toward the dock. In seconds he would be mush. But with only a few yards to spare he hit the water brakes and spun the skimmer— later he called it autorotating—into a complete 360 that killed all his speed. With a rush of water caused by his turn, he slid sideways and barely kissed the dock. Without missing a beat, he jumped out, turned back to us, made a deep bow and said, "You lose, mates."

We pulled up slowly in our skimmer. All I could do was applaud. Forget anything they've ever shown on those network stunt shows, this was hands down the most amazing thing I had ever seen.

"Oh, no," Uncle Press called out to him. He was trying to sound angry though I know he wasn't. "We all play by the same rules. We passed the buoy first."

"But the race was to Grallion!" answered Spader. "That buoy isn't Grallion. Almost doesn't count."

Spader was laughing. So was Uncle Press. Maybe this trip to Cloral was going to be fun after all.

"Spader!" came an annoyed voice from above the dock.

We all looked up to see a woman wearing what looked like some kind of uniform standing on a catwalk above the dock. She looked ticked.

"Wu Yenza," Uncle Press whispered to me. "Chief aquaneer."

"Spader's boss?" I asked.

"Yeah, Spader's boss."

"Uh-oh."

Yenza looked to be in her thirties. She had short black hair and was in pretty good shape. I guess all aquaneers had to be in good shape. She wore a black outfit that was similar to Spader's, but it had long sleeves with yellow stripes near the cuff that gave it a kind of military feel. I'd go so far as to say she was kind of hot, in an older woman way.

"Now, Spader!" shouted Yenza. She then stormed off.

Spader turned to us and gave a little shrug. He didn't look all that nervous about the slamming he was sure to get.

"Let's call it a tie, right, mates?" he said with a smile. "Sniggers on me at Grolo's, soon as I can make it!"

With that he turned and bounded up the stairs that led off

the dock and into the bowels of Grallion—and to deep trouble for him.

"He's doomed," I said.

"Nah. He'll get yelled at and told never to be so reckless again. But they won't do anything to him. Everyone likes Spader. He's the best aquaneer they've got."

We maneuvered the skimmer to the dock, tied it up, and stepped onto the floating platform.

"You didn't answer my question," I said.

"What question was that, Bobby? You've got so many."

"Is Spader the Traveler from Cloral?"

Uncle Press didn't answer right away. He busied himself getting our air globes and fins out of the skimmer. I knew he wasn't ignoring me, but the fact that I didn't get a simple yes or no made me nervous.

"Yes," he finally answered. "Spader is the Traveler from Cloral."

"I *knew* it!" I shouted.

"There's just one thing. Spader doesn't know it yet. He has no idea that he's a Traveler. We're going to have to tell him."

Uncle Press grabbed our gear and walked toward the stairs. I stayed there a moment, letting those words sink in. Here I had just met a guy who seemed to love everything there was about life—about *his* life—and we now had the job of telling him that it was all going to change. In my short time of being a Traveler, that was the hardest thing I had to deal with— finding out that my life wasn't what I thought it was, and having to leave it behind.

I didn't look forward to being the one who had to bring someone else's world crashing down around them.

CLORAL

From the moment I first left my home in Stony Brook, I'd been jumping from one disaster to the next. It seemed like I was always scared, or confused, or scared *and* confused. There were a few times when things didn't totally suck, but for the most part I was getting slammed every time I turned around.

But after spending some time on Cloral, I am very happy to write that the next few weeks were actually pretty great, for a change. From the second we stepped onto the habitat of Grallion, I felt safe. But it was more than that. As I learned about Grallion and how the floating habitats worked on Cloral, I felt as if I had found a place that had gotten it right. The Clorans had a society and a way of life that was like a perfect machine, where every piece and every person played an important part. Everyone relied on everyone else, and they respected each other for the roles they played.

That's not to say there weren't problems. The Clorans weren't mindless Disney animatrons who lived only to serve or anything like that. Far from it. They had their own opinions, and they didn't always agree with one another. It was the big picture that they kept in perspective. There were no wars and no tension between people of different races. There didn't seem to be any class distinction either. Meaning, though some people had more responsibility than others and got paid more salary, no one treated anyone like a second-class citizen. It was amazing.

I tried to figure out how such an ideal society could exist, when supposedly evolved societies like ours on Second Earth always seemed to be at one another's throats. The best theory I could come up with is that it was because each and every person on Cloral faced the same big challenge—they had to deal with living on the water. Yes, they had created these amazing boat cities that made you feel as if you were on dry land, but you weren't. You were floating. That meant anything could happen. A rogue storm could wipe out an entire city. Growing enough food to feed the entire world was an ever present worry. A simple virus could endanger an entire habitat. This was not an easy life. These people were united by a common cause—survival. Any other disputes were trivial compared to the larger challenges facing them every day.

But I'm getting way ahead of myself. Let me tell you what happened right after Uncle Press and I arrived on Grallion.

Since Uncle Press had been there before, he gave me a tour. As we climbed up from the depths of the docks, I noticed two things. One was that the inside of this barge was a labyrinth of machinery, pipes, engines, and pumps. I looked down long catwalks where workers busied themselves keeping the giant floating habitat running.

The second thing I noticed was that nothing seemed to be made out of metal. I'm not sure what the material was, I guess you would call it plastic or fiberglass or something. But all the walkways, pipes, supports, girders, and even the machines looked to be made out of the same kind of lightweight material.

When we walked on the stairs, rather than the sharp clanging sound of metal, our footfalls were almost silent, as if we were walking on carpet. I guess it made sense. You have to use light-weight stuff when everything has to float. And here's a weird thing: Even though the underbelly of Grallion looked like a vast factory, it wasn't all that loud. You could tell the place was alive, but it wasn't much noisier than Stony Brook Library on a busy Saturday. Pretty cool.

"What do they do here?" I asked Uncle Press as we climbed the stairs. "Do they just float around fishing and racing skimmers?"

"Every habitat has a specific purpose," was his answer. "Some manufacture materials, others process food, some are financial centers, others mine raw materials."

"And what about Grallion?" I asked.

"See for yourself."

We had reached the top of the stairs, where a door opened onto the main surface. We quickly stepped out into the sun and I got my first look at Grallion. Mark, Courtney, I'm not sure I can find the right words to describe it, that's how awesome a sight it was.

First, did I say Grallion was big? Well, big doesn't cover it. It was enormous. I felt as if I had reached dry land. But after having been below, I knew this wasn't dry land at all. This was a vehicle, but unlike any vehicle I had ever seen. Now, are you ready for this? Stretching out in front of me for as far as I could see . . . was farmland. I swear. I saw acre upon acre of flowering plants, fruit trees, and vines heavy with colorful vegetables.

Yes, Grallion was a giant, floating farm!

"This way," said Uncle Press, and walked off.

I didn't move at first. I couldn't. I wanted to get my mind around what I was seeing.

"You'll get a better view over here," called Uncle Press, laughing.

He knew I was blown away and he was enjoying it. I ran after him. I wanted to see more. He led me up the stairs of a tower, and from this higher vantage point I got a great view of the farms of Grallion. I saw that there were very distinct sections, broken up by walkways where farm workers could travel. There were even small electric vehicles that moved quickly and silently along roads that criss-crossed each other. To our far left I saw row after row of fruit trees. Many of them bore fruit that looked like apples and oranges, but there were trees with clusters of unfamiliar fruit as well. Some were bright green tubes that looked like balloons hanging from the branches. Other trees had great purple orbs the size of grapefruits. Others were covered with pure white fat berries. They all looked ripe and ready for picking.

Directly in front of us were rows of thousands of individual plants that grew out of the dirt. Yes, dirt. At least I think it was dirt. It was brown and looked soft, so if it wasn't dirt, it was a good imitation. Some plants bore small fruits and vegetables, others looked as if the whole thing would be picked like lettuce, or pulled out of the ground like a carrot or a potato.

To our right were aisles of fences where viney plants grew. This section held the same dark green, pickle-looking fruit that we had found in the cavern underwater. Another area of vines was covered with fruit that looked like round white disks. This odd fruit looked fragile and fluttered when the wind blew.

There was another whole section that grew beneath the shade of a gauzy tarp. These must have been plants that do better with indirect light. I'm guessing that the covered area took up a square mile. Another whole area looked to be planted with some kind of wheat. Unbelievable.

I watched as workers went busily about their jobs, tending to the crops. Some were pickers, others took water and soil samples. Still others did pruning.

The best word I can use to describe this vast farm full of lush fruits and vegetables is . . . perfect.

"This habitat feeds around thirty thousand people, give or take," Uncle Press explained. "The crating is done below and it's all transported forward. There's another dock near the bow where boats from other habitats arrive to transport the produce back to their homes. It's all very efficient."

"How many people work here?" I asked.

"I think about two hundred," he answered. "Only about fifty live here full-time: the habitat pilot and crew, some support people, the farm supervisors, and the agronomers."

"Agronomers?"

"Scientists. The guys who figure out what gets planted where. They're always experimenting with fertilizers and crop rotation and whatnot."

"Then there are about sixty aquaneers like Spader who keep the habitat running smoothly and coordinate the comings and goings of all the small boats. They live here in short shifts—maybe three months at a time. The rest of the people are like migrant farm workers. They come and go depending on the needs of the crops. That's where all the short-timers live."

He pointed far off to the left, where I saw a row of low houses running along the length of one side of the habitat. The houses looked like small, two-level homes.

"The homes on the other side are for the long-timers—the pilot and agronomers and whatnot."

I looked far to my right and saw another row of houses

along the opposite side that seemed to be a bit larger than the others. And why not? If these people were here permanently, they *should* have bigger homes.

"We're at the stern," he pointed out. "This is where most of the farm equipment is kept and where the agronomers work. In the bow there's a big wheelhouse where the habitat is controlled, but there are smaller control sheds on each side."

"This is a weird thing to say about a farm but, it's beautiful," I said.

"It's not weird at all. It *is* beautiful. Let's hope it stays that way."

Leaving that ominous thought hanging, Uncle Press started climbing back down the stairs to the main deck.

"What do you mean? What could happen?" I asked while following.

"Did you forget why we're here?" said Uncle Press tersely.

Oh, right. Saint Dane. The turning point. For a few seconds I actually stopped worrying about him. It was hard to imagine this place facing any kind of huge turmoil. Not like Denduron. That territory was a mess from the get-go. This place seemed more like, I don't know, Eden.

"So what do we do?" I asked, feeling kind of dumb for asking my previous question.

"I think we should live here for a while," he answered. "If Saint Dane is here, he'll be planning something. The best thing we can do is blend in, get to know the territory, and be ready if something strange happens."

"Which leads me to another question," I said.

"Of course it does," he replied. Wise guy.

"What do you tell people when you flume to a new territory? Don't they wonder who you are? Where you came from? Why you just happened to drop out of nowhere?"

"Ahhh," said Uncle Press knowingly. "Good question. Obviously you can't go telling people you're a Traveler from a distant territory and you're here to prevent their world from crumbling into chaos. That would be bad."

"Yes, that would be bad," I agreed.

"But there's another way of saying it," he went on. "I have told Spader that I'm from a distant habitat and my goal is to see all of Cloral. So I'm traveling around, going where my mood takes me and picking up work to help pay for my journey."

We had reached the bottom of the tower and Uncle Press stopped and looked at me.

"The thing is," he said with a sly smile, "that's not far from the truth. I just leave out the part about trying to prevent the collapse of their civilization. That would be hard to explain."

"Tell me about it," I said.

We continued walking along the perimeter of the farm.

"So we'll take jobs here. It's not difficult work. They're always looking for help. And we'll stay vigilant. The more you know about a territory, the better chance you'll have of helping them. That's what I did on Denduron."

"And when do we tell Spader that he's a Traveler?" I asked.

"When we need to," came the quick reply.

Uncle Press picked up the pace and I had to keep up with him. He suddenly seemed to be in a hurry to get somewhere.

"Where are we going now?"

"You heard Spader!" he answered, suddenly sounding all enthusiastic. "Sniggers are on him at Grolo's. You don't pass up an offer like that."

Sniggers at Grolo's. I guessed that would be a good thing.

We walked to the far side of the habitat where the temporary housing quarters were. Close-up they looked like small apartments. Nothing fancy, but nice enough. Men and women were hanging out, some were reading, others played with their kids. Two guys were playing catch with a curved tube that looked like a boomerang. I watched as they threw it far off to the side, only to have it circle back and land right in the catcher's hands. It was the Cloran version of playing Frisbee.

All these people wore the same lightweight, colorful clothing that Uncle Press and I now had on. We fit right in. Many smiled and waved a friendly greeting as we passed by. Uncle Press made sure to return every wave and I did the same. These people didn't know who we were, but it didn't seem to matter. They looked like a friendly bunch and that was okay with me.

After walking for what seemed like a mile, we came upon another row of low buildings that ran parallel to the homes along the edge. I didn't have to ask what they were. It was a minimall Grallion-style. There was a clothing store and a place to get haircuts. A small grocery store was next to a small library and that was next to a shop that carried a little bit of everything from tools to toys to cookware. On Second Earth we had a name for this kind of store. Target.

I wondered if there was a video arcade hidden somewhere, but then figured that was probably something unique to Second Earth. Oh, well. We got to the far end of the shops and finally arrived at our destination. A carved sign over the door welcomed all who came this way. It said simply: GROLO'S.

"Center of the Grallion universe," said Uncle Press. "And the finest sniggers ever pulled on any habitat this side of center."

"If you say so," I said, humoring him.

"Actually I have no idea," he said softly. "I haven't had sniggers anywhere else, but that's what they tell me."

He winked and entered the pub. I was right after him, excited about finally discovering the wonders of the much-talked-about sniggers.

As we walked inside, I saw that Grolo's was pretty much your standard tavern. I guess it doesn't matter what territory you're on, people like to meet and drink and swap stories and laugh too loud, because that's exactly what was going on here. There was odd music playing, though I'm sure to the good people of Cloral it wasn't odd at all. If I were to liken the music to something at home, I'd say it was kind of a New Age, techno, Japanese, string thing. How's *that* for a description? I know, it makes no sense, but if you heard it, you'd agree. I have to admit, I didn't hate it. It had kind of a dance beat and added a strong helping of feel-good to the place.

The pub was jammed. It was a mix of men and women of all ages, though I think I was the youngest there. I suddenly wondered if they would card me. That would have been embarrassing. Not only was I underage (at least by Second Earth standards), I didn't have any ID on me at all. If anyone asked, it would have gotten tricky. But they didn't, I'm glad to report.

Everyone seemed to be having a good time while drinking, or laughing, or telling stories, or doing all three at once. I noticed one table of people who weren't swept up in all the revelry though. There were four people, two men and two women, who were having an intense debate. The table they sat around was covered with large pieces of paper that looked like plans of some sort. They each kept jabbing their fingers at the plans while trying to make their point.

"Agronomers," Uncle Press said. "I think they're the only people around here who ever get stressed."

"How come?" I asked.

"It's their show. Grallion is about farming and if Grallion doesn't produce, then they're not doing their job."

I looked again at the agronomers, but now with respect. That's got to be some kind of serious pressure. If they fail, people don't eat.

"Press!" someone called out above the din. "What kept you? I thought you got into another natty-do with the sharkies!"

It was Spader. He had beaten us there. He sat on the bar, surrounded by a few other people who were laughing and drinking with him.

Uncle Press strode right up to the group.

"I thought you were in for a tum-tigger with Yenza!" exclaimed Press.

Sheesh, we'd just gotten here and Uncle Press was already picking up on the local jargon. I figured I'd better keep on my toes.

"Me?" laughed Spader with huge bravado. "Now why would dear Yenza have a row with me? I fill her life with happiness and joy!" He then added slyly, "And besides, I think she fancies me. If she were to kick me off Grallion, she'd die of a broken heart."

Everyone laughed at Spader's high praise of himself, but it was a friendly laugh. They knew Spader was joking. It was all just a goof.

"The chances of Wu Yenza dying of heartache over the sorry likes of you," shouted one guy jovially, "is about the same as old Grolo running out of sniggers."

Everyone hooted in mock horror. A quick look around showed me that everyone was drinking from clear mugs that were filled with a deep red liquid that I figured was the legendary sniggers. Spader leaned back over the bar and grabbed the handle of the tap that I assumed was where they drew the sniggers. He pretended to pull it, and his eyes went wide with shock.

"Empty!" he shouted in overblown horror. "Hobey-ho, he's run out of sniggers! Yenza *does* fancy me!"

Everybody laughed. A heavyset guy behind the bar, who must have been Grolo, playfully shoved Spader away from the tap.

"Don't go startin' rumors," he said, laughing, "or it'll be up to you to stop the riot!"

Spader laughed and rolled away. Grolo grabbed the tap and drew another mug of the frothy red liquid. Everyone was having a great time and Spader was the reason. He was the center of attention and he didn't disappoint those who wanted him to keep the party rolling. He grabbed a mug of sniggers and exclaimed, "So where is he, Press?"

"Standing right here, watching the show," answered Uncle Press.

Who were they talking about? Spader handed Press the mug of sniggers and quickly glanced around. In a second his eyes settled on me. Uh-oh. He was talking about me. I was sure that he had already told the story about how I got tangled up in the water sled and had to be rescued. I wanted to crawl away and hide. If I was going to live on Grallion, I didn't want people to think that I was a total loser. For a second I thought of turning and running, but that would have made it worse. No, I was going to have to face the ridicule. I could only hope that it would be fast.

"That's the guy!" shouted Spader.

All eyes turned to me. The best I could do was stand there and take it. I thought that maybe I could come up with something clever to make it all a joke. But my mind locked. I couldn't come up with anything funny about what had happened. My sore ribs and aching shoulder were a painful reminder of that.

"If it weren't for him," began Spader, "Press would be shark meat."

Huh? I looked to Uncle Press. He raised his mug of sniggers at me and winked.

"Press was trapped under the shelf," said Spader, spinning a dramatic tale that had everyone enthralled. "The nasty wogglie was nosing in on him. He was a big 'un, mind you. But then Pendragon here came flying by with the water sled. With no fear for himself, he distracted the beggar and gave Press the chance to slip away. Bravest thing I ever saw. Of course, I was lucky enough to be in the right place to put the finishing touches on the big wogglie myself."

He added this last bit with false modesty and everyone responded with hoots, like they didn't think he deserved any credit at all. No, in their minds, the real hero was me! I couldn't believe it. Suddenly, a mug of sniggers was thrust into my hand.

"To Pendragon!" shouted Spader. He raised his mug in a toast. Everyone else around the bar raised their mugs toward me as well. Uncle Press did too, with a huge smile on his face.

"Welcome to Grallion!" added Spader.

"Hobey-ho ho!" chimed everyone else as they raised their mugs to drink in my honor.

I couldn't believe it. Talk about snatching victory from the jaws of defeat, no pun intended. Of course, I felt a little guilty. It didn't exactly happen the way Spader described it. But still, it was sort of the truth. I looked to Spader and he gave me a little smile that told me he knew it was only sort of the truth too. But it didn't matter to him. He motioned for me to take a drink of sniggers, and I did.

I wasn't sure what to expect. I had tasted beer once before and I guess that's what I thought it would be like, but it wasn't. That was a good thing because I hated the taste of beer. To be honest, the first taste of sniggers that hit my tongue was totally nasty. It was like drinking carbonated cabbage juice. But in an instant the sour taste went away and what I was left with was an incredibly sweet sensation that actually left my mouth tingling. I once had this soda in Maine called Moxie. When Moxie first hits your tongue it tastes sweet, but after you swallow it leaves a nasty, bitter taste. This sniggers stuff was like reverse-Moxie. The first taste was foul, but it immediately went away and left a wonderful memory that lingered until your next sip. I liked this stuff! Hobey-ho ho!

"Put these on my tab, Grolo!" announced Spader as he jumped off the bar. "I've got business with my friends."

"You don't have a tab, Spader," barked Grolo.

"Then start one for me!" Spader shot back with bravura.

Grolo waved him off with a mock disgusted gesture. I didn't think he minded giving away a few pints of sniggers to Spader. The aquaneer was the life of the party here at the tavern. The more stories he told, the more everyone else drank sniggers. Spader was good for business. He put an arm around Uncle Press, his other arm around me, and led us away from the group toward the front door.

But when we reached the table of agronomers, he suddenly stopped and turned us to them. The scientists stopped their work and looked up to us expectantly.

"We just want you mates to know," said Spader, "we think you are doing a bang-up job. Really."

The scientists didn't know how to react. They just sat there and stared at us.

"Now get back to work!" snapped Spader and led us

toward the door. As we walked he whispered to us, "Scientists. They're brilliant but easily confused."

We blasted out of Grolo's into the sunlight, laughing.

I really liked this guy. But even though I was grateful for his story back there, I couldn't let it go without saying something.

"That story you told about me," I said. "You know that wasn't really how it happened."

"Says who?" Spader shot back. "That's how I saw it. There's always two ways of looking at things, Pendragon. In my few short years I learned that seeing what's positive about a situation is a lot more fun and gets you a lot further than looking for what might be wrong with it. That's my philosophy, for what it's worth."

Spader may not have been a wise old soul, but what he said made a whole lot of sense. I didn't think I had ever met anyone who was as full of energy and fun as this guy was. Without trying all that hard, he made you feel good. I could tell Spader had even gotten to Uncle Press. He said that Cloral was his favorite territory. I'm sure there were a lot of reasons for that, but I'm guessing Spader was a big one. It was fun to be around him. Over the next few weeks I learned a lot more about Vo Spader, and all of it was good.

He was the kind of guy who knew the right people to go to in order to get things done. He got Uncle Press and me set up in a small house near his. It was on the side of Grallion where the temporary workers lived, and since we had become temporary workers, we were right at home. The place was small, but comfortable enough. There were bunk beds (I got the top) and a small kitchen and some simple furniture. The best part about it though, was that the back window looked right out on the ocean. How great was that?

He got us jobs working on the farm. I was afraid this was going to be torture, but it wasn't. Not all of it, anyway. At home on Second Earth the big farms employ pickers who show up during harvest time, pick whatever needs to be picked, and move on to another. That seemed like pretty hard work, and not all that rewarding.

But that's not how it worked on Grallion. Rather than simply going out to pick whatever is ripe, the farm workers on Grallion are assigned to a quadrant. That's an area roughly the size of an acre. The workers are called "vators" and they have the responsibility of taking complete care of their quadrant, from feeding the plants to pruning, and yes, to picking the fruit. But the vators' responsibility doesn't end with the picking. They follow their crops all the way through the washing, sorting, and packing process right up until their crops are shipped out. It's very cool and gives you a real sense of accomplishment. I guess it's the difference between working on an auto assembly line where your whole job is to put the wheels on cars as they pass by you, versus staying with the same car from the very beginning and proudly watching it roll off the line.

Now, you may be thinking that I have no business running a farm, and you'd be right. Before coming to Grallion I didn't know the difference between weeds and worms. I didn't think Uncle Press did either. But it didn't matter because we weren't the only vators assigned to our quadrant. There were six other workers with us and each was pretty experienced. They showed us how to check plants for signs of disease and how to treat them with natural compounds brought up from the ocean floor. All the fertilizer was natural too. It seemed like even though Cloral was covered with water, much of what they used on the surface was brought up from below and processed for use on the habitats.

The fruit grew quickly on Grallion, so there was a harvest of some sort every few days. You would think this was the hardest part, and maybe it was, but it wasn't all that bad. It wasn't like we had to go out into the fields with baskets and fill them up with heavy fruit and lug them back to a central area or anything. It was way more civilized than that. Beneath every narrow walking path was an underground conveyor belt. All we had to do was pick the fruit and drop it on the ground, then lift the doors and drop the fruit down below. The conveyor belt would take it all to a central area where another of the vators from our quadrant would be waiting to wash, sort, and pack them up. It was all so simple.

Uncle Press and I went below several times to receive the harvested fruit from our quadrant and ensure that it was all cleaned and packed properly. We then used a forklift to bring the boxes of fruit all the way forward to the loading docks.

This is where we saw Spader at work. It was a busy place. There were all sorts of transport boats coming and going, bringing shipments of fresh fruits and vegetables back to their habitats. The habitats themselves were never allowed closer than a half mile to Grallion. That would have been dangerous. Instead they would send in small boats that would safely enter the docking area. Spader's job was that of traffic cop. He'd travel just in front of the incoming boats on his skimmer, calling back instructions to get them safely docked. He'd then jump on the dock, tie up the boat and signal the dockworkers to begin the loading process. Once a cargo boat was loaded, he'd reverse the process and guide the boats safely out of the docking area and send them on their way back to their habitats.

But that's not all Spader did. He was also on the pilot's crew. The pilot was like the captain of a ship. He was in charge of the vessel and its safety. Spader was still kind of a junior crew member, so most of his duties were of the lookout variety. At any given time there were ten lookouts stationed around the habitat to warn of any impending problems. It was a boring job, but an important one. It was probably pretty boring being a lookout on the *Titanic*, too. For a while, anyway. That will give you an idea of how important that job was.

I can guess what you're thinking. I made working on Grallion sound as if it were actually fun. Well, fun isn't exactly the word. It was work and some of it was hard, but I didn't mind it. I felt like I was an important part in keeping the wheels turning.

No, working the farm wasn't exactly fun, but there were plenty of other things to do that were *definitely* fun.

Spader took me on adventures. You know how much I like to dive, and on Grallion, hanging out *below* the water was a pretty normal thing. I already described how easy it was to swim underwater using the air globes. These gizmos made swimming underwater almost as natural as walking on the deck of Grallion. Actually, it was better. This is the closest to flying that I think a human will ever come. Spader and I would have races underneath Grallion. I really got the knack of using the water sleds. I found that by subtly shifting my body position, I could turn faster and move quicker. It was all about becoming aqua-dynamic. It didn't take long before I was almost as fast as Spader.

Spader took me fishing, too. I'm not much of a hunter, so he did most of the spearing. I acted more like a scout who found the larger fish and alerted Spader. I guess that makes me kind of like a hunting dog. Oh, well, that was my choice. But I have to tell you, I didn't mind eating the fish afterward. (Spader was a pretty decent cook, too.)

At first I was nervous about quigs, but Spader assured me that the sharks never came near Grallion. I knew that was because quigs only patrolled near gates and flumes, but I wasn't about to tell Spader that—yet.

Spader also showed me something that was really bizarre. Near where Grallion was anchored was another farm. An underwater farm! The people of Grallion didn't just farm on the habitat, they had crops growing on the ocean floor, too! This submerged farm had its own vators who tended the place wearing air globes. They grew everything from fruit, to long leafy vines that were cut at the base and brought up whole. Spader explained to me that these underwater farms were even more important to Cloral than farms like Grallion. He said there were farms all over the planet on the ocean's floor that had fed the Clorans for centuries. Growing food on habitats was a relatively new practice. The most important farms were underwater.

There was another underwater sport that Spader introduced me to, and once I got the guts to try it, I was hooked. Spader called it spinney-do and this is how it worked: A spinney was a kind of fish that traveled in small schools of maybe four or five and they looked like really skinny dolphins. I'm serious. Imagine a regular old dolphin, then imagine it being only about six inches in diameter and you'd have a spinney. At the backs of their heads they had these bizarro ridges. I had no idea what the spinneys needed them for, but they were crucial to playing spinney-do.

Spader motioned for me to be quiet and to watch. He then left me and swam cautiously up behind the spinneys, who were busily feeding on some kelp. They had no clue that he was there. They may have looked like skinny dolphins, but they were nowhere near as smart. Spader was able to sneak up right behind them. With one quick move, he jumped on the back of one and grabbed the ridge behind its head! Well, the spinney didn't like that at all and it started to bloat! It was like one of those puffer fishes that get all fat when you touch them. Only the spinney was so big, when it puffed up it got *huge*! It was strong, too! It had suddenly transformed from this sleepy, dopey fish into a water-going bucking bronco! Spader held on to the back ridge with both hands and wrapped his legs around its body as the fish started thrashing and bucking.

"Eeeyahhhaaa!" shouted Spader. You'd think he knew about Westerns and bronco busting, but I guess shouting like that comes naturally when your adrenaline spikes and you're holding on to an animal for all you're worth. Spader then got cocky and let one hand go, just to show off. The spinney twisted and spun and did its best to launch Spader, but Spader wasn't letting go. Finally, the big fish shot upward. Spader wasn't ready for that move because he did a somersault right off the fish's back. The real beauty of spinney-do was that even when you got thrown, you were still underwater so it wasn't like you were going to hit the ground and break a rib or anything.

"Next one's yours, mate!" exclaimed Spader, still flush with excitement.

I wasn't so sure I wanted to try, but it looked like fun. Two spinneys were poking around the kelp and Spader motioned for me to give it a go. To be honest, I was scared. But I wasn't going to let Spader see me chicken out, so I did my best.

My best was bad. I actually got as far as grabbing the spinney's back ridge and wrapping my legs around its body. But I hadn't expected it to be so strong. The thing bloated, bolted, and was gone. I just floated there, my hand still out, not sure of what happened. Spader swam up to me and patted me on the back.

"Gotta be faster than that, mate," he said, laughing. "You're on their turf down here."

Good advice. I'd remember it next time.

While Spader and I were having these adventures under the sea, Uncle Press was spending his off time learning more about Grallion and about Cloral. After all, we were here on a mission and the more we learned about this territory, the better prepared we'd be when Saint Dane made his move. I felt kind of guilty about having so much fun while Uncle Press was playing Sherlock. But he assured me that it was just as important for me to get to know Spader—he was the Traveler from Cloral, even though he didn't know it yet. At some point we were going to have to work together, so Uncle Press figured it would be a good idea for the two of us to bond.

That was okay by me. Spader and I were having a blast. The thought of battling Saint Dane was the furthest thing from my mind, most of the time. So after having spent a bunch of weeks on Grallion with Spader, I decided that my first impression of him still stood. He was a guy with a big personality and an even bigger sense of fun. He was a truly good guy who listened as much as he spoke. He also cared. He was quick to help out a friend, or even a stranger. He wasn't a slacker, either. He may have liked to have a good time, but he worked hard and he loved his job. This was a good guy to know. I'll remember those first few weeks on Grallion for the rest of my life. It was a great time.

But it was soon going to end.

One evening Spader made me dinner at his house. Uncle Press chose to hang at Grolo's instead. Spader had speared a couple of particularly tasty Kooloo fish that day and grilled them over hot coals in his backyard. Sounds like home, no?

The fish was golden and delicious. After dinner I cleaned up the dishes and Spader went to work cleaning up the rest of his house. There were clothes and pieces of equipment scattered everywhere. To be honest, it looked more like a garage than an apartment. Spader wasn't big on being neat, but tonight was different. He went around picking things up and putting things away and basically making the place look like someone actually lived there.

"What's the occasion?" I asked. "Got a date?"

I then noticed that Spader had more energy than usual. Believe me, for Spader that's really saying something. He was pretty much bouncing off the walls as he worked. It was like somebody took his power dial and notched it up a few amps.

"Big day tomorrow, mate," he said with excitement. "My father is coming by. Can't let 'im think I live like a dirty old crocker fish!"

This was the first I heard about Spader's family.

"Where does he live?" I asked.

"He's an aquaneer on Magorran," he said while continuing to clean up. "It's a manu habitat. Schedule has it swinging by tomorrow for supplies."

"Manu habitat?"

"They build things. Pieces for machinery and skinners and whatnot."

"Is that your home?"

"Home? No, mate. Home is Panger City. Lived there my whole life until I went to the Aquaneer Academy. My mum's still there. Haven't seen either of 'em for . . . hobey, can't remember. It's been a while."

I was beginning to get the bigger picture about what life was like on Cloral. These habitats were like cities and people left home to work, just like back on Second Earth.

"Dad's a real spiffer," Spader continued. "Gave me the aquaneer bug. Had me around skimmers my whole life. They wanted to make him an officer but he turned 'em down—didn't want to leave the docks. His tour's up soon so he can get back to Mum. Hobey, I can't wait to see his face again. Give me a hand here mate, would you?"

I helped him lift a couple of large water sleds he had been working on and put them into a closet.

"You never told me about your parents," said Spader.

Uh-oh. Up until now I'd been able to dodge questions about home. I'm not a good liar. Uncle Press and I made up a story about how we came from a distant habitat that was a university. We said it was full of intellectuals and professors, which explained why I needed to learn so much about working in the water and how the "real world" worked. Whenever Spader couldn't believe how little I knew about Cloral, I'd shrug and say: "I didn't get out much."

I hated lying to Spader, but I knew the truth would come out soon enough and hoped that when it did, he'd understand. But now he was putting me on the spot again by asking about my parents. I was going to have to come up with some version of the truth, because the whole truth would have blown Spader's head off.

"Dad's a writer," I said. "Mom works in a library."

That was the absolute truth, and it made my heart sink. This was the first time I had spoken about my parents in a long time. What made it worse was I had to pretend as if nothing was wrong. I couldn't tell Spader that they had disappeared, along with my sister and my dog. I think Spader must have sensed my anguish, because he didn't ask any more questions. That was good for all sorts of reasons.

"It's tough being away from loved ones," he said softly.

"Yeah, tell me about it."

"Tell you what, come with me to meet Dad tomorrow! You'll get a knock out of him, you will!"

"Sounds good," I said, but with a touch of sadness. I missed my family.

Uncle Press said that Spader was the Traveler from Cloral. I wondered if his parents had raised him to be a Traveler the same way Uncle Press said my family did for me. If so, did that mean they would disappear the same way my family had? Spader obviously cared about his parents. As we worked to make his house a little neater, I hoped that when the habitat of Magorran arrived the next day, his father would be on it.

The next day Uncle Press and I made the long walk forward to the transport docks to be there when Spader's father arrived. I could tell that Uncle Press was disturbed about something. As I told him of my previous day's adventures under the waters near Grallion, he stared straight down at his feet and didn't say a word. His mind was definitely somewhere else.

"What's up?" I asked.

"I don't know," came his thoughtful answer. "I'm feeling . . . uneasy, and I can't put my finger on it."

"What? Now you're psychic?"

"It's just a feeling. Don't you sense it?"

I thought. I felt. I looked around. Nothing.

"Uhh . . . no. Should I?"

"Maybe," he answered. "It's a Traveler thing."

"You mean we can predict the future, too?"

"No, but you'll start to realize you can pick up on things. It's like walking into a room and knowing right away that there's an argument going on, even though you haven't heard a word spoken. It's just picking up on the signals that people send out. No big deal."

"And you're picking up bad signals right now?" I asked, not really wanting to know the answer.

"I'm not sure. I just have this sense of . . . dread."

"I don't like dread," I shot back. "Dread is bad. Could this have anything to do with Spader's parents?"

"We'll find out soon enough," he said while pointing forward.

I looked to where he was pointing and saw it.

Magorran.

The manu habitat had appeared on the horizon and was steaming toward Grallion. Though it was still far away, I could tell that it was a different type of habitat than Grallion. It didn't seem as big. It might have been a third of the size. But the buildings on deck were taller. I guessed that these were some of the factories that Spader told me about. The closer it got, the larger these buildings loomed. It was pretty impressive. Uncle Press and I picked up the pace and hurried to the forward dock area to be there when the first advance boats arrived.

When we got there, we saw that several aquaneers stood on their skimmers, ready to shoot out to meet the advance boats. Uncle Press saw something down on the dock and pointed it out to me. I looked, and couldn't help but smile.

It was Spader. It wasn't weird for him to be down there or anything. It was the way he was dressed. Spader wasn't much for wearing his aquaneer uniform: the black long-sleeved outfit with the yellow stripes on the cuff. He normally wore his sleeveless shirt that was cut off at the shoulders. But today was different. Today Spader was here to greet his father and he was decked out in his best uniform. It was clean, too. I even think he took the time to comb his hair. To use one of his sayings, he looked pretty spiff.

As we stood above the docks, waiting for the first boat from Magorran to arrive, I began to have the same sense of dread that Uncle Press was feeling. I wasn't being overly insightful or anything, it was because I sensed a stirring among the aquaneers who were gathered below on the floating dock. Up until now they had been casually chatting and laughing. Suddenly their body language grew more tense. All eyes were focused out on the water and at Magorran.

I then looked up at Magorran. The habitat was drawing nearer. Most of the habitats that came to Grallion for supplies stayed far away. Grallion was anchored and stayed in place while the other habitats hovered about a half mile away. It was a safety thing. The habitats were so big that they didn't exactly turn on a dime and you never knew when the current would change. So all things considered, it was smart to keep the habitats far apart and send smaller boats between them.

But now something was wrong. There was confusion. It looked as if the aquaneers weren't sure of what to do. I didn't know what was going on, but whatever it was, it was bad. The answer came quickly. Wu Yenza, the chief aquaneer, ran out onto the upper platform near us. Her eyes were wild with excitement—and fear.

"Perimeter breach!" she barked out. "Warn them off!"

The aquaneers scattered. A moment later a piercing horn sounded long and loud.

"What's going on?" I asked Uncle Press.

Uncle Press didn't look at me. His eyes were focused on Magorran. When he spoke his voice was soft and calm. It was the voice of someone describing the inevitable.

"It's not stopping," was all he said.

I looked out onto the water and saw what he meant. Magorran, this giant habitat, was headed right for us. It had already passed the half-mile safety border and was showing no signs of slowing down. Even if it threw its engines into reverse, it was already too late. There was going to be a crash.

A second alarm sounded that was even louder and more piercing than the first. Where the first alarm sounded like a warning to Magorran, this new alarm sounded more like a warning to Grallion. Impact was inevitable. The only thing that could be done was to prepare for it.

The habitat of Magorran was looming closer. I could now look onto the deck and was surprised to see that there were no people. Wherever they were, I hoped they were doing whatever they could to slow themselves down.

The aquaneers below us began to stream up the stairs to get on deck. That is, all but Spader. Spader just stood there, staring at the oncoming habitat. It looked as if he were mesmerized by the behemoth that would soon crash into Grallion.

"Cast off lines!" shouted Yenza. "Everyone on deck! Move!"

Spader didn't move. Somebody had to kick him into gear. I started for the stairs to go down to him, but Uncle Press put a firm hand on my shoulder. I looked up to my uncle and saw that he was calm. He shook his head no, telling me not to go. But something had to be done.

"Spader!" Uncle Press called out to him.

Thankfully, Spader heard him. He turned around and looked up to us. On his face was a look of confusion. Not fear, just concern.

"Time to go, son," Uncle Press called to him. His voice was firm but unpanicked. It cut through the frenzied energy around us louder than any siren. Spader gave one quick glance back at Magorran to see that it was nearly on us, and then he broke for the stairs. He was the last one up.

"Let's get out of here," commanded Uncle Press. "We'll be safest on deck."

Spader joined the other aquaneers while Uncle Press and I ran for our lives. We climbed up the stairs as quickly as possible until we got on deck. I didn't dare look back. I didn't want to see what was about to happen. All around us was panic. Several different alarms were sounding. Aquaneers were everywhere, desperately trying to cast off the heavy lines that kept Grallion in place. Those who didn't have specific jobs in an emergency were doing the same thing we were—running back to get as far away from the impact zone as possible.

It was going to be ugly. I briefly wondered if both these giant habitats could withstand a collision without sinking. The thought of these huge vessels both going to the bottom was too horrible to even imagine, especially since I was on one of them. I tried to get that out of my mind. One thing at a time, and right now, the best thing we could do was keep running away from the impact zone.

On the deck in front of us I saw a frightening sight. The shadows cast by the buildings on Magorran were chasing us across the deck. It was right behind us. Impact was imminent. I finally couldn't stand it anymore and had to turn and look. What I saw made me gasp. The sheer size of Magorran was mind-boggling. The buildings on its bow must have been seven or eight stories tall, and they were headed right for us. Seeing something so big took my breath away. Knowing that it was going to hit us made me think I'd never take another breath again.

"Keep moving!" ordered Uncle Press.

I turned to continue running with him, and that's when it happened.

Magorran collided with Grallion, full steam ahead into a world that would never be the same.

END OF JOURNAL #5

◉ SECOND EARTH ◉

"How can he end a journal here?" shouted Courtney in dismay. "That's not fair. He can't leave us hanging like that!"

Courtney looked to Mark, expecting him to be just as outraged as she was. But Mark had other things on his mind. He had finished reading the journal several minutes before Courtney and was now busily leafing back through the pages of Bobby's Journal #5 and rummaging in his backpack. The frown on his face said that something was bothering him.

"He's messing with us," added Courtney. "He knows we pore over every word of his journals and he gave us a cliffhanger. That's just . . . wrong. This isn't a game. Why did he . . . What are you doing?"

Mark kept reading through the earlier pages, looking for something. Courtney was suddenly intrigued.

"You saw something, didn't you?" she asked. "Did you figure out who caused the habitats to crash? Was it Saint Dane?"

Mark didn't answer. The scowl of tension didn't leave his face either.

"*Mark!*" Courtney shouted with frustration.

This rocked Mark back into the room. His look of worry was replaced by the look of a small boy who just got caught doing something wrong.

"I-I'm an idiot. A total idiot, th-that's all I can say."

He was on the verge of tears. He held up the pages of Bobby's latest journal. "It's missing. The first page is missing."

Courtney jumped to her feet and grabbed the light green pages from him. She shuffled through them quickly, looking for the missing page.

"That's impossible. We read it together, in the bathroom at school. It's got to be here."

She flipped through the pages once, twice, a third time and then looked to Mark and shouted, "It's not here!"

"I know!" cried Mark.

"Don't panic. When was the last time we saw it for sure?"

"In the boys' room," whined Mark. "We were reading when Mr. Dorrico burst in yelling and I jammed all the pages in my pack and—"

Courtney dove at Mark's pack and frantically dug through it.

"Don't you think I already looked there?" said Mark with frustration. "Like five times already?"

Courtney threw the pack down and clicked into a different gear. She knew that being all frantic and pointing fingers of blame wouldn't help get the page back. They had to think clearly.

"We had it in the bathroom," she began, thinking out loud. "That's for definite. But we came right here. That means we lost it somewhere between the bathroom and here. It's gotta be here!"

Courtney started tossing the cushions on the sofa, desperate to find the lost page. Mark didn't help. His mind was already jumping ahead.

"There's another possibility," said Mark softly. "M-maybe it never left the bathroom."

"What?"

"I-I mean, everything happened fast with Mr. Dorrico and all. Maybe I didn't grab all the pages."

Courtney stared at Mark. For a moment Mark was afraid she would lunge at him and tear out his adenoids. But she didn't. Instead she glanced at her watch.

"School's closed," she said, all business. "If Mr. Dorrico found that page, he probably tossed it in the trash. That means it's either still in that trash can, or outside in the Dumpster."

The two stared at each other for a solid thirty seconds. Neither wanted to admit what the next step might be. Mark broke first.

"We're going through that Dumpster tonight, aren't we?" he said, sounding sick.

"Do you want someone to find that page and start asking questions? Like the police?"

That was a no-brainer. There would be way too many questions to answer if Captain Hirsch of the Stony Brook Police saw that page. Mark and Courtney hadn't been entirely honest with him about their knowledge of Bobby's disappearance, so if someone else found that page, they would look really bad.

"I'll meet you there after dinner," said Mark. "Bring rubber gloves. This is gonna be gross."

And it *was* gross.

Mark and Courtney met as planned, right after dinner. Both used the excuse that they were going to the library on the Ave. Instead they spent a solid two hours digging through the Dumpsters of Stony Brook Junior High. Neither could have imagined that one school could create so much disgusting ick in one day. Going through piles of discarded paper wasn't so bad. Paper was dry. Where it got tough was when they had to search through the stuff that *wasn't* dry. Their journey through garbageland couldn't have happened at a worse time. On that very day, the cafeteria had served spaghetti creole, the furnace had been cleaned and overhauled, and Miss Britton's biology class had the pleasure of dissecting frogs. That meant that the Dumpsters were loaded with sticky tomato sauce, greasy rags, and putrid frog guts.

It was not a happy two hours. Finally, after having wiped sloppy red sauce off yet another page for what seemed like the one zillionth time, Courtney had had enough.

"It's not here," she announced.

"It's gotta be," said Mark while wiping a smudge of grease from his chin. "Keep looking."

Courtney hauled herself out of the Dumpster. She was done.

"Look," she said. "If it's in here and we can't find it, then nobody else will either. It'll just end up at the dump and nobody will ever see it again."

"That's just it!" cried Mark. "Bobby trusted me with his journals. I could never face him again if I lost even one page."

He began digging again with even more energy. A tear grew in his eye. Not because the Dumpster smelled rank, which it did, but because he felt horrible for having let his best friend down. Courtney leaned into the Dumpster and put a hand on his shoulder. Mark stopped digging and looked at her.

"We're not going to find it here," she said softly, trying to calm Mark down. "The more I think about it the more I think it's gotta still be in the garbage can in the boys' bathroom."

Mark felt a spark of hope.

"You think?"

"We were in there just before last period, right? I always see the janitors emptying the garbage cans early in the day. I think there's a good chance Mr. Dorrico saw the page and stuck it in the can and it's still sitting there, waiting to get emptied tomorrow."

"I think you're right," he exclaimed, his spirits rising. "All I've got to do is get there first thing, before it gets emptied."

Mark felt much better. There was still hope, and a plan. Both were cautiously optimistic that they'd find the stray page the next day. The only thing they had to worry about for now was getting home and dumping their clothes before their parents caught a whiff of them. They both *really* needed a shower. It would be tough to explain why they smelled like rotten tomatoes, grease, and formaldehyde.

The next morning Mark was waiting at the front door of school as the janitors arrived for the day. He usually got to school early because he liked to hang out in the library and get some work done before classes, so the janitors didn't think it was odd that he was there. Mr. Dorrico was with the group. Mark knew that this was his chance to find out about the paper, but after what happened in the bathroom with Courtney the day before, he was totally embarrassed about approaching the man. Still, he didn't have any choice.

"Excuse me, Mr. Dorrico?" called Mark.

Mr. Dorrico stopped and looked at him suspiciously. The kids at Stony Brook almost never spoke to the custodians. It wasn't a law or anything, but the two groups didn't have much in common. Until today, that is. Mr. Dorrico stared at Mark. Mark could tell that he was trying to remember where he had seen him recently. Unfortunately Mark was going to have to remind him.

"My name's Mark Dimond," he said tentatively. "R-Remember yesterday? I was in the third-floor bathroom with Courtney and we were reading and—"

"*That's* how I know you!" exclaimed Mr. Dorrico.

At first he seemed happy for having solved the mystery of who this kid was, but his joy quickly turned sour as he remembered the scene from the day before.

"You kids think you're funny, don't you," he scolded.

Mark didn't feel like being lectured, but he figured it would be better to let Mr. Dorrico blow off steam. He might have a better chance of getting the information he needed if Mr. Dorrico felt like he had done a good job of telling him off. So Mark didn't interrupt him. He stood there and took it.

"I've been working at this school for the better part of fifty years," Dorrico went on. "There's nothing I haven't seen and nothing I haven't cleaned up."

Mark thought that was a particularly disgusting thought, but he let the guy ramble.

"So if you think you're being clever or original by trying to make me look foolish, then you've got another think coming!"

"You are absolutely right, sir," said Mark in the most respectful tone he could manage. "We both felt really bad about what happened. A girl should *never* be in the boys' lavatory. To make light of that rule is an insult to everything this school stands for. We felt so bad about it, we decided the best thing to do would be to apologize to you."

He ended his speech with a big, sincere smile. He was afraid he was laying it on a little thick, but he was on a roll and couldn't stop. Mr. Dorrico was thrown. He wasn't expecting a total apology.

"Uh, well," he fumfered. "You're right. Where's the girl? Shouldn't she apologize too?"

"She will," answered Mark quickly. "As soon as she gets to school."

"Okay then," said Mr. Dorrico with finality. "I'm glad we agree."

He started to walk off, satisfied with the knowledge that he had been shown the respect he deserved. But Mark couldn't let him go. He ran quickly in front of him.

"Uhh, there's one thing though," he said tentatively. "When we were in there, we were doing homework. I know, bad place to do homework. But I'm afraid I might have left one of my papers behind. You didn't see it, did you?"

Mr. Dorrico kept walking.

"I saw something," he answered thoughtfully. "It was a green piece of paper with writing on it. Didn't look like a normal piece of paper though. It was more like a piece of plant or something."

"Yes! That's it!" shouted Mark jubilantly. "Did you throw it in the trash?"

"I got a policy. Things get misplaced. If I find something that looks like schoolwork I'll leave it where I found it for a day in case the kid comes back to fetch it. If it's still there after a day then . . ."

Mr. Dorrico continued talking, but nobody was listening. Mark was already gone. As soon as he heard that the paper was left out in the open in the bathroom, he beat feet for the third floor.

Mark flew up the stairs, sprinted down the hall, skidded around the corner, and blasted through the swinging door that led into the lavatory. When he got inside he did a quick look around to discover there was no journal page to be seen. He dropped to his knees and looked on the floor. He checked all the stalls. He looked on the window ledges and under the sinks. No page. He then grabbed the wastebasket and turned it over. It was empty. Mark felt sick. Could one of the other custodians have thrown it away and then emptied the wastebasket last night? That wouldn't be fair. Courtney said they didn't empty them until the morning. But then where was Bobby's page?

Mark sat down on the floor of the lavatory, totally beaten. His last hope was gone. He dropped his head into his knees and closed his eyes. He knew he had to clear his head and think. What would he tell Bobby? He had let his best friend down. Bobby was able to flume all over Halla and stop wars but he couldn't even be trusted to hold on to a sheet of paper.

"'Hi, guys. I gotta apologize for taking so long to write. So much has happened since I left you two, I'm not really sure where to begin.'"

Mark heard those words being read aloud. They were the first words from Bobby's Journal #5—the first words on the missing page.

Mark raised his eyes from his arms. When he did, his heart sank even deeper than it had been a few moments before. Standing inside the door to the boys' lavatory, holding the missing page, was Andy Mitchell. Mark stared up at the kid with greasy dark-blond hair and a bad case of acne . . . and wanted to retch.

If it was possible to have a true archenemy in junior high, then Andy Mitchell was Mark's archenemy. Mitchell was the kind of guy who loved to pick on guys like Mark. The word "bully" always jumped into Mark's mind, but he was a little old to be afraid of bullies. Still, Mitchell loved to harass Mark. He'd cheat off of him in class—when Mitchell decided to show up for class, that is. He'd make fun of Mark's stutter for the amusement of his equally idiotic band of friends, and he never passed Mark in the hallway without giving him a quick punch in the arm. Mark always had to be looking over his shoulder for Mitchell because he never knew where the next bomb was coming from.

The only time Mark was completely safe was when he was with Bobby or Courtney. Mitchell never messed with those guys. Like all good bullies, he was also a coward. Of course, since Bobby left on his adventure, Mark found himself alone more often and at the mercy of the ever present Mitchell. Mark knew he was a classic creep whose power came from the fact that he wasn't afraid to intimidate and belittle. But he was also the kind of guy who would find that power ebbing as his peers grew up and stopped taking him seriously. Unfortunately that time wouldn't come for a while yet. For now, Mitchell was in charge.

Mitchell stood inside the lavatory door with Bobby's journal page in one hand and a burning cigarette in the other.

"There's two possibilities here, Dimond," said Mitchell as he gave a quick, juicy snort. Mitchell always seemed to have a cold. It added to his hideous mystique. "Either this is some lame story you're writing, or you know exactly what happened to Pendragon and you're not telling anybody."

Mark slowly stood up. His mind was in overdrive. What would he tell this guy to get him to give up the page and leave him alone? There weren't a whole lot of options open.

"Y-You g-got me, Mitchell," Mark said tentatively. "It's a s-story. For English. Where did you get it?"

"I found it in here after school yesterday," answered Mitchell. "What's the deal? You miss your buddy Pendragon so bad you gotta make up stupid stories about him?"

"I-I know. It's really s-stupid," said Mark.

This was going pretty well. Mitchell was making up all the answers. Mark didn't have to do anything. Now all he had to do was get Mitchell to give him the page.

"Thanks for finding it."

He held his hand out for the page. This was the moment of truth. Was Mitchell going to give it back?

"What'll you give me for it?" Mitchell asked.

"What do you want?"

Mitchell gave this some thought. This was tough for him. He usually didn't think much.

"Forget it," he answered. "Just take it. It's no fun messing with you anymore. It's too easy."

Mark had to try to stop from smiling. This was amazing. He was going to get the page back, no harm, no foul. He didn't want Mitchell to think he was too happy about it, so he just shrugged and held his hand out. However . . .

It was at that exact instant that his ring started to twitch. Mark felt the telltale movement, but it was such a surprise that he could only stand there, frozen. Then the gray stone started to turn clear and glow. Bobby's next journal was about to show up, and it couldn't be happening at a worse time.

Mark clamped his other hand over the ring to hide it. He made eye contact with Mitchell, hoping against hope that he hadn't seen the ring move. But one look into Mitchell's wide eyes told him the truth. Mitchell had seen it, all right. They stood there for a moment, staring at each other. Finally . . .

"Gotta go!" Mark put his head down and headed for the door. But he had to go past Mitchell, and there was no way Mitchell was going to let him get past. He caught Mark and shoved him back into the bathroom.

"What's going on?" shouted Mitchell, with a touch of fear.

"N-Nothing. I-I'm sick is all."

Mark tried to get by again, but Mitchell wouldn't let him pass.

"Show me that ring!" Mitchell demanded.

By this point the ring was starting to expand on Mark's finger. He couldn't keep his hand on it any longer. Though it killed him to do it, he had to take the ring off and lay it on the ground. As soon as it hit the floor, the dazzling flash from the stone lit up the dark bathroom with a sparkling spray of light.

Mitchell stood over the ring in wonder. He started to bend down to touch it.

"Don't!" commanded Mark.

His voice was so forceful, Mitchell backed off. It was the only time Mitchell had ever done anything Mark wanted him to. Mark didn't feel any victory though; his dominance would be short-lived.

The ring was now expanded to its full size and Mark saw the familiar black hole in its center. The two then heard some odd musical notes coming from deep within.

"Dimond?" yelled Mitchell nervously. "What is this?"

Mark didn't answer. He knew it would be over soon. If he were lucky, Mitchell would run in terror.

But Mark wasn't lucky.

Mitchell stayed. The light from the stone blasted out so brightly that both guys had to shield their eyes. The musical notes grew louder, and then a second later, it was over. The lights stopped flashing. The ring was back to its normal size. Sitting next to it on the floor was another roll of pages that Mark knew was Bobby's next journal. It had arrived the exact same way all the others had, only this time it couldn't have happened at a worse time.

Mark bent down and picked up the roll and the ring. He put the ring back on his finger, and hoping to keep whatever power he had over Mitchell going, he held out his hand.

"Give me the page," he said as forcefully as possible.

Mitchell was numb. He actually started to do what he was told. He held the lost page out for Mark. Mark reached for it, and just as he was about to grab it, Mitchell snatched it back. He was slowly getting his balance back.

"What just happened here?" he asked shakily.

"You wouldn't understand," said Mark, still trying to hold on to whatever leverage the bizarre episode had given him. "J-Just give me the p-page." Mark was losing it.

"I ain't giving you nothing!" declared Mitchell.

The power had shifted again. Mitchell was back in charge.

"I'm starting to think you didn't write this. I'm starting to think Pendragon's been writing about where he is, and he's sending letters to you, special delivery."

Mark didn't know what to say. Mitchell had hit the nail right on the head. How was he going to explain this? Mitchell looked at the page again, then smiled a sly little smile. Mark's heart sank.

"I'll bet there are a lot of people who'd like to know about these," he said.

"Andy, you can't," Mark pleaded. "This isn't stupid kid stuff at school. There are things going on here you can't even imagine. If you told anybody about it, you'd be starting something that I guarantee you'd regret."

This seemed to hit home with Mitchell. Mark realized it might be his one chance to gain some real leverage over the bully.

"There are only three people who know about these pages," Mark continued. "Me, Courtney Chetwynde . . . and now you."

"Chetwynde knows?" shouted Mitchell in disappointment.

This was good for Mark. Mitchell was just as afraid of Courtney as Mark was of Mitchell. Mark was beginning to realize he had more tools to work with than he thought.

"Yes, Courtney knows everything," continued Mark. "This is a serious thing. If you start telling people about it, then you might get in just as much trouble as we will. There's a lot at stake here. You want to go public with it? Go ahead. But your life will never be the same."

Mark felt as if he had laid that on pretty thick. He wasn't at all sure whether Mitchell would get in trouble if he revealed the journals, but he counted on the fact that Mitchell was dumb enough to *think* he could get in trouble. Mark knew that was the one weapon guys like Mark had over guys like Mitchell. They were smarter.

"Don't be an idiot, Mitchell," said Mark. "Give me the page, forget you saw anything, and I promise never to tell anyone that you know."

Mitchell stared at the ground, thinking about the offer. Mark knew that Mitchell was over his head. This was way too much for his brain to process.

"I'll make you a deal, Dimond," said Mitchell tentatively. "I'll give you the page, and I'll shut up about what I saw. But you gotta do something for me too."

"I asked you before, *what*?"

"This isn't before," said Mitchell. "This is now. Before I didn't see the hocus-pocus stuff. My offer is this: I'll keep quiet as long as you let me read what Pendragon sends you."

"What?"

This was probably the worst thing Mark could imagine. He didn't want to share Bobby's journals with anybody, let alone lame-wad Andy Mitchell. What was he going to say to Courtney? He didn't know what to do.

"That's my offer, Dimond," said Mitchell, suddenly sounding more confident. "Either you start showing me those letters, or I start blabbing to everybody about what's going on. I might get in a little trouble, but nothing like what you and Chetwynde will catch."

Uh-oh. Mitchell was being smarter than Mark thought possible.

"Okay," said Mark, though it killed him to do it. "But I can't let you read it before me and Courtney. The letters are being sent to us, not you. After we read 'em, I'll let you have a look. But the letters stay with me, and if you tell anybody and I mean *anybody* about what's going on, I'll make sure you get in every bit as much trouble as we do."

Mitchell thought a second, then handed the lost page to Mark. Mark grabbed it like it was his most valuable possession in the world. And at that moment, it was.

"Deal," he said. "When do I get to read what you got?"

Mark started for the door. He was feeling bold and lost at the same time. He no longer cared about Mitchell's bully tactics. Their relationship had just been kicked into a higher gear. It was a dangerous gear that was way beyond petty bully stuff.

"I'll let you know," declared Mark, and opened the door.

"You better, Dimond," threatened Mitchell. "We're partners now."

Mark stopped and looked back at the creepy Andy Mitchell. He was right. They *were* partners now, sort of. The thought made Mark's stomach roll.

A short while later Mark met Courtney near the gym, just as they had arranged the night before. Courtney was all sorts of excited to know if Mark had found the missing page.

"Well?" she asked impatiently.

Mark's mind raced. What was he going to tell her? He knew he was going to have to tell her the truth, but right now he felt as if he had failed her, and failed Bobby. It started when he left the page in the bathroom and continued when he didn't have the guts to stand up to Andy Mitchell. He felt like such a loser. Yes, he was going to have to tell Courtney the truth, but he couldn't bring himself to do it just then.

"I got the page," he said. "And this."

He pulled Bobby's newest journal from his pack. Courtney's eyes lit up.

"Double score! Excellent! See, I told you it was going to work out."

"You were right," said Mark with absolutely no enthusiasm.

Courtney didn't sense this. She had enough enthusiasm going for the both of them.

"That's weird," said Courtney.

"What?" Mark shot back, hoping that she hadn't sensed something had gone terribly wrong.

Courtney took the newest journal from Mark and looked at it.

"This isn't like the last one," she said with curiosity. "The last journal was written on that green, waterproof paper. This is . . . different."

She was right. Mark had been so nervous about Andy Mitchell, he hadn't even noticed it himself. This new journal was much more like Bobby's first journals that he wrote on Denduron. The pages were brown and crusty looking like parchment.

"You're right," was all Mark could say.

"Okay, we gotta wait till after school to read," she said, handing him back the pages. "Meet me out front after last period and we'll get back to my basement. Okay?"

"Sure. Sounds good."

"Man, I hope I can wait that long. I'm dying! Don't peek, all right?"

"No problem. I won't peek," said Mark, wondering how he was going to keep Andy Mitchell from peeking all day.

Mark and Courtney then separated and went about their normal school day. Mark did his best to immerse himself in schoolwork to get his mind off his dilemma. A few times while classes were passing, he caught sight of Andy Mitchell. Mitchell wouldn't say a word. He'd just give Mark this exaggerated wink as if to say: "We've got a secret, right, pal?" Mark would just turn away and cringe.

After school Mark and Courtney met up just as planned. They barely said anything to each other as they walked to Courtney's house. A dozen times Mark started to tell her about Andy Mitchell, but couldn't find the right words. He saw how excited Courtney was about reading the new journal, and didn't want to crash her mood.

When they got to the house, Mark decided that he wouldn't say anything about Mitchell until after they read Bobby's journal. In spite of all the extra stuff that was going on, Mark was excited to find out what happened to their friend. So without Courtney realizing that a momentous decision had been reached, the two sat down on the dusty couch to jump once again into the world that had become Bobby's.

"I'm shaking," said Courtney as she held the pages.

"Yeah, tell me about it," countered Mark, though he was shaking for a whole bunch more reasons than Courtney.

Luckily for him, the time for talking was over. It was time to read.

CLORAL

Oh, man, I gotta apologize to you guys. I didn't mean to leave you hanging like that. It's just that things are happening fast now and I haven't had many chances to write. That last journal was getting pretty long and I wanted to send it before something happened to it, or to me. I wasn't thinking. Sorry.

I'm writing this new journal from a place where I finally feel safe. At least for now, anyway. I won't tell you where it is yet because the events that led me here were pretty wild. I'd rather recount things as they happened and not jump ahead. It's easier that way. But I'll tease you a little by saying you're not going to believe where I am. Now let's get back to where I left you hanging.

When Magorran hit Grallion, I felt it rather than saw it. The impact sent a giant shockwave throughout the habitat that knocked most people off their feet, including me and Uncle Press. The habitat shuddered and shook and a horrible grinding sound filled the air as the two giant ships collided. I couldn't see it, but I could imagine the destruction that was happening at the point of impact. I could only hope that it wouldn't be so devastating as to send both habitats to the bottom.

Moments before the collision the aquaneers had thrown off most of the lines that secured Grallion, so that when the habitats hit, we would be pushed back instead of holding firm. If not for that move, there would have been way more damage. Also, the pilot of Grallion threw the engines into full reverse, which helped to soften the blow. Still, that wasn't enough to avoid the crash. Even after the collision, Magorran kept coming. The big habitat was powerful and moving fast. It pushed Grallion across the surface of the ocean like a toy. A really big toy. The only way to stop it was to stop Magorran.

Once we realized we weren't going to sink, Uncle Press helped me to my feet. There was a strong vibration from the force of the charging habitat and it was difficult to stand. Up till now I never even felt like I was on a ship. Now I felt like I was on the *Titanic*, and it was banging against the iceberg.

But there was one other thought that made me even more nervous. When something this huge and bad happened it could only mean one thing: Saint Dane was in the house. The look on Uncle Press's face told me he was thinking the same thing. This accident was classic Saint Dane. I could almost hear the wheels turning in Uncle Press's head as he calculated what the crash might mean to Grallion, to Cloral, to Halla, and to us. Finally he announced, "We're on the wrong habitat."

"You're kidding, right?"

He wasn't. Uncle Press took off running toward the impact point. This was insane. The safest place to be was far away from where the two habitats had collided. But being safe wasn't usually high on Uncle Press's To Do list. He was headed right for the most dangerous place on board, and I was right after him. We ran past several vators who were fleeing from the bow to a safer part of the habitat. There was a name for those guys. Smart. We weren't being smart; we were headed toward disaster.

The closer we got to the bow, the more damage there was. The deck had buckled and split. I could look down through jagged tears and see below to the pipes and struts that held Grallion together. It got tricky dodging around these open fissures. One wrong step and we could have fallen a few stories into the guts of Grallion. It was like running over a rickety old footbridge where the bottom could fall out at any moment. Still, Uncle Press wouldn't stop.

When we got near the bow, we saw the full extent of the devastation. Each of the two habitats were crushed where they impacted. It was a twisted mess of beams, girders, and decking. This no longer looked like a habitat. It looked like a vast, floating junkyard.

"Now what?" I asked.

Uncle Press pointed to several aquaneers who were leaping on board Magorran. They were led by Wu Yenza, the chief aquaneer. It was a daring jump because even though the decks of the two habitats were only a few feet apart, they were both still moving and grinding against each other.

"Follow them," said Uncle Press, which was the last thing I wanted to hear. But he didn't give me time to think. He ran to the edge of the deck, hesitated only a second, then leaped from Grallion onto Magorran.

"Let's go, Bobby!" he yelled.

Imagine standing on an ice floe as it hurtled down a river and you had to jump onto another ice floe that was going just as fast. That's pretty much what this felt like. The gap between the two decks was only a few feet, but it felt like a mile. I looked down. Big mistake. I could see through four stories down of twisted wreckage to the frothing white water. Falling would really, really hurt.

"It's cake, Bobby!" shouted Uncle Press. "C'mon!"

Cake. Yeah, right. I inched as close as I could to the edge without getting dizzy. The deck lurched under my feet. This was definitely *not* cake! I waited until Grallion settled, took a breath—and jumped.

I cleared the chasm by a good five feet. Okay, maybe it *was* cake.

"Now what?" I asked, trying to sound as if I were more in control of myself than I really was.

"The pilot house," answered Uncle Press. "Let's find out who's driving this bus."

The pilot house where the habitat was controlled wasn't far from which we boarded. Like the pilot house on Grallion, this was an enclosed structure where the pilot, the first mate, and a few other aquaneers would send the commands that controlled the habitat. Whatever the problem was with Magorran, the logical place to start looking for it was the pilot house.

We took off running, but it wasn't any easier over here than it was on Grallion. This deck was torn up from the impact as well. The whole habitat shuddered and heaved as it bounced against Grallion. It was like trying to run across a minefield during an earthquake.

The goal was to stop Magorran. I feared that when we got to the pilot house, we'd find none other than Saint Dane standing at the wheel wearing an aquaneer uniform and an evil, leering smile. But that would have been too easy. Saint Dane may have been responsible for this, but he wouldn't have done something as obvious as piloting the habitat himself. No, Saint Dane didn't work that way. He was a manipulator. This was an epic disaster that was worthy of him, but the cause of it would be far more diabolical. This was only the beginning. It wasn't just about two habitats colliding. There had to be something grander at stake. So as much as I feared seeing Saint Dane at the wheel, it was his overall scheme that I feared more.

Before we got to the pilot house, the habitat suddenly stopped shuddering. The aquaneers who boarded ahead of us must have reached the controls and shut down the engines. There was a strange calm. The horrible cracking sound of the two habitats grinding against each other stopped. The drone of the engines stopped. The rush of the water crashing between the two wrecked habitats stopped. The aquaneers must have slowed Magorran because after one last loud, twisting crunch, I saw Grallion pull away. The two habitats were once again separate.

As Grallion drifted away, I saw the extent of the damage, and it was pretty nasty. The entire bow end of the farm barge looked like a car after a head-on collision. Decking was bent and cracked. Geysers of water shot from burst pipes. Pieces of beams and struts floated in the water. The dock area was destroyed along with most of the small boats that were kept there. In a word, it was mangled. I'm sure that Magorran looked the same, though I couldn't tell because I was standing on it. The big question now was, why had the aquaneers on Magorran lost control? If our aquaneers could stop it so easily, what prevented the Magorran crew from doing the same?

Uncle Press and I reached the pilot house that was about a hundred yards back from the damaged bow. I was glad to see the collision hadn't destroyed it. It was a solid structure that was probably built that way in case something hairy like this happened. This was the first good news we saw. Magorran could still be controlled from here. The question was, why did it go out of control in the first place? The moment we opened the door, we had the answer. There were two aquaneers from Grallion at the controls. Yenza was at the wheel, the other worked the array of toggle switches for the many water-powered engines that controlled the habitat.

The aquaneer crew from Magorran was there as well. There was the pilot, the first mate, and three other aquaneers. I recognized their rank because they wore the same uniforms as the crew from Grallion. But there was one big difference between this crew and our crew.

These guys were all dead.

It was a creepy scene for obvious reasons, but it was made all the more so because the crew looked so . . . natural. It wasn't like there was a violent fight or anything. Just the opposite. The pilot sat in his chair, still looking forward with sightless eyes. The first mate was hunched over a map with a pen still in his hand as if he were in the middle of plotting a course, probably to rendezvous with Grallion. The other aquaneers were sitting on the deck near their stations as if they had simply fallen asleep. But these guys were definitely not asleep. Their eyes were wide open. There was something else. Uncle Press saw it first and pointed it out to me. Each of the poor dead aquaneers had a trace of something on the corners of their mouths. It was dry now, but it looked to have been a trickle of green liquid that had dribbled out of the corners of their mouths and crusted there.

They were dead all right. The mystery of the collision was solved. These guys died at their posts under full power. But the idea of five guys suddenly dying was tough to comprehend. It was then that I was hit with a thought that was even more horrific than the sight in front of me. It was like an alarm rang in my head. I reached out to Uncle Press, grabbed his sleeve and pulled him out of the pilot house.

"This wasn't a sudden crash," I croaked out through my dry mouth. "I mean, we saw it coming, right?"

"Yeah, so?"

"So if we saw it coming, how come nobody else on board Magorran did?"

Before I got all the words out, I saw in Uncle Press's face that he knew exactly where I was going with this. The crash happened because the pilot and his crew were dead. But somebody else on Magorran should have seen the crash coming and tried to stop it. That is, if anybody else on Magorran were alive to see it. The horrible realization hit Uncle Press just as it hit me. If nobody else tried to stop the crash, did that mean more people were dead? We both did a quick scan around and saw the same thing—nothing. There was no movement. No life. The sickening truth was setting in. There was a very good chance that everybody on Magorran had met the same fate as its crew.

This may have become a ship of the dead.

I turned away from Uncle Press and puked.

CLORAL

"**S**pader!" shouted Uncle Press.

I had my hands on my knees while tossing my lunch. I looked up to see Spader booking across the deck several yards away. He was headed deeper onto Magorran and I knew why. He was going to find his father.

Behind us Wu Yenza came from the pilot house and saw him too.

"Stop right there!" she commanded. "Do *not* go onto this habitat!"

Spader didn't even glance at her. There was nothing stopping him.

"We'll stay with him," said Uncle Press to Yenza.

"You are not authorized to be here," she said sternly.

"We're civilians," countered Uncle Press. "You can't stop us."

"We can't protect you either."

I didn't like the sound of that. Whatever caused this horrible disaster could still be out there. On the other hand, chances are it was Saint Dane, and that bad boy was our department.

"Understood," said Uncle Press. "We'll bring him back."

Yenza wanted to argue, but Uncle Press had already started to jog after Spader. I looked to the chief aquaneer and shrugged. She scowled at me and I turned and ran after Uncle Press.

Spader had a head start on us and it was tough keeping up with him. It didn't help that he knew exactly where he was going. We had to keep him in sight or he'd be gone. As we ran across the deck of Magorran I tried to keep an eye on him while taking in the new surroundings. This was a manu habitat, but the factories must have been toward the stern because the area we were running through seemed more residential. There were several tall structures that looked like apartment buildings surrounding a big park. This could have been a normal, downtown neighborhood back on Second Earth. It was strange to think that we were floating. Stranger still was the fact that the place was deserted. There wasn't a soul to be seen—living or dead. It gave me hope that everyone had evacuated Magorran before they met the same deadly fate as the crew.

Up ahead Spader hurried into one of the apartment buildings. When we entered after him, all my hopes that the habitat had been abandoned came crashing down. Sitting in the lobby were three more bodies. Like in the pilot house, it looked as if death touched them quickly and with complete surprise. They were three men who must have been factory workers because they all wore the same bright blue coveralls. They sat around a table that was covered with multicolored tiles. My guess was they were playing some kind of game when they met their fate. One still held a tile as if ready to make a play. He never got the chance. The whole scene was creepy and I didn't want to look too closely, but I did see that all three men had the same trace of dried green liquid on their chins. Whatever it was, it must have had something to do with the way they died.

I didn't want to be there anymore. This was getting dangerously gross. I was all set to turn and bolt back for Grallion, when we heard a crash coming from deeper in the building that sounded like breaking glass. Either it was Spader or somebody was still alive. Uncle Press took off toward the sound and as much as I wanted to run the other way, I stayed with him.

As we ran down a long corridor I tried not to think about what horrors lay behind each of the closed doors we passed. It was like running through a tomb. We finally came to a door that was open slightly.

"You ready for this?" Uncle Press asked.

"No, but we gotta do it," I answered.

So he pushed the door open and we both entered.

We saw right away that this was an apartment very much like Spader's on Grallion. It was small and simple, with molded furniture and windows that looked out on the ocean. Nobody was here, so we had to move on into the bedroom.

That's where we found him. Spader stood in the middle of the room. At his feet was a shattered vase. That was the sound we heard. Spader must have broken it himself, probably in anger. When we entered, he didn't turn to look at us. That was because he was focused on his father. The man was sitting at a desk with his head resting on the surface. Yes, he was dead. Like the others, it looked as if he had died peacefully. He wore his full aquaneer uniform. My guess was he wanted to look as good for his son as Spader wanted to look for him. My heart went out to my friend. I had expected Spader to discover that his father had disappeared, just as mine had. But this was worse. Much worse.

I think Spader was in shock. His eyes were focused on his father as if he thought he could change the sight before him by sheer willpower.

I had no idea of what to say or do. Uncle Press walked over to the fallen aquaneer and gently closed his eyes. He then looked to Spader and said in a gentle voice, "Don't be sad, this is the way it was meant to be."

Though he didn't know it yet, Spader was a Traveler. As I was told many times before, everything happens for a reason. I didn't quite buy it yet, but that's what I was told.

Spader looked into Uncle Press's eyes and I saw how bad he was hurting.

"This is the way it was meant to be?" he asked with a shaky voice. "I don't understand."

"You will," Uncle Press said gently.

"We're going to help you."

I knew what Uncle Press meant. Pretty soon we were going to have to tell Spader about being a Traveler. But I didn't think it was going to help him understand anything. I've known about being a Traveler for some time now, and I'm still pretty clueless.

Uncle Press looked down at the dead man, and saw something. Clutched in his right hand was a small folded piece of paper. Uncle Press gently took it from his hand and read it. He then looked at Spader, and handed the note to him. When Spader took it, I thought he was going to burst out in tears. That's because the letter was for him.

Scribbled on the sheet was one word: "Spader." In his dying moments Spader's father had written a note to his son. It was odd to see "Spader" written out in normal letters. Since Travelers understood all languages, I suppose we could also understand all *written* language as well.

As Spader took the note I saw Uncle Press put something quickly into his pocket. Spader didn't see it because he was looking at the note. But I did. Uncle Press had taken something else from the dead man's hand and didn't want Spader to see it. He looked at me and gave me a stern look which clearly said: "Don't say anything."

"What does the note say?" asked Uncle Press.

Spader showed the note to Uncle Press and I looked over his shoulder to see it too. It wasn't a written message; it was a drawing. It was a circular symbol about the size of an Oreo cookie. It looked to me like two interlocking letters from an Asian alphabet. I had no idea what it meant or what it represented.

"Do you know what this means?" asked Uncle Press.

Spader shook his head. Uncle Press handed it back to him and said, "If your father wanted you to have it, it's more important than we realize right now."

Spader nodded, folded the paper and put it in his pocket. He then looked to my uncle and I saw a change in the aquaneer's eyes. He was no longer in shock. He was totally in control.

"I'm going to find out what happened here," he said with certainty.

"Good. We're going to help you," Uncle Press answered.

The moment was broken by the sound of hurried footsteps. A group was headed down the hallway toward us, fast. Seconds later they entered the apartment and I saw it was a group of five aquaneers, headed by Wu Yenza. These guys looked as if they were on a mission. They were all business, and they carried guns. This was the first time I had seen weapons of any sort on Cloral, other than spearguns for fishing. These weapons were sleek, silver rifles with wide barrels.

I would have thought they were kind of cool, if I hadn't been so worried they might be used on us. Yenza had a gun as well, but hers was a silver pistol in a holster on her hip.

She strode purposefully into the bedroom and scanned the scene. When her eyes fell on Spader's father, she cringed with surprise and sorrow.

"I'm sorry, Spader," she said kindly. "I knew your father. There is much of him in you."

Spader acknowledged this with a nod.

"Magorran is being evacuated," she then said, clicking into business mode. "All nonessential personnel must return to Grallion."

"What's the point?" asked Uncle Press.

"We're sending in a medical team," she answered quickly. "The habitat will be quarantined until we determine what caused these deaths."

Good point. If a virus had done this, it could still be hanging around. It was best to leave this to the experts.

"When you get back to Grallion," she continued, "you will be disinfected. Do not take anything from here. Understand?"

I was sure that the same thought shot through all of our heads. What about the piece of paper with the round symbol on it? Was Spader going to leave it? The answer was *no*. He walked out of the room, past Yenza, without giving up the paper. Uncle Press and I shared glances, then followed him out.

We were escorted back toward the bow of Magorran by two armed aquaneers. We weren't under arrest or anything, they just wanted to make sure we got back quickly. Spader didn't say a word. He walked stiffly, looking straight ahead.

When we got near the crushed bow, I saw there was a

flurry of activity going on. Several more aquaneers had arrived and were putting on bulky suits that made them look as if they were getting ready to handle plutonium. I figured they wanted protection against any nasty microbe that might be on Magorran. I really hoped those suits weren't necessary, because if they were, it would have meant Uncle Press and Spader and I were already infected. Suddenly the idea of being disinfected was sounding pretty good. We had to get back to Grallion, fast.

One of the aquaneers stopped us and said, "We'll get you on a boat for Grallion. Wait here." He took off, leaving the other aquaneer to make sure we stayed put.

As we stood there I glanced over at the pilot house and saw something strange. Two agronomers were standing outside, away from everyone else. They were arguing. It was the man and woman whom I recognized from Grolo's. The man seemed to be pleading with the woman. He was angry and waved his arms to make his point, but the woman didn't want to listen and kept turning away from him. I had no idea what they were saying because we were too far away, but I wanted to remember what I saw.

A transfer boat brought the three of us back to Grallion. But we weren't allowed to go home right away. They first brought us to a medical building and made us give up our clothes. I think they burned them, because I never saw them again. We were given replacements though. We also had to empty our pockets. This was going to be tricky. It meant giving up my Traveler ring, not to mention Uncle Press's ring and whatever it was he took from Spader's father. I also wondered what Spader was going to do with the note. It could be a vital clue as to what happened on Magorran and I feared it would be destroyed.

The rings proved easy. They were sent through a sterilizer and given back to us. As for the other stuff, I wasn't sure. Before we got dressed we had to shower with some foul-smelling soap that stung my skin. Some medical personnel watched us the whole time to make sure we washed all the nooks and crannies. Nice, huh? To be honest, I didn't mind. I would have scrubbed myself with acid in Yankee Stadium if I thought I might be carrying a microbe that was deadly enough to do the damage I saw on Magorran.

Once we were released, all freshly scrubbed and stinging, we walked back toward Spader's house. Spader wasn't saying much and I figured it was because his thoughts were with his dad. Well, his thoughts may have been with his dad, but that's not why he was so quiet. As soon as we got away from the medical unit, I saw the real reason. He opened his mouth . . . and pulled out the note from his father. He had folded it and got it through without anyone knowing. Smart guy. We asked him to come for dinner, but he wasn't in the mood. He wanted to be alone. Can't say I blame him. Uncle Press and I went back to our apartment and I finally got the chance to talk with him in private.

"What happened over there?" I asked right away. "Was it Saint Dane?"

"It could have been," answered Uncle Press. "Or it could just have been a horrible accident."

"Accident?" I shouted. "How many people died on Magorran? Two, three hundred? That was no accident."

"You might be right, but we've got to look beyond the tragedy here. Saint Dane doesn't wreak havoc just for the sake of it. He always has a plan. If he caused those people to die, it's because it served some overall scheme. Remember, he's about pushing a territory toward chaos. If we're going to find his hand in this, we've got to figure out what his overall plan is."

"What about Spader?" I asked. "He's in bad shape. It's going to be hard to tell him about the whole Traveler thing."

"But he's got to learn soon. He's the only Traveler from Cloral now."

"You mean he wasn't before?"

"Up until he died, Spader's father was the Traveler. Now it's Spader."

"Oh, man!" I blurted out. "Spader's father was a Traveler too?"

"Yes," said Uncle Press softly. "And he was a friend."

He reached into his pocket and said, "I took this from him, but it belongs to Spader now." He held up the item he secretly took from Spader's dad and I instantly recognized what it was. It was a Traveler's ring just like mine. The band was made of heavy silver; the stone in the center was slate gray and there was some kind of bizarro engraving around it.

"I want you to give this to him. You'll know when the time is right," said Uncle Press, as he dropped it in my hand.

I nodded and put the ring in my pocket. I wasn't sure I wanted this responsibility, but Spader was my friend. How could I not do it?

Uncle Press then said, "Spader's father must have known something was going to happen."

"What makes you say that?"

"The paper he left for Spader. His last act was to get that symbol to his son, the Traveler. It's why I think the deaths on Magorran weren't an accident. There's something bigger going on."

"What do you think the symbol means?"

"I don't know, but I'll make you a bet: When we find that out, we'll find Saint Dane."

It was official. The game was on. It looked like Saint Dane had made his first move. But this wasn't like Denduron. There were no obvious good guys and bad guys here. At least not yet, anyway. There was nothing we could do but keep our eyes and ears open—and wait.

The next few days slipped by in a weird haze. Uncle Press and I went back to work, but our hearts weren't in it. It didn't seem like anybody else cared to be working either. Everyone wanted to know what the medical team would find on Magorran. I found myself stopping and staring out at the manu habitat that was anchored a mile away. It looked like a dark storm cloud looming on the horizon. The only signs of life were the several boats that would travel back and forth from Grallion to ferry medical personnel and repair crews.

Repairs were also under way on Grallion. The pilot brought us back to our original position and anchored us there. I heard that the collision with Magorran pushed us nearly ten miles over the ocean. It was important that Grallion return to its home because that's where the underwater farm was.

I tried talking to Spader a few times, but he didn't want company or conversation. I understood, but I also knew he shouldn't be totally alone. It was sad. The loss of his father changed him. He went from being a total extrovert to spending all of his time alone. This wasn't good, so one night I got two bottles of sniggers from Grolo's and paid him a visit.

When I knocked on his door, Spader didn't answer. But I knew he was in there so I let myself in. I found him lying on the floor, staring up at the ceiling. By the rank smell in there, I guessed he hadn't showered much in the past few days. I didn't say anything though, I just walked in and pressed the bottle of sniggers into his hands.

"Hobey-ho," I said.

Spader looked up at me and for a moment I didn't think he recognized me. His mind was miles away. But then he focused and smiled. He took the sniggers, too.

"Strange days, Pendragon, my friend," he said as he sat up.

"Yeah, strange days," I answered, and we both took a drink of sniggers. It tasted good. I don't think sniggers had alcohol in it, like beer. But it definitely had a sparkle, and that was good.

"What were you thinking about?" I asked.

Of course I knew he was thinking about his dad, but it was as good a way as any to start a conversation. Spader lifted his other hand and I saw that he was holding the piece of green paper with the round symbol. He waved it at me as if to say: "I'm thinking about this."

"Any idea what it means?" I asked.

"Not a clue," he answered. "But I know who might."

"Who?"

"My mum. She's a teacher. Sweetest lady in the world and twice as bright. I gotta get back there . . . tell her about Dad."

Spader closed his eyes. I wasn't sure if he was going to cry, but I looked away just in case. Things were about to get even worse for him. Here he was faced with the horrible task of telling his mother that her husband, his father, was dead. But there was more. There was the whole Traveler thing. When Spader went back to Panger City to find his mother, was she going to be there? Now that he had become the Traveler from Cloral, was she going to disappear the same as my family? Was he going to lose *both* of his parents? I felt like I had to say something to start getting his mind around the Traveler concept.

"Spader," I said cautiously. "There's something you should know."

Spader looked at me. His eyes were red. He wanted words of comfort from me, but I had none to give. As I sat there looking at him, I realized I had no idea of what to say. I needed to explain something that I didn't fully understand myself. Talk about the blind leading the blind.

"What, Pendragon?" he asked.

As I opened my mouth to say . . . I don't know what, Uncle Press entered the apartment. Whoa, big relief. He had bailed me out big time.

"I have news," he said. "About Magorran."

Spader and I both sat up in anticipation. We had been waiting for information for days. But one look at Uncle Press told me that it wasn't going to be good news. He looked nervous, and maybe even a little bit angry.

"Let's have it then," prodded Spader.

Uncle Press took a chair and sat opposite us. He spoke softly and clearly so we understood completely.

"The medical team made their report," he began. "They examined and tested every one of the victims."

"How many?" I asked.

"Two hundred and twenty."

Though I knew the number was going to be high, it was still a shock to hear it. Uncle Press let that information sink in, then continued.

"The test results came back exactly the same on each and every one of them." He took a breath and said, "They were all poisoned."

The news hit me like a hammer to the head.

"H-How?" I blurted out. "How can that many people be poisoned?"

"They aren't sure, but they think it may had something to do with a shipment of rice. It was bad, and they all ate it."

"What do you mean *bad*?" demanded Spader.

"They don't know," answered Uncle Press, trying to stay calm. "They can't tell. They said it was unlike anything they'd seen before."

Spader jumped to his feet and started to pace. "Bad rice? How can people die because of bad rice?"

"It gets worse," added Uncle Press. "The agronomers are afraid it may not be the only case. If there's a problem with the food supply, then what happened on Magorran is just the tip of the iceberg."

My thoughts immediately went back to the argument I witnessed between the two agronomers on Grallion. They knew something was wrong. The horrible reality was slowly beginning to sink in. Cloral was a territory covered by water. People relied on farmers to grow food both on the habitats and underwater. If something was poisoning the food supply, it would be beyond disaster. Compared to this, bubonic plague would seem like a nasty cold going around.

There could be only one reason for this . . .

Saint Dane. This had his stamp all over it. If the food supply went bad, there would be chaos throughout the territory, no question about it.

"We don't know the extent of the problem. Maybe it was a one-time thing and they caught it," Uncle Press said calmly.

"Not in time to save my father," snapped Spader. There was anger in his eyes. He wanted someone to blame for his father's death. Uncle Press and I knew who it might be, but now was not the time to share it.

It was late, so we left Spader alone. Uncle Press and I went home to form a plan. The next day was the memorial service for the victims on Magorran. We decided that after the ceremony we would join with Spader, get a boat, and travel to

Panger City to find Spader's mom. The only clue we had to go on to start tracking down Saint Dane was the strange symbol that Spader's dad left him, and Panger City was as good a place to start looking as any. With that plan in place, we tried to get some sleep.

I barely slept all night. The thought of territorywide famine made it a little hard to have sweet dreams. There were too many thoughts banging around in my head, so I decided to finish my journal to you. Writing always makes me sleepy, and this time was no different. I got as far as telling you that Magorran and Grallion had collided, and couldn't keep my eyes open anymore. So I rolled up the pages and sent them on to you. It wasn't until the next morning that I realized what a cliffhanger I had written. Again, sorry.

I laid back down on my bunk and finally got a few z's. But soon the sun was brightening the sky on a new day, the day we would leave Grallion.

The memorial service was scheduled for shortly after sunrise. I didn't know what to expect, but it turned out to be a pretty emotional moment. It took place on the stern of the habitat, away from the destruction up front. Everyone on Grallion was there. We stayed with the farm workers, the vators, who pretty much kept together in one large group. The aquaneers were lined up along the stern, shoulder to shoulder, in full dress uniform. Spader was among them. It had to be tough for him to stand there, but he did it. Good man.

The pilot of Grallion, a leathery-looking gray-haired guy named Quinnick, led the ceremony. I won't write down all that was said, but as you can imagine, it was pretty intense. He spoke about the dedication of those who serve others, and the harsh reality that all life must one day come to an end. He spoke glowingly of the crew and workers of Magorran, and about how they would never be forgotten.

Then an aquaneer stepped forward and began to play an instrument that looked to be made from a large piece of coral. It was a wind instrument, and though it seemed pretty crude, the sound it made was sweet, like an oboe. The tune he played was haunting and sad. It was a fitting send-off to the poor people of Magorran.

But it was short-lived because suddenly, without warning . . . *boom!*

An explosion rocked Grallion only a few yards from where we stood. The crowd didn't react immediately. Everyone just sort of looked around, stunned, not knowing what was happening.

Boom! Boom!

Two more explosions rocked the habitat, chewing up pieces of deck and dirt. People started to scatter and run for cover. We were under attack, but from where?

The answer came from Wu Yenza. She stood on the stern and yelled out, "*Raiders!*"

Raiders? What were raiders? The only raiders I knew were from Oakland. I looked off the stern and had my answer. There was a ship powering toward us. It wasn't a habitat, it was a battleship, and its giant guns were trained on us. These guys weren't from Oakland.

Things were turning very sour, very fast here on Cloral.

CLORAL

We were under attack.

Most people on deck scrambled for cover and I was one of them. Uncle Press and I stuck with a group of vators who fled to the building that held most of the farming equipment. That wouldn't give much protection, but it was better than standing out in the open with bombs raining down!

As we ran more missiles pounded the deck and blasted dirt and water everywhere. Yes, water. These weren't your everyday, ordinary cannonballs. Remember, this was Cloral. Everything here had to do with water. I soon found out that the giant guns on the battleship were actually huge water cannons that fired big, dense balls of water. But when these water missiles hit, they were every bit as destructive as a steel shell. And they could fire round after round without fear of running out of ammunition. After all, their ammunition was water, and there was an infinite supply around these parts. What made it even more frightening was that there was no sound. The guns didn't let out a giant roar when they fired, so it was impossible to prepare for a strike. The first clue that a water missile was about to hit was a faint whistling sound, and then it hit.

About a dozen of us crowded into the equipment shed and scrambled to the windows to look out on the action.

I looked to Uncle Press and said, "Raiders? What's the deal?"

Uncle Press didn't know. This was a wrinkle he wasn't prepared for.

"I have never seen them attack a habitat this large," one vator said with more than a touch of fear. "They usually prey on small vessels."

"What do they want?" I asked.

"Whatever we have," came the simple answer. "And they're not afraid to kill for it."

Gulp. I looked out the window to see that the aquaneers were scrambling to defend the habitat. These guys weren't just sailors, they were trained in using weapons as well. They moved fast and efficiently as they took up defensive positions facing the incoming cruiser. But the only weapons they had were the silver rifles I saw back on Magorran. They didn't have big cannons or missile launchers or firepower of any kind that could stand up to the barrage from the raiders' huge water guns. Their rifles seemed like, well, they seemed like water pistols compared to the mighty arsenal they faced.

"Why isn't Grallion armed?" I asked the vator.

"I told you," he answered. "The raiders have never been so bold. There was never a reason to be armed. Until now," added Uncle Press soberly.

All my romantic notions about pirates were just blown away, no pun intended. To me pirates were charming rogues who drank grog and chased wenches and shivered me timbers and were basically comical characters in search of treasure. But these weren't Disney pirates. The guys firing on us were killers. *Bold* killers. They were attacking an unarmed farming habitat with over two hundred people on board. But for what? There were no riches on Grallion. What could they possibly want?

Then the barrage of missiles stopped. We took a look at the battle cruiser and saw that it had pulled to within a few hundred yards of Grallion. Its guns were still aimed at us, but they were no longer firing for the time being.

The ship looked very much like a battleship from home, though of course there were no military markings. It was a light green color that made it blend in with the green water. I counted eight water cannons in all. Four front and four back. I wondered what their next step was. Were they going to board us? That wouldn't make sense because any advantage they had with their big guns would be lost once they set foot onboard. There were plenty of aquaneers with rifles to give them a hard time if they set foot on our deck. No, the advantage these bad guys had was from a distance.

Then, a booming, amplified voice came from the battle cruiser.

"Good morning, Grallion! I trust we have your attention."

It was a man's voice and he actually sounded cheery. He could have been calling to a neighbor over the backyard fence to talk about the Yankees.

"My name is Zy Roder, pilot and chief of the good ship *Pursuit*. Perhaps you've heard of me?"

The more I listened to this guy's booming voice, the more my stomach twisted. I looked to Uncle Press and his grim expression told me he was feeling the same way. Near us, a vator had been watching the cruiser through a spyglass. The moment we heard the voice coming from the raiders' ship, Uncle Press approached the man and asked if he could borrow the telescope. The worker obliged and Uncle Press took a closer look at our new nemesis.

"If you have heard of me," the voice continued, "then you know I am a fair man. I wish no harm on anyone."

Uncle Press saw what he needed to see, then handed me the spyglass. I took it and looked out at the cruiser. The crew of the ship he called *Pursuit* were all on deck. There was a mix of men and women, which meant that at least raiders weren't sexist. They weren't all torn up and scuzy looking the way you think of movie pirates either. No, just the opposite. These guys looked like an organized, buttoned-up crew. But the way they stared at Grallion made me think of a pack of hungry wolves, patiently waiting to strike. Their stares were blank and lacked any human emotion, except for maybe greed.

I moved the spyglass until I found the man called Zy Roder. He stood on the uppermost deck, holding something dark that I could only guess was a microphone. Like all the raiders, Zy Roder wore the same kind of lightweight clothing that everyone wore here on Grallion. He was a tall guy, with shoulder-length blond hair that blew around in the sea breeze. You might even call him handsome. He stood with his legs apart defiantly, with one hand on his hip. Pretty cocky. This was a guy who was used to getting what he wanted. I wondered what it was he wanted from us.

But the thing that struck me most about him was his eyes. Even though I was looking through a spyglass, I could see they were the same, icy blue eyes that I had grown to fear. There was no mistake.

It was Saint Dane.

He had arrived on Cloral and taken up with a band of outlaw marauders. The question now became, what was his next move? I handed the spyglass back to the vator. I didn't want to watch anymore.

"By now you must know of the horrible disease that is

spreading throughout Cloral," he continued. "Our food is being poisoned. Why? I have no idea. But I do know that safe food will soon grow scarce."

This was Saint Dane all right. He was doing what he did best, spreading fear.

"Our request is simple. The food on Grallion is safe . . . so far. You have so much, and we so little. These are my terms. Load ten of your largest transfer barges with grain, fruit, and vegetables. Send each barge out to us with a single aquaneer. We will take the barges and leave you in peace."

The farm workers around us erupted in protest. They complained that ten barges of food would wipe Grallion out for weeks. Worse, if they gave up all their supply of safe food, then what would be left for them to eat? Already, the fear of tainted food coming in from the outside was suspect. Who could blame them, after what happened on Magorran?

"If you refuse us," Zy Roder continued, "then we will resume our attack." The man now grew more intense. Gone was the pleasant voice of a fellow sailor. Saint Dane or Zy Roder—whatever he called himself here—wanted the people of Grallion to understand what he was capable of.

"We cannot sink Grallion, but that is not our intent. We will begin with your pilot house. It will be obliterated so that you will have no control of your habitat. Then we will destroy your docks so you will be trapped. We will target your engine rooms so you will have no power. You will be prisoners on your own habitat, with no means of escape. Trust me, friends, we know where you are most vulnerable and we will not leave until our demands are met."

This was pure Saint Dane. He probably didn't even care about getting the food. What he wanted was to cause panic. The word would spread quickly among the habitats that the food supply on Cloral was suspect, and that would create chaos as normally peaceful people would start to fight over the dwindling supply of fresh food. My guess is that Saint Dane probably had something to do with poisoning the food supply as well. His plan for toppling Cloral was beginning to become clear.

"I will give you one peck of time to begin the transfer," his voice boomed. "If I see no sign of your compliance, we will open fire. So until then, enjoy your day!"

What was a peck? Was that an hour? A minute? A second? Uncle Press read my mind and said, "Twenty minutes, in case you were wondering."

Saint Dane had one more thought. "Oh, one last thing," his voice boomed. "Welcome to Cloral . . . Pendragon."

Yikes. My knees buckled, which I'm sure was the exact reaction Saint Dane wanted. He knew we were here. Luckily, the other vators had more to worry about than why this pirate had given me a personal greeting. That would have been hard to explain. So instead of questioning me, they all started chattering at once. Half argued to give him the food, the other half wanted to fight. Neither choice was a good one.

"At least we know a little about his plan now," said Uncle Press, trying to sound positive.

"Yeah, big deal," I shot back. "What are we going to do about it?"

At that moment Spader burst into the shack. He looked around quickly until he saw us. "Press, Pendragon, come!" he shouted.

Neither of us knew what else to do, so we followed. Once outside we saw that Spader was off and running. He led us down to the same floating docks where we first arrived on Grallion. The area was deserted because all the other aquaneers were up on deck, ready to defend their habitat.

He ran to the end of one dock and jumped onto his skimmer. We finally caught up to him. I shouted, "What are you doing?"

While he spoke Spader busily prepared the skimmer for a trip.

"My father taught me everything there is to know about every ship on the sea," he said quickly. "I know about that raider cruiser, the *Pursuit*. There were only a few built, back when the aquaneers feared there might be a war between the habitats. They even built warships that traveled underwater. But the war never happened and the cruisers and submarines were never used—except for a few that got hijacked by raiders."

"What's the point, Spader?" asked Uncle Press.

Spader stopped working and looked up at us. "I know where she's vulnerable. I can scuttle the guns."

"How?" I asked in disbelief.

"Simple. There are two intake ports below the waterline. That's where they bring in water for power and ammunition. If I drive a skimmer into an intake port, it'll jam up the works. No water, no guns. It'll be dead in the water and we can take her!"

"Did you tell Yenza about this?" asked Uncle Press.

"She wouldn't listen. She thinks I'm off my cake."

"Are you off your cake?" I asked.

Spader jumped off his skimmer and back onto the dock. He stood across from us and spoke with sincerity.

"Ever since you turned up here, I've had a feeling," he said. "First you, Press, then later when you came back with Pendragon. I feel like you two mates are here for more than just picking fruit. Am I right? Are the three of us in for a natty-do, or am I just shooting fish?"

It seemed Spader had some rumblings about his future as

a Traveler after all. He didn't know much, he could only sense it, but it was there just the same. His father probably taught him many things to prepare him for this moment, just as Uncle Press did for me. Whatever it is that makes one a Traveler, it was starting to kick in.

"Are you with me?" Spader asked.

"More than you know," answered Uncle Press. "What's your plan?"

Spader jumped back down onto his skimmer.

"Press, stay here. Get to Yenza. Tell her what we're doing. When the intake ports are jammed up, I'll send up a signal with this flare."

He held up a small pistol that was probably a flare gun.

"This flare won't go up until the *Pursuit* is crippled," he added. "Then Yenza can take a crew and board her before the raiders figure out what happened."

"What about me?" I asked.

"You're getting pretty good under the water, mate," he said.

"Whoa! You want me to go with you? Under that cruiser?"

"I told you, there are *two* intake ports. I can't hit 'em both at the same time."

I looked to Uncle Press, hoping he'd bail me out of this suicide mission. He didn't.

"Are you up to this, Bobby?" he asked.

No! I wasn't!

"It'll be easy, mate," said Spader. "They won't be looking underwater. All we have to do is sneak up from below, wrench off the intake covers and send in a couple of skimmers. Snappy-do!"

It did sound easy. I spent a lot of time underwater with Spader and I was pretty confident down there. Maybe I could do this after all.

"I don't suppose there's a plan B?" I asked Uncle Press.

"Not this time," he answered. "Unless you've got one."

I didn't. I was going underwater.

"Wait for the flare!" shouted Spader.

"Be careful!" Uncle Press shouted back as he ran back up the stairs toward the deck.

Yeah, careful. That was a joke, right?

Spader opened the cargo carrier that was behind his skimmer and pulled out two water sleds and two air globes. He threw one air globe to me and stowed the two water sleds in the floor compartment of his skimmer. He then unhooked the cargo carrier so he wouldn't have to drag it along.

"Are those water sleds big enough to do the job?" I asked.

"Nah, those are for our getaway," said Spader.

"Then what are we going to use to jam the intake ports?"

Spader jumped from his skimmer onto another that was right next to it. He threw a few toggle switches and the engines whined to life.

"You take my skimmer," he said.

This didn't make a whole lot of sense. If we were going to sneak up on the raiders' cruiser from underwater, then why were we each taking a skimmer? They may be fast, but Saint Dane and his crew would see us coming for sure.

Spader put his air globe over his head and it instantly conformed to him. I did the same. I jumped onto the skimmer and started to power it up. Finally I couldn't take it anymore and asked, "Won't they see us coming?"

Spader pointed to a black toggle switch that was under the steering column.

"They would—if we were on top of the water."

He flipped the black toggle and a rush of air bubbles blew out from under his skimmer. Then it started to sink. Spader looked at me and smiled. I found the same switch on my skimmer, and threw it. The same thing happened. Slowly my skimmer submerged. As it turned out, these babies didn't just fly over the water, they traveled underwater, too!

Just before his head went under, Spader asked, "How do you know Zy Roder?"

"Long story," I answered. "I'll tell you later."

"You'd better. Hobey-ho!"

With that, my head sank below and we were under way. Spader had given me skimmer lessons before, so I was familiar with how it operated. But this was way different. Rather than stand up, I held on to the steering handles and my body floated parallel to the deck.

"You okay?" asked Spader.

"I think," was my answer.

"Then let's hit it!"

He cranked his throttle, dipped the nose of his skimmer, and immediately shot down to the ocean floor. I did the same, and we were off. This was a lot like using the water sleds, except they were much more powerful. I was too heavy on the throttle at first and the skimmer nearly pulled out of my grasp. I followed behind Spader but made sure to stay out of his wake because when I got too close, the jets from his skimmer's pontoons hit me like turbulence. It took me a few minutes, but I eventually got the knack of controlling the vehicle and staying clear of Spader. Now all I had to do was worry about the killers we were sneaking up on.

Spader hugged the sandy bottom. That was smart. The deeper we were, the less chance there was of us being spotted. Remember, the water was very clear on Cloral. Visibility had to be at least a hundred feet. I really hoped that from the deck of the *Pursuit,* we just looked like big fish.

In no time I could look up and see the dark shape of the cruiser floating above us. Everything looks bigger underwater, but even accounting for that, this ship looked immense. It was like a giant black cloud that blocked out the sun. Spader set his skimmer down in the sand directly beneath the massive ship, right in its shadow.

"I'll go up first," he said while taking out a wrench-looking tool from his back pocket. I'll pull off the intake covers, then come back for you. Get the water sleds ready to go."

I nodded and gave the "okay" sign. I still wasn't used to talking underwater. Spader took off swimming up to the *Pursuit,* and I swam to his skimmer to get the water sleds. So far so good, but time was running out. I didn't have my watch (since I wasn't allowed to have a Second Earth watch on another territory), but I guessed that we were getting close to the end of the twenty-minute time limit.

I got both water sleds and rested them down in the sand between our skimmers. A few moments later, Spader joined me.

"It was snappy-do," he announced. "Covers came right off. All that's left is for us to drop off our gifts."

"Tell me exactly what to do," I said.

Spader pointed up at the hull. "Right near the stern you'll see a big round opening. I left the cover hanging from it so you wouldn't miss. There's two of 'em. I'll take the one on the far side of the keel. All you have to do is bring the skimmer right up to the mouth, hit the throttle, and let her go. Soon as it's on the way, meet me right back here. I'll set off the flare, and we'll have a leisurely water sled ride back to Grallion while Press and Yenza start the natty-do topside."

"Got it," I said. It didn't sound all that hard.

"Then let's be heroes," said Spader, and hit the throttle of his skimmer.

He didn't speed to the surface; he traveled with more caution. Now was not the time to get cocky and make a mistake. I powered up and ascended just as cautiously. I kept looking up at the dark hull as I grew closer, expecting some alarm to sound and to have the raiders start firing their water cannons down at us. As long as we stayed directly under, we stood a good chance of pulling this off.

It only took a few seconds for us to reach the ship. A steady hum came from its engines. I glanced to Spader. He pointed up at the hull. I looked, and sure enough, there it was. There was a round opening about six feet in diameter with a metal cover hanging below it. The intake port wasn't flush with the hull, it was perpendicular to it. The metal cover that hung from the opening had narrow slits to let water in and debris out. Now that the cover was off, anything could get stuck inside and we were riding two very big pieces of debris. I was beginning to think this would work.

Spader and I now had to separate. He gave me a thumbs up sign—a Second Earth gesture he picked up from me—and glided his skimmer across the keel to the far side of the ship and the other intake port.

Now came the most critical part of the operation. I carefully guided my skimmer up toward the open port. The opening wasn't much bigger than the width of the skimmer, pontoon to pontoon, so I had to make sure the whole vehicle got inside. I also didn't want to bang the skimmer against the hull because that might alert someone that predators were lurking below. I carefully used the throttle to maneuver the craft into position. I had to bring it right up under the hull, then move parallel with the hull into the intake port. It was tricky, but I soon had the entire skimmer resting inside the port. The hard part was over. I was almost there. All I had to do was hit the throttle.

But I never got the chance.

That's because the ship came to life. The engines that had been idling quietly suddenly roared. I guessed the twenty minutes were over. The raiders were getting ready to fire on Grallion. The noise grew deafening, but worse than that, I felt a rush of water and realized with horror that I was being sucked into the intake port! The *Pursuit* was drawing in water for power and ammunition—and I was well within sucking range! The force of the intake pulled me into the opening. In seconds I would be splatter. There was nothing to grab on to. I was going in.

That's when a strange thing happened that I still can't explain. Even as I think back to what happened, it doesn't make sense. It felt like someone seized me by the hand and pulled me out far enough to grab on to the edge of the intake port. I wrapped my fingers around the lip then struggled to bring my other hand forward and grab on as well. I looked up, expecting to see Spader there, but he wasn't there. Whoever had saved me was gone.

Did I say saved? I wasn't saved yet. I held on to the lip of the intake port with the tips of my fingers. My entire body was still inside the tube leading into the ship. The force of the water grew stronger. I didn't have the strength to pull myself forward. I tried to find something with my feet to push off of, but the inside of the tube was smooth. I wasn't going to last much longer.

That's when I realized that the force of the intake pump wasn't just pulling on me, it was pulling at my skimmer, too. There was still hope! If I could hold on long enough, the skimmer would be sucked into the engine and jam it up just as if I had sent it in myself. All I had to do was hang on. But I didn't know how long I would last. It was torture. The only thing keeping me from being hamburger were the tips of my fingers. I watched as the skimmer slowly moved past me, headed deeper into the ship. It was taking too long. I wasn't going to be able to hang on much longer. The force of the water grew stronger, and the skimmer moved faster. But that meant it was even tougher to hold on. I screamed. Why not? Nobody could hear me over the roar of the engines.

My fingers had gone numb. I was done. Like a fiendish hungry beast, the intake pump finally won the battle. I lost my grip. I flew in toward the engine, knowing I was seconds away from death. I could only hope that it wouldn't hurt too much.

But an instant later I heard a horrifying grinding sound, and the pull of water stopped. The skimmer had been sucked into the engine! Spader's plan worked. Yes! I instantly kicked my fins and swam out of that hole as fast as I possibly could. I blasted out into open water and shot down toward the bottom, kicking for all I was worth.

Spader was already there, waiting for me. I was totally out of breath and probably looked as terrified as I felt.

"What kept you?" asked Spader calmly.

I wanted to scream that I was nearly sucked into the engine, but figured it could wait until later.

"Did you do it?" I yelled.

"Of course," was Spader's confident answer.

"Then shoot the flare!" I ordered.

He pointed the gun topside and fired. A screaming bright arc of light blasted from the pistol and shot toward the surface leaving a bright trail of light behind it. I looked up to see that the missile broke the surface and continued on into the sky. We had done it. We had crippled Saint Dane and the *Pursuit* and opened the door for Yenza and the aquaneers to defend Grallion.

But we had done something else, too.

A few seconds later I saw four splashes next to the ship. Four divers had just hit the water, and they were coming after us. Yeah, you guessed it. The raiders saw our flare.

"Uh-oh," said Spader. "Hadn't thought of that."

"We can't get back to Grallion," I said. "They'll get us for sure."

"Then let's give 'em a chase," said Spader as he grabbed his water sled.

We both powered up and sped off along the ocean floor headed for . . . I didn't know where. We flew over the bottom, inches from the coral, looking for a place to hide. It was a good thing that Spader and I had played all those games underwater, because my skills at handling the water sled were pretty good. Without slowing down, I looked back and saw the four raiders were right after us. They had water sleds too. I wondered if one of them was Saint Dane.

As we flew along the ocean bottom something caught my eye off to our right. Something was swimming alongside us, shadowing us. I only caught a quick glimpse because whatever it was, it darted below the coral. But what I saw didn't make sense. It couldn't have been a person because it was moving too fast. It might have been a big fish, maybe even a quig, but quigs were gray and black. This thing was green, like the water. Weird.

"The kelp!" shouted Spader.

I forgot about my strange vision and looked ahead to see the beginnings of the tangle of red sea kelp that grew from the coral reef and stretched up to the surface. If we could get into that dense jungle, we might have a chance of losing the raiders.

"Stay close," commanded Spader. "Don't want to get separated in there."

We hit the dense kelp but didn't slow down. The slimy leaves whipped at us as we sped by. Imagine running full tilt through a wet field of corn. That's what it was like. For a moment I thought we were home free, but it didn't last long because a second later, we popped out of the far side. Bad news. The kelp forest wasn't anywhere big enough to hide us. We had to keep going.

And that's when it happened. It was just a slight movement. I wasn't even sure what it was at first, but a moment later it hit me. It was my ring. It was getting warm and the gray stone was starting to glow. That meant that we were getting near the gate. I looked up ahead and saw the shelf of rock where the quig had nearly gotten us. It was the rock formation that held the gate to the flume. I knew instantly that it was our best and only hope. Spader was going to have to learn about being a Traveler sometime. I couldn't think of a better way to do it and save our butts at the same time.

"Follow me!" I shouted to Spader and changed my direction toward the rock overhang. Spader didn't question. He followed. The thought of running into a quig flashed through my head, but right now it was the least of our worries. When we were just about to shoot under the rock ledge, Spader yelled, "Stop!"

I did. He glided up to me and said, "Don't want to get trapped under there, mate. They'll have us for sure."

I looked back toward the kelp forest in time to see the four raiders break out of the vegetation and spot us.

"Do you trust me?" I asked.

"Well sure, mate, but—"

"Then c'mon!"

I hit the throttle and shot under the rock ledge. I did a quick look back to see if Spader was following. He was. For a change I could take the lead and he believed in me enough to follow. Now all I had to do was deliver.

The rock ceiling looked different, but only because the last time I was here I was going the other way. But that wasn't a good excuse for being lost. I had to find the gate. The raiders had already gotten to the rock ledge and were still coming fast. All they had to do was follow our bubbles and they'd have us. I could only hope that I'd find the gate before I hit the dead end of rock.

I started to panic. I was lost. I didn't know where the gate was. This rock ledge was huge. We could swim around here for hours without finding it. What was I thinking? I had led us into a trap. I had to calm down and think. Where was it?

The answer hit me instantly. I had been in such a rush to get in here that I wasn't thinking straight. There was an easy way to find the gate. It was my ring. I swept my hand out in front of me and saw that the stone would dim or grow brighter, depending on the direction I pointed. I carefully judged when the ring was shining brightest and that told me our course. It was like following a compass. I took off in that direction and seconds later, I saw it. The round hole in the ceiling was only yards ahead. I aimed my water sled toward it and gunned the engine.

A quick thought went through my mind. Maybe I shouldn't be leading the raiders to the gate and the flume. But I reasoned that it didn't make a difference. If it was Saint Dane behind us, he already knew about the gate. If it wasn't Saint Dane, then it wouldn't matter if the raiders found it. The flume didn't work for non-Travelers. No, this was the right move for all sorts of reasons.

I broke the surface inside the cavern and looked around quickly. It was exactly the same as we had left it. A moment later, Spader broke the surface next to me and looked around in wonder.

"Hobey, mate! How did you know about this?"

I pulled off my air globe and tossed it onto the ledge. I threw my water sled there too. There was no time to explain things to Spader. The raiders would be here in a second. So I yanked off his air globe and threw it and his water sled to the side. The two of us floated in the middle of the pool, treading water.

"I hope there's another way out of here," he said.

I laughed at that. I actually laughed.

"Spader," I said. "You have no idea . . . but you soon will."

I glanced up at the opening to the flume. I counted on the fact that we didn't have to climb up the sheer rock face to get there. We didn't have time.

"I'll ask you again," I said. "Do you trust me?"

"Of course, mate, but you better come up with something quick or we're going to have our own natty-do right here and—"

"*Zadaa!*" I shouted.

The flume came to life. The familiar bright light shot from the opening. The jumble of musical notes grew closer. Spader looked up in awe.

"Hobey, Pendragon," he said softly. "Where did you say you were from again?"

The water around us started to swirl. The light from the flume grew bright and the two of us were pulled up, together, out of the waters of Cloral.

A second later, we were on our way to see Loor.

END OF JOURNAL #6

☻ SECOND EARTH ☻

"Why did he go to Zadaa?" huffed Courtney. "Why didn't he bring Spader here to Second Earth? This is his home!"

Mark knew the answer. Loor was a Traveler. She would be able to help Bobby explain things to Spader. Things were getting hairy on Cloral and Loor was the kind of person you went to when things got hairy. Mark felt that Courtney should have realized this, but her jealousy toward Loor was clouding her thinking. Not that he'd point that out to her. No way.

Courtney stood up angrily and shoved the pages back at Mark.

"Well, if Bobby Pendragon thinks his new friend can help him better than we can, then *good luck* is all I have to say!"

"C'mon, Courtney," said Mark softly. "You know he did the right thing."

Courtney looked as if she wanted to argue, but backed off. She knew.

"Yeah, well, whatever," she said with a pout.

Mark now faced a dilemma. He had to tell Courtney about Andy Mitchell. He made a dumb mistake by leaving the page in the boys' bathroom and because of it, Mitchell knew about the journals.

"I'm sorry, Mark," added Courtney. She had calmed down. "You're right. You've been right about everything from the beginning. It's good that one of us thinks straight. At least now we know why these pages are different than the last ones. He wrote this journal on Zadaa, not Cloral, right?"

Mark wanted to scream. Courtney Chetwynde relied on him to be the brains of this duo and right now he was feeling like anything but. She trusted him and listened to his advice, which is more than anybody else ever did, except for Bobby sometimes. It killed him to have to admit he had screwed up royally.

"You okay?" asked Courtney, sensing that something was wrong.

"Yeah, sure, I'm f-fine," answered Mark quickly. "Just worried about Bobby is all."

"You'd better get those pages back to your house before anything else happens."

Mark looked at Courtney, saw the trust in her amazing gray eyes and made a decision. He couldn't tell her about Andy Mitchell. At least not yet. He wanted to work this out on his own rather than risk losing Courtney's faith. This was his problem and he was going to have to deal with it.

So he gathered the pages of Journal #6 together, put them in his pack, and left for home. Normally, once they finished reading a journal, Mark would stash it in the safest place he knew—an ancient rolltop desk in his attic. His parents hadn't gone up there in years and Mark had the only key. He wore it on a chain around his neck just to be safe. Every precaution had been taken. As soon as a journal was finished, it went into the desk.

Tonight was a little different though. Mark crept up to the attic and unlocked the desk drawer. He placed Journal #6 inside next to the brown rolls of parchment that were Bobby's journals from Denduron. But rather than lock them up, he took out Journal #5—the journal Andy Mitchell had seen the first page of. This was the journal he would show Mitchell. He hoped that maybe this would be enough. Maybe Mitchell would think it was all a crazy joke and get bored after reading these pages. It was the best Mark could hope for.

He spent a sleepless night, wondering how he was going to get out of this predicament. Sharing the journals with Courtney made sense. Courtney was Bobby's friend. Courtney could be trusted. But Andy Mitchell was different. He was an idiot. Worse, he was a bully-idiot. There was no telling what Mitchell would do with the information about Bobby once he got it. But as hard as he tried to figure a way out, he just couldn't find it. He had no choice but to show Mitchell the pages tomorrow.

At school the next day Mark did his best to avoid Mitchell. He held out the desperate hope that Mitchell had forgotten all about the journal page he'd found in the boys' bathroom. Mark got through the entire day without even seeing his nemesis. His hopes started to rise. He told himself that Mitchell didn't care enough to even show up for school! Maybe this would all blow over.

Wrong. No sooner had Mark stepped out of his last class than he felt a hand clamp down on his shoulder.

"Time for a little homework, aye, Dimond?" chuckled Andy Mitchell.

Mark's heart sank. The guy hadn't forgotten at all. It was time to deal with the devil. Mark shrugged Mitchell's hand off his shoulder and said, "Let's go."

Mitchell snorted and chuckled. He made Mark's skin crawl, but there was no way out of this. So Mark led him up to the boys' bathroom on the third floor. No one would bother them there, especially not Courtney. After her run-in with Mr. Dorrico, they decided not to read the journals there anymore. This was the best place Mark could think of to get some privacy, and to avoid Courtney. He felt guilty as hell about it, but there was no other way.

When they got inside Mitchell stood with his hand out. Mark stared at him. Mitchell snorted back a good one and hawked a lougie into a urinal. Mark nearly retched. He had a fleeting thought of barging past Mitchell and running away, but that would have been useless. No, this was the only way. So reluctantly he reached into his pack and pulled out the roll of green, slick paper that was Journal #5.

Mitchell reached out to grab it, but Mark pulled it away.

"You gotta read it here and you gotta give it right back when you're done," Mark said. Mitchell wasn't used to being ordered around like this, especially not from a geek like Mark Dimond. But Mark was intense. He was not fooling around. Mitchell snorted and chuckled, again.

"Whatever," he said, and swiped the pages away from Mark. He walked over to one of the stalls saying, "I'll read it in here."

"You will read it right here, where I can see you!" commanded Mark.

Whoa. If Mitchell wasn't sure about how important those pages were to Mark, he sure was now. Mark was not going to allow Andy Mitchell to control this situation any more than he had to. He already had too much control as it was. If Mitchell didn't do exactly as he said, Mark was ready to grab the pages away and take his chances with the police.

Mitchell chose to back off and gave another signature snort.

"All right, be cool," he said with a shrug. "I'll read 'em wherever you want."

Mitchell then walked to the far wall, turned his back to it, and slid down to the floor. With one last snort, he began to read the journal.

Mark didn't move. He stood by the sinks, staring at Mitchell. This was killing him. With each passing second he felt as if he were betraying Bobby a little bit more.

Mitchell took forever to read the journal. He wasn't exactly a rocket scientist and he constantly had to ask Mark the meanings of words. Mark would roll his eyes and explain to him what words like "submerge" and "erosion" meant. Worse, when Mitchell got to words that were specific to Cloral like vators or pecks, his total cluelessness made Mark want to scream. Mark felt bad for any teacher who was saddled with the likes of Andy Mitchell. He wondered who had the patience to teach him how to tie his shoelaces.

Finally, mercifully, Mitchell finished the journal and looked up to Mark. This was the critical moment. Mitchell's first reaction was going to tell Mark how much trouble he was going to cause from here on in. Mitchell stared at Mark for a moment, as if trying to pull his thoughts together. Mark figured that pulling those slim thoughts together couldn't take more than a nanosecond. It didn't. Mitchell snorted and laughed again.

"Who are you kidding?" he said with a sneer. "You made this up!"

Mark didn't react. He just stared at Mitchell. The truth was, he didn't care if Mitchell believed the journals were real or not. But Mark realized instantly that not reacting was the exact wrong move. He saw it in Mitchell's eyes. Mark realized that if he had argued with Mitchell and said something like "I didn't make it up! It's all true! I swear!" then Mitchell would have figured he was just some loser geek with a wild imagination and that would have been the end of it. But he didn't. By not arguing, he had done the exact opposite. His silence convinced Mitchell that everything in the journal *was* true. Mark wished he had a second chance to react, but it was too late.

Mitchell began to stand up. Before he got his balance, Mark swiped the journal pages out of his hand.

"Easy!" complained Mitchell.

"Are we done now?" asked Mark as he rolled up the journal.

"Done?" laughed Mitchell. "We're just starting! I want to read the other journals. The ones from that Denduroni place."

"Denduron. I can't let you—"

"And I want to read the journal that showed up here yesterday. I'm not stupid, Dimond. I saw it. It was brown, not green like this one. You already got another delivery from Pendragon and I want to see it."

"N-No way! I agreed to let you read the rest of—"

Mitchell lunged at Mark, grabbed him by the shirt, spun him around, and slammed him against the hard tile wall of the bathroom. He knocked the air out of his lungs and Mark nearly passed out. Mitchell wouldn't let him go though. He stuck his nose right in Mark's face and hissed, "Stop tellin' me what to do, you little freak. You wanna mess with me? I'll hit you so hard you'll be eatin' and fartin' out of the same hole."

Mark didn't believe that was possible, but he didn't want to risk it.

"Now listen to me. Do not tell Courtney Chetwynde I know about this. If you do, I'll go right to the police and fry both of your butts. Understand?"

"But—"

Mitchell slammed Mark against the wall again. This time Mark hit his head on the tiles.

"*Understand?*"

"Yeah, I understand."

"And I want to see the rest of them journals. We are sitting on a very big thing here. Someday we are gonna be famous, thanks to that weez Pendragon."

Mark was horrified. Mitchell, the village idiot, was already planning on how to release the journals to the world. This could not get worse.

"I want to see another one of them journals," he commanded, then threw Mark out of the way, and strode toward the bathroom door.

With one final snort, he then kicked the door open and left.

Mark sunk down to the floor, hurting in more ways than one. He had messed up worse than he could imagine. Mitchell now had complete control over him. Worse, if he told Courtney about it then Mitchell would make sure that the police knew everything. There was no one he could go to for help. He wanted to handle this on his own, but he was doing a truly bad job. He had let Bobby down, he had let Courtney down, and he had let himself down.

And then, just to add to his confusion, the ring on his finger started to twitch. In the past this had always been a moment of excitement because it meant he was going to hear from his best friend again. But now the idea of another journal arriving meant that it was going to be one more journal he would have to share with Andy Mitchell. One more journal that he would have to explain to the dimwit. One more journal that marked his total failure as a friend.

Mark took off the ring and put it on the floor. He then rolled over and turned his back to it. He knew what was going to happen. He didn't have to see. He closed his eyes and softly whispered, "I'm sorry, Bobby. I'm going to fix everything, I swear."

When he turned back around, the ring was lying right here he had left it. Next to it was another journal.

ZADAA

I have seen things that I never thought possible and most of it isn't good.

Since I wrote you last, things here have been pushed to the hairy edge of catastrophe and I feel as if it's up to me to bring it back. The worst part is I don't know how. Not a clue. I'm frustrated, freaked out, and most of all . . . scared. Definitely scared. Not only for me, but for the whole territory of Cloral. Whoever had the bright idea of making me a Traveler should be re-thinking that decision right about now. Did I mention how scared I was?

I'm writing this journal from a place that is both wondrous and frightening. As I think back on the events that led me here, I can't help but wonder where it's going to end. Every time I think I've got a handle on things, something new happens that turns me upside down. I thought I couldn't be surprised anymore, but I am. I guess that's why they call it surprise.

Once again we are on the verge of a battle. I don't want to sound overly dramatic or anything, but if things go south, this may be the last journal I write. I'm not trying to freak you out but, well, okay maybe I'm trying to freak you out a little. Why not? The whole point of writing this is for you to know what I'm going through, right?

I'm getting way ahead of myself. There's a lot to write about and I don't have a ton of time. I finished the last journal where Spader and I had hit the flume for Zadaa. There wasn't anything unusual about the trip, except for the fact I wasn't alone this time. Spader and I flew side by side. This was Spader's first flume ride and I wasn't sure how he would react. He was pretty tense at first, as you can imagine, but once I assured him everything was fine and that he could enjoy the ride, he simply looked forward and folded his arms. We flew along like that for a few minutes and I could tell he was starting to relax. He had been through a lot hairier situations than this under the sea. Maybe not as bizarre as this, but definitely not as hairy.

"What is this, Pendragon?" he finally asked. I could tell he was working really hard to stay calm.

"It's called a flume," I answered. "It's taking us to meet a friend of mine."

"And where is that?" he asked. "Your home habitat?"

"No, it's a place called Zadaa. She'll help me explain to you what's going on."

He nodded as if to say, "Okay. I'll wait until we get there to ask the eight hundred million other questions I have." He did ask one more question though.

"Pendragon, are we safe?"

Wow. How could I answer that one? I felt totally unsafe every second of every day. But I couldn't tell him that. I decided to play dumb to the more cosmic issue and only deal with the here and now.

"Yeah," I answered. "The flume is safe. I promise."

Moments later we arrived. The flume deposited us into an

underground cavern. Big surprise, right? Spader looked back into the flume that had now gone dark, his eyes wide with wonder.

"Don't worry," I said. "It works both ways. We can take it right back to Cloral."

"You mean we're not on Cloral anymore?" he asked in shock.

Oh man, this guy had a lot to learn and I didn't know where to start explaining.

"Let's find my friend," I said. "Then we'll try to answer your questions."

Try was the right word. There was only so much I was going to be able to explain to Spader. Once he started asking the big questions as to what all of this meant, I'd be just as lost as he was. I needed to find Loor as soon as possible.

I looked around the cavern and saw a pile of clothes. A quick exam showed me they were lightweight white robes, like those long togas they wore in movies about ancient Rome.

"We gotta wear these," I said. "It's what people wear around here."

Spader didn't question. We took off most of our Cloral clothes, but left on our shorts. Technically that was against the rules, but I wasn't going commando here. No way. There were also leather sandals and we each put on a pair. As we dressed, I hoped that Spader wouldn't ask me how these clothes got here because I wouldn't have a good answer. I supposed they came from the mysterious acolytes that Uncle Press had told me about, but that's all I could say. Luckily Spader didn't ask.

As I placed our Cloral clothes on the ground, I saw something that made me smile. There was another pile of clothing there. It was a pair of denim overalls and a pink shirt and a pair of Dr. Marten's boots—the clothes Loor wore when she came to Second Earth. Seeing these gave me confidence. Loor was definitely here. Of course the trick now was to find her. Up until now Uncle Press had been my tour guide. Now I was on my own. Gulp. I glanced around the cavern but saw no way out. We were surrounded by walls made of brown, sandy stone. A complete 360 showed no entrance, no door, no passageway, no nothing. But that was impossible. There had to be a way out. Then, just before I began to hyperventilate in panic, I saw it. There were footholds and handholds chiseled into the rock that led up toward the ceiling. I walked to the wall and looked up to see. Sure enough, the cutouts led up into a dark crevice. This was the way out.

I wanted to shout "Woo hoo!" but decided I should be cool. Like it or not, I was in charge and I wanted to show Spader I had total confidence, even though I didn't. So without a word, I began to climb. The cutouts led up into the dark crevice. In seconds, I was totally surrounded by rock. I knew this had to be the way out, so I didn't panic. After climbing for another few seconds, I hit a dead end—with my head. Ouch. That hurt. My first thought was that we were trapped, but then I realized my head didn't hurt as much as it should if I had just bashed it into hard rock. I carefully reached up and found that I was right. The ceiling wasn't rock, it was wood. A quick push up revealed that it was a trapdoor. We were out!

I scrambled up and out, followed right behind by Spader. Once he was out, I threw the trapdoor shut and saw that carved on the top of it was the star that showed this was a gate.

So far, so familiar.

We found ourselves in what looked to be a storage room. The walls were made of the same sandy stone as below, but there were large wooden storage bins that were filled with what looked like metal machine parts. The floor was covered with sand, which made me realize the trapdoor was normally buried. So I quickly covered it over with a few inches of sand.

Spader watched me but didn't say anything. I'm sure he was trying to process all this new information. His questions would come later.

"Okay," I said. "Let's find Loor."

A wooden door led out of this storage room and as soon as I reached to open it, it hit me that I had no clue what to expect on Zadaa. All I knew was that Loor was a warrior. Obviously that meant that Zadaa wasn't exactly a futuristic society. I could only hope that it wasn't like the Wild West and that we wouldn't have to fight for our lives every step of the way. That would suck.

As soon as we opened the door we heard a loud, steady sound. It was a constant, unwavering roar.

"It's water," Spader said.

That's exactly what it sounded like. Rushing water. But the sound was huge, so if it were rushing water, then there was a lot of it. We left the storage room and made our way through a labyrinth of tunnels cut into the rock. It reminded me of the mines of Denduron, but these passageways were more like corridors than wide mine shafts. Every few feet was another wooden door. We didn't bother to look inside any of them. This wasn't about exploration, this was about getting out and finding Loor.

The farther along the rocky corridor we walked, the louder the roaring water became. Finally we reached the mouth of the tunnel and stepped out into an awesome scene. We found ourselves on the bank of an underground river. It was about twenty yards across and moving fast. The cavern we were in was huge, with a high ceiling. To our left, about fifty yards downstream, the river split into three smaller rivers. Each new river disappeared into its own separate tunnel.

Upriver to our right was a waterfall. The water shot into the fast-moving river from a tunnel in the rock face about four stories above us. Mental note to self: Do *not* fall into this river. Swimming would be impossible because the water was moving so fast. There was no telling where the split rivers led.

"What are you doing here?" came a stern voice.

We both spun around to see a man wearing a similar white robe to the ones we wore. He was a small guy who wore a round gray hat that looked like a baseball cap without the brim. It looked hard, like it was for protection. In his arms were a bunch of rolled-up papers that could have been plans. He had come from the same tunnel we had, which meant he must have been behind one of the doors we passed. He was light skinned, which surprised me because both Loor and her mother, Osa, were very dark.

"I've never seen you two here," he said suspiciously. "What do you want?"

He seemed to be in a hurry and was all sorts of agitated as if our surprise appearance had thrown off his schedule. This was going to be tricky. I had no idea what kind of explanation to give the guy except to tell him the truth—sort of.

"We, uh, we're looking for a friend," I said. "Her name is Loor."

The guy's eyes widened further. Uh-oh. I must have said the wrong thing.

"Loor?" he said in surprise. "That is a Batu name. Why would you be looking for a Batu down here?"

Good question. Too bad I didn't have a good answer. Forget the truth. It was time to start lying.

"She, uh, she told me she might be coming down here," I said.

"Ridiculous!" the guy snapped. "No Batu would miss that barbaric tournament of theirs. If she told you she was coming here, she was lying. But they are all liars, no?"

With that the man hurried off, clutching his rolls of paper. Spader touched me on the shoulder and I saw that he had a look of total confusion on his face. Welcome to the club.

"What did he say?" he asked.

"You heard him," I answered. "Loor isn't down here."

"But how did you understand him? He was talking all gibberish."

At first I didn't know what Spader meant, but then it hit me: He was new to the Traveler game. He hadn't gotten to the point where he could understand all languages, yet.

"Long story," I said, and ran after the man with the scrolls. Spader followed dutifully. I caught up to the guy and walked alongside him.

"I'm embarrassed to say this, but my friend and I are lost. You know, all these tunnels and whatnot. Could you show us the way to the surface?"

The man stared at me suspiciously. This was a critical moment. If he started questioning me on who we were, we'd be sunk.

"You work in the manufacturing sector, don't you?" he asked.

"Uhhh, yes! Manufacturing. That's where we work."

"Let me give you a piece of advice," he said. "Do not make friends with a Batu. They cannot be trusted."

"Yes, good advice," I shot back. I figured I'd better agree with whatever this guy said if we wanted to get his help. "When I see Loor I'm going to just . . . call off our friendship.

No more lies! But I have to find her first, so how do we get out of here?"

"Follow me," he said, and walked off quickly.

Yes! We were on our way out. He led us along the riverbank and right up to the waterfall. As we got closer I saw that it was possible to walk behind the falling water. We climbed a few stone steps and passed right behind the wall of water. Very cool. We then saw that cut into the stone wall behind the falling water, was a tunnel. The man led us inside and after a few steps we came upon a room that had the coolest, strangest gizmo I think I had ever seen.

The best thing I can liken it to is one of those big pipe organs you see in church, but it was ten times the size. One whole wall was covered with pipes of every different size, ranging from about an inch in diameter to as wide as about ten inches. They ran from the ground, all the way up to the stone ceiling.

The guy put his rolls of paper down and stepped up onto a stone platform that faced a vast array of levers, switches, valves, and knobs. There must have been a couple hundred of these controls. I had no clue how he could tell one from another because none seemed to be marked. He walked back and forth on the platform, expertly flipping switches, tightening valves and loosening others. At one point he picked up one of the scrolls, unrolled it to check something, then tossed it down again and went right for a few more valves and opened them up. Whatever he was doing, it seemed very important. At least to him anyway.

Spader gave me a questioning look. I could only shrug. I had no idea what the guy was doing. I didn't want to ask him either or it would give away the fact that we didn't belong here.

"Uhhh," I interrupted. "Excuse me but, you were going to show us the way out?"

The guy kept working on his levers, but looked back over his shoulder at us. I could tell we were bothering him, but too bad.

"That way," he said, nodding toward an opening cut into the rock on the far side of the room. "Keep making rights, and remember what I said. Do not trust the Batu. Stay with the Rokador."

Ohhh-kay, whatever *that* meant. I didn't ask. "Thank you!" I said, and motioned for Spader to follow me. The man went right back to his work and we got the heck out of there.

We walked quickly through the doorway and, as instructed, kept making rights until we found a spiraling ramp that led up. We climbed and every so often we'd reach a new level and saw corridors that led off to places unknown. But, we didn't need to explore any more of this underground world. We needed to climb out.

After climbing for several minutes we finally leveled off and found ourselves in a room that was full of light. The walls were made of brown stone, but they were smooth, not like the rock below. It was clear that we were on the surface and the room we were in was man-made, not man-dug. A quick look around showed a doorway that led to the light. It was time to take our first look at Zadaa. I had no idea what to expect, but I was getting anxious to see the territory where Loor came from. I led Spader across the room, stepped out into the warm sun, and stopped short because the sight in front of us was absolutely breathtaking.

It was a sprawling city made entirely out of sand-colored stone. Imagine ancient Egypt before wind and time destroyed it and you'd have Zadaa. We stood on a rise that gave us a pretty great overview. There were soaring temples with sculpted figures that towered over the streets below. There were pyramids and tiered buildings with lush hanging plants draped over balconies. In the distance, beyond the boundaries of the city, there was nothing but desert. But the city within was alive with vegetation. It was like a vast oasis in a sea of sand. Running parallel to many of the streets were stone troughs that carried fresh water throughout the city. There were also ornate fountains everywhere. After having seen the river below, I knew what the source was. I wondered if the system of valves and switches that the guy down below was so busily working on had something to do with controlling the water flow.

This was a beautiful city, and I could easily imagine Loor walking the streets. Yes, this was Loor's home. It made absolute sense to me.

"Where is the ocean?" asked Spader.

His voice was shaky. After all of the bizarro experiences I had put him through, the sight of this city was the first thing that really rattled him.

"Where is the ocean?" he asked again, more nervously.

It suddenly made sense to me. Cloral was a hundred percent water. There was no dry land. Seeing a place that was just the opposite must have been pretty freaky.

"It's okay," I said, trying to calm him. "There is no ocean here. At least not one that I can see. These people live on dry land."

"That's impossible! How can you live on dry land? There isn't enough water for power or food!"

Okay, how weird was that? But I guess if you live in a place where everything comes from the ocean, having no ocean would be pretty scary.

"It's cool, I swear," I said. "It's just a different way of living. You'll see."

Spader didn't look so sure, but I wasn't worried about him. He'd get it soon enough. It was then that I realized something strange. I glanced back out on the city and realized that there was something very important missing. There were no people! This was a huge city, yet the streets were empty.

"Let's take a look around," I said, and started to walk. Spader didn't follow me this time. He was rooted to his spot. I had to go back to him and say, "C'mon! We have to find Loor."

Reluctantly he followed. We walked along one of the streets that was paved with stone. Towering statues loomed over us as we made our way through this strange and wonderful place.

"I'm having trouble walking," Spader said.

I didn't get what he meant until I saw that he looked kind of unsteady. He seemed almost dizzy and had trouble keeping his balance. I realized that he was going through the reverse process of getting used to being on a boat. My father called it "getting your sea legs." Spader had lived his entire life floating. This was the first time he was walking on solid ground and it was a strange sensation. Spader was trying to get his "land legs."

I tried not to laugh and said, "You'll get used to it pretty quick. But if you're going to barf, let me know." I didn't know how far this landsickness might go.

We continued on a little more slowly and started to see some people, but not as many as you'd think. The people up here on the surface had much darker skin than the guy we saw below. These people looked more like Loor and Osa. Their skin was dark, and they wore multicolored robes that were pretty spectacular.

"I wonder where everybody is?" I said. "Maybe it's some kind of holiday and——" That's when it hit me. The guy in the cavern below had said that the Batu would all be at the tournament! Maybe that was why the streets were deserted. Maybe everybody was at this tournament.

The very next person we saw, I stopped and asked, "Excuse me, which way to the tournament?"

It was a woman. She was tall and stern looking. She stared at me as if not sure why I would be asking such a simple question.

"Not many Rokador are interested in the tournament," she said coldly. "They do not have the stomach."

Rokador. That's what the guy down below had said. Maybe the guys who lived below were called Rokador and the people on the surface were Batu. We must look like Rokador. I wasn't sure if it was because of our white gowns, or the fact that we were pretty pale compared to the people on the surface.

"I think we can handle it," I said.

The woman chuckled, but I'm not sure if she was laughing with us or at us. She directed us to stay on this street and it would take us right to the tournament. Excellent. We were happening. Spader and I picked up the pace. I felt certain this would bring us to Loor.

As we continued walking Spader got stronger. He was adapting pretty quickly, so I figured it was a good time to start getting him up to speed on things. I began by telling him about the territories and about how they were all connected by flumes. I explained how Uncle Press and I came from a territory called Second Earth and that we were both Travelers who journeyed to the territories to help out in times of trouble. I explained how Loor was a Traveler as well, which is why I wanted her help. I didn't go into much more detail. It was better for him to get his mind around things a little at a time. For the first time I understood how Uncle Press felt when he explained things to me and I had so many questions. It really was easier to learn things as you went along.

Besides, the cheering up ahead told me that we had arrived at the tournament. Spader and I came to a building that looked like a coliseum. It wasn't as big though. I guess it was closer to a high school stadium than a pro ballpark. It didn't look as if we needed tickets either, because we walked right in.

The place was indeed a small stadium. As it turned out, my theory about why the streets were empty was correct. There were a couple of thousand people filling the stands. A quick look around told me that most of the spectators were Batu. They were dark skinned and wearing those colorful robes. But there were also a number of Rokador scattered throughout the crowd. They really stood out with their white robes and lighter skin.

There was a dirt playing field, and for an instant my thoughts went back to the Bedoowan stadium on Denduron and the gruesome quig battles where innocent miners were fed to beasts. I really hoped that they weren't doing anything nasty like that here.

Spader and I walked up to the railing and looked onto the field in time to see two teams marching in from opposite sides of the arena. They were all Batu—not a Rokador among them. They looked like warriors. Each and every one of these players was lean and buff. They weren't just men, either. It was half and half, men and women. They all wore these short leather tunics that showed a lot of skin, which is how I could tell they were all cut like athletes. They also wore lightweight protection on sensitive areas like elbows, knees, and the ever important groin. There were ten warriors to a side, and they marched in single file, carrying leather helmets under one arm while holding thin wooden clubs in the other.

"What's the do here?" asked Spader.

"I'm guessing there's going to be some kind of contest," I answered. "My friend Loor is—" That's when I saw her. The last warrior to march in was Loor. Though she was younger than the rest, she looked every bit as formidable.

"That's her," I said to Spader while pointing to Loor.

"That's your friend?" Spader asked with a mixture of surprise and awe. "She's . . . she's . . . amazing."

Spader stood staring at Loor, unable to take his eyes off her. I finally had to give him a shove to bring him back to reality.

"Don't even think about it," I said. "She's not your type."

"What type is she?" Spader asked.

"The type who has no interest in anything but kicking ass. If you think I'm kidding, watch."

The warrior teams stood on opposite sides of the arena and began the final act of suiting up. Here was the odd part. Each of them had these things that looked like wooden stakes that stuck out to the sides from their elbows and their knees. The stakes were about six inches long. One team had red stakes, the other had green. When they put their helmets on I saw that they also had a wooden stake that stuck straight up like those World War I German helmets. In all, each warrior had five wooden stakes sticking out of them. I had no clue what those things were for but I have to tell you, they looked pretty goofy.

Each team stood in a line, shoulder to shoulder, facing their opponents across the arena. A Batu guy wearing a bright yellow robe walked to the center, where he planted a stick in the ground. On the end of the stick he hung what looked like a necklace made of large, golden teeth. He then silently walked back and entered the grandstand. From the safety of the stands, he turned back to the playing field, raised a golden horn to his lips, and let out one short note.

Instantly everyone in the stands fell silent and focused their attention on the warriors below. I had a moment of fear for Loor. I had no idea how dangerous this was going to be. I knew she could handle herself, but what was the point of this game? I knew nothing of Zadaa and their customs and feared this would be one of those "fight to the death" type spectacles. There was nothing I could do but watch and hope she'd be okay.

The Batu in the yellow robe then gave one long, sustained blast from the horn. All the warriors raised their wooden clubs toward him in salute. Then Yellow Robe stopped blowing his horn, and the battle began. Instantly both teams of warriors let out war whoops and charged toward each other. Loor was right there with them. I wanted to close my eyes, but that would be disrespectful. Whatever was going to happen, I needed to see it.

The opposing teams clashed, swinging their clubs. I quickly saw the purpose of the wooden stakes that protruded from their bodies. They were the targets. This wasn't about knocking each other's heads off, it was about trying to knock their opponents' wooden stakes off. It was all about speed, and balance and blocking shots and returning shots that were well aimed. Of course, as good as they were, many shots missed their mark and there were a lot of painful body shots and whacks to the head. But this was not a blood feud. This was sport. I'm sure the shots stung and there would be dozens of black and blue marks the next day, but nobody was going to die here. Once I realized this I relaxed and tried to enjoy the spectacle.

Loor was on the red team. The green team was bigger and brawnier, but the red team seemed faster and more agile. I wasn't sure which was more important in a battle like this, speed or power.

It looked like it was going to be power. One red-team warrior had all five of his stakes knocked off in about five seconds. He dropped his club and ran off the field. Now I was starting to get the rules. You could keep fighting until all five of your stakes got knocked off. Then you were out.

Loor was brilliant. She kept to the perimeter of the fighting and took on all comers. She was being more defensive than aggressive, which really wasn't her style. But it seemed to be working because most warriors had at least one stake knocked off and she still had all five. She jumped and spun and knocked away attack after attack like some kind of fevered Jackie Chan clone.

"She's the smartest one out there," said Spader. "And quite beautiful, too."

I was beginning to think that Spader was really happy about coming to meet Loor.

Then one of the green warriors dove for the golden necklace and began to run off with it. Instantly three red warriors attacked him. The guy didn't have a chance. His stakes were knocked off immediately and he dropped the necklace. Now I understood the end game. This wasn't just about being the last one standing. My guess was that if someone grabbed the necklace and made it back to his area, then his team would win. It was like capture the flag. A really scary, painful version of capture the flag.

I then began to see that this wasn't just a wild clash. There actually was some strategy going on. Loor's red team took more of the defensive role and assigned a few warriors to guard the necklace. The green team, on the other hand, was all about attacking. It was every man for himself, and so far their strategy was winning. The red team had lost three warriors and several others had only three stakes or fewer. The green team had lost only one warrior and were pressing the attack. It looked as if the way to win this game was to attack with reckless abandon and overpower your adversary.

But that's when things changed. The remaining red team warriors had gradually worked themselves into a ring around the golden necklace. The green team was too busy slashing and hitting to realize they were being outmaneuvered. Also, the green team had been attacking so hard that they were beginning to get tired. Their swings weren't as forceful as they had been moments before. I guessed it took more energy to attack than to defend, and the red team still looked fresh.

The red now had formed a tight circle around the necklace and were able to fend off the attacking green warriors with much less effort. Every red-team member was in the circle except for Loor. She was still on the perimeter, playing it safe. Then one of the red-team warriors let out a loud yelp. It must have been a signal, because that's when Loor made her move.

She dodged around the green warrior she had been battling and sprinted for the circle. At the same time the red team broke open the circle just long enough for her to run inside. Loor scooped up the necklace and then the entire red team formed a wedge to protect her as they dashed toward their side of the arena. It was like a kickoff return right up the middle where the blockers formed the perfect wedge. They bowled over the green team, who were now so exhausted they could barely lift their clubs. In seconds the red juggernaut, with Loor in the center, rolled into their area, the winners.

Loor held up the necklace in victory.

I went nuts. I screamed, I shouted, I jumped up and down and cheered like my team had just won the Super Bowl with a touchdown in OT. It was awesome. Loor was awesome. Agility and skill had triumphed over brawn and might. It was a victory for the little guy and I was loving every minute of it.

Unfortunately nobody else in the stadium was as excited as I was. Here I was jumping up and down like some crazed fan from the Cleveland Browns Dog Pound, and everyone else just sat there, watching me, wondering who this idiot was who had lost control. Every eye in the stadium was on me, including the warriors down on the field. I felt like a total imbecile.

"Is this a custom where you come from?" asked Spader, who was just as surprised at my enthusiasm as everyone else in the stadium.

In fact it was, but that didn't make this nightmare any easier. I stopped yelling, looked down on to the field and made eye contact with Loor. She too was looking up to see where all the screaming was coming from. She saw me, but at first it didn't click for her. She was exhausted and still flush from the battle and the victory. Seeing me didn't compute. It made me feel even worse. She didn't even know who I was. I felt horrible. Then, a moment later, I saw it in her eyes. She finally recognized me; that's when something happened that I never would have expected. It was so shocking that I no longer cared about being embarrassed. It just didn't matter anymore, because as she stood there breathing hard, Loor looked up at me and smiled.

ZADAA

"It was a training exercise," Loor explained. "All warriors must take part. It is good experience to teach fighting as one, and as a team." For all of the mayhem she just went through, Loor came out fairly intact. Nothing broken, only a few bruises.

"Seemed more like football with weapons to me," I countered.

Both Loor and Spader gave me blank stares. They had no idea what I meant. That was okay. It didn't matter.

The three of us walked along the streets of the desert city, which Loor told us was called Xhaxhu (pronounced Zha-ZHOO). It was the capital city of Zadaa.

Spader walked behind us with his head down, listening to everything we said. Unlike the other people of Zadaa, he was able to understand her because she was a Traveler. Understanding everyone else would come in time, just as it did for me. I wished that Loor could have seen him the way he was when I first got to Cloral. She would have loved that guy. But as I wrote before, Spader had changed. Okay, he was pretty freaked out about our trip to Zadaa; can't blame him for that. The death of his father had turned him inside out. I could only hope that at some point he would deal with his anger and become his old self again.

"Why did you come to Zadaa, Pendragon?" asked Loor.

"Two reasons," I said. "Uncle Press and I think we know what Saint Dane is up to on Cloral and we could use your help, big time. The other reason is . . ."

I looked back at Spader, debating about how much I should blurt out in front of him. I decided it was time to jump in with both feet.

"The other reason is that Spader's father was the Traveler from Cloral. He's dead. Now Spader is the Traveler. The problem is, he has no clue . . . about anything. I've got to get him up to speed and I need your help to do it."

I looked back to Spader. He had stopped walking and was now staring right at me with confusion and what I thought might be a little bit of fear. I had just hit him with a boatload of information that didn't compute. Nothing I had just said made any sense to him. That was pretty obvious. Loor turned to him and said, "Tell me what you will remember most about your father."

Spader shot her a look. The question surprised him, but he wanted to answer. He looked down, remembering. He then looked back to Loor and said, "He was a great man, a great teacher, and I loved him." I think he was holding back a ton of emotion.

Loor touched him on the shoulder and said, "Then you will make a great Traveler. Come with me."

She turned and continued walking. Spader looked to me and I saw that the confusion was still there, but the fear was gone. I knew at that moment that coming to see Loor was the best move I could have made.

Loor took us to her home. The large building was made of

the same brown sandstone that all the structures were made of here on Zadaa. It was all on one level, with wooden floors and a thatched roof. The place was big, too. There were many rooms where others lived, like some big, sandy apartment building. Judging from the other muscle-types who were hanging out, I figured this must have been some kind of warrior dormitory. Loor's space had two rooms—one main room where the cooking was done and another that was a bedroom. The furniture was woven, like wicker. There were a few low chairs and a bed that were plain and simple. A community bathroom outside the apartment had a trough of running water for drinking and washing. Another trough of water that was the sewer ran underground. The place was crude, but efficient.

The three of us sat in the main room and Loor actually cooked for us. She baked three loaves of very tasty bread and we had crunchy fresh vegetables to go with it. She also gave us a sweet drink that was made from the sap of a tree. It reminded me of coconut. Uncle Press would have loved this. I wondered what he was doing just then, and if he was safe from the raiders on Cloral. But there was nothing I could do about that now, so I tried not to worry.

As we ate, Loor told us about her life as a warrior in training. She was part of the military here on Zadaa. The apartment she lived in was given to her by the military and she could live there for as long as she served. Because she was so young, she was pretty much a low-level soldier. But she hoped to someday become a leader. I had no doubt she would.

When we finished eating and cleaning up, we all sat there staring at one another. There was a very big issue hanging in the room and I had no idea how to attack it. Spader did it for me. He had been listening silently to our conversation and finally decided it was time to speak.

"You called me a Traveler," he said, breaking the ice. "What does that mean?"

Loor took the lead. She calmly explained to Spader how every territory had a Traveler who could fly through the flumes. She told him how each territory was about to reach a critical turning point and how it was the job of the Travelers to do all they could to make sure the outcome would keep the territory peaceful. To fail would mean the territory would fall into chaos. She also told him of Saint Dane, the evil Traveler who was working to do the opposite. His goal was to push the territories into bedlam.

This is where I jumped in. I told Spader that Saint Dane could change the way he looked. On Cloral, he was the pirate Zy Roder. Uncle Press and I felt sure that he was responsible for poisoning the crops. I said how a bad food supply on Cloral would cause a civil war when people fought over the food that was still safe—just the kind of thing Saint Dane would love.

Loor finished by saying how she and I still didn't understand why we had been selected to be Travelers, or who it was that chose us. But the job we were given was an important one. She said how the battles with Saint Dane weren't only about each territory, they were about all of Halla. She explained that Halla was everything—all territories, all people, and all time. Saint Dane's ultimate goal was to control Halla. The only thing standing in his way were the Travelers. That would be us.

Spader listened intently. This was some serious stuff we were laying on him. I had no idea how he would react.

"So?" I asked. "What are you thinking?"

I could tell he was trying to put this puzzle together in his head but was having trouble getting all the pieces to fit.

"This is . . . this is a lot," he said.

Yeah, no kidding.

"I'm sorry, mates," he added. "I'm an aquaneer. I know boats, I know water, I know how to fix them and have some fun along the way. That's pretty much what my life's about. But now you're telling me I've got to be responsible for the future of everything? Hobey, I'm not the best choice for that particular job."

"Tell me about it," I threw in. "Neither am I!"

Loor stood up and took something out of a wicker basket near the fireplace.

"Do you think your father was someone worthy of being a Traveler?" she asked Spader.

"Absolutely," Spader shot back without hesitation.

Loor handed Spader the item she pulled from the basket. I saw that it was a piece of green paper that was folded in two. It looked like the same kind of paper I was used to writing my Cloral journals on. Spader opened it up to reveal that it was a drawing. Actually, it was *half* of a drawing. It looked as if it had been ripped in two and this was the left half.

The drawing was in black ink. There was a solid, horizontal line about a third of the way up from the bottom. Below this line there was another line that started at the bottom near the lower left-hand side and curved up until it hit the right edge of the page, making a quarter of a circle. Above the horizontal line were a bunch of dots sprayed around in no particular pattern. In the upper right-hand corner were a series of five symbols. It looked like they continued on to the right half of the page that had been torn away.

I had no idea what this half drawing meant, until I noticed something that rocked me. In the upper left-hand corner of the page was a round symbol. It was the exact same symbol with the interlocking letters that was on the note Spader's father had left for him. I looked to Spader in shock. Spader's eyes were fixed on the paper. Finally, after an eternity, he whispered,

"Faar."

"Far?" I shot back, my pulse rate spiking through the roof. "Far what?" I looked to Loor and demanded, "Where did you get this?"

"My mother was a Traveler," she said calmly. "She knew Spader's father."

Whoa! Major twist.

"Before I knew of my destiny," Loor continued, "she returned from one of her travels with this drawing. She told me of a man whom she admired greatly. She said he knew answers when most did not yet know the questions. He had risked his life many times over to find the information on this page. He said it was important to the future of Cloral. But he feared it might be found by those with evil intent. That is why he tore it in two and gave half to my mother. Your father said that his time was growing short, and that his son would carry on his work. He asked my mother to pass this on to his son when he came looking for it. My mother is now dead, Spader. It is my duty to give this to you."

This was incredible. The web of Travelers was truly interconnected.

"This is the same symbol your father left you," I said to Spader. "If you know what it means, you gotta tell us!"

Spader stood up and paced. Things were happening too fast for him.

"It's a tall tale," he said nervously. "A children's story."

"What is?" I insisted.

"Faar!" he snapped back. "It's a legend. Everybody knows it."

"We don't," I said.

"Then I'll tell you," he continued. "The symbol represents

a mythical city called Faar that was built on the only dry land that existed on Cloral. It was supposed to be this amazing place full of scholars and music and scientists and art, like some kind of perfect place. But there was a tum-tigger of a disaster and this perfect place sank into the sea. The elders of the city saw the disaster coming and prepared for it. Somehow they saved the city, even though it sank into the ocean. The legend says the people of Faar will always live down below the water, secretly protecting all those who live on the habitats above."

"It was destroyed?" asked Loor.

"It sank, I didn't say it was destroyed," Spader said.

"Why didn't you tell us this when you saw the symbol on Magorran?" I asked.

"Because it's a fable. It was a bedtime story my father used to tell me. I thought he was giving me the symbol so I'd remember our time together. I didn't think it meant anything more than that! I still don't!"

"But, what if your father was trying to tell you something?" I said, attempting to keep my mouth from running ahead of my brain. "What if this is more than a children's story? What if your father discovered that Faar really exists?"

"That's impossible!" scoffed Spader.

"But if it isn't," I continued while holding up the half page. "This could be a map. Or *half* a map. Your father might have discovered Faar."

"But Faar isn't real!" he shouted back at me.

"But if it is," added Loor, "it would be just the kind of thing Saint Dane would want to destroy especially if it is important to the people of Cloral."

"Saint Dane!" shouted Spader. He was really worked up now. All the input over the last few days had finally gotten to him. "I don't know about territories or Travelers or Halla or flumes or any of that scutty-do magic, but there's one thing you've said that makes sense. If this Saint Dane is responsible for poisoning the people of Magorran, then I don't care *why* he did it. He killed my father and I'm going to pay for that. Pendragon, take me back to Cloral, now!"

This was going badly. After all we told Spader about being a Traveler and the mission we were on, there was only one thing he took away from it. He wanted revenge on Saint Dane.

I jumped up and said, "You don't get it. Saint Dane isn't just some *guy* you get even with. The dude is like . . . evil. And he has powers—more than you can imagine. He'd kill you before you even know you're in trouble."

"He couldn't be tougher than Loor!" countered Spader. "She's a warrior. She could come with us and use some of those natty weapons on him."

"It doesn't work like that," I said, trying not to get too frustrated. "You can't bring things from one territory to the next. We learned that the hard way."

"Fine!" he shouted. "There are plenty of weapons on Cloral. Let's just go after him!"

"You can't go after him!" I shouted back. "One on one, you'll be dead meat!"

"Then I'll be dead meat," said Spader with finality. "But I can't let my father's death go unavenged—no matter how big and bad this guy is. Take me back *now*!"

I had to think fast. Spader was out of control. I had to diffuse this situation, fast, before he did something dumb.

"No," I said with as much force as I could generate. "I'm tired and I'll never find the gate in the dark. If you want to go back on your own, knock yourself out. I'm not going back until tomorrow."

I sat down, picked up my coconut drink, and tried to act casual. It was a major-league bluff and I could only hope that Spader wouldn't go looking for the gate by himself. I didn't think he could find it, but you never knew. He stood with his feet firmly planted and his fists balled, weighing his options. Finally he said, "All right. We go back tomorrow. But then I'm going after Saint Dane whether you're with me or not."

With that he stormed out. I started to go after him but Loor put a hand on my shoulder.

"Let him walk alone," she said. "He needs to calm down."

I sat back down and dropped my coconut drink. I *hated* coconut.

"Well, that couldn't have gone any worse," I said with a false laugh.

"He has spirit," said Loor.

"Yeah, tell me about it. But if he goes after Saint Dane—"

"You must control him, Pendragon. You know as well as I that Saint Dane will kill him. I do not mean to sound uncaring, but he is no help to us dead."

"I get it. Between the two of us we can—"

"No," she said firmly. "I cannot go to Cloral with you."

That was *not* what I wanted to hear.

"What do you mean?" I asked incredulously. "We're Travelers. We help each other. You know 'the way it was meant to be,' and all that stuff. Don't bail on me now!"

"I have not yet found the turning point on Zadaa. But there is growing tension between the Batu and the Rokador. I want to try and stop the trouble before it grows worse. If I am successful then it will be one less battle we have to worry about in the future."

"Yeah, but what about the battle I'm fighting right now?"

"Your mission now is to control a passionate new Traveler and to solve the mystery of Faar. Think, Pendragon. You are better suited to that task than I. I would simply batter Spader senseless until he was unable to chase Saint Dane."

Good point. Diplomacy wasn't high on Loor's skill list.

"When you need a warrior," she added, "I will be there. You know that."

Of course she was right. Loor was always ready to fight, even if fighting wasn't the smartest way to go. I didn't need the responsibility of controlling *two* hotheads. Putting it another way, if she was the brawn of this team, then I was the brains. It was time to start using them.

"Is it possible?" I asked. "Could Spader's father have found a lost city?"

"After what we have been through," said Loor, "do you still think anything is impossible?"

The two of us looked to each other and shared a moment of unspoken understanding. We had been through a lot together and we knew there was much more to come. No, nothing was impossible in this new life of ours. The easiest thing to do was accept it.

Loor slept in her bedroom that night and I stretched out on the floor of the main room. She gave me a rough blanket and left an extra in case Spader came back. I'm happy to write that a few hours later, he did. He entered the apartment and lay down in front of the fire. I didn't say anything because I had no idea what kind of mood he was in. The last thing I wanted was to set him off again.

"Pendragon, you awake?" Spader whispered.

"Yeah."

"You're right, mate. I don't know all the rules of this game yet. Hobey, I don't even know what the game is. I'm willing to listen to what you think is best."

Whew, that was a relief. Now I could sleep.

"But you have to know something," he added. "I will learn from you. I will try and understand what it means to be a Traveler. But if I have a chance to hurt Saint Dane, I'm going to take it."

"That's the whole point, Spader," I said. "We all want to put Saint Dane out of business. But we've got to be smart about it. This might sound cold, but there is more at stake here than getting revenge for your father."

"But he was my *father,* Pendragon!" he said with emotion. "How can I look past that?"

I didn't sit up. I didn't raise my voice. I answered Spader as calmly as possible.

"You're not the only one who's been hurt here. Both my parents and my sister are gone. Loor's mother was killed. We both watched as Saint Dane's men shot her full of arrows. It hadn't been easy but we've been able to look past it. You'd better have the guts to do it too."

Spader didn't respond. I think I nailed him right between the eyes. Yes, we had all lost loved ones. Spader didn't have a monopoly on that particular horror. I could only hope that he now understood that the only hope we had of defeating Saint Dane was by fighting the larger battle, together.

I was too exhausted to think anymore. It had been an incredibly long day. I needed to sleep, so that's what I did.

We all got up before the sun. Loor started a fire and cooked us more of that incredible bread, along with a half dozen eggs. At least I thought they were eggs. They were green and looked more like something you would see in a Dr. Seuss book than on a menu at Denny's. Still, they were good and I was starving. We needed to eat every chance we had because we couldn't be sure where our next meal would come from.

It was now time to get going. Spader stood before Loor and said, "Thank you for helping me understand, and for holding my father's note. I guess we'll see each other again."

"We will," she said. Then added, "Trust Pendragon. He is the light we all need to follow."

That caught me by surprise. What did she mean by that? It sounded like a compliment, but it also sounded like she was expecting way too much from me. Spader looked to me and I'll bet he was wondering the same thing. He then nodded and left us alone.

"What was that about the light and the following?" I asked her.

She scoffed, saying, "I wanted to make sure Spader listened to you. That is all."

Oh. Okay. That was cool. I guess.

"When you need me," she added, "I will be there."

"Thanks for helping with Spader," I said. "I was lost there for a while."

"Your instincts are good, Pendragon," she said. "Someday you will realize that."

I nodded and backed out of the room. This was the second time I had to say good-bye to Loor, and it wasn't any easier. Still, I knew where to find her if need be.

Spader and I walked back toward the gate without saying much. I had to concentrate in order to retrace our steps through the city. It helped that my ring was doing a hot-cold thing to help guide us. With only a few wrong turns, we finally found the building with the ramp that led down to the underground river.

I really wanted to avoid running into that guy who worked the knob-and-lever gizmo. I didn't want to have to answer any more questions. But as luck would have it, the guy was there again, still checking his plans, still spinning his controls. What a boring job. We tried to sneak by without being noticed but—

"Are you lost again?" he said without looking at us.

"No," I said with authority. "Just passing through."

"Do you believe me now?" he asked.

"Uh . . . about what?"

"About the Batu. They are liars and barbarians. I hope you found that so-called friend of yours and told them I said so."

Loor was right. There was definitely bad blood between the Rokador and the Batu. I hoped she had luck in diffusing it.

"Yeah," I lied. "Thanks for the advice."

The man didn't say another word. I motioned to Spader and we continued on through the tunnel that led to the waterfall. Once we had gotten away from the roar of the water, Spader said, "I understood."

"What do you mean?"

"The guy back there. When he first started talking it sounded like: 'Shshaa shashaaa shashaaa' or something. But then all of a sudden he started making sense. I understood what he said about the Rokador and the Batu. What happened?"

I had to smile. "What happened is that you're becoming a Traveler."

Next stop, Cloral.

☻ SECOND EARTH ☻

The telephone rang, making both Mark and Courtney jump. When they were reading Bobby's journals they both became so immersed in the adventure that there own world seemed to slip away. But a jangling telephone is a surefire way to bring anyone back to the here and now.

Unfortunately for Courtney, they were reading the journal in Mark's bedroom. Though Mark did his best to excavate all of his crusty sweat socks and half-eaten cheddar cheese (extra sharp) sandwiches, the room was still in need of professional fumigation. The good news was that Courtney's gag reflex stopped when she got used to the putrid smell. The bad news was that she was afraid there were noxious gases eating away at her brain. Her goal was to read quick and get out fast.

They had been displaced from Courtney's basement because Courtney's father was actually going to attempt to make something in his workshop. That was always cause for worry in the Chetwynde house. Nothing good ever happened when Mr. Chetwynde decided to swing a hammer. Things usually got broken. When the telephone rang, Courtney's first thought was: "Dad hurt himself! He's headed for the emergency room." She had absolutely no faith in her father's handyman abilities.

Mark had to answer the phone because nobody else was home.

"Hello?"

"What's the deal, Dimond?" snarled a familiar voice.

The call wasn't about Courtney's father, it was Andy Mitchell. He was actually calling Mark's house. Mark wondered how Mitchell got his telephone number. Not that it was tough to get, but he couldn't picture Mitchell figuring out how to do something as complex as using a telephone book.

"Hey!" answered Mark with false friendliness. "How's it going?"

Mark was trapped. He didn't want to say anything that would make Courtney suspicious about what was going on with Mitchell. He knew she wouldn't continue reading the journal without Mark, so she had nothing to do but listen to his conversation. Mark fought his rising panic and pressed the phone closer to his ear so Courtney couldn't hear the other end of the conversation.

"You tell *me*," answered Mitchell. Mark could hear him snort and spit. "We have a deal, remember?"

"Uhhh, of course I do," answered Mark, trying to sound all innocent.

"So what's the problem?" asked Mitchell.

"No problem, everything's cool." He looked to Courtney and held up a finger as if to say: "I'll be off in a second."

Courtney shrugged. No biggie.

"So when am I gonna see the other journals?"

"Uhhh, let's see. How about . . . tomorrow?"

"How about in an hour?"

Mark's stomach twisted. "Okay, that's good too. Tell you what,

I'm kinda doing my homework now. But I should be done in an hour. Why don't you call me back then?"

Mitchell hung up abruptly. Mark didn't know what to do. If he just put the phone down, Courtney would wonder what happened. So he pretended to still be on the call.

"Uh-huh. Yeah. Sounds good. Okay, talk to you later. Bye."

Mark hung up the phone and hoped that Courtney only cared about getting back to reading the journal.

She didn't.

"Who was that?" she asked. Of course she did.

Mark hated lying. He wasn't good at it. He now had to get very good, very fast.

"Friend of mine," he answered, trying to sound casual. "He needs some help with homework. A-Algebra."

The instant Mark said that, he wished he hadn't. Up to that point he'd been cool, but when he made the full-on lie, when he said "algebra," he stuttered. Courtney caught it, too. He saw it in her eyes. Was she going to bust him on it? Courtney stared at him for a moment, then shrugged.

"Whatever," she said. "Can we get back to the journal?"

"Sure, yeah, of course."

Mark sat back down on the bed. He felt horrible. He hated lying to her, but was too embarrassed to tell her the truth. He was being blackmailed and had no idea how he was going to get out of it. If Courtney found out now, he was certain she'd lose all faith in him. It was a horrible position to be in. But for now at least, he could forget his own problem and lose himself in Bobby's problems.

"What do you think of this Faar place?" Courtney asked.

"If it's real, then destroying it would be the perfect, evil thing for Saint Dane to do. From what Spader said it's a legend that everybody on Cloral knows. It's part of their culture. If Saint Dane finds it and destroys it, it would be like pulling the rug out from under an entire territory. If the place is already a mess because of the food shortage, then the whole territory could crumble."

"Which is what Saint Dane wants," added Courtney.

"Exactly."

"Let's read," said Mark.

"Yeah, you've got an algebra lesson to get to."

This stung Mark, but he couldn't let it show. It was time to focus on Bobby.

CLORAL

We found the gate easily enough by following the signals sent from my ring. I opened the trapdoor and let Spader go down first into the crevice that led to the flume, then followed right behind.

When I was halfway down, I heard something off to my right. Remember, we were climbing down using footholds that were dug into the rock walls. It was like descending through a black cave. The crevice was only wide enough for one person, but it stretched off to either side for I don't know how far. It was too dark to tell. So when I heard something move off to my right, I froze. It wasn't a loud sound, it was more like a small pebble had been knocked into the crevice. Though it was a small sound, something had caused it. Something was out there in the darkness.

I cautiously looked to where I'd heard the sound, and was faced with two yellow eyes staring right back at me. Yikes! They were small, but that didn't matter. We were near a flume and that could mean only one thing: quigs. I had no idea what kind of beastie was behind those nasty eyes, but it wasn't going to be some harmless teddy bear.

My fear was that the slightest movement would push it into attack mode. My brain locked. I didn't know what to do.

Luckily Spader did. I felt him shoot up from below and reach out toward the yellow eyes. Before I could warn him, the yellow eyes were gone! I heard a loud *crack,* and that was it.

"W-What just happened?" I asked shakily.

"I got it, mate," answered Spader.

We both hurried down the rest of the way until we reached the cavern. There, lying at the foot of the rock wall, was the quig. It was the nastiest looking *snake* I had ever seen. It was about four feet long with a hooded head. All along its back were smaller versions of the sharp spines that the bear quigs had on Denduron. But most important, it was dead. Spader had snapped it like a whip.

"I'm used to those wogglies," he said casually. "They end up on the habitats every so often. All you gotta do is crack 'em good." He took a closer look at the fiendish thingy and frowned. "Never saw a sea snake looking like that before though."

And he never would either. Except here on Zadaa. The gruesome truth was that the quigs on Zadaa were snakes. I'd bet they were poisonous, too. I hated snakes more than anything. More than cannibal bears or wild dogs or even monster sharks. Snakes did something to me. Maybe because they were so quiet and sneaky. As I stared down at that creepy reptile, I hoped that Loor would do a really good job in keeping the Batu and the Rokador apart, because I did *not* want to come back to Zadaa.

Spader and I then changed back into our Cloral clothes and hit the flume. He went by himself this time. I showed him how to call out the name of the territory he was headed for, and just before the sparkling lights took him away, I warned him that the drop into Cloral was going to be wet.

Believe it or not, I was beginning to enjoy my trips through the flume because while I was flying I felt completely safe. Nothing to do but kick back and enjoy the ride. When I got to the end of this trip, I even spun around and tried to imitate Uncle Press's headfirst swan dive into the pool. But I timed it wrong and ended up landing on my back with a huge splash. It hurt, too. Hello, Cloral. So much for a cool entrance.

Spader was already standing on the edge of the pool.

"I'll lead from here," he said.

We were on his turf again, or should I say, in his water. He was back in charge. That was okay with me so long as we both agreed on the plan.

"What about the sharks?" I asked.

Spader grabbed his air globe and water sled.

"No worries there," he said. "Stay close to the bottom. Those beasties don't attack down. The only time you get into a natty-do is if you're on their level."

"Yeah? What if they come down to our level?"

Spader reached behind his back and pulled out his large, silver knife.

"Let 'em," he said with confidence.

"Whoa, did you bring that knife to Zadaa?"

"Didn't think I'd go someplace strange without my trusty, did you?"

"You gotta understand something, Spader," I said nervously. "Maybe I didn't explain this and if I didn't, it's my fault. But you can't bring things from one territory to the next. It's like . . . like . . . an infection. Believe me, I made that mistake and it was a disaster."

"It's just a knife, Pendragon," he said dismissively. "Couldn't do no harm."

With that he popped on his air globe and dove into the water. This was bad. Spader said he would learn from me, but the first thing I tried to tell him, he blew off. This was going to be tough.

But there was nothing I could do about it now, so I popped on my air globe and followed him under. I didn't want him to get too far ahead of me. After all, he had the knife. We both skimmed the bottom, traveling side by side with our water sleds. I kept glancing around, looking in the distance for the shadowy killers. And it wasn't just quigs that worried me. When we left for Zadaa there were four raiders after us. I had a brief hope that maybe the quigs ate the raiders, but that would have been hoping for too much. When we broke out into open water from under the rock overhang, I felt even more vulnerable. I kept glancing around, checking our backs. At one point I thought I saw a shadow moving several yards off to our right. I was about to tell Spader, when the shadow suddenly twisted and shot away. There was definitely something there all right. But if it was a quig, or a raider, it had decided to leave us alone.

Once we had traveled a few minutes I began to relax. As Spader said, the sharks only hung around that reef. I stopped worrying about getting eaten and began to worry about what we might find back on Grallion. When we left, we had just jammed up the raiders' battle cruiser and signaled to the aquaneers that the big guns wouldn't fire. The question now was, what had happened after that? Had the aquaneers boarded the cruiser? Had the raiders boarded Grallion? Had there been a battle between the good guys and the bad guys? Most important, was Uncle Press okay?

At least one answer came to us quickly. As the water sleds sped us closer to Grallion I saw something in the distance that wasn't there when we left. At first I didn't know what it was because we were so far away. It just looked like a dark mass. But as we got closer it began to take shape, and it was big. Really big. Spader recognized it for what it was first.

"Hobey-ho!" he exclaimed. "They had a natty-do all right!"

We sped closer, and that's when I saw the eight long tubes sticking out from the huge mass. Though the proof was right before my eyes, I could barely believe it. The long tubes were cannons. The dark mass . . . was a sunken ship! It was the raiders' battle cruiser. A minute later we glided and slipped right by the immense hulk. It was lying on its keel, tipped to one side. Being that close to something so big always took my breath away. It reminded me of the video footage I'd seen from the wreck of the *Titanic*. But this ship had only been on the bottom for a short time. It hadn't rusted out yet.

Whatever happened topside after we jammed up its guns, it was pretty clear that the raiders had gotten their butts whipped. Now I wanted to get to Grallion as soon as possible to hear the victory story.

We drove our water sleds past the huge sunken ship and continued on to Grallion. We stayed underwater the whole way and didn't surface until we had slipped into the dock area where we had launched the skimmers.

An aquaneer was on the dock, tinkering with an engine. He saw the two of us surface and his eyes grew wide.

"Spader?" he said with awe. "Spader!" The guy jumped up and started yelling for joy. "They're back! They're alive! Hobey-ho, Yenza, they're back!"

We were greeted with a hero's welcome. The aquaneers mobbed us on the docks and all but carried us topside. I got smacked on the back so much, I ended up with black and blue marks. No kidding. But I didn't care. This was great. When we got up into the sun, I took a quick look around to see there was absolutely no hint that a battle had taken place here. That's because it all happened on the water, and on the raiders' cruiser. The aquaneers took turns telling us what happened.

Just before the deadline that Zy Roder had given them for firing his guns again, Yenza quickly passed an order to every aquaneer. She said they were to attack soon as they saw a flare fire from beneath the water. The aquaneers thought she was crazy, but they followed orders. Sure enough, they saw our flare and went after the raiders with everything they had. They sent several boats loaded with aquaneers to swarm the cruiser and caught the bad guys completely by surprise. The *Pursuit*'s big guns were useless and the raiders weren't prepared for close-in fighting. Before they could rally to defend themselves, the aquaneers had boarded the cruiser and had little trouble taking command.

The only bad thing was that so many of the raiders escaped on small speedboats. Worse, their pilot, Zy Roder, had escaped as well. Yeah, Saint Dane got away. When I heard this, I glanced to Spader. I could tell that this news had tweaked him. He knew that Roder was really Saint Dane, and I'm sure he hoped to hear he had been captured. No such luck.

The aquaneers then scuttled the battle cruiser so no one could use it in anger again. While listening to them recount their victory, I split my attention between the aquaneers and Spader. I wanted to see Spader's reaction to what had happened. What I saw, I didn't like. This wasn't like the time at Grolo's where he was the center of attention, telling tales and buying everyone sniggers. No, if Spader was happy about the victory over the raiders, he didn't show it. He listened to the group intently, then after they finished their story he gave them polite congratulations. The old Spader would have jumped up and shouted: "Hobey-ho! Nobody challenges Grallion! Sniggers are on me!" But not this new Spader. This was a darker Spader, and it had me worried.

That's when I saw a welcome sight behind the group of ecstatic aquaneers. It was Uncle Press. He smiled and waved me over. I ran to him and the two of us hugged.

"You're becoming a legend around here," he said with a chuckle. "Next they'll be writing songs about you."

"Trust me, I wasn't all that heroic," I said. "I almost bought it down there." It sounded modest, but I meant it.

"Where have you been?" he asked.

I gave him a quick rundown on our trip to Zadaa and our meeting with Loor. I explained how Spader was getting up to speed on being a Traveler, but he wasn't handling it well. I said how his one and only concern was to get revenge on Saint Dane, and it was going to be hard to hold him back. I also told Uncle Press about the most important discovery of our trip: the symbol and the half of a map that might lead to the Lost City of Faar, as the legend referred to it. Uncle Press agreed that Faar, if it indeed existed, would be a perfect target for Saint Dane.

Spader then broke away from the celebration and joined us.

"Saint Dane got away," he said with no emotion, though I knew he was burning up inside.

"Don't worry," said Uncle Press. "We'll see him again."

I had been thinking a lot about what our next move should be, and it was as good a time as any to throw it out there.

"I think we should go to Panger City," I said.

Spader shot me a surprised look and said, "No. Leave my mum out of this."

"I'm afraid your mum may already be in it," I said, trying not to sound too harsh.

"Why? How?" Spader demanded.

"Spader's dad gave half of the map to Osa to give to Spader. That means the other half is still out there somewhere. We didn't find it with Spader's dad, so I'll bet you anything it's with Spader's mum."

Spader reached into his pocket and pulled out the half map. Uncle Press took it and examined it.

"These numbers on top," he said. "They could be partial coordinates."

Spader grabbed the map back angrily.

"I don't care about your fantasy games. Leave my mum alone."

"You don't get it," I said urgently. "Maybe this whole Faar thing is a fable and we've got nothing to worry about, but if it isn't and Saint Dane is trying to find that lost city, then he'll want this map. If your mum has the other half, she's in trouble."

This hit Spader hard. I couldn't have shocked him more if I had thrown ice water in his face. I hated to do it, but he had to understand what was at stake here. He looked at the half map, then jammed it into his pocket.

"Yenza," he said. "She'll give us a boat. We can be in Panger City by nightfall."

He took off running toward the aquaneer barracks. Uncle Press watched him run off and then said, "He's hurting."

"This is bad. When he finally comes face to face with Saint Dane—"

"We'll worry about that when it happens. Right now let's get ready for a treasure hunt."

CLORAL

Uncle Press and I followed Spader to the far side of the aqua-neer barracks. As we got closer, we heard yelling coming from the building. "I warned her, yes I did! I saw this coming but no one believed me!"

It was coming from Wu Yenza's office. When we peeked in the door, we saw Yenza behind a desk, looking stern, as usual. Spader stood to the back of the room, listening. All the hubba was coming from two agronomers who stood in front of Yenza's desk. They were the same man and woman I had seen outside the pilot house on Magorran shortly after the crash. They were arguing then, and they were still arguing now. At least now I had the chance to hear what it was all about. The man was a short, balding guy with an elflike face named Ty Manoo. In another life, he could have easily gotten a gig in Santa's workshop. The guy paced, flailed his arms for emphasis, and spit when he talked.

"We set something in motion that must be stopped!" he shouted.

The woman didn't seem all that worried. Her name was Po Nassi. She was tall and slim with sharp features that reminded me of a sly cat. She stood with her arms folded, looking bored, as if Manoo were nothing more than an annoying kid.

"You are overreacting again," she said while rolling her eyes.

"Overreacting!" Manoo shot back. "There are hundreds dead on Magorran! We were attacked by raiders! What kind of reaction would you suggest?"

"What is the problem?" asked Spader.

"The problem is we caused the poisoning on Magorran," Manoo spit out.

Whoa. New development. Uncle Press and I looked at each other and entered the office. It was time to get involved. Yenza saw us and stood up. She looked kind of flustered, like she was losing control of the situation and from what I saw of Yenza, she did not like to lose control.

"Spader, get your friends out of here," she ordered.

"No," Spader shot back. "They're here to help us."

"I don't want to cause a panic," Yenza argued. "Until we find out exactly what happened, we don't need rumors circulating."

Uncle Press spoke to Yenza in a calm, controlled voice. "If I may, Commander. Pendragon and I have come from a long way off because we heard there might be some . . . difficulty here. We won't spread rumors; we won't cause a panic. Our only goal is to help see you through this crisis."

Yenza looked into Uncle Press's eyes, and I could see her relax. It was kind of creepy, actually. Uncle Press's soothing words had taken the fight of her. It reminded me of the quiet way that Loor's mother, Osa, had a calming effect on people. It was almost hypnotic. I wondered if this were some kind of Traveler trick and made a mental note to ask about it later.

"They already helped save Grallion once," Spader added. "They're friends."

Yenza looked us over. Finally she sat back down and said to the agronomers, "Tell them what you told me."

Immediately the little guy, Manoo, took over.

"It was an experiment," he started. "The population of Cloral is growing. The demand for food is always getting greater."

Nassi didn't want to be left out and added, "We calculated that at the present rate, there was a good possibility the day would come when the demand for food would be greater than the supply. So we set out to perform an important service."

"We started looking for ways to increase plant growth," Manoo continued. "We figured if we could get crops to grow bigger and faster, we'd never have to worry about having enough food. We experimented with fertilizers and crossbreeding and found ways to change the very cell structure of plants. But it was wrong!"

"It wasn't wrong!" countered Nassi. "It's a work in progress!"

"But we were changing nature!" cried Manoo. "I tried to tell them we were headed for disaster, but no one listened."

"That's because we were successful!" Nassi argued.

"Successful?" shouted Manoo. "We changed nature! We created plants that grew faster but turned poisonous!"

Manoo was a mess. He wiped his sweaty forehead with his sleeve and continued.

"It was the fertilizer," he said. "We created a fertilizer that affected the normal growth cycle of plants and changed their genetic structure. It was incredible. Plants grew seven times faster and yielded twice as much fruit. We were all so excited that we wanted to share the discovery with everyone. But we moved too fast. We didn't test the results."

"It was only recently that we discovered an unfortunate . . . side effect," Nassi said, trying to sound casual, as if it were no big deal. "Some of the mutated crops became poisonous. We never actually used the fertilizer on Grallion's crops. We're safe here."

"But, we had already sent a sample of the fertilizer to the Agronomy Society. We only wanted them to study it, but they were so impressed they immediately began manufacturing it and sending it all over Cloral!" shouted Manoo.

Yenza jumped to her feet. "You're telling me that a fertilizer is being used all over Cloral that turns crops deadly?" she screamed, trying to control her horror.

"Yes!" shouted Manoo. "What happened on Magorran is just the beginning!"

This put a whole new spin on things. Could it be that Saint Dane wasn't responsible for the poison crops after all? Was he simply taking advantage of the situation? The creation of this killer fertilizer seemed to be the turning point on this territory, but it looked to be the people of Cloral who brought it on themselves.

"The Agronomy Society is on Panger City," Spader said. "We've got to get there and stop them from sending out more fertilizer."

"That's *exactly* what we have to do!" squealed Manoo.

"Give us a speeder craft," added Spader. "We can be in Panger City before nightfall." Spader was being very clever. Stopping the fertilizer was critical, but the main reason he wanted to get to Panger City was to protect his mum. There was a whole "two birds with one stone" thing happening.

"I'm going too!" added Manoo. He then turned to Nassi,

stuck a finger in her face and spit out, "You are too. I'm not going to take full blame for this."

Nassi shrugged and said, "Fine, whatever you want. I don't mind taking the credit. Once we perfect the process, we'll be heroes."

"But right now, we're killers," Manoo said angrily.

This got a reaction from Nassi. Up until then she was only looking at the problem as a science experiment. Being called a killer was a whole 'nother ballgame. She actually looked shaken.

"I'll go," she said, cowed.

Yenza came around from behind her desk heading for the door.

"Meet me at the stern dock in two pecks," she ordered. "I'll prepare a speeder. We're *all* going to Panger City." Then just before she left the office she turned back and lifted a finger.

"Do not mention this to anyone," she commanded sternly. "Any of you. If Grallion is safe, there's no need to cause panic."

She then left. Nassi and Manoo followed after her, leaving us alone with Spader.

"Is it possible?" he asked. "Could Saint Dane have nothing to do with this?"

"It's possible, but it doesn't matter," answered Uncle Press. "He may not have started it, but he'll take advantage of it."

"And there's still the stuff about Faar," I added. "How does that fit in?"

"Hopefully we'll find out on Panger City," answered Uncle Press.

Forty minutes later, or two pecks, depending on where you come from, the six of us were at the dock, ready to leave for Panger City. I stood with Uncle Press, Spader, and the two agronomers, Nassi and Manoo. The speeder we were going to take was a coolio-looking powerboat that looked about forty feet long. It was painted the same sea-green color as the raiders' battle cruiser. It had a cabin up front that was big enough to hold a galley and some bunks. The wheelhouse was on top of the cabin. Wu Yenza was already there, powering up. The deck was large, with seats along the rails. It kind of reminded me of the dive boats Uncle Press used to take me on. But unlike dive boats, this baby looked like it could do some serious haul ass.

We all boarded and Spader cast off the lines. Yenza powered up the engines, which as usual weren't all that loud. These water-powered engines were great! Yenza then expertly guided the boat away from the docks of Grallion and out into open water. Moments later, once we had passed the marker buoy, Yenza hit the throttle and this boat showed us why it was called a speeder. I was nearly thrown over by the sudden surge of power, in seconds we were flying over the water like a seagoing jet.

Like the skimmers, the ride was smooth and pretty quiet. The only way I could tell we were moving so fast was from the wind whipping at my face. When I stood up I had to lean forward or it would have knocked me back down.

The two agronomers kept to themselves during most of the trip. They stayed in the cabin up front and argued. What else was new? They had pads of paper where they scribbled out equations and formulas. I assumed they were trying to figure out how to undo the harm done by their mutant fertilizer.

Yenza stayed at the controls. Spader acted as navigator. He had charts and plotted a course to Panger City. Uncle Press and I had nothing to do except worry. Would it be too late to recall

all the fertilizer? How far had it spread? Had it already started a chain reaction that would infect all the crops of Cloral? Stranger still was the mystery of Faar. What was so important about this mythical city that the dying wish of Spader's father was to tell his son about it? How did this all tie in with Saint Dane? Hopefully, all of these questions would be answered on Panger City.

"This makes perfect sense," said Uncle Press softly. He was looking out onto the water, thinking.

"What does?" I asked. I wasn't used to hearing that things were making sense.

"The agronomers went too far," he said thoughtfully. "Their intentions may have been noble, but they created a monster. It's just the kind of thing that Saint Dane would take advantage of. He'll do everything in his power to keep the poison spreading and turn Cloral upside down. This is the turning point. This is why we're here."

"Then what about this lost city of Faar?" I asked.

"I don't know where it fits into this puzzle, but if Spader's father was concerned, then I'm concerned too."

I looked up to the wheelhouse and saw that Spader was staring at the horizon. I wanted to know what was going through his mind. He was a great guy. A friend. But I was afraid his anger over the death of his father was going to get him into some serious trouble and make things worse for all of us. Hopefully his mother was safe. But then Spader would have the tough job of telling her that his father was dead. But as rough as this would be, what I really feared was that something might have already happened to his mother, like it happened to my family. If Spader lost his mother, then I was sure he'd go off the deep end.

The trip took most of the day. I tried to get some sleep but my mind was racing with worry. I watched the sun as it traveled across the sky on its way to the ocean. Then, just as I was finally nodding off—

"There!" shouted Yenza.

I quickly climbed the ladder to the wheelhouse and looked forward to where she was pointing. I didn't see it at first because it was only a gray speck on the horizon. But as we drew closer and the speck grew bigger, I saw it for what it was.

Panger City.

Even though we were flying over the water at an incredible speed, it must have taken us another two hours to get there. That's how big this city habitat was. The closer we got, the larger the buildings grew. It soon became clear to me that this habitat was every bit as big as Grallion, but unlike Grallion, it was covered with buildings. It really was a city! I was staring at skyscrapers! Some of them must have been over forty stories high. This looked every bit like a big city from home, but cities at home weren't floating on the ocean. It was incredible!

As we got closer I saw more detail in the buildings. Like I told you before, there was no steel on Cloral. Everything was made from some kind of hard plastic compound. Rather than familiar building colors of gray concrete and silver steel, these buildings were white and light blue or green. But other than that they looked very much like office buildings at home.

When we got inside the safety buoy and slowed down, I had to strain my neck back to look up at the huge buildings that towered over me. Only one thought came to mind: How can this thing possibly stay afloat?

Yenza carefully drove our speeder into the dock area, which was very much like Grallion's. Two aquaneers to guide us in and tie us up. They immediately stood at attention and saluted Yenza as she jumped off the boat.

"We may be leaving at any time," she said with authority.

"Yes, sir!" responded both aquaneers professionally.

Yenza then turned back to us and barked to Manoo and Nassi, "Where is the Agronomy Society?"

Manoo scrambled over the rail of the boat, nearly fell in the water, but caught himself and stood up straight as if nothing were wrong. Nassi rolled her eyes and gracefully got off the boat.

"We'll take you there," he said sharply.

The little man waddled past Yenza and headed up the stairs toward the surface. The rest of us got off the boat and followed. I walked with Spader and asked, "When was the last time you were home?"

He didn't answer. He kept looking ahead and picked up the pace to get away from me. So much for small talk. Spader's mind was somewhere else.

When we arrived on the surface, we stepped out of a building and onto a scene that looked pretty much like any busy city street. The sidewalks were full of people hurrying to wherever they were hurrying; small vehicles traveled on the streets; and vendors sold food from wheeled carts. It was like being back in New York City, except everything looked more colorful, and *way* cleaner.

There was one other detail that made it very different from home. There were water canals that ran parallel to every street. They were around twenty feet across, which was about the same width as the streets, but that was plenty big enough for the many small water-powered boats that traveled quickly along, speeding people on their way. I'd never been to Venice, Italy, but from the pictures and movies I'd seen, this was kind of like that. One quick look around showed me that these canals crisscrossed the entire city habitat. Every so often there were footbridges that stood like half circles over the waterways so that boats could glide under them. At each bridge was a beautiful fountain that sent up sprays of water in various patterns. The fountains had no function except to look good.

I have to say, Panger City was a beautiful place.

But I didn't have much time to hang out and appreciate it. When we all regrouped on the street, Spader didn't stop. Without a word of explanation he kept walking toward one of the canals.

"Spader!" called Yenza. "Spader, get back here. That is an order."

Spader wasn't listening. I knew where he was going and nobody was going to stop him.

Yenza was about to run after him, but Uncle Press stepped in front of her saying, "He's going to see his mother."

This made Yenza soften for a moment, but just as quickly her hard look returned.

"I understand, but that's not why we're here," she said angrily. "He knows that."

"He does," said Uncle Press calmly. "We'll stay with him. It's more important that you get to the Agronomy Society."

Yenza looked at Nassi and Manoo. Nassi was getting impatient. Manoo just looked like he wanted to pee.

"We can't waste any more time!" Manoo squealed.

Yenza looked back to Uncle Press and said, "Let him talk to his mother, then bring him back to the speeder."

"Understood," replied Uncle Press.

Yenza definitely had a soft spot for Spader. I think he got away with a lot of things Yenza would never allow from her other aquaneers. On top of that, Spader had saved Grallion, with our help of course. So I guess he deserved a little slack.

I saw that Spader had already jumped onto a skimmer and was powering it up.

"Uhhh, Uncle Press," I said. "We're going to lose him."

"Go!" shouted Yenza.

Uncle Press and I took off on a run toward the canal. It seemed as if all the skimmers were community property because people were getting on and off randomly and just leaving them, kind of like bicycles in China.

Spader kicked his skimmer into gear and sped off. We were losing him.

"Uncle Press!"

"There! Got one," he announced, pointing. He saw an empty skimmer and we both jumped on. Uncle Press quickly powered up, hit the throttle, and we were off.

Luckily there was a speed limit on the canals. It was pretty crowded and to go too fast meant a guaranteed accident. Spader was already far ahead of us, but I could tell he was having trouble going as fast as he wanted to because it looked like rush hour had hit Panger City. Uncle Press maneuvered our skimmer around the slower traffic and only managed to tick off a few people by cutting them off.

We traveled quite a ways through the canyons of towering buildings. We couldn't stop to appreciate the tour though; we had to keep up with Spader. Spader knew exactly where he was going and made several turns down different canals. I kept watching him and directed Uncle Press who was busy avoiding other skimmers.

Finally Spader turned off into a narrow canal that ran between two smaller buildings. I saw where he dumped the skimmer and kept watching to see which building he was going toward. I had a strange sense of déjà vu. This is exactly what happened when we followed Spader to his father's apartment on Magorran. I could only hope that we wouldn't find the same kind of horror here on Panger City.

We landed our skimmer and quickly jumped off. When we ran up onto the street, Spader was standing there, waiting for us.

"I just saw you," he said, sounding a little embarrassed. "I didn't know you were following me."

"Yeah, well, we're sort of in this together whether you like it or not," I said.

"I'm sorry," he said. "I'm glad you're here. I'm a little . . ."

He didn't finish his sentence. I could tell he was afraid of what he might find.

"It's okay, Spader. We're with you," said Uncle Press.

Spader nodded, then turned and led us into the apartment building where his mother lived. This place looked like any apartment building at home, except for the fact it was light yellow. It was five stories high with around ten apartments to a floor. Spader knew exactly where he was going. We climbed the stairs to the top floor and walked to the door on the far end of the corridor. That's where Spader stopped, caught in the moment. Soon he would find what he came for, and I could tell that as much as he wanted to go inside, he was afraid to. He looked up to us. Uncle Press gave him an encouraging nod.

Spader knocked on the door. "Hobey-ho!" he called happily.

There was no answer. He knocked again.

"Mum?"

There was no sound of footsteps coming to the door. No one called from inside to ask who it was. I hoped that his mother was out shopping or taking a nap or visiting friends.

Spader glanced at us again and tried the doorknob. It was open. His heart must have been racing because mine sure was. He then took a deep breath and stepped inside. Uncle Press and I followed him, stepping into his mother's home.

I have to tell you guys, I never thought I'd have this feeling even *once* in my life, but to go through it twice was, well, it wasn't fair.

The apartment was totally empty. Not a piece of furniture or picture or any other sign that anyone had ever lived there. It was just like the feeling I had when we all went back to 2 Linden Place in Stony Brook and I saw that my house was gone. Well, it wasn't exactly as bad as that because what I saw back on Second Earth with you was that my own family had disappeared. I knew exactly what Spader was going through.

He stood near the door, staring at the empty home, unbelieving. Uncle Press walked up to him, put a hand on his shoulder and softly said the magic words, "Try not to be sad. This is the way it was supposed to be."

Spader pulled away from him angrily.

"How can that be?" he shouted. "Where is she?"

"She's not dead, Spader," said Uncle Press. "You're a Traveler now. That meant it was time for her to move on too."

Spader shot a look of total confusion to Uncle Press. I have to admit, I was still confused about this whole family-disappearance part of being a Traveler myself.

"So then where is she?" I asked. "And while we're at it, where's *my* family?"

Uncle Press looked uncomfortable. I think he knew exactly where they were, but for some reason he didn't want to say.

"Spader, I'll tell you the same thing I told Bobby when he found out his own family was gone," he said calmly. "You were always destined to become a Traveler. Your family was here to raise you and teach you and help you become the person you are today so that you could begin your journey. But they've begun a journey of their own now. Someday you'll see them again, I promise."

"What about my father?" demanded Spader. "He didn't go anywhere. He was killed!"

"He was a Traveler," answered Uncle Press. "He had other duties. I promise you both, as time goes on you will understand everything, but for right now, you must know that nothing horrible happened to your mother."

This was bringing up all sorts of old, horrible feelings in me. I was getting frustrated over not knowing all there was to know about being a Traveler. I could only imagine what Spader was feeling. This was still very new to him. We stood in the room for a few moments, then Spader suddenly ran farther into the apartment. We followed him as he ran through the empty home, into what was probably once a bedroom at one time.

He stood in the middle of the room and said, "This was my room. I lived here from the time I was born until I left to become an aquaneer. I don't believe that my entire childhood can be wiped away as if it never existed."

He went into a closet. "Pendragon, help me," he said. I shrugged and followed.

"Help me up?" he asked.

I clasped my hands together and held them out. Spader put his foot in and I hoisted him up.

"I had a hiding place nobody knew about," he said while running his hands along the wall over the closet door. "It is where I kept the things that were most important to me."

I felt bad for him. Spader was doing the same thing I did when I walked onto the empty lot at 2 Linden Place. I looked over every inch of that empty space, desperate for any sign that proved I had lived there. But there was nothing. Even the scar on the tree that had been made by our swing was gone. I knew that Spader's secret hiding place would be empty.

Over the closet door was a piece of wall that had been neatly cut out and replaced. Spader knew exactly where it was. He pulled away the piece and reached into the compartment. Of course it was empty. I could tell by the pained look on his face.

But then, just as he was about to climb down, his face changed. He had found something after all.

"Let me down," he ordered.

I awkwardly bent down and dropped his foot. He banged his shoulder against the door frame as he came down, but he was okay.

"What did you find?" I asked. I couldn't believe that some hint of his past life had actually been left behind.

Spader held the treasure in his hand.

I knew instantly that it wasn't something he put there himself. It was a piece of green paper, folded in half. Written on the outside in black letters was: "For Spader. I'm proud of you and I love you. Hobey-ho!" I could only guess that it was his mum's handwriting.

Spader unfolded the paper and I saw his mum's final gift to him. It was the other half of the map that led to the lost city of Faar.

"She may be gone," he said softly. "But I guess her job wasn't finished until I got this."

"Hello? Anyone home?"

The bright voice came from the entrance to the apartment. It was a woman's voice. For a moment I thought Spader's mother had returned. Spader did too. He ran for the entrance. Uncle Press and I were right behind.

But when we got there, we saw that it wasn't Spader's mother after all. It was Po Nassi, the agronomer. What was she doing here?

"Here you boys are! Why did you run off like that?" she asked like a scolding but jovial schoolteacher.

"Why aren't you with Yenza and Manoo?" asked Uncle Press.

"Those two are on a futile quest," she answered with a huff. "My time is better spent elsewhere."

This was weird. Had she followed us?

"Now," she said. "Young Spader. Did you find what you came for?"

Spader answered her with a confused look. Uncle Press and I did the same. What was she talking about?

"I didn't think it was possible, myself," she explained. "Like all you wet little Clorans, I thought the lost city of Faar was a myth. That is, until I saw the symbol your father had drawn for you. He was a resourceful Traveler. I'm guessing he discovered the city was real and knew its location. Now I think you know it too."

Uh-oh. Uncle Press stiffened beside me. The hair began to stand up on my neck. I was afraid I knew exactly where this was going and it was a very, very bad place.

"How could you know?" Spader asked, dumbfounded. He had no clue what was going on, but he was about to find out.

Nassi looked to Uncle Press and gave him a catlike grin.

"Ahh, Press. Don't you just love them when they're young?" she asked. "Such . . . innocence."

And then it happened. The agronomer Nassi began to transform before our eyes. Her face contorted, her body shifted, her whole figure grew watery and unformed. It only took about five seconds, but I guarantee they were five seconds that Spader would replay in his mind for the rest of his life. I probably would too, but I had seen it before. Her hair grew long and gray. Her body rose to a solid seven feet tall. Her clothes changed from Cloral blue to the black suit that was all too familiar. And again, what stood out most were the eyes. They became icy blue and charged with an evil fire.

"Does it make more sense to you now, water boy?" snarled the tall, ominous figure.

Spader looked at me with total confusion.

"It's Saint Dane," I said with no emotion. "He's been playing with us all along."

CLORAL

"You naughty boys, you sank my battleship," Saint Dane said playfully, as if he really didn't care.

Spader looked to me and to Uncle Press. I think he was in shock. Nothing had prepared him for seeing Saint Dane transform the way he did. I wasn't exactly comfortable with it either, but at least I had seen it before so I didn't go into total mind lock.

"The poison fertilizer?" asked Uncle Press. "Was it your doing?"

Saint Dane let out an evil laugh. Here we go again. I hate it when the bad guys laugh. It always means they know more than you do.

"You give me too much credit, Press, my friend," Saint Dane said. "You know I don't initiate anything."

"But you don't mind helping it along," Uncle Press added.

"Of that, I am guilty. That weasel Manoo and his agronomers would have abandoned their experiments years ago if I hadn't convinced them otherwise. It was so easy to feed their egos. I told them they would be heroes for saving Cloral from starvation for generations to come!" He laughed ironically.

"They were too blinded by visions of glory to realize they were brewing up the means to kill every living soul on the territory. Surprise!"

"So you *did* kill my father," Spader spat at Saint Dane.

"Indirectly, I suppose," Saint Dane said, beginning to sound bored. "But we're all much better off with one less Traveler, don't you think?"

This pushed Spader over the edge. He lunged at Saint Dane, ready to grab his throat. But Saint Dane pulled a quick draw from under his coat and jammed a silver pistol into Spader's chest, stopping him cold. Spader's eyes were wild with hatred, but there was nothing he could do.

"Talk to Pendragon," Saint Dane said calmly. "He knows you can't defeat me."

"No?" I jumped in. "What about Denduron?"

Saint Dane turned to look at me for the first time. His cold blue eyes gave me a chill.

"A minor inconvenience," he said. "This game has only begun, Pendragon."

"Game?" shouted Spader. "You killed hundreds of people. This isn't a game!"

"But of course it is," answered Saint Dane. And with that he began to transform again. His body grew liquid, he shrank slightly, and when the change was complete, standing before us was Zy Roder, the raider pilot.

"This is very much a game," he said with a different, raspier voice. "And the stakes are high indeed!"

At that moment the door flew open from the hallway and several more raiders entered the apartment. They all held silver guns like the one Roder/Saint Dane had. Any thoughts we had about escaping had just gotten very dim.

"Now," said Roder/Saint Dane. "I have a question for you.

Tell me what you know about this place called 'Faar.'"

We all did our best not to look at each other.

"Faar is a children's story," Spader finally answered. "What is it you want to know?"

Roder/Saint Dane jammed his silver gun into Spader's chest, making him wince in pain.

"Please don't waste my time trying to be coy," Roder/Saint Dane said. "I saw the symbol of Faar on your father's desk."

"I knew that he'd been searching for Faar," he continued. "But when I saw the symbol, I knew he'd been successful."

"You were there?" I said, stunned. "On Magorran?"

"To be precise, Po Nassi was there," he chuckled. "Only seconds before you three arrived."

I got the feeling that Saint Dane loved fooling people with his little charades.

I really hated this guy.

He then looked directly into Spader's eyes and said, "Your father discovered Faar and passed the information to you, didn't he?"

Spader didn't move. He wasn't about to give Roder/Saint Dane the two pieces of map. No way. But Roder/Saint Dane flashed forward with his free hand and grabbed Spader around the neck. Both Uncle Press and I made a move to stop him, but the other raiders jumped between us, holding us back.

"Tell me," Roder/Saint Dane seethed. His strength was incredible because he lifted Spader off the ground with only one hand. "Tell me what you know, or I'll first kill Pendragon, then Press, and then I'll go back to Grallion and see what mischief we can get into there. The only one I won't kill is you. You'll have to live knowing they died because you wouldn't tell me what I will find out soon enough anyway."

Spader was turning blue. Both Uncle Press and I struggled

to get away from the raiders, but it was no use. There was nothing we could do to help Spader.

Then, slowly, Spader reached into his pocket for the map.

"Don't!" I shouted. But it was too late. Spader pulled out the two map halves and tossed them on the ground. Instantly Roder/Saint Dane threw him down and Spader collapsed on the floor, gasping for breath. Another raider picked up the two pieces of paper and handed them to Roder/Saint Dane. The evil Traveler held the two pieces together and studied them for a few seconds.

He then let out a smile and said, "It's so simple. Thank you, Spader. Now Cloral has absolutely no hope of fighting off the plague I've nurtured for so long."

Huh? What did a mythical lost city have to do with the killer fertilizer that was spreading across the territory?

Boom! A gunshot sounded from out in the hallway that sent the raiders scrambling for cover. I can't believe I acted as fast as I did, but in the one second of confusion, I lunged forward and grabbed the two pieces of the map from Roder/Saint Dane.

Boom! Boom! Two more gunshots. Though they weren't exactly gunshots. Remember how I described the way the water cannons on the battleship fired compact missiles of water? As it turned out, that's exactly what *all* the guns on Cloral fired. And right now, standing out in the hallway was Wu Yenza and two aquaneers. I wasn't sure how they knew we were in trouble, but I didn't care.

The water bullets they fired hit the walls and exploded, doing more damage than any bullet could.

"Drop your weapons!" shouted Yenza.

While Roder/Saint Dane and the other raiders ducked for cover, Uncle Press grabbed Spader and me and pulled us into the back room. The raiders were too busy defending themselves to come after us.

"Is there another way out?" Uncle Press shouted.

"There's a ledge, all the way around the building," gasped Spader, still trying to get his breath back from nearly being strangled.

"Show us!"

From the other room I heard the booming sounds of more water missiles hitting the walls. One shot blasted right through a wall and into the room we were in, missing me by a foot. These weren't like any water pistols I'd ever played with!

Spader threw open a window and leaped out. Uncle Press pushed me toward the window to go next. I hesitated. I was never good with heights and we were on the fifth floor. Yikes. But there was no other choice. There were more raiders than aquaneers outside. As soon as the bad guys realized that, they'd be coming after us. So I put my fear aside and climbed out the window.

There was a two-foot-wide ledge that went all around the building. Normally two feet would be plenty wide enough to walk on. But when you're five stories in the air, it feels more like two inches. I looked down and started getting dizzy.

"Go!" shouted Uncle Press. "He was already out behind me and pushing me to follow Spader.

Spader was moving quickly ahead of me, approaching the corner of the building. I took two steps and—

Boom! A piece of wall blasted out in front of me, spewing splintered bits of building everywhere. Suddenly I wasn't worried about the height anymore and started to run. More blasts of water missile blew out chunks of building just behind Uncle Press. If we stopped, we'd get blasted off the ledge.

Spader reached the corner and made the turn. I was right

behind him. We were now on the far side of the building from where the battle was taking place. Spader found a window and jumped inside. For a moment I thought we were going to drop in on some unsuspecting guy taking a nap or something, but luckily we found ourselves in a stairwell.

"Go down the stairs!" Spader ordered. But rather than lead us down, he headed back toward the corridor where the fight was going on. Uncle Press grabbed him.

"What are you doing?" he shouted.

"Going after Saint Dane!"

He tried to pull away from Uncle Press, but my uncle held him firm.

"Listen, Spader," Uncle Press said. "You just had a taste of what we've been telling you about. Saint Dane has powers that you are no match for."

"Not to mention the gunfight going on," I added. "You go back there, you're history."

Spader was torn. His blood was boiling and he wanted a piece of Saint Dane—bad.

"We told you before," Uncle Press continued with a calm voice, trying to talk Spader down. "There's a bigger battle to be fought here. You heard what he said about Faar. It could be the last piece in the puzzle for destroying Cloral. Which do you think is more important? Going back in there and getting killed, or doing what your father wanted you to do?"

Spader looked up at my uncle with questioning eyes.

Uncle Press then said, "Let's go find the Lost City of Faar."

Boom! Like an exclamation point on his sentence, a water missile ripped through the door to the corridor. The raiders were coming after us. But Spader was with the program now. He knew what we had to do.

"C'mon!" he yelled, and bolted down the stairs. We all flew down, taking three stairs at a time. I thought I was going to take a tumble and break my neck, which would have been a really stupid thing to do at this point. But speed was everything now, so I kept going.

We blasted out a side door to the apartment building and went on a dead run for the canal and the skimmers. As we rounded the building, I saw that Yenza and the two aquaneers were backing out of the front door, still firing their water guns at the raiders. I really hoped there were no innocent bystanders in the way.

"Yenza!" yelled Uncle Press.

The chief aquaneer looked up and saw that we were out of the building. She immediately gave a command to the other aquaneers. They gave up on the fight and joined the sprint for the skimmers. As we ran across the grass toward the canal, small water bombs kicked up the dirt at our feet. I didn't have to turn around to know the raiders were now out of the building and after us. I could only hope that we were far enough away that their guns wouldn't be accurate enough to do any damage.

We all hit the canal at about the same time and jumped on the skimmers to make our escape. Nobody had to say a word. Uncle Press and I were on one, Spader and Yenza on another, the two aquaneers on a third.

The skimmers all whined to life. We were seconds away from blasting off. Then Spader turned around and actually gave me a smile.

"Last one back to the speeder buys the sniggers." For a second, the old Spader had returned. He gunned the engine and took off. Uncle Press gunned ours, too, and the aquaneers were right behind. With the water around boiling from the incoming rain of water missiles, all three skimmers blasted off and away from the raiders.

The dash back to the dock was hairy, but not because of the raiders. As I wrote before, the canals were busy. But this time nobody cared. With Spader in the lead, we all flew over the water, dodging other skimmers like gates in a ski race. I wondered if there was a Panger City highway patrol that would pull us over for reckless skimming. Luckily, there weren't any accidents, though we had a ton of close calls.

It wasn't until we made it back to the canal near the docks that we could all finally take a breath. Or at least a half breath because this race was only just beginning. We tied up the skimmers and headed for the dock.

"How did you know to follow us?" Uncle Press asked Yenza as we ran.

"It was Nassi," she answered. "I never trusted that woman. As soon as you left to follow Spader, she went after you."

"You saved our lives, Yenza," he said. "Thank you."

Yenza then stopped on the side of the busy street and faced the three of us. The aquaneers stood behind her, ready for anything. Yenza was used to calling all the shots and I didn't think she liked being out of the loop, especially when it meant having to battle raiders. "You were talking to Zy Roder like you knew him. What is going on?"

The three of us exchanged looks. How could we possibly explain any of this to her? It was Uncle Press who took a shot at it.

"Po Nassi was working with Zy Roder," he explained.

Technically, Po Nassi *was* Zy Roder, but Uncle Press made the wise decision not to go down that road. Good thinking.

"She knew exactly what she was doing," he continued.

"She knew the fertilizer was poison. Spader's father was working with me to investigate this horror . . . until he died."

"Po Nassi was deliberately trying to poison Cloral?" she asked in shock. "Why?"

"That's tougher to answer, but it's true. We've got to leave Panger City right away. Where is Manoo?"

"I'm right here!"

The little elf-man hurried to us from the building that led to the docks. He looked all sorts of angry and upset.

"Where have you been?" he demanded.

"Did you get to the Agronomy Society?" Yenza asked, ignoring his question.

"Yes," Manoo answered nervously. "But it's too late!"

"What do you mean?" Yenza demanded.

"The fertilizer," whined Manoo. "It's been sent all over Cloral. Almost every underwater farm is using it right now. Our entire food supply is going to be poisoned! It's a total disaster!"

How's *that* for a horrifying news item? Saint Dane's plan had kicked into high gear and Manoo was out of his mind with worry.

Welcome to the party, Manoo and I've been out of my mind for a while now.

"Get back to the Agronomy Society," Uncle Press ordered Manoo. "Make sure they track down and stop every shipment. Can you do that?"

"I suppose," answered Manoo. "But who are you to tell me—"

"Just do it, Manoo!" barked Yenza.

She called to the two aquaneers, "Make sure this man gets back to the Agronomy Society safely."

The aquaneers both offered a crisp salute and stood ready

to go with Manoo. Yenza took Manoo by both arms in a warm gesture of trust and friendship.

"Do what you can, Manoo. Hobey-ho."

Manoo stood up straight as if the entire fate of Cloral were now resting on his shoulders. He was now on a mission, and he took it seriously.

"Let's go!" he shouted to the aquaneers, and the three took off.

Yenza then turned back to Uncle Press and said, "And why must we leave Panger City?"

Uncle Press looked to me and held out his hand. I knew exactly what he wanted and handed him the two pieces of map.

"Ever hear of the Lost City of Faar?"

In minutes we were back on the speeder boat, blasting away from Panger City, bound for, well, the plan was to head for the Lost City of Faar, but at the time it seemed like we were chasing a fairy tale.

When we put the two pieces of the map together, this is what we saw: The horizontal solid line that was a third of the way up from the bottom on the left half of the map continued on to the right half of the map all the way to the far side. The curved line that began at the lower left corner formed a complete semicircle with another curved line on the other half. It was now a wide, upside-down smile beneath the horizontal line. The spray of dots that was above the horizontal line on the left half of the map was also on the right half. Finally, the series of numbers from the left half continued on to the right.

We had no idea what the horizontal line or the semicircle beneath it or all the dots meant, but Spader and Yenza knew what the numbers meant. They were map coordinates that marked a very specific point in the ocean. We now had a location, but it was a long way off from Panger City. Their best guess was that it would take us all night to get there, even with the speeder boat throttled up to the maximum. Spader set the course and locked it into the speeder's automatic pilot to make sure we wouldn't stray. When traveling that long of a distance, even a minor error could have sent us way off course. Unless something bizarro happened, by morning we would be at the exact spot where the map said we would find the Lost City of Faar.

I was excited, but also pretty doubtful. The idea of finding a lost, sunken city seemed pretty far-fetched. But as Loor said, after all we'd seen, nothing was impossible.

I also hoped that Saint Dane had a lousy memory. He had only looked at the map for a few seconds before Yenza and the aquaneers came in with their water-guns blazing. Hopefully he'd forget a number in the coordinates, or switch two, or mess up something else that would send him in the wrong direction. That's what I hoped for, but I didn't think for a second that it would happen. I knew that Saint Dane now had the same information we did. The real question was how quickly he could catch up. It was going to be a race, but a race to what?

It was a beautiful night and the water was so calm that the stars were reflected in the water in front of us. I was standing on the bow looking out on this awesome sight, when I sensed that someone was behind me.

It was Spader.

"Tell me about where you come from," he asked.

"That's a lot of ground to cover," I answered.

"It's called Second Earth. Don't ask me if there's a First Earth or a Third Earth because I don't know. I live in a town called Stony Brook. We have big cities and farms and small towns just like Cloral, the only difference is they don't float on the water. I think something like four-fifths of the planet is covered with water; the rest is dry land."

"So how do you get around if you can't use skimmers and speeders?" he asked.

"Well, we have cars . . . vehicles that can go long distances on land, and big trains that travel on rails. And, oh yeah . . . we can fly."

"What?" he asked in shock. "You can fly?"

I laughed. "Sort of. We have vehicles that fly. Some are small and hold only two people, others are big enough to carry four hundred."

"Hobey, that's magic!" Spader said in awe.

I guess to someone from another territory that didn't have airplanes, the power of flight was pretty amazing. It was almost as amazing as being able to breathe underwater with plastic globes that molded to your head. Every territory was unique in its own way and believe it or not, I was beginning to like the idea that I was going to see more of them.

"And you have a family?" he asked me.

"Yeah. Mom, Dad, and a little sister named Shannon."

We both fell silent for a while. We knew what we were both thinking. What had happened to our families?

"You know something, Pendragon?"

"What?"

"I believe Press," he said with confidence. "We're going to see them again. But not before some amazing adventures come our way."

I had to smile. Maybe he was beginning to accept our fate.

For the rest of the night Spader and Yenza took turns at the controls and keeping watch. We all tried to get some sleep, but it wasn't easy. We went below to the cabin, where there were some bunks. As excited as I was, I really needed some sleep, and konked out as soon as my head hit the pillow. I planned to sack out for only an hour or two, but as it turns out I slept through the entire night!

What finally woke me up was the sound of the engines slowing. I immediately sat up in the hammock, banged my head on a beam of course, swore to myself, then headed topside.

Uncle Press, Spader, and Yenza were already standing on deck. We must have made some pretty good time because the sun hadn't come up yet. It was still pitch dark and the stars still shone off the water. It was very quiet, especially now that the engines were killed and we weren't moving. I did a complete three-sixty and saw nothing but water.

"Are we here?" I asked.

"Right on the spot," answered Spader.

"It's strange," Yenza said. "According to the charts we're over a huge trench, one of the deepest on Cloral. But my instruments show it to be fairly shallow. I don't understand."

"Could we be in the wrong spot?" I asked.

Spader answered the question. "Not a chance."

I walked up to the bow of the speeder and looked out onto the water. It was so calm that it was tricky to find where the horizon stopped and the water began. Especially since the stars reflected off the water.

The stars. The stars reflected off the water. That's when it hit me.

I ran to the others and shouted, "Give me the map!"

Spader had it. He had glued it together using some kind of, well, glue. I held it up toward the horizon. Then I slowly turned, still holding the map out in front of me until everything lined up and—

"That's it!" I exclaimed.

"What's it?" asked Uncle Press.

"Look," I said, pointing to the map. "The horizontal line represents the horizon. And all these dots above it are—"

"Stars!" shouted Spader. "Hobey-ho, look!"

It was incredible. The dots on the map lined up perfectly with the constellations in the night sky. There was no mistaking it. We were in the right spot.

"Good thing we got here at night," Uncle Press added.

"So then what's this big half circle below the line?" I asked.

I think it hit all four of us at the same time because we all looked at one another cautiously. We knew exactly what that semicircle was supposed to be. If the straight line was the horizon, then anything below it was water. And there was only one thing that was supposed to be below the water in these parts.

"Could it be?" Spader asked in awe.

"I've heard about Faar since I was a girl," said Yenza with reverence. "It's supposed to be the most wonderful place that ever was. It's where Cloral was born. To think that it could be real . . ." She couldn't finish the sentence. The idea was too incredible to her.

"One way or another, we're going to find out," said Uncle Press.

I could tell from his tone of voice that he wanted to treat this as any other expedition. He probably wanted Spader and Yenza to get rid of any childhood fantasies and fears that might get in the way of our solving this mystery.

"Let's all eat something," he said. "Then get ready to dive. As soon as it's light enough to see, we'll have a look at what's down there."

There was a stock of dried fruits and vegetables on board. The thought crossed my mind that these might be poisoned like the rest of the food on Cloral. But since they were dried, they had probably been here for a long time and were safe. So we all sat on deck and ate breakfast. To be honest, it was disgusting. That stuff tasted like shoes. Not that I've ever eaten shoes before, but if I had, I'm sure they would taste like this. But we had to eat something so I pretended like they were Pop-Tarts. Shoe-flavor Pop-Tarts.

Gradually, the sky grew brighter and then the sun began to peek up on the horizon. Soon we were bathed in its warmth and light.

It was time to start our mission. Since this was an aquaneer speeder boat, it was well equipped. There were air globes and spearguns and water sleds. It was decided that Yenza would stay on board while the three of us went sunken city hunting. So Uncle Press, Spader, and I got geared up. We each popped on an air globe and strapped on spearguns.

I didn't have my watch, but I was pretty sure we were past the twenty minutes that you're supposed to wait to go swimming after you eat. I had to laugh to myself. Here I was about to search for a mythological underwater lost city on the other side of the universe, and all I could think about was some old wives' tale my mother told me about getting cramps at a picnic. It was times like this that I really missed her.

"If we see something, we'll surface and let you know," Uncle Press said to Yenza. "But understand one thing. Zy Roder has the same information we do and I guarantee he'll be headed this way. Whatever you do, do not take him on yourself, understand?"

"You're talking to a chief aquaneer, Press," said Yenza with a little bit of an attitude. "I can handle things."

Uncle Press smiled in apology. "Sorry, my bad. Just be careful. Please."

"I'll say the same to you," she said with a little smile.

I was beginning to think that Yenza was developing a "thing" for Uncle Press. Bad idea for her. He wasn't the kind of guy you'd want to start a relationship with. He was on the road a little too much.

"Spader, take the lead," Uncle Press said. "We'll follow on either side of you." He then smiled and said, "Look for a really big city."

"Hobey-ho," said Spader with a laugh.

"Hobey-ho," I echoed.

We all grabbed our water sleds, gave a quick wave to Yenza, and did a giant stride into the water. A few seconds later we were all settled and floating next to each other on the surface.

"Everybody set?" asked Spader.

We were. He dove underwater and Uncle Press and I followed right behind him. We descended in V formation for several feet, then took a look around. Yenza was right. The water wasn't all that deep here. I'm guessing it was maybe sixty feet to the bottom. That isn't very deep at all and certainly no place to hide an entire city. The bottom was fairly barren. For as far as I could see there was nothing but blue-green water and a huge field of low, brown coral. No city. No nothing.

"Let's head this way," said Spader. "It's the way Pendragon lined the map up with the stars."

As we sped along with our water sleds, I saw that this area of the ocean was much less interesting than the ocean bottom around Grallion. There were no plants or kelp fields. There were no farms. There didn't even seem to be any fish. This was the Cloral equivalent of our moon. We traveled for a long way with nothing to see but more nothing. I hated to be the killjoy and say that we should give up, but I was beginning to think we were wasting our time.

I was just about to say something when I saw movement out of the corner of my eye. Quick movement. I looked to my right, but nothing was there. I figured it must have been an eyelash or something . . . until I saw it again. Something moved out there. I saw it a little better this time and thought it was a fish. It made me think back to the big fish that was shadowing Spader and me when we were making our escape from the raiders under Grallion. It was the same kind of thing.

Then I saw it again, and again.

"Did you see that?" I asked.

Spader slowed to a stop and we pulled up.

"What was that?" he asked.

"I saw it too," said Uncle Press.

Phew. I wasn't crazy and hallucinating. But that meant there were strange fish out there who were smart enough to be shadowing us. They were fast, too. And big. Not Moby Dick big, but at least as big as a man.

"There!" shouted Uncle Press.

We all looked to see a green shape moving off to our right. It was far enough away that we couldn't make out exactly what it was, but it was moving a little more slowly than the others so we could at least confirm that it was real.

"I say we follow, mates," said Spader.

"Hobey-ho," answered Uncle Press.

Oh, swell. I really hoped this wasn't a bad idea. We all gunned the water sleds and took off in the direction of this strange green fish. We were at full throttle, but the fish far enough ahead of us that we really couldn't get a good look at it. I felt like it was teasing us and luring us forward. But that was impossible. Fish don't lure people—people lure fish.

"Are you seeing this?" Spader asked.

We all looked ahead to see that the bottom was beginning to fall away. It was getting deeper.

"Stay near the bottom," said Uncle Press. "Don't lose that thing."

I felt the water pressure build around me. At home it wasn't smart to dive any deeper than, say, sixty feet. Going deeper caused all sorts of problems with water pressure and decompression sickness and a nasty thing called "the bends" that you got if you stayed down too deep for too long. But that wasn't a problem on Cloral. I guessed it had something to do with the rebreathing devices in the air globes that kept the right mix of gases in your system. But still, this was deeper than I had ever gone before. It was getting dark, and the bottom kept falling away. We were chasing a big, smart fish into the dark unknown and I was getting scared.

"There's a ridge up ahead," announced Spader.

About thirty yards ahead of us it looked like there was going to be a drop-off. Yenza had said this was the deepest trench on all of Cloral, and I had the feeling we were about to see it. But I was sure this was the end of the line for us. There was no way we were going to go any deeper. We didn't have lights, the water was getting cold, and who knew what was down there?

I also saw that the fish thing we were chasing reached the edge and shot down over the side. I had no plans to follow it.

"Take us to the edge," said Uncle Press. "We'll stop there."

Phew. It was official. The edge was as far as we were going. Uncle Press and I pulled up even with Spader so that the three of us were now traveling shoulder to shoulder. Whatever we were going to see over the edge, we would see it together. A few seconds later we reached the end and looked down into the abyss.

Mark, Courtney, yeah, I'll say it again. What we saw was impossible. It was a vision like I had never encountered in my life and I can't imagine I ever will again. There are unique things in every territory. Some are evil, some are beautiful, and some are just plain spectacular. What we saw fell into the spectacular category. The three of us could only hang in the water and stare in wonder.

"Hobey," said Spader dumbly. "This is a dream, right?"

"If it is," said Uncle Press with the same dumb feeling, "we're all having it."

The bottom fell off into black. We were on the edge of a trench that rivaled the Grand Canyon. As clear as the water was, we couldn't see the bottom or the far side of this trench—its expanse was breathtaking. But what we saw before us made the immense size of the trench seem inconsequential. For what we were seeing was a magical water ballet.

The water below the edge was full of *hundreds* of the same green fish like the one we were just following. But now that we were closer, we saw that they weren't fish at all. They were people. At least I thought they were people. They were certainly people-shaped, but they were covered in a green skin that made them look like they were also part fish. Though they had arms and legs, these looked as much like webbed fins as they did regular old human appendages. Their faces were also covered by the same green skin. I know that sounds gross, but it wasn't.

It was an incredibly graceful sight. They were all twisting and swimming and diving and generally looking as if they were having a great time. It was like watching an amazing aquarium with scores of twirling fish dancing in the water.

Several lights shone up on them from somewhere below. These beams swept back and forth as the fish-people swam in and out of their light. I was totally mesmerized. I felt as if I could watch them forever. It was just plain beautiful.

But then three of these fish-people left the larger group and swam over toward us.

"Uh-oh," I said. "Time to get scared."

"Don't move," commanded Uncle Press.

I didn't, but instantly switched from rapture into near-panic mode. What did these fishies want with us?

Each of the fish-people swam gently up to one of us and motioned for us to follow. Whoa, these things really could think. Maybe they were more "people" than "fish" after all.

"What do we do?" I asked nervously.

"I say we follow," said Uncle Press, already swimming forward.

Gulp. I didn't have time to argue. Spader and I followed. I had no idea what these creatures wanted. Did they expect us to join in their dance? Would it be some kind of insult if we didn't?

I then saw that we weren't joining the main group. These guides were actually leading us deeper into the trench. I had a moment of panic, but Uncle Press said in a calm voice, "It's okay. Just go slow."

Then, below us, something caught my eye. It was the wall of the trench. I first heard a small rumble, and then I saw a crack of light beginning to appear out of the rock face.

"What is that?" asked Spader, his voice cracking with tension. Good. I wasn't the only one who was chicken.

The crack of light grew larger and larger and we soon saw

that it was actually some kind of rock door that was opening up. Then, as if on cue, all of the dancing fish-people gathered together like, well, like a school of fish, and all swam together *into* the light! They dove as a group, sped down, and disappeared into the rock wall.

Our three guides were still with us. They motioned for us to follow, and then they, too, dove down toward the light.

The three of us stayed where we were. Even Uncle Press seemed a little reluctant.

"What do you think?" I asked.

Uncle Press looked down at the three guides who had stopped again and were gently motioning for us to follow. He then looked up to us and said, "I think the Lost City of Faar . . . isn't lost anymore."

CLORAL

If I had only one sentence to describe what it was like to be a Traveler, it would be this: "Just when you think you've seen it all . . . you haven't."

As if fluming from one bizarre territory to another wasn't enough, within each of these territories I kept finding new and different places that had my head swimming—no Cloral analogy intended. I guess I shouldn't be so surprised. It would be the same thing for a first-time Traveler coming to Second Earth. To go from a city like Chicago to the rainforests of South America to a tundra village in Siberia would be just as rattling. Still, what we found under the ocean of Cloral went way beyond my imagination.

As strange and exciting as it was for me, it must have been a hundred times more bizarre for Spader. To him the Lost City of Faar was a fable. Could you imagine walking through the forest and finding a hut where seven dwarves lived with a beautiful princess? Or stumbling upon Noah's Ark? Or finding the Garden of Eden? Every culture has its myths and legends. I can't imagine what it would be like to discover that one of them was true. But that is exactly what Spader experienced when we swam through the rocky entrance to the Lost City of Faar.

I wasn't totally convinced it was a good idea to follow these fish-people into the opening in the wall of rock. So far they hadn't done anything but frolic, like playful sea lions. But still, they could have been luring us to our deaths. Did these strange creatures feed on excited divers who followed them without a question, convinced they were about to discover the truth behind a myth, only to be served up like reverse-sushi? As always, my mind went to the worst possible outcome.

What changed my thinking was something I saw just below the opening. It was partially hidden by a tangle of sea-weed, but there was no missing it because it was about five feet across. It was an ancient carving. Some of the detail had been eroded away by time, but there was no mistaking the strange, interlocking letters. Spader saw it too and smiled at me. It was the symbol his father had left for him. It was the symbol of Faar. We were in the right place.

With a glance and a nod to each other to show we were all prepared to go to the next step, the three of us swam together, shoulder to shoulder, into the light that blasted from the large opening.

We found ourselves in an underwater tunnel that was big enough to drive a car through, if you happened to have a car that could drive underwater. We passed by the big lights that were shining out into the open sea. Once past them, my eyes adjusted to the dark and I saw that the tunnel led far back into the rock. Every few feet were small marker-lights that showed the way. That was a relief because I wasn't so sure I would have had the guts to swim into a pitch-dark tunnel. I then heard a loud, scraping sound that made me quickly look back. The rock door was shutting behind us. A loud *crunch* told us the door was locked into place and we were closed in. Gulp. We had to go forward whether we liked it or not.

"Everybody cool?" asked Uncle Press.

"I guess," was my shaky answer.

Spader just floated there with wide eyes.

"Spader, you okay?" Uncle Press asked.

"Just a little nervous," he answered.

Good. I'm glad he said it first. Truth be told, nervous didn't quite cover it for me. My heart was thumping so hard I was surprised the others didn't hear it. Then something touched my shoulder.

"Ahhh!" I screamed, and spun around.

It was one of the fish-people. Man, those guys were quiet. Like snakes. That's why I hate snakes—too quiet. Did I tell you that?

The fish-guy motioned for us to follow and swam into the tunnel. The three of us had no choice but to follow. We swam close together. It felt safer that way. The tunnel was pretty long and not all that interesting. It gave my mind time to wander and I started to think about what this lost city was going to be like. I wondered if it was completely underwater. That would be weird, like living in one of those fish tanks that people decorated with little castles and sunken ships.

So far the fish-people hadn't tried to communicate with us other than with hand signals. I wondered if that meant they couldn't speak. I hoped that a Traveler's ability to understand all languages included sign language.

These questions, and a whole bunch more I hadn't thought of yet, would soon be answered, for I saw that the tunnel was growing brighter.

A few moments later the water level began to drop. We were soon able to raise our heads above the waterline. The farther we traveled, the lower the water got. We went from swimming underwater, to swimming on the surface, to walking along the bottom. That answered my first question. Faar may have been underwater, but it was dry. That was cool. I didn't like the idea of hanging out in a fish tank.

The water got low enough so we felt comfortable taking off our air globes. We were now standing in the tunnel with only a few inches of water lapping at our feet. I looked forward and saw that the tunnel was about to make a right turn. The bright light that came from around the bend up ahead told me that we were soon going to see the Lost City of Faar.

We took off our fins and our spearguns, placing them in a safe pile along with our water sleds.

The fish-man we had been following then walked back to us. Yes, I said walked. On two legs. I had a brief memory of *The Creature from the Black Lagoon,* that goofy old black-and-white horror movie. But if this guy wanted to do us any harm, he would have done it back in the water so I wasn't scared. Much. He reached up to his head and began to peel away the green layer of skin that covered his whole body. It made a wet, sucking sound as he tugged on it. For a second I thought I would puke. If this were some kind of snakelike skin-shedding ritual, I'd rather not have to see it, thank you very much.

But after a few seconds I realized what was really happening. As the light green layer of skin came off, it revealed a guy who was very much human. The green stuff wasn't skin after all; it was some kind of fish suit. It reminded me of those tight suits that speed skaters wore in the Olympics. It was absolutely formfitting. But unlike speed skaters, this suit also gave the swimmer webbed feet and hands. Once the suit was pulled off, I saw that the guy's hands were normal too. No webs, no scales. Underneath the fish suit he wore a blue, also formfitting, suit that went from his neck to almost his knees. It wasn't all that different from the clothes we had on ourselves.

As it turned out, there was nothing unusual about the guy at all. He was short, not much over five feet. But he looked strong. Not a lot of fat on those bones. I couldn't tell for sure how old he was, but I'd guess he was around thirty, in Second Earth years. He was also completely bald. Michael Jordan bald. That wasn't all that weird, but something about his face wasn't quite right. I couldn't figure it out at first, but then it struck me: He didn't have eyebrows. You never think about eyebrows until somebody doesn't have them. It's kind of freaky-looking. Not horrible, just freaky. Adding to the freaky quotient was the fact that his eyes were the lightest color blue I had ever seen. I actually had to look close to see that there was any color in them at all. His skin was also very white, which didn't surprise me since he lived underwater.

In all, he was a fairly normal-looking guy, with a few strange characteristics. But nothing that would give me nightmares or anything. Things were looking up.

The guy finished pulling off his suit—it was all in one piece—and walked up to us. "My name is Kalaloo," he said with a warm smile.

"Are we in . . . ?" Spader asked, a little dumbfounded.

"Faar?" the guy said. "Yes. This is Faar."

We all exchanged quick glances that said, "We made it!"

Uncle Press said, "My name is—"

"Press, yes, I know," said Kalaloo. "And you're Pendragon," he said to me. "And you're Spader. You look like your father."

Whoa! Underwater-guy knew who we were?

"You knew my father?" Spader asked in wonder.

"I was sorry to hear of his death," the guy said with sympathy. "He was a friend."

"Time out," I said. "How do you know us?"

"Spader's father told us there would be others. We have been expecting you for some time, and watching you as well."

"I knew it!" I blurted out. "I saw one of you under Grallion when we were escaping from the raiders!"

"Yes, that was me," he answered. "I wanted to make sure nothing happened to you. I almost failed when you were being pulled into the engine of their ship."

"That was you?" I said in shock.

He smiled and nodded. "It was very close."

"Well, uh, thanks," I said.

"Thanks" didn't cover it.

The guy had saved my life. My head was spinning. It felt like we were three steps behind, again.

"How do you breathe underwater?" I asked. "You don't have gills or anything, do you?"

Kalaloo let out a warm laugh and said, "No, but sometimes I wish we did."

He lifted up the green suit and showed us that built into the fabric was a small, shiny silver mouthpiece.

"This pulls oxygen from the water; it's very efficient."

This looked like a smaller version of the harmonica thing on the back of the air globes.

"I was hoping that Osa would be with you," Kalaloo said. "Will she be joining us soon?"

I looked to Uncle Press, who answered the tough question.

"Osa is dead," he said solemnly.

Kalaloo looked genuinely hurt. "She had a daughter," he said.

"Her name is Loor," I said. "And she's everything her mother wanted her to be."

"I am saddened to hear of Osa's passing," said Kalaloo. "She will be missed."

There was a silent moment of respect for Osa, then Kalaloo said, "We should go. They're waiting for you at The Council Circle."

"Who is?" asked Uncle Press.

"The Council of Faar," he answered. "They are anxious to hear from you."

The three of us exchanged looks. They were waiting for *us*? This was all very strange, but there was no reason not to play along, so we followed Kalaloo toward the light.

As we walked I noticed that the ground was now completely dry. When we rounded the corner of the tunnel we stepped into an area that looked like a locker room—Faar-style. There were several people there, all pulling off their green fish skins. They must have been the swimmers we saw outside. They all had the same look as Kalaloo: light skin, bald, no eyebrows, and bluish eyes. It was kinda freaky, but I was already getting used to them. What should I call them? I wondered. Faarites? Faarmers? Faarbarians? I soon learned to refer to the people there as "Faarians."

They hung their swim skins on hooks and then put on these soft, white tunics that had a little bit of an ancient Roman feel. These gowns pulled down over their heads and went to above their knees. They tied them tightly at the waist with pieces of cloth that varied in color from rich green to deep red. Nobody wore shoes, not even sandals.

As Kalaloo led us past them, many of the people smiled and welcomed us.

I said "hi" back as many times as I could. I wanted to show them that I was cool too. It got to the point where I was walking backward to keep eye contact with them. I kept walking backward until I walked right into Uncle Press.

"Oops, sorry, didn't mean to—" I turned around and froze. The words caught in my throat. That's because I had just gotten my first glimpse of the Lost City of Faar. Or maybe I should call it the Found City of Faar. Maybe I'll just call it Faar. Or maybe I'll just call it . . . phenomenal.

Where should I start? Yet again, I was about to enter an entirely new and amazing place. I had to keep telling myself that according to legend it once existed on the surface. If that were true, then this city would be plenty cool. But when you factor in that we were sitting hundreds of feet below the ocean—well, then it became unbelievable.

As strange as this may sound, I was looking out at a rocky mountain. I know, that's impossible, but that's what it was. The city was built into and around the craggy ledges of a small mountain. The mouth of the tunnel was closer to the top than the bottom so we were actually looking down at most of Faar.

The city had an ancient feel to it. There were no modern buildings, no cars, and no sign of technology anywhere. But there were plenty of birds. Can you believe it? Birds were flying in this underwater cavern!

The buildings had an ancient Greek look with marble staircases that led up to the columned entryways of domed structures. They were perched all over this craggy mountain and ranged in size from huge, impressive monuments like you'd see in Washington, D.C., to small simple stone houses made of whitewashed stucco. I saw many Faarians strolling along gentle pathways that snaked in and around and up and down and everywhere in between. There were beautiful, hanging vines draped over most of the city and several waterfalls cascaded from springs hidden deep in the mountain.

Far below, at the base of the mountain, I saw lush, green

fields. There were some larger buildings down there that didn't seem as elaborate as the ones that dotted the mountain. I made a mental note to ask what they were later.

Remember, we were underwater. A major detail that I've left out is that the whole place was protected by a glittering dome. There was no sky, only a vast dome that allowed filtered light to make this city as bright as day. I now understood what the upside-down smile on Spader's father's map was. It represented the dome that protected Faar.

Kalaloo let us stand there for a while to soak in this wondrous sight. He must have known how amazed we were. Finally he asked Spader, "Is it what you imagined?"

"Hobey," Spader said in awe. "It's like someone reached into my mind and pulled out everything I ever thought about Faar and made this."

"I have to admit," said Uncle Press, "I'm not familiar with the legend."

"Let's walk," said Kalaloo.

He led us along a gently winding path made of soft sand. That was good, since none of us wore shoes.

"I think the myths have grown larger with time," he began. "But I can give you the simple story. In the beginning Faar was the only dry land on Cloral. The myths say that it sank after a cataclysmic event, but that isn't exactly what happened. The simple truth was that the waters of Cloral rose. Luckily it took a very long time to happen. The Council of Faar knew the water was coming and had time to prepare. A giant dome was erected over the center of the city. What you see here was only a small part of Faar. It wasn't possible to save it all. The waters began to rise even as the dome was being constructed. It was a race. By the time Faar was completely sealed and safe, the water was nearly to the top."

I thought back to our swim to get here and realized that while we were skimming across the shallow reef, the city of Faar was down below us, hidden by a skin that looked like coral.

"Why does the dome look like coral from up above?" I asked.

"Because it is," Kalaloo answered. "At first the dome was crystal clear, but over time the coral grew and enveloped it. For the longest time it was kept clear, but eventually the Council of Faar thought it best to allow the coral to hide us. However, we keep the covering thin so that light can find its way through."

We continued to walk through this amazing city. People strolled by us and always gave a friendly wave. They were all pretty mellow. I heard soft music coming from one of the buildings we passed. It sounded like that New Age stuff you hear in the dentist's office that's supposed to calm you down before they drill into your head. Not exactly my taste.

"Why did you decide to hide?" asked Uncle Press.

"Faar was the beginning of life on Cloral. It grew into an advanced civilization that used water for power and created building materials from the silt under the seabed. But people eventually grew restless. Long before the water rose, adventurers built ships and left to explore the rest of our world. They went in search of other dry land, but there was none to be found. Those people lived with many hardships as they struggled to survive on the ocean. Generations passed and because Faar was the only civilized place on all of Cloral, it became a target. The sons of Faar who left in search of adventure now returned as enemies in a desperate search of food. Faar was in danger of being destroyed. So when it was discovered that Faar was going to be swallowed by the sea, it was considered a miracle that gave us our only hope of salvation."

"So when the city sank, you stayed hidden underwater to protect the city from the descendents of people who were born here?" I asked.

"Exactly. The people in the ships above had to create an entirely new world from nothing. Many died to pave the way for the mighty habitats you see today. The fact that they've come as far as they have is due to their undying spirit to survive, and because of the people of Faar."

"What do you mean?" asked Spader.

"From the time the Council of Faar decided that we would remain hidden, it was declared that we would do all we could, secretly, to help those who remained living on the surface of the water. How could we not? They were our brothers. It became the principal goal of all Faarians. The Clorans, which we call the people above, needed all the help they could get to help them. We would secretly tend their underwater farms. We led them to mines which held material for building. We even saved many from drowning as they struggled to build the habitats."

"Just for the record," I interrupted, "you keep saying *we* like you were there. You're not like, ancient, are you?"

Kalaloo laughed and said, "No, not at all. Most of what I am telling you was passed down to me by my ancestors. There are at least two hundred generations separating me from the Faarians who built the dome."

"Okay, cool, just wondering."

"Make no mistake," Kalaloo continued. "If not for the people of Faar, the Clorans would not have survived to become the great society they are today. We are all very proud of this, and still do all we can to help our brothers above."

Uncle Press asked, "What do you know of the trouble that's facing them right now?"

"This brings us to the meeting we must attend at the Council Circle," said Kalaloo. He suddenly became serious.

"We first heard of the problem from Spader's father. It is a very rare occasion that a Cloran stumbles upon Faar, but your father was not a typical Cloran. It was like he had a much greater sense of . . . purpose."

I knew exactly what Kalaloo meant. Spader's father was a Traveler. He totally had a greater sense of purpose.

"And I sense that you three are much the same," he added.

Right again, fish-man.

"What did he tell you?" asked Uncle Press.

"He said he feared a great plague would soon come to Cloral that would endanger every living person."

I shot a look to Uncle Press and Spader. It seemed as though Spader's dad saw Saint Dane's plan coming. The horrible thing was that he became a victim before he could stop it.

"Did he know exactly what was going to happen?" Uncle Press asked.

"He was afraid that something might damage the crops," answered Kalaloo. "From what we have seen, he was right. We are receiving word from all over Cloral that underwater farms are now producing poisonous crops."

"It's the fertilizer," I said. "It makes plants grow faster, but they become poisonous."

"Why did my father come to you?" asked Spader. "Was he trying to warn you?"

"Yes," Kalaloo answered quickly. "But he also came looking for help. Our knowledge of the life cycle is far greater than the Clorans'. He wanted to know if we could do anything to help prevent such a disaster."

Kalaloo fell silent. The big question hung in the air. Was Spader's father right? Could the answer to battling the deadly chain reaction be found right here in Faar?

"Well?" Uncle Press finally asked. "Can you help?"

"Absolutely," answered Kalaloo with a smile.

He pointed down to the bottom of the mountain of Faar and to the large buildings I described before.

"Those buildings contain the life of Cloral," he explained. "For hundreds of generations we have studied every variety of plant that exists here. To put it simply, we know how Cloral works."

"So, what about the poisonous plants?" I asked.

"We have already analyzed samples of the mutated plants. We found that their cell structure was changed and their chemistry corrupted. This new fertilizer created a very complex problem, but we have the means to undo it. Even now we are preparing to send hundreds of Faarians out to the underwater farms of Cloral with a simple chemical compound that will reverse the damage. It is a large task, but we have the means. But the Clorans must stop using the fertilizer."

"That's already happening," said Uncle Press. "They know the damage they've done and they're going to stop."

Kalaloo broke out in a big smile.

"Then you are giving me wonderful news!" he said happily. "Once the Faarians reverse the damage, the crops will be safe again!"

Kalaloo was thrilled that everything was well on the way to being put right.

But we knew differently.

Uncle Press looked worried. So did Spader. An absolute feeling of certainty came over me that made me shiver. I knew what the final act of this conflict was going to be.

These brilliant, ancient people held the key to saving all of Cloral. There was no doubt about what that meant. Saint Dane was going to attack Faar to prevent them from saving the territory.

The people of Faar had been protected for centuries by the waters of Cloral, but they couldn't hide any longer.

Saint Dane knew where they were, and he was coming.

I had no idea if these brave people were capable of defending themselves, but we were going to find out. I'm going to end this journal here, guys, because, whatever is going to happen, I'm sure will happen soon. This journal was written and sent to you from Faar, an amazing city of guardian angels that is hidden hundreds of feet below the waters of Cloral.

Unfortunately, it won't be safe much longer.

END OF JOURNAL #7

● SECOND EARTH ●

Mark finished reading the journal before Courtney and sat down on the floor with his back leaning against his desk. Of course he feared for Bobby and Press and Spader and for the battle that was soon to erupt on Cloral. Actually, he wondered if the battle had already taken place. Was Bobby on Cloral in the past? Or was it the distant future? Or was everything happening at the same time as events here on Second Earth? The whole relative timeline thing was one of the many great mysteries of Bobby's adventures as a Traveler.

It was also tough to read about Bobby's troubles without being able to do anything about them. Not that he had any ideas. And even if he did he wasn't allowed to interfere. Not after what happened on Denduron. His entire job here was to be a librarian for Bobby's journals.

Which was the other thing that was upsetting him. As a keeper of the journals, he was doing a lousy job. He kept glancing at his watch, hoping that Courtney would hurry up and finish and get out of there before Andy Mitchell called back to ask about reading them.

Finally Courtney finished the journal and looked up at Mark.

"Those people can't defend themselves," she said somberly. "From what Bobby described, they're totally peaceful."

Mark stood up and gathered the stray pages together. "Yeah, well, we'll see."

"Aren't you worried?" Courtney asked.

"Of course I'm worried, but what can we do?"

Courtney dropped her head. Mark was right. There was nothing they could possibly do to help.

"It's getting late," he added. "I got stuff to do."

He wanted her out of there because the phone was going to ring any second. She took the hint.

"Right," said Courtney. "The algebra guy."

"Huh?" Mark didn't know what she was talking about. But a second later he remembered his lie and tried to cover.

"Right," he said quickly. "Algebra. Gotta help m-my friend."

There it was again. The stutter. Mark tried not to wince.

"You okay?" she asked curiously. "You're acting all nervous."

"I-I'm just afraid for Bobby.

Mark hated to lie to Courtney, but he didn't know what else to do. Besides, it wasn't a total lie. He *was* afraid for Bobby.

Then the phone rang. Mark shot a look to it as if he wanted it to explode. Courtney caught this look, but didn't react.

"I'm out of here," she said, getting up to leave. "You'll call me when—"

"Soon as the next journal shows up."

Ring. The phone sounded like thunder to Mark.

"See ya," said Courtney, and left Mark alone in his room.

Mark answered the phone before the horrible bell could stab at him anymore. "Hello?"

"Well?" came the dreaded voice from the other end of the line.

"Hang on," Mark said. He glanced out of his window to make

sure Courtney was gone. Moments later he saw her walking down the sidewalk, away from the house. His gut rumbled. He felt like a traitor.

"Let's meet on the Ave," Mark then said into the phone. "That pocket park below Garden Poultry."

"Fifteen minutes," snorted Mitchell.

"Could you make it a little later—"

Click.

"Guess not," said Mark to himself as he put the phone down. He was trapped. He had to bring Journal #6 to Mitchell. Or Mitchell would tell the police about Bobby. There was no way out of this.

So Mark went upstairs to his attic and opened the old desk that was his safe place for keeping Bobby's journals. He took out Journal #6 and replaced it with the one they had just finished reading—Journal #7. He had a brief thought that he should probably just take *all* the journals to Mitchell so he could read them at once and get this torture over with. But he didn't even like carrying around one journal. What if he got hit by a bus? Putting them all together would give him a nervous breakdown.

No, he had to play this out slowly. Hopefully Mitchell would lose interest and just leave him alone. That was his best and only hope. So he slid the drawer closed, made sure it was locked, placed Journal #6 in his backpack and started on his way to Stony Brook Avenue.

It was late Saturday afternoon by the time Mark arrived at "the Ave," as all the kids called it. It was a busy street, full of shops and restaurants and people strolling the sidewalks in search of bargains and their next latte. But it was just past six o'clock, closing time for most stores. The crowds were getting thin.

Mark hurried along the sidewalk, past his favorite shop, a

deli called Garden Poultry. They made the best French fries in history. The smell of hot cooking oil always hovered around the place like a delicious, salty cloud. Normally Mark couldn't resist the temptation and would always go in for a box of fries. (They always came in boxes, like Chinese food.) But not today. Today he had other things on his mind.

He got to the pocket park that was a few doors down from Garden Poultry. They called it a pocket park because it was nothing more than a space between two buildings, like a pocket. At one time there was probably another building there, but Mark couldn't remember seeing one. The town had turned the space into a miniature park with grass, a stone walkway, flowering trees, and several wooden benches where people could eat their · boxes of French fries from Garden Poultry.

It was a pretty little place except for one thing: Andy Mitchell was sitting on one of the park benches, waiting for him. Actually, he was sitting on the back of the park bench with his feet on the seat.

"You're late!" shouted Mitchell the instant he saw Mark.

"You didn't give me much time," answered Mark.

"You got the—" He didn't finish his own sentence. Instead he grabbed Mark's knapsack away from him and dug inside to get the journal.

"Take it easy!" scolded Mark. "You gotta treat these with respect."

"Yeah, yeah, whatever."

Mitchell unrolled Journal #6 and began to read. Mark sat down on the bench next to Mitchell's feet, settling himself in for a long wait. He knew Mitchell was about the slowest reader in history.

As with the last journal he read, Mitchell had to ask Mark the meaning of several words. Mark still couldn't believe that a guy could live to the age of fourteen and still not know the meaning of words like "manipulate" and "elaborate." What a loser. It killed Mark to watch Mitchell clutch the valuable pages with his greasy, nicotine-stained fingers like a week-old newspaper. It also turned his stomach every time Mitchell pulled in one of his signature snorts and hawked it out on the sidewalk. Didn't this guy ever hear about Kleenex?

Finally, after what felt like forever, Mitchell was done.

"Jeez," he said with a touch of awe.

Mark's first sarcastic thought was *Could you be any less articulate?* But he wouldn't dare say it for fear of getting pummeled.

"You think this is all really happening?" Mitchell asked.

"I do," was Mark's simple, honest answer. He wanted to be home.

"Did you get the next one yet?"

Mark thought of how to answer this question, but came to the conclusion that it wasn't worth lying. He was tired of lying.

"Yes."

"Well, I don't want to read it," Mitchell said.

Huh? Mark suddenly perked up. Could it be true? Was Mitchell actually losing interest? Maybe reading the journals was too hard for him. Maybe all the big words were taxing that raisin-size brain of his beyond capacity. Or maybe he was getting freaked out by what the journals meant and wanted to pretend like he had never seen them, like the ostrich who sticks his head in the sand. Whatever the reason, it didn't matter so long as Andy Mitchell left Mark alone and never asked to see another journal again.

"I don't want to read it until I see journals one through five. I feel like I'm picking up a story in the middle. I want to know how it all started."

Mark was crushed. The little bit of hope he had that Mitchell would go away, just went away.

"And I want to read 'em all at once," added Mitchell.

"No way!" shouted Mark. "I am not going to bring all the journals out at the same time. I can't let anything happen to them. The best I can do is show you one at a—"

Mitchell tossed the pages of Journal #6 into the air.

"Hey!" shouted Mark in horror as he dove for the pages that scattered across the park.

Mitchell laughed as Mark frantically chased the pages now blowing around in the wind. Finally Mark got them all together and brushed off the bits of dirt.

"You don't get it," said Mitchell. "You only got two choices— do what I tell you, or I go to the police."

This was going from bad to worse to total disaster. Andy Mitchell wasn't going to go away. That much was clear now. He had gotten a taste of Bobby's adventure and he wanted more. All Mark could do now was try to control the situation as best as he could.

"Okay," Mark said. "But I don't care what you say, I'm not taking all those journals out at the same time. The best I can do is have you come over to my house to read them."

The idea of Andy Mitchell setting foot in his house made Mark feel like termites were digging into his flesh. It was a nightmare of untold magnitude. But he couldn't think of any other solution.

Mitchell smiled. "Okay," he said. "I can live with that. When?"

"I don't know," answered Mark. "It's gotta be when my parents are out. I'll let you know."

Mitchell walked over and stuck his nose in Mark's face. Mark could smell his stale cigarette breath and nearly gagged.

"I like this," he chuckled. "We're becoming regular partners."

Mitchell then snorted, wheeled, and walked away. Mark couldn't take it anymore. The snort put him over the edge. He gagged a couple of dry heaves. He then sat down on the park bench and looked at the rumpled pages of Journal #6. *I'm a failure.*

The next week in school Mark did everything in his power to avoid Mitchell. He went to school late because Mitchell knew he usually went early. He went in a different door every time, just to avoid following any patterns. He carried all his books with him so he wouldn't have to go to his locker. He didn't even go close to the Dumpster area behind the school where so many kids went to smoke. That part wasn't so hard; he never went back there anyway—unless of course it was to jump in the garbage and search for a lost page of a journal sent to him by his best friend who was on the other side of the universe. He didn't like remembering that little adventure.

With all of his planning, Mark had actually gotten through an entire week without seeing Andy Mitchell. But the stress was crushing him. His schoolwork was going south, too. Something was going to have to give soon.

On Saturday it did. Mark's parents had both left for the day and he was looking forward to a long morning of cartoons. It was a guilty ritual he was sure most of the kids at school still practiced, but would never admit to. He had just settled down into the couch, ready for anything Bugs Bunny, when the doorbell rang. For a second he considered not answering it, but if it were a Federal Express delivery for his father, then he'd be in trouble. So he went to the door and opened it. It wasn't FedEx.

"I'm getting sick of you ditching me," Andy Mitchell said as he backed Mark into the house. "What is your problem?"

Mark knew exactly what his problem was. It was Mitchell.

"M-My parents have been around all week," stuttered Mark nervously. "There w-wasn't any g-good time."

"Where are they now?" asked Mitchell.

Mark considered telling Mitchell that they were both upstairs, but he realized he couldn't take another week of dodging Mitchell.

"They're out," said Mark.

"Good! Where are the journals?"

"W-Wait in the living room," Mark said. "I'll get them."

There was no way he was going to show Andy Mitchell his secret hiding place in the attic. Having him know the journals were in his house was bad enough. So while Mitchell sat in front of the TV laughing at Pepe Le Pew, (Who laughed at Pepe Le Pew? Nobody thought Pepe Le Pew was funny!), Mark went to get the journals.

He tried to be as quiet as possible so Mitchell wouldn't know where he was going. Mitchell was the kind of guy who was a step away from juvi. Mark wouldn't put it past him to break into the house and steal the journals. But there was no way he would do it if he didn't know where they were. So Mark quietly went up into the attic, opened the desk drawer, took out the four brown scrolls that were Bobby's first journals, and quickly went back downstairs. He got as far as the second-floor hallway near his bedroom when—

"You got a bathroom?" Mark jumped and yelped in surprise. Mitchell was upstairs, in his face.

"Of course we got a bathroom," answered Mark. "Downstairs, near the—"

Mark felt his ring twitch. Oh, no. He couldn't believe it was happening now, in front of Mitchell. Again.

"What's the matter?" asked Mitchell. "You look sick. You gotta use the can too?"

Mark had to think fast. He didn't want Mitchell to see the next journal arrive. The less this creep knew, the better.

"Use the bathroom in my room," Mark ordered. "It's closer."

Mark would sooner drink acid than let Andy Mitchell go into his room, but it was the only thing he could think of quickly.

"Lemme read the journals while I'm sittin' on the can," snorted Mitchell.

Mark didn't need that image. But then he felt his ring move again. It was starting to grow. There wasn't any time so he handed the four precious journals over to Mitchell and pushed him into his room.

"Let me know when you're done," said Mark, and pulled his bedroom door closed.

Mark had pulled it off. Mitchell would be occupied long enough for Bobby's next journal to arrive. Mark ran down the hallway, yanking the ring from his finger. It had already grown to its largest size and was getting hot. Mark ducked into his parents' bedroom so that when the light show started, there would be no chance of Mitchell hearing or seeing anything.

Mark closed his parents' door, placed the ring on the floor, and backed away. Instantly the glowing lights told him the doorway to Cloral was opening up. With a quick tumble of the familiar musical notes and a final, blinding flash, the delivery had been made.

Mark looked at the floor to see the ring had returned to normal and another roll of green paper had been deposited next to it. For a moment the excitement of getting Bobby's next journal made Mark forget about his problems with Mitchell. He knew that the pages on the floor were going to tell them about the battle for the Lost City of Faar. He wanted to grab the pages, pull them open, and start reading right away. But he couldn't do that for two very good reasons. One was that Courtney wasn't here. They never read the journals without each other. He had messed up a lot recently, but that was one thing he wouldn't fail on. The other was that Andy Mitchell was sitting on his toilet, reading the journals from Denduron. The thought made him shiver.

He didn't want to risk going up to the attic to hide the newest journal, so he ditched it under his parents' bed. The journal would be safe there until Mitchell left. Of course, at the speed that Mitchell read, it might take a week to get him out of there. But that was a risk Mark would have to take.

After stashing the journal under the bed, Mark went back to his room to begin the long ordeal of explaining every other word of the first four journals to Mitchell. He opened his bedroom door and saw that the bathroom door was closed. That was good. He didn't want to catch a glimpse of Andy Mitchell sitting there with his pants around his ankles. Gross.

"Do me a favor, Andy," Mark called out. "Finish what you're doing and read the journals out here, okay?"

Mark didn't want to risk getting the journals wet, with water or anything else.

"All right?" Mark called out.

Mitchell didn't answer. Mark went to the bathroom door and knocked.

"You okay in there?" he asked.

Still no answer. Mark began to panic. Could Mitchell have fallen down and hurt himself? Could he have gotten sick? How would he explain any of this? He had no choice, he was going to have to go inside. But then he feared Mitchell was just being Mitchell and choosing not to answer. The last thing he wanted to do was open the door and catch him sitting on the toilet. But still, he had to make sure nothing was wrong. So he opened the door.

"Are you all—"

The bathroom was empty.

"Andy?" Mark called out in confusion. "Mitchell!"

Mark backed out of the bathroom, totally confused. What had happened? He looked around his bedroom, trying to see any telltale clue that would explain what was going on.

That's when he saw it. His window was open. With rising panic he ran to it and looked out. The roof of the first-floor porch was just below the window. There were many times when Mark and Bobby used this route as a secret way to get in and out of the house. The roof led to a rose trellis on the far side of the house. Climbing down the trellis was like climbing down a ladder.

Mark went into brain lock. The evidence was all before him. He didn't want to accept it, but he had to.

Andy Mitchell had just stolen Bobby's journals.

CLORAL

It's over.

I guess I don't have to tell you guys that I made it, since I'm writing this journal. I'm back on Grallion now, where I'm feeling safe for the first time in a long time. But the sad truth is that not everybody was as lucky as I was.

As I sit here in my apartment reliving the events of the last few days, I'm feeling a little numb. Maybe this is what they mean when they say somebody is in shock. Everything that happened seems like it was a dream. Maybe that's a good thing. When you feel as horrible as I do, then pretending it was all a dream makes it a little easier to handle.

Many people acted bravely, even in the face of death. I think that's what I'll remember most about the ordeal I've just been through. I have met some special people here on Cloral. I hope they think the same of me.

This is what happened.

Kalaloo led Uncle Press, Spader, and me along a winding path that brought us higher up on the mountain. The path ended at a giant outdoor shelter that was perched on a plateau near the peak. We walked up several marble steps to a large, round platform that had all sorts of tile work on the floor. We're talking intricate stuff here. There were elaborate scenes of people building ships and swimming with schools of colorful fish, and even one scene that showed the dome being built over Faar mountain. I guessed this incredible mosaic showed the history of Faar. I hated to walk on it. It was like walking on art.

Around the perimeter of this platform were massive round columns that supported a giant, marble dome. It felt like we had just arrived on Mount Olympus! Above the stairs that led to the platform, attached to the dome was a large, marble symbol. It was the familiar symbol of Faar that Spader's father had drawn for him.

In the center of the platform was a circle of bleachers that were also made out of marble. People were sitting there, gibbering with animation. I counted twelve in all. Men and women, all wearing the same tunic-looking outfits that everyone else on Faar wore. Of course, they were all bald, too. Even the women. Weird. I figured this was the Council of Faar that was waiting to meet with us. Kalaloo led us into the circle and everyone immediately fell silent. It was kind of creepy. We stood at the dead center, surrounded by all these bald people who looked at us with sour expressions, as if we were strangers intruding on their perfect world. The fact is, we were.

We stood there like dopes, not sure of what to say. Finally Kalaloo took the lead.

"We have news," he announced to the group. "Not all of it is good. These brave voyagers are continuing the work of our good friend Spader, who died so tragically."

He walked behind Spader and put a hand on his shoulder. "In fact," he continued, "this is the son of Spader. We must welcome them all."

The twelve members of the council applauded politely, but they didn't have a whole lot of enthusiasm. It was all so stiff and formal. I really wanted to start screaming, "Wake up, people! Saint Dane is coming to kick your teeth in! Hel-lo! You gotta get ready!" But that wouldn't have been cool.

Uncle Press then brought the council up to speed. He told them of the tragic mistake the Clorans made by creating a fertilizer that turned the underwater crops into deadly poison. He told them how thrilled we were to hear that the good people of Faar had the means to undo the harm and make the crops safe again. I have to admit, he was good. He strode around the circle like a lawyer presenting his case. Nobody could take their eyes off him.

Uncle Press then gave them the bad news. He told them that a raider had discovered the location of Faar, and was probably headed this way to attack them at this very moment.

This caused a big hubbub. *Finally,* the council was showing some life.

"How did this happen?" one woman demanded. "How could a raider learn of Faar?"

Uncle Press didn't back away from the truth.

"I'm afraid he learned of Faar's location at the same time we did," he answered. "The elder Spader had a map to guide us here, and the raider pilot saw it."

Spader dropped his head in shame, but I gave him a shove. He had nothing to feel bad about. He didn't have any choice but to show the map to Saint Dane.

"Trusting the elder Spader was a mistake," shouted one man angrily. "We should never have let him leave!"

This caused another uproar. The crowd was getting hostile. It was true, we were the ones who were bringing the boogeyman to their doorstep. I couldn't blame them for being angry, but I was beginning to like them better when they sat there like boring, bald statues.

"Please!" shouted Uncle Press, trying to restore order. "There is a larger issue here!"

"Larger than the safety of Faar?" yelled a councilwoman.

"Yes!"

The crowd grumbled, but they wanted to hear what Uncle Press had to say.

"The man who is coming to attack Faar is the same man who poisoned the crops," Uncle Press said. "He wants nothing less than the destruction of Cloral. Spader's father realized that. If he didn't come here, you wouldn't have learned about the disaster until it was too late. Now there's a chance to stop it."

"But he brought the shark to our very door!" a man yelled angrily.

"The shark was already at your door!" Uncle Press shot back. "Did you think the people of Faar would be immune? You eat from the underwater farms, don't you? How many of you would already be dead if you hadn't been warned?"

No one said anything because Uncle Press was right. If Spader's father hadn't gone to Faar and sounded the alarm, there would be many more dead than the people of Magorran.

I saw the council members exchange worried glances. Their perfect world was looking a little bit shaky right about now.

"I beg you," said Uncle Press with passion. "You must send out the Faarians to begin the process of saving the farms as soon as possible. That's what this man is coming for. He wants to prevent you from saving Cloral."

"And who will save Faar?" one woman demanded to know. "We are not warriors. Our sole defense has been secrecy. We have no weapons to fight with, no shields to protect us."

Good question. Nobody had a good answer.

Finally someone spoke up. "Maybe there is a way," Spader said to the group. "Right now floating above us is an aquaneer from Grallion. I can swim up in a jiff and tell her the score. It wouldn't take long for her to get back to Grallion, gather a force of aquaneers, and return to stop the raiders. It would be a real natty-do, but I trust my aquaneers against a band of raiders any day!"

"That will never do," said Kalaloo. "You would have to reveal the existence and location of Faar. Think of what we would be giving up in exchange for their protection."

"Think of what you'd be giving up if you don't get any protection," Uncle Press countered.

It was a tough choice. Nobody was quick to offer an opinion. The decision that would be made in the next few moments, no matter what it was, would change the future of Faar and of Cloral forever.

That's when an elderly man who had been quiet up until now, stood up. This must have been out of the ordinary, because every one of the council members seemed to snap to attention. It was clear that this guy had their respect. I got the feeling that he didn't speak much, but when he did, the others listened. In other words, he was the *man*. He spoke slowly and with a soft rasp.

"We have been preparing for this day since the waters closed over our city," he began. "No one, not even the builders of the dome, expected us to hide until the end of time. Cloral is a changed world. Mostly, for the better. I believe it is time for us to rejoin it."

This caused some quiet murmuring among the council members. Finally a woman stood and said, "Are you suggesting we transpire?"

I'm not sure what "transpire" meant, but the woman said it with such horror that I'm guessing it was a pretty dramatic thing.

"No," the elderly man answered. "Nothing that drastic. I am suggesting we move slowly and reintroduce ourselves to our brothers above."

"Can I remind you?" interrupted Uncle Press. "We have to move quickly to save the underwater farms. If we don't you may not have any brothers left up there to reintroduce yourselves to."

The council members shared troubled looks. They were about to make the most important decision in the history of this city since they discovered the waters were going to rise up and swallow them. It was pretty intense.

I finally got the guts up to say something.

"You've been helping the Clorans forever," I said, trying not to let my voice shake. "Maybe it's time you let them help *you*."

The elderly man locked eyes with me. He may have been old and frail, but those fierce eyes told me he was a force that shouldn't be taken lightly.

"What is your name?" he asked me.

"Pendragon."

He seemed to be sizing me up, and it was giving me the creeps. I suddenly wished I had kept my mouth shut. But then he gave me a small smile.

"Much has been said before this council today, all of it well-intentioned. But the words of the youngest ring the clearest."

He then turned to the council and continued with conviction. "It is time to accept help from those we have helped for so long. All in agreement with sending young Spader to return with his aquaneers, say 'ho.'"

The responses didn't come all at once. Nobody wanted to go first. But eventually each council member responded with a "ho," and with every response, they became louder and more assured.

"All against, say 'no.'"

There wasn't a single "no" to be heard. The elderly man then turned to us and said, "We have set a new course. Young Spader, please go now. We must act swiftly."

Spader looked to Uncle Press and me. His eyes were alive with excitement. He was born for this moment.

"Will Yenza do this?" Uncle Press asked him quietly.

"You know that answer," Spader said with absolute conviction.

"Then what are you still doing here?" Uncle Press said with a smile.

"Hobey-ho!" I said, and gave him a reassuring clap on the shoulder.

"Don't start the do without me, mates!" he said, then turned and bounded off the platform.

I could only hope that he got to Yenza fast, and that her help wouldn't be too little, too late.

"Now," said the elderly man. "There is the matter of the underwater farms. Kalaloo, are we prepared?"

"I believe so," he answered. "The crafts are being loaded."

"Then off you go," the man commanded.

Kalaloo said to us, "Come. You'll want to see this."

We definitely wanted to see how the Faarians were going to save the underwater farms. It seemed pretty impossible to me, but as I've learned, nothing is impossible.

After a respectful bow to the council members, we started off the platform.

"Pendragon!" called the elderly man.

I stopped and turned back to him.

"This fellow who wants to harm us . . . should we truly fear him?"

Now *there* was a question. What he was really asking me was if Saint Dane were capable of destroying Faar. I had to answer this question as truthfully as possible. I didn't want the council to second-guess their decision. I held the old man's gaze so he knew how serious I was.

"I could just say yes," I began. "But the absolute truth is that he is evil beyond your imagination. You can't back down from him. The biggest mistake you could make would be to not fear him enough."

The old man nodded in understanding. He looked tired. He raised his hand to me in thanks and to tell me to get going.

Kalaloo hurried us off the council platform, along a different path down the mountain and into a tunnel that brought us into Faar's mountain. We walked along a narrow hallway that brought us deep inside the city. I was amazed to see wonderful works of art hanging on the walls. Most were posed portraits of stern-looking men and women. I figured they were past council members, but didn't bother to ask. We had more important things to do than study art history.

"We must go to the base of the mountain," explained Kalaloo. "That is the staging area."

"It's a long way down," said Uncle Press.

"Not the way we're going," answered Kalaloo.

We arrived at a big tube. It came down through the ceiling and disappeared into the floor. There was a door in the tube right in front of us, and I imagined there were more doors if you walked around. Kalaloo led us through the door into a small room that was no bigger than an elevator. As it turned out, that's exactly what it was. The big tube held four elevators.

Kalaloo grabbed a lever on the side of the room and pushed it forward. I heard a *whoosh* of air, and a moment later we were on our way down. We were hauling, too. There wasn't any door on this thing and seeing the floors fly by made it seem even faster. I held on to the side of the car nervously. Kalaloo laughed.

"Do not worry, Pendragon. You are floating on a cushion of air. That is how we power so much of Faar, with air that is compressed through channels built into the mountain."

That was cool. But until we were on firm ground again, I had to hope this aerovator wouldn't spring a leak. We descended so fast my ears popped. Kalaloo then eased up on the throttle and we began to slow. A moment later we gently touched down.

"Like floating on a cloud," I said, trying to sound casual, but my voice cracked.

Uncle Press laughed. He knew I was freaked out.

Kalaloo led us out through another long corridor that soon brought us back into daylight. As soon as we stepped outside I looked up to see that we were at the base of Faar's mountain. It was a pretty majestic sight, this mountain city with the glittering dome covering it.

We hurried along a pathway that led to the large buildings I described to you before. We passed many other Faarians along the way. I couldn't help but notice that the people down here were moving a little more quickly. Where everyone else was kind of strolling around, enjoying the weird music, these guys down here had jobs to do.

"The mutated crops may be deadly," Kalaloo explained, "but the cellular change that occurred was a fairly simple one. We have prepared a chemical compound that when spread over the living plants will quickly reverse the process."

That sounded good, but we weren't talking about sprinkling plant food on a rose bush. We were talking about thousands upon thousands of acres of farmland. I didn't care how advanced these guys were, that was a big job.

"How can you possibly spread the chemical over such a vast area?" Uncle Press asked. Great minds think alike. He didn't believe it was possible either.

"That is the easy part," answered Kalaloo with a proud smile.

We were now at the door to the large building. Unlike the ancient, marble structures farther up on Faar's mountain, this building seemed a bit more modern. It reminded me of a big airplane hangar.

When we stepped inside, I saw that my first impression wasn't far off. It wasn't an airplane hangar, but it could have been. The space inside was vast. The ceiling was high and there were no walls or partitions to divide up the space. It was just one big garagelike room. But the building itself wasn't the impressive part. What my eye first went to was every science fiction geek's fantasy. Since I thought it was pretty cool, maybe that means I'm a science fiction geek too.

Lined up in front of us side by side was a fleet of small submarines. I counted twenty in all. My first thought was that they looked like those helicopters where the pilots sit in big, clear bubbles. They were about the same size and the fronts had similar-looking bubbles. Inside one bubble, I saw seats for two pilots, surrounded by the vehicle's controls. Attached in front was a long mechanical arm that I guessed must be used for grabbing things, kind of like what they have on the space shuttle. Behind the bubble the body of the submarine was light green, which I figured made it tough to see underwater.

Each sub floated in its own individual pen. I looked below

the waterline and saw two large cylinders attached to the bottom of the sub that could only be the engines. Each sub pen had its own big door that I was sure would open when it came time to launch.

The place was pretty busy. Faarians were swarming over the submarines, preparing them for their mission. It looked like they were being fueled up because many of the vehicles had thick hoses attached to the back. These hoses came down from giant bins that were up near the ceiling. But I knew they didn't need fueling, since they used water for power. I wondered what these snaky tubes were for, but waited for Kalaloo to explain. In all, it was a pretty impressive operation.

"We call them haulers," Kalaloo said proudly. "They may not look like it, but at full speed they move so quickly they are nearly impossible to see."

If that were true, then "haulers" was the perfect name because it sounded like they could really haul.

Kalaloo motioned for me to get inside one of the subs. I thought that was cool. The bubble had a door on top that was open, so I slipped down into the pilot's seat. I felt like I was at the controls of a jet fighter, especially since the main control was a stick near my right hand, just like a jet.

"One pilot drives the hauler," he continued. "The other navigates, controls the arm, and delivers the cargo."

"Cargo?" asked Uncle Press.

Kalaloo pointed to the tube that ran from the bins in the ceiling down to the haulers.

"That is the main purpose of the haulers. We have used them to secretly tend Cloral's underwater farms for generations. The back is a cargo area where we carry seed, or fertilizer, or minerals, or anything else that is needed. Right now we are loading the chemical that will save the mutated crops."

Now it made sense. The hoses weren't loading fuel, they were filling up on the chemical that would save the farms. These haulers were like underwater crop dusters.

"How far can they travel?" asked Uncle Press.

"With these twenty vehicles, we can cover all of Cloral," answered Kalaloo.

That was pretty impressive. These guys knew exactly what they were doing. I was beginning to think they were going to pull this off. If their counteracting chemical actually worked, and I had to believe it would, then they were going to bring Cloral back from the brink of disaster. I couldn't wait to see these haulers pulling out of their pens and getting on their way.

"When will you be ready to launch?" asked Uncle Press.

"Soon. They are nearly loaded and final repairs are—"

"Press!"

We all looked up to see Spader running toward us. Uh-oh. He was supposed to be on his way to Grallion with Yenza. What was he doing back here? He ran up to us all out of breath and wild-eyed.

"She's gone," he said, gulping for air.

"What do you mean gone?" asked Uncle Press calmly. "Is Yenza headed back to Grallion?"

"No. I mean she wasn't there when I surfaced. Something's happened to her."

This was bad. My mind already jumped to the worst possible conclusion. Could Saint Dane have gotten to her? She was tough, but she had been alone up there. She would have been no match for a team of armed raiders. I pulled myself out of the hauler and jumped down between Uncle Press and Spader.

"Do you think Saint Dane got to her?" I asked.

A second later I had my answer, but it didn't come from

Uncle Press. There was a low, far-off rumble. It sounded like an explosion. We all exchanged looks, then Uncle Press turned to Kalaloo.

"Get the haulers out *now*!" he shouted.

Kalaloo turned to his team and started barking orders. "Don't load them all! We have to launch!"

Uncle Press ran for the door. We followed right behind him. The three of us blasted outside just as two more explosions sounded. They were coming from outside the dome. They sounded close, too.

Several Faarians stood still, looking around in confusion. They had never experienced anything like this before. As I looked at their faces, my heart went out to them because I knew it was only going to get worse from here.

"He's here, isn't he?" I asked.

"I'm afraid the party just started," said Uncle Press.

CLORAL

The booming explosions were coming closer. There were more of them now, and it was getting scary. The ground began to shake under our feet with each new blast.

"What is Saint Dane doing?" I asked nervously. "Does he have some kind of depth charges or bombs or something?"

Uncle Press said to Spader, "Did you see anything on the surface? Any ships?"

"No, mate," Spader answered quickly. "Nothing!"

More explosions followed. Saint Dane was trying to rip Faar apart.

"Bobby," Uncle Press said. "The Faarians have to get out now."

"Excuse me?" I said, not sure if I believed what I was hearing.

"They've got to get out of Faar. If they stay here, they could die."

"But . . . where are they going to go?" I asked. "There's nothing but water out there."

"You've seen them in the water, you think they'll have any trouble?"

He was right. These Faarians were part fish.

"They've got a better chance out in the water," he added. "If they stay here, they're targets."

"Why are you telling me this?" I asked.

"Go back to the council. Convince them to . . . to . . ." He was having trouble finding the words.

"To abandon ship?" I finished the thought for him.

"Yes, abandon ship," he said sadly. "Spader and I will do what we can to help them launch the haulers."

This was getting intense. He wanted me to tell these people to leave Faar . . . to leave their home. It was a city that for centuries had battled back everything that man and nature had to throw at it. But now they were being threatened by something far more dangerous than people desperate for food, or rising floodwaters. They were now being attacked by pure evil. Even as we stood there, the explosions were getting louder. Uncle Press was right. The Faarians had to get out.

I started to run off but—

"Bobby!" Uncle Press called. "Get your air globe first."

At first I wasn't sure why he was telling me this. About a second later, it hit me. We were stuck in here just like the Faarians. If we had to abandon ship, we didn't have any of those spiffy fish suits with the built-in breathers. We needed our air globes if we wanted to survive . . . and we definitely wanted to survive.

"What about you guys?" I asked.

"We'll do what we can down here then meet you up at the tunnel we entered through. Understand?"

I nodded.

Spader gave me a nervous smile. "We're in a tum-tigger now, Pendragon."

"Yeah. Let's not stay long, all right?"

The two of them headed back for the hauler hangar as I ran for the tunnel that led to the aerovator. Using this elevator didn't thrill me. I always thought you weren't supposed to take an elevator if there was an emergency like a fire or an earthquake. Being attacked by raiders probably qualified as an emergency, but I didn't have time to run all the way up the mountain's paths. I'd probably get lost anyway. So I had to take my chances on the elevator.

I had to circle the big elevator tube until I found a car. When I jumped inside, I realized I wasn't sure of how it worked. I only saw Kalaloo do it once. I grabbed the handle, pulled it toward me and—whoa! I rocketed off the ground so fast my knees buckled. I nearly got knocked to the floor from the force! I was afraid this aerovator was going to launch off the mountain like a missile, so I quickly backed off on the handle and slowed down. Whew!

The next challenge was to figure out which floor to stop on. I first had to get my air globe, then climb back up to the Council Circle.

After rising up for a few minutes, I took a wild guess and stopped the elevator on one of the floors. When I ran out, I passed a lot of Faarians who looked stunned. There were women gathering their kids together and pressing against the rock walls of the mountain. A few people ran past, pulling on their green swimskins. I guess they figured out for themselves that it would be safer outside in the water. But mostly people just stood around, looking confused, and scared. I thought about screaming, "Get out! Get out! Abandon the city!" but figured they'd think I was a nut job. No, if there was going to be an official evacuation order given, it would have to come from the council.

When I got out of the corridor into the open air, I saw that

I was only one level below the rocky entrance to the tunnel we had used. I had made a great guess! So I sprinted up the winding pathway toward the entrance.

That's when another huge explosion hit Faar. This was the closest yet, and it nearly knocked me off my feet. A few Faarians screamed. They had never experienced anything like this before. Hey, neither had I, but at least I knew where it was coming from, sort of. I'm not sure which was worse, being clueless, or knowing that someone totally evil was out there who wanted to destroy Faar.

Back in the submarine hangar, Uncle Press and Spader were doing all they could to help Kalaloo and the Faarians launch the haulers. Obviously I wasn't there to see what I'm about to write. It was explained to me afterward.

The Faarian submariners scrambled into their ships. They all pulled on their green swimskins and lowered themselves into the clear cockpit domes. There were two submariners in each hauler. The whole time explosions rocked the hangar, but they couldn't speed up the process for fear of damaging a hauler.

Finally the first hauler was ready for launching. The airlock door opened behind it and the small craft eased out. Once the hauler was beyond the door, the outer compartment flooded and the ship floated free.

The first hauler was on its way to save the underwater farms of Cloral.

As I ran for the tunnel where we left our gear, the explosions started coming faster. It was like Saint Dane had found his target and was zeroing in. I had no idea what his weapon was, but it was pretty powerful. I could only hope that the

Faarians had built this place tough so it could withstand the attack.

I found our gear right where we had left it and grabbed my air globe. For a second I thought I should bring the other two down to Uncle Press and to Spader, but that wasn't my mission. I had to get to the Council Circle and convince them to abandon Faar. That was the plan; I had to stick to it.

I ran back through the tunnel and made my way out into the light. I quickly debated about the best way to get up to the Council Circle. Should I take the aerovator or just run? Since the aerovator scared me and I had already traveled the paths to the platform once before, I decided to run. It wasn't easy though. Every time an explosion rocked the place, I was nearly knocked off my feet. Once I almost stumbled off the path and would have fallen down the steep, craggy mountain if a Faarian hadn't grabbed me. He saved my life. But I didn't stop to give him more than a quick "thanks." I had to get to the council.

I retraced the route we took before and was soon running up the marble steps that led to the fancy platform and the Council of Faar. I didn't know what I'd find there. For all I knew these people had already left. But when I got to the top of the steps, I saw that they were all still sitting on the round bleachers. They seemed to be in heated debate. I didn't want to step into the middle of it, but I had to. I had to somehow convince these people that the best thing they could do was announce to all of Faar that it was time to leave.

Down in the submarine hangar, the second hauler was ready for launching. The cargo hold was loaded with the precious chemical and the submariners were at the controls, ready to go. Slowly the door at the rear of their pen began to rise. In a few moments the second hauler would be out and on its way The other eighteen haulers wouldn't be far behind. Things were looking good . . .

. . . and then there was an explosion. A big one. It was a direct hit to the air lock behind the hauler that was on its way out. A wave of water blasted in that rocked the hauler forward. The submariners were bounced around like they were in a washing machine. Worse, the half-open door to the sea stopped moving. Several Faarians desperately tried to work the controls to get it moving again, but it was no use. The door was jammed.

Then they discovered something even more ominous. The explosion had done more harm than they first realized. The Faarians discovered that *none* of the doors behind the haulers would open! This last explosion had done some major damage. If they couldn't repair it, then the rest of the haulers would be stuck in their pens, unable to be launched.

While the Faarians frantically tried to repair the damaged controls, Uncle Press told Spader to get out of there and bring back their air globes. Spader refused. He didn't want to leave Uncle Press. But Uncle Press insisted. He reminded Spader that the Faarians had breathers in their suits. If they had to abandon Faar, they would be fine. But as for he and Spader, the Travelers wouldn't be doing much more traveling.

Spader got the point. He didn't want to leave, especially when things were looking the bleakest, but he knew he had to go. So, reluctantly he left the hauler hangar and started up toward the tunnel where the last two air globes were waiting.

At the Council Circle I approached the bleachers and heard some of the arguments that were being made.

"We must protect Faar at all costs!" one woman yelled.

"Cloral cannot afford to lose our knowledge and support."

"It was a breakdown in security," another man jumped in. "We should never again allow an outsider to enter Faar."

Another woman yelled at this man, "Wake up! The secret is out. They know we're here."

"We can recover from this," another argued. "We can lock down. We are impenetrable!"

They were arguing in all different directions and getting nowhere. More important, they were missing the big point. Faar was in mortal danger now. I was about to step into the circle, when I felt a hand on my shoulder. I turned quickly and saw that it was the old man who everyone listened to before.

"What is happening below?" he asked.

"They're starting to launch the haulers," I answered.

"This . . . demon who is attacking Faar," he continued. "What is his goal?"

"That's a tough one to answer," I said truthfully. "But right now, he wants to send Cloral into chaos. That's why he poisoned the crops. The only thing stopping his plan from working is Faar."

"What kind of person would destroy a city so that he can destroy an entire world?" he asked with pain.

"You said it yourself. He's a demon. And he's capable of a lot worse, trust me."

The old man closed his eyes. I guessed he was processing the information. He seemed hurt by the fact that such hatred and evil could exist. For all of his wisdom, the evil that Saint Dane brought to his doorstep was beyond anything he could imagine.

"This is going to sound horrible," I continued, "but you have to abandon Faar."

His eyes snapped open and he shot a look at me like I had just slapped him across the face.

"I don't think he's going to stop until this place is rubble," I added.

"This is our home," he said defiantly. "It is the home of our ancestors. We will not leave our home."

I knew exactly what it was like to be asked to leave home, but I didn't want to go down that road with him.

"I know, it's a horrible thing," I said, trying to sound reasonable. "But if your people stay here, they might die."

"And what if this attack is unsuccessful?" he asked.

"Then they come back," I answered quickly. "Simple as that."

Two more explosions rocked the dome. The old man lost his balance, but I grabbed his arm and held him up before he could spill. The council members fell silent. That last jolt was pretty hairy.

"I don't think there's much time," I said.

The old man looked at me. I saw the pain in his eyes. He had made his decision. He stood tall and walked back into the council meeting. All eyes were on him. No one said a word. He walked directly to the center of the circle and addressed the crowd.

"It is time to act," he said.

He then knelt down to the floor and lifted up a piece of tile. He reached into the space that the tile had covered, and he must have turned a switch or pushed a button or something because the floor began to move. A two-foot-round section of floor rose up and up and up until it became a podium in front of the old man.

The council members watched in awe. Some whispered to each other, but most just stared. I had no idea what was going on.

The podium looked like some kind of control panel. There were four chunks of crystal on top that were about the size of baseballs. One was clear, another green, a third yellow, and the fourth was reddish.

"We have been prepared for such a disaster," the old man announced to the council. "We must not ignore the inevitable."

"No!" a man shouted. "You cannot transpire!"

There was that word again. What was transpire? It sounded like some kind of last resort.

"We will not transpire, at least not yet," the old man responded. "Faar is strong. We may still withstand this attack. But I am ordering the evacuation."

With that, the old man put the palm of his hand over the yellow crystal, and pushed it down. Immediately, it began to glow yellow, and an alarm sounded. At least I think it was an alarm. It was a loud horn sound that I guarantee was heard everywhere on Faar. From what I could tell, this was a signal. It was telling everyone that it was time to abandon Faar.

The council members hung their heads in defeat.

"Go," said the old man with compassion. "Join your families. Be sure they get out. If you hear the safe command, then return. But if you do not, my love is with you all."

Slowly the council members started to file off the bleachers.

One woman called out to the old man, "Come with us. My family will care for you."

The old man just shook his head. "My place is here," he said. "There is still the chance we may need to transpire."

The old guy was going to stay at his post, no matter what. It felt kind of like the sad resolve of a captain going down with his ship. Moments later the council had left the platform and the old man and I were alone.

"What's your name?" I asked him.

"I am Abador," he said proudly. "Senior to the Council of Faar." The guy shuffled over to the bleachers and sat down. He looked tired.

"What is this transpire thing you keep talking about?" I asked.

The old man looked at me with a sly smile. "You have learned much about our world here, Pendragon," he said. "But there are some secrets that are best kept that way. I will tell you this much: The grand city of Faar is a wonderful miracle. Since we were hidden below the sea, we were never attacked by enemies, we never sought to expand our land, we never wanted more than to better ourselves and be the guardians of Cloral. I truly believe this was possible because we were hidden. We did not face the same difficulties or temptations that control the lives of so many above."

He took a deep, tired breath and continued, "There have been preparations. We knew the day would come when our existence would be revealed. It was inevitable. Now that the day is here, I face a dilemma. Should we reveal ourselves fully and become part of Cloral once again? Should we allow this perfect world to be infiltrated and corrupted by the petty concerns of the Clorans? Or is it better to cherish what we once had and not allow the dream to be corrupted?"

"I'm not sure I get the problem," I said. "You're saying you've got a choice between joining the rest of Cloral or being destroyed?"

"That puts it simply," he answered.

"Then if you're asking me, I say it's a no-brainer. You may think the people of Cloral are these horrible boneheads who aren't as advanced as you guys, but from what I've seen it's a great place. People live in peace. They work hard, they have fun, they respect one another, and compared to where I come from, they pretty much have it all figured out."

A few distant booming explosions erupted. Abador looked up.

"And what of this . . . attack?" he asked. "Is this what we have to look forward to?"

"No," I said as strongly as I could. "This is a different enemy. This attack isn't just about destroying Faar. It's about destroying the Cloral I just described to you. And if you call yourselves guardians then you won't roll over and let it happen. Look at it this way, if you give up now, then you've failed all those generations of Faarians who helped Cloral become the place it is."

Abador looked right into my eyes with that same powerful stare that I had seen before. I hoped I hadn't pushed the guy too far. But I felt strongly about what I had said. Here he was thinking Faar was such a special place that he wouldn't want to become part of Cloral. But I didn't think he truly appreciated what a great place the rest of Cloral was. And now that Cloral was in deep trouble, it wasn't time for the Faarians to give up. I didn't know what this transpire thing was, but it sounded to me like it was a self-destruct plan. It sounded like he wanted to destroy Faar rather than let it become part of Cloral. That was dead wrong.

"You must go," Abador said. "I will think about what you have said."

"So . . . you're not going to transpire or anything dumb like that, right?"

Abador glanced over at the control podium with the four crystals. The yellow alarm crystal was still glowing. He chuckled and looked back to me.

"You are very wise for someone so young," he said. "But

do not make the mistake of thinking you know all there is to know."

What did that mean? Before I had the chance to ask him, another explosion hit that made all the others seem like minor fireworks. It was deep, it was loud, and it knocked me off my feet. The marble bleachers shifted and Abador was thrown to the platform as well. I got up and helped the old man to his feet, but he pulled away from me and shouted, "Go! Now!"

"You can't stay here! Let me take you out."

"Pendragon, my place is here," he said with absolute authority. "If the worst comes to pass, and Faar is in danger of being destroyed, I must be here to transpire."

He glanced back at the podium. I now understood, sort of. That podium was the last resort. He said how they had planned for this day, and if all else failed, he needed to be at those controls. I still feared what "transpire" would do, but if this was his destiny, it wasn't my place to challenge him. No, I had said all I could and now it was time to go.

"Good luck, Abador," I said. "I know you'll do the right thing."

"Thank you, Pendragon. You have helped an old man see things more clearly."

There was nothing else to say, so I turned and ran off the platform. When I got to the edge I looked down on Faar and saw what the alarm had set in motion. Hundreds of Faarians were streaming along the paths, flowing out of the mountain like ants from their hill. They were all pulling on their green swimskins, ready to hit the ocean. There were men and women of all ages. Many helped the elderly and the very young to pull on their skins. There was no panic; there were no fights. I wondered if they had practiced this before, like a fire drill.

They were going to get out in an orderly manner, and that was good.

Then something happened that wasn't good. It was a very small thing that didn't mean much to me at first. But a few seconds later the horrible reality hit me like a shot to the gut. It was something that I felt on my arm. It was a little tickle that I scratched without giving it a second thought at first. But then I lifted my arm up and saw it for what it really was, and my heart sank.

It was a drop of water. Nothing more, just a single drop of water. But then, another drop fell on my arm. Just a drop. No biggie, right? Wrong. I slowly looked up and realized with horror that this single, innocent drop of water came from the dome overhead. That could mean only one thing.

The dome that had protected Faar for hundreds of generations was starting to crack.

CLORAL

As I stood on the steps of the council platform I looked up at the glittering dome that had kept the oceans of Cloral away from Faar for hundreds of generations. What I saw looked like rain. The droplets glistened in the light as they fell. Believe it or not it looked beautiful, like thousands of small, glittering diamonds falling from the sky.

But these beautiful gems brought some seriously bad news. If the dome were cracked and letting in water, where would it stop? Could the pounding that Saint Dane was delivering weaken the dome? If that was the case, then the pressure from the millions upon millions of pounds of water might eventually crack it—like an eggshell. That image was too horrifying to even imagine. I could only hope that the alarm was sounded early enough so that Faar would be evacuated.

And the explosions continued. Saint Dane's attack was relentless. The entire mountain shuddered with each new blast. I couldn't imagine what kind of weapon he had that could destroy something that had been rock solid for centuries.

Then I thought of Spader and Uncle Press. I didn't yet know of the disaster that had happened in the hauler hangar. The only thing I could do was stick to the plan. So I ran for the tunnel that would lead us out of Faar and to my rendezvous with Uncle Press and Spader.

It was getting treacherous. Enough water was now falling from the dome that the pathways were getting slippery. Since many of these paths were right on the edge of humongous cliffs, I had to be careful or a simple slip would mean *splat*. So I moved quickly, but carefully. Soon I joined the flow of Faarians headed for the tunnel, and safety. It was still orderly, but people kept looking up at the falling water and I could tell they were on the edge of panic. Still, they held it together and kept moving toward the tunnel.

Then, just as I was about to enter the tunnel, I saw something that totally lifted my spirits.

"Hey!" I yelled.

Spader was coming out of the tunnel, carrying the other two air globes. It was a struggle for him because he was working against the tide of people flowing in the other direction. I stepped to the side of the path, out of the stream, and waited for him. When he finally got to me, he was all out of breath and excited.

"Where's Uncle Press?" I asked.

"It's a tum-tigger down there, Pendragon," he blurted out. "They launched one hauler and then there was an explosion. They can't open the doors to launch the rest."

Oh, yeah, things were getting worse. Faar was on the verge of collapse, and the haulers weren't on their way. Saint Dane was winning.

"Press is still down there," he said. "I think we've got to get him out."

We both looked up at the dome. The water was coming down harder now. Whatever cracks were made by the explosions were getting bigger.

"Let's go get him," I said, and we both ran along the path back into the mountain to get to the aerovator.

It wasn't easy. There were hundreds of Faarians moving in the other direction. We tried to be respectful, but ended up having to push our way through. Now was not the time to be polite. When we finally got into the mountain and to the tube with the aerovators, we saw a pretty huge Faarian guy directing traffic. He was making sure that as each aerovator arrived, everyone got off quickly and kept moving toward the escape tunnel.

Another aerovator arrived and people flooded out. As soon as it was empty, we tried to jump into the car. But this big guy grabbed us both and pulled us back.

"No passengers," he said firmly.

"But we've got to get down to the hauler hangar!" I shouted.

"Don't you hear the alarm?" the man said. "This is an emergency. These lifts can only be used for the evacuation."

This guy was big and he wasn't kidding around. There was no way Spader and I could push past him and force our way onto the aerovator. But we also couldn't take the time to run all the way down to the bottom of the mountain. We were stuck. I had to make this guy understand how important it was that we get down there, so I grabbed him by the arm and forced him to look right at me. When I spoke, I tried to do it slowly and calmly.

"Listen to me," I said. "There are people down there who are in danger. It's really important that we get to them. We have to use this lift. Please let us pass." I didn't act all frantic or threaten the guy or anything. I just tried to get across how important this was. At first, I thought he was going to shove me out of the way, but a strange thing happened. He kept looking at me and I sensed that he was relaxing. It was totally weird. He went from being a brick wall in our way to a puppy dog. He then stepped out of the way, leaving the path open for us to enter the aerovator.

"I understand," he said softly. "Good luck."

Spader and I walked past him, not sure what had just happened. But we weren't about to question it. We got on the aerovator, I grabbed the controls, and we headed down.

"What was that about, mate?" Spader asked. "It's like you hypnotized him or something."

"I have no idea," was all I could answer. I was just as confused as he was. The only thing I could think of was the way Uncle Press had done the same thing to Wu Yenza back on Grallion. She was all ready to throw us out of her office, until Uncle Press talked her out of it. I was thinking now more than ever that the ability to get through people's toughest defenses might be a special Traveler ability, like understanding all languages. This was something I was going to have to learn more about, no doubt about it.

But that would have to wait, for we were almost at the base of Faar's mountain.

"We've got to get them out of there," I said. "This place is going to get very wet, very fast."

"They're all working on the water doors," Spader said. "I'll bet they don't even know what's going on out here."

The aerovator hadn't even stopped moving when the two of us jumped out and ran through the tunnel to get out of the mountain and reach the hauler hangar. One thing I noticed right away was that there were no more Faarians evacuating down here. That was good. Maybe it meant that the city was nearly empty. I could only imagine what it looked like outside of Faar, in the ocean with thousands of green swimmers in the water. I knew they would be okay out there, but if the dome over Faar continued to crack, they wouldn't have a home to come back to.

It was a sad thought, but there were bigger problems to deal with right now. Spader and I ran out into the open to find that it was pouring rain. Water was now flooding through the cracks in the dome.

I looked up at Faar's mountain and was relieved to see that the paths weren't clogged with people anymore. That meant everyone was getting out. From the looks of things, it was none too soon.

We continued running toward the hauler hangar. Spader held the two air globes, and I had mine. I hoped that when we got inside we would find that they had fixed the damage and that the haulers were all on their way. Once that was done, we could get the heck out of Faar and deal with Saint Dane. That wasn't a happy thought.

We were about twenty yards away from the entrance to the hangar, when we heard it.

It sounded like thunder. It was different than the explosion sounds. The explosions were a low rumble. This new sound was like the sharp peal that comes right after a nasty bolt of lightning strikes. But it wasn't short and sweet. No, this sound continued as if it were the longest crack of thunder in history. Unfortunately crack was the perfect word to describe it.

Spader and I froze and looked up to see a sight so horrifying, I hate to even remember it long enough to write about it. The dome that protected Faar from the ocean above was beginning to crack. I saw long slits of light starting to spiderweb their way across the coral-covered surface. In seconds the force of the water would smash through and flood the rest of Faar.

"Uncle Press!" I shouted, and started to run for the hangar.

"No!" yelled Spader, and pulled me back.

It was a good thing, too, because an instant later, a section of dome caved in. It wasn't the whole dome, just one section, but it was directly over us. If I had kept going, I would have been crushed by the torrent of water that was on its way down.

"We gotta get out of here!" Spader shouted.

I couldn't move. I looked up at the broken pieces of dome and the tidal wave of water that was now plummeting toward us. I then looked to the hangar. Uncle Press was in there.

"Pendragon, move!" shouted Spader, and pulled me back toward the mountain. We had maybe ten seconds before the water would hit. Would it be enough time to get to the aerovator? The two of us booked back toward the mountain tunnel on a dead run. We got inside, but we weren't safe yet. As soon as the water hit, it would flood the tunnel and keep coming. This was the beginning of the end of Faar.

I heard a deafening *boom* outside behind us as the pieces of dome and water crashed down. Immediately the water came surging through the tunnel, headed for us. All we could do was run and stay ahead of the torrent that was quickly shooting through the tunnel to get us.

We made it to the tube and saw that our lift was still there. That was huge, because if it hadn't been, we'd be dead. We both dove in and turned back to see the flood of water was rushing toward us. I grabbed the control stick and slammed it all the way forward. The aerovator blasted off so quickly that the two of us were thrown to the floor. I had a death grip on the control lever. There was no way we were stopping. Now our biggest concern was if the rising water would destroy the aerovator tube before we got out. I held my breath, expecting the speeding car to suddenly stop. But it didn't. We kept rising. Moments later we were back to the escape-tunnel level.

The Faarian guy who was guarding the lift a few minutes before was gone. No other Faarians were around. Spader and I ran through the empty corridor. I feared what we would find outside of there. Would the dome have totally collapsed? If that had happened, we might as well stop running because it would be over for us. The weight of the water would be too much. The whole mountain would probably be crushed.

As we got closer to the end of the tunnel that led out of the mountain, the sound of rushing water was deafening. It sounded like Niagara Falls out there. This gave me hope. It meant that the whole dome hadn't collapsed, just the one section that we saw crumble. If that were the case then we still had a shot at getting out. The two of us reached the entrance and cautiously looked outside.

What we saw was both horrifying and wondrous. So far the dome was holding. But there was a huge, jagged hole that must have been thirty yards wide. Water was pouring down so hard, it looked like it was coming from a powerful hose. Imagine a hole thirty yards wide with a solid stream of water powering through. It was awesome, and frightening.

"Pendragon, look," said Spader.

He was pointing down. What I saw made me catch my breath. The water was rising inside Faar. It was only a matter of time before the entire city would be underwater. But that's not what hit me. Spader was pointing to the hauler hangar. The water was rapidly rising and would soon cover the huge building. If this weren't bad enough, the sight that really made my heart sink was near the door where we had been only a few minutes before. There was a pile of rubble that must have been pieces of the collapsed section of dome. It had fallen right in front of the hangar, blocking the entrance. I had hoped that Uncle Press and the Faarians would be protected inside the hangar. Their only hope would be to wait until Faar was submerged, then swim out. Uncle Press could even buddy breathe with one of the Faarians in their swimskins. They would make something work.

But now that the entrance was blocked under a ton of rubble, there was no way they'd get out of there. Now their only hope would be if they could repair the pen doors and escape that way.

"This is bad, Pendragon," Spader said solemnly. "If they don't get those hauler doors open—"

"Yeah, I get it," I said.

The two of us stood there in a daze. There was every probability that the hauler hangar was going to be a tomb for those brave Faarians, and for my Uncle Press.

"We gotta go," Spader then said.

I looked up toward the tunnel that led out of Faar and saw that we had actually caught a break. The rush of water that was powering down from the dome was on a free fall to the bottom. If it had hit any of the paths, it would have wiped them out. But as it was, the paths weren't being hit and we could still make it up to the escape tunnel. There was some rubble from the crumbled dome lying around, but nothing we couldn't jump over or run around. But we had to do it fast. The water level was rising.

There wasn't a single Faarian left. They had all made it out. We got to the tunnel safely, but before ducking inside I remembered something and stopped. I turned around and looked up toward the Council Circle where I had left Abador. I briefly wondered what he was going to do. It was clear now, Faar was doomed. Did that mean he was going to transpire . . . whatever that meant?

One look up at the distant platform told me that whatever transpire meant, it wasn't going to happen. That's because the white marble roof that had protected the Council Circle was gone. It must have been knocked over by pieces of the falling dome. That could only mean one thing—Abador was dead. If he had stayed at the podium, which I was pretty sure he had, then the crashing marble would surely have killed him. And since nothing else dramatic had happened to Faar, I could only assume that it had gotten him before he had the chance to transpire. My heart went out to the old man. His love for Faar and all that it stood for was huge. He had saved his people from a horrible death, but he failed in his last important act. After seeing the dome collapse, he would surely have begun to transpire but he never got the chance. I felt sad for the man who wasn't able to help Faar through to the final destiny that his ancestors had so carefully planned for.

"Uh, Pendragon, can we leave now?" asked Spader.

I turned away from Faar for what was sure to be the last time and followed my friend into the tunnel. We ran past the empty locker room and right to the spot where we had left our gear. Spader put Uncle Press's air globe down next to his water sled.

"You never know, right?" he said.

Yeah. You never know. But you usually have a pretty good idea. I didn't think Uncle Press would be needing his air globe anymore. For a moment time stood still. Seeing that air globe did it. It didn't matter to me that Faar was crashing down, or that Saint Dane was about to destroy Cloral. All I could think about for those few seconds was that I had lost my Uncle Press. After telling everybody else how they had to be strong and do the right thing and make tough choices, all I wanted to do was stand there and cry.

Spader must have realized what I was going through, because he put a hand on my shoulder, and said, "Time for that later, mate. We have to go."

Right. We were outta there. We both grabbed our water sleds and headed back through the tunnel. We soon hit the water. It quickly got deep, first covering our ankles, then our knees, our hips, and then finally became so deep that we had to start swimming. We popped on our air globes, triggered our water sleds and submerged into the waters of the tunnel.

Luckily the lights were still on so we could see where we were going. It would have been tough trying to find our way in the pitch black. We sped along, back through the tunnel, without saying a word. I can't speak for Spader, but I knew where my thoughts were. Though it looked as if we were about to escape the destruction of Faar alive, we were about to enter another mess. No doubt waiting for us in the ocean outside were Saint Dane and his raiders. I only then realized that once the dome cracked, the explosions had stopped. I guess Saint Dane had done all the damage he needed. He had destroyed Faar and kept the haulers from saving the underwater farms. His mission was complete.

The sad truth was that we had failed Cloral. Saint Dane's plan for pushing the territory into chaos was about to succeed. Food would grow scarce, people would fight to get whatever safe supply was left, and who knew how many thousands would die from either starvation or poisoning.

And still, we had to face Saint Dane. He was out there,

waiting for us, I was sure. All we could hope to do now was escape to fight another day.

We swam back to the large rock door that led to the open ocean. The door was wide open, and why not? This wonderful city was history. Why bother to close it? Spader and I shot out into open water, not really sure what we would find.

"Gotta be careful, mate," said Spader. "Don't want to get sucked back into that hole in the dome."

Good point. There were millions of tons of water flooding into that hole. It was like a giant, open drain. It would be easy to get sucked in. I hoped that the Faarians realized this and were keeping their distance.

As we rode our water sleds away from the tunnel to get away from the dome, I actually felt a slight tug, as if we were swimming against a strong current. I knew it was the pull of the water being sucked into the hole in the dome. Luckily we were far enough away that our water sleds kept us moving forward and safe. Did I say safe? Yeah, right. Real safe. I looked ahead and began to see shapes. They were hard to see at first because they weren't much different than the color of the water, but the closer we got, the more distinct they became. In a few moments I realized what they were.

It was the people of Faar. There were thousands of them, all floating in the water, looking back at the coral reef dome that had protected their city and kept it hidden. It was gut wrenching. These people were now all homeless and stranded in the middle of the ocean.

And we were stranded right along with them. I began thinking about how we could find the closest habitat and get the word out to the aquaneers to start picking up these people, when something caught my eye.

At first I thought it was a shadow. But it was really big,

like a shadow from a cloud when it crosses the sun. It was far away and blurry, so I couldn't tell what it really was. What I could tell for certain was: It was coming toward us.

"You see that?" I asked Spader, and pointed toward the moving shadow.

Spader spun around and looked.

"Never seen any fish that big," he said.

"Maybe it's a school of fish, or a whale . . . or . . ."

The words stuck in my throat. As the shadow drew closer, it became very clear how Saint Dane had attacked Faar. I also knew why Spader hadn't seen it coming when he was on the surface.

Saint Dane was in a submarine. It was a huge, black, monstrous-looking craft with a flat bottom and rounded body. My guess was that it fired underwater missiles, just like the battleship he used to attack Grallion. There was no doubt about it, this was a weapon of war, and it was at Saint Dane's command.

"About time you two showed up!" came a voice from behind us.

Spader and I both spun around to see four raiders floating there, each with a water sled and holding spearguns on us.

"Looks like you were the last to leave the party," one laughed. "There's somebody wants to see you."

Two of the raiders moved to either side of us, while the other two trailed from behind, guarding us with their spearguns. They motioned for us to swim along with them. There was nothing we could do. We were trapped and on our way to Saint Dane's submarine.

◉ SECOND EARTH ◉

The phone rang next to Mark's bed.

"Don't answer it," ordered Courtney. She was too involved in Bobby's adventure to stop reading, even for a moment.

"I have to," answered Mark. Though he didn't want to. He was afraid of who might be calling.

"Hello?" Mark answered tentatively.

"Mark Dimond?" came a familiar man's voice over the phone.

"Yes," Mark answered. He wasn't giving up any more information than necessary.

"This is Captain Hirsch, Mark. Stony Brook Police."

Mark's heart instantly started beating faster. This was it. This was the call he was dreading.

"Hi, Captain, how are you?" Mark asked, trying to sound more together than he felt.

At the sound of the word "captain," Courtney's ears pricked up.

"Mark, you're aware that there's a reward out for any information that would lead us to finding the Pendragons, right?"

"Yeah. Twenty-five thousand dollars."

"That's right. Do you know where Courtney Chetwynde is?

I called her home but her parents said she was out."

"Well, yeah. She's here with me."

He looked at Courtney. Courtney raised her eyebrows as if to say, "He's asking about me?"

"That's good," Hirsch said. "I wonder if you two would mind coming down to the station. There's something here I'd like to show you."

Uh-oh. Mark thought he knew exactly what Captain Hirsch wanted to show him.

"Uhh . . . I guess. We're kind of in the middle of something now though."

"How about an hour?" asked Hirsch. "We could send a car for you."

"An hour? Uh . . . y-yeah, okay. I guess we could be finished in an hour. You have my address?"

"Yes, I do," answered Hirsch. "Oh, Mark, one more thing. Do you know a guy named Andy Mitchell?"

That was it. The door holding back Mark's fears was blown wide open. Andy Mitchell had stolen Bobby's journals and it took him all of one day to take them to the police, figuring he'd collect the reward money. The only thing that truly surprised Mark about it was that he'd thought it would take Mitchell a week to read those first four journals.

"Mark, you still there?"

"Y-Yeah, I'm here."

"Do you know Andy Mitchell? Is he a friend of yours?"

Two completely different questions. Mark wondered what Mitchell had said to the police about their relationship. He wondered if Mitchell admitted that he was a bully who had black-mailed Mark into showing him the journals, only to steal them and turn them in for a reward. No, Mitchell probably didn't go into that kind of detail.

"Yes, I know him. But he's not exactly a friend of mine."

"Okay then, we'll see you in an hour."

"Bye." He hung up the phone.

"That was Hirsch? What did he want?" asked Courtney.

"He wants us to come down to the station to show us something."

"Did he say what it was?"

"No," answered Mark. "He's sending a car here in an hour. I figured we'd be finished reading by then."

Mark's mind raced. The drama with Andy Mitchell was going to end in an hour, one way or another. But as anxious as that made him, it didn't even come close to the drama that was playing out on the pages of Bobby's journal.

Courtney said, "I don't want to think about the police until we finish. My mind's not there. That okay?"

That was *more* than okay with Mark. His mind wasn't there either. He didn't want to have to discuss Andy Mitchell or the missing journals or his being an idiot who got blackmailed until they found out what happened to Bobby and Spader and Uncle Press.

"Yeah," Mark answered. "We gotta read."

Mark got back on the bed. He and Courtney stretched out on their stomachs, side by side, with the journal in front of them, ready to discover what happened on that dark day under the oceans of Cloral.

CLORAL

Y ou'd think things couldn't have gotten any worse than they were at this moment: Faar was destroyed. Its entire population was now homeless and floating in the ocean. All but one of the haulers were stuck under tons of water and rubble, unable to save the underwater farms of Cloral. Uncle Press, Kalaloo, and several Faarians were trapped down there as well. If they weren't dead already, they would be soon.

And now Spader and I were being escorted into an ominous-looking submarine full of killer raiders that was commanded by Saint Dane.

As the raiders brought us toward the hovering sub, I said to Spader, "I didn't know they had these on Cloral."

"Same as with the battle cruiser," answered Spader. "Warships were built long ago in case there was a territory war between the habitats. They never had to use them, and a few were hijacked by raiders."

"Quiet!" shouted one of our guards.

It now made sense. Saint Dane was able to fire under-water missiles at Faar. He just kept pounding away at the dome until it couldn't take it anymore.

We were now directly underneath this war machine. I wasn't sure where we were going until I saw a large door slide open in the bottom of the hull. It led up to a large, flooded chamber. It was probably big enough to bring a truck inside. The raiders directed us to swim up and in. I looked into the black chamber above me and stopped. I didn't want to board this evil boat. But a sharp jab in my ribs from a raider's speargun told me we didn't have a choice. So Spader and I swam up inside Saint Dane's city-killing submarine.

We floated in this dark chamber while the hull door slid closed below us. We were now inside, in pitch darkness. A hiss of air told me that they were pumping the water out of the chamber. It didn't take long. Soon we were standing on the hull door that had just closed. The water level kept going down until the chamber was dry. That's when the lights kicked on and I saw something that made this horrible situation even worse.

Sitting next to us in this large chamber was the one and only hauler that had been launched from Faar. Saint Dane must have captured it the instant it left the underwater city. This was totally depressing. Now there was no chance for any of the underwater farms. Saint Dane had won a complete victory. He didn't leave any loose ends.

I looked to Spader, who seemed as deflated as I was.

"Drop your gear!" ordered one of the raiders.

We took off our air globes and dropped our water sleds.

"Let's go. He's waiting for you," commanded the same raider.

With another jab in the side from his speargun, Spader and I were escorted out of this chamber and through the submarine to meet Saint Dane. I had never been in a submarine at home. I had only seen pictures and movies. But compared to the high-tech subs from Second Earth, this vehicle looked pretty simple. I expected to see all sorts of tubes and pipes and valves all over the place, but there were none. It was cramped and the walkways were narrow, just like you'd imagine, but there were very few signs of the technology that ran the thing. It was just like walking down a narrow corridor, with rooms off to either side. I guess that made sense. The Clorans definitely had water technology down cold.

Suddenly there was a jolt. The submarine shuddered and we all nearly lost our balance.

"What was that?" I asked.

"We're surfacing," answered one of the raiders. "Keep moving."

We got to a ladder that led up. Two raiders went up first, followed by us, followed by the other two. They were taking no chances with us. I wasn't exactly sure why. It wasn't like we were going anywhere.

The ladder led us up to what looked like the control room of the sub. Again, it wasn't as high-tech looking as the submarines we know. There were two raiders sitting at dual steering wheels forward. Three other raiders manned various control stations. I'm sure one of them controlled the weapons that were fired at the city of Faar. There was only one other person there, and I'm sure you can figure out who that was.

It was Roder, the pirate pilot. Of course, we knew that it was really Saint Dane. He stood between the two guys steering, looking out of a narrow window at the underwater seascape.

"We found only two," said one of the raiders to him.

Saint Dane turned to us.

"Welcome aboard, my friends," he said with a warm smile. "I just love the toys they've got here on Cloral, don't you?"

We didn't say anything. What was the point? I glanced at Spader and saw that he was grinding his teeth in anger. His hatred for Saint Dane because of what he did to Spader's father had come flooding back. I really hoped he wouldn't do anything stupid.

"And where is my friend, Press?" he asked. "Not still on Faar, I hope."

I didn't answer. But Saint Dane walked up to me and looked me right in the eye. I didn't want him to think that he scared me, so I looked right back at him. It was like he was searching my mind. After a few seconds he shook his head slowly.

"It's all in your eyes, Pendragon," he said. "Press is dead. I am sorry. He was a worthy adversary, but as I've told you before, I cannot be beaten. This is the way it was meant to be."

"No, it isn't," I shot back at him. I couldn't stand hearing those words. "Cloral isn't done yet."

Saint Dane chuckled like I was some kind of stupid kid who didn't know what he was talking about. I hated that. Mostly because he was right.

"Is that what you think?" he asked. "Let me show you something."

He pointed forward and I now saw light outside through the window. We were no longer underwater.

"All clear," announced one of the raiders at the controls.

A raider who had been guarding us stepped to the rear of the control room to a round door in the wall. There was a wheel on the door that he spun to disengage the locking mechanism. He then pulled the door in on its hinges and sunlight flooded into the submarine.

"Please," said Saint Dane, gesturing for us to go outside.

I walked to the door and stepped out, followed by Spader.

The control room was inside the tower above the main body of the sub, so when we went outside, we stepped right onto the top of the hull. The sub was big. I'm guessing from the bow to the tail it was about fifty yards long. The control tower was about two-thirds of the way forward. I also noticed that there were long guns jutting from the control tower. They weren't as big as the battle cruiser's, but I'm sure they were just as deadly.

Saint Dane walked past us and strode toward the bow of the ship.

"Come," he ordered.

Spader and I had no choice but to follow. Saint Dane walked almost to the bow of the ship and the three of us stood there, alone.

"Do you see that?" he asked.

We looked ahead and I didn't see anything at first, but once our eyes adjusted to the light, we saw what he was talking about. It was a giant whirlpool. And I mean, giant. There was no question as to what was causing it. This was the spot directly above the shattered dome of Faar. The swirling water was pouring into the doomed city, creating this monstrous whirlpool. Saint Dane stood there with his arms folded in front of him, smiling, enjoying his handiwork.

Spader said, "Where are—" but Saint Dane held up his hand to quiet him.

"Please, a moment more," he said.

We all looked back to the swirling water to see that he was right. A few moments later the whirlpool stopped. The water was still for a moment, and then a giant bubble of air erupted on the surface.

"That's it," Spader said softly. "Good-bye, Faar."

It was heart-wrenching. That bubble of air was Faar's last

gasp. The city was now completely underwater. The ocean surface was once again still.

Saint Dane then turned to us.

"Now, what were you saying?" he asked Spader politely.

"Where are the pilots from the hauler?"

Saint Dane waved his hand as if this were an insignificant detail.

"We threw them back in the sea," he said. "Two small little fish of no consequence. But they did help us quite a bit."

"How's that?" I asked.

"The moment we saw them launch from Faar, we knew the exact spot to target our missles and cripple their fleet. No more bubble boats emerged," he added with a laugh. "So we must have been successful!"

"You trapped a dozen men down there!" Spader spat out in anger.

"And destroyed the heart and soul of Cloral," Saint Dane replied calmly. "Not bad for an afternoon's work, don't you think?"

I could feel Spader's tension. He was out of his mind nuts with hatred for Saint Dane and was a hair away from lunging at him. But that would have been a huge mistake. So I put a hand on his shoulder. Spader jumped. He really was a raw nerve.

"Calm down," I said as softly as possible.

Spader forced himself to take a breath and seemed to relax a bit.

"Pendragon, I am impressed," said Saint Dane. "You've grown wiser since our adventure on Denduron."

"I beat you on Denduron," I shot back.

"So you think," Saint Dane said. "Honestly, do you really

think I care which territory is my first domino? Cloral will do just as nicely as Denduron. As I told you before, once the first falls, the rest will tumble in turn."

"Cloral hasn't fallen," Spader spat out.

"But it will," Saint Dane replied smugly. "Eventually they will find a way to purify the crops, but not before thousands have died and thousands more go to war. It was a delicate balance here, with all the habitats existing together. But now with Faar gone, the scale just tipped."

Saint Dane then walked over to me and leaned down. Our eyes were on the same level and he was so close I could smell his breath. It was sour. I wasn't surprised. But I wouldn't back off. No way.

"It is all happening exactly as I planned," he said softly. "Even if you managed to stop me here, I would simply move on to another territory. You have no idea what is waiting for you, Pendragon. If you continue to fight me, you will certainly go the way of all the pitiful Travelers who came before. Is that what you want? Do you want to die in futility like Spader's father? Or Osa? Or Press?"

This last comment stung, but I wouldn't let him know it.

"The offer still stands, Pendragon," he said with a tempting smile. "When Halla is mine, there will be grand rewards for those who helped me. You seem to enjoy splashing around Cloral. I'll give it to you. Do what you want with it. Restore their farms, make Spader an admiral, be their hero, make them love you. Whatever you want. It would be so easy and the fight would be over. What do you think?"

This is going to be hard to explain, but at that moment something changed for me. Yes, I was still afraid of Saint Dane. I still didn't know much about being a Traveler or even why I was chosen to be one. There was still a ton for me to learn, but at that moment, something became very clear and it filled me with a sense of confidence that I hadn't felt since, well, since I was on the basketball court at Stony Brook.

"You want to know what I think?" I asked Saint Dane. "I think if you truly knew what was going to happen, if you really believed this was all part of your plan and that you couldn't be beaten, then you wouldn't keep begging me to join you."

Saint Dane blinked. I saw it. I had hit a nerve.

"What do I think?" I added. "It might not be here, it might not be today or even on this territory, but for the first time since I met you on Second Earth, I think that when this is all over, I'll be the one who's beaten *you* . . . because *that* is the way it's supposed to be."

Something clicked in Saint Dane's eyes. It wasn't huge. He didn't gasp or shout or anything like that, but I saw it: Saint Dane was afraid of me. I was sure of it.

The two of us stood there for a moment, not knowing who would make the next move. And that's when I heard it. It was a far-off sound and hard to make out. But it was definitely a sound I had heard before. It was a faint whistling sound. It was coming closer, too. Fast. Where had I heard it before? It took me exactly two seconds to remember.

I turned to Spader and shouted, "Incoming!"

I grabbed him and dove down onto the deck. An instant later the submarine was rocked by an explosion. The control tower was hit by a water missile—just like the ones that Saint Dane had launched on Grallion. The sound I heard was that of an incoming bomb.

Boom, boom! Two more missiles hit the control tower and the submarine rocked in the water. But where was this attack coming from?

"Look!" shouted Spader, pointing off the port side of the sub.

I looked and saw such a wonderful sight, for a moment I thought I was dreaming. But it was no dream. It was a fleet of speeder boats full of aquaneers, and they were attacking.

"Hobey, Pendragon! It's Yenza," Spader laughed. "She was a step ahead of us."

That had to be the answer. When we didn't resurface, Wu Yenza must have gone to get her rescue team. And they were coming in full force. Some of the speeders looked more like gun ships. They weren't as big as the battle cruiser, but they would definitely stand up to this submarine.

There was frantic activity on the deck of the submarine.

"Dive!" shouted Saint Dane. "Get us below!"

A raider shouted, "Sir, we can't!" He pointed to the control tower and sure enough, the first few missiles from Yenza's aquaneers had blown a hole in the skin of the tower. If they tried to dive, they'd sink. Saint Dane looked at the damage, then spun to look back at the approaching fleet. He looked angry. I liked that. When he got angry, it meant things weren't going his way, and that didn't happen too often.

"The guns!" he commanded. "We'll fight them off."

He then ran along the deck and disappeared into the control tower. Spader and I were left flat out on the deck. Saint Dane no longer cared about us. And why should he? We were targets too.

"Time to go, mate," said Spader. "Let's slip over the side and we'll swim for it."

Three more missiles struck near the sub, sending up waves of water that splashed over us. The raiders were now on the guns and firing back. This was going to be a fierce battle—a natty-do, as Spader would put it—and I didn't want to be floating in the water in the middle of it.

"I have a better idea," I said.

I got up and ran back toward the control tower. Two more shots hit the hull, rocking the sub and nearly knocking me off. But Spader caught me and kept me going.

"No place to run, Pendragon," he said.

"Sure there is," I answered.

I ran inside the control tower. Spader was right after me.

We had to push past a bunch of raiders who were scrambling to get to their battle stations. They didn't care about us anymore. Remember, they were raiders. They knew nothing of Saint Dane's grand plan to conquer all the territories and control Halla. All they knew was that they were being attacked.

Even Saint Dane wanted a fight. He stood at his station, barking orders, turning the submarine so it wouldn't be such a wide target. If there were ever a time to get out of there, it was now.

I led Spader back the way we came, down the ladder into the hull of the ship and back toward the water tank we arrived in. I figured there was only one way we could get off this sub and survive in open water. We had to get to the hijacked hauler.

As we ran through the submarine we kept getting knocked around by the force of the missiles that were hitting the hull. Yenza was really pouring it on. That was cool, as long as Spader and I were off by the time she sent it to the bottom the same way she had the battle cruiser.

Luckily it's kind of hard to get lost in a submarine, so we found the tank chamber pretty easily. When I threw the door open and we saw the hauler, Spader smiled.

"Why didn't I think of this?" he laughed with surprise.

"You know how it works?" I asked.

"Pendragon, if it moves in the water, I can drive it."

"Okay," I said. "But can you get it out of here?"

Spader gave me a "don't ask dumb questions" look, and ran for the hauler.

"Get our gear, then go over to those levers," he instructed as he climbed up onto the bubble.

As Spader lowered himself into the bubble, I ran to get our air globes and water sleds. I grabbed them all, then threw each up to Spader, who stood with half of his body out of the top of the bubble.

"Now what?" I asked.

"Four levers," he said. "One floods the chamber, another empties it, third opens the hatch, fourth closes the hatch. We don't have to flood the chamber because we're already on top of water. The pressure keeps the water out. All we have to do is open the hatch, and we're gone."

"Okay, which lever opens the hatch?"

"Hobey, Pendragon. I don't know *everything*!"

He then slipped into the bubble and started powering up. This was the old Spader, the one I knew before his father was killed. It felt good.

I went to the four levers. None of them were marked. There was only one way to figure out which was the right one. I had to call upon all my Traveler experience and special powers to figure it out. It's called . . .

"Eenie, meenie, miney . . . *mo*! I pulled on "mo" and with a grinding screech, the floor began to move. The hatch door was sliding open! Go, mo! Unfortunately, as soon as the hatch began to open, it set off an alarm. A shrill, blaring horn blew, which said only one thing: "Someone is trying to escape in the hauler." My guess was at least one of the raiders would come to find out who it was.

"Better hop in," Spader shouted.

I ran across the moving floor and leaped on to the bubble

craft. I dangled my legs down into the cockpit and was just about to drop in when Spader said, "Hold on, mate. We gotta release first."

He was right. The floor hatch was now all the way open, but the hauler wasn't free. The craft was suspended from two hooks that kept us dangling over the water below.

"So how do we release?" I asked.

"I'd say you should swing that lever right there."

Sure enough, there was a lever right over my head. I grabbed it, pulled it toward me and—whoa! The hauler fell free and splashed down in the water. I lost my balance and fell into the globe, right in Spader's lap.

"Thanks for droppin' in, mate," Spader said. "Close 'er up, please."

I stood up and pulled the bubble closed over us. With Spader in the left pilot's seat and me in the right, we were ready to go.

That's when the door to the chamber flew open and two raiders jumped in with guns.

"Dive, please," I said.

"Right!"

Spader hit four toggle switches, air bubbles hissed through the water around us and we began to sink. The raiders shouldered their rifles and took aim. All I could hope was that the bubble on this hauler was strong enough to take a direct shot from a water rifle. I didn't have long to wonder. The raiders opened fire on us. I ducked, expecting the bubble to shatter to pieces. But it didn't. Their water bullets splattered against the clear shield without leaving so much as a scratch. Score another one for the genius of the people from Faar.

We were now almost submerged. The raiders had stopped firing and watched us helplessly as we sank below the surface.

Then, just before the water closed over us, someone else entered the tank room. It was Saint Dane. For an instant I actually thought I saw a look of worry on his face. That's the last image I saw of him, then we slipped underwater.

Spader took control of the vehicle like he had been a hauler pilot his whole life. We descended well below the submarine, then he hit the throttle and we left the dark shadow behind.

"What about the big guns?" I asked. "The ones they used on Faar. They can blow Yenza's boats out of the water."

"They can, but they won't," Spader answered. "They only fire when it's submerged. Yenza knows what she's doing, all right. She nailed that control tower so they can't submerge again. Saint Dane made a big mistake. On the surface, he's no match for my mates. There's only one problem."

"What's that?"

"It's going to be over too fast. I want to join up with them and take a couple of shots at Saint Dane myself before the natty-do's all done!"

I looked back at the dark submarine. If Spader was right, the battle above was as good as over. Yenza would handle the raiders, and with a little luck, Saint Dane would go down with his ship. I was no longer worried about what was happening up there. My thoughts were elsewhere entirely. So I reached forward and killed the engines.

"Hobey, mate, what're you doing?"

"You really know how to pilot this thing?" I asked seriously. "Don't get all macho aquaneer on me. I want the truth."

"This is a fine piece of machinery," he said, looking around. "It's way more advanced than anything I've ever seen. But that just makes it easier. All modesty aside, I can move this little beauty through a mile of kelp and not break a single leaf."

My mind was working hard, figuring the possibilities.

"What are you thinking, Pendragon?" Spader asked. "You think we should start dumping this cargo over some of the farms?"

"Good idea, but no," I said. "We can do that later. Right now, I got something else in mind."

"What?"

"I want to go after Uncle Press."

Spader's eyes opened wide with surprise. He hadn't expected me to say that.

"Hobey, mate!" he said in awe. "Do you know how dangerous that would be? You're talking about finding our way down through that submerged city; poking through who knows what that's floating around in there waiting to get us all tangled up and trapped. Then if we're lucky enough to make it to the bottom we'd have to dig through the pile of rubble that's covering the door with a mechanical arm we've never used before and for all we know can't even lift that kind of weight. And it's all on the chance that Press and the others are still alive down there. Do you know that's what you're asking?"

"Uh . . . yeah, that pretty much sums it up."

"You're crazy!" he said. A moment later, he smiled. "I like that."

"Then why are we still here?"

Spader fired the engines back up, banked hard to the right, dipped the nose, and we were on our way back toward the coral reef for one last visit to the city of Faar.

CLORAL

Descending into Faar wasn't exactly like diving into the unknown. We had just come from there. But to say that things had changed a little would be a major understatement. We sort of knew the geography of the place, but now that it was underwater it would be like traveling through the dangerous insides of a giant sunken ship. The whole space would be filled with water and that meant stuff would be floating all around.

Still, I didn't think we had a choice. There were a dozen Faarians down there who could still be alive, and Uncle Press was with them. We had to give it a try.

Spader drove the hauler back toward the coral reef that was the dome over Faar. He kept making slight maneuvers he didn't need to so he could get used to the controls of the hauler. Smart idea. Better to get totally familiar with the craft out here in open water than down in the murky depths.

As we approached the coral reef, I looked for the hole that Saint Dane had blown open. It would be our doorway into Faar. It wasn't hard to find. There were long, parallel lines dug into the reef that must have been caused by the huge volume of water that was pulled across it as it was sucked toward the hole. It was like a road map. All we had to do was follow it.

A few moments later we both saw our goal. The huge, jagged hole stood out like a black scar on the reef. It looked even bigger up close than it had from down below. Spader stopped the hauler just shy of the edge and we hovered there, looking at the damage in silence. A moment later something floated up from down below. It was a white tunic, the kind the people of Faar always wore. The piece of clothing rippled and moved in the current. It looked like a lonely spirit leaving the city forever.

"Pendragon, I want to get 'em out as bad as you do," Spader said. "But we have to be smart. If it's a tum-tigger down there, we'll have to pull out."

"I understand," I said.

Spader then pushed the little sub forward and soon we were hovering directly over the middle of the black hole. He looked to me. I nodded.

"Let's give it a go," he said.

He toggled a switch on the control panel and we began to sink straight down. We passed the jagged edge of the hole, dropping from the bright blue-green of the ocean into the dark tomb of the sunken city. We first traveled through a debris field of clothes, books, and memories. Everything on Faar that wasn't attached was free to float around. There were constant bangs and thumps against the bubble of the hauler as we knocked into all this lost junk. I hate to call it junk though, because not long ago these were important possessions. We passed lots of clothing and dishes and we even saw a small doll that a child must have left behind. That one was tough. It made me think of my little sister, Shannon.

Soon it got so dark I lost all sense of direction. I couldn't tell up from down or if we were even moving.

"Must be some lights on this beauty," Spader said.

That was important. We had to descend quite a ways before we reached the peak of Faar's mountain, but before we got there we needed some kind of light to guide us or we'd surely crash into it. Spader scanned the control panel and chose a switch.

"Let's try this one."

He toggled the switch and instantly a series of lights sprang to life below the bubble. They weren't headlights, but they sent out a bright cocoon that allowed us to see a few yards in every direction. It wasn't much, but at least now we would know if we were about to hit something. I looked to my right and—

"Ahhh!" I screamed, and nearly jumped into Spader's lap.

It was one of the portraits from the corridor leading to the Council Circle of Faar. I was staring out at a stern-looking guy who gazed right back at me with a sour puss.

"It's like diving through an underwater junkyard," Spader said.

"Or *graveyard*," I added.

The portrait floated away and I got my nerves back under control. Spader tried another switch and this time another light kicked on. This one was attached outside of the bubble on my side. It was the headlight we were looking for. Excellent.

"Try that knob there," Spader instructed.

Next to my right arm were two controllers that looked like video game joysticks. I grabbed the smaller of the two and moved it. Sure enough, the searchlight outside moved too. We had found our eyes!

"Let's see where we're going, then," instructed Spader.

We could only see what the headlight was shining on. Everything beyond fell off into darkness. I directed the light forward and we got our first view of the top of Faar's mountain. It appeared out of the distance like a ghost. It was an incredibly eerie sight. Luckily the water was pretty clear. I expected there to be sand kicked up and floating around, but it wasn't too bad. Also, the layer of junk seemed to have thinned out. Most everything that could float was headed to the surface. We were now traveling below the debris field.

"Let's get moving," said Spader, and we plunged deeper.

The best thing about having the lights was that we could navigate. Spader dropped the nose of the hauler so we weren't sinking blindly anymore. We had to descend in circles, like a corkscrew, so that we could drop as straight down as possible.

"I want to see something," I said and pointed to our left.

Spader directed the hauler to where I pointed and soon our headlight was moving across the platform that had held the Council Circle. As I described before, the marble roof had been knocked off when the water began to flood through the dome. It was on its side now, half covering the platform. The round symbol of Faar had broken off and it lay on the platform, cracked in two pieces. How's that for symbolism? Most of the marble pillars still ringed the platform, but they no longer had anything to hold up. A few had tumbled over, and now crisscrossed on top of one another.

"Closer," I asked, and Spader dropped us in for a better look.

We were now hovering only a few feet above the platform. I played the light over the wrecked surface until I saw exactly what I was looking for, but hoped I wouldn't find. The podium that held the four crystal controls had been knocked over. It was still functioning because the yellow crystal continued to blink. Even now it was sounding the alarm to evacuate Faar. But that's not what I was looking for.

"Oh, no," Spader said sadly. He had just seen it too.

From beneath the toppled ceiling, an arm was reaching out. There was no doubt in my mind that it was Abador. He had stayed at his post until the end and was killed when the marble dome crashed down. It seemed as though in his last moments he was reaching for the control podium in the desperate attempt to transpire. He had failed. Of course it was tragedy enough that this brave man had died, but I hated to think that he died knowing he had failed. I could only hope that he knew that Faar had been safely evacuated.

"Let's move on," Spader said with respect.

I nodded and he steered the hauler away so we could continue our descent into Faar. All the way down I kept the headlight trained in front of us, looking for any danger in our way. We passed by some familiar sights. We saw the pathways we had walked along. We saw the entrance to our escape tunnel and all the smaller entrances that led deep into Faar's mountain. As of now the crushing water hadn't done any major damage to the city. The buildings seemed intact and the paths weren't washed away. This was great news because if some of these big marble buildings had fallen down and piled on top of the hauler hangar, this rescue would be over before it got going.

I had a brief feeling like we were inside one of those snow globes that you shook to create a storm. I wondered how long it would take for erosion to start doing its worst. Eventually the city would turn to sand, but for now it was intact. It was hard to believe that only a short time ago it had been completely dry and busy with people.

"There we go!" announced Spader.

We were nearing the hauler hangar. I was thrilled to see that it looked pretty much the same as when we saw it last. The building hadn't collapsed under the weight of the water. There was the pile of dome rubble in front of the entrance, but other than that nothing new had fallen down that would stop us from getting through. Now the question was whether the mechanical arm could move the stuff away.

Spader put the hauler down on the same path we had run along just a while ago. We landed so gently that only a small cloud of sand was kicked up.

"Give it a go, mate," he said.

He meant the mechanical arm. I grabbed the other joystick that was at my right arm and twisted it. The mechanical sound around us proved the arm was activated and working. The long, white tube of an arm had about four joints so it could move in pretty much any direction. On the end was a large, white mechanical hand. It had three fingers and a thumb, like Fred Flintstone. Swiveling the joystick made the arm move easily. It took me all of thirty seconds to figure out how to move it. Finally I discovered that pulling the trigger on the joystick made the hand close shut. I maneuvered the arm out in front of the hauler, brought the hand back, and right in front of Spader, released the trigger so the hand opened wide—and waved at him.

Spader laughed.

"I guess you've got it figured out," he said.

I was totally ready to begin the excavation.

Spader gently lifted the hauler off the bottom and got us in position over the pile of rubble in front of the hangar entrance.

"Go slow," he said. "Once you grab on to a piece, I'll pull

us back. I gotta be careful though, I don't want to start kicking up sand or we'll be blind down here."

I rubbed my hands together, grabbed the joystick, and made my first attempt. I reached the long arm out and found a small piece of rubble. This was just a test. I maneuvered the hand over the chunk, squeezed the trigger, and the hand clamped on. I then lifted the piece away and dropped it off to the side.

"That was spiff," said Spader, as if he expected it to be harder.

"Let's try something a little bigger," I said with confidence.

I saw a chunk of coral sticking out of the pile. It looked perfect to grab on to. Spader didn't even have to move the hauler. I eased the arm over toward it and latched on with no trouble. But as I tried to pull back, there was some serious resistance.

"It's not moving," I said.

"Let's use hauler power," said Spader.

He started to ease the hauler backward, but the piece still wouldn't budge. Spader hit the throttle, the engines whined, but still the piece wouldn't budge.

Spader said, "Maybe you should try a smaller—"

Suddenly the piece broke free, and so did the pile of rubble. It seemed as if half the pile had been leaning against this one little piece and when we pulled it loose, it was like pulling a card out from the bottom of a house of cards. Huge pieces of dome tumbled toward us and hit the bubble of the hauler. The impact knocked us back and we twisted over on our side. Then another piece hit us from the other side and spun us back the other way. Sand was swirling everywhere. It was impossible to see. Then with a jolt, we hit the bottom on our side and two more heavy pieces fell down on us. There was nothing we could do but hold our breath and hope we wouldn't spring a leak. We finally ended up on our side with a bunch of broken dome all over us.

"Wrong piece," said Spader.

"Yeah, no kidding."

We didn't move for a while and let the sand settle so we could see what the deal was. I was convinced we were now pinned here on the bottom of Faar and was already making plans to put on our air globes and abandon ship, when Spader gently gunned the engine. I was thrilled to see we could move. He slowly backed us away from the pile of rubble and let it fall down in front of us. We were completely free now, so Spader righted us and we were hovering once again.

"Let's pick our pieces a bit more scientifically this time, right?" Spader said.

I gave him a sideways "give me a break" look, then started scanning the pile of rubble to choose my next victim. After what had just happened, it was obvious that this wasn't going to be a quick task. We were going to have to start at the top and only move pieces that were completely clear. We couldn't afford to have another collapse. This was going to be like playing a game of Jenga . . . a really *dangerous* game of Jenga.

So we went about the painstaking task of moving the pile. Of course the little pieces were easy. The bigger pieces took a lot more power. One good thing was that because we were underwater, they were a lot lighter than they would have been on land. Many of these pieces were wide, thick chunks of material that withstood centuries of pressure. We pulled off a few pieces that were bigger than a car. I was afraid those pieces would be too much for the hauler, but the little vehicle proved time and again that it was up to the task.

I don't know how long we were digging. It could have been hours. I tried to focus on the job and not think about the worst, which was that we were too late for Uncle Press and the Faarians.

Finally, with one final tug from the hauler, we pulled over a huge chunk of dome and revealed the doorway to the hangar.

"Yeah!" I shouted.

"Hobey!" added Spader.

It was unbelievable that we had gotten this far. But our victory celebration was short-lived because almost immediately our thoughts went on to the next step. We had no idea what we were going to find beyond that door.

"Uh-oh," said Spader ominously.

I hated "uh-oh." Nothing good ever happened after "uh-oh."

He pointed to a gash that was cut in the wall that must have been made by a falling piece of dome. The gash was so big, it went right through the wall. That meant that as soon as the rising water got high enough, it would have flooded the hangar. We could only hope that the Faarians had their swim-skins, and that they could buddy-breathe with Uncle Press. If not, the hauler hangar was now a tomb.

Spader gently touched the throttle and the hauler eased closer to the door. I shone the headlight on it so we could see exactly what we had to deal with. The door itself was bent. I hoped that didn't mean it was jammed or anything.

I reached for the joystick of the mechanical arm and was about to go after the door handle, when something caught my eye. It was a flicker of movement. I quickly looked to see that it had come from the gash in the wall. Something was moving in there!

"Don't stop now," said Spader with excitement. He'd seen it too.

I had to force myself to keep calm. We were too close now for me to blow it by doing something dumb. So I slowly moved the mechanical arm over to the handle and grabbed on. I tried to tug it open using just the arm, but it wouldn't budge.

"Back it up," I said to Spader.

The engines of the hauler began to whine. But the door still wouldn't budge. Spader throttled up. I could hear the engines strain, but the door wouldn't move.

"I'm going to really gun it," said Spader. "If the door pops, release it quick or—"

Crack!

The door gave way. I instantly released the trigger and we went sailing backward. Spader threw on the water brakes and stopped us before we slammed into anything from behind.

"Go back, go back!" I shouted.

Spader reversed the engines and we moved right back to the hangar and to the now open door. I shone the light on it, hoping that whoever was inside would see it and know that this was the way out. We hovered there, and waited.

"C'mon," I begged. "C'mon!"

"We saw something move in there, right?" Spader asked.

"Yeah, I thought that—look!"

Something moved inside the open door! I held my breath. Was someone still alive in there, or was it a floating corpse?

Then a Faarian in a green swimskin poked his head out of the doorway. He was alive! He held his hand up to shield his eyes from our bright light and looked around the sunken city in wonder. He then gave a wave, and with a kick, began swimming to the surface.

I couldn't stop smiling. We had saved at least one of the

Faarians, but were there more? And what about Uncle Press?

One by one, more Faarians in swimskins began to float out of the door and swim to the surface. It was kind of eerie. They were like green ghosts floating up and out of a grave. Then again, this wasn't a grave. This building had saved them from being crushed and drowned—or drowned and crushed. It wasn't a tomb at all; it was their lifeboat.

I kept waiting to see Uncle Press. Since he didn't have his air globe, I expected to see him emerge from the doorway while buddy-breathing with one of the Faarians. But after counting fourteen swimmers, there was no Uncle Press. I started to get nervous again. Could all the Faarians have survived because they had swimskins, but Uncle Press have died because he didn't have the right gear? That wasn't fair. But still, nobody else was coming out! I was all set to put on my air globe and figure out a way to get out of this hauler to go look for him, when a knock came on the outside of the bubble. I turned to my right and came face-to-face with a Faarian in a swimskin. "Ahhh!" I jumped again.

Since the skins completely covered their heads, they were kind of creepy looking. Imagine Spider-man as a frog, and you'd pretty much have a Faarian in a swimskin.

This guy clung to the bubble of the hauler and was pointing at something.

"What does he want?" Spader asked.

"He's trying to tell us something," I said.

The Faarian was pointing to something inside the hauler, behind my head. I spun around and saw that perched on a hook behind my seat was a pair of headphones. Spader had a pair behind him as well. I pointed to the headphones and looked at the Faarian. He nodded.

Spader and I both shrugged and put the headphones on.

We then looked back to the Faarian and heard a familiar voice say, "What took you so long?"

It was Uncle Press!

"Yeah! All right! Hobey-ho!" we shouted. Spader and I were over the moon. I guess the Faarians had an extra skinsuit in the hangar.

"How did you end up with this hauler?" Uncle Press asked.

"Long story," I answered.

"How bad is it?" he asked.

"Faar is underwater," I said. "Saint Dane blew a hole in the dome. But the entire city was evacuated. As far as I know there was only one casualty—the old man from the Council of Faar. What about the other haulers? Were they launched?"

"No, they're all still in there," Uncle Press said. "The outside doors were buried."

That was horrible news. The underwater farms of Cloral couldn't be saved. Saint Dane was still going to win.

"We should get out of here, mates," said Spader. "Find something to hang on to, Press. We'll give you a ride."

Uncle Press couldn't get inside the hauler because we were watertight. He would have to hitch a ride to the surface. He found a spot behind the bubble and grabbed on.

"Watch out," I said. "There's a lot of junk floating around."

Spader pushed the throttle, lifted the nose and we began our final ascent from Faar. We had to go slowly because we didn't want Uncle Press to get swept off. Besides, we weren't in any hurry. It gave me time to fill him in on all that had happened since we split up. The hard truth hit him the same as it did me. We had totally failed. The underwater farms were still producing poison crops, Faar was destroyed, and Cloral was on the verge of chaos. Even if Yenza had a complete victory over Saint Dane topside, it wouldn't matter. The damage was done.

The three of us fell silent during our final stage of the ascent. I wanted to take one last look around at the city that died trying to be the salvation of Cloral. The last chapter in the legend of the Lost City of Faar was a tragic one. And no figure was more tragic than poor Abador, Senior to the Council of Faar, who died trying to fulfill his destiny. Whatever transpire was, it would never happen. Instead it would be just one more unexplained mystery in the myth.

That's when a thought came to me.

"Stop," I commanded.

"What?"

"Stop right here," I said.

Spader stopped our ascent and we hovered in midwater.

"What's up, Bobby?" asked Uncle Press.

"Faar is dead. There's nothing we can do to save it. And there's nothing we can do to bring the rest of the haulers up to save the crops, right?"

"Yeah, that's about how the day has gone," said Spader. "What's your point?"

"My point is there's nothing else to lose."

"You getting philosophical on us, or is this leading somewhere?" Uncle Press asked from outside the hauler.

"I think we should take it all the way. We should complete Faar's destiny."

"Which is . . . ?"

"Transpire," I said sharply. "I say we finish what Abador couldn't."

Uncle Press said, "But we don't even know what that is. You said yourself it might be a self-destruct mechanism."

"So what?" I shot back. "If that's the way the Faarians

wanted it, then I think they deserve to end things the way they planned. It can't make things any worse for Cloral, right? Abador said they had been preparing for this moment for generations. Who are we to deny them?"

I looked to Spader for an opinion. He only shrugged.

"Why not?" he added.

I looked outside the bubble to Uncle Press, but it was impossible to read any expression on his face since it was covered by a green swimskin.

"Do you know how to do it?" he asked.

"I think so."

"Then you're right. There's nothing to lose," he said. "Let's do it."

"Get us back to the Council Circle," I said to Spader.

Spader took control and we started moving again. In a few minutes we were once again hovering over the platform and looking down at Abador's hand that, tragically, had fallen only a few feet short.

"You have no way of knowing this, old man," I said to Abador. "But we'll finish it for you."

"What do I do?" asked Uncle Press.

"You see that blinking yellow light?" I asked.

"Yeah."

"There are three other crystal switches. One of them must be the control to transpire."

"Okay, which one?"

"Beats me," I answered. "If in doubt, eenie, meenie, miney, mo. I'm partial to mo."

"Great," scoffed Uncle Press, and swam off toward the panel.

He looked at the three other switches: green, red, and white. He first reached forward and pushed the green one. All that happened was that the green crystal started to glow, and the yellow light stopped blinking.

"That must be to turn off the evacuation alarm," I said.

There were two choices left. From where I sat, the white crystal looked as if it had already been pushed down.

"I think the white crystal raises and lowers the podium," I said. "It must be the red one."

"Red it is," said Uncle Press.

He reached forward, touched the red crystal, and glanced back to me. I gave him a nod, and he pushed it down.

And that's when the party *really* started.

First, the red crystal flashed brightly. That much I expected. The next thing we knew we were surrounded by sound. It started as a low whine, but then grew in volume. It sounded like giant engines were powering to life. Then the mountain rumbled. The waves it sent out from its movement started to buffet the hauler.

Uncle Press shot back to us and grabbed on.

"I think now's a good time to be someplace else," he said.

"Hang on!" shouted Spader.

He hit the throttle and we began rising again. The monstrous sound grew louder. The hauler was being buffeted so hard that it was making my teeth chatter.

"You okay, Press?" called Spader.

"Get us outta here!" he shouted back.

Then I heard something new. It sounded like cracking, but it was immense.

"Uh-oh," said Spader.

There it was again. "Uh-oh." I *hated* "uh-oh."

Spader was looking up. I looked up too and saw that we were getting closer to the hole in the dome, and safety. But that's not what the "uh-oh" was about. The trouble was, the rest of the dome was cracking! The rumble was sending shock waves through the water that were so strong, we could actually see cracks traveling across the surface of the dome. But unlike the last time the dome cracked, this wasn't in one single place. Now, the entire dome was beginning to shatter!

"It's breaking up," shouted Spader.

"Get under the hole!" I shouted back. I figured that if it all came down, humpty-dumpty-style, then our only chance of not being crushed would be if we were under the hole.

"I gotta pick up speed!" shouted Spader.

"I'm okay," answered Uncle Press. "Go!"

Spader pushed us faster. It was a race to make it out of that hole before the whole world came crashing down on us.

"Come on, come on!" Spader coaxed the hauler on.

I killed the lights because we didn't need them anymore and could use every last bit of power for speed. We then hit the field of floating debris. Pieces of everything hit the bubble. I wasn't worried about the glass breaking. If the raiders' waterguns couldn't shatter it, then I didn't think a chunk of floating junk could. I was more afraid that something would hit Uncle Press.

"We got it!" Spader yelled.

And a second later we shot up out of the hole and into the light of open ocean. Unbelievably, the dome had held. But we weren't safe yet. The sound of the roaring engines was even louder outside of the dome. The water was still vibrating like crazy, and there was something new. All around us were massive jets of air bubbles shooting up from around the perimeter of the dome.

"Keep moving!" shouted Uncle Press.

Spader hit the throttle and we sped away. It didn't matter where we went so long as we didn't stay here. The jets of air shot up all around us, like fissures opening up somewhere deep below and letting off pressure. There was no way to avoid them. They kept hitting us and knocking us around. This was probably the closest I will ever come to being inside a washing machine.

"Press?" called Spader.

"Don't talk, drive!" shouted Uncle Press.

Finally we got past the fissure jets and Spader was able to put us right. The water just beyond them was absolutely calm. In seconds we had gone from being tossed in heavy seas to floating as calmly as if we were in a bathtub. It was a strange feeling. I wasn't complaining.

"Now *that* was a tum-tigger," said Spader.

But it wasn't over yet. The roar of the engines, or whatever they were, was still growing louder even though we were out of the turbulent zone. The air fissures had suddenly stopped erupting, and as soon as the bubbles stopped shooting up, the engines whined louder.

Then we heard another cracking sound.

"The dome's collapsing!" Spader shouted.

We all looked back at the coral reef, expecting the dome to collapse in. But that's not what happened. It erupted. Yes, it started to expand upward.

"I don't believe it," Spader whispered in awe.

Believe it.

A moment later we saw. Something was pushing the dome up from below. It was the top of Faar's mountain! In that one amazing moment, it all came clear to me what transpire meant. When Abador and the council debated about whether to reveal themselves to Cloral or remain hidden, they weren't talking about self-destruction. They were talking about rejoining their world, literally. The preparations that had been going on for centuries were all about pushing the Lost City of Faar back to the surface. The three of us watched in shock as the top of Faar's mountain broke through the weakened dome and continued to rise toward the surface.

Luckily one of us had the smarts to do a little mental calculation.

"Faar is a big place, gentlemen," said Uncle Press. "We are still in the wrong spot."

Good thinking. If Faar was coming up, we were still too close.

"Outta here!" shouted Spader, and hit the throttle once again.

As we sped away I looked back around at the spectacle. The mountain continued its impossible rise up through the shattered dome. In a few moments, the peak would break the surface of the sea. It was awesome . . . but we weren't home-free just yet.

"Slight problem," Spader said while scanning the instruments.

"What?"

"We're not moving."

Whatever force was being used to power this city's ascent had gotten hold of us. It felt as if we were fighting a wicked current coming right at us.

"More power!" I shouted to Spader.

"I'm trying! It's pulling us back."

Spader pressed the throttle to full power, but it didn't help. We were being sucked back toward the mountain. It was like being sucked into a rip-current. But then, suddenly, everything reversed. I didn't know if the force of the mountain rising was now stronger than the pull of the engines that were forcing it up, but in an instant we went from being pulled back to being pushed forward by a tidal-wave force of water. Our hauler suddenly shot forward faster than it was ever designed to go.

This underwater wave ride lasted a full minute. Finally Spader was able to get control and slow us down.

"I'm taking us up," he announced, and we shot topside.

A few moments later we broke the water's surface. I quickly opened the bubble top and pulled myself out to get to Uncle Press. He was exhausted, but okay. He pulled the swimskin off his face and looked up at me.

"Are you sure it was the red button?" he said with a smile.

I had to laugh. Man, this guy was cool.

We then heard something that sounded like a giant whale breaching the surface. But it wasn't a whale, of course. It was Faar's mountain. Spader joined us on the top of the bubble and the three of us watched in wonder.

The mountain rose slowly from the water. It was impossible, yet there it was. We were far enough away now that we were safe, but close enough to see detail on the mountain. As it rose higher the marble buildings were revealed along with the paths that wandered between them. Bit by bit the city that had been hidden for hundreds of years was once again feeling sunlight.

"Look!" shouted Spader.

We looked around us and saw green heads popping up in the water everywhere. The Faarians were coming up to witness the rebirth of their home. There were hundreds of them stretched out on either side of us. They all pulled off their swimskin hoods so they could see this miracle through clear eyes.

Faar's mountain continued to rise. Of course the higher it got, the larger it became. I was beginning to think that maybe we were still a little bit too close. If this thing kept getting bigger, pretty soon we'd be lifted up with it. The mountain now towered over us. What emerged next from below was the hauler hangar that was the lifeboat for Uncle Press and the brave Faarians.

It suddenly hit me that with Faar rising, the haulers came up with it. They could now be pulled from the hangar and sent on their mission after all. This was incredible! There was still a chance to save the underwater farms.

With a final shudder, Faar's mountain stopped moving. One last wave of water hit us—we rode up and over it, and then settled. The three of us sat there on the floating hauler, in complete awe. We were now looking at a huge island, and a city.

All around us the Faarians began to cheer. They screamed and laughed and hugged each other and they cried. They had gone from losing everything to starting an incredible new life on Cloral. This was their destiny and they welcomed it.

I couldn't help but think of Abador. I hoped he somehow knew what had happened. It may not have been his hand that brought Faar back to life, but it was definitely his spirit.

There was one other amazing fact. We were now looking at the only dry land on the entire territory of Cloral. As Saint Dane had said to us earlier: "Not bad for an afternoon's work, don't you think?"

CLORAL

The sea was now calm. The three of us sat on the bubble of the floating hauler, staring at the reborn city of Faar. None of us could say anything for the longest time. There were no words that could truly describe the spectacular sight we had just witnessed. Well, maybe there was one.

"That was . . . cool," I said, knowing it was the biggest understatement of all time.

The three of us exchanged glances and started to laugh. It was an incredible moment. We helped the city of Faar complete its destiny and probably saved Cloral at the same time. If there was a lesson here it would have to be that you should never, ever lose hope. We had given up. Thrown in the towel. The fat lady had not only sung, she had left the stage. Saint Dane was already doing his victory lap. But we pulled it out. Unbelievable. The only way we could show our disbelief was to laugh. It felt great.

We watched as the Faarians swam toward their city and tentatively crawled up on the shore. One by one they emerged from the water, gathered together, and stood looking up in awe at their mountain city. It was the first time the sun had touched their buildings in centuries. Water still poured from the beehive of tunnel openings that dotted the mountain. The transpire was complete.

As we sat, watching this wondrous sight, we heard the sound of waves slapping against a hull. All three of us turned to see that the black submarine was cruising toward us. My first thought was to jump back in the hauler and get the heck out of there, but a closer look told us there was no reason to be afraid. The deck of the submarine was lined with aquaneers. They were all staring at Faar with the same look of wonder. Just as Spader had predicted, his mates had won. They now commanded the raiders' sub.

Stepping from out of the control tower was Wu Yenza. She walked out into the sun and stood with her hands on her hips confidently, watching as they drew closer to us. She was very much in charge.

"She's good," Uncle Press said.

"She's better than good," I added. "If not for her . . ."

I didn't have to finish the sentence. We all knew where we'd be right now if Yenza hadn't gone for help. I turned to Spader and said, "Maybe you'll get a promotion for this."

An odd thing happened. Spader didn't smile and make a clever comeback. He just watched the approaching submarine intently. His mind was somewhere else. Even though we had just pulled out an incredible victory, there was now a dark frown on his face. Without a word, he dropped back down into the hauler and powered up so we could rendezvous with the sub. I looked at Uncle Press. All he could do was shrug.

As Uncle Press pulled off his swimskin, Spader guided our hauler right up alongside the sub. An aquaneer tossed us a rope so we could tie on. Spader handed me the two air globes and water sleds and I tossed them up to the aquaneer. We then all climbed aboard the sub and were reunited with Yenza.

"I guess you found Faar," she said with a wry smile. Another understatement.

"What made you leave?" asked Uncle Press.

"A hunch," she said. "When you didn't surface, I assumed you had found the city. And if Zy Roder was right behind us, I didn't want to take him on myself. I'm good, but not *that* good."

"Where is he?" asked Spader with no emotion.

Uh-oh. Now I knew what was in Spader's head. The sight of the sub approaching had reminded him of Saint Dane. I was afraid that he would still be looking for revenge.

"He's in the brig down below," answered Yenza. "I won't let him get away again."

Spader walked past us toward the control tower.

"Spader, let it go," I called.

But Spader kept walking. What was he going to do? Uncle Press and I followed him.

Spader entered the control tower. He grabbed an aquaneer by the shirt and demanded, "Where is the brig?"

"Below, halfway to the stern," answered the aquaneer, a little intimidated.

Spader pushed him aside and headed for the ladder.

Uncle Press called, "Spader, stop. Take a breath."

Spader wasn't listening. He slid down the ladder. We were right behind him. We hit the main deck and had only taken a few steps when we heard a scream come from the back of the sub. It was a horrible, pained howl. Without a word we all began running toward the sound. Spader was a few feet ahead of us and glancing into each doorway as he passed, looking for the source. Finally he saw something and entered a doorway. We followed right behind.

This was the right place. The room was split in half. We had just entered the front half. The back half was closed off by prison bars. On the floor in front of us was an aquaneer. Another aquaneer was behind the bars of the cell. Roder/Saint Dane was nowhere to be seen.

"He killed him!" shouted the aquaneer behind the bars. He was all sorts of excited and out of breath.

Uncle Press immediately went to the fallen aquaneer.

"Who did?" demanded Spader.

"Zy Roder! We were putting him in the cell when he suddenly turned on us. The guy is strong! He threw me in here and closed the door, then grabbed him and choked him and— I think he's dead." The guy was out of his mind with panic.

Uncle Press checked the aquaneer's pulse.

"He's not dead, but he needs help," said Uncle Press. "I'll get Yenza." He blasted out of the door and turned left to get back to the control room.

"Where's Roder?" asked Spader.

"I don't know! He ran out. Let me out of here. We've got to find him!"

I pulled a set of keys from the belt of the fallen aquaneer and threw them to Spader. Spader unlocked the door to the cell and the other aquaneer ran out.

"I've got to report this to Yenza!" he shouted, then ran out and turned to the right.

"Help me," I said to Spader, and the two of us moved the aquaneer into a sitting position so he was more comfortable. His eyes opened slowly and focused on me.

"Are you all right?" I asked.

"Roder . . ." the guy gasped. "I got too close to the cell. He grabbed me."

"We know," I said. "Your friend told us."

The aquaneer focused on me and frowned. "What friend?"

"Roder locked the other aquaneer in the cell after he attacked you."

The aquaneer shook his head and said, "Roder was already in the cell. He reached out and grabbed me. Nobody else was here."

Spader looked at me with confusion, but I knew instantly what had happened. Saint Dane had transformed himself again. That wasn't an aquaneer in the cell, it was Saint Dane, and we had just freed him.

"He took a right," I said. "The control room is to the left."

"He's going for the launch chamber," shouted Spader.

"Let him go," I begged.

Spader wasn't listening. He bolted from the room, hot after Saint Dane.

"You okay?" I asked the aquaneer.

He nodded and waved for me to get going.

"Spader!" I shouted. "Spader, stop!"

I ran after my friend, but there was no stopping him.

Moments later we both got to the door of the launch chamber that had once held the hauler. Spader pushed on the door, but something was keeping it closed from inside. He pushed harder and the door finally gave way. Someone had put a barrel against it. We both jumped into the room in time to see Saint Dane about to make his escape.

He had transformed back into his normal self. His steely blue eyes flashed at us as we tumbled into the room. He was on a skimmer, like the underwater skimmers we used to sabotage his battle cruiser. We saw him a second before his head went under the water. His long, gray hair billowed out, like a spiderweb in the water around him. Our roles had reversed.

This is how Saint Dane had seen us as we made our escape on the hauler.

Saint Dane shot us a look of such hatred that I thought my hair would ignite. Then his head sank below the surface. Spader made a move as if to dive for him, but I held him back.

"Let him go," I begged Spader. "You'll get another chance."

Spader threw me aside and ran back out into the corridor. I followed, but had trouble keeping up because he was running flat out.

He got to the ladder, scrambled up into the tower, then jumped outside, onto the hull. As I was climbing up the ladder after him I kept yelling, "Stop him! Somebody stop Spader!"

Things were happening so quickly no one had time to react. Spader ran across the hull and headed right for the hauler we had arrived on. Before anyone could stop him, he cast off the line, jumped on board, and dove into the bubble.

Uncle Press and Yenza came running.

"What is he doing?" Yenza asked.

"Saint Dane, I mean Roder, escaped. He's got a skimmer."

Spader was already submerging in the hauler. Uncle Press watched him sink below the surface, his mind turning. He then looked to the deck, grabbed an air globe, and threw it to me. We were going after him.

"I know where he's going," he said.

"How? Where?" asked Yenza.

I wanted to ask the same thing, but I figured Uncle Press would tell me on the way. He grabbed his own air globe and one of the water sleds. I grabbed the other.

Yenza said, "I'll send a team of aquaneers with you."

"No!" commanded Uncle Press quickly. "We can handle it."

Something about the way Uncle Press snapped at Yenza made me realize where we were going. It all made sense. I should have figured it out myself. We were headed for the gate. Saint Dane was going to try and escape through the flume. It was the only option left to him. The aquaneers didn't need to see this. It was a Traveler thing.

"Ready?" asked Uncle Press.

"Close enough," I answered.

We both splashed down and plunged below the surface.

"You know which way?" I asked.

Uncle Press looked around and said, "There!"

I looked and saw a thin trail of bubbles left by the hauler. We both triggered our water sleds and followed the trail like breadcrumbs in the forest.

"This could take hours," I said to Uncle Press as we shot along side by side.

"Maybe," he answered. "Or maybe Saint Dane knows about another gate."

I hadn't thought of that. On Denduron there were two gates. Who's to say Cloral had only one? But neither of us knew for certain, so all we could do was follow the trail of bubbles.

"Spader is going to be an important ally to you, Bobby," Uncle Press said. "But he's got to learn how to control his emotions."

"Yeah, no kidding," I said.

"Killing Saint Dane isn't the answer," he continued. "I wish it were that simple, but it's not."

"You mean . . . he can't die?" I asked.

"His body can die," Uncle Press explained. "But he would just come back in another form."

"What is he? Some kind of . . . ghost?"

"Not like you're thinking. His spirit is evil, Bobby. Killing his body won't stop him from his quest."

"Okay," I said, not really understanding. "What *will* stop his quest?"

Uncle Press didn't answer at first. I wasn't sure if he didn't want to tell me, or he didn't know. Finally he said:

"It won't end until he thinks he's won. That's when he'll fail."

O-kay. That meant almost nothing to me. But I was used to that. The truth was, things were actually getting less confusing . . . sort of. When I thought back to how clueless I was the first time I hit the flume, I was amazed at how far I had come. But there was still a long way to go and much to learn. I had to accept that. So I didn't push Uncle Press anymore. Besides, getting too much information just freaked me out.

We traveled for a long time and my arms were getting tired from holding the water sled out in front of me. I kept having to change my grip, sometimes holding on with only one hand to rest my other arm. I didn't think it was going to be possible to keep going at this pace and hang on for the hours it would take to get back to the flume near Grallion.

And that's when my ring started to twitch. We were nowhere near the rock shelf where we had first arrived, so that could only mean one thing: There was another gate.

The bubble trail from Spader's hauler led us deeper. It was getting darker too. And cold. Up ahead I saw a rock formation rising up from the bottom. It looked kind of like a mesa you'd see in a Western movie, but of course it was underwater. It rose up to a flat top, with steep cliffs on either side. My glowing ring told me the gate must be hidden in this formation somewhere.

Something else made me think we were almost there. On

the far side of the rock formation I saw a fat stream of air bubbles rising toward the surface. Whatever was causing this was on the other side of the formation, out of our sight. It could have been Spader's hauler, but I didn't know why it would be spewing so much air. Uncle Press and I directed our water sleds toward the bubbles, and as soon as we passed over the top of the formation, we had the answer.

It was Spader's hauler all right, but Spader wasn't in it. The hatch was open and it was now filled with water. Jets of air spewed up from inside. But that wasn't the most dramatic part. There had been an accident. Okay, maybe accident wasn't the right word because it looked like Spader had meant to do what he did.

It was an unbelievable sight. Jammed between the bubble of the hauler and the rock wall was a dead quig. It wasn't as big as the others, but it looked plenty nasty just the same. Spader had no weapons to protect himself, so he rammed it with the hauler. The shark had fallen onto a ledge, with the hauler right on top of it.

"Nice shot," said Uncle Press.

The quig's tail twitched. Maybe it wasn't dead after all. We kept our distance.

"So where's the gate?" I asked.

We had to be in the right place. Not only was my ring going nuts, but the quig was a dead giveaway. I hoped that it was close because Spader didn't have an air globe. Once he got out of the hauler, he was going to have to hold his breath. The two of us scanned the steep wall of the rock formation, but saw no opening.

Then I caught something out of the corner of my eye. It was a bubble no bigger than a golfball that rose up near one section of the wall.

"There!" I announced, and drove my water sled toward it.

When we got close to the wall I saw that the whole rocky face was draped with a curtain of red sea kelp. I tried to remember the exact spot where I saw the bubble rising and started pushing the kelp aside, looking for an opening. But there was nothing behind the kelp but rock. No opening, no tunnel, no gate. The whole time I was looking, I kept glancing over at the quig that was pinned by Spader's hauler. If that thing suddenly sprang to life, I was out of there.

Finally I grabbed a handful of kelp and pushed it aside to reveal a star dug into the rock.

"Got it!" I shouted.

Uncle Press joined me and we dug through the vines until we found a narrow opening. It wasn't much wider than a human body, but it had to be the gate. I don't know why I was feeling so brave all of a sudden, but I went first. I entered the dark crevice and pulled myself along by grabbing on to the rock walls. It only took a few seconds before I saw a shaft of light streaking down through the water ahead of me. A second later I surfaced into another underwater cavern. Uncle Press surfaced right behind me and we both pulled off our air globes.

I didn't know what to expect. What I really hoped was to find Spader there alone and safe, with no Saint Dane to deal with.

The cavern itself was much smaller than the one near Grallion. The pool of water that we now floated in was barely big enough for the two of us. Directly across from us was the flume. We were definitely in the right place. None of this was a surprise. What was hard to believe were the two people inside the cavern.

One was Spader. He was sitting on the rocky floor to our left, crying. And it was pretty obvious why. The other person in the cavern . . . was his father. I had only seen the guy once, and he was dead at the time, but I remembered him. Dead guys tend to leave an impression. The question was, how could he possibly be here? Alive?

When Uncle Press and I threw off our air globes, Spader's father turned to us and said, "Look, your friends have arrived."

The two sat together looking like they were having a quiet, father-son heart-to-heart. There must have been a hundred emotions fighting for Spader's brain time.

He looked at us through his tears and cried, "Hobey, Pendragon! He's alive! Saint Dane kept him here, like a prisoner! Can you believe it?"

The truth was, I couldn't. But my mind wasn't firing on all cylinders at that point either. It was Uncle Press who kept a clear head and gave Spader the bad news.

"It's not him, Spader," he said. "Your father is dead. You saw him on Magorran. He was poisoned."

Spader looked at Uncle Press in confusion. If he had been thinking clearly, he would have realized the truth on his own. But seeing his father alive again had done a number on his head. It sure messed with me for a second, but I soon understood the truth as well. It made me hate Saint Dane even more, if that were possible. He was truly an evil being to have done this to Spader.

"Oh, Press, you are such a killjoy," Spader's father said. "And I thought you were dead."

He turned to Spader and said with a sigh, "Your daddy *is* dead, Spader. And you will be too if you don't back off."

Spader's brain wasn't computing. He watched with wide eyes as his father stood up, walked to the mouth of the flume, and announced, "*Veelox!*"

Instantly the flume sprang to life with light and sound.

Spader's father then looked back to Spader and said, "Who knows? Maybe I'll find your mother along the way and kill her, too!"

Spader fell back against the wall like he had just been punched in the stomach. Spader's father then made a quick transformation back into Saint Dane. He then looked right at me and stared into my brain with such an intense look, I wanted to sink back under the water to escape it.

"Until next time . . . ," he said with an evil grin. Then with a slight bow, he was enveloped by the light and sucked into the flume. I looked at Spader. His eyes were huge. He was only now starting to realize what had happened.

Uncle Press and I pulled ourselves out of the pool of water and went to him.

"His evil reaches out in a lot of ways," said Uncle Press. "He takes as much pleasure in causing you this kind of anguish as wiping out a territory or murdering hundreds of people. It's all the same to him."

I could see Spader's anger growing. His look went from one of confusion, to realization, to rage.

"I'll kill him," he seethed, and went toward the flume.

Uncle Press held him back. "Don't," he said firmly. "This isn't about your own vendetta. This is about protecting the territories, and Halla."

Spader shoved Uncle Press aside. He pushed him with such force that Uncle Press slammed into the rock wall and fell to the ground.

"I don't care about the territories, or Halla, or whatever it is you say I'm supposed to be fighting for. He killed my father and he will die for that."

He strode toward the flume. That's when I heard the faint sound of the musical notes coming back.

"*Veelox!*" called Spader.

The light began glowing from the flume and the notes got louder. But something was wrong. I had heard them coming *before* he said "Veelox." The flume had already been activated. Something was coming our way.

Uh-oh. I thought back to the mine tunnel on Denduron when Saint Dane had sent back a quig shark through the flume that nearly ate Loor and me. Spader stood in the mouth of the flume, expecting to be taken away, oblivious to the danger. The musical notes grew louder and light blew out from deep inside.

"No!" I shouted. "Something's coming back!"

I started to run for Spader, but Uncle Press grabbed me from behind and pulled me back so hard I tripped and fell on my butt.

"Spader, get out of there!" he yelled, and ran for the flume.

Spader wasn't moving. There was only one thing on his mind, and that was revenge. I scrambled back to my feet in time to see Uncle Press headed for Spader. The light was so bright now that whatever was coming would be here in a second. Spader stood at the mouth of the flume, waiting for a ride that wasn't coming.

What happened next took only a few seconds, but they were the longest seconds of my life. I will never forget them. They were seared into my brain forever. Uncle Press dove at Spader and knocked him out of the way. Spader crashed against the far wall, out of the light, away from the flume, and safe from whatever was coming back. But now Uncle Press stood there alone. He had saved Spader, but whatever was coming through the flume was going to hit him.

I heard a whistling sound, then a scream, and an instant later the rock wall opposite the tunnel exploded. At first I thought it was some kind of bomb that had come through, but there wasn't one big boom; there were several smaller, sharp cracks. Bits of rock were blasted off the wall and rained down on me. There was no mistaking what it was—these were bullets. It was like someone had fired a machine gun into the flume and the bullets traveled all the way through, only to be spit out here.

Another second went by and it was over. The lights stopped, the musical notes stopped, and the storm of bullets ended.

"Uncle Press!"

He was lying on the ground, right at the mouth of the flume. I ran to him to see if he had been hit, but I already knew the worst. There was no way that many bullets could come flying out of the flume and miss him completely. It would have to be a miracle. But since my life had been one miracle after another lately, that's what I was hoping for.

When I knelt down next to my uncle, I saw that my miracles had run out. Uncle Press had been hit. More than once. His eyes were unfocused, but they still had life. I looked quickly to Spader, who was crouched in the corner where he had fallen. He, too, looked at Uncle Press in shock. He had no idea what could have happened.

"Get the hauler," I screamed at him. "We've got to get him back to Grallion."

"Bobby, no," Uncle Press said, grabbing my arm.

"You are *not* going to die!" I shouted. My uncle was lying in front of me, mortally wounded. My invincible uncle. The uncle I loved and who took me on more adventures than any kid deserved . . . and that was *before* I became a Traveler.

"Listen, Bobby——," he said weakly.

"No! You are not going to tell me this is the way it's supposed to be! Not like this. Not you!"

Spader crawled over to us and listened. He was in even more emotional agony than before. I knew what he was going through. Uncle Press was going to die because he saved Spader's life, the same as Osa died saving mine.

"You've asked me a lot of questions, Bobby," Uncle Press whispered. "But there's one you never asked."

"What?" I said, tears streaming down my cheeks.

"I've told you there is only one Traveler from each territory," he said. "You never asked why there were two from Second Earth."

He was right. I never did. I don't know why, but the thought never crossed my mind. It was so obvious, but I never thought about it. Or maybe I didn't want to.

"Are you going to tell me?"

"The answer is, there *can't* be two Travelers from Second Earth. I knew my time was short. That's why I brought you from home. It was your time. It was Loor's time, and Spader's, too. You are the next Travelers."

I couldn't think straight. I didn't care about Traveler rules or Halla or Saint Dane or anything else, only that my uncle was lying here, dying.

"I'll tell you something else," he said. "You are the last. All that has gone before is prelude. The fight is yours. You will take it to the end. You are the last Travelers."

He was growing weaker by the second. He looked to Spader and said, "Spader, I know this is hard to believe, but you will see your father again. Your mother, too."

He then slipped his hand down my arm and held my hand. "And I promise you, Bobby Pendragon, you will see your family again. And when you do, I'll be there. Remember that and don't be sad . . . because this is the way it was meant to be."

He then closed his eyes, and he was gone.

CLORAL

The ceremony was everything it should have been.

The Council Circle was loaded with people. The marble bleachers held the entire Council of Faar. Seated next to them was a group of aquaneers in full dress uniform. Among them was Quinnick, the pilot from Grallion, and Wu Yenza, the chief aquaneer.

The rest of the bleachers held an assortment of others. Some were from Faar. Others were from the Agronomy Society and had made the trip from Panger City. Seated with them was Ty Manoo, the agronomer from Grallion. There were also dignitaries from other habitats. Word was spreading quickly about the reemergence of the city of Faar. It had only been two days since the city rose, but the haulers had already been lifted from their hangar and sent across the territory to rescue the farms.

Cloral had reached its turning point—and survived.

Of course, no one seated in that circle had any clue about the bigger picture. They had no idea that Cloral was only one territory of many that Saint Dane was trying to spin into chaos. To them, victory was having ducked a huge ecological disaster. Nothing more, nothing less. And there was an added bonus in that this near-catastrophe had triggered the discovery of their own ancient roots. The raising of the city of Faar was an amazing event. Imagine if Atlantis had suddenly appeared back at home. How cool would that be? Well, this colossal discovery was all the people of Cloral could focus on now. They didn't know about the larger evil that had almost destroyed their world.

But I did. So did Spader.

I had mixed feelings about Spader after what happened to Uncle Press. I knew it wasn't his fault. If he thought his actions would have put Uncle Press in danger, he would have backed off. I'm sure of that. Still, I couldn't stop thinking that if Spader had listened to us, Uncle Press would still be alive. Spader *had* to learn to control his emotions. He and I were very much in the same place right now. I still feel guilty because Osa died while protecting me. And now I knew what it was like to lose a loved one to death, and Saint Dane. But if we were going to work together as Travelers, we had to move past this. As I stood on the council platform waiting for the ceremony to begin I wasn't sure if that was possible. I would always remember how Spader ignored our warnings and because of it, Uncle Press was dead.

I hadn't seen Spader since we got back to Faar. Maybe that was a good thing. It gave us both a chance to chill out and get our heads together. But I was beginning to worry. He should be here for this ceremony. He was the Traveler from Cloral now. I really hoped that he hadn't bailed.

I stood alone on the edge of the platform, outside of the Council Circle. The marble ceiling had been repaired and hoisted back onto the pillars right away. The round symbol of Faar was rejoined and placed back in its prominent spot. The rest of Faar was still pretty much a mess, but I think restoring the Council Circle was important because it represented the heart of Faar. From here, decisions about the future of Cloral would be made.

The sun was setting on the ocean. Sunsets are always beautiful and this one was no different. There were a few long clouds on the horizon. The warm sun lit them up like blazing arrows shooting across the water. The amber light washed over the marble buildings of Faar, making the city look like a painting. As I looked down on Faar's mountain I saw that there were hundreds of people standing on the paths, watching the beautiful sunset. For them it must have been extraordinary. Faar had not seen sunsets in hundreds of years.

Kalaloo had explained to me how the transpire had been planned for generations. The scientists of Faar had devised an ingenious mechanism that when triggered would pump air into vast chambers below the city. The pressure built up in the chambers and lifted the city high enough to allow the sea to rush in and force the city even higher. The chain reaction continued until the surrounding seabed collapsed into the chambers, creating a base. It was like a controlled earthquake, where all the force was funneled upward.

It may have been physics that brought Faar to the surface, but to me it was pure magic. Seeing the people of Faar enjoying this sunset made it seem even more so. In spite of how horrible I felt right now, something good had come out of this adventure.

"Pendragon?"

I turned to see Spader standing there. He was dressed in his full aquaneer uniform, the same as on the day he thought he was going to meet his father. What a relief. Though it was going to be tricky working through what happened, at least I knew he understood that his place was here.

"I've thought a lot about what to say to you," he said quietly. "But there's nothing I can think of to tell you how sorry I am for what happened."

I said, "How about 'I'm sorry for what happened'?"

He dropped his head.

"I wish I could change what I did."

I just nodded and said, "If I told you it was cool and to not worry about it, I'd be lying. But the thing is, now I know how you felt when your father died. Saint Dane killed Uncle Press, just like he killed your father. I want him stopped now more than ever. But there's something you gotta understand. Getting revenge on him isn't the answer. If you understand that, we're cool. If not, then I'm going to have to go forward alone."

"He understands, Pendragon," said a familiar voice.

Walking up to us was Loor. I was stunned. Seeing her here, on Faar, was totally out of context. She was wearing a light green Cloral suit that really showed off her athletic body. She looked more beautiful than ever. I wanted to throw my arms around her and give her a hug, but that wasn't Loor's style. She stepped up to me and put a hand on my shoulder. That's about as warm as Loor got.

"Spader came for me. He was confused, and afraid to speak with you," she said.

I could understand that. If he needed help, the last person he could go to was someone who blamed him for getting his uncle killed.

Loor continued, "We have all lost the ones we loved most. Press always said how this is the way it was meant to be. I believe him. Spader was no more responsible for Press's death than you were for the death of my mother. When she died, I hated you, Pendragon. But I came to see how this is the course we were destined to follow. It will often be a tragic one, but there is a greater purpose. I understand that. I believe Spader does too."

I looked at Spader, who finally looked back to me, waiting for a reaction. I could see how genuinely pained he was.

"I can't tell you that I don't want revenge on Saint Dane," he said. "But I believe the only way to do that is to complete our mission. I'm with you, Pendragon."

We shared eye contact for a moment. I could tell that he was aching for me to say something to make him feel better.

I didn't say anything at first. That's because there was something I had to do. I had thought long and hard about it, and after all that had happened, I wasn't sure if I could go through with it. But now, with Loor's help, I realized that it was the absolute right thing to do. So I reached into my pocket and pulled something out that I had been holding on to for weeks.

"You're a Traveler now," I said to Spader. "This was your father's. Now it belongs to you."

It was the ring that Uncle Press had taken from Spader's father. The Traveler ring. Uncle Press told me I would know the right time to give it to Spader. This was it. I reached out and dropped it into Spader's outstretched hand.

Spader looked at the large ring and I could tell he was holding back tears.

I then smiled and said, "You realize it's going to be a tum-tigger."

Spader smiled. "Hobey-ho," he said.

The two of us hugged. Our friendship was going to survive this, as it should. I looked at Loor, who winked at me. I always thought that I'd have to call on her for help with some kind of nasty battle. When you needed a warrior to bail your butt out of the fire, call Loor. As it turned out, the first time she came to my rescue, it was to help me work through an emotional crisis. Funny thing, this Traveler business.

Kalaloo then walked up to us and said softly, "We're ready to begin."

I saw that now standing on the edge of the platform were two small groups of people. One group was made up of six Faarians, the other six aquaneers. Each group carried a long, yellow container on their shoulders. These were the bodies of Abador, and my Uncle Press. At home you'd call them coffins, but they didn't look like anything I'd seen on Second Earth. They were more like oval-shaped tubes made out of yellow plastic. The coffin held up by the Faarians had the words *"Ti Abador"* written in black letters on one end. The coffin carried by the aquaneers had my uncle's name *"Press Tilton."* (Did I ever tell you that Uncle Press's last name was Tilton?)

The two groups of pallbearers stood with the coffins up on their shoulders. They each walked slowly toward the Council Circle. Abador's coffin was first, followed by Kalaloo. Then came Uncle Press's, followed by Spader, Loor, and me. As we walked slowly into the circle everyone stood up. Soft music was playing too. It wasn't all sad like the church music you hear at funerals. No, this was nicer than that. It kind of reminded me of the mellow New Age music I wrote about before, but somehow it felt right to me now.

The pallbearers placed the two coffins next to each other on pedestals that were in the center of the circle. Kalaloo stood by them while the three of us walked to seats in the marble bleachers. When we had gotten to our places, Kalaloo raised his hands. The music stopped and everyone sat.

"Today is a sad and glorious day," Kalaloo began, addressing the group. "Here, amid the splendor of a Faar that has been reborn, we must also face the realities of death."

He went on to give a very nice speech about Abador. He spoke about how he had dedicated his life to serving Faar and its people. He was often the voice of reason when others had trouble finding the truth. And finally, it was his vision and bravery that saved Faar from destruction. He finished by saying that not only was Faar reborn, but for generations to come, people would remember Abador as the father of the new Cloral.

When he was finished, he turned and raised his hand for me to join him. This was going to be tough. I had to say a few words about Uncle Press. I had never done anything like this before. It wasn't that I didn't know what to say. Far from it. The problem was, I was afraid that I wouldn't be able to get through it without crying. Uncle Press deserved better than that.

I walked up next to Uncle Press's coffin as Kalaloo stepped back. I stood there and looked around at the group. Only a few of them even knew Uncle Press. Most had simply heard about how he helped save Faar and Cloral. To them he was a faceless hero. But he was more than that and I wanted them to understand.

"People have called my uncle brave," I began. "And he was. But that can be said of many people. Many of you here today have shown incredible bravery. But that's not what made Press Tilton special. The thing is, Uncle Press cared. Where most people can't see past their own personal problems, Uncle Press always looked beyond. He helped many people in times of trouble in ways you will never know. Even I don't know most, and that's the way he wanted it. He didn't do it for glory or for riches or to be honored at a wonderful ceremony like this. He did it because he cared. It's what helped save Cloral, and Faar, and why he's not with us today. But you know, that's not really true. He *is* with us today. I know he's with me. And I know that as long as I keep his vision alive, he will never truly be gone. As I say good-bye to him, there's one thing I hope for above all else. I hope that when the time comes that I see him again, he'll be half as proud of me as I am of him today."

That was it. I couldn't say anymore. I touched Uncle Press's coffin and walked back to my place. As I walked everyone stood up. It was time to pay their last respects. I stood between Loor and Spader, trying to be brave. Loor actually reached over and held my hand.

The music began playing again. It was soft and soothing, but began to feel very sad. The two groups of pallbearers gathered around the coffins and lifted them up as the pedestal lowered away. Each group walked their coffins over to a different section of the platform and gently placed them down on the tile. The groups then stepped away, leaving the coffins on the floor of the platform. A moment later the coffins began to sink below. There were panels beneath them in the platform that acted like elevators to gently lower them down.

Kalaloo had come to me the day before and asked if I would honor them by allowing Uncle Press to be buried in the Grand Mausoleum of Faar. This was a place where only the most revered people in Faar's history were laid to rest. It was right under the ornate, mosaic platform we had been standing on. Of course Abador would be buried there. Having Uncle Press there as well was proof of the Faarians' gratitude for all he had done for them.

As much as I knew this was a great honor, my first thought was that he should be brought back home, to Second Earth. But if he were on Second Earth, he would be alone. My family was gone. There would be no one to visit his grave or even remember who he was. But on Faar, he was a hero. I remembered his first words to me after he made that perfect swan dive into the pool of water below the flume. He told me that this was his favorite territory. What better place to stay forever?

I humbly accepted Kalaloo's offer. Uncle Press would stay here on Faar. He'd be remembered as a hero, though the people here wouldn't even come close to knowing how great a guy he really was.

Shortly after the ceremony we returned to Grallion. Loor came with us and we showed her around the amazing farm habitat. We even raised a glass of sniggers to Uncle Press at Grolo's.

I was happy that Cloral was out of danger. We had done our job. But I still felt kind of numb. Of course, most of that was because of Uncle Press. Not having him around was . . . strange. That's the best word I can use. Of course I missed him and the sadness was like a heavy weight on my chest, but there was more. The sadness was about looking back. Losing him was also losing the final link to my family and my life on Second Earth.

The strange part came when I thought about the future. Uncle Press had been my guide. Though I wasn't freaking out twenty-four-seven anymore, I still didn't know much more about being a Traveler than when I started. Up until now, if I was confused about something, I could turn to Uncle Press. He wouldn't always give me the answer, but I always felt as if he was pointing us in the right direction.

Now I was on my own. The biggest question now was, what next? I seriously thought about getting back to Second

Earth and hiding under your bed, Mark. You could feed me leftover mac and cheese, nobody would know where I was, and I'd never have to think about anyone named Saint or Dane again.

But that wasn't going to happen. The real question was, should I chase Saint Dane to Veelox? That's the last territory he flumed to. I wasn't sure if it was the right step or not, but if it was, I didn't want to go alone. Loor was gone. After spending a few days on Grallion, she returned to Zadaa. Tensions there were growing worse, and she feared that something nasty could happen anytime. She wanted to be there and I didn't blame her.

That left Spader. He would be a great partner. We had become friends before things went south and now that things were calm again, we rekindled our friendship. I knew he would go with me, but I was still nervous about how he would handle Saint Dane. I didn't want him getting all out-of-control crazy again. I figured the best way to deal with my worries was to put them on the table. So one evening after dinner, Spader and I took a walk through the farm.

"I have to leave," I said. "Cloral is past the turning point. There's no reason to stay here."

"Even for the great fishing?" asked Spader with a laugh. He was kidding. I knew it. He then said, "Where will you go?"

"Veelox, I guess," was my answer. "That's where Saint Dane went." Of course, I'd rather go someplace where Saint Dane *wasn't,* but that's not how it works.

"Ever been there?" he asked.

"Nope. Don't have a clue about the place. Uncle Press was always my tour guide but now, well . . ." I didn't have to finish my sentence.

We walked along in silence for a while. I wasn't sure how to ask him if he wanted to go with me. More important, I didn't know how to ask him if he was going to be a loose cannon and get us both killed.

"I want to go with you," Spader said. That took care of that problem. "I'm a Traveler, right? That's what Travelers do. If Cloral is safe now, there's no reason for me to be here either."

"Spader, I—"

"You don't have to worry about me, Pendragon," he said sincerely. "I'm with the program. I meant what I said before. It's not about getting revenge on Saint Dane. It's about stopping him from hurting the territories. Look, mate, it was a rough time. I was out of my head. But I'm back now, and I want to go with you."

That pretty much covered all the points I didn't know how to bring up with him. That was easy. The question was, did I believe him?

"You need me, Pendragon," Spader added.

That brings me to where I am right now, sitting in my quarters on Grallion, writing this journal. Tomorrow, Spader and I are going to leave. Our destination: Veelox. Whatever *that* is.

Writing this all down was hard, but believe it or not, it's made me feel a little better. Looking back on the events that led to the salvation of Cloral made me realize how important our mission is. Uncle Press always told me this, but it took seeing it for myself, again, to understand. I have no idea what we'll find on Veelox, or how we should begin hunting for Saint Dane. I guarantee he won't be walking around with a sign saying: HI, BOBBY, HERE I AM! I'm sure he'll take on some disguise and be working his evil magic just as he did with Denduron and Cloral. The biggest difference will be that I won't have

Uncle Press to rely on. Welcome to Traveler life . . . chapter three.

As I finish writing this journal, I have to say how Uncle Press's last words are really helping keep my head together. He said, no, he *promised* that we would be together again. I'm not sure how that's possible, besides meeting up in heaven or something. But I don't think that's what he meant. The more I think about it, the more I realize he was talking about actually being together again. For real. In this lifetime.

Of course, that raises the biggest question of all. Where exactly is here? For that matter, when is now? That all depends on what territory you happen to be on. For the first time I'm beginning to see some amazing possibilities. I wonder how many territories there are? Are they all like the ones we've been on so far, or is it possible to flume into a whole 'nother plane of existence? The potential is incredibly exciting, and makes my head hurt.

This is where I will end it, guys. I'll send this off to you and then get some sleep. Please know that I miss you both. I hope I can get back there soon. Thank you again for reading my journals and keeping them safe. You are the light of reality in my otherwise dark and confused new life.

Hobey-ho.

Bobby.

END OF JOURNAL #8

◉ SECOND EARTH ◉

Mark and Courtney rode in the back of a black-and-white police cruiser on their way to the Stony Brook Police Station. They had been picked up at Mark's house by a nice cop named Officer Wilson. When he showed up at the door, Mark half expected him to say: "You're under arrest, slimeball!" and slap the cuffs on him. But that didn't happen. He was all friendly and as they rode along he even offered to put the siren on for them. Mark had to fight back the urge to say: "Yeah, go for it!" The kid in him thought it would be cool, but this was serious business, not time for fun. It also didn't help that Courtney gave him a sharp look that said: "If you say yes to the siren, I'll clock you." They rode in silence.

Both were a little bit stunned. They had finished reading Bobby's last journal and had just learned that Press was dead. They had met Press a few times and gotten to know him better through Bobby's journals. Hearing about his tragic death was a shock. Of course it helped that Bobby and company had kicked some serious butt on Cloral. It took some of the sting away. They were already anticipating what they would hear from the territory of Veelox.

But riding above these thoughts was the reality they faced in their own world, here and now.

Mark had a pretty good idea why Captain Hirsch had called them. It was about the journals Andy Mitchell had stolen. He was sure that Mitchell had turned them in to the police to get the reward. Why else would Captain Hirsch want them to come in?

Mark and Courtney had met the captain months before. They were the first ones to alert the police that Bobby and his family were missing. But since that meeting, they learned the truth about what had happened to Bobby through his journals. Though they didn't have any idea where the Pendragons had gone, they knew now *why* they had disappeared. They were here to raise Bobby to become a Traveler, and their job was complete. That's why they left to go . . . somewhere.

Mark and Courtney never told the police what they knew. It was just too unbelievable. They were afraid they would be locked up in some hospital for the mentally deranged, or become suspects in the investigation they started themselves. Worse, they were afraid if people found out about the truth, it would make it harder for the Travelers to complete their mission—especially when it brought them here to Second Earth. So after lots of discussion and thought, Mark and Courtney decided to keep the truth a secret.

But now, with Andy Mitchell bringing the journals to the police, it was possible this whole thing could blow up in their faces.

Those were the worries going through Mark's mind as Officer Wilson pulled into the parking lot of the Stony Brook Police Station. Both he and Courtney tried to act all casual, as if nothing were wrong. They had to be very careful about what they said to the police, or they could find themselves in deep trouble.

Officer Wilson led them through the precinct and had them

wait in the same conference room where they first met with Captain Hirsch months before.

The room was empty except for two thick file folders sitting on the end of the long conference table. Both Mark and Courtney had a pretty good idea of what was in those folders. It was the reason they were here. They gave each other a look, but didn't say a word. There was no way to know if they were being watched and listened to from behind the two-way mirror that ran the length of one wall. Mark wondered what was going through Courtney's mind. She looked pretty calm. That was good. She would have to be calm for both of them, because Mark wanted to hurl.

"Hi, guys. Thanks for coming in," said Captain Hirsch as he walked quickly into the room. "Sit down, please."

Mark and Courtney took seats next to each other on one side of the conference table. Captain Hirsch sat down at the far end, in front of the two file folders. He was dressed in his usual gray business suit, with his tie loose around his neck. Mark wondered if he slept in that suit. Hirsch looked to Mark, then to Courtney, as if he wanted them to say something. They didn't.

"So, you both know Andy Mitchell?"

"Yes," they both said.

"What do you think of him?"

Mark wanted to say he thought Mitchell was an obnoxious slug, but he didn't want Hirsch to think he had a negative attitude.

Courtney said, "He's an obnoxious slug."

Obviously, Courtney couldn't care less about what other people thought of her attitude.

Hirsch nodded. He then reached for one of the file folders.

"This look familiar?" he asked, as he pulled something out and held it up for them to see. It was the first page of Bobby's first journal. It looked *very* familiar. Courtney shot a look to Mark. Mark had to stay cool, even though his worst fear had come true. It was official. Mitchell had turned the journals in. Mark had kept the journals rolled up and tied with a cord, the way Bobby had sent them. Mitchell must've flattened them out and stacked them up so they could fit in a folder. Mark hated Mitchell all the more for being so disrespectful.

"Yeah, it's familiar," said Mark, trying not to appear angry.

"It sure is," added Courtney, sounding a little bit more upset than Mark would have liked. He was afraid Courtney would go ballistic when she saw the journals, but thankfully, she didn't.

Captain Hirsch put the page back in the folder.

"Andy Mitchell brought this in about an hour ago," he said. "He's still here. I'd like to have him join us."

"He's here?" said Mark with surprise. "Now?"

"Yeah. Is it okay?" Hirsch asked.

"Sure," said Courtney. "Bring the slime in."

Captain Hirsch nodded to the mirror, which meant they were being watched. That was a totally creepy feeling. A few seconds later the door opened and Andy Mitchell strode in looking like a guy who had just won the lottery. He walked all cocky and had a smug smile on his face. When he saw Mark and Courtney, the smile fell off. But he got his act back together quickly.

"Man, that was fast," he said with a sneer. He then said to Mark and Courtney, "You guys feeling the heat yet?" He snorted and gave an obnoxious laugh.

"Sit down please, Andy," said Hirsch.

Mitchell threw one leg over a chair and sat on the far end of the table. Mark half expected him to spit on the floor.

"Why's this taking so long?" Mitchell asked. "You guys gonna buy me lunch or what?"

Hirsch didn't respond. He turned to Mark and Courtney,

saying, "Andy brought these pages to our attention. He tells us they're proof of what happened to Bobby Pendragon. If it's true, he's going to get a large reward."

"You got that right!" snorted Mitchell. "Twenty-five big ones."

Mark saw Courtney's hand clench. He knew she was fighting the urge to jump over the table and pummel this weasel. Or maybe she wanted to pummel Mark. He wasn't sure which.

"Andy," Hirsch said with a friendly smile. "Could you tell me how you gained possession of these papers?"

"I told you," Mitchell answered, pointing to Mark. "He had 'em! The two of 'em were keeping them secret so nobody would know what was really going on. I figured it was my civic duty to bring 'em in."

Mark closed his eyes. This was horrible. *Civic duty, yeah right.*

"That's not what I asked you, Mr. Mitchell," said Hirsch politely. "I asked how you gained possession of these pages."

"You mean . . . how did I get 'em?" Mitchell asked. Clearly he wasn't sure of the meaning of the word "gained." *What a tool.*

"Yes," answered Hirsch patiently.

Mitchell began to squirm. He started to answer a few times, but stopped himself as if he wasn't sure he was saying the right thing. Finally, he just blurted out:

"I took 'em, okay? I just took 'em. But so what, man? You would have done the same thing! This kinda stuff shouldn't be secret! People gotta know!"

Hirsch continued calmly, "So you're telling me you stole them from Mark Dimond?"

It was clear that Mitchell didn't like where this was going. "Yeah, I stole 'em. But that's not the point!"

Hirsch nodded. He then reached for the second file folder on the table. Mark and Courtney watched without saying a word or showing any emotion. Hirsch opened the second folder to reveal a thick stack of white paper with lines of typing on it. The lines were single spaced and traveled neatly from margin to margin.

"I'm going to read something to you, Mr. Mitchell," said Hirsch. "I want you to tell me if it sounds familiar."

"Knock yourself out," responded Mitchell.

The police officer looked down at the top page, and began to read aloud.

"I hope you're reading this, Mark.

"Heck, I hope anybody's reading this because the only thing that's keeping me from going totally off my nut right now is getting this all down on paper so that—'"

"That's from the journal," said Mitchell, a little confused. "The first one. That's how it starts. What are you reading that from?"

Hirsch held the thick stack of clean printed pages up for Mitchell to see. "Mark and Courtney brought me this story last week," he said.

"What?" gasped Mitchell, stunned. "I don't get it."

Hirsch put the pages down and chuckled. "Yeah, that's pretty obvious."

"What's goin' on?" demanded Mitchell in confusion.

"This is a story they wrote," said Hirsch, trying to hold back a smile. "A story. It's fiction. Do you know what that means? They made it up."

Mitchell shot a stunned look at Mark and Courtney. The two sat there looking like innocent angels.

"No. No they didn't!" shouted Mitchell. "Pendragon wrote it! It's all true!"

Courtney shook her head and spoke to Hirsch, saying, "Like we told you, it may be childish, but it was our way of dealing with Bobby's disappearance."

"Yeah," added Mark quickly. "I even wrote it out in long hand on those brown pages, as if Bobby wrote it himself. It makes the whole thing seem more real that way."

"But we also typed it on the computer, so it was easier to work on," said Courtney. "It's just a fantasy, but it felt good to pretend that Bobby was on some big adventure instead of, well, instead of being wherever he really is. Now that we're sitting here talking about it, it's kind of . . . embarrassing."

"Don't be embarrassed," said Hirsch kindly. "People deal with loss in a lot of ways. You two were very creative about it."

"You gotta be kidding me!" screamed Mitchell as he jumped up from his chair. "They are lying! Ly-ing! I . . . I saw pages appear from nowhere in a big flash of light through . . . through his ring. Look at his ring!"

Mark shrugged and held up his fingers. He had no rings.

Mitchell was in full-on panic mode. Mark could see that he had gone from thinking he had twenty-five thousand dollars in his pocket to being treated like an idiot thief who believes in fairy tales. He desperately tried to turn it around.

"Okay, okay," he stammered. "Answer me this: Why did they bring you those printed-out pages? Huh? I'll tell you. They were trying to beat me here and get themselves off the hook, that's why."

"No," said Hirsch patiently. "They came here to report their handwritten pages had been stolen. They brought the typed pages to prove the story was theirs. Quite frankly, I never thought the stolen pages would turn up, but then you walked in out of the blue. How very convenient!"

"No!" shouted Mitchell in anguish. He was losing badly.

Hirsch looked at Mark and Courtney and said, "Do you want to press charges against Mr. Mitchell?"

Mark and Courtney looked at each other, then Courtney said, "No, just getting the pages back is enough."

"Yeah, in a way we feel kind of bad for him," said Mark sympathetically. "We never thought somebody would believe our story was good enough to be true!"

"Really!" added Courtney with a laugh.

"But it *is* true!" shouted Mitchell, on the verge of tears. "Isn't it?"

"You're free to go, Mr. Mitchell," said Hirsch. "But I first want you to apologize to these two for what you did."

Mitchell flashed a look of anger and hatred at Mark that rocked him back in his chair. It didn't seem to bother Courtney, though. Mitchell didn't scare her. Mitchell got all red in the face, like he was in horrible pain, then he squeezed out a weak, "I'm . . . sorry."

"It's okay, Andy," Courtney said sympathetically. "Let's forget this ever happened."

"Yeah," added Mark.

"Thank you, Mr. Mitchell. Now go away," ordered Hirsch.

Mitchell stood there for a second, desperately thinking of something he could say to turn this around. But he wasn't smart enough to do that. He looked at Courtney. Courtney gave him a tiny little smile and a wink. That was it. Mitchell couldn't take it anymore.

"Ahhhh!" he shouted, and stormed out of the conference room.

Hirsch said, "You're right. He *is* an obnoxious slug."

"Thank you, Captain," said Courtney in her most polite voice. "I knew you would be the right person to come to for help."

"No problem, that's my job. I do have a favor to ask though."

"Anything," said Courtney quickly.

"Would you let me read this story? It's really pretty good!"

Mark and Courtney exchanged glances, then Mark said, "Sure, but could you read the printed pages? We'd like to hold on to the handwritten ones."

Hirsch quickly slid the folder with Bobby's journals over to Mark.

"Of course, here you go," he said. "That Mitchell guy's a piece of work. Did he really think this story was true?"

All Mark and Courtney could do was shrug innocently.

A few minutes later Mark and Courtney were out of the police station and walking down the Ave. Bobby's first journals were safely tucked into Mark's backpack. They had politely turned down a ride home from Officer Wilson, saying they'd like to walk. They said the whole ordeal was pretty stressful and they needed to cool down.

They went right to Garden Poultry and bought two boxes of French fries, along with a Coke and a Mountain Dew. Mark did the Dew. They brought the food to the pocket park and sat on a bench to enjoy their feast. Neither one had said anything from the time they left the police station. They just kind of drifted toward Garden Poultry without even discussing it.

Finally, as he finished his last crispy golden fry, Mark said, "I'm sorry, Courtney."

Courtney gulped down the rest of her Coke, then said, "Losing that page from the journal was an accident. It was as much my fault as yours. But not telling me right away that Mitchell found out about the journals . . . Mark, that was bad."

"I know, I know," was all Mark could say. "I thought I could handle the guy. I . . . I was embarrassed to tell you how bad I screwed up. But man, when he wanted to see all the journals and started talking about how we were going to be famous when we showed the whole world what we had—I didn't know what to do."

"You should have come to me before it got that bad," said Courtney. Mark could tell she was angry.

"Yeah," said Mark guiltily. "But your plan was awesome." He

thought back to the moment when he finally fessed up to Courtney about what had happened. It was right after Mitchell demanded to see all of the journals. Courtney didn't get angry. Instead she came up with the idea to turn the tables on Mitchell. She knew he would tell the police about the journals to claim the reward. That was a no-brainer. But they figured they could beat him to the punch by pretending they wrote the story themselves. It took Courtney three late nights of grueling typing to get Bobby's first journals into her computer. Then they printed out the pages and took them right to Captain Hirsch. That's when they told him the bogus story about their handwritten version being stolen. The key to the whole thing was showing the story to the police *before* Mitchell did. Neither of them liked to lie, but the situation was desperate. Mitchell had to be stopped from exposing Bobby's story to the world.

As it turned out, it became only half a lie when Mitchell came to Mark's house and ended up stealing the journals after all. Still, if Mitchell had just read the journals and returned them, that would have been the end. But they knew Mitchell wouldn't do that. He was too greedy. They knew he'd take the journals to the police—and walk right into their trap. The sting worked beautifully. They got Bobby's journals back and Mitchell couldn't demand to see them anymore by threatening to go to the police.

It was a beautiful thing, but Mark still felt bad for not having been totally honest with Courtney.

"You brought me into this when you showed me the first journal," Courtney said. "If you want me to stay in, you've got to be honest with me, always."

"I will, I promise," Mark whined.

The two were silent for a second, then slowly, Courtney smiled a devilish smile. "But it sure was sweet seeing Mitchell squirm!"

Mark laughed too and they slapped high-fives. Mark then reached around his neck and pulled out the chain that held the key to his secret desk. Dangling next to it was Mark's ring. He took it off and put it right back on his finger, where it belonged.

There was nothing left to do now but go home. They walked together until Courtney reached her street.

"So, you'll call me?" asked Courtney.

"Soon as the next journal shows," answered Mark, as he always did.

The two then gave each other a hug and separated.

They wouldn't get back together for another five months.

Both went back to their normal lives at home and at school. Since the only friend they had in common was Bobby, that meant neither of them saw much of each other. Occasionally they'd pass in the hallway. Courtney would look at him as if to ask: "Well?" Mark would just shake his head. Nothing yet.

Courtney played softball for the Stony Brook team. It was fast-pitch and she was the pitcher. The team went undefeated that spring, and Courtney was MVP of course.

Mark's big project was to build a battling robot for a county science fair. He had a real knack for mechanics and physics. The robot was killer. It destroyed the competition with a combination hook, buzz saw, sledgehammer package. He took first prize and started to investigate how to get on the TV with his battling robotic baby.

Courtney had a birthday on March 6. She turned fifteen. Mark sent her a card with the greeting: "Happy Birthday, Hobey-ho!"

The two did get together once, on March 11. Bobby's birthday. They went back to Garden Poultry on the Ave, got some fries, and toasted Bobby in the pocket park with Coke and Dew.

Both wondered if Bobby had any idea that he had just turned fifteen.

The next big event was graduation from Stony Brook Junior High in June. Mark was valedictorian and was supposed to give a speech. But he was too nervous and let the runner-up take his place on the podium. He was still the valedictorian, though, and got a huge dictionary as a prize. The next stop for these two was high school—a big, scary step. They would soon be going to Davis Gregory High, the big public high school in Stony Brook. Nobody knew who Davis Gregory was, but they figured he must have been somebody important. Mark wondered if someday there'd be a school called Bobby Pendragon High.

The summer went along lazily. Courtney played baseball and got her junior lifeguard certification. Mark tinkered with his killer robot, getting ready for the big state competition. He had gotten an invitation and everything. His reputation was getting around.

Mark always wore the ring, waiting for the day when the next journal would arrive. The truth was, both Mark and Courtney tried not to think about Bobby, because the longer it went without getting a journal, the more they feared that something nasty had happened to him. That was something they didn't even want to consider, so it was easier to put Bobby out of their minds entirely.

Then, on August 21, two things happened. First, it was Mark's fifteenth birthday. He celebrated in his usual way: getting some creepy new clothes from his mother and a gift certificate from his father that would be spent wisely at the local electronics store.

The other thing that happened was Mark got a strange phone call at home.

An official-sounding woman's voice said, "May I speak to a Mr. Mark Dimond, please?"

"That's me."

"This is Ms. Jane Jansen, vice-president of the National Bank of Stony Brook. Are you familiar with us?"

The woman sounded like somebody's idea of a pruny old schoolteacher.

"Uh . . . sure," he said. "You're on the Ave . . . uh . . . Stony Brook Avenue."

"Correct," she answered. "Do you know a Ms. Courtney Chetwynde?"

"Yes, what's this about?"

"Mr. Dimond, would you and Ms. Chetwynde please come down to our branch as soon as possible? With some identification? I believe this may be an issue of some importance."

This really threw Mark. He didn't even have a bank account. What could they possibly want with him and Courtney? He was just about to tell this wacky woman that he wanted to call his parents first, when she dropped the bomb.

"It has to do with a Mr. Robert Pendragon."

Those were the magic words.

"We'll be right there," Mark said, and hung up the phone before she had the chance to say good-bye.

Mark immediately called Courtney and was relieved to find her home. Half an hour later, the two of them were standing outside the large, gray cement building with the big brass letters that read: NATIONAL BANK OF STONY BROOK.

Mark never understood how Stony Brook could have a national bank, but it had been around forever so he figured they must know what they were doing. The bank itself was old-fashioned. There was a huge lobby with a high ceiling capped by a glass dome. This was not like the modern banks that Mark had been in with his mother. This looked like the bank from Mary Poppins. There was lots of dark polished wood, brass hardware, and leather furniture. There were a lot of customers, too, and they all whispered when they spoke. It was like a library. Mark thought this bank probably looked exactly the same as it did the year it was built. Based on the cornerstone he saw outside, that year was 1933.

Mark and Courtney told the receptionist they were there to see a Ms. Jansen. They were asked to have a seat in the waiting area, so the two of them sank into the cushy leather chairs to wait for this mysterious woman who had some news about Bobby.

"You have any clue what this is about?" Courtney asked Mark.

"None, zero, nada," Mark answered.

A second later they both saw a rail-thin woman walking toward them. She wore a gray suit and had her hair up in a bun. Her glasses were black with perfectly round lenses. Mark knew immediately that this must be Ms. Jane Jansen. She looked exactly like her voice sounded. She was old, too. Mark wondered if she had been working here since the bank opened.

The woman walked up to the receptionist and asked her a question that Mark couldn't hear. The receptionist pointed to Mark and Courtney. Ms. Jansen looked at them and frowned.

"I guess we're not what she was expecting," Courtney whispered.

Ms. Jansen walked over to them quickly. She had perfect posture and a stiff neck that didn't turn. Whenever she looked in a different direction, she moved her whole body.

"Mr. Dimond? Ms. Chetwynde?" she asked with a snippy tone.

"That's us," answered Mark.

"Do you have some form of identification?" she added suspiciously.

Courtney and Mark gave the woman their student ID cards. Jansen looked at them over her glasses and then frowned again.

"You two are quite young," she said.

"You needed our ID's to figure that out?" Courtney asked.

Mark winced. Courtney was being a wise-ass, again.

Ms. Jansen shot Courtney a sour look and handed them back their ID's. "Is this the way young people dress today to attend a meeting?" she asked, sounding all superior.

Mark and Courtney looked at each other. They were both wearing shorts, T-shirts, and hiking boots. What was wrong with that?

"We're fifteen, ma'am, what did you expect?" said Courtney. "We don't have snappy outfits like you're wearing."

Jansen knew this was a cut, but let it go.

"Please follow me," she said, then turned and walked toward the back of the bank.

Courtney rolled her eyes at Mark. Mark shrugged and the two of them followed the stiff, skinny little woman. A minute later they were sitting across from her at a large oak desk.

"We have been holding an envelope for the two of you," she explained. "We assume it must be some sort of inheritance from a relative of yours. Are either of you related to Mr. Robert Pendragon?"

That was a tough one to answer. Mark was about to say that they were just friends, but Courtney jumped in first saying, "Yeah, he's a distant relative."

Jansen continued, "Well, it doesn't matter actually. The instructions are quite clear."

She then handed the envelope to Mark. It was an old, yellowed letter that had two names written on it: "Mark Dimond" and "Courtney Chetwynde." It was Bobby's handwriting. Both Mark and Courtney had to force themselves to keep from smiling.

Jansen continued, "We were instructed to deliver this

envelope to you on this date. We were also instructed to have you open it right away."

Mark shrugged and opened the letter. He pulled out a sheet of paper that was folded in half. It was old and yellow too, like the envelope. There was a header engraved on top that read: "National Bank of Stony Brook" in fancy lettering. Below it were the words: "Safety Deposit Box #15-224."

There was one other thing in the envelope: a small key.

Mark and Courtney had no idea what to make of this, so they showed it to Ms. Jansen. She looked at the note and the key, then said quickly, "Follow me, please."

She got up and walked off again. They followed her.

"This is freaky," whispered Courtney.

This time Ms. Jansen led them into a place Mark had always wanted to go—the huge bank vault. Since the bank was open for business, so was the vault. There was a giant, round door that looked like something you'd see in Fort Knox. When this baby closed, there was nobody getting in. Or out, for that matter.

Mark wondered if inside they would see big bags of money with dollar signs on them. Or stacks of clean crisp bills. Or maybe even bars of gold.

But there was none of that. Ms. Jansen led them to a room full of brass lockers. Some were as big as the lockers at school, others were no larger than a few inches wide. These were the safe deposit boxes of the National Bank of Stony Brook.

Ms. Jansen walked along one row of doors, scanning the numbers inscribed on each. She finally arrived at the one marked: 15-224. She stopped and handed the key to Mark.

"You both are now the owners of the contents of safe deposit box number 15-224. I will leave you alone to inspect the contents. When you are finished, please relock the box and return the key to me. Any questions?"

"I'm kind of confused," said Mark. "Who set this up?"

"I told you, a Mr. Robert Pendragon."

Courtney asked, "He came in here? Did you see him?"

The look on Ms. Jansen's face got even more pinched, if that were possible.

"I know you consider me to be a fossil, Ms. Chetwynde, but I assure you, this account was opened long before I was employed here at National Bank."

"So when was that?" asked Mark.

"I'll have to double check the exact date, but I believe it was sometime in May."

"He was here three months ago?" shouted Courtney in surprise.

"Please, Ms. Chetwynde," said Jansen testily. "I'm not a fool, so do not try to play me for one. This account was opened in May of 1937."

Mark and Courtney went into stunned brain lock.

"Do you have any more questions?"

Both Mark and Courtney could only shake their heads.

"Then I'll be at my desk."

Jansen gave them a last annoyed look and hurried off.

Mark and Courtney couldn't move. They both tried desperately to get their minds around the incredible information.

"Is it possible?" Courtney finally asked.

"There's one way to find out," answered Mark.

He inserted the key into the deposit box marked 15-224. This was one of the larger boxes compared to the others. It looked to be about two feet high. The door hinged outward, revealing a handle attached to a steel box. While Mark held the door open, Courtney pulled on the handle. The steel box slid out easily. It was roughly the size of two shoe boxes.

"Take it over there," said Mark.

Built into one wall was a row of four desks set up with partitions between them, kind of like the study carrels in the library at school. These wooden desks looked ancient, just like everything else at this bank. Courtney put the box down on one of the old desks and they each pulled up a chair. Mark was happy nobody else was here.

The two looked at the steel box. The lid was still closed so they couldn't see what was inside. Mark's heart was racing. He knew Courtney's was too.

"I can't breathe," Mark said finally.

"Then open it. This is killing me!"

Mark reached for the lid, hesitated a moment, then lifted it up.

They saw that the deep box was mostly empty. But lying on the bottom was a stack of four books, each bound in dark red leather. They were about the size of a piece of computer paper: 8x10 inches. Each looked to be about a half-inch thick. The weird thing was that they didn't have any titles. There were no markings on the covers whatsoever.

There was something else in the box too. Sandwiched next to the stack of books was an envelope. Mark's hands were shaking as he pulled it out. It was a business-size envelope with a printed return address in the upper left corner. It was the name and address of the bank. Whoever wrote this letter wrote it here in the bank. There was something else on the envelope. In Bobby's handwriting were the words: "Mark and Courtney."

"That's us," said Courtney with a weak smile.

Mark nervously opened the envelope and pulled out the single page inside. He unfolded it to reveal a letter written on National Bank of Stony Brook stationery. The words were written in Bobby's handwriting.

Dear Mark and Courtney,

I gotta make this fast. I don't have much time. Here's the deal. I lost my ring. I haven't had it for months now. That's why you haven't been getting my journals. I've been writing though. Every thing that's happened I put down on paper, just like always. But it's been making me crazy. I hate having all the journals together. They're not safe with me. I can't believe it took me as long as it did to come up with a solution.

I came to Stony Brook. I knew the National Bank was around forever and sure enough, here it is. What a rush. The Ave is a totally different place, though. I was kind of hoping Garden Poultry was here to grab a quick box of fries, but no such luck. You know what's there instead? A barbershop. Same building, different business. Weird.

I could go on forever about how strange this is, but I don't have time. If my plan works, and I can't think of why it won't, you'll be sitting in the same spot where I am right now, reading this letter.

I've put all four journals in the safe deposit box. The whole adventure is contained here. Hopefully, the next time you hear from me it will be through the rings. I think I might know where mine is now, and that's where I'm headed.

Thank you, guys. I miss you.
Bobby
May 31, 1937

P.S. If they still have these wooden desks in the vault, look under the one to the far right.

Courtney and Mark both read the letter a few times to make sure they understood. Somehow Bobby got here in 1937 and left his journals. It made sense. Bobby knew the National Bank would still be here in the present, so there was no reason why it wouldn't work. The bigger question was, how the heck did he get to 1937? It began to raise all sorts of questions about the flumes sending Travelers through time as well as territories.

They both turned their attention to the desk they were sitting at. They looked pretty old and were probably the same desks that Bobby had sat at. They both got down on their knees to look under the desk on the far right. They had no idea what they should be looking for until—

"Oh, man, look!" Courtney said.

She pointed to a spot underneath the desk. Something was carved into the woodwork. The only way you could see it was to be down on the floor, looking straight up. The words said: "Happy Birthday, Mark."

As they lay on their backs, looking up, Mark and Courtney started to laugh. This was so perfectly Bobby. Mark wished he had a camera with him so he could take a shot and keep it with the journals. He planned on coming back and doing just that.

The two then pulled themselves out from under the desk and stood up. They stared at the open safety deposit box and the four journals inside.

"I can't believe there's a whole story here," said Courtney.

"We should bring them home," Mark said.

"Yeah," agreed Courtney, "but this is killing me. Let's just look at the first page."

Mark couldn't think of a reason not to, so he reached inside and took the first journal off the pile. It was nicely bound, like a book that had never been opened.

"Not exactly old parchment papers," Mark said.

He then carefully opened the cover to the first page.

Unlike the stories from Denduron and Cloral, Bobby had typed this journal. The pages were the size of regular computer printer paper, but they were heavier and cream colored. Also, the typing looked all messy. This wasn't like a clean page from a printer. This had actually been typed on an old-fashioned type-writer. Neither of them had ever seen something like this—it was like looking at a piece of history. In a way, that's exactly what it was.

"Let's at least see where he was," said Courtney.

"Okay," agreed Mark.

The two sat down at the desk and began to read.

to be continued

PENDRAGON

Journal of an Adventure Through Time and Space

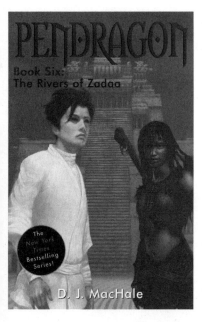

Bobby Pendragon continues his pursuit of Saint Dane in **The Rivers of Zadaa**

Bobby Pendragon has followed Saint Dane to the territory of Zadaa, where Saint Dane's influence has fueled the fire of discontent between two warring tribes: the Rokador and the Batu. This is also the territory where the Traveler Loor lives, and together she and Bobby work to thwart Saint Dane's efforts to destroy Zadaa.

D. J. MacHale is a writer, director, and producer of several popular television series and movies, including *29 Down; Are You Afraid of the Dark?; Encyclopedia Brown, Boy Detective; Tower of Terror;* and *Ghostwriter*. Pendragon, his first book series, became an instant hit that included a *New York Times* bestseller. He lives in Southern California with his wife, Evangeline; his daughter, Keaton; a golden retriever, Maggie; and a kitten, Kaboodle.